THE
HOTEL QUADRIGA

THE
HOTEL QUADRIGA

Jenny Glanfield

Macdonald

A Macdonald Book

Copyright © Jenny Glanfield 1988

First published in Great Britain in 1988
by Macdonald & Co (Publishers) Ltd
London & Sydney

British Library Cataloguing in Publication Data

Glanfield, Jenny
The Hotel Quadriga.
Vol. 1.
I. Title
823'.914 [F]   PR6057.L25

ISBN 0-356-15150-6

Typeset in Times by Leaper & Gard Ltd, Bristol, England
Printed and bound in Great Britain by
Richard Clay Ltd, Bungay, Suffolk

Macdonald & Co (Publishers) Ltd
Greater London House
Hampstead Road
London NW1 7QX
A Pergamon Press plc company

Dedication
To Colin

Acknowledgements

The Hotel Quadriga is a historical romance. The Hotel Quadriga has never existed except in my imagination, but I extend a debt of gratitude to the Hotel Adlon as the inspiration behind the creation of this establishment. Likewise, the Jochum, Kraus, von Biederstein and other principal families and characters in this novel are imaginary. Necessarily, however, in telling a story set in a historical context, real personages are mentioned and quoted. Every effort has been made to ensure that these factual references are correct and the informed reader will be able to differentiate between those who existed in real life and those who lived only on paper.

I should like to thank the following people for their support during the long period that it took me to research and write this book: my editor, Helen Anderson, whose expertise and understanding made *The Hotel Quadriga* into the book it now is, and my agent, Bill Hamilton, whose assistance and encouragement were invaluable; also — Michael Downs, Lilo Friepan, the Groves family, Roger Hicks, Ilse Kricke, Julie and Leon Rose, the late Hanny Rudolph, Len Warran and the librarians at Meopham Library and the Goethe Institute, London. Most of all, however, I should like to thank my family — my late mother, Joyce Gay, without whose inspiration I might never have commenced it; my brother, Tony, for his technical assistance; and my husband, Colin, for use of his unending fund of knowledge and his patience. Finally, I want to thank our three cats, Timmy, Tiger and Darli-Darli, who kept me company and never once criticized.

Jenny Glanfield
Summer 1987

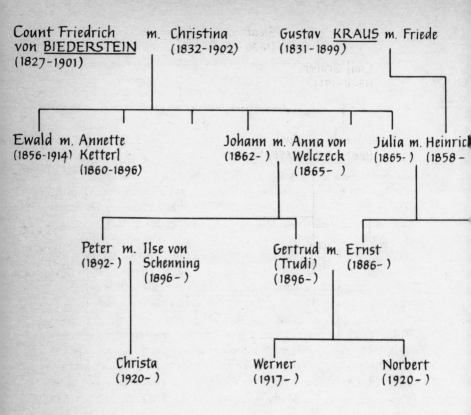

Count Friedrich von **BIEDERSTEIN** (1827-1901) m. Christina (1832-1902)

Gustav **KRAUS** (1831-1899) m. Friede

Ewald (1856-1914) m. Annette Ketterl (1860-1896)

Johann (1862-) m. Anna von Welczeck (1865-)

Júlia (1865-) m. Heinric... (1858 –

Peter (1892-) m. Ilse von Schenning (1896-)

Gertrud (Trudi) (1896-) m. Ernst (1886-)

Christa (1920-)

Werner (1917-)

Norbert (1920-)

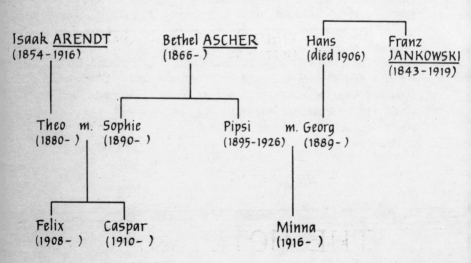

Isaak **ARENDT** (1854-1916)

Bethel **ASCHER** (1866-)

Hans (died 1906)

Franz **JANKOWSKI** (1843-1919)

Theo (1880-) m. Sophie (1890-)

Pipsi (1895-1926) m. Georg (1889-)

Felix (1908-)

Caspar (1910-)

Minna (1916-)

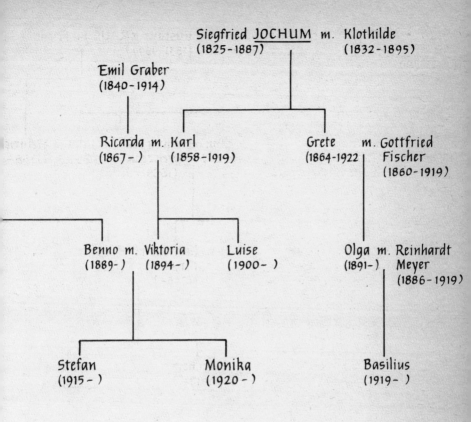

Siegfried JOCHUM m. Klothilde
(1825-1887)   (1832-1895)

Emil Graber
(1840-1914)

Ricarda m. Karl   Grete   m. Gottfried
(1867-) (1858-1919)   (1864-1922)   Fischer
                                          (1860-1919)

Benno m. Viktoria   Luise   Olga m. Reinhardt
(1889-) (1894-)   (1900-)   (1891-)   Meyer
                                               (1886-1919)

Stefan   Monika   Basilius
(1915-)   (1920-)   (1919-)

Eitel TOBISCH m. Liese Kaufmann
(1857-1910)

Otto m. Anna Feldmann
(1893-) (1891-)

·THE HOTEL QUADRIGA·

PART ONE
1871-1894

Prologue — Berlin 1894

The atmosphere inside the Hotel Quadriga was tense with expectation. None of the staff shifted from their allotted positions, but their eyes followed Karl Jochum as he pulled his heavy, old gold, fob watch from his waistcoat pocket, glanced at it thoughtfully, then strode across the fine Savonnerie carpet covering the Tuscan marble floor of the foyer towards the glass doors of the hotel entrance.

He cut a resplendent figure in his black cutaway morning coat and finely striped trousers. A substantial man in his mid-thirties, with broad shoulders and powerful thighs, his thick flaxen hair immaculately combed across his high forehead and his fair moustache impeccably curled and waxed above a wide, good-humoured mouth, he reflected both the grandeur and the elegance of his surroundings.

In his mind he was reviewing the arrangements, assuring himself that no detail, however seemingly unimportant or trivial, had been overlooked; for if any one thing went badly today, the result could spell total disaster. He forced himself not to look again at his watch, not to let his nervousness show, not to let anyone suspect that he was concerned by his visitor's late arrival.

Behind, him, Eitel Tobisch, the hotel's General Manager, was standing stiffly to attention; only his eyes betrayed his tension, as they constantly scanned his assembled troops. For over an hour now the Hall Porter had been waiting in position behind his desk, the Reception Manager and his clerks at their posts, and the pages lined up in military formation like toy soldiers. In the restaurant, Max Patschke was surveying his kingdom of unoccupied tables, flanked by his platoon of waiters. Arno Halbe, in the bar, every last glass sparkling, was in command of a corps of uniformed stewards. Overseeing his band of chefs and kitchen staff, Maurice Mesurier was poised for action in the shiny, spotlessly clean kitchen. Upstairs, the Housekeeper, in her long starched skirts, had her army of chambermaids, cleaners and laundry maids competently organized.

Standing rigidly erect on the wide flight of steps in front of the hotel, attired in the deep cobalt blue uniform that Karl's wife Ricarda had chosen as the house colours, their brass buttons gleaming in the afternoon sun and their top hats erect, two commissionaires were on watch for the important guest.

The colonnaded entrance to the hotel spanned the wide pavement of Berlin's Unter den Linden, the broad avenue of lime trees that gave the street its name. Some citizens had protested that Jochum had appropriated municipal property in extending the portico of his hotel to the kerbside, but the Emperor had waved their objections aside. Now crowds of people were waiting in the brilliant June sunshine, staring, as Karl and his two porters were doing, in the direction of the Imperial Palace. The people of Berlin loved a spectacle but, above all, they loved a sight of His Majesty, Wilhelm II, King of Prussia and Emperor of Germany.

His Majesty was scheduled to arrive at the Hotel Quadriga at four o'clock and already it was thirty minutes past, a fact not wasted upon the good-naturedly bantering crowd, who were passing the time calling out ribald comments to the immobile commissionaires and to each other.

'The Emperor's not going to come.'

'No, he's just late. HM can be late if he wants to, can't he? That's what being an Emperor is all about.'

'How would you know what Emperors can do?'

'I saw him riding in the Tiergarten the other morning. He stopped and asked me how I was.'

'Ach, that's nothing new. I was ...'

'Look at that character there in his uniform. Thinks he's a blooming general!'

'More like my old sergeant major!'

'They say you can eat anything you want at the Quadriga.'

'Did you know the baths are made of solid gold?'

'Rubbish! Nobody would waste their money on solid gold baths, not even an Austrian!'

'Jochum was born in Berlin, wasn't he?'

'Yes, but his father came from Vienna.'

'Well, your old man came from Silesia, didn't he?'

'All true Berliners come from Silesia, my friend.'

'It cost ten million marks to build this hotel ...'

'The beds alone cost two thousand marks each ...'

Their voices were drowned by loud cheers and waving handkerchiefs. 'His Majesty! The Emperor!'

Karl breathed a deep sigh of relief. If the Emperor had failed to turn up, he would never have been allowed to forget it. Word would have spread like wildfire around Berlin that Jochum's supposed friendship with the Kaiser was nothing more than a fabrication, a pack of lies. After all, what was he but the son of a Viennese sweetmaker and an ex-private in the First Brandenburg Guards? Yet, for all his humble beginnings, he was now on intimate terms with the highest aristocracy in the land and was the owner of the most luxurious hotel in Germany!

The royal carriage drew up at the kerbside and the two commissionaires moved grandly forward to open the doors to allow Their Majesties to descend. A bevy of officers, court officials and other attendants surged out of their respective coaches and gazed wonderingly at the façade of the hotel.

His broad face spread in a wide, welcoming smile, Karl approached his royal patron and took Kaiser Wilhelm's outstretched hand. Then he bent low over the Empress's glove and saluted the Court Marshal and other senior officers. Finally, with a deep bow, he said proudly, 'Your Majesty, it is my great honour to welcome you as the first guest of the Hotel Quadriga.'

Chapter One

Under the Brandenburg Gate they rode and marched in triumphant procession, that glorious morning in June 1871, rank upon rank of soldiers in full dress uniform, the finest cavalry, infantry and artillery regiments of the world. Their helmets gleamed, their plumes danced, their lances shone and their cuirasses flashed. In strict tempo, burnished black boots goose-stepped over the cobbled roadway. The hooves of horses with lustrous coats and resplendent trappings clattered on the flagstones. Drums rolled, trumpets blared and blazing torches were brandished in the air. They heralded a new era of history. They proclaimed the birth of a new country — the nation of Germany!

Karl Jochum was thirteen that summer. He stood with his parents and sister amidst thousands of other Berliners on the pavement of Unter den Linden, shouting himself hoarse with excitement, as they welcomed the victorious German armies. On and on they marched, these magnificent soldiers who had won the war against France, who had marched out as Prussians and who now returned as Germans.

Eventually, the parade was over and the delirious crowds started to disperse, but Karl stood rooted to the spot, staring up at the Brandenburg Gate and the statue of the Quadriga that rose above it — a chariot drawn by four prancing horses, driven by Viktoria, the Goddess of Victory. Sculpted by a man called Gottfried Schadow, the Quadriga had originally been created to commemorate peace between France and Prussia in 1795. Only eleven years later, however, Napoleon had captured Berlin and taken the Quadriga back with him to Paris, a shameful memory that Berliners vowed should never be repeated. So, in 1814, the Prussians soundly beat Napoleon and reclaimed the Quadriga, adding an iron cross and a Prussian eagle before she was re-erected, facing west this time towards France, to bring victory to the Prussian troops whenever they marched to war; and this time she had brought victory with a vengeance, for their triumph over the French in the recent war had been overwhelming.

A man standing beside Karl followed his gaze. 'From now on,' he prophesied, 'that gate will symbolize not Prussia, but Germany.'

Karl turned to him, his blue eyes shining. 'Yes, I am a German now.'

It was all Chancellor Bismarck's achievement. For the first thirteen years of Karl's life, there had been no Germany, merely an alliance of some 350 sovereign states, dominated by Prussia's military superiority. Now Bismarck had united them, so that the new empire reached from East Prussia to the borders of Denmark and Holland; incorporated the French provinces of Alsace and Lorraine; and swept right down to include Bavaria. In a dramatic ceremony in the Hall of Mirrors at Versailles, the King of Prussia had become Emperor of the German nation.

Reluctantly, Karl turned away from the Brandenburg Gate and joined his family slowly making their way down Unter den Linden in the wake of the troops. The memory of their resplendent uniforms lingered still before Karl's eyes, particularly the white with scarlet decorations of the First Brandenburg Guards. He turned to his father. 'Papa, I'm going to be a Guards officer, when I'm grown up.'

Sigi Jochum put his arm lightly round his son's shoulder. 'I'm sorry, son, but that won't be possible. To become a Guards officer you have to belong to the nobility and have a long military tradition in the family. I only came from Vienna just before you were born and even if you were eligible to go to Military School, I still couldn't afford to give you the kind of financial allowance you'd need. Guards officers are the elite of the country, personally chosen by the Emperor himself. No, my boy, you'll have to do your military service, but it will be as a humble private, like I was.'

Karl narrowed his eyes, then nodded, for his father's answer came as no real surprise to him. He came from lowly peasant stock, very different from the backgrounds of the aristocratic officers leading the ranks of soldiers they had just seen.

They strolled on towards the Schlossplatz, where they ran their small shop, but as they passed Café Kranzler Karl stopped for a moment to look at it. 'If I can't be an officer, I'll serve the Emperor in some other fashion. Papa, we'll make our sweet shop into the biggest and best confectionery shop in all Berlin. And then — we'll open a café.'

His father stared at him in astonishment. 'Like Kranzler?'

17

'But better, with a bigger terrace and more space.'

His mother snorted. 'And who's going to run it?'

'I will,' Karl told her seriously. 'And it's going to be such an excellent café, even the Emperor will come to dine in it.'

From the age of eight, Karl had been getting up at four in the morning to help his father bake the dark brown rye bread, the pastries and cakes that had established Sigi Jochum's reputation in Vienna and achieved it in Berlin. He now made feather-light pastry, marzipan that melted in the mouth, and creamy smooth chocolates.

'Well, you're certainly going to be a fine sweetmaker, son,' Sigi said, 'but running a café — I don't know.'

Karl smiled at him knowingly, but said no more for the moment. He had so many plans in his head, so many dreams he wanted to fulfil.

Eventually, they crossed the bridge over the River Spree and stood in front of the Imperial Castle. It was a grim, forbidding building, where the Emperor spent little time, preferring his castles outside the city at Charlottenburg and Potsdam, but it still epitomized Karl's dream.

'I'll serve in the Guards,' he vowed. 'And one day, I shall open a café where the Kaiser will come to dine.'

By the time Karl was conscripted at the age of eighteen he was as fine a patissier at his father, but had lost none of his restless ambition to do more with his life than run a small, rented sweetshop on the Schlossplatz.

Already slightly taller than Sigi, Karl was big-boned and muscular, his physique as well as his blond colouring betraying his Austrian ancestry. Even-tempered, with a shy smile, he was beginning to attract admiring glances from young girls in the street, but his awkward approaches usually attracted only rather mocking ripostes, leaving him embarrassed and tongue-tied.

To his incredulous delight, he was posted to the First Brandenburg Guards at Karlshorst, where, after his induction period, he was made batman to First Lieutenant Count Ewald von Biederstein. As soon as he met his officer, Karl realized what his father had meant by the military elite, for the Count was by far the most elegant and distinguished gentleman he had ever met.

Although he stood nearly a head shorter than Karl, Count Ewald still managed to appear to look down on him. He was dark

as Karl was fair, with beady brown eyes and a nearly curled mous-"
tache over delicate, almost feminine lips. His cultured voice
immediately impressed upon Karl that he had been brought up to
give orders in the expectation that they would be obeyed. Standing
in his officer's quarters, he described in clipped tones a batman's
duties: 'I expect my uniforms to be clean and pressed at all times,
Private, and my boots to be polished so that I can see my face in
them. Do you get that?'

Karl saluted, 'Yes, sir!', experiencing a slight feeling of disappointment. He had entered the army expecting to learn to fight,
not to be a servant.

Count Ewald stared at him searchingly, then he suddenly
grinned. 'Damn it all, Private, you'll pick up the domestic duties
quick enough. Now come and meet Elvira — she's the only thing
that *really* matters.' He marched the rather perplexed Karl out of
the room, down the stairs, and across the parade ground to a
splendid stable block. 'Know anything about horses?'

Karl shook his head. 'I'm sorry, sir.'

Count Ewald turned in his stride, gazed at him in blank amazement, then sighed. 'Do you think you can learn?'

Karl looked him straight in the eye. 'Yes, sir. If you give me
time, sir, I think I can learn anything.'

'Hummph.' The Count sounded less certain, then stopped at a
box containing a black mare with a white blaze on her forehead.
She whinnied when she saw him, lowering her head to be petted.
Karl watched carefully how his officer stroked the beast, then,
determined to prove he was not afraid, he too raised his hand and
stroked her velvety coat. Elvira stared at him unblinkingly, then
gave him an approving snort. Karl felt he had passed his first test.

Evidently Count Ewald did too, for he smiled at Karl, a smile
that extended for the first time to his eyes, which crinkled at the
corners. 'What are you in civilian life, Private?'

'A sweetmaker, sir. My father runs a confectionery shop on the
Schlossplatz.' He sensed the Count comparing his own delicate
fingers with their manicured nails to Karl's broad, rather clumsy-
looking hands. 'I actually make very good sweets,' he added hesitantly.

'A sweetmaker, eh? Well, maybe that will come in useful one
day. Who knows?'

It took Karl very little time to realize that Count Ewald von
Biederstein possessed a wealth of experience it would take him a

lifetime to accumulate. The Count enjoyed talking and found in his new batman a receptive audience. In languid tones, he confided that he had been born in 1856, which made him two years Karl's senior, and was the eldest of six children. 'The Kaiser's my godfather, of course,' he mentioned casually.

Karl tried to conceal his awe, still finding it incredible that one of Count Ewald's godlike stature should talk to him in such familiar terms. 'Where does your family live, sir?'

'Fuerstenmark, Karl.' Although Karl would never have dreamed of calling his officer anything but 'sir', Ewald now called him by his Christian name whenever they were alone. 'That's in Pomerania. Have you ever been to Pomerania, Karl?'

'No, sir. But I'm sure it's a delightful country.'

'It's good hunting and riding country, but that's about all I can say for it. Fuerstenmark Castle itself is a dank, dark hole dating back to the thirteenth century, with nobody except peasants living within twenty miles of it.'

'Has your family always lived there, sir?'

'Since it was built,' Count Ewald sighed. 'And I've no doubt they'll still be there in the twenty-sixth century. To tell you the truth, Karl, I can't stand the place, although, damn it all, it is the family seat and all that. I simply find it the most boring place on earth. No, the army's my home and I intend it always will be.'

In vain, Karl attempted to walk like Count Ewald and even to dress like him, openly imitating the First Lieutenant's mannerisms and manner of speaking, for he knew that if he wished to do business with the cream of Berlin society in his café, he must learn to behave like an aristocrat himself. His clumsy efforts did not escape the notice of the Count who did not try to conceal his amusement. 'Damn it all, Karl,' he drawled, tapping his highly-polished black boot with his swagger stick. 'It's taken generations to breed men like me. A peasant can't hope to become a gentleman overnight.'

Karl was not offended, 'I see no reason why I should not try to better myself, sir.'

The Count gazed at him critically, then a wicked twinkle appeared in his eyes. 'Damn it all, Karl, you amuse me. Let's see if we can't make a gentleman of sorts out of you, after all. It would be good sport, if nothing else.'

Under Count Ewald's excellent tutelage, Karl's education improved rapidly. Very soon he knew how to behave in the presence of aristocratic ladies, how to hand them in and out of carriages, the presents they preferred and the compliments they should be paid. He knew the few good restaurants in town, although he had never eaten in them, and the best vintages of wine and champagne, although he had sampled only the dregs left in bottles. He knew all the court scandals and all there was to learn about the Emperor, although he never met him.

Karl soon realized that his First Lieutenant enjoyed life in the army not so much for the potential glory that might be his on the battlefield, but for the victories that could be won elsewhere: on the racecourse, at duelling, and in a lady's boudoir. It was when he was asked to deliver an important note for his officer, and saw that it was addressed not to General Hofer but to his niece, that Karl had his first idea of how to turn Count Ewald's flirtations to his own advantage. On the next occasion, he asked for an evening pass and permission to add a little something that might make the Count's missive quite irresistible to the lady. 'Irresistible?' the Count drawled. 'Don't you think I already am?'

Karl merely inclined his head, then went home and made some heart-shaped, chocolate-covered cherries, which he packed into a small box. It was the Count's turn to regard Karl with respect. 'Damn it all, Karl, you're a genius,' he declared next day. 'Never seen anything like it in my life! I gave her your chocolates and she almost had her clothes off before I was inside the door! I know I said your being a sweetmaker might come in useful, but I didn't really believe it.' He gave Karl an envelope containing the princely sum of four five-mark gold pieces, more than his week's pay.

It was the beginning of a very lucrative small business. Karl used his gold marks to buy more ingredients and employed his time off, for which he now had no difficulty in obtaining a pass, in his father's kitchen, making sweets not only for his Count, but soon for other officers as well. A man in the Molkenmarkt, in the old town, made up special boxes and a nearby farmer from Karlshorst gave Karl a lift back from Berlin after market. Karl paid for his fare in Sigi's famous poppyseed cake. It was an arrangement in which everybody profited, not least Karl.

Within a year, Karl's life had settled down to an even, if busy, pace. When he was not valeting the Count or making sweets, he was taking care of various other sadly neglected areas in his learning. To the scoffing amusement of the other men in his barracks, he spent all his meagre private's pay on the purchase of books and was studiously teaching himself French, English and book-keeping.

Although the Count now admitted grudging admiration for Karl's industriousness, he could not resist trying to tempt him away from his studies. His favourite ploy was to offer him theatre tickets and the company of various attractive young ladies, most of whom seemed to be called Anna — the maids of his many mistresses. Although he was often tempted, Karl always refused, for women were a luxury he simply couldn't afford. Even if the theatre tickets were free, the maids would expect to be bought supper after the theatre and his budget did not extend to such extravagances, nor were his ambitions to be realized by dallying with ladies' maids.

'Damn it all, Karl, you're becoming a bore with your studies,' the Count grumbled one evening, after Karl had turned down tickets for *Romeo and Juliet* at the Royal Theatre. 'Why not have some fun for a change? I've never known a fellow like you — turning down an evening with a pretty filly in favour of book-keeping! Pfui, if any one of those girls stepped into *my* bed, I wouldn't turn her away, I can tell you!'

Karl was not put out. Indeed, he had a fairly shrewd idea that the Count often bedded the maid after he had satisfied her mistress. He and his officer, he reflected, quite simply had different aspirations.

Count Ewald was not one to harbour a grudge either. 'I've given my theatre tickets to Sergeant Kraus,' he grinned, the next day. 'He was delighted to do me a favour. Poor old Kraus, heir to an enormous fortune, but more than anything in the world he'd like to have a title. I suppose now he'll go round telling everyone that he and I are bosom friends. Well, if it keeps him happy and Countess Bensheim's maid out of the way for the evening, I suppose it doesn't matter!'

That evening, as Karl handed him a carefully wrapped box of chocolates before he rode off to meet the Countess, he clapped him on the shoulder. 'Better make some more tomorrow, Karl. Judging by the effect they're having on the Countess, perhaps they'll pave the way to the heart of the Princess Ida Czerevill!'

Karl saluted as his officer rode away on Elvira, his face disclosing none of his inner excitement. Karl Jochum chocolates for the Princess Ida Czerevill! His chocolates being given to a Princess! He was achieving fame beyond his wildest dreams!

Princess Ida was Polish and her husband something in the diplomatic service. She was probably forty, but Ewald did not mind. He preferred his women to have a little experience. Her maid smiled knowingly when he arrived, allowing her eyes to run appreciatively over his slim, upright figure and linger on his handsome, slightly tanned face. Then she turned with a saucy swing to her hips and led him up to her mistress's boudoir, where she stood for a moment, giggling, in the doorway.

A single oil lamp lit the boudoir. The maid pointed towards the open bedroom door, then brushed herself against Ewald. He just had time to cup her breast in his hand before she disappeared.

Princess Ida was lying naked on the bed, her black hair spread across pink lace pillows, her legs very slightly apart. Ewald walked across the room to her, his eyes clouding with desire, the blood coursing hot round his body. What a filly!

'Touch me here, darlink,' she murmured. 'Touch me here, with your dagger.'

He laid the cold steel between her legs and watched her writhe. 'I know something else I should much rather put there,' he said huskily, bending down to kiss her painted lips.

The Polish were obviously a very inventive people, as well as being indefatigable. Before the night was over, Princess Ida claimed to have had forty-nine orgasms, achieved not only in bed, but on the carpet, in the bath, over the living-room table and in the kitchen — when they went downstairs to seek refreshment. As she poured him a large glass of neat vodka, she candidly informed him that she had once come a hundred times in a single night. Ewald, already feeling weak, paled at the thought, not daring to ask how she kept count. Then she opened Karl's chocolates stating that sweets always restored her energy. At this point, Ewald was forced to beat a retreat.

'Have a chocolate before you go, darlink.'

He picked her up and carried her back to bed, where she lay glassy-eyed, staring at her reflection in the huge mirror in the ceiling. With a languid hand, she reached down and stroked herself. 'Well, if you won't help me, darlink, I shall have to help myself.'

As if by magic, the maid appeared from nowhere. Mesmerized, Ewald watched as she took off her night-dress and lay down beside her mistress. 'Next time, you like both of us?'

Ewald let himself out of the house, jumped onto Elvira and started on the long trek back to Karlshorst. The image of the two women refused to leave his mind. If he slept all day to conserve his energy, then had a good meal before he left, he could manage both of them. He thought of the Princess's full breasts and the maid's small pointed buds. Two pairs of hips — one ample and one narrow. Two triangles of hair — one dark and one blonde. He had never been to bed with two women, but his imagination was fertile enough to picture what he could do with them.

It was six o'clock when he got back to Karlshorst and, despite the fact that he hadn't slept a wink all night and was so exhausted that he nearly fell off Elvira several times, he still felt a tingling in his loins at the memory of Princess Ida and the house in the Wilhelmstrasse. He removed Elvira's saddle, gave her a quick rub down, then went up to his rooms, where he flung himself on top of the bedclothes without bothering to undress. When Karl came to wake him at seven, he opened a bleary eye and said, 'Fifty boxes of chocolates, Karl, as quickly as possible.'

'Fifty, sir?'

'Fifty, Karl. They give the Princess energy. Now, damn it all, Karl, turn out the light and let me go to sleep.'

The next day Karl was in the kitchen behind the family shop on the Schlossplatz. Smiling proudly, he stood back to admire his handiwork. On lightly greased paper were arrayed rows of delicately sculpted marzipan roses with dewdrops on their curling petals, perfumed violets, sugar-encrusted snowdrops and chocolate-covered crystallized fruit. He nodded in satisfaction.

'You're an artist, son,' Sigi Jochum declared. 'In all the years I've been making sweets, I've never produced anything as beautiful as those. You're wasting your time in the army, that's certain.'

'No, Papa, it's not wasted time. I've learned a lot — and I'm earning some money.'

'Ach, money, that isn't the most important thing in the world. You're young, Karli, you should be out enjoying yourself.'

'I'll enjoy myself later, when I've made enough money to buy the things I want,' Karl told him, wiping his hands on his apron and walking across the small room to the pile of boxes standing on the dresser. He laid them on the table and, with a pair of tongs, lifted the fragile sweetmeats into them.

Her arms deep in a bowl of hot water, Karl's mother, Klothilde, was scrubbing the sticky saucepans and dishes Karl had used. A short, wide-hipped figure in a voluminous black skirt, her grey hair knotted at the nape of her neck, she had to stand on tiptoe to reach into the sink. 'Your father's right, it's wrong for you to spend all your free time working. You should have a young lady friend, Karli, go walking with her along Unter den Linden or in the Tiergarten.'

'A lady's maid, perhaps, from one of the fine houses you visit when you deliver your sweets,' his sister suggested, looking up archly from the button she was sewing on Karl's uniform jacket. 'After all, you're quite a handsome figure now your moustache is growing.'

Karl felt a hot flush colour his cheeks. 'Haven't you sewn that button on yet, Gretchen? I'm due back at the garrison at seven, and we still have to pack these sweets into their boxes.'

Grete smiled sweetly and stabbed her finger with the needle. Blood marked the white woollen cloth. 'Now look what you've made me do!'

'Cold water,' Klothilde commanded. 'Quickly, Grete, before it stains.'

'Fifty boxes,' Sigi Jochum counted. As each box was filled with its contents of twelve sweets, he reverently put on the lids, some covered with silk, others with lace threaded through with satin ribbons, all imprinted with the legend, in discreet, Gothic lettering, *Karl Jochum.*

'All these are for Lieutenant Count Ewald,' Karl told them, his eyes glowing. 'He's going to give them to the Princess Czerevill.'

'The Princess Czerevill ...' Sigi murmured admiringly, while Klothilde glanced proudly at her son.

Only Grete remained unimpressed. 'What's so special about the Princess Czerevill?'

'But, imagine, Gretchen, Karli's chocolates are going to a Princess,' Klothilde said.

'It's only her title makes her different from us and it certainly makes her no better. All Berlin knows the Princess Czerevill is little more than a whore!'

'Gretchen!' Sigi's voice rang out across the kitchen. 'You will not talk like that!'

Karl frowned at his sister, wondering not for the first time how he and she could be so dissimilar. Grete lived in some dream world of her own, where all people were equal. She had some naïve notion that the aristocratic Junker classes should be abolished and that one day the Jochums would be the social equals of the von Biedersteins. She was an inveterate reader of French history, particularly of the French Revolution, and Clemenceau, the revolutionary mayor of Montmartre during the Paris Commune six years earlier in 1871, was her greatest hero. But how nice it would be, Karl thought, if she could for once forget her crazy political ideas and congratulate him on his good fortune. Still, Grete was Grete and one day she would learn the realities of life.

There was a knock on the door and Klothilde, with an annoyed look at her daughter, bustled across the room to open it. 'Karli, Farmer Pleiger's arrived. Grete, where's your brother's jacket?' The unrepentant Grete stood up to help Karl into his coat and Klothilde, scarcely reaching her son's shoulder, peered critically at the damp patch. 'Well, well, it will dry by the time you get back to your barracks.'

He bent down to kiss her. 'Don't worry, Mama, it will be all right. Thank you for your help.'

Grete smiled at him mischievously. 'Bye-bye, Karl, give my love to Ewald!'

Karl slapped her gently on the behind, incapable of being angry with her for long. 'You behave yourself, young lady.'

Sigi accompanied him outside, placing the boxes of sweets carefully in the empty cart, folding some sacks around them to stop them bumping about. Karl jumped up beside the farmer, then, as always, looked across the square at the Imperial Palace. Sigi followed his gaze. 'Still thinking of your café, eh, Karl?'

'When I leave the army, we'll open it, Papa. You wait and see, we'll have a restaurant where even the Kaiser will come to dine.'

Farmer Pleiger flicked his whip and his ancient mare moved slowly between the shafts, then ambled gently down the cobbled roadway. The gnarled old man sucked noisily on his evil-smelling pipe and said, 'The Kaiser, eh? The Kaiser won't eat in any restaurant, boy. He only ever eats in the castle. He won't mix with us common folk.'

On the pavement outside Haus Jochum, Sigi Jochum waited until the cart had disappeared from view. He was so proud of his young son but he also felt slightly frightened for him. Karl did not seem to understand that he was only a lowly peasant. Both he and Grete appeared to believe they could become the equals of Count Ewald von Biederstein. He felt Klothilde take his arm. 'Come on in, Sigi. There's still work to be done.'

Sigi shook his head. 'What will become of our two children, Klothilde?'

She smiled at him wisely. 'They're only young, Sigi. You wait and see, they'll get married and settle down, then they'll forget all their bright ideas.'

He looked across to the Imperial Palace. 'A café where the Kaiser will come to dine? The Jochums entertaining the Kaiser? What will the boy think of next?'

'Disgusting meal,' Gustav Kraus stated, pushing the remains of a congealing pork cutlet into cold potato purée and laying his knife and fork down on his plate. 'Berlin is supposed to be the capital of Germany, yet nowhere is there a restaurant serving anything like edible food. How does the government expect to attract foreign trade when these are the kind of facilities it offers them?' He stared contemptuously round the dining room of the Konrad Hotel, where he was staying during his brief visit to the city.

His son, Heinrich, thankfully put down his knife and fork too. Like Gustav, he was a big man with a healthy appetite. Leaning back in his chair, he knew he made an impressive figure in the distinctive white uniform of the First Brandenburg Guards, although he still found it hard to stomach the fact that not even Gustav Kraus's wealth could buy him an officer's commission. 'Even the food at the sergeants' mess at Karlshorst is better than this,' he agreed.

He studied his glass of beer fastidiously, decided it was clean and took a sip. 'Have you been down the Wilhelmstrasse recently? New houses, embassies and palaces are going up all along it. And the Arendt Bank has opened a new head office in the Behrenstrasse. Perhaps we should think of building a hotel of our own.'

Gustav studied his son shrewdly. 'You may be right, but property is something I know nothing about. I'm an engineer, boy, don't forget. And Kraus is a mining and manufacturing company. That's where we've made our money.'

Heinrich nodded, for the story of Kraus Industries was one his father never tired of telling. In his early twenties, Gustav had inherited a derelict silesian steel works through his wife. He had sacked most of the staff, and employed those remaining to make cheap cutlery. Within two years, the factory was making a profit and was renamed grandiosely 'Kraus Industries'. From then on, the company had never looked back, for Kraus had been in the right place at the right time — in a steel works during the railway age.

27

He obtained a state contract to build seamless wheels for railway engines and carriages that would not crack under high speeds. He diversified into armour plating for all kinds of vessels and vehicles, and then developed Krupp's idea of a cannon made, not of bronze, but of cast steel. In the early 1870s he was officially appointed an armourer to the German nation. With his profits, Kraus Industries acquired a vast works in the Ruhr and a chemical plant in Wedding, a small village on the outskirts of Berlin.

'Take our works in Wedding,' Gustav continued. 'I took a risk when I bought them ten years ago. A calculated risk, but still a risk, because, Heinrich, I knew nothing about chemicals. Many people thought I was mad, buying a factory making paints, dyes, glue and polish. What does old Kraus think he's going to do with that, they asked themselves. But I reckoned that it'd be more profitable to produce explosives ourselves than buy them in. And I was proved right, of course. There's nobody can beat a wily Silesian!'

Heinrich gave a thin smile. In the intervening ten years the Kraus chemicals plant had grown so large it had become a local landmark and been nicknamed Kraus Village. From miles around one could see its tall chimneys belching forth clouds of sulphurous, black smoke. Already it provided work for several hundred men.

This was not, however, the future that Heinrich envisaged for himself. He was proud of his father's achievements but refused to be limited by them. When he left the army and returned to Kraus Industries, he was determined that a lot of changes would be made. He had already made up his mind to diversify, not necessarily into the hotel business, but certainly into land and property, from which he was confident a lot of money could be made.

He also had certain other plans, in which he was determined his military service at Karlshorst should play a useful role. 'I'm pleased to say that Count Ewald von Biederstein and I are becoming close friends,' he told his father. 'We had tickets for the theatre the other evening.' He neglected to explain that he had accompanied Countess Bensheim's maid while Biederstein bedded her mistress.

'Count Ewald is godson to the Kaiser,' Gustav said thoughtfully. 'His family may own a vast estate in Pomerania but they don't have our money, Heinrich. You'd do well to keep in with the Count.'

Heinrich stared at him, amazed at his father's unexpected perspicacity. He knew that First Lieutenant Count Ewald von

Biederstein regarded him as a parvenu, a nouveau riche, a commoner of no greater importance than his orderly, Karl Jochum, or his black mare, Elvira, but he was determined that this would not always be the case. 'Count Ewald has three sisters. I have heard the first two are already promised in marriage, but the youngest, Julia, is only thirteen. It's my intention to marry her, Father.'

Before his father had chance to reply, a waiter appeared beside them, coughing nervously to attract their attention. 'Herr Konrad sends his regards, Herr Kraus, and wonders if the two gentlemen would care for a brandy after their meal. With his compliments, of course.'

Heinrich looked at the waiter's dirty white gloves with distaste. When the man turned round, he noticed his trousers were slicked with grease. He dreaded to think about the condition of the kitchens.

The waiter placed two brandies in front of them. Their contents slopped onto the tablecloth. When Heinrich picked up his glass, the liquor was stone cold. He sniffed it, then cradled it in his hands, hoping against hope to improve its aroma. He tried to imagine bringing Countess Julia von Biederstein to a place like this and shuddered.

When he had a controlling say in the management of Kraus Industries, he would investigate the hotel business, for he was certain there was a lot of money to be made that way.

On a mellow September afternoon in 1878 at the end of his second year in the Guards, Karl stood at the end of the Leipziger Strasse staring across the Potsdamer Platz. This, he was convinced, was the site for Café Jochum, for here lay the very heart of the city. Carefully, he made his way across the square to avoid being run down by the heavy traffic of horses, carriages and horse-drawn omnibuses.

He stopped in front of a building set back from the pavement, tall wrought-iron gates set in a high wall ensuring privacy for its front garden. Peering through the railings, he visualized the wall pulled down and the lawns paved over and dotted with white tables, shielded from the sun by colourful umbrellas. He imagined the sturdy front door standing wide open and a stream of people entering the indoor café-restaurant over which would stand the legend *CAFÉ JOCHUM*.

The house appeared lifeless, for its blinds were drawn, but the garden was well kept and the exterior in good repair. He wondered to whom it belonged. Most probably to a Junker landowner, who seldom visited Berlin. Dragging himself away from the gate, he looked at the adjoining building, Loewe, the city's most prestigious tobacconist, which fronted the pavement. He hesitated for a moment, then summoned up his courage and walked into the shop. At the sight of his uniform the middle-aged shop assistant stood upright, making the beginning of a salute, then, noticing Karl's private's button, relaxed. 'Can I help you, sir?'

Karl could not afford to smoke and certainly not cigars from Loewe. 'I'm afraid I don't want to buy anything but I wondered if you knew who owns the house next door? It appears empty.'

'Like our shop, it belongs to the Duke of Altweg-Pommern. The Duke is very old and it's many years since he was last in Berlin. Why, is your officer interested in the property, sir?'

Karl latched onto this excuse. 'Yes, that's right. Well, thank you for your help.'

He left the shop and, deep in thought, made his way back up the Leipziger Strasse, the Wilhelmstrasse and into Unter den Linden. Berlin was growing beyond all recognition. Everywhere, new streets were being laid out and new houses rising up. Wealthy industrialists were moving into luxurious apartments around the Tiergarten, huge mansions were being constructed on the Wilhelmstrasse, prestigious head offices for banks, newspapers and insurance companies in the Behrenstrasse and the Kochstrasse. It was a city of growth.

With a surge of frustrated impatience, he stared down the wide avenue of Unter den Linden, with the tall lime trees — now over two hundred years old — which gave the street its name. He was a child of Berlin, growing up in the city. Its future and his were inextricably interwoven. He had plans for it — but how could they be realized?

Money, that was the problem. Profitable as his business was, his income as sweetmaker to the First Brandenburg Guards was far from sufficient to buy him the property on the Potsdamer Platz, even if it were for sale. Even the sale of the lease of the shop on the Schlossplatz would make scant inroads into the capital needed to establish Café Jochum. The marks hoarded in a locked box under his bed in the Karlshorst barracks were pitifully few compared to the expense he was planning. He wanted a lot of money — and he wanted it as quickly as possible.

The officers of the First Brandenburg Guards knew none of his financial worries. They had their considerable private incomes, which they sometimes augmented by gambling. Karl strode down Unter den Linden, arguing with himself the pros and cons of gambling — at cards or on the racecourse. There were vast fortunes to be made that way, as he knew from watching Count Ewald.

There were also vast fortunes to be lost, as other officers demonstrated. He thought about First Lieutenant Eitel Tobisch and shivered. Lieutenant Tobisch's batman had told him that his officer's debts were now so high that he was soon going to be forced to resign his commission and, since his father had lost most of his fortune in the stock market crash of '73, he would be unable to bail him out.

Yes, the problems of gambling in the form of stocks and shares were even more manifold, for one was dependent upon the advice of bankers, accountants and stockbrokers, most of whom were Jews. In other words, horses, cards and stocks all contained an equal degree of risk. Karl looked around him. He needed a commodity on which to gamble to which no risk was attached. What was definitely going to increase in value?

He passed an open building site in which the foundations of a house had just been dug. Workmen hurried backwards and forwards, carrying hods of bricks. He was certainly right to be thinking of buying a property, but even better than that would be to buy land!

He turned and looked back through the Brandenburg Gate and in his mind's eye saw the fields of the Pappelallee stretching west of the city towards the villages of Steglitz and Wilmersdorf. As Berlin outgrew itself and new suburbs were created, whoever owned those fields was going to make a fortune. Karl determined that he was going to participate in the making of it.

A week or so after Private Karl Jochum had made his momentous decision about his financial future, the Amateur Chase took place on the course at Karlshorst. It was a superb day for racing, the ground not too hard, the sun shining in a cloudless blue sky. The stands were full, as the top ten thousand of Berlin society flocked to watch one of the greatest events in the racing calendar.

Clad in his white silk breeches, close-fitting boots and his scarlet and gold racing silks, First Lieutenant Eitel Tobisch emerged from the weighing-in room carrying his racing saddle. His horse, Romeo, stood patiently with the stable lad waiting to be saddled up ready for the parade ring. A four-year-old chestnut gelding, Romeo was a strongly-built horse and lifted his head proudly as the stable lad led him round the ring before the critical spectators.

Eitel's eyes skimmed the crowd: officers, many of them from the First Brandenburg, businessmen, city dignitaries, and ladies with long, sweeping dresses and broad-brimmed hats. An excited hum of voices carried across to him on the breeze. Programmes were waved. Hands pointed knowledgeably at the horses parading round the ring. How many of them, he wondered, had placed their money on himself and Romeo?

The odds had been twenty to one when his batman had placed Eitel's bet on Romeo, which meant that he stood to gain twenty thousand marks, as well as the prize money, if he won the race. It was against the rules, of course, for a jockey to bet on his own horse, but Eitel Tobisch was desperate and rules meant nothing to him any more. Anyway, his orderly had placed the bet, so there was no reason for anyone to ever discover his secret. Not even Isaak Arendt who, with great misgivings, had the previous day extended Eitel's loan by that very thousand marks in the belief that it was needed to help his sick mother.

Beads of sweat formed on Eitel's forehead and he felt his knees tremble. Well, tomorrow the Arendt Bank would be repaid, not only that thousand, but a substantial portion of his other indebtedness. He would also be able to settle his debts with his fellow officers, including the five thousand he owed Count Ewald von Biederstein from last Saturday's poker game. Yes, his future would be settled within the next twenty minutes. By this time tomorrow, First Lieutenant Eitel Tobisch could start afresh.

'Good boy, Romeo,' he said, patting his horse's mane, then he mounted and cantered down the course to the first fence, just to show Romeo what was expected of him. Then they joined the other horses and circled while their girths were tightened. Eitel glanced nervously at the other jockeys. In his opinion, there was only one other horse in the field to match Romeo and that was a roan gelding called Tsar Niklaus, a superb jumper but less fast on the flat. That was where Romeo would gain his advantage!

Tense with excitement, the horses lined up ready for the start. The roll was called, the starter's hand swept down on the lever, the tape flew up and they were off!

There were at least a dozen horses ahead of Romeo after the sixth fence, but Eitel did not force Romeo's pace, knowing the danger of exhausting his mount too early. From the corner of his eye, he could see Tsar Niklaus drawing alongside him, then pulling a little ahead.

Over the fences they soared, safely across the open ditch and the water jump. Romeo cleared the fences with effortless ease and gained a couple of lengths on Tsar Niklaus by his long stride. Then they were neck and neck again. Along the course the crowds were cheering and Eitel could dimly hear voices shouting, 'Romeo! Romeo! Romeo!' Others were screaming, 'Tsar Niklaus! Tsar Niklaus!'

The roan drew ahead of them and Eitel felt Romeo gather up his reserves of strength to catch up with him. They jumped that fence simultaneously.

The stands could now be seen again in the distance and the winning post was not far off. There were only four horses ahead of Romeo and Tsar Niklaus now and Eitel knew Romeo was in his element. He could see his way to lead the field and, Eitel, crouched, almost standing, over the horse's withers, felt as if they were flying above the ground. He flourished his whip, muttering through clenched teeth, 'Come on, boy, come on.'

It happened within fractions of a second. The four horses bunched at the fence and, just as Romeo was projecting himself into the air, Tsar Niklaus, taking fright at the confusion, collided with him, causing him to catch his leg on the brushwood. He crashed down to the ground and Eitel felt the reins pulled from his hands.

As he was hurtled earthwards, he could hear the pounding of hooves as the other horses galloped on towards the distant winning post. Instinctively, he lifted his hands to protect his head, rolling into a ball as he landed. Like a dead weight, Romeo's massive body fell across his legs. He felt a searing pain, then he lost consciousness. consciousness.

Count Ewald and Karl returned home from the racecourse in sombre mood. Tsar Niklaus and his jockey had escaped the accident relatively unhurt, but Romeo had had to be shot, while Eitel Tobisch had been brought by ambulance to the regimental infirmary where even now his crushed leg was being operated on.

'He'll have to resign his commission, of course,' Count Ewald said, leaning back in his chair and extending his legs, so that Karl could remove his boots. 'Man was a damned fool. Never occurred to me that he was playing to pay off his gambling debts. Always gave the impression that money was no problem. Damn it all, why didn't he say something? Does the regiment no good, this sort of thing. If the Kaiser gets to hear of it, there will be all hell to pay. Frankly, the man would have done better to kill himself while he was at it. As it is, he'll always walk with a limp, won't be accepted anywhere in society and will probably gamble even heavier to pay off the money he owes.'

'Perhaps he'll have learned his lesson, sir.'

'I doubt it. Once a gambler, always a gambler. Tobisch was born that way. He'll never reform.' Then he frowned. 'I hope the news hasn't reached Fuerstenmark. If my father learns Tobisch owes me five thousand he's going to be furious. He made me promise not to play poker. He'll probably stop my allowance.'

Karl put the boots outside the door, ready to take away and polish. He tried to imagine for a moment what it must be like to be Count Ewald and be able to write off five thousand marks with scarcely a second thought. Thank God, his own money was safely locked away and not lost in one dramatic gesture on something as uncertain as a horse's ability to jump a fence or a hand of cards.

Almost as if the Count were reading his thoughts, he suddenly asked Karl, 'What do you do with your money? You must have quite a tidy sum saved up by now. I suppose you're like all peasants and hoard it under the mattress.' At Karl's affirming nod, he snorted. 'Open a bank account, man, so that it earns some interest. Why not open one with the Arendt Bank? My family has banked there for several generations.'

'Surely the Arendt Bank wouldn't want to be bothered with a small account like mine?'

'Why not? Gustav Kraus was nobody when he opened his account and look at him now. Owns half Silesia, most of Essen and a substantial portion of Berlin, so far as I can see.'

'But the Arendts are financial advisers to Chancellor Bismarck himself.'

Count Ewald waved his hand expansively. 'I'll give you a personal reference. Banks aren't interested in who you are, Karl. They're just interested in making money. Financial adviser to Bismarck or not, Herr Arendt would rather have your account earning him money, than Tobisch's, which is losing it.'

Isaak Arendt's office at his family's bank's new headquarters was panelled in dark oak, on which hung portraits of Arendt ancestors. The huge oil painting of his great-grandfather took pride of place in the long conference room, which opened off Isaak's office. It depicted a rather short gentleman in a black frock coat, curls framing his very Jewish face, with cavernous eyes and a hooked nose. To look at, Isaak seemed to bear scant resemblance to the eighteenth-century Arendts. In spirit, however, he was very similar. Jakob Arendt had been a very determined man. So, too, was Isaak.

Isaak pushed Eitel Tobisch's file to one side of his desk and opened another, empty except for a letter of introduction from Count Ewald von Biederstein and wondered what old Jakob would have made of this new city of Berlin and the new generation of Arendt customers.

The old man had founded the banking house in the late eighteenth century. The son of a Cologne shoemaker, he had started a second-hand clothes business, diversified into money-lending and had eventually been appointed banker to the Prince of Rhein-Pfalz. While he remained in Germany, his three sons went to open up Arendt Banks in London, Paris and Vienna.

Jakob's grandson, Isaak's father, was responsible for trying to introduce the Arendt Bank into Russia, but in St Petersburg he came up against the powerful German banking family of Stieglitz. Stieglitz wanted no competition in a country where they held a virtually monopolistic position. A few words whispered in the right ears, some palms suitably greased, and the potential usurpers of Stieglitz power were cast out of Russia. The Arendt Bank was not the only one to suffer. The great Rothschild banking dynasty was also refused permission to open an office. They were all told that it was forbidden for Jews to run a business in Russia employing more than five clerks and that it was illegal for a Jew to take up permanent residence either in St Petersburg or Moscow.

With hatred in his heart, Isaak's father returned to the Rhineland, an area that had always been more tolerant of the Jews than anywhere else in Germany, and passed on to his son his account of his treatment at the hand of the Tsar. In London, his cousin conferred with Baron Lionel Nathan de Rothschild, who offered Lord Halifax one million pounds, interest free, to support British troops against the Tsar in the Crimean War.

It was one of the many stories upon which Isaak had been

weaned. When he married, as he shortly hoped to, and had children of his own, they too would learn of the perfidy of the Tsar. They would learn about the endless persecution of the Jews in Russia, the pogroms and the slaughter of innocent men. Like Isaak, they would be taught never to forget. Not they, nor their children, nor their children's children.

A knock on the door aroused Isaak from his reverie. This was not Russia, nor even Cologne. This was Berlin in 1878, a metropolis of ambition and activity, a city where new fortunes were to be made. No longer did the Arendts have to struggle to achieve modest wealth but were now in a position to help others. Who knew what other enterprising young men were even now working to leave small, cramped quarters to build up vast international businesses?

'Come in,' Isaak Arendt called. He glanced down again at Eitel Tobisch's file, then pushed it into a drawer. There was no fortune forthcoming from Tobisch. Not only had his leg been broken in the Karlshorst Chase, but his name was disgraced and he had been forced to resign his commission.

'Private Karl Jochum is here,' a clerk announced.

'Please show him in,' said Isaak Arendt.

Karl followed the clerk nervously into Isaak Arendt's office, for he had expected to be interviewed at the tellers' counters in the main hall of the bank, not in this prestigious first-floor suite. The banker came round from behind his desk, smiling confidently, extending his hand to Karl, then motioned him to take a seat. Karl did as he was bid, glancing apprehensively at the sombre portraits of swarthy Jewish gentlemen, presumably Arendt forebears, hanging on the panelled walls, fulfilling the conventional image of Jewish moneylenders.

Other than serving Jewish customers in his father's shop, Karl had little experience of Jews, for none were permitted in the army. Everyone had blamed the stock market crash of '73 on Jewish greed, but since the Jochums' entire investment was in their shop and they had no stocks or shares with which to speculate, the vagaries of the financial world had left them unscathed. Indeed, if anything, they had profited, for in the ensuing recession, people had seemed to eat more sweets than ever.

Karl was, therefore, slightly but not unduly prejudiced against Jews and felt intimidated by, rather than resentful of, the Jew sitting before him. Isaak Arendt looked only a few years older than himself, though very different in appearance, being as dark and slim as Karl was blond and broad. His black hair, moustache and beard were neatly trimmed in the German fashion and his elegant suit had evidently been made by the Court tailors. Karl shifted uneasily in his standard-size private's uniform, feeling a discomfort he seldom experienced even in the presence of Count Ewald.

'Well, Private Jochum, and how can I help you?'

'Count Ewald von Biederstein recommended that I open a savings account with your bank.'

'We should be delighted to welcome you as a customer, Private Jochum. Now, if you would kindly give me some information about yourself.'

Karl watched the banker write down, in a slanting spidery hand, his personal details. He told him how his father had moved from Vienna to Berlin in the early 1850s, about the shop on the Schloss-platz and his own military service. The arrangements for the savings account were finalized, the sum to be deposited handed over, and, after Karl had given two specimen signatures, the banker leaned back in his chair. 'That seems very satisfactory, Private Jochum. Do you intend to remain with the First Branden-burg Guards?'

Karl shook his head, fingering the small button in his collar. 'No, Herr Bankdirektor. Rewarding though I find it to be serving His Majesty the Kaiser and First Lieutenant Count Ewald von Biederstein, I shall leave the army when my three years are up. That will be in about a year's time.'

'You'll be helping your father, in his shop?'

There was an encouraging smile on Isaak Arendt's face. Karl bit his lip. It seemed premature to divulge his grandiose plans, yet, when the moment came to fulfil them, he was going to need this man's assistance. He made a swift, intuitive decision. 'For a short while, Herr Bankdirektor, but I don't intend to remain a shopkeeper for the rest of my life. My ambition is to open a café-restaurant.'

'At your premises on the Schlossplatz?'

'They are only leased and very small, Herr Bankdirektor. I intend to buy the freehold of a very much larger property, with a terrace and a large dining hall.'

'Have you already identified a site?'

Karl smiled ruefully. 'There's a house on the Potsdamer Platz that would be ideal. It belongs to the Duke of Altweg-Pommern and it isn't even for sale. But that's where Café Jochum should stand.' He paused and added, 'If I could afford it.'

'Come and see me again, Private Jochum, when you leave the Guards. Banks don't just take deposits. They lend money too — for the right venture. It could well be that Café Jochum will be one of those.'

'It's going to be a very fine café,' Karl blurted out. 'I know exactly how it will look and precisely the clientele I want to welcome there. I can assure you already, Herr Bankdirektor, that it will be the best café-restaurant in Berlin. One day, the Emperor himself will dine there.'

Isaak Arendt stood up. 'It's been a pleasure meeting you, Private Jochum.' He pointed to the full-length portrait of an old man with side curls and a flowing white beard. 'That was my great-grandfather, Jakob Arendt, who founded this bank. He started from a small, dirty room in Cologne. His grandson, my father, is now financial adviser to Chancellor Prince Otto von Bismarck. If you are prepared to work for them, Private Jochum, your dreams can come true. There is absolutely no reason why you should not own a café at which the Emperor comes to dine. If you have faith in yourself, others will believe in you also.' He held out his hand. 'I hope that I, too, shall be present when the occasion occurs.'

Karl grasped the outstretched hand. 'I shall make certain that you are,' he promised.

Karl's military career reached its peak in the early summer of 1879, when the Emperor himself announced his intention of visiting Karlshorst with his grandson, Wilhelm, to inspect the troops at the passing-out parade. For weeks in advance of this royal visit, the entire garrison was in a state of uproar as officers and ranks prepared to be reviewed by the 'Supreme War Leader'.

In order to witness this great event, Count Ewald's family advised that they would make one of their rare journeys to Berlin from Fuerstenmark. Ewald greeted this news with something less than joy. 'Damned nuisance,' he expostulated, taking a cigar from the cedar-lined humidor on the sideboard, while Karl cleared up after the previous evening's poker game. 'My mother always fusses around me as if I were still in napkins and my father expects me to account for every penny I've spent. Arrangements will have to be made for reunions of family and friends, including a number of very suitable young women, one of whom I shall be expected to marry.'

'Would you not like to marry, sir?'

Ewald blew a cloud of blue smoke into the air. 'What's the point when I'm having so much fun being single? Father's worried about an heir, of course, but in my opinion, there's time for that. A wife, whoever she is, is an encumbrance, while childen are a drain on the emotions. No, with five brothers and sisters, I've seen enough of family life to know it's not for me. What do you think? I suppose you'd like to get married and breed. Peasants always do.'

Karl had grown used to his officer teasing him about his lowly birth. 'One day I hope to get married, sir, but I doubt it will be soon. I don't anticipate having much time for women in the immediate future.'

The Count leaned back in his chair, one elegant leg crossed over the other. 'You amuse me, Karl. When are you going to learn that women are the only things in life worth finding time for? Damn it all, what else is there other than women and horses?'

'Perhaps our different circumstances lead us to have different aspirations?' Karl suggested hesitantly. 'In your position, sir, you can do almost anything you want, whereas I shall always have to struggle to achieve my ambitions.'

The expression on Ewald's face became serious for once. 'Nothing I've ever really wanted to do that much, other than bed as many women as possible, keep a stable of thoroughbreds and possibly have one good skirmish with the French. Doubt if I'm even going to see that now, after Bismarck's peace congress. Imagine — over eight hundred diplomats, military attachés and officers from virtually every European country meeting in Prussia of all places, to settle a dispute. In the olden days, we'd have gone out and fought with swords and cannon. Now, we fight with words!'

Personally, Karl was relieved that the unrest in the Balkans had been settled peaceably, for a war would have interfered greatly with his plans. However, he had been long enough in the army to realize that to young officers like the Count, war meant both excitement and the chance of promotion. It could take five years for a first lieutenant to attain his lieutenancy in a peacetime army and another long six for his captaincy. 'Prussia has a reputation for being warlike. Perhaps it's not a bad thing for us to demonstrate that we can also live in peace with our neighbours.'

'Getting quite a philosopher, eh, Karl?' The Count tapped the ash from his cigar onto the carpet. 'You'd get on well with my youngest sister, Julia. She always says things that she hopes will comfort me.' Then he smiled. 'Mind you, she spends the rest of her time arguing with everyone else! Well, that's one thing to look forward to, at least, seeing Julia again. Bright little spark!'

As Karl stood at attention on the parade ground the following day he momentarily forgot all about the von Biedersteins and even about his café. Like the hundreds of other soldiers lined up beside him, he was aware of only two people — the Emperor and his grandson in full dress uniforms sitting on horseback and facing the parade. When Karl's division marched past in the distinctive drill step of the Prussian Guards, eyes right to acknowledge their Supreme Leader, Karl felt that he would burst with pride.

He quickly came down to earth again when he stood at the door of the Count's quarters that afternoon as the von Biederstein family swept regally past him. By far the most formidable was Ewald's mother, the Countess Christina. A portly lady, with voluminous flowing skirts, she peered critically at the room and its contents through her lorgnette, carefully dusting the seat of her chair before she sat down. Her husband, Count Friedrich, was also stout, with bushy red whiskers and a weather-beaten face from the winds that swept across his estate.

They had brought three of their children with them: Hannelore, Johann and Julia. Hannelore appeared to be a mirror image of her mother, and was, Karl knew, promised in marriage to a Duke of Saxe-Cobourg, an excellent match in her mother's eyes, for he was distantly related to Prince Albert, Consort of Queen Victoria of England. Johann favoured his father and was much more to Karl's liking. Karl knew from his officer that Johann hoped, one day, to take over the management of Fuerstenmark. 'He's welcome to it as far as I'm concerned,' Ewald had once commented. 'Who wants to live at Fuerstenmark? So long as I get my income from it, he can have it.'

Only one member of the family seemed to have anything in common with Ewald and that was Julia. She was only thirteen but it was impossible to ignore her bouncing curls, her vivacious features and dancing brown eyes. Karl took one look at her and lost his heart. She alone smiled at him and acknowledged his presence, thanking him when he took her coat, pulled out her chair and offered her something to eat and drink.

To begin with, the conversation, very naturally, turned on the Emperor and the parade. Count Friedrich demanded details of the officers who were passing out that day. The Countess intensified her search of her son's quarters for signs of a profligate existence. Hannelore sat silently, while Johann fiddled with the buttons on his jacket. Julia devoured her sandwiches with a most unladylike haste, then cried, 'Oh, Ewald, please persuade Mama that I should attend the ball this evening!'

Ewald smiled at her affectionately. 'Julia, my dear, you know it's an impossibility. You'll have to be patient. After you've made your debut, like Hannelore, you can attend garrison balls.'

Countess Christina ignored them both. 'The Countess Waldheim is going to be present at the ball this evening, Ewald. You have apparently made a very favourable impression upon her and Rosalinde.'

'It would be an excellent match,' Count Friedrich stated. 'Rosalinde's dowry will be quite considerable and the Waldheim estate is only fifty miles from Fuerstenmark. The Count's stables are renowned.'

'Rosalinde has a wart on her nose and thick ankles,' Ewald retorted.

'Ewald!' His mother sat upright in her chair, her nostrils quivering. 'You are not required to make personal remarks.'

'Mama, you are talking about a very personal aspect of my life. In the first place, I don't want to marry, and in the second, I shall not marry an ugly woman.'

Julia's eyes twinkled and she looked expectantly at her mother. Count Friedrich snorted and the two older children shifted uncomfortably in their seats. Karl took a deep breath and for the first time, the Countess showed her awareness of his presence. 'This is not a subject to discuss in front of the servants,' she said coldly.

Even Karl was given the evening off, not to attend the officers' ball, of course, but to attend festivities in his own mess. It was a quite splendid occasion, with unlimited beer and no guard duty. For once he gave himself over totally to pleasure and did not think once about his studies, business or the Count.

Judging by the groans around him, he was not the only private to wake the next morning feeling as if he were at death's door. His head throbbed, his limbs ached and his tongue felt thick and swollen. Sitting up in bed was a most unpleasant sensation. Getting

41

out of it was even worse. He pulled on his uniform and tottered weakly out to the latrines, then put his head under a cold tap. He shouldn't have had that last stein of beer at two o'clock in the morning. That really had been a mistake.

Bleary-eyed, he made his way across the courtyard, wondering how the Count was feeling. Did champagne cause as bad a hangover as beer? Ewald always claimed not. Well, he would soon see for himself.

The first objects that met Karl's eyes in the officers' quarters were trunks belonging to newly-commissioned officers standing outside their doors, ready to be taken to the railway station later that morning, as their owners were posted to garrisons at Danzig, Stuttgart, Munich or Breslau, or even to the War Academy to train for a position on the General Staff. Orderlies, evidently feeling as fragile as himself, arranged their officers' belongings in silence, grimacing at any noise.

He let himself into the Count's room, fetched hot water and prepared his officer's shaving equipment — cut-throat razor, strop and dry towels — then, knocking gently, he opened the bedroom door. What he saw gave him the shock of his life. Snaking across the floor was a pair of silk stockings. White petticoats and lady's undergarments had been flung over a chair. The Count's dress uniform, his sword and even his shako with its flowing plumes, instead of hanging neatly, lay in an untidy heap beside the wardrobe. But, by far the worst, in the single bed, the sheet scarcely covering their naked bodies, lay two people: one, Ewald himself, and the other, a red-haired girl. Stupefied, Karl stood for a moment, open-mouthed, his throbbing head forgotten, gazing at the first nude woman he had ever seen. She had loosened her hair, so that it spread across the pillow. Full-breasted, she lay close to the Count, one arm flung across his hairy chest. Their legs were intertwined. Both were sound asleep.

Then, with horror, Karl realized the immensity of his officer's crime. The Count might be heir to the von Biederstein estate and godson to the Kaiser himself, but neither of these social qualifications would stop him being court-martialled and probably cashiered if he were discovered to have spent the night with a woman in his rooms. And now that he studied the face of the lady herself, she too was familiar to him, as the sister of one of Ewald's fellow officers.

He put the pitcher of water and shaving equipment down on the marble-topped dresser. If she were seen, her reputation would be ruined, and possibly her brother, too, would be forced to resign his commission. Karl turned the key in the bedroom door, then strode across to the bed. 'Sir, Lieutenant, wake up, sir!'

Count Ewald groaned and, without opening his eyes, grunted, 'Karl, go away. I'm asleep.'

The young woman woke with a start, gazing at Karl in panic. She snatched at the sheet, pulling it round her neck. 'What are you doing here?' Then she stared at the unfamiliar room and Karl watched as realization of her terrible situation dawned on her. 'What's the time?' she whispered.

'It's nearly eight, my lady.'

'Oh, do be quiet,' Ewald groaned.

The woman grasped him by the shoulders, shaking him. 'Ewald, Ewald! It's eight o'clock. I must go home. I'm going to be in the most terrible trouble. If my parents discover that I'm missing, they'll call the police.' She looked appealingly at Karl. 'What am I going to do?'

'If you'll permit me to suggest it, I think the first thing you should do is get dressed, my lady,' Karl said, and let himself out of the room.

Waiting for the couple to dress, Karl racked his brains for a means of getting Ewald's visitor out of the garrison unnoticed. In his desperation, he even helped himself to one of the Count's cigars to aid his thoughts, but quickly stubbed it out at the nauseous feeling it aroused in his stomach. It was impossible to think of her simply walking out, for the guards would immediately spot her. Perhaps if she dressed up as a man, as a private like himself? If there were not too many people about, she might pass unnoticed.

Cautiously, Karl opened the door. There was only one person in sight, but that one could not have been worse, for it was Sergeant Kraus. If anyone would spot a stranger, Kraus certainly would.

Almost as if he had been waiting for him, Kraus approached Karl, smiling with unusual affability. Karl stared at him. The man's small eyes were clear behind his glasses, showing no sign of a hangover, but, of course, Kraus considered himself above the other non-commissioned officers, so he was hardly likely to have spent the night drinking in the sergeants' mess. He had probably been the only man in Karlshorst to go to bed at ten and get a sound night's sleep. 'Good morning, Private Jochum. Is something the matter?'

43

Karl's eyes rounded in horror. Was it possible the man already knew their secret? Why else should he be prowling in this particular corridor on this particular morning? Forcing himself to appear calm, he replied, 'No, Sergeant, nothing is the matter. Can I help you, sir?'

'I happened to be passing and I wondered if the Count's family were well. I believe they are in Berlin?'

The man's gone mad, Karl thought. At a time like this, he asks about the Count's family? But he replied, 'Yes, sir, they appeared very well when they were here yesterday.' Now run away and leave me alone, he thought.

'And was the Countess Julia present?' Kraus persisted.

What on earth? There's a naked woman in the bedroom and he asks about Countess Julia? What possible interest could he have in her? 'Yes, she was here,' he replied shortly.

'They're staying in the Wilhelmstrasse, I believe?'

It was then that Karl received his inspiration. Looking past the sergeant's bulky figure, his eyes lit once again upon the trunks waiting to be taken to the station. Trunks large enough to carry a human body. Trunks large enough to convey a lady who needed to be smuggled out. 'That's right, they're staying in the Wilhelmstrasse. I'm just getting some of First Lieutenant Count Ewald's belongings together, so that they can travel back with them to Fuerstenmark.'

'If I can be of any assistance,' Sergeant Kraus said ingratiatingly.

'Actually, Sergeant, I should be most grateful if you could help me carry the trunk downstairs to the cart.'

Five minutes later, the two men were staggering down the stairs and across the courtyard to the gate, where a loaded cart was already waiting to leave for the station. Perspiration was pouring down Heinrich Kraus's red face and even Karl, strong though he was, felt weak. 'What on earth's in there?' Kraus stuttered.

'A body,' Karl replied, feeling very much better now that the lady had almost left the garrison.

Kraus gave a thin smile and left hurriedly.

'Where's this one for?' the driver asked.

'To be taken into Berlin.'

'I haven't got no orders to take trunks into the city,' the driver grumbled. Karl reached into his pocket and slipped a gold five-mark piece into his hand. The driver's expression brightened. 'Where do you want it delivered, sir?' Karl whispered a few words

44

in his ear and he grinned. 'Makes no difference to me, sir. Just hope there aren't too many people around in the Tiergarten to witness a lady escaping from a trunk.'

'Pretend you're a magician practising your vaudeville act,' Karl suggested, giving him another gold coin.

'Your officer doesn't make a habit of this sort of thing, does he?' the driver mused. 'Much more profitable business than carting luggage to the station.'

Karl frowned. 'We're relying on your discretion. This is a serious matter. People's lives are at stake.'

The driver shrugged, climbed onto his seat, unhitched the reins and switched his whip around his horse's rump. 'Gee up!'

The guards on the gate ignored another cartload of luggage leaving the garrison. Karl watched until the lumbering vehicle with its human cargo was out of sight, then went slowly back to his officer's room. He didn't envy the lady her journey, and he doubted that she would ever be tempted to spend another night in an officer's rooms.

A white-faced Ewald was waiting for him on his return. 'Has she gone?'

Karl nodded. Now that the drama was over, his head throbbed dreadfully again and he was starting to feel very unwell.

'How did you manage to get that trunk downstairs, Karl?'

'Sergeant Kraus very kindly helped me, sir.'

'Kraus? Well, that was kind of him, I suppose. Most unexpected ... And you saw the cart leave?'

'Yes, sir.'

'Karl, if ever I can render you any service in return for what you've done for me this morning, you know you have only to ask.' The Count sank wearily down on a chair. 'God, what a fool I was. If anyone else had discovered that wretched woman had spent the night in my room, my career would have been over, my father would have disowned me and I'd be like old Tobisch, trying to make my living in the cardrooms of some terrible hotel in Baden-Baden.'

'I'm glad I was able to be of service, sir. And now, if you'll excuse me, I must go and get a breath of fresh air. I don't feel at all well.'

At the end of September that year, Karl polished his officer's boots for the last time. He restocked the mahogany humidor. He bade

45

his farewells to the black mare, Elvira. In his barracks, his suitcase was packed, his bunk ready to be occupied by a new recruit. His three years in the First Brandenburg Guards were over. Until the age of forty-five, he would be expected to serve two weeks every September in the Reserves, but to all extents and purposes, unless war broke out, his military life was ended.

Dressed in his civilian clothes, he stood at the door of Count Ewald's quarters and saluted. 'I've come to say goodbye, sir.'

He felt very real regret at the parting. He had entered the army as a raw recruit, a peasant with boorish manners and knowing no social graces. Now, in everything but his rank, he moved, spoke and even thought like an officer. There was a clipped preciseness to his gait, as there was to his features. His full moustache was neatly waxed and curled. His blue eyes gazed steadfastly upon the world, subject to few of the embarrassments he had known three years ealier. With Count Ewald, he had learned to show deference, but not servility. Thanks to his mentor, Karl Jochum had become a man.

The Count frowned. 'Damn it all, Karl, I'm sorry to see you go. It won't be the same, somehow, without you.'

'I trust we'll meet again.'

'Meet again? Of course we will! I shall visit you at this café of yours. That's what the city needs, a decent restaurant where officers can dine in comfort. I can see it now, Karl, with velvet hangings, crystal chandeliers and an orchestra playing in the corner. Oh, and Karl, have a few private dining rooms, won't you?'

Karl smiled, for it was a feature he had already considered, recognizing the need for gentlemen like Count Ewald to have somewhere to dine with their lady friends away from the public gaze. 'Yes, sir.'

'Do you really intend to open this café, Karl?'

'Certainly, sir. First of all, I must increase the business of my father's shop, but then I shall open my café.'

The Count walked across to his writing bureau, pulling open a small drawer and extracting an envelope. 'I'm very grateful to you, Karl, for everything you've done for me. I hope you'll accept this small gift as a token of my estimation.'

Karl obstinately shook his head. 'It's been a pleasure serving you, sir. I don't want any presents.'

'It's only a cheque. Damn it all, man, if it hadn't been for you, I might have been cashiered.'

'I'm glad I was able to be of service, sir, but your thanks are all I require.'

The two men stared at each other for a moment, then the Count threw the envelope down on the table. 'Karl,' he cried, slapping him on the back, 'you really are a rather splendid fellow, despite the fact that you're a peasant! Well, if you won't accept my money, will you at least allow me to help you in other ways, like recommending Haus Jochum to new officers here at Karlshorst?'

'Your patronage is the greatest gift you could offer me, Count Ewald, sir.'

'And isn't it about time you stopped calling me Count? You're no longer in my service, damn it all. You're my friend! My name is Ewald, Karl!' He extended his hand to Karl, who shook it warmly.

Chapter Two

Karl's determination to make his mark on Berlin did not falter when he returned to his parents' small shop on the Schlossplatz, even though he found the transition from army to civilian life harder than he had imagined. He missed the discipline, the manoeuvres, but, most of all, the camaraderie of men — especially First Lieutenant Count Ewald.

Nothing, he soon realized, had changed at home, except that his father had grown older and more set in his ways, while Grete was a more convinced socialist than ever. His mother, always neat, always spotlessly clean, but just a little plumper, still kept their flat near the Rosenthaler Platz, serving every morning in the shop, while Sigi baked or made deliveries.

The goods sold in the shop had not changed either, still the same bread, pastries, cakes and tarts that Sigi had always made, which were, he declared, what his customers wanted. And they were the same old customers, Karl thought despondently — simple housewives like Klothilde, who complained if prices went up and counted every pfennig in their change. There was a comfortable living, but no fortune, to be made from them.

So, while Sigi baked dark rye bread and apple tarts, Karl continued to make his delicately packaged sweets, delivering them personally to Karlshorst every week. The officers of his old regiment were all men from influential families, the sons of generals and cabinet ministers, landowners and archbishops. These were the men with whom it was essential he remained in contact, for these were the kind of people he eventually wanted to attract to Café Jochum.

Gradually, word spread round Berlin and soon elegant carriages were stopping outside the shop on the Schlossplatz and distinguished ladies, accompanied by their maids, were descending to buy Karl Jochum's chocolates. Unlike ordinary housewives, they were not worried about price. Wealthy industrialists purchased boxes for their mistresses. City dignitaries called in to buy sweets for maiden aunts. Haus Jochum was becoming fashionable.

For Karl, they were headstrong and satisfying days. Up at four in the morning and seldom in bed before ten at night, his youth and animal energy carried him forward, positive that his family was behind him. At long last, he felt he was nearing his goal.

Then, in 1882, three years after he had left the army, two events occurred which convinced him that all his dreams could come true. The first was that the Duke of Altweg-Pommern died and his house on the Potsdamer Platz came up for sale. The second was an announcement in the newspaper that set his blood racing even faster. 'That's the opportunity for which I've been waiting!'

It was nine o'clock in the evening and the Jochums were sitting round the tiled stove in the living room of their small apartment. Grete was immersed in a sentimental novel by Hedwig Courths-Mahler, Klothilde was knitting, and Sigi, who, like Karl, had been up since four, was nodding over his accounts books. The turnover of Haus Jochum had increased dramatically since Karl's return — but so had the paperwork. At fifty-seven, Sigi Jochum should have been looking forward to his retirement, instead of which he was working harder than ever before in his life. He looked wearily towards his son. 'What is it now?'

'Chancellor Bismarck intends to create Berlin's equivalent of the Champs Elysées, an avenue called the Kurfuerstendamm, fifty yards wide and over two miles long, along which fashionable houses, apartment blocks, shops and cafés will be erected and purchasers are invited for shares in the Kurfuerstendamm Company.'

Klothilde glanced up from her knitting. 'I've never heard of the Kurfuerstendamm. Where is it?'

'It doesn't exist yet, Mama,' Karl cried, pacing up and down the room. 'It's going to be where the Pappelallee is now. You know the lane that runs from the Tiergarten out to the villages of Steglitz, Wilmersdorf and Charlottenburg? Well, that's going to be the Kurfuerstendamm! The Cabinet has apparently approved an order that it be built and now the land alongside it is for sale at ten pfennigs a square metre!'

Sigi gave an exasperated grunt add returned to his ledgers. 'Steglitz, Wilmersdorf, Charlottenburg! They're all miles away. Who's going to want to go there, Karl?'

'Before very long, Berliners will be living there, Papa. They won't be separate villages any longer, they'll be suburbs of Berlin.

The time will come when it won't be possible to build upwards any more and the city will grow out, towards the west. Shares equivalent to ten pfennigs a square metre! They'll be worth a fortune!'

'Listen, son, you've worked hard for your money. Don't gamble it away. You don't know what the price of that land will do. The Kaiser's old and must die soon. His son is a sickly fellow. People are already grumbling about the fact that Bismarck seems to be running the country. He could lose office and his Kurfuerstendamm Company be dissolved. Don't be over-ambitious, Karli.'

'I'm not being over-ambitious, Papa, I just know that Bismarck is right. I looked at the meadows along the Pappelallee a long time ago and knew that there was a fortune to be made for whoever owned them. Now, I'm going to back my own judgement.'

Without removing her eyes from her book, Grete asked, 'I thought you wanted to buy a building so that you could open a café, Karli?'

Her brother stopped in mid-stride and surveyed his family. 'I'm going to do both. I'm going to put in an offer for a property on the Potsdamer Platz and I'm going to buy shares in the Kurfuerstendamm Company!'

Sigi shut his ledgers with an irritated bang. 'And where do you think you're going to find the money?'

'I shall go to see Herr Arendt. I'm sure he will help me.'

Sigi rubbed his head wearily across his forehead. 'I'm sure he'll think you're crazy, but if it makes you happy, go and see him.'

Karl was not the only person to be excited by the news of Bismarck's Kurfuerstendamm Company, nor the only one interested in the demise of the Duke of Altweg-Pommern. As soon as Heinrich Kraus, now in charge of Kraus Chemie in Wedding, heard the news, he wrote to his father asking if he would come to Berlin.

Once again, they dined in the Konrad Hotel, where Heinrich had a room. Nothing had changed in the hotel in the intervening five years. The rooms were still small and dingy. There was still only one bathroom to each floor. The food in the restaurant was still unimaginative. The waiters' clothes were still slicked with grease.

But on this occasion, neither man was concerned with such trivialities. Earlier that day they had visited the properties on the Potsdamer Platz and studied at length the Chancellor's plans for the proposed Kurfuerstendamm.

Pushing aside his bowl of congealing pea soup, Gustav

muttered, 'I'm not sure, son. What do we want with a house and a tobacconist shop?'

Heinrich stifled a sigh. 'We'll have nothing to do with either the house or the shop. We'll continue to lease the shop to Herr Loewe and find a new lessee for the house. All we shall be are landlords, receiving rent.'

'And this Kurfuerstendamm Company? What makes you so certain people will want to buy land that far out of Berlin?'

'Berlin is growing. When they can't build upwards any more, they'll build out to the west.'

Gustav Kraus nodded doubtfully. 'You've made an appointment with Herr Arendt to discuss this?'

The waiter took away their soup plates and thumped two plates of meat and potatoes down in front of them. Heinrich grimaced. 'We're seeing him at ten o'clock tomorrow morning.'

'Well, let's see what he has to say. But if we do go ahead with this scheme of yours, then it must be your responsibility, mind. You're responsible for any losses as well as any profits.'

Behind his thick spectacle lenses, Heinrich's eyes glittered. He was making the first step towards transforming Kraus Industries into the company he wanted it to become.

Karl arrived early at the bank for his appointment with Isaak Arendt. The banker's male secretary told him to take a seat, gave him a newspaper to read and offered him a cup of coffee, both of which Karl refused, nervously clutching the attaché case containing the pages of figures on which he had been working night after night in preparation for today's meeting.

The door to Isaak Arendt's office opened and Karl heard the banker say, 'Gentlemen, I look forward to seeing you again.' Two men emerged, one of whom Karl immediately recognized as Heinrich Kraus. He stood up, exclaiming, 'Herr Kraus!' and extending his hand in greeting.

Both men stared at him blankly, then Heinrich's eyes showed a flicker of surprised recognition. 'Jochum,' he said, ignoring Karl's outstretched hand. 'Didn't know you banked at Arendt!' As the secretary led them away, Karl heard him explaining to his father, 'Jochum was batman to Count Ewald von Biederstein.'

'Herr Jochum, please come in,' Isaak Arendt invited smilingly then, when they were both seated, he asked, 'You and Heinrich Kraus served in the same regiment?'

Still smarting a little from his rebuff, Karl nodded.

'An interesting young man,' the banker commented. 'I shall be intrigued to see what he does with his life.' From his tone, it was impossible to tell whether he liked Heinrich Kraus or not. Then he emerged from his brief reverie and said, 'Well, Herr Jochum, I'm sure you have other things on your mind than Herr Kraus. How can I help you?'

Karl opened his attaché case and extracted his papers, trying to appear casually confident, but unable to ignore the pounding of his heart. 'I have two projects that I'd like to discuss with you.'

'Let me guess, Herr Jochum! You've decided to open your café and you've found a suitable property to rent?'

'I've found a suitable property to buy.'

'If the price is right, why not?' He opened the file on his desk. 'Your account stands at two thousand marks. What property do you have in mind?'

'A house on the Potsdamer Platz, next door to Loewe,' Karl told him, hoping his inner nervousness was not revealed in his voice.

'The same one you mentioned at our first meeting? So you haven't changed your mind, Herr Jochum? And your second project?'

'I should like to buy shares in the Kurfuerstendamm Company.'

Isaak Arendt picked up a newspaper cutting announcing the sale of the shares and fingered it pensively. 'The Kurfuerstendamm Company certainly seems to be generating a lot of public interest. Tell me, Herr Jochum, have you discussed your plans with your father?'

Karl hesitated, then admitted, 'Yes, I have, and he's worried about them. He says I would do better to use my savings to buy the lease on the Potsdamer Platz building, not worry about the freehold, and certainly not gamble with the Kurfuerstendamm Company.'

'And why don't you? It would certainly seem the most cautious approach to starting up a new business.'

For a moment, Karl was tempted to concede, then he pulled himself together. He had not slaved day and night to relinquish his dreams without any fight. 'I believe that the most valuable commodity for the next few decades is going to be land. Not just the fields along the Pappelallee, but even the forest at Grunewald and the land around the villages of Dahlem and Steglitz.' He glanced at the banker, but the man's expression betrayed none of his thoughts.

'Café Jochum will be the starting point of my restaurant business and I'm certain it will be profitable, but it can't compete with the return I could make on owning shares in the Kurfuerstendamm Company.' Still Isaak Arendt said nothing, so he floundered on. 'I'm not a financier, Herr Arendt, I'm a sweetmaker, but I'm not going to remain a sweetmaker all my life. And in order to build the businessI want, I need money.'

Isaak Arendt's gaze remained inscrutable. 'And how much money do you think you need to borrow to buy the lease on the Potsdamer Platz property?'

Karl handed him the sheets of paper covered with columns of neatly pencilled figures, over which he had laboured for so many midnight hours. His surprise evident, the banker took them and cast a quick eye over the calculations. 'Did you do these yourself?'

Karl felt a momentary burst of anger, which he quickly stifled. 'I'm a businessman, Herr Arendt, and business is about money.'

Isaak Arendt glanced up from his closer study of Karl's figures, stared unblinkingly, then returned to the financial projections his client had made. Suddenly, he leaned back in his leather armchair, clasped his hands behind his head and smiled. 'You can have your loan, Herr Jochum. You're absolutely right about the future value of land around Berlin. Buy into the Kurfuerstendamm Company and I shan't be surprised if we don't see Café Jochum itself on that street in the not too distant future.

'Now, about the Café Jochum you plan to open on the Potsdamer Platz. I know for a fact that you are not alone in your interest in that property. My advice to you is to move quickly, before it is bought by somebody else. Do you have a lawyer, Herr Jochum?'

Dazed, Karl shook his head, scarcely able to believe his good fortune. His own father greeted his plans with scepticism but an unknown banker agreed to them with enthusiasm.

Isaak Arendt took a sheet of the bank's embossed notepaper and scratched a few lines of writing. 'Here's a letter of introduction to Dr Erwin Duschek. He's a graduate in law from Dresden University, an extremely capable advocate, specializing in company law. Duschek and Duschek is a family firm, with whom we have enjoyed very good relations for a long time. I have absolutely no hesitation in recommending Dr Duschek to you.'

'Thank you, Herr Bankdirektor.'

'You'll also need an accountant. Let me see.' He pursed his lips. 'Now, what about Israel Silberstein? Another good man, recently arrived in Berlin from Frankfurt. Yes, I think he'll look after your affairs very competently. The Silbersteins are also customers of the bank. Here's his address. After you've been to see Dr Duschek, make an appointment to meet Israel Silberstein. A café where the Kaiser will come to dine, you once told me, Herr Jochum?'

Speechless, Karl nodded.

Isaak Arendt smiled. 'That is the kind of business that will appeal to Herr Silberstein, I think.' He stood up. 'Herr Jochum, it's been a very real pleasure meeting you again and I wish you every success for the future. However, I don't think you need my best wishes. Your success is already assured.'

Sigi's first reaction to Karl's news was mixed incredulity and dismay. At last, he was forced to accept that Karl was absolutely serious about opening a café. 'But I still don't like it, Karli. Now, a café in Vienna, that I could understand, but a café in Berlin, that's another matter. To a Viennese, the café is an extension of his home. He goes there to meet his friends, to play cards, to listen to good music. But the Berliner, Karli, that's a different animal. He'll drink maybe one cup of coffee, several glasses of water and sit all day reading newspapers provided free of charge by the management. There's no profit in that, son.'

'The Berliner has a sweet tooth, Papa. Think of the profits we've made just here, in your shop. At Café Jochum, we'll sell the same sweets and cakes but at twice or three times the price. Then, think of the profit we can make on tea, coffee and ice creams, which are made from little more than water. How many cups of coffee can you make from one bag of coffee beans, Papa?'

'Yes, I suppose you're right. But, Karl, do we have to move from our shop here on the Schlossplatz? Your mother and I have been here nearly thirty years. It's our life, son.'

Karl knew he ought to feel sorry for him but all he felt was a surging impatience. Why were old people so obstinate and stuck in their ways? 'What's the point, Papa? We can still sell bread and cakes and Haus Jochum sweets and chocolates from the café. You'll still be in charge of all the patisserie.'

'And our customers, all our old friends, will they come to the Potsdamer Platz?'

Karl privately hoped that a lot of them would not, but he said consolingly, 'Of course they will.'

His father shook his head doubtfully, then he suddenly brightened. 'Well, you've still got to buy the property. I'm not going to do anything about our lease here until this lawyer fellow of yours has everything signed and sealed. When are you seeing him?'

'Tomorrow, Papa. But don't worry, there won't be any problems.'

Sigi stared at his son, then said, rather plaintively, 'Please understand Karli, I don't want to hold you back. You're young and you've got your life ahead of you. But I'm getting old and rather tired, and sometimes I feel the world is moving too quickly for me. Now, you do what you think is right.'

In Dr Erwin Duschek, Karl found a man after his own heart, quick to understand his client's needs, brisk without being discourteous, and keen to get ahead. Karl guessed his age at about thirty and was grateful to Isaak Arendt for having introduced him to a young lawyer and not an old greybeard, who would inevitably have poured cold water over all his plans.

A few days after their first meeting, Dr Duschek asked Karl to come back to his office. 'I have news for you, Herr Jochum. I don't think we shall have much trouble in obtaining a lease on the property in which you are interested, but buying the freehold appears to be a rather more difficult matter. As you are probably aware, the late Duke owned the freehold of the tobacconist shop as well as the house next door. Apparently his executors would prefer to sell both freeholds as one title, and, what is more, they have an interested buyer for the whole.'

'But there's nothing to stop them selling the house to me and the shop to someone else, is there?'

'Nothing at all,' Dr Duschek assured him, 'except that it's an easier transaction as far as they're concerned.'

Karl frowned. 'Do you have any idea who the other interested purchaser is?'

'All I've been able to find out is that it is a nominee property company. There are quite a few of them, buying up large sections of Berlin. Rather than operate under their own names, they set up special companies for the purpose. Their interest is the ground rent, of course, and the fact that the property increases in value.'

Karl nodded grimly. 'The exact reason why I want to purchase the freehold, Herr Doktor. You see, I believe there's nothing else in life quite so secure as land. Gold, money, precious stones, they could all lose their value, but land is part of the world itself. That's why I was so keen to invest in the Kurfuerstendamm Company. My money is buying something concrete. Land has a tangible value, Dr Duschek, land is real.'

'I suppose you don't have any influential friends who could intercede on your behalf? The late Duke's executors might be swayed by a personal plea from, say, a member of the aristocracy.'

'Do you think Count Ewald von Biederstein might be able to help?' Karl asked tentatively.

'It would most certainly be worth talking to him.'

So Karl drove out to Karlshorst and sought an interview with his former officer.

'Begad! I know old Willi well!' Ewald exclaimed. 'Bit of a simpleton actually, I've always thought, but he's got a kind heart. So, they're selling off some of the old Duke's property, are they? Just goes to show — you can be a Duke and still not have enough money. Leave it to me, Karl, I'll tell him to instruct his lawyers to sell the house to you. Now, let me tell you about the new love of my life. She's Hungarian ...'

With a broad smile of satisfaction on his face, Karl sat back to listen to the virtues of Ewald's latest conquest.

A few days later, he heard from Dr Duschek that the freehold of the property on the Potsdamer Platz was his to buy.

Karl's next port of call was the accountant recommended by Isaak Arendt, but whereas he had instinctively liked and trusted Erwin Duschek, he felt uneasy with Israel Silberstein, who was short, rather plump, with fleshy lips, and the hand he offered Karl to shake was slightly damp to touch. His office was on the third floor of an unprepossessing old building and it was sorely in need of a coat of paint.

Noticing his look, Israel Silberstein waved a deprecating hand. 'I'm twenty-six, Herr Jochum. I have to start somewhere and I see no sense in loading my overheads unnecessarily. Now, why don't we talk a little and see if we can't do business together?'

Still filled with misgiving, Karl outlined his plans for Café Jochum to the accountant, who nodded shrewdly, all the time making notes. 'And you have brought your forecasts with you, Herr Jochum?'

Karl hesitated, then reached down to his attaché case. 'You realize these are very confidential?'

Silberstein leaned back in his chair and sighed. 'Ach, Herr Jochum, I understand now what is the matter. You do not trust me, because I am a Jew. I am a member of a different race, Herr Jochum, and that makes you afraid.'

Suddenly, Karl felt embarrassed, because that was exactly what he had been thinking. 'No, I ...'

'Don't deny it, Herr Jochum. It doesn't matter. What does matter is whether I am a good accountant. And I am, Herr Jochum. I am a very good accountant. So, now we have got that little awkwardness out of the way, shall we look at your forecasts?'

Silently, Karl handed over his working sheets. For a long time, Israel Silberstein poured over them, nodding occasionally in approval, but more often shaking his head. At last, he said, 'You seem to think it is going to cost a lot of money to fit out your café, Herr Jochum. I believe it could be done very much more cheaply than this. What is going to cost so much money?'

'Kitchen equipment, cutlery, crockery, furniture, fittings ...'

'But so much? Ach, Herr Jochum, I know where we can buy cut-price tablecloths and very cheap cast-steel cutlery.'

Karl leaned across the table to snatch back his figures. 'Herr Silberstein, this is my café and it is going to be run my way.'

'Herr Jochum, I am only trying to be helpful. You see, you have never run a café before and I'm afraid you don't know what you are doing.'

'And how many cafés have you run, Herr Silberstein? What personal experience do you have?'

'I have a lot of business experience, Herr Jochum.'

It seemed they had reached an impasse. They sat glaring at each other across the table, until Silberstein lowered his eyes and said, 'Herr Jochum, explain to me what will cost so much.'

Karl took a deep breath. 'Very well. The cutlery and condiment sets will be made of solid silver. The tablecloths will be of the finest linen from Breslau. The porcelain is to be hand-painted, burgundy and gold on white, by an artist from Meissen. The chairs will be covered in maroon sateen to match the heavy velvet curtains. From the ceiling, we shall hang gold chandeliers. No expense will be spared to make Café Jochum the finest café in Berlin.'

Beads of perspiration glistened on the accountant's forehead. 'You're taking a very great risk, Herr Jochum. A very great risk.'

'That is my business, Herr Silberstein.' Karl tried to remain polite. 'However, if Isaak Arendt considers it a risk work taking, I don't see that you have any great cause for concern.'

'You have shown these figures to Herr Arendt?' Karl nodded. 'And he agrees with them? He is willing to advance you this money?'

'Yes.'

'Well, in that case ...' The accountant pulled out his handkerchief and wiped his face. 'And who do you think will frequent your café, Herr Jochum?'

'The cream of Berlin society.'

'You have entrée to Berlin society?'

Karl knew that Silberstein was wondering how the son of a Viennese shopkeeper could be so confident. He knew nothing about Count Ewald and the First Brandenburg Guards. He knew nothing of Karl Jochum chocolates. 'Yes, I have entrée to Berlin society.'

'Well, in that case, I'm sure these figures are right. I didn't know about your family connections, Herr Jochum. Why, if you are correct, we could soon be thinking about expanding your business.' His eyes roved hungrily over the estimated profits.

Karl smiled inwardly. Now that Silberstein could see several noughts added to the profit account, his attitude was changing. Yes, he could do worse for an accountant than this greedy little Jew.

'Our offer for the freehold of the house on the Potsdamer Platz has been refused,' Heinrich Kraus told his father next time they met, once again at the Konrad Hotel. 'Karl Jochum is buying it.'

'Jochum? Never heard of him. Who's he?'

'You met him briefly at the Arendt Bank.'

'What's he going to do with it?'

'Make it into a café, I understand.'

'But you've bought the freehold of the tobacconist shop?'

'Yes, Father. And I've bought two hundred thousand shares in the Kurfuerstendamm Company.' Heinrich frowned. 'One of my confidants told me that Jochum also bought some. Got thirty thousand at ten pfennigs each. Now, where did a man like that get three thousand marks? His family has no money. His father only rents his shop on the Schlossplatz.'

'Must have borrowed it. Maybe you'd better keep an eye on him. The man must have vastly overextended himself. When he's bankrupted, we'll buy the Potsdamer Platz property at below market value and get his shares in the Kurfuerstendamm Company. Young men — they always think they know best, when all the time they know nothing. Well, you can't put an old head on young shoulders.'

Heinrich stared at him, open-mouthed. It appeared that his father had already forgotten that it had been his, Heinrich's, idea to diversify into property and land. Suddenly, he found himself hoping that Jochum would do well, if only to prove to his father that business acumen was not the sole prerogative of old age. Then he shrugged. What did it matter, if it made the old man happy? Gustav was over fifty now and must soon be thinking of retiring, at which time control of Kraus Industries would pass to Heinrich.

'What sort of café?' Gustav asked suddenly.

'I understand no expense is to be spared to make it into the best café in Berlin.'

'We'll go and have a look at it, once it's opened. I'm sick to death of Konrad's food.'

On 1 January 1883 Dr Duschek handed Karl the key to the house on the Potsdamer Platz. 'If there's anything else I can do for you at any time, please don't hesitate to call on me, Herr Jochum.'

Karl shook the lawyer's hand firmly. 'Thank you, Dr Duschek, I won't forget, and I'm sure it won't be long. The next property I'll be after will be Loewe. Think what I could do if I owned that as well!'

Dr Duschek smiled. 'It would give me the greatest pleasure to act for you again. Now, good luck, and remember my invitation to the opening of Café Jochum!'

Now Karl could get down to work in earnest. Six months' notice was given to the landlord of the shop on the Schlossplatz, who expressed regret at their departure, but assured them it would be no problem getting new tenants for such a prime site. 'Well, son, that's the end of an era,' Sigi said sadly.

Karl put his arm round him, 'No, Papa, it's the beginning of a new one.' Now that he had got his own way, he felt slightly guilty at causing such disruption at this stage of his parents' lives, but he was positive they would be happy again once Café Jochum was opened. 'Come and look at our new property, Papa, and let me explain what we're going to do.'

Together, they made their way to the Potsdamer Platz and let themselves into the empty house. 'We must take down the front wall,' Karl explained, 'so that people can step onto the terrace from the square, and we'll pave over the garden. Then we must open up the front, with low windows, or even sliding glass doors; but for the rest there's very little that needs doing. See, the Duke's banqueting hall makes a superb restaurant; and the kitchens — look, Papa, they're enormous.'

Gradually, Sigi became more enthusiastic. 'If you made these two reception rooms into one, you'd have another dining room.'

'And upstairs, Papa, the bedrooms can be made into private dining rooms. There's already a laundry lift that can be converted into a dumbwaiter.'

'Yes, I see now what you're trying to do, Karli. But do you think you can get all this work finished in six months?'

Karl smiled confidently. 'It will be finished by the end of June if I have to work all night and all day.'

The following six months were the happiest of Karl's life. He was twenty-five years old, physically in his prime and filled with the almost supernatural energy that comes to a person who is doing the thing he wants to do more than anything else in the world. Gradually, Café Jochum began to take shape. The front wall was ripped down and the terrace paved. Low glass windows were fitted into the old house's façade. The rooms were refashioned and redecorated. The kitchens were fitted out. Furniture and equipment started to arrive. Chandeliers were hung.

At the end of May a chef was engaged, a man called Fritzi Messner, who came with excellent references from the Spa Hotel in Baden-Baden. Fritzi had, however, been born in the oldest part of Berlin, in Neu-Koelln, and cooked the city's specialities to perfection. Never had Karl tasted green eel fresh from the Heiligensee with gherkin salad or dill sauce, or Havel perch baked in the oven until it was crisply brown, served with potato salad, as fine as Fritzi prepared them. And Fritzi's boulette, called Hoppel-Poppel, was not just a simple dish of meatballs in gravy, but a gargantuan feast, served in gargantuan helpings.

It was decided that Fritzi would prepare all the savouries, while Sigi was in charge of the sweets and desserts. 'I think I shall enjoy that, Karli,' Sigi said, that evening, when they all gathered together in their flat on the Rosenthaler Platz. 'Messner seems a good man and it will be nice to have a bit more room to cook in.'

A meagre staff of kitchen helpers and waiters had also been taken on, but until they found a head waiter they could trust

Klothilde volunteered to be in charge of the till. 'It has to be one of us. We can't entrust our takings to a total stranger. But I hope you find someone soon. You need someone younger than your old mother.'

'If you'd spent less money on chandeliers, you'd be able to afford more staff,' Sigi grumbled. 'It's not that we don't want to help you, son, but we're getting old.'

'And what am I going to do in this wonderful establishment?' Grete asked. 'I'm quite willing to help, you know.'

Karl smiled at her impishly. Grete was nineteen now, her light brown hair piled high on her head, her cheeks round and rosy like her mother's and her figure beginning to plump out in the same way. 'You can do the washing-up.'

'Washing-up!'

'Somebody has to do it, and since as a socialist you sympathize so much with the workers, who better than you?'

Grete gave an exasperated sigh. 'Oh, well, if it helps. But make sure it's not for long, eh?'

Karl bent down and gave her a peck on the cheek. 'Thank you, Gretchen.'

'There's one thing still worries me,' Sigi said. 'We should have an orchestra to play in our café. Music is good for business. I know that from Vienna.'

Karl suddenly remembered Ewald's words. He, too, had mentioned an orchestra. 'But we can't afford one, Papa.'

'A quartet, then. Karli, listen, it shouldn't be difficult. Offer the musicians free meals and free publicity until you're established. There must be lots of people in this city who'd jump at a chance like that.'

Karl took his advice and advertised in the newspaper, but already June was drawing towards its close and out of the hundreds who replied, he chose four at random, uncertain as to whether or not they could actually play.

Those last days were hectic in the extreme, but finally the shop on the Schlossplatz was closed and the stock moved to the Potsdamer Platz. Posters were affixed to advertising columns and handwritten invitations sent out to all the officers of the First Brandenburg Guards, city dignitaries and old customers of Haus Jochum.

All night before the great day, Karl and Sigi were up, baking, icing, decorating and filling an amazing variety of sweets and cakes to titillate the Berlin palate. Karl, himself, made the marzipans, chocolates and truffles, packing them in silk-covered boxes or arranging them in disciplined lines on burnished silver platters. From dawn, Fritzi Messner stood in the kitchen, cutting vegetables, roasting huge joints of meat, filleting fish and preparing vast cauldrons of soup. From first light, the three waiters put the finishing touches to the gleaming interior of the café-restaurant, aligning cutlery, polishing cut-crystal glasses, laying out delicate Meissen porcelain on stiff damask table linen from Breslau. Above them, glittering gold chandeliers hung from the ceiling, the crystal in them reflecting the red from the furnishings, so the lights resembled rubies rather than diamonds.

In the gentlemen's cloakroom, Karl shaved, changed into a well-fitting cutaway morning coat, ran a comb through his hair and gave a final twirl to his moustache. Then he walked out to the front of the café. On the terrace, white-painted cast-iron tables, covered with gay blue and white checked cloths, were each adorned with a small vase of flowers and a parchment menu, encased in a glass frame. Sliding glass doors led from the terrace into the café's interior. Above the entrance was a sign, reading *CAFÉ JOCHUM*.

Karl looked up at it and smiled. Then he put out a big board, saying, *CAFÉ OPEN*.

'What happens if nobody comes?' Sigi's voice asked.

'They'll come,' he promised, but for a dreadful moment he wondered whether they really would. He stared out across the square, where a few people were already gathering to watch the day's events, for curiosity had been growing for weeks as Café Jochum neared its opening day. These humble townspeople could never afford Café Jochum prices, but what would happen if they were his only visitors?

'You seem so young to be taking on so much. Karli, I do hope you know what you're doing.'

Firmly, Karl banished his doubts to the back of his mind. 'Papa, I know I'm doing the right thing.'

The people came, one of the first of them First Lieutenant Count Ewald von Biederstein. Karl grasped him firmly by the hand, then conducted him to a corner table bearing a 'reserved' notice. 'This is your own table, Ewald. Nobody else will ever sit here, except at your invitation. No matter how full Café Jochum is, this is your *Stammtisch*.'

'Damn it all, Karl, that's extremely civil of you.'

'If it weren't for you, Ewald, I might never have been able to open Café Jochum.'

As the morning passed, the crowds on the pavements outside grew denser, for increasing numbers of carriages arrived, many bearing coats of arms, and all containing well-known Berlin personages. Karl Jochum personally greeted each newcomer, bowing them into his café, helping them to be seated and taking their orders. To each, he presented a small box of Karl Jochum chocolates.

Isaak Arendt arrived with his wife and small son, Theo. 'Congratulations, Herr Jochum,' he said, looking round the overflowing café. 'I think you have every reason to be happy.'

Dr Duschek brought his wife. 'I think I can safely say, Herr Jochum, that you have today contributed to the history of Berlin.'

Israel Silberstein was mentally counting the profits. 'We shall have to order a bigger safe, Herr Jochum. At this rate, you will have repaid your loan within a year.' He rubbed his hands together. 'The restaurant business is obviously a very good business.'

But soon, Karl was too busy to notice either the crowds or the identity of his customers. As the quartet played on the podium, he and Sigi were soon forced to help the overburdened waiters. With trays balanced high above their shoulders, they hurried to and fro between tables.

In a far corner, in a white silk blouse and full black skirt, her eyes proudly scanning the room, sat Klothilde Jochum, scarcely able to believe her son's dream was coming true and that all these fine and distinguished people were vying with each other to be the first to visit the new Café Jochum. As customers paid for their meals, the waiters brought their bills to her and she handed out the change, ringing up the amounts on her till.

In the kitchen, Grete Jochum, clad in a long white apron, stalwartly doing the washing-up, listened to the hum of excited conversation emanating from the café. She was glad to be able to help Karl, but she could not forget the many thousands of people in Berlin to whom the price of a meal in Café Jochum was the equivalent of a week's wages. Somehow, she felt she was betraying her socialist cause.

Karl's enthusiasm, however, was infectious. Although his family and meagre staff worked that day as never before, not a cross word was heard. Even Fritzi Messner, renowned at Baden-Baden for his outbursts of temperament, hummed as he worked and did not grumble, even when orders were mixed up and returned.

At midnight, the last customers left. Every single piece of food had been consumed, every last cake, chocolate, canapé and pastry gone. They had run out of cream and butter. There were no more eggs, cheese or meat. There was just enough coffee to last until the shops opened next day.

Klothilde and Grete sat behind the till counting the takings, while Karl and Sigi were making a list for the next day's provisions, when a small dark-haired man of about Karl's age entered the café. 'Herr Karl Jochum?'

Karl looked at him curiously. 'Yes, what can we do for you?'

The stranger held out his hand. 'I'm pleased to meet you, sir. My name is Max Patschke and I come from Vienna. May I congratulate you on your first successful day?'

Karl shook his hand. 'Thank you, Herr Patschke.'

'I won't beat about the bush, Herr Jochum. From what I've heard you need a first-class head waiter. I should like to offer you my services.'

Karl studied him more closely. Shorter than he was, Max Patschke had the upright stance of a man who had completed his military service. He was obviously self-assured and when he smiled, as he suddenly did now, his face displayed an unexpected, almost boyish, charm. Karl glanced at his father, who had stopped writing and was also studying the Austrian, then he shook his head ruefully. 'I'm sorry, Herr Patschke, but I'll be quite honest with you and tell you straight away that even if we wanted to employ you, we simply cannot afford to pay you.'

Max Patschke's brown eyes lit up, as his smile intensified. He waved a hand, brushing aside Karl's objection. 'I think I'm right in saying that this is your first venture into the restaurant business, Herr Jochum?'

'Well, yes . . .'

'Then I hope you'll pardon my saying that you still have a lot to learn.'

Karl opened his mouth indignantly, but his father broke in, 'Herr Patschke, we're always ready to listen to advice. What is your proposal?'

'It's very simple. I don't want a salary, but I want to be paid a percentage of the takings every day. That way, if business is good,

I live well, and if it's bad, well, then I'll be looking for a new job anyway.'

Klothilde Jochum nodded shrewdly. Sigi went across to the bar and started to open a bottle. 'Sit down, Herr Patschke, and please take a glass of wine with us.'

'Thank you.' He took a seat but addressed himself again to Karl. 'Herr Jochum, I know how you feel. The first day is always the worst and until you've been open for several months, you can have no idea how well your business is going to run. But I will say this. You couldn't have picked a better chef than Fritzi Messner. I've worked with him before and he's excellent.'

'You know Fritzi Messner?' Sigi asked, pouring the wine into glasses and handing one to Max Patschke.

'We worked together at Baden-Baden. Allow him full control of your kitchen and you'll have no problems.' Then he turned to Karl. 'And with your Herr Papa making the sweets and Max Patschke on the restaurant floor, your business will run like clockwork.'

Karl felt as though control of his business had been snatched away from him. 'And how do you see my role?' he asked in a disgruntled tone.

Again the urbane smile. 'But, Herr Jochum, you are the business brain. You make sure we're doing what the public wants and we'll keep them supplied. It needs more than just the actors to put on a play. You, Herr Jochum, are the Herr Direktor!'

Suddenly, Sigi Jochum laughed. 'Herr Patschke, you have the cheek of the devil, but I for one am pleased that you arrived. Apart from anything else you'll be a match for our Karl here, be able to keep him in order! Karli, I propose we take Herr Patschke at his word and see what he can do.'

'I promise you that is a decision you will never regret,' his fellow countryman promised him earnestly.

Karl shrugged. 'Mama?'

Klothilde's reply was written on her face. 'Herr Patschke, I think we need all the help we can get. We can't continue like this on our own.'

Max bowed towards her. 'Thank you, Madame. Now, if you will permit me to say one more thing, with which I am sure you, as a fellow Viennese, will agree — you should employ a different violinist. The one you've got is terrible. He doesn't do justice to this establishment.'

'But ...!' Karl expostulated.

'I happen to know someone who would be delighted to play for you. With your permission, I'll send him a message asking him to come and see you. His name is Franz Jankowski.' He drained his glass and stood up. 'Now, I shan't detain you any longer.' He bowed low over Klothilde's hand and kissed it. Then he turned to Grete, who had sat silently throughout the conversation, and lifted her hand to his lips. 'Fraeulein, I beg you to take care of your hands if you insist on doing the washing-up. Better still, let us find someone else to do such a menial chore and free you for pursuits more fitting to your great beauty.' Grete looked up at him tiredly, but could not help smiling.

Finally, Max took his farewell of Sigi and Karl. 'Goodnight, Herr Jochum. Good night, Herr Direktor. I shall be here at seven tomorrow morning.'

'Good night, Herr Patschke,' Klothilde said gratefully, 'I shall look forward to seeing you tomorrow.'

Sigi walked with him to the door. 'Good night, Herr Patschke. I have the feeling we have just concluded a most satisfactory arrangement.'

Karl stared at them both in astonishment. 'What?'

Klothilde chuckled. 'He's quite right, Karli. The violinist is appalling.'

True to his word, Max Patschke arrived early the following morning and rapidly proved himself worth his weight in gold. A true professional, he made an excellent impression on the customers, to whom he always referred as guests, and combined just the right degrees of authority, servility and dignity. Soon guests were greeting the head waiter in familiar terms as they would an old friend. But Max, bowing graciously, never sought to presume upon their familiarity, nor did he ever take it for granted.

Within a week, he introduced more staff, all paid, as he was, from the fifteen per cent service charge, thus releasing Klothilde and Grete from their arduous tasks and allowing them to spend their days at home. Sigi too was no longer forced to combine the job of waiting with his main function as patissier. All in all, Max achieved many changes for the better in a very short space of time.

But the principal change he effected was in the introduction of Franz Jankowski. Franz arrived at the café at about six o'clock one glorious Saturday evening, when the terrace was crowded with people drinking coffee and watching the sun set over the rooftops. Max Patschke hurried across to him and led him to Karl's private office. 'Herr Direktor, this is Herr Jankowski, the violinist I mentioned.'

Karl's immediate reaction was disappointment, for he was very different from the suave, elegant musician he had imagined. Franz Jankowski was about forty and already quite bald, with a rather large, aquiline nose and deep set, cavernous eyes. Not very tall but very thin, he looked as if he had not eaten a good meal for a long time. His clothes, though scrupulously clean, were obviously quite old, and the violin case, which he clutched possessively to him, was extremely battered. However, since Max was hovering expectantly, he greeted him politely and asked him a few questions about himself.

'The violin is my great love, Herr Direktor, and I should welcome the opportunity to play more often. But it is not my only occupation, because I also work for Ullstein.'

'The newspaper and publishing house?'

'That's right. I work there as a printer. But because I work in the early mornings my evenings would be free to play at your café. You see, Herr Direktor, I am not married. My time is my own.'

Karl thought for a moment. Although Franz's appearance was not exactly prepossessing, it was finally his ability that counted. 'Why don't you come into the café and play something?' At least the interior of the café was fairly empty, so little damage would be done if the man were no good.

'Thank you, Herr Direktor.' Franz followed him out of the office and made his way to the podium where he opened the battered case and extracted an old violin and bow. Tucking the instrument affectionately under his chin, he played a few notes, adjusted a string, then launched into the first movement of *Spring* from Vivaldi's *The Four Seasons*.

To Karl's astonishment, Franz Jankowski's whole appearance seemed to change, the haunted expression on his face being replaced by one of rapt joy, as he became one with his music. Suddenly, Karl became aware that the hum of conversation from the terrace had gradually died and customers were crowding to the open windows to listen. The kitchen doors opened and Sigi appeared, closely followed by Fritzi Messner and the other kitchen staff. Waiters quietly put down their trays and stood in awed attention. Then, to his even greater amazement, he realised total strangers were walking in from the street and crowding in the café entrance.

When Franz Jankowski eventually put down his violin, there was a thunderous burst of applause. Mesmerized, Karl walked up to the podium and held out his hand. 'Herr Jankowski, you have the job.'

Within days, the news of Franz Jankowski's playing had spread round Berlin and every evening the café was crowded as customers poured in to listen to him. Israel Silberstein rubbed the palms of his hands happily. 'People are saying that at Café Jochum not only can you drink excellent coffee and eat the finest food in Berlin, but you can listen to music better than in any theatre or concert hall. Herr Jochum, that man is worth a fortune. You must put up your prices.'

When Ewald heard him, he was ecstatic. 'Damn it all, Karl, that man should be playing for the Emperor in the Court orchestra. He's wasted here.'

Sigi, the Viennese love of music in his veins, agreed. 'What have we done to deserve such talent? Karli, that man could be a virtuoso player. Why does he choose to work for us?'

In the end, Karl asked Franz that same question. 'Why are you playing for us here in Café Jochum, Franz? Have you ever considered trying to obtain a position at Court?'

Franz Jankowski looked embarrassed. 'Herr Direktor, I am a Jew. I would never be permitted to play at Court. Jews are second-class citizens, you see.'

Karl stared at him, comparing him in his mind to Israel Silberstein and Isaak Arendt. It seemed there were as many different classes of Jews as there were of Germans, but at that moment, he felt that talent such as Franz Jankowski possessed ought to transcend all barriers, racial, religious and political. Finally, he said slowly, 'One day, Franz, the Emperor will visit Café Jochum. Then you will play for him.'

By December, Café Jochum had become such an integral part of the Berlin landscape that it was hard to remember a time when its terrace had not graced the Potsdamer Platz.

Those last years of the reign of Wilhelm I were gracious, elegant and romantic times. In his carriage and pair, the Emperor, warmly wrapped in a travelling rug, his spiked helmet on his head, rode through the snow-covered streets for his morning excursion along the tree-lined avenues of the Tiergarten park. Ladies in flounced, bustled dresses, snugly attired in fur hats and muffs, curtsied as he passed, while beside them their husbands, in Astrakhan coats, raised their top hats and bowed. Their constitutional over, the Emperor's loyal subjects repaired for coffee and cream cakes at Café Jochum.

But, however many of his subjects dined at Café Jochum, the Kaiser never paid the establishment a visit. Wilhelm I, Emperor of Germany and King of Prussia, accepted the obeisance of his people. He did not mix with them.

Karl Jochum resigned himself to this fact. The Emperor was an old man, while he himself was still young. There would be other Emperors. And one of them would dine at Café Jochum.

Chapter Three

Since its opening, Karl had been too busy running Café Jochum to pay much attention to his young sister, so he was flabbergasted when, that winter, she announced her engagement to Gottfried Fischer.

A rather angular individual, with a shock of untidy hair and a serious expression constantly haunting his weak eyes, Gottfried came from Munich, where he studied ancient German literature. A carpenter's son, he had gained a scholarship to university, then succeeded so well in his studies that he had been sent to Berlin for a year to read at the Friedrich-Wilhelm University as part of his doctorate. Introduced by one of Grete's girlfriends, the couple had fallen in love and now, three months later, Gottfried had proposed marriage.

Karl was appalled. It was not to the young man's academic life that he objected, but to his political views, for even during their brief encounters it had been obvious that Gottfried, like Grete, was a convinced socialist. When he mentioned this to his mother, she said, 'Karli, Gottfried seems a very gentle man, he'd be the last person to mean any harm to anyone. Come, dear, be broad-minded. It takes all sorts to make a world, and if Grete is happy with him, that's all that matters.'

'Grete's always had these stupid notions about all people being equal. Gottfried will just encourage her.'

'She's marrying a man, not a politician. And if you had any sense, you'd get married too. I should like to see my grandchildren before I die.'

This was not the turn he wanted the conversation to take. 'But, Mama, I can't marry just anyone in order to give you grand-children to dandle on your knee!'

'Well, it's not natural, a healthy young man like you and not interested in marriage.'

'Mama, it's not that I'm not interested — I just haven't got the time.'

'Then make time. Your father worked hard, but he still found the time to marry me and bring up you two children.'

Perhaps it was better, after all, to talk about his sister. 'I'm sure Grete will have children very soon.'

'But Karli, Grete will be in Munich and I'll be in Berlin. I just wish Gottfried were a local boy. I'm going to miss her so much.'

The wedding breakfast was held in one of the private rooms at Café Jochum, a small affair, since the Jochums had no relations in Germany and most of Gottfried's family lived in faraway Bavaria. For the first time, Karl sat as a guest, waited upon by his own staff. To his surprise, it made him feel rather uncomfortable and he had to stifle an ingrained urge to get up and help.

Despite all his socialist convictions, Gottfried Fischer was obviously suffering from no such inhibitions. As a waiter piled his plate high with food, the bridegroom was treating the wedding guests to a lecture on his pet subject. 'I believe that everyone, man or woman, should have the opportunity to equal education and access to governmental positions of power, something that simply doesn't exist at the moment. The man in the street is entitled to a say in how his country is run. We desperately need political reform, so that power is taken out of the hands of the Junkers and placed fairly, in the hands of the people.'

Karl thought of the von Biedersteins, most typical of all Prussian Junkers. 'But surely the Junkers have a right to rule?'

'No more right than the Kaiser. By what right does a Prussian Emperor rule over us Bavarians, for instance? My family and I were always totally against the inclusion of Bavaria in the German Empire and I, for one, lost any remaining respect for Ludwig II when he allowed himself to be bought off so easily by Bismarck. Bavaria has always been a free state and it should have remained one. We don't want anything to do with *Sauer Preuss* — with hard Prussians!'

Any criticism of his Kaiser was guaranteed to make Karl's blood boil, but he was reluctant to let the conversation get too heavy. 'Nevertheless, you've married a Prussian girl,' he pointed out, in what he hoped was a jovial tone.

'You're not Prussians, you're Austrians. That's very different. Austria and Bavaria are both Alpine countries. Their people have a lot in common. That's why I fell in love with Grete.' He glanced tenderly at her.

Karl looked at her too, wondering if she realized what she was

71

letting herself in for, marrying this socialist hothead. If so, she seemed unperturbed. 'Karli,' she said, 'Gottfried and I share the same ideals. We want to make the world a better place in which to live. It isn't right that aristocrats like the von Biedersteins and industrialists like the Krauses should live in luxury while their workers live in poverty, dying through malnutrition, poor sanitation and disease.'

'But a lot is being done for them,' Karl argued. 'The state sickness insurance schemes being introduced by Bismarck are designed to help just those people. Bismarck isn't a socialist, but he still has people's welfare at heart.'

'He was forced into that move by fear,' Gottfried claimed. 'He thinks that by introducing compulsory insurance against sickness, accident, incapacity and old age, he can stop the growth of the Social Democratic Party.'

'I'm going to join the Social Democratic Party when we go to Munich,' Grete informed her family proudly.

'But Grete, dear, you're a woman ...' her mother said mildly. 'Surely you don't want to become actively involved in politics?'

Gottfried ignored them both. 'The workers of Germany live in hovels. They are the backbone of our country and they deserve to be better treated.'

Karl was starting to feel extremely angry. 'What about the *Mietkasernen*, the rental barracks, put up in Wedding and the Prenzlauer Berg to house the workers from factories like Kraus Village? They aren't exactly hovels.'

'Have you ever been into one of those flats? The only light they receive is from the back yard. Your apartment, Karl, is a mansion compared to them, while this café is a palace.'

'The world is changing too quickly,' Sigi interjected. 'Every day, it seems to me, something new is invented. First we had the steam train, now we have the electric train. Then there is Herr Benz talking about a motorized automobile. We are changing from an agricultural, rural country to an industrialized, urban nation. I suppose that's bound to bring problems.'

'Yes, and there must be social — and political — reform. Have any of you read the Communist Manifesto?' They all shook their heads. 'It ends,' Gottfried closed his eyes as he recalled the words, '"Let the ruling classes tremble at a Communist revolution. The proletarians have nothing to lose but their chains. They have a world to win. Working men of all countries, unite!" The Manifesto was drawn up by two Germans, Karl Marx and Friedrich Engels, living in exile in England in 1848. One day they will be proved right. There will be a communist revolution by the German people.'

Karl shuddered. 'I know nothing about communism and I don't want to. So far as I'm concerned, the English are welcome to Herr Marx.'

'He died last year,' Gottfried said sadly.

'Then let's hope his ideas died with him.'

His new brother-in-law shook his head. 'Marx's ideas won't die, Karl, because they are based on common sense. As the world about us changes, so the status of people must change. You wait and see, as the country grows more industrialized, so the working classes will rise against the capitalists. Through their struggle, they will gain power. Before you and I go to our graves, Karl Jochum, we shall have witnessed the proletarian revolution!'

There was silence after this as they all stared at him, then through the open door they heard the strains of Franz Jankowski and his orchestra striking up a waltz. Sigi turned to Klothilde. 'Young people today are very different from how we were, aren't they, my dear? I know that on my wedding day, I wanted only to take you in my arms. Over thirty years later, I feel no differently. Shall you and I go downstairs and dance?'

Gottfried had the grace to look embarrassed. 'I'm sorry, Herr Jochum, I didn't mean to be rude. Grete, I'm afraid I don't dance very well, but will you be my partner?'

Karl watched them leave the room, took a deep breath, then found relief for his pent-up feelings by starting to clear the table. Thank God, Gottfried wasn't a local boy. Munich was welcome to him!

In the five years since Heinrich Kraus had left the army and been able to devote his energies full-time to Kraus Industries, the company had grown apace, and even his father was slowly coming to respect his ideas and innovations. While the Silesian steel works still remained under Gustav's sole directorship, Heinrich addressed himself unflaggingly to expanding the chemical factories in Wedding, to supervising the now considerable Kraus property investments and, most importantly, to increasing the output of the mills, smelters and huge gunshops in the Ruhr. Because this was where he now spent most of his time, he was having a magnificent new villa constructed on a hillside above Essen.

Perhaps his greatest ability was the capacity to think through an idea to its end, make a decision and then act upon it. Heinrich was a realist and an opportunist, but, most importantly, he was ruthlessly determined to achieve his ambitions. Among these, he still counted the Countess Julia von Biederstein. For five years, he had waited patiently for her to come of age and, that autumn, his patience was finally rewarded, when he learned that she was going to make her debut at the Court Ball.

Heinrich planned his campaign with the precision worthy of any general. Few commoners were received at court, but even the Kaiser recognized his indebtedness to Kraus Industries, armourers to the German nation. A few hints dropped in the right ears at the Palace and a discreet mention of the Biederstein name procured Heinrich his invitation. Now he must trust in Count Ewald's good nature and hope the Lieutenant would not cut him.

His large figure impeccably dressed in a dinner jacket and trousers fashioned by the Court tailors, he experienced no nervousness as he entered the imposing ballroom, for he knew Kraus wealth made him more than equal to the aristocratic throng attending Berlin's greatest social event. The only thing that differentiated him from them was his lack of a title, and, before too long, he was resolved to have acquired one of his own!

Purposefully he set his course straight for the von Biedersteins and, once again, fortune smiled upon him. Count Ewald greeted him very cordially, with a glint of amusement in his eyes. 'Why, damn it all, Kraus, didn't expect to see you here! Father, allow me to introduce Heinrich Kraus. Served in the Guards with me, you know.'

'Kraus?' Count Friedrich snorted disparagingly, giving a curt bow, obviously intended to demonstrate that he had never heard of his family and that he could therefore be of no importance. Countess Christina scrutinized him disdainfully through a diamond-encrusted lorgnette, then deliberately turned away to continue her conversation with a dowager duchess on the best spa at which to take a cure for rheumatism. Count Ewald grinned cheerfully and placed an affectionate arm round the shoulder of the young lady standing beside them. 'Julia, allow me to introduce Heinrich Kraus.'

She was even prettier than he had expected, a petite little figure dressed in pink tulle, her brown curls piled intricately high and decorated with a small tiara made up of diamonds and pearls. She gazed up at him from round hazel eyes, a faint flush colouring her cheeks. Then she gave him her hand. 'Herr Kraus, I'm delighted to make your acquaintance.'

'If you will excuse me for a moment ...' Obviously relieved to have discovered an escort for Julia and an opportunity to escape from his parents, Ewald disappeared in the direction of a very beautiful young debutante.

'Will you permit me ...?' Heinrich took Julia's arm and led her to a nearby velvet-covered ottoman. 'This is your first Court ball?'

'Indeed, yes, and I've been looking forward to it for so long.'

'Your family does not often come to Berlin?'

Julia pouted very prettily. 'Unfortunately not. My father much prefers to devote his time to our estate in Pomerania. He does not like the city.'

Heinrich felt a surge of excitement. 'But you do, esteemed Countess?'

She was appealingly frank. 'Herr Kraus, I love the city. I love its modernity, the theatres, shops and cafés.'

With a conversational dexterity he had not known he possessed, Heinrich found himself discussing the plays of William Shakespeare, fine art, opera and the latest fashions in ladies' bonnets.

'How wonderful to be able to talk to somebody who understands these things,' Julia sighed. 'Herr Kraus, you cannot imagine how bored I get at Fuerstenmark and how I long to escape from it. I hate the countryside — and, above all, I find our home most distressingly uncomfortable compared to the modern apartment we have taken in the Wilhelmstrasse.'

Heinrich was not normally a good dancer, but that evening, with the little Countess in his arms, he seemed to be floating on air, for he knew he had discovered the way to her heart. So confident was he that she would marry him that, at the end of the evening, he ventured to tell her that he would write to her the next day inviting her and her family to dinner the following evening. Then, bending low over her hand, he kissed it and made his departure.

He was up early the next morning, for he had an extremely busy day ahead of him. His first task was to have a huge bouquet of pink roses delivered to the Biederstein apartment in the Wilhelmstrasse. Attached to them was a note, reading *To Countess Julia, with the respectful greetings of Heinrich Kraus.* An hour later, he dispatched two dozen pink carnations.

The next thing was to decide where to entertain the Biedersteins

75

that evening. Unlike them, he had no rented apartment — and it was obviously impossible to invite them to the Konrad Hotel. In Heinrich's mind there was only one suitable place, but it was an establishment he had never personally visited — the Café Jochum.

Upon his arrival at the café, he paused in the doorway, taking in the luxurious velvet hangings, the crisp white tablecloths and the smart young waiters hurrying to and fro, silver trays balanced high above their heads.

'Can I help you, sir?' The head waiter materialized at his side.

'My name is Kraus, Heinrich Kraus. I should like to see Herr Jochum.' He handed the man his card.

'If you'll take a seat for a moment, sir, I'll see if the Herr Direktor is free.'

It was a strange sensation for Heinrich to see Karl Jochum approaching him confidently across the floor of his own restaurant in the building that Heinrich had tried, and failed, to buy. Gone was the rather lumpish private from the First Brandenburg Guards; in his place was a tall, self-confident, rather elegant man. With a start, he realized that his was not the only career to flourish. Karl Jochum, too, for all his humble beginnings, seemed a candidate for success.

Immediately Heinrich discarded the rather superior tone he had been intending to adopt and extended his hand in a friendly manner. 'Herr Jochum, it's good to see you again — and let me contratulate you on your restaurant. I am impressed.'

Gratified, Karl beamed. 'Thank you, Herr Kraus. It's kind of you to visit me. Will you take a cup of coffee?'

'Thank you.'

Max Patschke, who had been discreetly hovering nearby, led them to a corner table and took their order. Then Heinrich said, 'Herr Jochum, I believe you have private dining rooms here. I am inviting some guests to dinner this evening and I wish to entertain them in the most fitting style.' He saw no necessity to inform Jochum of his guests' identities.

'But of course, Herr Kraus. I believe we can guarantee you both an excellent meal and the privacy you desire,' Karl told him politely. He signalled to Max, asking him to bring their parchment menu folders, then handed one to Heinrich. As Heinrich studied it, his admiration grew. As well as Berlin's fish and pork specialities, there were wild boar and venison from Bohemia, crayfish 'Jochum', turbot from the Baltic and rack of lamb from Holstein.

Why the devil couldn't the Konrad provide such facilities? 'Fine,' he said. 'Now, may we inspect the dining rooms?'

The arrangements made, Heinrich returned to the Konrad Hotel, where he penned another letter to Julia. *Esteemed Countess*, he wrote. *Since I first saw you from afar at the garrison at Karlshorst, I have greatly admired you. To be able to enjoy your company last night at the Court Ball was an honour exceeding my wildest expectations. Please accept the flowers I have taken the liberty of sending as a token of my humble respect. If you and your family would be kind enough to dine with me tonight at Café Jochum, I should be eternally grateful. Your devoted servant, Heinrich Kraus.*

He rang for a page boy to deliver the letter. Then he sat back to wait.

The arrival of the flowers caused consternation in the Biederstein household. 'Herr Kraus shows a distinct lack of refinement. No officer or member of the aristocracy would behave in such a manner,' Countess Christina informed her daughter. 'He is no gentleman!'

Heinrich's letter created an even greater furore. 'You will destroy it!' the Countess ordered. 'We are not going to have anything to do with this vulgar commoner.'

Julia merely shook her head dreamily. 'What shall I wear?'

'We shall not have dinner with a stranger at some common coffee house.' Countess Christina turned to Ewald. 'What were you thinking of to introduce Julia to such a man?'

Thoroughly enjoying the situation, Ewald smiled. For one thing, he was grateful for any situation that drew his parents' attention away from himself, and, for another, he wanted Julia to be happy. He had been pleasantly surprised by Heinrich Kraus's demeanour the previous evening. Away from the army, the man seemed to have become less obsequious and brash. 'He may not be an aristocrat, Mama, but he is extremely wealthy, even if he has made his money in commerce.'

She frowned sceptically. 'Papa has never heard of him before.'

'Should have done. His company's rapidly becoming one of the wealthiest in the country.'

'Is he very rich?' Julia breathed.

'Rich enough to build you a fine villa and buy all the fur coats you desire,' Ewald replied sardonically.

Countess Christina looked thoughtful. 'One of the wealthiest companies in the country ...?'

'If His Majesty thinks highly enough of him to invite him to the Court Ball, I don't think we Biedersteins can afford to dismiss his attributes out of hand,' Ewald added.

'I shall instruct the Count to make some enquiries,' his mother conceded. 'However, I had never thought that Julia would ever ...'

But Julia ignored her. 'I've made up my mind, Mama. I'm going to marry Heinrich Kraus.'

At six o'clock that evening, Karl took a final look at the private dining suite reserved for Heinrich Kraus's party, adjusted a knife here, a glass there, then, wondering as to the identity of the guests, he went downstairs to await their arrival. Who could be important enough to bring Kraus to Café Jochum for the first time?

His question was soon answered, for at that moment Kraus arrived and, simultaneously, a carriage bearing the von Biederstein crest drew up in front of the Café. Descending from it, he saw the Count, the formidable Countess, Ewald, and an elegant little person who could only be Julia. Struggling to conceal his astonishment, Karl hurried out to greet them.

Ignoring both Karl and Heinrich Kraus, Countess Christina took her husband's arm and, her furs almost literally bristling in indignation at finding herself in such barbaric surroundings, marched into the café. Ewald shook Karl's hand and winked.

Although he bowed to them, Karl, however, had eyes only for Julia. Very petite, she looked ravishing in a high-necked cerise gown, with crimson sashes, a matching bonnet perched cleverly on her curls. As if they were old friends, she greeted him. 'Herr Jochum, how nice to see you again. What a lovely café you have here. Ewald says the sweets you make have won more ladies' hearts than any duel.' Then she stopped to listen to Franz's music. 'Isn't that beautiful?'

Heinrich Kraus frowned at Karl and took Julia's elbow possessively. 'I have reserved a private dining room for us.'

Karl turned to find Max waiting with an impish expression on his face. 'Max, take our guests upstairs, will you?' he ordered sternly.

So that was the purpose of this evening's dinner. Somehow or another, Heinrich Kraus had inveigled his way into the Biedersteins' favour and was paying court to Julia. Strangely depressed, Karl made his way towards the kitchens.

Max served their esteemed guests. 'I've fallen in love,' he declared to Karl, when he met him in the kitchen. 'What's Heinrich Kraus got that we haven't, Herr Direktor?'

'Money,' Karl said succinctly.

'Don't you think she's lovely?'

'I thought she was beautiful five years ago, when I first saw her; but she's too good for the likes of me.'

'She's too good for the likes of Herr Kraus,' Max commented darkly.

Never in his life before had Heinrich Kraus worked as hard as he did to make a success of his dinner party with the Biedersteins. Throughout the excellent meal, Countess Christina sat stiffly upright, the feathers in her hat quivering with anger. Count Friedrich stared superciliously down his nose, constantly referring to the good marriages his other two daughters had made. Count Ewald contributed little to the conversation, watching the scene with languid amusement.

But Heinrich was confident of success. Countess Julia, her chin cupped in her hand, hung on every word he uttered, gazing at him from beneath long, dark lashes. 'Your company is involved in the supply of electricity to Berlin?' she asked admiringly.

'And to other parts of the country. At the villa I am building outside Essen, I shall have my own electricity generator. It will provide lighting and heating throughout the house.'

'You'll have electrical heating in every room, including the bedrooms?'

'Julia!' her mother admonished.

'The bedrooms at Castle Fuerstenmark aren't heated?' Heinrich asked.

'They're bitterly cold,' Julia informed him. 'Herr Kraus, you've no idea how I long for a modern, comfortable house!'

'Julia, Castle Fuerstenmark is your home!' her father exclaimed.

Heinrich merely smiled at Julia. He could offer her no grand title or aristocratic family tree, but he could offer her wealth and the home of her dreams. And in return, by marrying him, she would give him what he most desired — her aristocratic connections, Count Ewald as a brother-in-law, access to Fuerstenmark as 'his' country estate, and, above all, the prestige these would give him in social and business circles. Her parents would never accept him as their equal, but her parents did not matter. All he desired was a connection to them by marriage, the first step towards obtaining a title of his own.

'Seems like Julia's decided to marry Heinrich Kraus,' Ewald told Karl next day, as he settled himself down at his reserved table and accepted the glass of champagne Max automatically brought him. 'Not altogether surprised. For all her charm, Julia's always been a calculating little wench and never made any bones about her intention to marry a rich businessman. The parents don't like it, of course, but then, times are changing. There aren't many aristocrats with Kraus's kind of money.'

Karl grunted, struggling to come to terms with the thought of the pretty little Countess marrying a gross individual like Kraus. Not that he had ever entertained any idea of marrying her himself, simply that for the past five years she had somehow epitomized for him feminine beauty and perfection. So engrossed was he in his reverie that he almost missed Ewald's next words.

'Kraus must have been in a bit of dilemma to know where to invite us. When he's in Berlin, he stays at the Konrad Hotel. Well, he couldn't ask us there, although it would have been much simpler for him. Now this is no reflection upon Café Jochum, Karl, but I've thought for a long time that what this city needs is a really first-class hotel with a restaurant of this standard. Take my family as an example. Every time they come to Berlin they have to bring almost their entire household with them, causing no end of an upheaval. Imagine how much simpler life would be if they could stay in a really fine hotel.'

Suddenly all thoughts of Countess Julia vanished from Karl's mind as he saw the possibilities of such an establishment. A luxury hotel, that could accommodate all the aristocrats who attended the Court Ball. A prestigious hotel with a first-class restaurant, where wealthy industrialists like Heinrich Kraus could entertain their guests without leaving the premises. He grasped Ewald's hand, shaking it fervently. 'Thank you, Ewald, it's a marvellous idea. I'll do it!'

'You'll do it? But, damn it all, Karl . . .'

Karl smiled confidently. 'I don't know how I'll do it, but one of these days I'll build a hotel in which your family can stay whenever they visit Berlin.'

He suddenly felt so excited that the prospect of Julia marrying Heinrich Kraus did not seem nearly so depressing.

By the time the marriage took place a year later, he had totally recovered from his disappointment and was able to view it dispassionately. He felt slightly envious of Kraus, but nevertheless had to admire his initiative. His main surprise was that Julia could stoop to marry a commoner in order to achieve her ambitions, an event almost unheard of in previous generations. Perhaps it meant, as Grete was always hoping, that the great social divide between the aristocracy and the ordinary people was slowly narrowing. Whether this was a good or a bad thing, Karl wasn't sure.

In the meantime, however, he was busy, he was happy and his loan from the Arendt Bank was steadily diminishing. Soon, he would be able to begin saving and put the next stage of his plans into effect, for not a day went by when he did not think of the hotel that he would one day build and, before that, the restaurant where the Kaiser would come to dine.

As Berlin continued to grow in international significance, new companies opened their offices in the city, foreign embassies were established and an increasing number of foreigners were seen on the streets, many of whom found their way to Café Jochum. One, in particular — a German diplomat called Emil Graber, from the Commercial Section of the German Embassy in London, who spent a lot of time in Berlin meeting with German industrialists — seemed to enjoy not only the ambience of Café Jochum, but Karl's company as well.

A man in his mid-forties, with a head of flaming red hair, he gave Karl vivid descriptions of restaurants and hotels in Paris, Rome, Monte Carlo and London. 'Yours is the only restaurant worthy of the name in Berlin,' he told Karl one evening, as he drank his after-dinner brandy. 'But you could do with more space — and you need a more international menu. German food's all right for Germans, I suppose, but after so many years abroad, I find it a bit heavy — and a bit monotonous. All that meat and potatoes. You need more vegetables, more light courses — a greater variety.' He paused for a moment, then asked, 'Have you ever heard of the great chef, Maurice Mesurier?'

'But of course, everyone's heard of Mesurier.'

'You need a chef like him. He'd cost you a fortune, but he'd be worth his weight in gold.'

'Would Mesurier ever move from Paris?'

'Even chefs get restless and look for a new challenge. You could always ask him. Well, think about what I've said, Herr Jochum.'

Karl repeated the conversation to his father later that evening. 'Herr Graber's right. Why should people go out to eat exactly the same food as they would at home? Café Jochum should offer them something different — a culinary experience.'

Sigi passed a tired hand over his forehead. He was just over sixty now, but he was beginning to look very old. 'Are you never going to be content, son? We're happy as we are. Why not stay that way?'

Karl opened his mouth to argue, then shut it again. His father didn't understand. It was a waste of time talking to him. But when he mentioned the diplomat's suggestions next day to Max, his head waiter said thoughtfully, 'I think he's right, certainly about the space. If we could take over Loewe, we could fill it in no time.'

'Do you think Loewe would sell his lease?'

'You could ask him.'

Karl made an appointment to see his neighbour and, after a few moments' polite conversation, came out point blank with his question. 'Herr Loewe, I'm thinking of extending Café Jochum. Would you be willing to sell your shop?'

Loewe, a grizzled sixty-year-old grinned. 'Herr Jochum, I have been thinking of extending my garden for my retirement. How much do you want for Café Jochum?'

Karl smiled weakly. It seemed he had no option but to continue as he was.

Then, a couple of months later, Max Patschke rushed into Karl's office almost beside himself with excitement. 'Loewe's had a heart attack and died!'

Karl carefully added a tenth coin to the pile of gold five-mark pieces he was counting and narrowed his eyes. 'Poor old boy,' he said, but his mind was racing. 'Do you think Frau Loewe will keep the business on?'

'I shouldn't have thought so, but who can tell?'

'I want to buy it. I don't care how much it costs me, I'm going to have it. Max, we'll convert the first floor into a restaurant, the shop into a confiserie and, during the summer months, meals will be served in the garden. I'll go and see Dr Duschek right away!'

'Aren't you being a little precipitate?' Max asked in alarm. 'Loewe only died last night.'

'It's the early bird that catches the worm. I'd never have wished the old boy dead, but now he is I'm going to make Frau Loewe an offer she can't refuse. Come, Max, don't you want to run the best restaurant in Berlin?'

'I thought I already was.'

Karl grinned at him. 'This is only the beginning. It's nothing to what we're going to do.'

Dr Duschek smiled when Karl explained the purpose of his visit. 'I guessed this would happen one day. Now, I suppose you would also like to purchase the freehold of the property.' When Karl nodded, he warned, 'It may prove difficult, if not impossible. If you recall, it was bought by a property investment company. However, I'll see what I can do.'

A couple of weeks later, Karl was back in Duschek's office. 'Buying the leasehold of the property presents no problems,' the lawyer informed him. 'Frau Loewe has decided to move to Leipzig and live with her married daughter. And she'd be delighted if the property went to you. But the freehold is another matter.'

'I want the freehold, I want to own that land.'

'I knew you'd say that, Herr Jochum, so I've been looking into the situation and written to the property company care of their bank.'

'Who runs this property company? Don't waste time writing letters. Let's talk to them face to face.'

'I'm not certain yet, but I believe it could be Heinrich Kraus.'

Karl's mouth hung open. Images of Kraus flickered through his mind. Sergeant Kraus lifting the heavy trunk down the stairs at Karlshorst. Herr Kraus wooing the Countess Julia. Heinrich Kraus, so he had recently learned from Ewald, the father of a baby boy called Ernst. No, to hell with it, he'd force Kraus to sell him the freehold. He'd show him he couldn't have everything his own way — not always!

'Karl Jochum wants to buy the leasehold and freehold of Loewe,' Heinrich Kraus told his father, holding out Dr Duschek's letter.

'Thought you said he'd overextended himself and would soon be bankrupted,' Gustav grumbled.

'No, Father,' Heinrich said icily, 'you said that.'

'What's our annual income from it?' Heinrich told him and he did some scribbled calculations on his blotter, then sat back and studied them. 'What's your opinion of Jochum as a businessman now?'

'I'm impressed with him,' Heinrich said. This was only a formality that he was going through, in order to make his father feel important. These days it was Heinrich who ran Kraus Industries. His father was only a figurehead.

'We'll sell,' Gustav decided, which was what Heinrich had already made up his mind to do. 'You never know, this man Jochum may be useful to us one day. But we're not in the charity business, Heinrich. This is what the freehold's worth. Add twenty-five per cent to this figure and see how serious he is.' And that too coincided with Heinrich's own decision.

When Dr Duschek received Heinrich Kraus's letter, he suggested to Karl that it was time to hold a meeting together with Israel Silberstein and Isaak Arendt. They met in the bank's conference room, with the portraits of Arendt ancestors staring down at them.

'The freehold belongs to Heinrich Kraus,' Dr Duschek told the meeting. 'And he certainly seems intent on making it expensive for Herr Jochum to extend Café Jochum.'

'Has Kraus really added twenty-five per cent to the value of the freehold?' Karl demanded.

'On current values, it appears so. But you have a choice, Herr Jochum. You don't have to buy the freehold.'

'I'll buy it, but it's the last time I'll ever do business with Kraus.'

'It is robbery, daylight robbery!' Israel Silberstein cried. 'He thinks my client is made of money.'

'He's not doing badly,' Isaak Arendt smiled, looking first at the statement of Karl's account, then at Karl himself. 'Herr Jochum, if you buy this property, what do you intend doing with it?'

As Karl launched into his pet theory, he felt a sudden surge of confidence. These three men all believed in him and, unlike his father, they wanted to see his business grow. He explained concisely his plans for refurbishing, furnishing and fitting out the extended Café Jochum. Then he told them about Emil Graber. 'He's a diplomat from the German Embassy in London.'

'Oh, yes, Herr Graber and I are old friends,' Isaak said. 'A man of sound common sense.'

Pleased, Karl went on. 'Well, it was Herr Graber who pointed out to me the lack of any restaurant serving an international cuisine in Berlin. He advised me to try to engage a chef of the standing of Maître Mesurier.'

Isaak Arendt rubbed his hand thoughtfully across his chin.

'Mesurier, eh? Well, why not? I'm going to Paris next week to see my cousin, who's sure to have contacts in the restaurant business. Would you like me to approach Maître Mesurier on your behalf, Herr Jochum?'

'Do you really think he'd be willing to leave Paris and come to Berlin?'

'Why not?' Isaak Arendt echoed Diplomat Graber's words. 'Mesurier is well known for his love of a challenge.'

'Can we afford him?' Silberstein asked.

Isaak Arendt laughed. 'Herr Silberstein, don't forget: one day, the Kaiser will dine at Café Jochum. Only the best is good enough for him.'

Karl's joy knew no bounds when Isaak Arendt returned from Paris with the news that Mesurier was willing to come to Berlin, although the salary the Frenchman was demanding seemed exorbitant. 'Do you think he's really worth that?'

'It's seldom that I encourage my customers to be extravagant, but I believe when you have tasted one of his meals — as I have — you won't begrudge a pfennig of his salary. You wait and see, you and Mesurier will change the face of Berlin.'

Mesurier certainly changed Café Jochum. A tiny, volatile Frenchman, unable to speak a word of German, he took command of its kitchen from the first day of his arrival. 'You Germans have no taste, no style. Look at what you eat!' He pointed to Fritzi Messner preparing a heaped plate of Kassler ribs with potato purée and pickled red cabbage. 'From now on, we are going to do things a little differently. Instead of two courses, we shall serve six or seven course meals. All courses will be small. All will be exquisitely prepared. Nobody shall leave the table hungry — but they will not be bloated!'

'Why did you come to Berlin if you dislike the Germans so?'

'Pfff, I am a chef not a politician. I have nothing against the Germans, only against their food. I am like a missionary, with food as my religion. I must go out into the world and convert the heathens. That is why I accept your job, Monsieur Jochum. I cannot stand barbarism.'

As an army of workmen started turning the former tobacconist shop into a restaurant, Mesurier gathered his forces together. From Italy came Luigi Cassati, who made Neapolitan ice cream with wonderful new flavours and containing pieces of real fruit, topped with whipped cream and served in silver goblets. He entertained his colleagues incessantly with arias from *Tosca*, *Rigoletto* and *Trovatore*. A new vegetable chef came from Madrid. A saucier arrived from Piedmont.

'I think you had better get a new patissier, too,' Sigi told Karl quietly one day, as they watched Mesurier volubly directing his staff.

'But, Papa ...'

'No, Karli, it's all right, I'm an old man and I can't take in any more new ideas. For a start, son, I can't speak French.'

Karl bit his lip and listened to the hubbub in the kitchen, which occasionally reached such a pitch of excitement that he wondered how any food was ever produced. Although, when the different chefs all spoke their own language, it appeared a veritable Tower of Babel, in fact, French, being the international culinary language, did provide the common tongue. 'But Fritzi can manage.'

'Fritzi's young, like you and Max,' Sigi said. 'It's no good, Karl, I think it would be better if I retired.'

Looking at his father's worn, lined face, Karl experienced a sudden remorse. In devoting every minute of his waking day to his café, he had given little thought to his parents and their feelings. If he were honest with himself, he knew he did not need Sigi any more in the kitchen, that his father was slow in his ways. And yet, he was still an integral part of the business. Without him, it would not be the same. 'I'm sorry, Papa, I've been very thoughtless. If you want to retire, I do understand, but I don't want you to go entirely. Listen, why don't we take on another patissier, as you suggest, but you come in whenever you want to?'

'All right, son, if that's what you would like. I must confess that I'd miss my work if I retired altogether. It's my life, really.'

But as the day approached for the new Café Jochum to be opened with its Restaurant Français under Maître Mesurier's direction, Sigi's anxieties returned. New menus were set out and advertisements prepared for newspapers and display around the city. 'This is a terrible risk you're taking,' he told his son.

Karl put his arm round the old man's stooped shoulders. They felt thin and bony to his touch. 'You said that when we opened Café Jochum three years ago, but everything turned out all right then. Don't worry, I know I'm not making a mistake now.'

This time, his confidence was not assumed, for he genuinely believed he was making the right move. He was realistic enough to know that he could not change the ingrained habits of conservative Berliners overnight, but with time, and with experienced travellers like Diplomat Emil Graber to set an example, they would soon follow the new fashion.

Emil Graber came to Berlin a couple of weeks after the new restaurant was opened and as soon as Max told him of the diplomat's arrival, Karl hurried from his office to greet him. With a pang, he saw that many tables still remained unoccupied, although each day a few more courageous souls ventured in to try the 'foreign food'.

'I see you took my advice,' Emil Graber said, his green eyes twinkling, when Karl reached his table and bowed. 'I also hear you have tempted Mesurier away from Paris.'

'Herr Diplomat, I am indebted to you for your good advice and I hope that in recognition of that you will permit me to invite you to your dinner this evening on the house.' He was very conscious of the honour extended to him by the diplomat's friendship.

'Thank you, Herr Jochum, but there's no need.' Then he saw Karl frown and said, 'I shall be delighted to accept, and may I say that from now on I shall spare no effort to tell everyone about the excellence of Café Jochum in Berlin.' Karl bowed again, in no doubt that the diplomat would keep his word.

Gradually, Karl's judgement was proved correct. As foreign diplomats and visiting businessmen learned about Café Jochum's French cuisine, the tables started to fill, and then Berliners cautiously began to follow suit. Each morning, Karl awoke hoping that this would be the day copious helpings of homely German food would go out of fashion completely. But each day it didn't quite happen.

Then, about six months after Mesurier's arrival, a miracle occurred. It was early evening and the whole of Berlin had turned out on the streets to enjoy the last rays of the sun and ice cream or coffee at Café Jochum.

Karl was in the kitchen, watching Mesurier prepare a roast capercailzie, when voices rising from the café in a hubbub of excitement caught his attention. Perplexed and concerned, he excused himself and nearly collided with a waiter, who tumbled through the swing doors in his agitation. 'Herr Direktor, it's the Prince!'

Emerging from the kitchen, Karl saw nobody was seated in the interior of the café any more, but were pressed up against the windows, peering out through the glass at the scene being enacted on the terrace. 'It *is* him! It's the Prince!' someone cried. 'No, it can't be,' Karl heard another voice say scornfully, 'it's just someone who looks like him.' 'I tell you, it's Prince Wilhelm. Look, he's sitting down.'

His heart thumping, Karl hurried past them to where Max Patschke and a bevy of white-coated waiters were helping the new guests to be seated. Extra chairs were swiftly found for the officers and attendants in the Prince's party. Hoping his nervousness did not show, Karl bowed to Prince Wilhelm, the Emperor's grandson, a young man of about his own age. 'Your Royal Highness, you do me a great honour.'

The Prince leaned back in his chair. 'I've been hearing extraordinary stories, Jochum. They tell me your restaurant serves twenty-course dinners.'

'Well, not usually twenty, Your Highness, but certainly six or seven.'

The Prince turned to his entourage, among whom Karl suddenly recognised Ewald, grinning broadly. 'You see!' Prince Wilhelm exclaimed triumphantly, then turned to Karl again. 'Furthermore, I've heard your ice cream contains chips of ice from the North Pole.'

'With every respect, somebody has been telling Your Highness fairy stories. The ice is made of water from Berlin.'

'Huh! Then I hear your chef has truffles imported specially from Périgord. Jochum, what is wrong with German truffles?'

Karl hesitated for a moment, his mind racing, for he knew the dangers of seeming to praise anything French to a member of the Prussian royal House of Hohenzollern. He studied the Prince's face, the dark moustache trimmed with military precision, the unfaltering stare from his brown eyes. Then he noticed Ewald winking at him from across the table. He knew how much this encounter meant to Karl and would not lead him into trouble.

Summoning all his courage, Karl replied, 'As Your Highness knows, truffles grow in the ground and are routed up by wild boar. Well, since the French are notoriously mean, they eat their pigs' food and call it a delicacy, while we in Germany prefer to fatten up our pigs and eat them as a delicacy. That is why German meat is so tender and full of flavour.'

There was a momentary silence, then the Prince threw back his head and roared with laughter. Immediately, his courtiers joined in. Then the laughter spread to adjacent tables, where customers who had been straining their ears to hear what was going on, laughed too, simply because their Prince was laughing. 'Very good, Jochum, very good! Germans feed their truffles to the pigs, eh? Ever hear anything like it? To the pigs!'

With a great sense of relief that everything appeared to be all right, Karl waited until the laughter had subsided, then asked, 'May I offer Your Highness something to eat or drink?'

'Do you have beer, Jochum, good *German* beer?' There was still a mischievous glint in the Prince's eyes.

'Certainly, Your Highness.' Karl bowed.

The Prince waved an arm to include all his colleagues. 'Then we'll have some beer.'

The Prince's visit assured the success of Café Jochum. At the speed of light, word spread round Berlin that Prince Wilhelm had sat on the terrace of Café Jochum and drunk beer with his attendants. Every table in the restaurant was reserved for weeks in advance and for days people actually queued to obtain a seat in the café where Prince Wilhelm had drunk. Seldom if ever before had it been known for a Prince of the House of Hohenzollern to arrive unannounced and sit drinking among the ordinary people. They loved their Prince and they loved Café Jochum.

'You see, Papa, I told you we would build a restaurant where the Kaiser himself would come to dine!'

'He isn't Kaiser and he didn't dine,' Sigi said flatly.

Karl stared at him in perplexity, surprised at his lack of enthusiasm. 'Papa, what's wrong? Why aren't you pleased?'

Sigi sat down heavily on a chair. 'I'm sorry, son, of course I'm pleased. I just don't feel too well today.'

Looking at him closer, Karl saw his father's face had a yellowish tinge. 'You're doing too much. Why don't you and Mama take a holiday — go to Munich, perhaps, and see Grete?'

Klothilde, gazing anxiously at her husband, nodded. 'That would be nice, Sigi. A change would do you good.'

'Maybe,' Sigi agreed, but as the days passed, he said nothing more about the proposed holiday. Karl and Klothilde watched him worriedly. He no longer went to the café, but stayed in the apartment, listlessly reading the newspaper or just gazing vacantly out of the window.

When he complained about lack of appetite and pains in his

stomach, Klothilde insisted upon calling the doctor. Dr Blattner was a young man who took a keen professional interest in his patients. 'I'm sorry, Frau Jochum,' he told her after examining Sigi, 'but your husband will have to come into hospital, so that we can do some tests on him.'

'What do you think is the matter?'

'I fear very much that it's a tumour.'

'Can you cure it?'

'I'd like a specialist to look at him first.'

Sigi's condition deteriorated very quickly after that and it came as no great surprise to Karl when the specialist asked himself and his mother into his office and told them that Sigi's end was very near. 'He's a very sick man, I'm afraid.'

'Can't you operate?' Karl asked helplessly.

The surgeon shook his head sympathetically. 'It's much too late, I'm afraid. The tumour has probably been growing for months, if not years.'

'Do you think that's why he was always so tired?' Suddenly, Karl remembered his impatience with his father and desperately wished he had been gentler with him.

Perhaps the specialist read his thoughts, for he said, 'It could well be, Herr Jochum, but you mustn't blame yourself. Even if we had discovered the tumour earlier, there's little we could have done, except maybe relieve the pain a little.'

Karl bit his lip, trying to fight back tears, then he felt Klothilde's hand on his arm. 'No, you mustn't blame yourself, Karli. Your papa has enjoyed every minute of his life. That's the important thing. Now, let's go and sit with him.'

That afternoon, Sigi spoke to them for the last time. A pale gaunt figure, propped up high against the pillows of the hospital bed, Klothilde's hand grasping his, he turned his head towards Karl and said, 'I'm very proud of you, son. I'm proud that I lived to see Prince Wilhelm visit your café. You know, you and the Prince are about the same age. I wouldn't be surprised if you don't both rule in Berlin for a while. But Karli, you must be careful. You mustn't rush too quickly.' Then, as if he had used up his last energy, Sigi's eyes closed.

It was so like his father to think more of others than himself, even when he was dying, that Karl felt tears rise once again in his throat. He bent over him and kissed him tenderly on the forehead, fearful of his shallow breathing. 'Thank you, Papa. Thank you for everything.'

90

Two days later, Sigi Jochum passed away in his sleep, his wife and son beside him. In a daze, they left the hospital after completing the necessary formalities, and Karl put his arm around his mother. Silently, they returned to the empty apartment. They sat down and, in a quiet voice, Klothilde said, 'He was a good man, Karli, he was a truly good man. I don't know how I'm going to live without him.'

Grete and Gottfried travelled from Munich to attend Sigi's funeral. Reunited with her daughter again, Klothilde confessed how greatly she was dreading the lonely years stretching ahead of her. 'Karl is away from the apartment all day long, often not coming home until long after I've gone to bed. Somehow, now your father's dead, Gretchen, Berlin holds nothing for me.'

'We've got a spare room, Mama,' Grete said gently. 'Why don't you come and live with us? I'm often alone too, for Gottfried spends more and more time at the university or on his political work. We should be so pleased to have you near us.'

Klothilde looked across at her son. 'Would you mind if I left you, Karli?'

'Of course I wouldn't, if you want to go.' But Karl knew he would miss her desperately.

'Then I think I will. I can always come back again, if I change my mind or if you find you need me, can't I?'

A couple of days later, Klothilde returned to Munich with Grete and Gottfried. Karl went with them to the Anhalter Station to see them off on their journey to Bavaria. For a long while after the huge steam locomotive had disappeared from view, he stood on the platform, watching the distant trail of its smoke. For the first time, he realized, he was totally alone.

Chapter Four

In the autumn of 1887, Ewald von Biederstein realized sadly that his bachelor years were almost over when his father came to Karlshorst and issued him with an ultimatum. While Ewald lounged in his leather-covered saddle chair, Count Friedrich stood in front of the fire with his hands under his coat tails. 'I came to Berlin, sir, because I believe it is time that you and I had a serious talk.'

Ewald sighed. 'Yes, sir.'

'You are thirty-one, Ewald, and it is time you were married. Now Johann has taken a wife, you are the only one of my six children to be single! That, sir, is a disgrace!'

Ewald chose a cigar from the humidor. His brother Johann had recently married Anna Welczeck, a nice enough girl, he supposed, but she would doubtless prove, like all other wives, to have only two topics of conversation — her children and the servants.

'All your three sisters have children. Even that man Kraus has fathered a son.'

Even Julia had changed since marrying Heinrich, Ewald reflected. Her old vivacity seemed to have disappeared and her letters from her new villa at Essen were full of her husband and baby Ernst.

'I have therefore made a decision. You will marry the bride of my choice, Ewald. You will marry Annette Ketterl.'

Ewald jumped from his seat. 'No, sir, I protest!'

'I suggest you do not protest too loudly. Allow me first to list the advantages of marrying Annette Ketterl. Her father, as you know, is dead. Her mother is an invalid. The estate is sadly neglected, being looked after by an inefficient and unscrupulous manager. Added to our Fuerstenmark estate it could be made very profitable again.'

'But, Papa, Annette is old. She must be thirty if she's a day!'

'She's twenty-seven, no spring chicken, certainly, but then, neither are you. You will make a good couple.'

'And if I refuse?'

'You will lose your allowance, which will mean you'll have to resign your commission. And here I would also point out, sir, that after fourteen years in the army, you have still not been selected for the War Academy, and you are still only a lieutenant.'

'But that's not my fault, sir. Germany is at peace ...'

His father ignored him. 'Not only will you lose your allowance, but I shall publicly disown and disinherit you if you do not marry Ketterl, and the estate will pass to Johann.'

'Damn it all, sir, that seems rather unjust!'

'Don't argue with me! Which will it be, Ewald?'

Ewald saw that this time his father was in deadly earnest. 'I'll marry Annette Ketterl.'

There was no relaxation of his father's expression, no clap on the back, no 'Thank God you've seen sense at last, man.' The old Count was made of sterner material than that. 'Now we shall set the date, Ewald. Your mother and I think next March would be a suitable time, and Annette's mother is in agreement.'

What did Annette think about it, Ewald wondered? Then he realized he had exactly six months of freedom left.

'The wedding will take place at Fuerstenmark,' Count Friedrich continued, 'and we shall, of course, invite the Emperor.'

But Ewald wasn't listening to him any more, he was thinking about how to make maximum use of his remaining six months.

No wedding took place at Fuerstenmark in March 1888, for Wilhelm, Emperor of Germany and King of Prussia, died at the great age of ninety. So, instead of celebrating his marriage, Lieutenant Count Ewald von Biederstein was among the officers of the First Brandenburg Guards who accompanied the Emperor's coffin in the long funeral cortège from the Charlottenburg Castle through the streets of Berlin.

It was a cold, misty morning and with thousands of other Berliners Karl Jochum stood on Unter den Linden to watch, in quiet homage, the funeral procession as it passed under the Brandenburg Gate. Sombrely, he recalled that other morning, seventeen years earlier, when he had stood in that same place with his family and watched the triumphant troops returning home from the Franco-Prussian War. He remembered the stranger who had said to him, 'From now on, that gate will symbolize not Prussia, but Germany.'

Karl looked up at the statue of the Quadriga, the chariot of the

Goddess of Victory. *Vale Senex Imperator* read the banner beneath the prancing hooves of the Quadriga's horses, and on the other side of the great gate, *May the Lord Bless His Departure.* Yes, under Kaiser Wilhelm, this gate had indeed become the symbol of a united and powerful nation.

Seventeen years, Karl thought, seventeen years in which so much has happened. It was then he had vowed to his father that he would open a café at which the Emperor would come to dine. He had opened the café, but now, not only the Emperor but his father was dead.

On and on the troops and mourners moved in front of him and the damp mist touched his face with clammy fingers. Karl shivered and pulled his coat collar closer around his neck. What would happen next, he wondered, and he knew that thought was in the minds of everyone else standing around him.

The old Emperor's son, Friedrich, who was married to Victoria, the eldest daughter of Queen Victoria, became the next Emperor of Germany, but Berliners were hardly aware of his existence, for he came only once to the city during his brief reign, spending his days at Charlottenburg and Potsdam. Already suffering from cancer when he came to the throne, he died a scant ninety-nine days after the death of his father.

Germany's third Emperor in a year was Wilhelm II, Friedrich III's twenty-nine-year-old son. Waving his handkerchief ecstatically, Karl Jochum once again stood on the streets of Berlin with his fellow citizens and cheered the new Emperor as he passed in glorious procession to address parliament. 'Less than two years ago he was in Café Jochum,' he cried to Max Patschke, 'and now he's Emperor! Max, that is the man who'll help me achieve my ambitions! He's *our* Emperor, Max!'

Wilhelm II heralded his rule with ringing words to his people: 'I shall lead you to glorious times!' When Karl heard this, his face lit up, more convinced than ever that a new era was beginning. He thought of his father's prophecy that he and Prince Wilhelm would both rule in Berlin. Yes, that time was coming. The future suddenly looked very bright.

The deaths of two Emperors in such swift succession had meant an extended period of Court mourning, to which the von Biedersteins, as members of the aristocracy, had necessarily adhered. But when Wilhelm II succeeded to the throne, the Prussian court could shed its black and plans forged ahead for the wedding of Count Ewald to Annette Ketterl.

'Damn it all, Karl, no more reprieves,' Ewald grumbled, at his *Stammtisch* in Café Jochum. 'The date's set for April.' Then he fished in his pocket and extracted an envelope. 'Here, you'd better have this. It's your invitation.'

'You mean you're inviting me to your wedding?'

'Damn it all, Karl, a condemned man must have one friend present when he's walking to the gallows. Of course I expect you to be there!'

Karl kept the invitation prominently displayed on his desk and, scarcely able to believe his good fortune, impatiently counted off the days until April.

Finally the great day arrived. His precious invitation securely packed in his new hide travelling bag, Karl gazed out of the train window onto the flat Brandenburg countryside as he travelled for the first time towards Fuerstenmark. But now that he was actually underway, he started to feel extremely nervous, and, as the journey progressed he was haunted by strange fears that he might, inadvertently, behave in a manner that would offend his Junker hosts. If only he were not alone, if only there weree someone with him who could guide him with a sure hand around the pitfalls lying ahead.

A carriage was waiting to meet him at the railway station to take him on the last stretch of his journey to the Castle Inn in Fuerstenmark village, where he was to spend the night.

Rather than eat alone among strangers, Karl asked the innkeeper if he could have some bread and sausage in his room, then set out to explore the village about which he had heard so much from Ewald. It consisted of one long cobbled street, dominated by the adjacent castle and the church. The castle was square and squat with tiny windows deepset into thick stone walls, built to withstand not only the chill winds that swept across the plains from Russia, but also, in distant times, marauding bands of invaders from the North and East. As Ewald had said, it was not a handsome building, but its very solidity was impressive. It had stood there for many centuries and it would stand for many more, for nothing could shake its strength, any more than the power of the von Biedersteins could be shaken.

He walked slowly back down the road so that he could stare through the low archway leading into the stabled courtyard. Tomorrow he, Karl Jochum, would walk through that arch and enter the main door of the castle. Tomorrow, he would join the von Biedersteins.

On that thought he went to sleep, waking early next morning tense with anticipation. At breakfast, it was evident all the guests of the inn were members of the wedding party and all appeared to know each other, for they talked excitedly together about the day ahead, taking no notice of the solitary Karl. Only when the carriages pulled up outside the inn to take them to the church did Karl realize another person had joined their group, a young woman he hadn't seen before and who also appeared to be on her own.

Karl bowed slightly, holding out his hand to help her into the carriage. It was but a short distance from the inn to the church, but it afforded Karl ample opportunity to study the stranger sitting opposite him. She was dressed in a vivid emerald green tailored costume, which had a somewhat foreign look, but showed off her neat figure to great advantage and reflected her green eyes. Her wide-brimmed matching hat was extremely modish, but again it was not a Berlin fashion. Under her hat, her hair was immaculately pleated, gleaming deep copper against the brilliant green, little curls dancing over her forehead and in front of her shell-like ears. Karl stared at her with the perplexed feeling he had seen her somewhere before.

Then the carriage drew up at the church and it was time to descend. The lady in green stayed beside him and they took their seats together at the back of the church, where they were excellently situated to watch the other guests arrive. Karl recognized one or two friends of Ewald, officers from the Guards who had dined at Café Jochum, then his heart jumped, for he saw Heinrich Kraus with Countess Julia on his arm, leading a small boy by the hand. At that moment, the organ, which had been playing quietly until then, swelled out in a triumphant march.

'The Emperor's arrived,' Karl's beautiful neighbour whispered, and, as one, the congregation rose. Regally, nodding occasionally at acquaintances and surrounded by his entourage, Kaiser Wilhelm II made his way to the pews reserved for the royal party beside the bridal couple's parents. Standing ramrod stiff, Karl felt his heart thump with pride. Never had there been such a triumphant day as this, when he was an invited guest to the same wedding as the Emperor. It did not matter that Karl was accommodated at the local inn, while the Kaiser stayed at one of his nearby castles. He was near his Emperor, kneeling when he did, standing when he did, and later they were going to sit at the same table and eat the same meal!

A fairy-tale bride in shimmering white, Annette Ketterl now made her way up the aisle, leaning on her uncle's arm. Holding up her long train were half a dozen small bridesmaids and page boys. As she reached the altar rail of the small church, Ewald, magnificent in his white uniform, stepped out to stand beside her.

For the first time in his life, Karl felt envious of his old friend and rather angry with him. Annette was not the ugly old hag Ewald had described. She was tall and very elegant, rather like a swan with her slim, cream neck and the smooth folds of her dress. Instead of complaining about his loss of freedom, Ewald should be grateful for such an attractive woman with whom to share his life. Karl suddenly found himself wishing that this were his wedding day, so that from now onwards he would have someone with whom to share his dreams and aspirations, and who would take away his loneliness. Without realizing what he was doing, he turned to look at the lady in green. Simultaneously, she glanced at him and smiled. Karl felt a hot flush mount to his cheeks and looked away again.

Eventually, the service over, they walked out of the church into the mellow April sunshine. A regimental guard of honour from the First Brandenburg Guards stood outside, their rifles forming an arch under which Ewald, Annette and their guests processed, then they made their way through the archway, across the gravel courtyard and into Fuerstenmark Castle itself.

A major domo announced them and it was then that Karl learned his new friend's name. 'Fraeulein Graber,' the major domo boomed. 'Herr Jochum.' But Karl had no time to pay attention to her name at that moment, for Kaiser Wilhelm was standing just inside the entrance to the huge beamed hall, surrounded by his attendants, waiting to receive the acknowledgements of his subjects. Karl bowed low. Was it possible that Wilhelm would remember him? Would he recall the day he and his courtiers had dropped in on Café Jochum, exchanged pleasantries and drunk beer on his terrace? If so, the Emperor showed no sign of it, for he seemed to ignore Karl's presence, turning instead to address one of his adjutants.

Then they moved down the formidable line of Biederstein and Ketterl families, shaking hands and murmuring greetings, Karl feeling rather daunted, Fraeulein Graber obviously totally at ease. The formalities over, a butler handed them each a glass of sparkling wine and they turned to look at the high vaulted room, containing a hundred or so people, of whom, Karl realized with a nervous pang, he was acquainted with only Ewald and Heinrich Kraus. If Fraeulein Graber left him, he would be totally alone.

At that moment, she said, 'Perhaps we should introduce ourselves? My name is Ricarda Graber.' Her voice was pleasingly low, with a hint of a foreign accent.

He bowed. 'Jochum, Karl Jochum. I'm delighted to make your acquaintance.'

'You are perhaps related to the Biedersteins?'

'No,' Karl hesitated for a second, then, with an assumed confidence, said, 'Ewald and I are old friends. I was in the Guards with him.'

Ricarda Graber nodded, 'Annette and I are very distantly related. Poor dear, she doesn't have much family, so the least I could do was travel across for her wedding.'

Across from where? He glanced again at her foreign-looking clothes. 'You don't live in Germany?'

'Oh, no. I live in London, Herr Jochum.'

'You're English?' he blurted out in astonishment. 'But, Fraeulein Graber, you speak excellent German!'

She laughed. 'But I am German, Herr Jochum. In fact, I was born near Berlin, although I fear I've lived so long in England I've almost forgotten how to speak German. You see, my father is in the diplomatic service and I've lived there since I was ten. But my grandmother still lives in Heiligensee, just outside Berlin. Unfortunately ...'

At that moment, a woman's voice broke in on them. 'Ricarda! How lovely to see you!'

'Anna! How lovely to see you again, my dear, and how well you look. Marriage obviously suits you. And where's Johann?'

Karl stared at the two women joyfully embracing each other, his mind in turmoil. So that was why her features were so familiar! The same green eyes, the same red hair — and the same charming manners. She was the daughter of Emil Graber, the diplomat who had befriended him and suggested that he invite Maurice Mesurier to Berlin!

Taking a step backwards, he watched Johann von Biederstein join the small group, bowing over Ricarda's hand and kissing it. He bit his lip in an attempt to fight back his disappointment. For a brief while, he had thought he had found a friend, a kindred spirit, another alien in a foreign environment, but he had been wrong.

This was Ricarda's social circle; he was the only outsider, the only peasant among the nobility. Suddenly, he wished he could take off the black morning coat he had had made at such great expense by the Court tailors, and join the servants, handing out drinks. That was where he belonged — with the servants, not with the guests.

'It's been such a long time since I've seen you,' Ricarda was saying to Anna von Biederstein. 'Let me see, it must have been at Hannelore's debut.'

'My dear, Hannelore's eldest is ten now! She's got five altogether. And did you know that Julia's had another son?'

'Julia?'

'Yes, he was only born last week. Look, she's over there. Oh, and she's got the baby with her!'

Karl felt his misery increasing by the second. He saw Julia making her way towards them carrying her baby in her arms, Heinrich Kraus walking stiffly beside her, holding his first son by the hand. Would they acknowledge him or would they cut him?

Ricarda kissed Julia, shook hands with Heinrich, leaned over to admire the baby, then crouched down to say hello to the little boy. 'So you're Ernst.' The child stared unsmilingly at her and Karl saw with a start that he had the same sandy hair and pale eyes as his father. So Heinrich's first-born was breeding true to type.

Then, to his astonishment, for he thought she had forgotten him, Ricarda stood back. 'Herr Jochum, do you know my old friend, Countess Julia? She, Anna and I were all young girls together.'

'Why, Herr Jochum!' Julia exclaimed. 'How very nice to see you again.'

'You know each other?'

'Herr Jochum is an old friend of Ewald's,' Julia said. Karl would willingly have died for her out of sheer gratitude. 'Herr Jochum, I believe you already know my husband, Herr Kraus?'

He felt Heinrich's cold eyes flickering over him and was certain that, like him, the man was remembering the freehold of the Potsdamer Platz building. 'Yes, we are already acquainted.'

As if she sensed the hostility between the two men, Ricarda asked quickly, 'What are you going to call your new son, Herr Kraus?'

'We've decided upon the name Benno.'

'Benno, eh?' Ewald voice rang out from behind Karl. 'Not a Biederstein name!'

'My grand-grandfather was called Benno,' Heinrich said frigidly.

'I think Benno is a most attractive name,' Ricarda stated. At that moment, Benno Kraus opened his eyes and gazed at the strange faces peering at him. Then he puckered his face, opened his mouth and screamed.

Perhaps, Karl thought hopefully, Benno wouldn't become a typical Kraus. He started to feel a little better.

His mood improved even more when Ricarda Graber made it obvious that she had no intention of forsaking him, but took his arm for him to lead her into the galleried dining hall for the wedding breakfast. 'So, Herr Jochum, you were in the Guards,' she asked in her fascinating accent, as they started on their soup. 'What do you do now?'

He wondered if her father had ever mentioned his restaurant to her. 'I own the Café Jochum on the Potsdamer Platz,' he said, his heart thumping.

Abruptly, she put her spoon down on the table and gazed at him. 'But I didn't realize you were *the* Herr Jochum! Why, you must know my father, Emil Graber! Herr Jochum, he's often talked to me about you. In fact, I think I know almost everything there is to know about you, about Max Patschke and, of course, Maurice Mesurier ...'

Her enthusiasm was so evidently genuine that Karl felt all his previous misgivings fading away. Before he could stop himself, he found himself saying, 'Fraeulein Graber, if you would permit me to call on you, I should be delighted to invite you to Café Jochum as my guest.'

'Why, that would be wonderful. I should enjoy it so much. But tell me, Herr Jochum, how did you come to own Café Jochum?'

To his surprise, Karl found himself telling her about his family, the way he had built up the business, Sigi's death, Klothilde's move to Munich and even some of his plans for the future. So engrossed did he become in the conversation, he even forgot about the Emperor's presence until the last course had been cleared away and silence was requested for His Majesty to speak.

After the speeches and toasts, the assembled company rose and moved back to the hall, where an orchestra was playing. Ewald and Annette led off the dancing, then the Kaiser danced with Annette and soon all the young people were on the floor. Karl held out his hand to Ricarda. 'Would you like to dance?'

She was a very graceful dancer and Karl found himself, once again, giving silent thanks to Ewald's tutelage all those years ago. Whatever else Ricarda Graber thought of him, she could not fault his manners. Reflecting on this — and also wondering why it was so important that she should think well of him — Karl's self-congratulatory reverie was interrupted by the Emperor's voice. 'Herr Jochum!'

With Ricarda's arm still in his, Karl turned and bowed, suddenly aware of being the centre of interest, as people's heads turned curiously in their direction. 'Your Majesty,' Karl breathed.

'Herr Jochum,' the Emperor leaned back in his chair, a mischievous twinkle in his eyes, 'since we last met, I've been taking a very great interest in truffles and I learn that there are very few in Germany. Do you know why?'

Karl stifled a smile, conscious of a sudden silence in the vicinity, as onlookers strained to hear what the Emperor was saying. 'No, Your Majesty.'

'The French keep popping over the border and taking them to feed to their own pigs, so they can sell their truffles to us at a profit!' The Kaiser roared with laughter at his own joke.

Those attendants who had been present on the occasion at Café Jochum laughed too. Others stared in mystification, but obediently chuckled.

'With Your Majesty's permission, I shall inform Maître Mesurier.'

'That's it, never let the French forget who's who!' His Emperor grinned, then turned back to his courtiers.

'Herr Jochum, you are the most surprising man,' Ricarda Graber told him, as they made their way back to their table, followed by many envious eyes, 'You appear so reserved, indeed almost shy, yet you are on intimate enough terms with His Majesty to share a private joke with him.'

The very last of his nervousness disappearing, Karl smiled at her. He knew a social rift still existed between himself and the nobility, but Ricarda, Countess Julia and the Emperor himself seemed intent on helping him to bridge it. The rest of the wedding passed in a daze, as total strangers came up to make his acquaintance and he and Ricarda were made to feel like two of the most important guests.

When he thought back over the day's events, he realized that the only person to have actually treated him coldly was Heinrich Kraus, a mere commoner, like himself.

Nothing seemed more natural than that he and Ricarda should travel back together to Berlin. Whereas the outward journey had seemed interminably lonely to Karl, the return trip passed like a flash. 'It's a shame your parents couldn't accompany you on this visit,' Karl commented politely.

'My mother died last year,' Ricarda explained. 'I think that's one reason why my father has been particularly glad to have a daughter. Mama was ill for a long time and at least I have been able to act as hostess at diplomatic dinners and functions since I was about sixteen. Papa was hoping to come with me, but, unfortunately, he was delayed at the last moment. However, he may still be able to join me.'

'I hope so.' But the thought of Emil Graber reminded him of the social gulf between them. Herr Graber belonged to the upper classes that patronized Café Jochum, where Karl Jochum was their servant.

They were both silent for a moment, then Ricarda asked, 'Was this your first visit to Fuerstenmark, Herr Jochum?'

He nodded.

'I hadn't been there before either, although I've heard a lot about it from Anna and Julia. I suppose it's very impressive, because it's so old, but I did find it a dismal place.' She shuddered. 'All those long, draughty corridors; huge rooms with small windows and cold, stone floors; those terrible, threadbare tapestries. No wonder Julia couldn't wait to leave it.'

'Ewald doesn't like it either,' Karl confided.

She laughed, her green eyes sparkling. 'Ewald and Julia are the only two in that family with any taste.'

But, for once, Karl didn't want to talk about the Biedersteins. He wanted to learn more about Ricarda. 'What is your taste, Fraeulein Graber?'

'In houses? Oh, I like space and light. I like clean, bright colours and uncomplicated shapes. A house should be a living thing, with plants and flowers, books and pictures. It should be welcoming, not oppressive.'

'You must live in a very fine house in London.'

'Yes, I suppose it is, but it isn't ours, Herr Jochum.' She leaned forward. 'Do you know what my dream is? It's to have a house of my own that I can decorate exactly as I'd like it. Imagine, a whole house, that I could make into my own and call home! That's why I so enjoy staying with my grandmother. Do you know Heiligensee, Herr Jochum?'

102

He knew of the village, situated on the edge of a lake formed by the River Havel about fifteen miles from Berlin's city centre.

'My grandmother has a beautiful little house on the shore of the Heiligensee itself. When my grandfather died many years ago, she sold the dairy herd and farmland that they owned but stayed on in the house. Now, that house is old, but it's full of family mementoes.' As she spoke her face grew soft. 'It's much more beautiful than Fuerstenmark Castle.'

Karl could scarcely believe it as the train pulled into Berlin. 'Is someone coming to meet you?'

'Certainly not. I shall take a cab.'

He found her independence both daunting and challenging, but she was certainly the most intriguing woman he had ever met. 'You will come to dine with me at Café Jochum?' he asked, as he carried her bag to the taxi rank.

'But, of course, I'm looking forward to it.'

'Shall I call for you at seven tomorrow evening?'

'Thank you, Herr Jochum, that would be most acceptable.' She handed him a card. 'This is my grandmother's address.'

All next day Karl whistled as he moved round the café. 'I'm inviting a very special guest to dinner this evening,' he told Mesurier. 'I want you to prepare something quite unique.'

The little Frenchman studied him. 'Eh, with tomatoes, maybe?' At Karl's blank stare, he grinned mischievously. '*Pommes d'amour*, love apples.'

'So Cupid's arrow has struck,' Max Patschke commented knowingly.

'Fraeulein Graber is the daughter of Herr Diplomat Graber,' Karl told him stiffly, but he knew there was more to it than that. The hours until he was due to meet Ricarda passed very slowly indeed.

He dressed very carefully that evening, dreading that he would cut himself shaving, polishing his shoes until they shone like Ewald's boots had in the olden days, and buttoning his collar so tightly it cut into his neck.

He drove out to Heiligensee in a first-class Droschke, the horse's hooves echoing the beating of his heart. Never, he told the cabby, had he seen Berlin looking so beautiful. Not for a long time had a spring evening been so mellow. 'There's snow in the air,' the driver retorted gloomily, but nothing could dispel Karl's happiness.

They drove through the fishing hamlet of Heiligensee, and pulled into a drive lined with dense shrubs. Then round a bend they saw the house itself. Nestled against a backdrop of tall oak trees, the building was just two storeys high, looking over striped lawns that stretched down to the water's edge, and fringed with flower borders massed with narcissi and tulips. Across the width of the house was a south-facing verandah, glassed in at the sides to keep out the wind, a riot of colour with ranked tubs of geraniums.

Gazing at it, Karl suddenly understood what Ricarda had meant about Fuerstenmark Castle. Where that had intimidated him, this house seemed to welcome him. At that moment, the front door opened and Ricarda emerged, a stunning figure in turquoise, running across the drive towards him. 'Herr Jochum, you're so punctual!'

'I hope I'm not too early?'

'Not at all, I seem to have been dressed for hours!' She was bewitchingly frank. She looked at the cabby. 'Will he wait while you meet my grandmother?'

At the sight of Ricarda, the cabby had brightened considerably. 'Course I will, miss. Take your time.'

So Karl stepped for the first time into the Graber cottage at Heiligensee, ducking under low beamed doorways into the homely living room where Grandmother Graber was sitting in front of a log fire. Once she must have had the same flame-coloured hair as her son and granddaughter, although age had now turned it white, but she still had the same green eyes, which peered at him keenly. Her features were strong and she gave the impression of indomitable toughness. 'So you are Herr Jochum,' she said, holding out her hand.

Karl bent low over it. 'I trust you don't mind my inviting Fraeulein Graber to dinner.'

She appeared to be considering the matter, weighing up his character while he stood there, as if she could decide upon the spot whether her only granddaughter would be safe with him. So this is how Ricarda will look when she's old, Karl reflected, and suddenly he knew that he was falling in love with Ricarda, and was sure that his feelings would never change, not even when her hair no longer flamed.

'I'm absolutely delighted,' the old lady said decisively. 'Now, run along, children, and enjoy yourselves.'

'Isn't she a wonderful person?' Ricarda asked, as they drove back through the country lanes towards Berlin.

'She certainly is. And, Fraeulein Graber, you were right about her house. It's very beautiful.' Now, as they approached the Potsdamer Platz, Karl was filled with a new apprehension: what would happen if Ricarda did not like Café Jochum?

He handed her out of the Droschke, paid the cabby, then led her across the terrace and in through the front door. Max Patschke hurried out to greet them. 'Good evening, gracious lady. Good evening, Herr Direktor. If you'll follow me ...'

But Ricarda did not move. Her eyes danced round the crowded restaurant, taking in the velvet curtains, the gold candelabra, the gleaming silverware, the orchestra led by Franz Jankowski and the bustling waiters. 'Did you design this yourself, Herr Jochum?'

'Yes, Fraeulein Graber.' Suddenly, he knew everything was all right.

'But it's so elegant! Why, I don't think I've ever seen such a beautiful restaurant, not even in London or Paris. No wonder you're proud of it.'

Max gave Karl a sly wink, then led them upstairs to a private room. When they were seated, Karl asked, 'Will you permit me to order for you, Fraeulein Graber?'

'Oh, please!'

'We'll have the menu I arranged earlier with Maître Mesurier, Max.'

Their conversation flowed easily as they dined from a succession of small, appetizingly prepared courses of melon in port wine, soup and turbot. When Max brought in the meat course, Ricarda was telling him that her father was, after all, able to come to Berlin and would be arriving in a month's time. Then she broke off to gaze at the partridge on her plate, intricately wrapped in fresh vine leaves. 'How beautiful!'

Maurice Mesurier himself followed Max. In his hand he held a sauce boat, which he held out to Ricarda for her inspection. 'A little sauce, Madame?'

'Please.'

Another waiter served the vegetables onto a side plate and still Mesurier hovered discreetly in a corner of the room. Ricarda cut into the meat, added a little sauce and tasted. Her eyes widened and she ate some more. Then she turned to the chef. 'But Maître Mesurier,' she exclaimed in fluent French, 'this is excellent. Please accept my compliments.'

The diminutive chef beamed. '*Merci*, mademoiselle.'

Karl stared at Ricarda. 'You speak French?'

'But, of course, I'm a diplomat's daughter, don't forget.'

She was full of surprises! With his still rather guttural French, Karl turned to Mesurier. 'Maître, please join us in a glass of wine and tell Mademoiselle Graber the secret of fine food.'

They could see he needed little encouragement. 'What differentiates a good cook from an artist is the same that distinguishes a dressmaker from a couturier, Mademoiselle. It is how he embellishes the basic commodity he is working on to transform it into a work of art. In this case, for instance, the partridge is marinaded for two days in white wine, adding a little of this and a little of that, until it has a fine flavour. Then it is wrapped in vine leaves to contain the juices and finally it is roasted. But on its own, Madame, the partridge is nothing!'

The rapt expression on Ricarda's face showed that not only was she having no problem keeping up with his French, but she was entranced. 'As you will have realized,' Mesurier continued, 'it is the sauce that completes the dish. The sauce, Mademoiselle, is everything! It is like the frills on a woman's dress, the feathers on her hat, the little touch of rouge on her cheeks, the curl over her forehead. It is the finishing touch that beautifies and perfects.'

Ricarda stared in awe at her dish of food. 'And what is this sauce called, Maître Mesurier?'

He rose to his full height of five feet two inches. 'I have taken the liberty of naming it Sauce Ricarda, Mademoiselle.' Then he took her hand, and, bowing low over it so his tall white cap brushed her arm, he kissed it.

'Maître Mesurier, I have never been paid a finer compliment.'

'What other languages do you speak?' Karl asked, when the chef had gone.

'Italian, Spanish, a little Russian and, of course, English.'

She made his own linguistic accomplishments seem very modest. 'I could do with someone like you in my hotel,' he blurted out.

'Hotel, Herr Jochum?'

Suddenly, he found himself confiding in her his plans for building a hotel select enough even for the Emperor.

'Have you thought what you'll call it?'

'There will be time enough to give it a name if it's ever built.'

She stared at him seriously across the table. 'Oh, it will be built. That is something of which I'm absolutely certain.'

'And what makes you so certain?' he asked sceptically.

'Because you're a man who succeeds in everything he sets out to do. Look at Café Jochum, as fine a tribute as any to your ability. Yes, Herr Jochum, if you say you're going to build Berlin's most luxurious hotel, then I'm in absolutely no doubt that you will do so.'

'It won't be easy.'

'The most worthwhile things in life never are.' She frowned. 'What do Berliners call the statue on top of the Brandenburg Gate?'

'You mean the Goddess of Victory? The Quadriga?'

'Yes, that's it. That's what you should call your hotel, Herr Jochum. The Hotel Quadriga!'

It was an inspired suggestion. As all its implications filtered through Karl's mind, he smiled admiringly at her, then reached across and took her hand. 'That's wonderful. That's what we'll call it. The Hotel Quadriga!'

Simultaneously, they realized what he had said. For a few moments, they were silent as the word 'we' hung between them, then, still clasping her hand, Karl asked, 'You will be helping me, won't you?'

For the next four weeks they were seldom apart, except at night when Ricarda returned to Heiligensee. For the first time in his life, Karl took time off from his work, so that they could explore Berlin together. They visited art galleries and museums, went to the theatre and the opera, and often simply drove into the countryside with a picnic. Every evening, they dined at Café Jochum. They were halcyon days, except for the dark cloud that hung over Karl's horizon, drawing steadily closer with the expected arrival of Emil Graber in Berlin. The diplomat, Karl was convinced, would be no more in favour of Ricarda marrying a commoner, than the Biedersteins had been regarding Julia's choice of Heinrich Kraus. But where Kraus had at least been able to offer wealth, all Karl could offer was devotion and he doubted Diplomat Graber would consider that sufficient.

Ricarda was not only beautiful, she was highly intelligent, cultured and articulate. There must be any number of young men, from her own class, waiting to ask for her hand in marriage. The more he thought about it, the more certain he became that he stood not a chance. All he represented to her was a holiday romance, while her father, immediately seeing the danger he represented, would whisk her post-haste back to London.

As the dreaded day approached, Ricarda grew even gayer, while Karl became morose. 'Karl, is something wrong?'

But he couldn't tell her. Instead, he bit his lip, looking, Ricarda thought, just as he must have done as a small boy.

The night before her father arrived, Ricarda Graber lay awake for a long time, thinking over all the things she had to tell him. There was no doubt at all in her mind that he would welcome Karl as a son-in-law, for he had always spoken admiringly of him and his achievements. Nor was she in any doubt at all that Karl was the man she wanted to marry, for never before had she known anyone to whom she instinctively felt so close, with whom she honestly believed she could spend the rest of her life. The only problem was that, during their entire time together, Karl had never once mentioned the word love. Never once given her any real indication that he wanted to marry her. Never once even given her an opening to declare her feelings for him.

She closed her eyes and smiled. Tomorrow, her father was coming. He would find the solution. Everything, she was certain, would be all right.

It was wonderful to see him again. She sat impatiently on the arm of his chair, while he talked to his mother, then dragged him out into the garden, so they could talk in private. By the water's edge, there was a fallen oak tree that had been fashioned into a kind of seat and it was on this that they sat while she told him all about Ewald's wedding, meeting Karl and his plans for an hotel. When she had finished, Emil Graber laughed. 'I've always liked Karl Jochum, but I must confess that I'm not clear whether you and he are going into the hotel business together or if you're getting married.'

Ricarda signed. 'I think he loves me, Papa, but it's as if he's worried about something.'

'You're a very unusual young woman, Ricarda. Perhaps he's frightened of you. Or, maybe, he quite simply fears he isn't good enough for you.'

'But that's rubbish, Papa! He's a wonderful man. Think of all the things he's done with his life.'

Her father chuckled. 'You are a diplomat's daughter, Ricarda. He is the son of a sweetmaker, as you've told me several times during the last hour.'

108

'You think that could be the reason?'

'I shouldn't be a bit surprised.'

'But what can I do?'

Emil looked out across the calm water, where a few boats were fishing for eels. 'You really want to marry him?'

'More than anything in the world.'

'Then I suggest you propose to him,' her father said.

Karl had never felt so miserable in his life as when he drove out to Heiligensee that Sunday lunchtime, for this, he was convinced, would mark the end of his relationship with Ricarda. Emil Graber, who had spoken to him so friendlily in the past as a guest of Café Jochum, would now stare superciliously and dismiss him from the house. He almost felt inclined to ask the cabby to wait so that he could take him straight back to Berlin.

Yet Heiligensee looked as welcoming as ever, grey smoke curling up from the kitchen chimney, its garden massed with flowers. Then the front door burst open and Ricarda came out, her face wreathed in smiles. 'Karl! We thought you were never coming!' She linked her arm in his and led him into the house.

'Herr Jochum, how nice to see you again.' Emil Graber stood up from the armchair where he had been reading a newspaper.

Stunned, Karl shook his hand. Grandmother Graber bustled in, wiping her hands on her apron. 'Ach, excuse me, Herr Jochum, it's the maid's day off. I'm afraid you're going to have to put up with my cooking today.' Karl gazed at them all in bewilderment. This was not at all the reception he had been expecting.

'Can I offer you a drink, Herr Jochum?' Emil Graber asked. Then he laughed, 'It's usually the other way round, isn't it — you offering me a drink?'

Karl smiled weakly. Was the diplomat making fun of him or was he trying to put him at his ease?

'Perhaps a cognac, Herr Jochum?'

'Thank you,' Karl said, but his suspicions remained.

Karl said little during lunch, but the Grabers, practised at making conversation from the many functions they had attended, did not make his silence seem conspicuous. Then, the meal over, Grandmother Graber announced she was going to take her normal afternoon nap, while Emil said he would take his newspaper to the verandah. 'Why don't you two go for a row on the lake?'

This was it, Karl decided. Everything had been arranged beforehand. Since they had invited him to lunch, they did not like to turn him away before he had eaten, but now the formalities were over, Emil and his mother had discreetly withdrawn, leaving Ricarda to tell him her father's decision.

Heavy-heartedly, he made his way down to the rowing boat tied up to the simple jetty. Ricarda's face was serious, as he handed her down, then cast off. Slowly, he rowed out towards the centre of the lake, watching the cottage recede until Emil Graber was a mere blob on the verandah. All the time, Ricarda sat, knotting her handkerchief nervously in her fingers, not saying a word. Eventually, Karl laid down the oars. 'It's all right. I know what you want to say. I do understand.'

Her wide green eyes stared across at him, then she gently laid her hand on his. 'Do you, Karl?'

'You want to tell me that you're going back to London and that we shall never meet again.'

'Is that what you want, Karl?'

'Of course it isn't, Ricarda. But I know it's what your father wants. He doesn't want his daughter to marry a common café proprietor. I do understand.' He paused. 'Oh, Ricarda, I'm going to miss you so much.'

To his surprise, she clasped both his hands in hers. 'Karl, what about the "common café proprietor", as you call him? Would he like to marry Emil Graber's daughter?'

Surely his feelings were obvious? 'But of course he would.'

'Then why doesn't he ask her?'

Suddenly, he realized she was smiling at him. 'You mean ...?' he asked disbelievingly.

'I mean that if you won't ask me to marry you, then I'm going to have to ask you.'

Forgetting they were in a fragile rowing boat, Karl slipped off the seat and knelt at Ricarda's feet. 'Ricarda, will you marry me?'

'Of course I will,' she said, tears glittering in her eyes.

He took her in his arms and, as the boat rocked dangerously, kissed her for the first time.

The marriage of Karl Jochum and Ricarda Graber took place at the end of July 1889 in the small parish church of Heiligensee, followed by a magnificent reception at Café Jochum.

The Grabers were there, of course, and Klothilde, Grete and

Gottfried travelled up from Munich to be present. Count Ewald was Karl's best man and brought the graceful Annette with him. Isaak Arendt, his wife and Theo came, as did Israel Silberstein, Dr Duschek and his wife. There were also many old guests of Café Jochum, friends from Berlin, who had known Karl Jochum for many years and held him in high esteem.

For the occasion, Maître Mesurier produced a magnificent spread. The guests sat down to one of the seven-course meals for which the French chef was renowned, each course excelling the next in looks, taste and rarity. They drank Rhenish hock, French claret and fine champagne. When the dinner was eventually over, Franz Jankowski's orchestra, which had been playing quietly for the duration of the meal, burst into a quick Viennese waltz. Karl turned to Ricarda, 'Will you dance?'

As he took her in his arms, he was certain there was no happier man in the world that day. He had his café, he had his plans for the future and he had, for his wife, the most beautiful woman he had ever met. He held her close, her luxurious auburn curls soft beneath his chin, and vowed he would never ever let her go.

At six they slipped away from their guests to change in upstairs rooms set aside for the purpose, before they left for their honeymoon. Emil Graber was returning to England that evening and taking his mother with him for a holiday, so that the newly-married couple could spend their honeymoon at Heiligensee. 'It's a family tradition,' the old lady had told them. 'I spent my honeymoon there and so did Emil. Now, my dears, so should you. And, when I die, the house will be left to you in my will.'

Everybody crowded out onto the pavement to watch them depart. Klothilde kissed her son affectionately. 'I think Ricarda is a lovely girl, Karli. Your father would have liked her very much, I'm certain, my dear.'

'You must come and visit us in Munich,' Grete told them.

'It's been a most satisfactory visit,' Emil Graber declared. 'I'm delighted to have you as my son-in-law, Karl. And I shall continue to tell everyone about Café Jochum!'

Maître Mesurier in his tall chef's hat, Fritzi Messner, Max Patschke, Franz Jankowski, all the waiters and kitchen staff, stood and cheered as Karl and Ricarda mounted into the horse-drawn carriage that was to take them to Heiligensee. Passers-by stopped to watch and they, too, waved and shouted ribald comments.

'I feel a bit like the Kaiser,' Karl laughed to Ricarda.

'We have so many friends,' she said, wonderingly.

'But, most important of all, we have each other.' As the coach left the Potsdamer Platz in the direction of the Tiergarten, Karl put his arm around her shoulder, drew her to him and kissed her.

It was a blissfully happy time, the honeymoon at Heiligensee. For the first time in his life, Karl lay in bed until eight or nine in the morning, rising for a leisurely breakfast that Ricarda set on the verandah overlooking the lake. Then, hand in hand, they strolled by the lake, gathered wild flowers, paddled in the water, prepared a simple lunch, and often, revelling in their wanton luxury, went back to bed in the afternoon.

'Are you going to find Berlin boring after London?' he asked his wife, as they sat in front of a log fire.

She took his hand in hers. 'Bored? With a hotel to build, how can I be bored?'

'It's going to be a while yet before we can build the Hotel Quadriga, I'm afraid. In the meantime, you have to occupy your time.'

'I don't think that's going to be any problem. I'm going to enjoy keeping house for you, Karli. It will be such fun to have an apartment of my own.'

Karl thought doubtfully about the flat on the Rosenthaler Platz in which he had lived all his life. Since his mother had left, he had kept it clean, but it had become very much a bachelor apartment. 'We must find somewhere bigger.'

'Why? If it was big enough for all your family, it must be big enough for us. And then, when the hotel's built, we'll move there.'

'You really do believe we'll build the Quadriga, don't you?'

'Of course.'

Karl was silent for a moment, then he asked, 'We might have children, mightn't we? Would you like children, Ricarda?'

She moved closer to him. 'More than anything in the world.'

That night they made love with renewed intensity. As he later drifted into sleep, Karl hoped they would have a son, a boy whom he could bring up in the same way as Sigi had reared him. A boy, who would serve in the First Brandenburg Guards, then learn to run Café Jochum and, eventually, the Hotel Quadriga.

With frightening speed the honeymoon passed and they were back in the city, Ricarda accustoming herself to life as a Berlin house-wife, Karl back at the reins of Café Jochum. Although Max had done an excellent job in his absence, he was obviously relieved to see Karl back. 'Don't have too many honeymoons, Herr Direktor,' he quipped, 'it's hard work managing the shop on one's own.'

Karl believed him. With its private dining rooms and two large downstairs restaurants, Café Jochum could accommodate over two hundred people at one sitting, while the café-concert seated a further hundred. It must have been an almost impossible task for Max to combine the organization with his position as head waiter. Grimly, he realized that it would be quite a long time before he and Ricarda could take another holiday.

'Isn't there anything I can do to help you?' Ricarda asked, when he explained the problem.

'You help me best by being here, at home. You've no idea how wonderful it is to know that you are waiting for me.'

But as the first year of his marriage sped by, Karl became increasingly aware of the toll demanded of him by Café Jochum. Try as he might, he seldom managed to be home much before midnight. Although Ricarda never complained, he knew she must find the long days lonely. However much they hoped and tried, she did not become pregnant and their childlessness disappointed him for her sake as much as his own. Besides providing him with an heir, a son would fill in those long hours while he was away.

In the meantime, however, Ricarda seemed happy pottering round his family's old apartment, buying bits and pieces of furniture, pictures and ornaments that caught her fancy. Once again, the flat began to look like home and it was evident that she had a great talent for interior decoration. 'This is in preparation for the Quadriga,' she would say. But sometimes Karl doubted the Hotel Quadriga would ever be built, although he was more convinced than ever that the timing was right. Under the rule of the new young Emperor a fresh impetus had been given to building work in the city. The Reichstag building, to house parliament, was completed on the Koenigsplatz; work commenced to refurbish the Imperial Palace; and plans were put underway to construct a Memorial Church to Kaiser Wilhelm I between the new Kurfuerstendamm and the Tauentzienstrasse.

The value of Karl's shares in Bismarck's Kurfuerstendamm Company was steadily rising, as imposing new buildings rose from the meadows along the former Pappelallee. When he sold those shares, they were going to be worth considerably more than the ten pfennigs each he had paid for them.

Yes, the moment was right and he would probably even be able to raise the money, but he lacked the time to do anything about it. Quite simply, Café Jochum consumed his every waking second.

In July 1890, after Karl had been married for a year, an unexpected visitor walked into Café Jochum. At first glance, Karl did not recognize the tall, balding man with a monocle in his right eye, who limped towards him. Then his mind went back to the Amateur Chase at Karlshorst on a clear September day in 1878. He saw a group of horses bunch at a fence and a chestnut gelding throw his jockey, only to fall heavily on top of him. 'Lieutenant Tobisch!' he said, with a certain feeling of misgiving. Then politeness got the better of him. 'How are you, sir? Please do sit down and have a drink.'

Eitel Tobisch sipped appreciatively at the glass of beer. 'This is a fine place you've got here, Herr Jochum.'

'Thank you sir,' Karl replied, but he sensed there was more to Eitel Tobisch's visit than mere curiosity. Although he was reasonably well dressed and wore his monocle with a confident air, there was something uneasy in the former lieutenant's manner that roused his suspicions. Since Tobisch had never before sought him out for a social visit, Karl could only assume that the man wanted a favour of some kind. But why come to him?

The lunchtime trade was slowly building up and Karl had more important things to do than watch Eitel Tobisch drink a glass of beer. 'Has your visit a particular purpose?' he asked bluntly.

Eitel Tobisch looked distinctly uncomfortable at this. 'Actually, I was wondering if you could offer me some kind of job.'

Karl was staggered, for it was the first time he had been approached by someone from a superior social background and, what was more, by an officer from his former regiment. But he remembered Tobisch's fondness for cards and could only assume he had once again lost all his assets at the gaming tables. Apart from anything else, he certainly could not afford to employ gamblers on his staff.

His suspicions appeared justified, for the man continued, 'I've just returned from Monte Carlo.'

'I'm sorry, Herr Tobisch, but I'm not looking for any personnel at present.'

'From the Hotel du Palais at Monte Carlo,' Tobisch added swiftly. 'I was working there as General Manager. I've been in the hotel business ever since I was forced to resign my commission.'

Karl looked at him sharply, for this put a whole new complexion on things. 'So what brings you to Berlin?'

'My father's ill. The doctors don't give him long to live. My mother, who is herself an invalid, wrote to ask me if I'd come home to look after them both. What else could I do?'

'I'm sorry,' Karl said mechanically, then asked, 'Where else have you worked?'

'Baden-Baden, Rome, Paris and Cairo. One way or another, during the past thirteen years, I've worked in almost every side of hotel life.'

Karl tapped the ash from his cigar thoughtfully into the ashtray. If the man's story were true — and it would be easy enough to verify — he was just the person he was looking for to ease some of the burden of Café Jochum from his shoulders. And, eventually, of course, when the Hotel Quadriga was built, his knowledge of hotel management would be invaluable.

In the meantime, however, one big question mark still hung over Eitel Tobisch. Could he be trusted not to return to the card tables? It was not something Karl felt in a position to ask, yet he knew the subject had to be brought into the open before he employed him. Then he had a moment of inspiration. Ricarda was the finest judge of human character he had ever met. 'My wife and I run this business together, so I suggest Ricarda meets you before we come to any decision. Perhaps you could dine with us tomorrow evening?'

Evident relief etched itself across Eitel's face. 'I'll do anything,' he promised. 'I'll even wait on tables.'

'I'm sure that won't be necessary.'

That night, he told Ricarda all he knew about Eitel Tobisch's background.

'Do you think he's a good manager?' she asked him.

'I think he'd have made a good officer if he could have stayed away from poker and horses, so I can only assume he'd make a good manager.'

'Would you like me to ask him about his gambling?'

'I'm sure you could do it more tactfully than I could.'

They ate the next evening in one of the private dining rooms. Eitel Tobisch proved an interesting conversationalist, telling little anecdotes from his life in some of Europe's most prestigious hotels with humour, as well as giving an illuminating insight into the way a hotel was run. Without divulging any more than was necessary of

115

his plans, Karl told him of his intention to open one day a first-class hotel in Berlin. Tobisch's eyes lit up. 'What a wonderful challenge!'

'You would be interested in helping us run such a hotel?' Ricarda asked, laying her napkin on the table.

'Interested? Frau Jochum, I can assure you there is nothing I should like to do more.'

'My husband tells me you were forced to resign your commission because of gambling debts. You must understand, Herr Tobisch, that if we place you in a position of trust — as we are contemplating — then we must have some kind of undertaking from you that your gambling will not interfere in any way with your duties within our business. Can you give such a guarantee?'

Eitel Tobisch's cheeks paled and two pink spots appeared on each side of his mouth, as he stared at her. Then he slowly took his monocle out of his eye and relaxed. 'Frau Jochum, I could offer you references to put your mind at rest, but I admit they could be worth no more than the paper on which they would be written. All I can do is give you my word of honour as an officer of the First Brandenburg Guards that I shall never do anything dishonest or damaging to my employer's business in any way. What I cannot promise is that, when I am in a position to again, I shan't take up poker and go to the races. But that, I hope you will agree, is my own business.'

Ricarda held out her hand. 'Thank you, Herr Tobisch, I appreciate the honesty of your reply. And now I'll leave you to discuss your business together.' She stood up and both men sprang to their feet.

But later that evening, she confessed to Karl, 'I'm sure he means everything he says, but I can't help feeling he's essentially a rather weak man. If temptation is put in his way, he won't be able to resist.'

Karl suddenly remembered Ewald saying, 'Once a gambler, always a gambler. Tobisch was born that way. He'll never reform.' But he wanted somebody to help him run Café Jochum. 'Apart from your reservations about his gambling, do you think he'd make a good manager for Café Jochum?'

'Oh, I don't doubt his abilities at all in that sense.'

'Then I suppose what he does in his own time with his own money is his own business. I propose we take him on. Don't you see what a difference he'd make to our lives? For the first time

116

since our honeymoon, we'd be able to spend some time together.'

Forcing her doubts to the back of her mind, Ricarda relented. 'It would be nice to see a little more of you,' she admitted.

Eitel Tobisch gradually took over many of the tasks that had, until then, necessitated Karl's almost constant presence on the premises. He got on well with Max Patschke and was wise enough to let Maurice Mesurier reign supreme over his kitchen kingdom. As time went by, Karl relaxed and almost forgot he had ever doubted the former lieutenant.

So far as Eitel Tobisch was concerned, he considered himself an extremely lucky man. Walking into Café Jochum to ask for a job had turned out to be one of the wisest moves he had ever made, although it had been humiliating at the time to seek assistance from a former private.

As he got to know him better, however, he had only admiration for Karl Jochum, who obviously possessed an inborn flair for the restaurant business. It was evident that his staff, from the lowliest kitchen assistant to the head waiter, adored their Herr Direktor and would willingly go out and die for him, should this ever be demanded of them.

Eitel had smarted under Ricarda Jochum's question about his gambling, but as the first year of his employment passed, he knew that he would keep his word. Thanks to the Jochums he had a respectable and responsible position with a good salary, with even greater prospects ahead if they did open their hotel. At long last, Eitel Tobisch felt he could hold his head high among his fellow men.

His one regret was that his parents could not have lived longer to witness his success, for they had died within a few weeks of each other shortly after his return to Berlin. But at least he had been near them, able to take care of their last months, and they had ended their lives proud of their only son.

Unable to afford the rent on his parents' house, Eitel had taken lodgings with a Frau Kaufmann in the old town, where he was not long in meeting his landlady's daughter, Liese. In her late twenties, Liese was no beauty, but she was a good housekeeper and seemed endowed with sound common sense. Eitel was tired of his previous nomadic existence and Frau Kaufmann was keen to see her daughter married. It was not long before they all assumed that a marriage between the two would one day take place.

Gradually, Eitel's savings were mounting to the point where he would be able to afford to rent and furnish a flat of his own. Not once since his return to Berlin had he been near the racecourse or the gaming tables, and he finally felt sufficiently self-confident to confess his weakness to Liese.

She didn't look shocked or surprised, but merely said, 'That's all right. I'll look after all our money once we're married.'

Eitel hesitated, then acquiesced. Perhaps, it would be best that way, although he had a feeling that, by giving Liese control over his money, he was giving her control over his life. Together, he thought, he and Liese would build a good home together and, hopefully in the not too distant future, have children. Eitel hoped he would have a son, a boy who would follow in his own footsteps and enter the army, although he would make sure the boy never disgraced his family in the way he had done.

Eitel Tobisch and Liese Kaufmann were married in December 1891 in a quiet civil ceremony in the old town. When they stepped into their new apartment, Eitel put his arms round her and kissed her.

Liese submitted to his embrace with stony features. She supposed she would have to put up with his attentions until she had borne him a child, but that did not mean she had to enjoy them. She had achieved all she wanted — to get away from her mother, have a home of her own and enough money to live well.

The first two years of Ricarda's married life were full and satisfying, with only one disappointment — the fact that, so far, they were still childless. Early in 1891, Grete wrote from Munich to tell them that she had just given birth to a baby daughter, whom they were calling Olga. A shadow flickered over Ricarda's face when she read the news, then she reassured herself with the thought that there was still time. Karl might be thirty-three, but she was only twenty-four, young enough to bear a dozen children if she wanted to.

In the meantime, since there was little she could do to help Karl at Café Jochum, she spent much of her time thinking about the Hotel Quadriga and finally, that spring, discovered its site. A quarter of the way down Unter den Linden was a large building, a former ducal palace, now converted into apartments which, in their turn, were falling vacant as rising rents forced their inhabitants away from the city centre to live in villages like Wilmersdorf,

Steglitz and even Charlottenburg, just as Karl had forecast would happen so many years earlier.

Filled with excitement, but saying nothing to Karl, Ricarda paid a visit to Dr Duschek, who smiled when he heard her plans. 'Herr Jochum has certainly found a kindred spirit in yourself! Of course, I can make enquiries for you.' A couple of days later, he was able to tell her that the landlord, who was not, he was pleased to say, Heinrich Kraus, would indeed be prepared to consider a reasonable offer for the property. 'But it's going to be very expensive, Frau Jochum, and the refurbishment that will be necessary is going to cost even more. I think you should be thinking of the whole operation costing somewhere in the region of five million marks.'

Five million was an impossible figure for Ricarda to conjure with, but she did not let it daunt her. Day after day, she stood on Unter den Linden, looking at the building's façade and even, on a couple of occasions, persuading the hall porter to allow her into the main entrance hall. Slowly, in her imagination, the hotel began to take shape. She would, she decided, leave the palace's elegant frontage fairly well as it was, but she would add a colonnaded portico along its entire length, over which balconies would lead off from the first floor suites and apartments. Inside, the foyer would be clad with white Carrara marble, spread with cobalt blue carpets.

Gradually, she began to make enquiries about furniture, bathroom fittings, linen, kitchen equipment and beds, so that when the long-awaited moment finally arrived and the Hotel Quadriga actually began to take shape, she, at least, would be prepared. Not a word of all her preparations, however, did she breathe to Karl.

It was two years now since her father had returned to London promising to sing the praises of his son-in-law's café but, apart from the occasional Englishman specifically mentioning that he had been recommended to the restaurant, there was no noticeable increase in trade. Karl was not unduly worried. Café Jochum was full — that was all that mattered. But, as he sat at his desk each morning, he wondered how to achieve his greatest dream — that of having the Emperor as a guest in his restaurant.

Then, one morning, the unprecedented occurred. Busy working out the seating for a banquet that evening, Karl was disturbed by a waiter bursting into his office without knocking. 'Herr Direktor! The Kaiser!'

Karl leapt up from his chair, then stopped to brush an imaginary speck of dust from his black coat and collect his thoughts. The

Emperor! He hurried into the entrance hall where Max Patschke was already greeting their royal visitor and his two attendants. He bowed. 'Your Majesty, what an unexpected honour.'

Emperor Wilhelm did not smile. 'Jochum, there's a matter of some importance we must discuss in private.'

Karl went pale. Something was obviously wrong. He led the gentlemen into his office. 'May I offer Your Majesty a little refreshment?'

The Emperor nodded impatiently. 'Perhaps some Rhine wine.' He waited until Max Patschke had served the wine, then announced, 'A British trade delegation is coming to Berlin and they have specifically requested that their meal be prepared by Mesurier. It appears your chef's reputation has reached even London. Jochum, you must lend me Mesurier.'

Karl stared at him, open-mouthed, unwilling to believe that fate could deal him such a blow. Instead of the Emperor dining at Café Jochum, Mesurier was to cook at the Palace!

'Well, Jochum, can I have Mesurier?'

Karl remained silent, knowing his whole future depended upon his reply. If he once allowed Mesurier to go, he could lose him for ever. But to refuse the Emperor's request could cause the most terrible repercussions. Never had he found himself in such a dilemma. Then he took his courage in both hands. 'Your Majesty, I am very reluctant to let you have Mesurier, who is employed by Café Jochum. I greatly regret it, but either the British trade delegation must eat here or they must eat without Mesurier.'

There was a shocked silence, then the Emperor rose from his chair, his face turning purple with rage. 'Jochum,' he roared, 'do you dare to disobey me?'

Inwardly trembling, Karl stood his ground. 'If you give me an order, Your Majesty, I cannot refuse it. But since I believe Café Jochum to be the best restaurant in Berlin and since Mesurier is employed here, it would obviously be preferable to me if the meal took place on my premises.'

The Emperor stared at him, then slowly his colour subsided and a smile spread across his face. 'Jochum, you have always been an enterprising man. Evidently, you are a brave one as well. Not many of my subjects would show personal courage such as you have just done.' He sat down again. 'So, do you believe Café Jochum capable of providing the venue and the menu worthy of very important visitors?'

'Of course, Your Majesty.'

'And what would you propose as a suitable dinner?'

'That is a matter I should have to discuss with Maître Mesurier, Majesty.'

The Emperor sighed. 'My Court Marshal will write to the head of the British delegation, informing them that their wish will be granted. Mesurier will cook for them.'

'May I ask if you will yourself be present at this dinner, Majesty?'

Kasier Wilhelm stood, signalling to his aides that he was ready to leave. 'Be present, Jochum? Of course I shall be present. These people are coming to see me, damn it all. You don't think they're coming all this way just to eat at Café Jochum, do you?'

It was only after he had escorted the Emperor and his aides to their carriage and watched it drive away that the implications of the risk he had taken fully penetrated Karl's mind. By refusing to comply with His Majesty's wishes, he could have been arrested, accused of lese-majesty or even high treason! His legs grew weak at the thought and a muscle twitched nervously in his face. He seldom drank during the day, but right now he needed a stiff drink!

Composing his features, he marched through the café into the kitchen, where he poured himself a glass of cooking brandy. Then he turned to his chef, who was eyeing him with open astonishment. 'Maître Mesurier, you are going to prepare a meal fit for the Emperor!' And, damn it all, it had better be the best you have ever prepared or we'll all end up in prison, he added mentally.

Mesurier listened to the details of the dinner, then asked disdainfully, 'You want me to prepare a meal fit for the gods that will also titillate the palates of Englishmen and Prussians? But, Monsieur le Directeur, the English have no knowledge of good food, and the Prussians ...'

'Herr Maître ...'

'*Eh bien*, le rosbif, perhaps, and le plum pudding ...' The chef's face was a picture of gloom. 'Maybe a little Sauerkraut ...'

Slowly, Karl relaxed. The brandy was taking its effect and Mesurier at his most gloomy usually turned out to be Mesurier at his most creative. 'I think His Majesty has something a little different in mind. He wants to show his British guests Mesurier's genius. He wants to give them a gastronomic experience they will never forget.'

'I think you expect Mesurier to perform a miracle.'

'Yes,' Karl replied succinctly, 'I do.'

Mesurier looked at him from large, sorrowful eyes. 'I feared so. Very well, Monsieur le Directeur, I will think.'

For twenty-four hours, Mesurier brooded round the kitchen, sniffing at herbs, staring at pieces of fruit and toying with vegetables. From time to time, he muttered, 'Kaiser! *Anglais! Merde alors!* Then he summoned Karl to his presence. 'Tenderloin of Venison Kaiser Wilhelm,' he announced dramatically.

'But there's nothing unusual about venison,' Karl objected, with a feeling of disappointment. 'The Emperor is probably served venison wherever he goes.'

'Ah, but that is because it is one of his favourite dishes, I believe. And the English, they eat it too, so we shan't be giving them some unknown foreign food that might upset their delicate stomachs. But, Directeur, never will they have eaten Tenderloin of Venison *à l'Empereur*, because until today it has never existed!'

Not even to Ricarda, whom he adored, would Maurice Mesurier reveal the secret behind his new dish. 'Well,' she laughed, 'I trust you will remember to honour Queen Victoria in some way as well.'

'Mais oui, for Her Majesty, I shall prepare a *tarte aux prunes Victoria*, made with Victoria plums specially imported from England for the occasion.'

To Ricarda's great delight, her father was the German official accompanying the British trade delegation on its visit to Berlin. Leaving his bags at the Konrad Hotel where they were staying, Emil Graber made his way straight to the Rosenthaler Platz. He took Ricarda in his arms fondly, then stood back to study her. 'You look well and you appear happy. Are you?'

'Happier than I've ever been in my life.'

Karl arrived home early from Café Jochum, leaving Eitel Tobisch in charge of the evening's business. He greeted his father-in-law affectionately, then said, 'I believe I'm in your debt, sir.'

'What do you mean?' There was a mischievous twinkle in Emil Graber's eyes.

'The British delegation apparently expressed a desire that their meal be prepared by Mesurier. This wasn't by any chance due to your recommendation?'

'You know I promised to recommend Café Jochum, Karl. I simply carried out my promise.'

When he heard how his plan had nearly misfired, he was horrified, then he asked, 'So what is Maître Mesurier preparing that is worthy of such important guests?'

'Ah,' Ricarda told him, 'that's a secret, one that not even Karl is allowed in on.'

Emil Graber could not stay long. 'I must get back to my colleagues at the Konrad Hotel. After all, I'm supposed to be in charge of this mission. But, one thing I will say, Karl, is that the sooner you open your hotel the better. The Konrad is dreadful.'

It was a sentiment Karl heard echoed among both the British and German businessmen the following evening, as they sat over aperitifs, waiting for the Emperor to arrive.

The table for twelve in the large private banqueting room on the first floor of Café Jochum was impeccably laid. Silver cutlery and goblets gleamed on the stiff damask tablecloth and silver holders displayed the name of each of the distinguished guests; the table plan had been approved by the Kaiser himself, who would be seated at the head of the table.

'I always say a good breakfast is the right way to start any day,' one Englishman was commenting to Heinrich Kraus. 'At home, I get up to porridge, followed by bacon and eggs. Maybe a kedgeree on Sunday. Not just a couple of bread rolls and some jam.'

'It must be a mile and a half from my room to the lavatory,' another grumbled. 'What happens if a man gets caught short, eh? Not even a wash basin in my bedroom.'

'Your cousin runs the London Arendt Bank, doesn't he?' a third man asked Isaak Arendt. 'Well, he must know the Savoy, opened last year. If Berlin wants to pick up international trade, it needs a hotel of that quality. Perhaps you should tell your Emperor.'

'Er-hmm,' the British Ambassador coughed, rising to his feet, and signalling his colleagues to do the same. 'His Majesty has just arrived.'

After supervising the serving of the first course of the meal, Karl left the room and did not return until the meat course. These was a hush as Max Patschke took from the commis the huge silver salver containing the venison. The meat had been cut into octagonal slices and between each two slices lay a little pâté de foie gras, spread with glacé, meat-jelly from the venison. It had then been gently fried in butter, so that it gleamed golden brown. Now, placed on croutons of toasted bread, these little tournedos, garnished with sprigs of parsley and thin slices of lemon, looked exquisite.

Max presented the platter before His Majesty, then expertly served a portion onto his plate. So far, the Emperor had made no comment upon the quality of the meal. Now, he looked down at the delicately browned rounds of meat, nodded in satisfaction, gazed down the table towards the Ambassador and announced, 'Venison! My favourite dish!'

As a bevy of waiters served the other guests, Mesurier advanced from the doorway where he had been waiting, dressed in an elegant black frock coat, but still with his tall white chef's hat on his head. In his hand he held an elaborate sauce-boat on a small gold tray. He gave a little bow, then spooned some of the sauce onto the Emperor's plate. From the steaming, rich brown gravy wafted an unusual but appetizing aroma. The texture of the sauce was not smooth, but slightly mushy. The Emperor dipped his fork into it and tasted.

It was as if everyone in the room knew that this was a decisive moment. Karl held his breath. Mesurier took a step backwards. They all waited. Then the Emperor declared, 'But Mesurier, this is excellent!' Slowly, he lifted a little more sauce onto his fork and raised it to his mouth, glancing, as he did so, at the British Ambassador. 'It is quite superb. I'm sure you have never tasted anything like this in London.'

Mesurier's face remained impassive, but Karl sensed the little Frenchman's inner elation. After weeks of tension, he himself started to relax. All was well!

Now the British Ambassador tasted the sauce, then looked up at the Maître in amazement. 'I have dined in many places in the world, but never have I eaten anything as exquisite as this.'

The other gentlemen took up their knives and forks and from all round the table came gasps of delight. Mesurier calmly bowed and left the room. Karl followed him. 'My congratulations, Maître,' he said, once they were safely in the kitchen. 'Now tell me what was actually in that sauce.'

The chef allowed himself a cunning smile, but shook his head mysteriously and returned to his cooking pots. 'I am pleased to have found favour with His Majesty.'

When the meal was over, Mesurier was summoned back to the banqueting room. Again, Karl accompanied him, hovering discreetly in the corner of the room. 'Monsieur Mesurier,' the Ambassador said, puffing contentedly on a large cigar, 'any time you would care to come to England, may I assure you of a very great welcome. Such talent as yours would be prized at the Court of St James. In the meantime, however, may I ask you the name of the sauce that added such piquancy to the venison?'

'I took the liberty of naming it after His Majesty, Your Excellency. The dish is called Tenderloin of Venison Kaiser Wilhelm.'

'And what made you think you could take such a liberty?' the Kaiser demanded, not looking at all displeased.

'The ingredients reminded me so much of you, Your Majesty.'

The Ambassador leaned forward eagerly. 'Yes, Maître, please tell us what gave the sauce its distinctive flavour.'

Karl smiled inwardly, as Mesurier rose to his great moment. His hands clasped behind his back, he bowed towards the Ambassador, then explained, 'Your Excellency is perhaps referring to the few grains of caraway added during the very last moments of preparation?' He paused, then, as the room was silent, he smiled and continued, 'But the real secret of the sauce, the ingredient without which it cannot succeed, is dependent upon the quality of the truffles, and those truffles, Your Excellency, can only be obtained from certain remote spots in the oak forests of Périgord!'

'Truffles!' the Emperor roared.

Mesurier bowed and made his triumphant exit.

Chapter Five

Word of the Emperor's dinner at Café Jochum spread like wildfire round Berlin, and by the time the British delegation departed a week later, there was scarcely an empty seat to be found in any of its restaurants, day or night.

Karl was sitting in his office when the royal carriage once again drew up in the Potsdamer Platz. On this occasion, the Kaiser's behaviour was markedly different. He marched into the entrance hall, clapped Max Patschke familiarly on the back, then pushed past him to burst, unannounced, into Karl's office.

Karl leapt up swiftly, knocking over his chair in his confusion. 'Your Majesty!'

'That showed 'em!' the Emperor declared. 'Haven't got anything like Café Jochum in London!' He sat down and Karl, righting his own chair, followed his example. 'Now you and I have matters of importance to discuss, grave matters.'

'May I offer Your Majesty a little refreshment? Some sparkling Rhine wine, perhaps?' Karl asked, knowing his Emperor's predilections.

'Excellent, Jochum.'

As he rang the bell for Max, Karl tried to conceal his triumphant happiness. The dinner had obviously been an unmitigated success!

Max served the wine, closed the door discreetly behind him and they were alone again. Kaiser Wilhelm sipped his glass, cleared his throat, and sipped again. Karl started to look at him rather anxiously. Eventually, the Emperor said, 'The British trade mission was a great success, Jochum. Kraus Industries obtained an extremely profitable export order, as well as an agreement for a British company to manufacture their armaments under licence over there. And the whole deal is being financed by the Arendt Bank. Yes, very profitable.'

Karl inclined his head. He was glad for Isaak Arendt's sake, although he was less sure of his feelings about Kraus.

'You see, the head of the Commercial Section of our embassy in

London is a very enterprising gentleman, Herr Jochum.' He shot him a piercing glance. 'I believe you know Herr Graber?'

'I am honoured by having him as my father-in-law, Majesty.'

'So I gather,' the Emperor intoned drily. 'Well, it was Herr Graber who brought to my notice a very disturbing aspect of the British trade delegation's stay in Berlin. It appears, Jochum, that the hotel in which they stayed was less than satisfactory, being far inferior in quality to many London hotels. Did Herr Graber discuss this with you, by any chance?'

'We did discuss the matter briefly, Majesty.'

'We must remedy this matter and we must do it quickly.'

Karl took a deep breath. 'It has long been my plan to build a hotel, Your Majesty, one which will be the most elegant and luxurious in Germany and, hopefully, in all Europe.'

'Then you must build it, Jochum. Berlin needs such a hotel. It must be built! Have you thought what name you will give it?'

'My wife and I have thought of the "Hotel Quadriga", Your Majesty.'

'Hmmm, not bad. Quadriga, eh?' Abruptly he stood up. 'Build your hotel, Jochum. And no scrimping, mind! Devil take 'em, we'll make our English cousins green with envy yet!' Then, before Karl could reach the door, he swept regally out.

Unable to contain his excitement, Karl hurried straight home to the Rosenthaler Platz to tell Ricarda. 'We can build our hotel!' he exclaimed exultantly, as he burst through the door. He told her about the Emperor's visit, then ended, 'Now, all that remains is to find our site.'

She was already putting on her hat and coat, and to his great surprise, informed him, 'I found that months ago. Come on, Karli, let me show you!'

Outside their apartment, they boarded an electric tram travelling westwards and, while Karl was still demanding to know what she was talking about, Ricarda took tickets for Unter den Linden. In next to no time, they were disembarking outside the former ducal palace. 'Well, what do you think of that?'

He stared at it, then stepped backwards into the road, while the busy traffic swirled, irritated and honking, around him. 'It's perfect,' he said slowly. 'But I'm sure it's not for sale.'

'At the right price, it is, and now you have the Kaiser's blessing, I'm sure there will be no problem.'

He looked at her incredulously. 'You mean ...?'

She smiled innocently. 'Well, I just asked Dr Duschek to make some enquiries.'

In a rare public display of affection, he took her hand. 'You have always believed in our hotel, haven't you?' He stared up Unter den Linden towards the Brandenburg Gate, with its central arch, through which only the Kaiser was allowed to pass, the statue of the Quadriga prancing high above it. 'The Hotel Quadriga,' he murmured. 'We'll build it, Ricarda, the finest hotel in Berlin, we'll build it!'

Their first port of call was Dr Duschek. 'So you've admitted your husband to your secret, have you, Frau Jochum?' he smiled. Then he turned to Karl, 'You have a wife in a million. I don't know of many others who have their husband's interests so much at heart.' He leafed through a file. 'Here are all the particulars, Herr Jochum. Let me know when you want me to make your offer.'

Karl read carefully through the correspondence, and raised an eyebrow when he saw the approximate price of the building. 'First,' he said ruefully, 'we have to pay a visit to Herr Arendt. Café Jochum is profitable, but not that profitable.'

The banker was all smiles, when he saw them. 'So, you achieved your ambition, Herr Jochum. You always vowed the Emperor would one day dine in your restaurant and now he has.'

'I also promised you would be present when he did, and you were.' Then he repeated his account of the Kaiser's visit and described the property on Unter den Linden.

'I had a shrewd suspicion you might have something like this in mind,' Isaak Arendt said, opening a folder on his desk, 'so I've taken the liberty of doing a little homework on your behalf. Now, your deposit account stands at about one and a quarter million marks, with another thousand or two on your current account. Tell me, do you still have your shares in the Kurfuerstendamm Company?'

Karl nodded.

'How many did you buy?'

'Thirty thousand.'

The banker gave a wry smile. 'A very good investment, if I may say so. Do you remember how much you paid for them?'

'Ten pfennigs each,' Karl said, remembering his father's comments at the time. 'You don't know what the price of land will do,' Sigi had said. 'Bismarck could lose office.' Well, old Bismarck had retired, but his Kurfuerstendamm Company still remained.

'They're worth just over forty marks each now,' Isaak Arendt told him, doing rapid calculations on his blotter. 'Which means your shareholding is worth about one and a quarter million marks.'

Karl gasped. He knew the shares had gone up in value, but not that much!

'The market is very buoyant now. You should have no problem selling them. So, Herr Jochum, your assets seem to amount to about two and a half million marks. How much do you think it will cost to build your hotel?'

'About five million at a guess,' Karl said cautiously.

'Well, tell Dr Duschek to start his negotiations, for the bank will have no hesitation in matching your own investment. So if you put two and a half million into your project, the bank will lend you a further two and a half million as a mortgage.'

Three months later, Karl had sold his shares in the Kurfuerstendamm Company and become the owner of the former ducal palace on Unter den Linden. Ricarda watched him as he selected a key from a large bunch, opened the front door, then turned, picked her up and carried her over the threshold. 'Welcome to your new home, Frau Jochum, welcome to the Hotel Quadriga!'

Laughing, she remained in his arms, snuggling her head against his shoulder. 'Oh, Karl, isn't this wonderful? Are you happy?'

Gently, he let her down to the floor. 'Yes, I don't deserve to be as happy as I am. All this, and you.'

Still leaning against him, she said, 'This will be the foyer, and over there, next to the reception desk, will be the main staircase. The foyer is floored in white marble, Karl.'

Amused, he said, 'You sound as if it's already built.'

'In my mind, it is. Shall I give you a guided tour?'

'Why not?' he decided to humour her.

'Then we have to go outside again.' Ricarda disengaged herself from his arm and took his hand. 'Ideally, we should have a sweeping drive, but there simply isn't room, so I think we should have a colonnaded portico over the pavement, with a balcony above it.'

'A portico, eh?'

'It would shield our visitors from the weather and give us a degree of privacy. Our commissionaires can stand here on the steps and help people from their carriages.'

'And overhead we'll have a big sign saying "Hotel Quadriga".'

'No big sign, Karl. After all, the Emperor doesn't have any signs on his palaces, does he? And this is our palace.' Then she continued enthusiastically, 'We should have wide glass revolving doors to let light into the foyer and the porter's lodge should be here ...'

'You seem to have given this a lot of thought.'

'But of course I have, darling! What else have I had to do all day, while you were at work? Oh, Karl, you are going to let me help design the hotel, aren't you?'

'It's going to mean a lot of work.'

'Somebody's got to do it, so why shouldn't it be me?'

'But you're a woman,' her husband said disparagingly. He made his way down the hall. If the reception desk were here, and the hall porter's lodge there, and the staircase came down here ... Hmmm, it seemed to make sense. But white marble was going to show the dirt dreadfully. They needed carpet and what colour should that be? Burgundy, as in Café Jochum, or some other colour? 'Ricarda!'

She was no longer beside him. Astonished, he turned to see her still standing near the front door, blowing her nose, her eyes glittering as if she were crying. But Ricarda never cried! 'What's the matter?'

'Nothing,' she sniffed, trying to smile.

He studied her. He'd obviously upset her in some way, which was the last thing he intended. Then realization dawned. She actually wanted to help design the hotel and he had hurt her by curtly refusing her offer. Damn him for being an unthinking fool! 'Please stop crying,' he said, putting his arm round her again. 'This is supposed to be the happiest day of our lives, remember? Now then,' he forced a stern note into his voice, 'if you are designing the interior of this hotel, would you mind telling me what colour the carpet is going to be?'

Her green eyes widened. 'Do you mean it, Karl? Can I really do it?'

'I asked you a question. What colour will the carpet be?'

'Blue,' she whispered, 'cobalt blue. And the uniforms of the commissionaires and page boys will be the same colour. Blue with gold trimmings. Oh, Karl, thank you.'

'Cobalt blue, eh? Well, that sounds very smart. Yes, Frau Jochum, you have the job.'

'Oh, Karl, how long do you think it will take to complete it? When will we be able to open the hotel?'

'In about two years' time, I should think,' he replied ruefully, 'but by the time we've finished, Ricarda, we're going to have the finest hotel in the world.'

They were united in their choice of an architect. Dr Hubert Hedler was a stocky man of about forty, with grey whiskers and twinkling grey eyes. Before committing himself, he trudged over every inch of the building, making copious notes, then he led Karl and Ricarda out onto the pavement. 'It would be nice to have a sweeping drive, but that's impossible. Instead I think we should have a granite portico the length of the pavement, with a balcony above it.'

Karl and Ricarda exchanged glances.

'Here, we should put glass doors and I think white marble might be very impressive in the foyer. Now, let me show you how I see the reception area.' He made some rough sketches. 'If the reception desk were here, the main staircase could sweep down ...'

They both laughed and Dr Hedler looked at them puzzled. 'Is something the matter?'

Karl shook his head. 'Tell me, Dr Hedler, do you have any objection to working with a woman?'

'It would be a most unusual experience, Herr Jochum, but if you mean your gracious lady wife, then I'm sure it would be a most pleasurable one.'

'In that case, you are hereby appointed architect of the Hotel Quadriga.'

Under Dr Hedler's supervision, a demolition team was contracted. They erected scaffolding and hung tarpaulins over the front of the building and started to rip down the inner walls. All day long, for weeks on end, a pall of dust hung over Unter den Linden, as cartload after cartload of rubble was carried away.

Every day, Karl and Ricarda arrived at the site, to inspect progress made the previous day and to discuss the next stage of the work with the architect. It was Ricarda's dearest wish to have a garden, but space no more permitted this than it did a grandiose drive. 'Why not have a Palm Garden Room?' Dr Hedler suggested.

'You mean like the Palm House at Kew Gardens? Oh, that would be wonderful! We could grow exotic tropical plants and have a small fountain playing!'

'I've been thinking rather more about the cellars,' Karl said. 'Dr Hedler, do you think there is any way of extending them out under the pavement?'

'Why do we want more cellar space?' Ricarda asked.

'Storage space is valuable. We need every bit we can get.'

'We'd have to obtain permission from the Kaiser,' Dr Hedler said, 'but we could request it at the same time as we ask about the portico over the pavement.'

'Let's do it.' Karl scribbled a few figures. 'With that extra space, I estimate we could store up to a million bottles of wine.'

'A million bottles of wine,' the architect breathed reverently. 'I think His Majesty might approve of that.'

It was two months before the last wall came down and the work of reconstruction could begin, but that very day a letter arrived from the Court Marshal's office advising Herr Jochum that His Majesty was in agreement with the alterations he wanted to make to Unter den Linden. At long last the real work could commence!

Ricarda has never enjoyed herself more, spending every day at the site. Regardless of dirt and dust, she picked up her long skirts and strode confidently across uneven floors, climbed up rickety ladders to look at perspectives and ventured fearlessly into the cellars. She found a fellow enthusiast in Dr Hedler. The architect had a temporary office erected on the ground floor and here he and Ricarda spent many happy hours pouring over designs and plans, catalogues and samples.

At this point Karl called a meeting in his office at Café Jochum with himself, Ricarda, Dr Hedler and Israel Silberstein. 'If we're not careful, we could find ourselves in a great deal of confusion. Dr Hedler is already ordering large quantities of building materials and soon Frau Jochum is going to be placing orders for fittings and furniture. Somebody has to co-ordinate all these and I think Herr Silberstein would be the best person, if he has time.'

'I should be most pleased to help, Herr Jochum. Indeed, I've already given the matter some thought. If all orders are centralized through myself, then I can reconcile them to the invoices when they arrive and keep a daily check on our expenditure.'

'Good, and you'll report to me how often?'

'Weekly, Herr Jochum?'

Dr Hedler delved into his bulging briefcase. 'Well, let me give you these for a start, Herr Silberstein. These are the orders for bricks, timber and cement, all from local suppliers. And these are for the granite for the portico, which is coming from Finland, and the marble for the foyer, from Italy.'

'I've been thinking about the bathrooms, Karl,' Ricarda said. 'We've already agreed that there should be a private bathroom for every room, each with its own lavatory, but while we're about it, why don't we have all the bathroom fittings gold-plated?'

Karl frowned. 'Surely a rather unnecessary extravagance?'

'Our guests will expect nothing but the best.'

Silberstein coughed. 'Excuse me, Herr Jochum, but I don't believe the gold fittings need actually cost us anything, if we take the quantity discounts into account that we should obtain from our suppliers. After all, with about one hundred and fifty rooms to be fitted, we should be able to buy very favourably.'

Ricarda looked from one to the other. They seemed to be making a lot of fuss about a few taps, when they had five million marks to spend. What was important was that the hotel should contain every conceivable luxury.

'Would you be prepared to negotiate on our behalf, Herr Silberstein?' her husband asked.

'It will be a pleasure, Herr Jochum.'

Slowly, oh, so slowly, the building work progressed. Huge blocks of granite were shipped from Helsinki, then trundled by railway to Berlin. Slabs of white marble came from Tuscany. Curious Berliners lined the pavement outside and watched as they were moved behind the tarpaulins, speculating as to how His Majesty's hotel was going to look when it was finished.

Eventually, the portico was completed and the low archways linking the vast cellars finished. New walls were erected on the ground floor to house restaurants, the bar, a ballroom, a gentlemen's smoking and reading room, a ladies' retiring room, the kitchens and the Palm Garden Room. In late November, when the shell of this latter room was completed, Ricarda led Karl enthusiastically into it. 'Isn't it going to be charming? Imagine it, with its plants and fountain, and filled with Louis XVI furniture. Green, white and gold!'

'It sounds very expensive to me,' Karl commented drily.

She took his hand. Dear Karl, he was always worried about money, not seeming to realize that it was individual touches like gold-plated taps and the Palm Garden Room that were going to give their hotel its unique character. 'I'm sure Herr Silberstein will be able to obtain a discount on the furniture, dearest.'

'Hmmm, well, just keep away from the Empire Room. I don't want any white and gold furniture in there! That's going to be a man's room and I'm the one who's going to decide how that's furnished!'

Ricarda submitted readily, for she had no feeling for the heavy

133

oak panelling and dark furniture she knew Karl wanted there.

'But you're agreed that the restaurant should be papered in blue, with gold candelabra, aren't you, Karl?'

'If it makes you happy, my love,' he replied absently.

It was February before the main staircase and the first floor suites, designed to accommodate the hotel's most important guests, were completed. As the builders repaired to the second, third and fourth floors, the Jochums stood in one of the apartments over-looking Unter den Linden, admiring the spaciousness of the rooms.

'No two rooms should be the same,' Ricarda said thoughtfully. 'Each one should be decorated in different colours, each with the furniture arranged in a different manner, each bearing its own, individual identity.'

With this, Karl did agree, taking her ideas a step further. 'We need an emblem for the hotel, insignia to go on our stationery and in all the public rooms. Perhaps it could even be woven into the carpets? And why don't we have it included in the bedheads?'

'And you have some particular emblem in mind?'

He smiled at her. 'What about a horse, copied exactly from one of the prancing horses of the Quadriga?'

'Then we should order the carpets and bedsteads immediately. If they're to be handmade, they'll take ages to complete. I know we're far from being ready to open for business, but we won't be able to open at all without any beds!'

'Tell Silberstein what you want.'

Ricarda made a long list of all her requirements, then, at a meeting with the accountant, gave him detailed sketches of the beds. They were to be black japanned, with burnished brass knobs, the figure of a prancing horse wrought into each headboard, and fitted with Terry springs from England. At the same time, deep feather mattresses were placed on order, as were voluminous quilts filled with gossamer-light, pure eiderdown. All the sheets and pillows were to be edged with real Brussels lace.

'We shall need two thousand pairs of sheets. Herr Tobisch tells me there should be six pairs for each bed. One actually on the bed, one held in readiness by the chambermaid, two coming and going from the laundry, one in reserve and one in the linen cupboard. Then, of course, we'll need simpler bedlinen for the staff rooms.'

Israel Silberstein noted her requirements, adding them to his existing list of solid silver cutlery, lead crystal glasses, fine linen tablecloths and napkins.

134

'I've also made up my mind about carpets,' Ricarda continued. 'In the foyer we shall have Savonnerie — in the house colours, Herr Silberstein, and with the figure of a prancing horse woven into the pile. In the first-floor suites, we shall have Aubusson, while in the corridors and the remaining rooms, I think Persian will be perfectly satisfactory. The colours will match the decor of the rooms. Ah yes, and curtains. They will, of course, be brocade, drawn by a brass rod attached to a fine gold cord. Each room will also be provided with silk dressing gowns for our guests. Is all that perfectly clear?'

The accountant inclined his head obsequiously. 'Perfectly, Frau Jochum. I shall let you know delivery dates.'

Now that the cellars were finished, Karl turned his attention to the wine, for the sort of wine list he desired could not be compiled overnight. He had a long business relationship with Hugo Keppel of Keppel und Sohn, licensed victuallers, and it was to him that he entrusted many of his requirements. But not even Keppel could supply all the wines he wanted and Karl spent many long, happy hours contacting distant, and often obscure, vineyards to obtain their lists and deciding upon the vintages to purchase. As he made his selections, he gave his lists to Israel Silberstein to deal with.

Israel Silberstein also met with Maurice Mesurier, Max Patschke and Eitel Tobisch, each supreme in their separate kingdoms and each determined to lack for nothing. Mesurier wanted the very latest in kitchen equipment, Max enough covers to serve a thousand customers in an evening, while Eitel had the unenviable task of deciding what was required for the administration of a hotel that was not even halfway built.

The first workman had set foot in the palace on Unter den Linden in May 1892. By the summer of 1893, the façade was still shrouded with tarpaulins, there were piles of bricks in the bedrooms, gaping holes where the plumbing was yet to be fitted, windows with no glass and doorways with no doors, but in spirit at least, the Hotel Quadriga was starting to take shape.

Israel Silberstein had never been happier. The Hotel Quadriga was the biggest project with which he had ever been connected, compared to which paying the bills and doing the accounts for Café Jochum paled into insignificance. No expense was being spared to make the Hotel Quadriga into Europe's finest and most luxurious hotel. There were five millon marks available to pay for

135

the best and Silberstein was resolved to obtain the best possible value for them.

It was not long before he realized that he, too, could profit from his transactions. 'We are highly delighted at the privilege of being able to supply Herr Jochum's hotel and we shall, of course, give you an introductory commission, Herr Silberstein,' the carpet dealer told him. 'Would ten per cent be acceptable to you?'

Silberstein did not bother to conceal his disappointment. 'On an order such as this, I was expecting at least twelve and a half per cent.'

'But of course you shall have the twelve and a half per cent. Your ten per cent is on top of that.'

The accountant rubbed his hands. 'In cash?'

'Naturally.'

For a brief second, Israel Silberstein wondered if he ought not to pass on the concession to Karl Jochum, but he did not hesitate long. He paid it into his personal bank account.

Very soon, he had similar arrangements agreed with most of the suppliers to the Hotel Quadriga. His bank balance was rapidly increasing and he left his old flat, taking a new one in the city centre. Then he went to see his brother-in-law, Moses Schwarz. 'If these middlemen can afford to give me twenty-two and a half per cent, their margins must be much higher.'

'About fifty per cent,' Moses agreed knowledgeably.

'So,' Israel suggested cunningly, 'why don't you and I set ourselves up as distributors? Then, instead of the profits going to these other suppliers, it all comes to us?'

'But we'd need warehousing, staff, transport ...'

'No we wouldn't. We just place the order with the manufacturer and ask him to deliver when the goods are needed. That way we have no overheads.'

'But I have no experience in trading,' Moses objected.

'You have nothing to do. You set up the business in your name and I'll run it. I'll give you two per cent of our profit for doing nothing.'

It seemed a highly satisfactory arrangement. Shortly afterwards, a new distributor started supplying the Hotel Quadriga. Karl Jochum did not so much as raise an eyebrow when he signed the cheque. The amount on it tallied perfectly to the order and the invoice. Schwarz Trading was just one of the hundreds of companies from whom the hotel was now buying.

By the summer of 1983, when the hotel itself was still an empty shell, Israel Silberstein's apartment was beginning to resemble a suite in it. Samples of Savonnerie carpet lined his floors from wall to wall. He had a bath with gold-plated taps. His table was decked with the finest linen and was laid with solid silver. Furthermore, he had moved his office to plush new ground floor premises in the financial sector near the Behrenstrasse, engaged an assistant to deal with his other clients, and taken on a secretary.

His rapacious hunger now knew no bounds. Greedy for yet more money, Silberstein could see a way of becoming even wealthier. He had already proved that people would pay almost anything in order to have the privilege of supplying the Hotel Quadriga — the Kaiser's hotel. Furthermore, most of them knew of Karl Jochum even if they had never done business with him before, for Café Jochum had been in existence for ten years and Karl's credit standing had never been called into question. It was on this that Silberstein decided to gamble.

The next time he went to see Karl he took with him a series of cheques made out to Schwarz Trading, the amounts on them corresponding exactly to the invoices relating to them. As always, Karl signed them without a question. Then Israel paid them into his bank account, but did not pay the suppliers.

In a very short while, his bank balance showed a credit of five hundred thousand marks and by September 1893 it had reached the magic total of one million marks. Israel Silberstein instructed his bank to transfer all his funds to a Swiss bank account. Schwarz Trading's account was empty.

There were many occasions, during those hectic months, when Karl simply did not know whether he was coming or going, for it seemed he was always trying to be in two places simultaneously. His presence was constantly needed at Café Jochum, while at the same time, Ricarda, Dr Hedler, bricklayers, carpenters, tilers and plasterers were demanding his attention at the steadily rising Hotel Quadriga. Then there were his weekly meetings with Israel Silberstein, when the accountant presented him with an intimidating pile of invoices, orders and cheques. Karl knew it was wrong, but now he simply signed them, cutting short any explanation Silberstein tried to make.

So the first knowledge he had of the hotel's real financial situation was when he received a discreetly worded letter sent to his home address by Isaak Arendt, telling him that his loan facility was now fully extended and his current account was approaching a million overdrawn. For Karl, tired and overwrought, it was the final straw. 'What the devil?' he demanded angrily.

'Karl, what's happened?' Ricarda asked, pouring his morning coffee, her own face pale, with bags under her eyes from too little sleep.

'Your gold-plated taps and lace-edged sheets!' he snapped. 'Do you realize that the hotel is only halfway finished and we're already a million over budget?'

His accusation caught her on the raw. 'Not just my taps and sheets. What about your Empire Room?'

'What about your Louis XVI chairs in the Palm Garden Room?'

'What about your million bottles of wine?'

They left the apartment separately, Karl to go straight to Café Jochum, Ricarda to the hotel. It was the first time they had quarrelled since their marriage. They were both puzzled and angry, neither quite sure what had happened.

At Café Jochum, Karl greeted his staff curtly, ordered a waiter to bring him a coffee and told Eitel Tobisch that he didn't want to be disturbed by anybody. Then he sat down to think. His first reaction was to wonder why Silberstein had not alerted him to their financial situation and to curse him for a fool. Then he realized that whatever he did about the accountant, he still had to talk personally to Isaak Arendt and try to raise an additional loan.

About ten o'clock there was a hesitant knock on his office door. 'Yes?' he barked.

'Herr Hugo Keppel asks if he can see you, Herr Direktor,' a waiter said nervously. 'He says it's very important.'

'All right,' Karl sighed.

The wine merchant entered apologetically. 'I'm sorry to disturb you, Herr Jochum, but there's something I must talk to you about.'

Filled with foreboding, Karl waved him to a seat. 'What's the matter?'

Hugo Keppel placed five invoices on the table made out to Schwarz Trading. 'We supplied on your behalf, Herr Jochum, but Schwarz hasn't paid. Three months is a long time to allow a bill to go unpaid and since we've had no dealings with Schwarz before, I've had the company investigated. It appears it has no funds with which to pay its debts.'

138

Karl stared at him puzzled. 'What is this company, Schwarz Trading?'

Hugo Keppel nodded. 'I was certain you would know nothing about it. I hate to tell you this, Herr Jochum, but Schwarz Trading was formed shortly after you started building your hotel and is owned by your accountant, Israel Silberstein and his brother-in-law, Moses Schwarz.'

Karl rubbed a weary hand across his forehead. 'Oh, dear God …'

Hugo Keppel gave a sympathetic grunt. 'Your accountant has been double-crossing you, Herr Jochum. The police will have to be informed of course, but I felt I owed it to you as an old friend to tell you first. Herr Silberstein is a crook.'

After Israel Silberstein was arrested and his affairs investigated, the full extent of his fraudulence came to light. To Karl's horror, he learned that during the year and a bit that the hotel had been being built, Silberstein had milked his client of about a million marks. Steps were being taken to recover the money from Switzerland, but in the meantime Karl's financial situation was worsening by the minute.

'Oh, Karl, I'm so sorry,' Ricarda said, when he explained to her all that had happened. 'And I'm sorry I was angry with you that morning.'

He put his arm round her and drew her to him. 'It was my fault.'

It seemed they had never been closer than during those misty autumn days as disaster confronted them. When Isaak Arendt requested a meeting, Karl asked Ricarda for the first time if she would come with him. 'After all, it's only fair that you should know what's happening. It's your future at stake as much as mine.'

The banker's manner was more frigid that day than on any previous occasion and the portraits of the Arendt ancestors seemed to glare down disapprovingly from the panelled walls. He listened to Karl's account of what had happened, then said, 'Well, since the bank has some responsibility, since it introduced you to Silberstein, and since you are an old customer, Herr Jochum, there seems to be no alternative but to increase your mortgage by another two and a half million. But I won't pretend to be happy about the situation.'

Afterwards, they made their way to the semi-finished hotel, where they gazed at the desolate scene about them. The foyer floor was half covered with marble and there were cavernous holes where the lift shafts had been sunk. Rolls of carpet lay waiting to be laid and wallpaper ready to be hung. Their footsteps echoed emptily on bare floorboards as they wandered between piles of furniture covered in dust sheets. 'The extra two and a half million Herr Arendt is lending us still isn't going to be enough,' Karl said, despondently.

'Do you think we'd do best to cut our losses at this point rather than allow ourselves to be dragged deeper into debt?' Ricarda asked.

Karl was silent for a long time, then he turned decisively. 'No, damn it all, I'm not going to be beaten. What we are doing is right. One way or another, we'll see this hotel built, whatever it costs!'

That night they clung tightly together in their flat in the Rosen-thaler Platz; then very gently, Karl kissed Ricarda. She drew closer to him, burying her face in his shoulder, and suddenly he felt hot wet tears on his bare skin. 'Hush, my darling, it will be all right.' He stroked her back until her weeping ceased, then, very tenderly, he started to make love to her.

Ricarda gave herself absolutely to him that evening, for it seemed to her that there were just the two of them alone, isolated, with all the rest of the world against them.

Reluctant though he was to presume upon an old friendship, Karl knew only one person to whom he could take his troubles and who might be able to help him. Since their respective marriages, he and Ewald had seen much less of each other than in former days, for the Count had become almost a reformed character, spending his evenings with his wife rather than in cafés and gambling clubs.

So, fairly certain of finding him at his married quarters, Karl took a taxi to Karlshorst. In appearance, Ewald had changed little over the years. Even off-duty, he was still dapper and elegant, his boots highly polished and his neat moustache waxed. He appeared delighted to see Karl, but horrified to hear his story.

'You see, the additional mortgage won't be sufficient,' Karl said, after he had finished explaining the hotel's ghastly predicament. 'It's going to cost about ten million in total to build the Quadriga, which means I still need another two and a half million.'

Ewald let out a low whistle, then he said thoughtfully, 'I know one person who could help you, if you'd let him, and that's Heinrich Kraus.'

Karl stiffened. 'I'd prefer not to have any more business transactions with him! I haven't forgotten the freehold of the Potsdamer Platz, even if he has!'

'He's my brother-in-law, remember. Karl, I know he's greedy, but I also happen to know that there's something he wants very much more than money at the moment. Will you leave the matter with me, Karl? I think I know how to solve your problems.'

'I want no favours from Kraus.'

The Count stood up and sauntered over to the sideboard. 'Kraus does nobody any favours. Now then, old man, what about a drink? You look as if you need one.'

The following day, Count Ewald sought an interview with his Emperor, during which he told him there was a grave danger that the Hotel Quadriga might never be completed.

'What?' the Kaiser cried. 'Jochum's hotel not finished? But it's due to be the finest hotel in Europe! Biederstein, I think you'd better tell me exactly what the problem is!'

Ewald explained.

'But this is terrible. We've been taking a very great interest in it. We've granted royal permission for the portico to extend over the pavement and the cellars to reach under Unter den Linden. It must be completed.'

'Herr Jochum is unfortunately lacking sufficient capital.'

The Emperor felt in his pockets. 'Biederstein, the royal coffers are empty. We can't help Herr Jochum. But surely there must be somebody else. Have you no suggestions?'

Ewald smiled. Then he described his idea to the Kaiser.

When he had finished, his ruler rubbed his hands together in glee. 'Excellent, Biederstein! Excellent!'

In Essen, in the heart of the industrial Ruhr, that black basin of belching factory chimneys, smelters, mines and clanking railway marshalling yards, Heinrich Kraus was already becoming known as 'The Steel King'. Local people pointed out to strangers his stucco and red brick villa, built on a hill overlooking the town, with the words, 'That's the Steel King's fortress.'

From the baronial splendour of the 'Fortress', Heinrich Kraus could watch the whole panorama of the Ruhr, the jets of flame that illuminated the sky day and night from Kraus furnaces, the smog that hung like a low cloud over the valley, the piles of slag and debris from the pit heads, the sooty shop roofs, smokestacks, and colliery headgear. If he opened a window, he could hear the roar of the steam sirens, engines shrieking on Kraus rails, the endless snorting and groaning of heavy equipment and he could smell the foul soot and sulphur in the air, as it crept even up to his hillside sanctuary.

Not that he minded it, for it was from this that his fortune was made, from the rifles, howitzers, field guns and mighty cannons produced in the Kraus factories which he overlooked; from the steel rails over which the steel, Kraus wheels of the steam trains thundered; and from the steel plating for the battleships of His Majesty's growing navy.

Nor was Essen the limit of his kingdom. This same scene could be observed again in Silesia, where his father still lived, and in Wedding's Kraus Village. Kraus weapons were exported to Japan, Turkey and Bulgaria, to South Africa and South America. Even the British were manufacturing Kraus arms under licence, unable to keep up with German technology. One day, Heinrich was determined, Kraus would rule the world.

That autumn in 1893, Heinrich Kraus was thirty-five years old. Realizing how vital it was to keep up his connections with the army, he had bought himself a commission in the Reserve Officers Corps, which entitled him to wear an officer's uniform. Generous donations to his regiment had been acknowledged from the right circles and, needless to say, he always fulfilled his reservist duties. One day, he hoped his services to his country would come to the ears of the Kaiser, who would realize that it was time to honour him in the accustomed manner.

For despite all his riches, despite his marriage to the charming Julia von Biederstein and his two small sons, there was still one thing missing in his life. He might be known as the 'Steel King', but he still had no real title. He was still not of equal rank to his wife and his aristocratic in-laws.

When a message reached him at the Fortress from Berlin, summoning him to the Kaiser's presence, he scarcely dared hope that the long-awaited moment had arrived; but about what else could His Majesty wish to speak to him with such urgency?

In his reserve officer's uniform, he presented himself at the Imperial Palace, prepared graciously to acknowledge his Emperor's recognition and accept the title he would be given — hopefully nothing less than a baron. He was, therefore, extremely surprised when the Kaiser said, 'We believe you are acquainted with Herr Jochum, Herr Kraus?'

Jochum? What the devil?

'Herr Jochum is building a very fine hotel on Unter den Linden, but he is apparently experiencing — er — financial difficulties. Now, you realize, Herr Kraus, that this is a project in which we have a very great interest?'

Remembering the fiasco at the Konrad Hotel, Heinrich inclined his head.

'Let me put it this way. Anybody who helped Herr Jochum out of his current difficulties would be considered as rendering a very great service to the country, Herr Kraus.'

Heinrich listened very carefully. A service to the country? And it sounded to him as if His Majesty had stressed the word 'Herr'.

'So confident do I feel about the success of the Hotel Quadriga, that I would buy shares in it myself. Unfortunately, Kraus (not even a Herr this time), the other building work that we are undertaking in the city has rather undermined our resources.'

'If I had known Herr Jochum was in such grave trouble, I would have immediately hurried to offer him my support.'

Two imperial eyes bored into his. 'We want that hotel finished at all possible speed. Oh, and Kraus, am I right in believing that you have applied to set up an electrical company to supply electricity to the city of Berlin?'

With bated breath, Heinrich replied, 'That is correct, Your Majesty.' It was a contract he was determined to obtain, although several companies were competing for the privilege.

'Is it not possible that the Hotel Quadriga might profit from having its own private electricity supply? The Savoy Hotel in London has its own generator, as well as its own Artesian well. We are reluctant to appear to lag behind our English cousins.'

Heinrich bowed. 'I am sure that can be arranged, Your Majesty.'

'Thank you, er, Herr, er, Kraus.' Then the Emperor laughed. 'If only I weren't so poor!'

Heinrich Kraus made his way slowly from the Palace, across the River Spree, down Unter den Linden towards the Hotel Quadriga. There he stood for a long time, looking at the tarpaulins shrouding the unfinished building. He still had no guarantee of being given his coveted title, but it was obvious he would never obtain it unless he fulfilled his Emperor's wishes. There was no twenty-five per cent profit to be made from Jochum this time. On the contrary, he expected this whole enterprise was going to cost him a great deal of money. Without entering the hotel, he turned towards the Behrenstrasse.

The following afternoon, four gentlemen met in the first-floor conference room of the Arendt Bank. Karl Jochum and Heinrich Kraus shook hands rather coolly, while Isaak Arendt and Erwin Duschek shuffled their papers in a slightly embarrassed manner. Isaak came straight to the point. 'Herr Kraus has heard of your difficulties, Herr Jochum, and would like to help you. Do you have any objection to my divulging to him your current situation?'

Karl flushed angrily, but shook his head. He had told Ricarda that they would build the hotel no matter what the cost, and if the price he had to pay was Kraus, then he supposed that was the way it had to be.

When Isaak had finished speaking, Kraus nodded. 'So your own investment in the hotel is seven and a half million marks, Herr Jochum, five of which is on a five-year mortgage from the Bank? And you need another two and a half million? Well, I am willing to lend you that money, at a very low interest rate, on two conditions.'

He took his spectacles off, cleaned them with his handkerchief, then continued, 'The first is that Herr Arendt extends the period of his mortgages to twenty-five or even thirty years, so that my loan can be quickly repaid, and the second, that a suite at the Hotel Quadriga is made available to myself and my family for our sole use at all times.'

Karl stared at him, wondering what Kraus hoped to gain by such a deal. Isaak Arendt and Erwin Duschek also had puzzled expressions on their faces, then the lawyer said, 'That seems a very fair proposal to me.'

'I believe the Savoy Hotel in London has its own electricity generator and independent water supply,' Kraus continued. 'It would be Kraus Industries' pleasure to install similar facilities for the Hotel Quadriga, free of charge.'

Isaak Arendt leaned back in his chair. 'In view of such generosity, it would seem churlish of me to refuse your terms, Herr Kraus. When will your sixty-fifth birthday take place, Herr Jochum?'

Still stunned, Karl had to stop and think. '1923.'

'Very well, your mortgages become repayable in 1923. And how soon do you think you could repay Herr Kraus's loan?'

As soon as he could, Karl vowed inwardly, wishing he knew why Kraus was suddenly so eager to be of service. 'Certainly by the turn of the century.'

His face expressionless, Heinrich Kraus turned to Dr Duschek. 'My lawyer will be in touch with you, confirming all the details.' Then he stood up and offered his hand to Karl. 'My engineers will come to see you very soon. Good day, Herr Jochum.'

A few weeks later, Ewald sent Karl a newspaper cutting, announcing that His Majesty Wilhelm II, King of Prussia and Emperor of Germany, in recognition of his loyal servant's contribution to his country, had conferred a baronetcy upon Heinrich Kraus, who would henceforth be known as Heinrich, Baron von Kraus zu Essen. 'I told you there was something he wanted more than money, didn't I?' the Count had scrawled on the bottom.

When Eitel Tobisch heard the good news that the future of the Hotel Quadriga was assured, he breathed a deep sigh of relief. Unlike Karl Jochum, who hurried straight up to the hotel to tell Ricarda, Eitel poured himself a large brandy to steady his nerves. He had not dared tell Liese about the problems threatening his employer, for he knew she would only have screamed at him and told him to find another, more secure job.

In his innermost heart, he knew he had made a terrible mistake in marrying Liese Kaufmann. What he had taken for common sense had turned out to be sheer petty-mindedness. After two years of marriage she found fault with everything he did, blaming him for every small problem. And she was not only bad tempered, but mean with it. When Eitel handed over his week's wages to her, she took it all except for a few coins, hardly allowing him enough for his omnibus fare to work. She scrimped and save on the housekeeping, putting the rest into a savings account for their old age.

Now, Eitel lied to her about his earnings, not admitting to his last salary increase and keeping his own money in a desk drawer in his office. It would only require the slightest excuse, he knew, for him to take up gambling again.

In recent months, the atmosphere at home had grown even worse, for Liese was pregnant with their first, and she vowed only, child. Eitel put down his empty glass, tidied his papers and left Café Jochum with lagging steps. At least Karl would not be forced to sell the café, as Eitel had feared, and the hotel would be completed. Things could be much worse.

He was greeted at his apartment door by a neighbour. 'Herr Tobisch, you must hurry. They've taken your wife to hospital. She's having her baby!'

Eitel stared at her anxiously, his previous bitter thoughts about Liese forgotten. 'Is she all right?'

'She was in terrible pain,' the woman said, an expression of joy on her face.

By the time Eitel arrived at the hospital, his son had been delivered. 'There wasn't time to try to find you, Herr Tobisch,' the doctor told him. 'Your wife had obviously been in labour all day, unable to attract anyone's attention. It was fortunate your neighbour went in to see her.'

'Is Liese all right?'

'She's very weak. We had to deliver the baby by Caesarean section and it was a very difficult operation. She won't be able to have any more children, and she'll be very frail for a long time.'

'Can I see the baby?' He had no desire to see Liese, but he did want to see his son. A nurse led him to a cot where a small baby was yelling lustily. Eitel Tobisch put down a timid hand. 'We're going to call you Otto.' Otto stopped crying and eyed him belligerently.

With their financial worries behind them, hopefully for ever, the Jochums turned the full force of their energies towards getting the Hotel Quadriga finished. Valuable time had been lost through the Silberstein fiasco, when deliveries had been held up because of non-payment, and other creditors had been reluctant to supply in case they were never paid. Now, a new accountant had been appointed, with very limited powers, the old debts had all been paid, and goods came pouring in.

Under the supervision of Dr Hedler and an engineer from Kraus Industries, the Artesian well was sunk and the electricity generator installed in the cellar not far from the huge central heating boiler. This whole area was then walled off, so that the fluctuating temperatures would not affect Karl's wine.

Ricarda seemed to be on her feet all day long, supervising the hanging of wallpaper and pictures, the laying of carpets, and the arrangement of furniture. On top of this, she was busy organizing their own apartment, for they had decided to move from the Rosenthaler Platz into the hotel as soon as they could. Standing in it, one early December morning, she remembered talking to Karl on the train journey back from Fuerstenmark. 'Imagine, a whole house that I could make into my own and call home!' she had said, little imagining that nearly five years later she would have a whole hotel to call home.

This apartment was going to be their real home. A first-floor suite at the back of the hotel, it overlooked a small courtyard and consisted of four rooms, a bathroom and a small kitchen. The largest room would be their living room, with their bedroom next door, while the other two served as guest room and dining room for the time being.

For the time being, Ricarda thought, glancing at the watch she wore on a long gold chain round her neck. Who knew, perhaps before they moved in, the guest room would already have to be redesigned as a nursery? She'd know for certain when she went to see Dr Blattner in a couple of hours' time. Impatiently willing the time to pass quickly, she left the apartment to find Eitel Tobisch and maybe help him for a while.

By now, Eitel was spending more time at the hotel than at Café Jochum, for ultimately the smooth running of the establishment was going to be his responsibility. Far from being distrustful of him, Ricarda now had implicit faith in the General Manager, for he had worked like a Trojan to help Karl keep Café Jochum running and organize the hotel. Yet, these days, she thought, as they supervised workmen carrying the handmade bedsteads up to the third floor, he had a rather downcast look, which was strange considering he had just had a baby son.

She thought of Eitel Tobisch again, as she sat in Dr Blattner's waiting room. Surely, this time, it was no false alarm? Surely, if women like Liese Tobisch could have babies, she could too! Grete's little girl, Olga, was two now. Baron Heinrich von Kraus's two boys, Ernst and Benno, were seven and four respectively. Countess Anna von Biederstein's small boy, Peter was one. Only Ewald's wife, Annette, and herself remained childless. Dear God, she prayed, please let me have conceived this time. Please let me give Karl the son he wants.

The doctor's surgery door opened. 'Frau Jochum, come this way please.'

She knew immediately that her prayers were answered. 'Yes, Frau Jochum, the tests are all positive. Your baby is due in June next year. My congratulations to yourself and your husband.'

She waited until the workmen had all gone home for the day and Karl came to collect her from the hotel, before she told him her news. Then in the peace of the empty building, she asked, 'Will the hotel be finished by June, Karli?'

'Just about, I should think.' He looked at her closely. 'Why?'

147

'Because we're going to have a baby, Karl. It's due in June.'

He took her hands and, for a long time, gazed at her, his eyes misted over. Then he drew her close to him, kissing her hair. 'Oh, my dearest, what wonderful news.' His voice was husky, choked with emotion. 'After all we have been through, after so long, and now, the hotel and a baby ...' He gazed out across the white marble floor of the foyer, towards the wide sweep of the staircase. 'The Quadriga must be completed by June. Our son will be the first of the Quadriga Jochums, the start of a dynasty. He must know the Quadriga from the day he is born, for one day this will be his hotel.'

At the beginning of June, the huge tarpaulins were taken down from the façade of the Hotel Quadriga, the scaffolding dismantled and the public allowed its first glimpse of the city's new landmark. All day long, eager faces were pressed against the windows, peering in through the glass revolving doors. 'That's His Majesty's hotel, that is.' 'Didn't think it would ever be finished, did you?' 'Takes time to build a blooming 'otel, mate.' 'Do you think the Kaiser will actually visit it?'

That last question also occupied Karl's mind. 'The ancient Kaiser', people had called Wilhelm I; 'the sickly Kaiser', they had called his son; 'the travelling Kaiser', they had nicknamed Wilhelm II, for His Majesty could not stay long in any one place, but had to be constantly on the move. Karl could only pray he would be in Berlin when the Hotel Quadriga opened. He personally delivered a letter to the Imperial Palace, inviting His Majesty to open the hotel officially on the fifteenth of that month. The days went by and there was no reply.

Karl and Ricarda moved into the hotel a week before it was due to open. By then, Ricarda was so huge she could do very little, but her condition did not prevent her from taking an interest in everything that went on. She watched their furniture moved into their new apartment, treasures she had brought with her from England, family heirlooms belonging to the Jochums, and pieces she had bought during the early years of their marriage. Then, of course, there was the new nursery suite in blue.

Nurse Bauer moved with them into the hotel. A voluminous figure, formidable in her starched uniform, but highly recommended by Dr Blattner, she viewed her new surroundings with disapproval. In her opinion, it was not done for a refined lady to give birth to her first child in an hotel, even one as superior as this one.

To Ricarda, those days, everything around her, even including Nurse Bauer, was beautiful. Every day, she waddled round the building, watching the last, finishing touches being put to the rooms in preparation for the great opening. 'You ought to be resting,' Nurse Bauer constantly admonished, but she could not rest. She had to see everything, touch everything, convince herself, time and time again, that it was all real.

On 14 June, the day before it was due to open, His Majesty sent a note saying that he would be at the Hotel Quadriga at four o'clock the following afternoon. As everyone heaved a sigh of relief, Karl marshalled his troops for a full rehearsal.

First he lined up the twelve page boys in descending order of height. 'Don't forget, His Majesty is a Colonel of the Death's Head Hussars. You will stand strictly to attention and only move when you are ordered.' Proudly watching from a seat in the foyer, Ricarda reflected how smart they looked in their blue and gold uniforms, blue caps on their heads and white gloves on their hands. One by one, Karl described their duties. 'You, Fritz, will accompany us to the Palm Garden Room.' He marched off in that direction and Ricarda followed them. It was a glorious room, bright and airy, with its glass roof and clambering tropical plants, including a magnificent collection of orchids. On a podium, erected facing the doorway, Franz Jankowski was practising with his orchestra. Ricarda smiled at him, glad that he was going to achieve his life's ambition and play for the Emperor.

Double doors led from the Palm Garden Room into the restaurant, where Max Patschke was detailing his waiters. 'When His Majesty arrives with the Herr Direktor, you will stand here and here,' he was saying. Karl nodded in satisfaction. Beyond the restaurant lay Maître Mesurier's domain. No food had yet been cooked in the new kitchens, but the staff were all ready to prepare the banquet intended for His Majesty the next day.

Karl, Ricarda and Fritz returned to the foyer, then entered the bar, where the new barman, a Westphalian called Arno Halbe, was polishing his crystal glasses and tumblers. It was a strange room, Ricarda thought, impersonal, as if it had no character, yet it looked comfortable with its deep leather settees. How many evenings shall we sit here in the future, she wondered. How many strangers will pass through here? What great events will this room witness?

'Heini!' she heard her husband's voice again in the foyer, summoning another page. 'You will conduct us up to the first floor in the lift!' This time, she did not accompany them, for she was feeling tired. The baby was moving restlessly inside her. She would take her last look at the bedrooms later that evening, on her way to bed. She returned to the Palm Garden Room, sank down in a chair, and listened to Franz.

It was quite late when Karl woke her. 'There you are, my dear. I've been looking for you everywhere. Well, I think everything is organized for tomorrow.' He looked tired, she thought. And then, 'If only the baby were born I could help him more.'

He took her hand and eased her out of the chair, asking, 'Do you want to inspect the suites now or tomorrow morning?'

'Oh, let's look now. Has Herr Tobisch put flowers in each room?' Then she bit her lip as a searing pain shot through her side, causing her to gasp aloud. But Karl hadn't noticed, already opening the lift door for her. They were halfway down the corridor on the first floor when the pain cut through her again, making her reel sideways against the wall.

'Ricarda! What's the matter?'

'I think it must be the baby,' she whispered through clenched teeth.

There were no bells in the Hotel Quadriga, no loud sounds to disturb the guests. The button that Karl pressed on the wall set a light flashing at the end of the corridor and, within seconds, a page boy was at their side. 'Hurry! Have Dr Blattner fetched to the hotel immediately.' White-faced, the boy scurried away.

'It's all right,' Ricarda said. 'I'm all right now.'

Within ten minutes, Dr Blattner was with her in their bedroom, feeling her pulse and giving Nurse Bauer her instructions. 'Oh, damn it,' Ricarda muttered to the nurse's horror, 'I'm going to miss the Emperor. All that effort and I'm not going to be there!'

Anxiously, Karl paced up and down the hall, trying to catch words from the mumbled conversation going on in the bedroom. After a quarter of an hour, the doctor emerged, took Karl's arm and led him into the drawing room. 'It will be some time yet.'

The hours that followed were even more anxious for Karl than the terrible days when it had appeared the hotel would never be built. Dr Blattner stayed with him, keeping him company and helping him to drink a bottle of wine, brought from the cellar. 'I understand the Emperor is coming to christen the Hotel Quadriga tomorrow.'

But, so worried was Karl about his wife, he could hardly think even about His Majesty.

It was one o'clock in the morning of 15 June 1894 that Ricarda gave birth. To Karl's stunned disbelief, he found himself the father of a baby girl.

There was no sleep for Karl Jochum the night before the Hotel Quadriga opened. While his wife, daughter and Nurse Bauer dozed fitfully in the early hours of the morning, Karl's mind worked overtime, allowing him no rest. A thousand worries plagued him. Already he did not mind that his son was a girl, but what if there were something wrong with the child? What if Ricarda had overtired herself and should become ill? Perhaps even now she was bleeding to death? He went in and out of the bedroom and nursery a thousand times, until Nurse Bauer, still in her uniform, took pity on him and made him some hot chocolate. 'Go and look at your hotel, Herr Jochum,' she said, not unkindly. 'Your wife and baby need their sleep. I'll call you when they wake.'

Somehow, the morning passed. Everybody except him seemed to have something to do. Mesurier was immersed in clouds of steam and the perfumes of roasting meats. Max was supervising the laying of tables, so that every piece of cutlery was perfectly aligned. Franz had taken the whole day off from Ullstein and the sound of his violin flooded the foyer. Eitel was here, there and everywhere, confirming arrangements with the housekeeper, checking paperwork, signing letters, ordering pages out on last-minute errands. 'We already have thirty reservations for tomorrow night, Herr Direktor.'

Karl nodded. Until the Emperor's visit was over, he could concentrate on nothing.

Two o'clock found him dressed in his new cutaway morning coat and striped trousers, pacing up and down the blue Savonnerie carpet. At half past two, the commissionaires were posted on the steps and the crowds started to gather. At three, the page boys were lined up. What if the Emperor did not arrive? What if he did arrive and something went wrong? Was Ricarda all right? What about the baby? Four o'clock came and went and the crowd, growing bigger by the minute starting calling out ribald comments. Karl stood between the two commissionaires in their top hats and blue uniforms, gazing towards the Imperial Palace.

Suddenly, a cheer went up. 'His Majesty! The Emperor!' Karl

breathed a sigh of relief. His broad face spread in a wide, welcoming smile, he approached his royal patron and took his outstretched hand. Then he bowed low over the Empress's glove and shook hands with the Court Marshal and the other attendants, among whom he was delighted to recognise Ewald. Finally, with a deep bow, he said proudly, 'Your Majesty, it is my great honour to welcome you as the first guest of the Hotel Quadriga.'

The Emperor gazed wonderingly down the arched colonnade. 'So this is the famous portico. Made, I am told, from granite blocks.'

'Cut to size and shipped from Finland, Your Majesty.'

'No other hotel in the world has such a prestigious entrance as this, Jochum?'

'Indeed not, Your Majesty.'

As the commissionaires bowed deeply, the royal couple, followed by their retinue, moved through the glass doors into the foyer, its white marble polished to such a finish that it reflected the images of the august visitors as they passed. The Emperor glanced around him in open admiration, then he marched up to the page boys, standing, as Karl had anticipated, by the flankman, as if he were inspecting the troops of the Death's Head Hussars. 'Excellent!'

At Karl's signal, Fritz marched forward and opened the door into the Palm Garden Room. Gradually, Karl found himself relaxing. Everything was going exactly to plan. 'What a delightful room,' the Empress said, her eyes lingering on Ricarda's Louis XVI furniture. 'And just look at those orchids!'

'If Your Majesty permits?' Karl signalled to Fritz, who snipped off some of the flowers, deftly wrapped their stems in a small napkin and handed the bouquet to him. Karl presented it to the Empress, who held it close to her nose to catch the perfume, then passed it to one of her ladies-in-waiting to carry.

The Emperor wanted to see everything. In the restaurant, after Max Patschke had presented him with a commemorative menu, almost a work of art in the head waiter's superb handwriting, he had to demonstrate all the subtle electric lighting effects he could achieve in the room, picking up the shimmering gold flecks in the heavy blue wallpaper.

'Well I'll be damned,' the Kaiser exclaimed in admiration. 'I'm sure they haven't got anything as good as this in London, eh, Jochum?'

Karl inclined his head modestly.

In the bar, the Emperor looked around him with an air of perplexity. 'Such an ordinary room, Jochum ...' He sat down in one of the deep, padded, leather armchairs that were grouped around low tables. 'But comfortable and somehow friendly.'

'Thank you, Your Majesty. You see, I don't believe a bar should be too intrusive or overwhelming. Its atmosphere should come from its occupants and it should be adaptable to the occasion of the moment. Too many bars make their customers feel intimidated, when they should feel at home. The Quadriga bar will develop its own atmosphere with the people who pass through it.'

'I shall come again and test the truth of your words,' the Emperor promised, with a twinkle to his male companions. Count Ewald nodded enthusiastically. The Empress frowned.

In the vast ballroom, the Kaiser said, 'New Year's Eve is going to be a splendid occasion here, Jochum!' His Empress, however, was far more interested in the pink ladies' salon. Then, Karl conducted the party into one of the hotel's six hydraulic lifts, taking them to the first floor. 'Quite remarkable,' the Emperor declared, examining the raised buttons indicating the different floors. 'Just wait till my Uncle Edward hears about this! I understand you even have your own electricity generator, Herr Jochum?'

There was something in His Majesty's voice that made Karl wonder, not for the first time, quite how indebted he was to his sovereign for Kraus's apparent munificence. Was it really possible that the Emperor had bartered a loan, electricity and water for the Hotel Quadriga for a title? 'Baron Heinrich von Kraus zu Essen has indeed been kind enough to install a private electricity supply for us, Your Majesty. Indeed the hotel is considerably indebted to the Baron's generosity.'

The Emperor quite definitely smirked. 'Delighted to hear it. And where will the Herr Baron stay when he visits the hotel?'

Yes, the Emperor knew every detail of that transaction! 'The Herr Baron has a suite permanently reserved for his use on the first floor. If you'll come this way?' He opened the door with the new Kraus coat of arms emblazoned on it, then stood aside to let the royal party enter. As he did so, Ewald winked at him, and suddenly the whole scenario became clear.

Ewald was at the root of his good fortune! Ewald had told the Emperor of Karl's troubles and suggested that in return for a baronetage, his brother-in-law Heinrich Kraus would be certain to help out. And the Emperor, wanting the Hotel Quadriga to be superior to any other in Europe, had stipulated that it should also have its own electricity and water supplies ...

The Emperor strode through the three-roomed suite, pulling open cupboard doors, peering out onto the balcony overlooking Unter den Linden, then eventually going into the bathroom, where he stopped still in astonishment at the sight of the massive bathtub with its gold-plated fittings. 'And does the hot water actually work?'

The page boy leapt forward to turn on the tap, but the Emperor motioned him imperiously away, bending down to turn the faucet himself. A torrent of steaming water gushed out, swirled, splashed up into the imperial face, then disappeared in a surging eddy down the waste pipe. 'Well, I'll be damned! Did you see that?' He turned to Karl with a disarming smile. 'You know, I'm rather glad now I made that fellow Kraus a baron!'

In a daze, Karl led them round the rest of the hotel. The day was turning out to be a fraction too exciting for his tired mind. First the baby, then the Emperor and now this revelation about Kraus!

But the Emperor was obviously not a bit tired. Entering the lift that was waiting for them on the fourth floor, he positioned himself next to the lift buttons. 'Now we're going to the cellars, eh, Jochum? The famous cellars that stretch out under the road?'

'Certainly, Your Majesty. Heini, the cellars!'

'No, Heini,' the Emperor cried. '*I'm* going to drive the lift.' With a mischievous grin on his face, he pressed the button, sending the elevator hurtling towards the basement. 'Jochum, how do I stop it?' His finger hovered on the red emergency button.

'This one, please, Your Majesty,' Karl said, just in time, stopping the lift.

'Now we're going back to the top again.'

After three trips up and down, the Empress said, 'Wilhelm, that's enough! I feel quite faint.'

With obvious reluctance, the royal lift operator conveyed them to the cellar. Here, a smile of anticipation on his face, Karl led them into his series of caverns, stacked floor to ceiling with racks of bottles wrapped in tissue paper and nestled on beds of straw. Kaiser Wilhelm looked around him with awe. 'Good God, Jochum, how much wine do you have here? Are you expecting a siege?' Then he clapped Karl on the back. 'We must give a reception, help you empty some of these!'

'I should be greatly honoured, Majesty. In the meantime, if you will allow me to offer a little refreshment, Maître Mesurier has prepared a light repast. But first, we must visit the Empire Room.'

'Mesurier! Still got that French devil with you, eh?'

Karl heard Ewald chuckle, for the story of Mesurier's truffles had become a legend in Berlin. But, as the door to the Empire Room was opened, all voices were stilled. The Emperor strode in, then stopped. The room was dominated by a huge stone fireplace in which, despite the summer month, a vast log fire was roaring, and over which a massive bronze bust of the Emperor was displayed. The furnishings were a clever mix between those to be found in an English gentlemen's club and the traditional dark oak of Wilhelmine Berlin. Upon the walls, in heavy gilt frames hung, in deference to the Kaiser's love of the navy, magnificent oil paintings of German battleships.

'Ah, a man's room,' the Emperor breathed contentedly. 'Now, Jochum, this is a room in which I can feel at ease. You wait until the English see this! They won't be able to say Berlin is a provincial backwater any more, will they? Won't be able to say we lack glamour and interest now! They think London is the only city in the world to have handsome hotels, but from now on, damn it all, they're going to have to eat their words!'

Karl thought his heart would burst with pride. He had done it! He had achieved his and his Emperor's dream!

He led them now into a private banqueting room, with wide windows, concealed by lace curtains, that looked up Unter den Linden towards the Brandenburg Gate. As they entered, the Emperor asked suddenly, 'And Frau Jochum? Why isn't she here?'

Karl bowed. It was well known that the Kaiser held women, including the Empress, in scant regard, so his enquiry was truly gratifying. 'My wife and I deeply regret her inability to be here, but I am honoured to tell Your Majesty that she gave birth early this morning to our first child, a daughter!'

The Emperor shook his head sadly at the news that the baby was a girl, but declared, 'Spendid! And what are you going to call her?'

In all the confusion, Karl had given no thought to the child's name. He glanced up the road towards the statue of the Quadriga, driven by Viktoria, Goddess of Victory, as if seeking guidance. Then he turned back to the Emperor, grandson of Queen Victoria of England, son of her eldest daughter, Princess Victoria, and father of a little girl himself, the Princess Viktoria Luise. 'We are going to call her Viktoria, Majesty.'

PART TWO
1894-1919

Chapter Six

On a bitter December morning just before Christmas in 1899, Baron Heinrich von Kraus zu Essen stood with his sons on the derelict quayside of a deserted dockyard on the mouth of the River Weser between Bremerhaven and Cuxhaven. His red, fleshy cheeks bloated beneath his peaked cap, and the uniform he wore as an Officer of the Reserve encasing his immense girth, the Baron's massive figure dwarfed the two boys. The 'Steel King' was forty-one that year and finally the head of Kraus Industries, for his father had died of a heart attack some months earlier.

Physically a mirror image of his father at that age, even to the steel-rimmed spectacles perched on his podgy nose, Ernst, now thirteen, was studying the shipyard intently. Benno, just ten, slim, with his mother's dark curling hair and brown eyes, was looking dreamily out across the North Sea.

'I'm sure you can see why the previous owner of this dockyard went bankrupt,' Baron Heinrich told them. 'For one thing, it lacks all the deep water advantages of, say, Kiel, which means it could be very difficult to build large ships here.'

'A longer slipway would remedy that problem, wouldn't it, Father?' Ernst asked.

'Indeed it would.'

'It's much nearer the Ruhr than Kiel is, and, of course, it's very near to Wilhelmshaven,' Ernst continued, with the air of having done his homework well. Across the bay, they could see the cranes, derricks and masts of the country's premier naval base.

'There should also be a lot of marine labour easily available,' Baron Heinrich added. 'This has always been a traditional shipbuilding area. Benno, what do you think?'

His youngest son did not move, still gazing out across the choppy waves. The Baron grunted in exasperation. Ernst was a true Kraus, serious, intelligent and with the makings of a good business brain, but Benno was a different matter. Although he was intelligent, he seemed to have inherited some of the wilfulness that had led his mother to oppose her family's wishes and marry him.

'Benno, what do you think?' he repeated.

'What kind of ships are you going to build here?'

'Flat-bottomed barges and tugs to begin with. Then, in due course, a battleship.'

To Baron Heinrich's astonishment, Benno, instead of looking excited at the prospect, pulled a disappointed face. 'Oh, I thought you might build a transatlantic liner, one even bigger and faster and more luxurious than the *Wilhelm der Grosse*, so that Kraus could win the Blue Riband for Germany.'

Baron Heinrich shook his head. Benno wasn't such a fool after all. By winning the Blue Riband a couple of years earlier, the *Wilhelm der Grosse* had won considerable prestige for German passenger shipping and Germany herself.

Ernst looked at his younger brother scornfully. 'You don't win wars with passenger liners. One day the British will try to force us into a war and we have to be ready to prevent it. If we have battleships as big, or bigger, than theirs, they won't dare to take us on. Isn't that so, Father?'

Baron Heinrich nodded. Down in South Africa, the Boers were fighting a battle for survival against the British, a fight in which every right-minded German sided with the courageous, tenacious Boer farmers pitting their miserable strength against the might of the British Empire. It was a war in which nobody else could intervene — for one very simple reason: no other country in the world had the naval power of the British. So long as Britannia ruled the waves, she ruled the world. This was something the Kaiser recognized, which was why he had passed the Navy Bill earlier that year; and so did Baron Heinrich von Kraus, which was why he was standing on this desolate quayside. Germany might have the arms and the soldiers, but before she could hope to beat the British in any war, anywhere, she had to have a navy of even greater strength. Baron Heinrich's ambition was to help her build it. He had the steel, he could buy the expertise. Now, he believed, he had found the shipyard.

The first shower of sleet slanted across the quayside, whipping their faces icily. Baron Heinrich turned abruptly. 'We shall buy this shipyard and we shall rename it Kraushaven. Now, let's go to Berlin and finalize the arrangements.'

They made their way among the deserted wharves, the Baron, despite his bulk, striding along in military fashion, Ernst trying to ape him, and Benno, dragging his feet through the debris.

160

Very little went on in the Hotel Quadriga of which Viktoria Jochum was not aware. The first thing she noticed that morning just before Christmas, when she slipped out of the apartment after her governess, Elli Zimmer, had dressed her and given her breakfast, was the tremendous activity going on at the other end of the corridor. Under the personal supervision of the housekeeper, three chambermaids were carrying piles of bedlinen and towels into the Kraus apartment. While she watched, a page boy arrived laden down with flowers, followed by another bearing vases. Surely all these preparations could not be just for the Baron?

Thoughtfully, Viktoria made her way downstairs towards her father's office, situated just behind the reception desk at the foot of the main staircase and marked *PRIVAT* in big letters. If the door was open, she knew she was allowed to knock and enter, then sit listening to him as he gave his staff their orders for the day. If the door was shut, as it was on this occasion, she had to continue to her next source of information: either Herr Tobisch, the General Manager, or Herr Quitzow, the Reception Manager.

Both men were standing behind the reception desk, discussing the day's room allocations, and Viktoria slipped on to a tall stool beside them to listen to their conversation and to watch the busy foyer. Many people smiled and said good morning to her as they passed, for, although she was only five, she was easily recognizable as Karl Jochum's daughter, with her blonde hair, blue eyes and squarish, obstinate jaw. Viktoria, too, knew them all, if only by name and room number.

'The Countess Julia is arriving this morning,' Herr Quitzow was telling Herr Tobisch. 'We are sending a carriage to the railway station to meet her.' Viktoria pricked up her ears. 'And the Herr Baron and the two sons are travelling from Bremen sometime this afternoon.'

Herr Tobisch consulted his schedules. 'They are staying two nights, then they are returning for the New Year's Ball.'

Viktoria smiled happily, her curiosity satisfied. So the entire Kraus family was coming to the Hotel Quadriga for the first time! The Herr Baron was frequently here on his own, visiting the vast chemical factory he owned in Kraus Village in Wedding, but this would be her first opportunity to see his two sons, Ernst and Benno.

She was about to slip down from the stool, when Herr Tobisch said something even more exciting. 'Now, you haven't forgotten

161

that the Count and Countess Johann von Biederstein and their children are also staying for the New Year, have you, Quitzow? You have reserved the Brandenburg Suite for them?' Viktoria's eyes widened. The Brandenburg Suite was situated on the first floor next to the Kraus apartment and was one of the finest in the whole hotel.

She knew Count Ewald, of course, for he was one of her father's oldest friends, and she was extremely fond of him, but she had never met the Count's younger brother, Johann, nor his wife Anna and their two children, Peter and Trudi, for they seldom came to Berlin, apparently preferring to live in the country at Fuerstenmark. Viktoria knew all about Fuerstenmark, for she had been brought up on the story of her parents' meeting at Uncle Ewald's wedding and was thrilled to think that these aristocratic Junkers were coming to stay at the Hotel Quadriga.

She looked round the bustling foyer, at the page boys in their blue uniforms carrying guests' luggage out to waiting taxis, at the Hall Porter giving directions, at Max Patschke hurrying out of the restaurant with a menu in his hand and an anxious frown on his face, at guests — dukes, counts, barons, generals, diplomats and industrialists, their wives, servants, children, nannies and governesses — and glowed with pride. This was her hotel, for hadn't she and the Quadriga been born on the same day, five and a half years ago? Hadn't she and the hotel been the focus of the Emperor's attention and hadn't she been named after the Emperor's daughter?

She wriggled on her stool, attracting Eitel Tobisch's attention. 'I shan't be long, Miss Viktoria, but this is a busy time for us, you know, what with Christmas and New Year.'

Viktoria smiled at him, then jumped down from her stool. She knew she could twist him around her little finger and she believed she understood why. Firstly, of course, it was because she was her Papa's daughter and Herr Tobisch admired her Papa greatly. Time and time again, he had told her the story of how the Hotel Quadriga had nearly failed to be built and how, in the nick of time, Papa and Baron Heinrich von Kraus zu Essen had rescued it from disaster. 'And that very day, Miss Viktoria, my son Otto was born. Can you imagine it? That very day!'

Viktoria had her own ideas about Otto, and they weren't very kind, but she never spoiled Herr Tobisch's story.

'After Otto, my wife became very ill and she couldn't have any more children. Poor Liese.' Herr Tobisch was a rather tragic figure, Viktoria always felt, and was certain he was so fond of her because he would have liked to have had a daughter like her and not a son like Otto, which was very understandable in her opinion.

Her head full of the exciting news she had learned at the reception desk, Viktoria wondered where to go next. If she returned to the family apartment, Mama and Elli Zimmer would insist that she did some lessons, so she decided to go to the room she loved more than any other in the hotel — the Palm Garden Room. She loved the furniture her mother had chosen for it, she loved the music Franz Jankowski played there in the evenings, and she loved the tall, trailing tropical plants, among which she could imagine herself in a jungle.

Immersed in her thoughts, she quietly pushed open the double doors, but as she made her way across it a movement caught her eye and she realized she was not alone. To her horror, she saw the stocky, blond figure of Otto Tobisch peering out from behind one of the plants.

'What are you doing here?' Karl Jochum's rules on staff and their relatives were very strict. Employees were not allowed on the premises except to work, and neither were their families encouraged to visit either the hotel or Café Jochum. Some staff whose homes were not in Berlin actually lived in the hotel, but they were forbidden to use the bars, restaurants or any other of the hotel's facilities. They spent their off-duty hours in their rooms or in the staff kitchen. But, sometimes, Eitel Tobisch, because of his position, enjoyed special concessions and, when his wife was feeling poorly, his six-year-old son was allowed to come to work with his father.

'I've as much right to be here as you have,' Otto said defiantly.

Then she saw what he was doing. His trousers undone, he was piddling into one of the huge plant pots. Despite herself, Viktoria felt her gaze riveted upon his small penis, from which issued a steady stream of water. So that was how little boys did it! Then she reddened, as she sensed him staring insolently at her. 'Stop it, stop it immediately!' she cried.

'You haven't got one of these, have you?' Otto sneered. 'Here, want to take a closer look?'

Suddenly frightened, Viktoria turned and started to run across the slippery parquet floor. 'I'm going to tell Papa! He'll make you stop, he'll turn you out of the hotel!'

Before she could reach the door of the room, Otto had caught up with her, his hands roughly grasping hold of her arms, pinioning them behind her. 'Don't you dare tell your father!'

'I will, I will!' she muttered through clenched teeth, for Otto's hands were hurting her, his nails digging into her skin. Although he was only a year older, he was considerably bigger and stronger than she was.

Suddenly he loosened one arm and put it round her neck, twisting her head back so that he was leering down at her. 'If you tell your father, I'll break your neck.' His arm tightened against her windpipe and silver stars danced before her eyes. 'Now, promise you're not going to tell him or anybody else.'

Never in her life had she been so terrified. She was convinced that Otto could and would break her neck if she did not promise. Incapable of nodding her head, she grunted, and Otto released her. For a moment or two the two antagonists faced each other, then Otto opened the door and slammed out of the room. Lifting her hands to her aching throat, Viktoria burst into tears. After her promise, she dared not tell her mother or father what had happened, for Otto would be sure to find out and then her life would be in constant danger.

Gradually, the pain receded and she wiped her eyes and blew her nose. She was just going to have to be very careful in the future and make certain she was never alone again with Otto.

Fortunately, her parents were taking luncheon in the main restaurant with Countess Julia, so she ate alone with Elli Zimmer, who was too preoccupied with her Christmas plans to notice Viktoria's unnatural silence. That afternoon, however, instead of going back downstairs to witness the arrival of the Krauses, Viktoria stayed in her room.

Christmas was her favourite time of the whole year, Ricarda thought, as she helped Karl hang candles and small presents on the tree in their private living room. It was the tradition for parents to decorate the tree as a surprise for their children and, since Viktoria's birth, it was one of her greatest pleasures. Unlike the English, Germans preferred to keep Christmas simply, then welcome in the New Year uproariously, and so Christmas was the only occasion that they were ever together as a family and not at the beck and call of anyone and everyone in the hotel.

This was also the first Christmas they had spent with her father, who had just retired to a small flat in Charlottenburg and whose presence in Berlin seemed to make up in a way for the loss of Karl's mother, who had died in Munich just after the hotel was completed, and for her own grandmother, who had passed away at about the same time. Viktoria loved Emil Graber, 'Opa', as she called him in nursery talk, a name now adopted by the whole family.

More times than she cared to remember during the past five years, Ricarda had left Viktoria, first with Nurse Bauer and then with Elli Zimmer, while she devoted herself to her hotel duties. She passed her hand across her waist in a swift gesture and smiled. Her second child was due in May and after it was born she was determined things would change.

She looked up at Karl affectionately. 'Ready?'

He nodded, turned off the electric light and, opening the door a fraction, called out, 'Viktoria! Opa!'

Ricarda watched their expressions as they entered the room, hand in hand, Opa quietly smiling, the little girl's eyes full of wonder. How lucky they were to know such peace and such happiness. 'Happy Christmas, darling,' she said, bending down and kissing Viktoria on the forehead.

'Happy Christmas, Mama. Oh, isn't the tree beautiful?'

Ricarda took her hand and, since their group was too small for them to stand in a circle round the tree, they held hands in a row, Karl, Ricarda, Viktoria and Opa. While the candles flickered, they sang the old Christmas hymns such as *Stille Nacht, heilige Nacht* and carols she and her father had learned in England like *The Holly and the Ivy*.

Once Christmas was over, the hotel gradually started to fill again, reaching its busiest time on New Year's Eve, as guests arrived from all over the country to attend the traditional Quadriga Ball, being held this year not only to welcome in a New Year but also a new century!

'Please let me stay up and watch the new century arrive,' Viktoria pleaded, gazing from one to the other of her parents. 'Please, Mama, I'm not a baby any more.'

'You won't be able to stay awake so late.'

'Oh, I shall, I'm so excited, I couldn't possibly sleep.'

Karl ruffled her fair curls. He might have wanted a son, but this little daughter of his was a true Jochum with her square jaw and

165

love of the hotel. 'Why not? The other children will be there.'

Ricarda knew when to give in. 'All right, but you must sit quietly and be good.'

'Oh, thank you, Mama. Papa, can I come with you now on your tour?'

As she watched them set off, hand in hand, Ricarda smiled. It would be good for Viktoria to mix with some other children, particularly from families such as the von Biedersteins and the Krauses, with whom they had been invited to sit that evening for the ball. Of course, the Kraus boys were both much older than Viktoria, but the two Biederstein children were nearly contemporaries of her daughter, Peter being seven now and Trudi nearly four.

Thinking of them reminded her to go up to the Brandenburg Suite and check that everything was in readiness for them. Lifting her long, green skirts, she hurried up the main staircase.

Karl and Viktoria went first to the kitchens, where Maître Mesurier and his chefs were busy making last minute preparations for the gala dinner. A blast of heat hit them from the ovens, and steam issued from dozens of boiling pans. Smilingly, the diminutive Frenchman stopped his work, exchanged a few words with Karl, then gave Viktoria a piece of chocolate cake. She reached up and kissed him on the cheek, 'Happy new century.'

'And to you, *chère* Mademoiselle.'

Their tour of inspection continued through the restaurants, where Max Patschke was gazing anxiously at his list of table reservations and waiters were rushing round, moving tables to make room for last-minute guests. Then they went to the bar, where a large throng of elegantly dressed men and women was already gathering, sipping sherry and madeira. Arno Halbe nodded to Karl and smiled at Viktoria as they continued on their way into the huge ballroom.

'Oh, Papa, doesn't it look pretty!'

The room did, indeed, look superb. On each of the small circular tables around the dance floor candles flickered and paper streamers garlanded the walls and ceiling. Father and daughter walked across the waxed floor to the musicians. 'Good evening, Franz. It's going to be a busy one.'

'Good evening, Herr Direktor. Good evening, Miss Viktoria,' Franz Jankowski greeted them. 'It's a night we're only going to see once in our lifetime!'

Viktoria looked at her father anxiously. 'How shall we know when the new century arrives?'

Karl laughed. 'When the twentieth century arrives, you'll know all right. There'll be fireworks and big cannons will be fired and every church bell in the city will ring. Now, come along and have some supper. I haven't got time to stand around chatting, you know, not tonight of all nights.'

A couple of hours later, Karl stood with Ricarda and Viktoria, proudly welcoming his guests to the last New Year's ball of the old century and the first of the new. Impeccably dressed as ever, he knew he made an imposing figure, as he bowed to old friends and greeted new ones. He had achieved his dream, for during the past five years, the Hotel Quadriga had become a truly cosmopolitan centre and for many, a home away from home, a place where their every whim was catered for, where nothing was too much trouble, and where people knew they would be given a service equal to none.

'The compliments of the season to you and a happy New Year, Herr Jochum.' Isaak Arendt's voice interrupted his reverie.

Karl shook his hand warmly. 'And to you, Herr Arendt.'

'Good evening, Herr Jochum. I am Theo Arendt.' Karl turned in astonishment at the voice. Damn it all, the last time he had seen the boy had been at his wedding eleven years ago! Now he was a young man of about twenty. How time did fly!

'And may I present an old friend of our family, Professor Bethel Ascher?' Isaak Arendt said, indicating a man in his mid-thirties, holding two young girls by either hand.

Professor Ascher bowed. 'I'm pleased to make your acquaintance, Herr Jochum. These are my daughters, Sophie and Pipsi.'

The two girls curtsied politely and Karl could not help staring at them. Probably aged about ten and five respectively, they were undeniably Jewish, with very dark eyes and jet black hair that reached down to their waists. Dear God in heaven, Karl thought, they are going to be beauties when they grow up!

He glanced at Ricarda and Viktoria, his wife so elegant with her auburn hair piled on top of her head, her bare shoulders pale against the emerald green of her gown, and his daughter so pretty with blonde ringlets, wearing a pink taffeta dress and new white boots. What an extraordinary city Berlin was, he thought, that it could produce such different children.

'Herr Jochum, good evening!' a familiar voice boomed, and

Baron Heinrich von Kraus zu Essen loomed beside him in his Reserve Officer's uniform. Since he had worked out how the Baron had acquired his title and now that his loan was fully repaid, the last vestiges of Karl's antipathy to the 'Steel King' had vanished. Indeed, he felt a sneaking respect for the man. 'Good evening, Herr Baron. Good evening, Countess.' Julia had aged over the years, he thought sadly. Those once so vivacious brown curls were turning grey and her face appeared drawn.

'Let me introduce you all to my two sons, for you'll be seeing a lot of them in years to come,' the Baron said. 'This is Ernst.' Still looks just like his father, Karl decided. 'And this is Benno.' Karl suddenly remembered the little baby crying at Fuerstenmark Castle and how he had hoped the child would take after his mother. And I do believe he has, Karl thought. Same dark curls, same dark eyes, much more Biederstein than Kraus.

'Karl, old friend! Happy New Year!' A hand clapped him on the shoulder and Karl turned with a delighted smile to greet Ewald. Poor Annette had died in childbirth just over four years ago, a shock from which the Count had recovered remarkably well, mechanically resuming his old bachelor ways, although, Karl suspected, he was no longer the philanderer he had once been. 'You remember my brother, Johann, and his wife Anna, of course?'

While Karl and Count Johann shook hands and Ricarda and Anna embraced, Viktoria became conscious of a small girl studying her dress critically. 'Hello, I'm Viktoria Jochum,' she said.

'I'm Countess Gertrud von Biederstein.' Viktoria stiffened. She had hoped she would become friends with the Biederstein children, but Trudi's airs and graces made her suddenly doubtful.

'And I'm Peter,' a boy's voice said. 'I'm very pleased to meet you, Viktoria.'

He was taller than she was, with dark brown hair and brown eyes. He held out his hand and she took it in her own. Then he smiled and, for no reason at all, she suddenly felt shy. She let his hand drop and clasped her mother's instead. She felt safer that way.

Now that they had all been introduced, they followed the master of ceremonies over to the large table that had been reserved for them; only Karl remained at the ballroom door to continue welcoming his guests. Waiters brought champagne for the adults and freshly-pressed apple juice for the children.

168

The ballroom was crowded now, nearly every available inch of floorspace taken up with couples dancing to the music directed by Franz Jankowski. Viktoria sat close to her mother, watching the dancers and letting the grown-ups' conversation waft over her.

'What do you think of the Boer successes in the South African war, Heinrich?' Ewald asked. 'Damn good thing, eh, the British garrisons besieged in Ladysmith, Mafeking and Kimberley? Roberts and Kitchener are never going to succeed in relieving them. The Boers will win the war! I say we ought to give them a hand!'

'There's got to be an end to British imperialism,' Johann stated flatly. With his ruddy cheeks, red hair and bushy whiskers, he took after his father, the old Count Friedrich. 'With the triple alliance between Austria, Italy and Germany, and the treaty between Russia and France, England seems to have become a kind of balancing factor. She seems to hold all the power now.'

'She holds the power because she rules the waves,' Heinrich said drily. 'And because she rules the waves she has gained colonies, which add to her strength.'

'That's why you've bought the dockyard near Wilhelmshaven, is it?' Johann asked him shrewdly.

'That's quite right.'

'Things could change a lot if Queen Victoria died,' Ewald said. 'After all, she's over eighty now. She can't last for ever. We all know His Majesty doesn't exactly see eye to eye with the Prince of Wales. And he's got a very strange relationship with the Tsar.'

'I don't believe His Majesty wants war,' Heinrich told them. 'On the contrary, he wants to be in a position to prevent one. Indeed, I'd go so far as to say that the only people who actually want war are the military.'

They all stared at Ewald, who admitted slowly, 'Yes, promotion does come slowly in peacetime, that's true, and it's bad for army morale to be inactive for a long time, but to say that the military is advocating war would be going too far.'

Viktoria shifted restlessly in her chair. It was always the same when grown-ups got together. All they could ever talk about was politics and war. She looked around the table. Peter and Trudi were talking in low undertones to each other, while Ernst Kraus was following the discussion seriously, but Benno was staring at her smilingly. Then, to her surprise, he stood up and walked round the table. 'Would you like to dance?'

She looked up at her mother, who nodded encouragingly, then, feeling very adult, she allowed Benno to take her hand.

'I'm afraid I don't know how to dance,' he confessed, as they approached the dance floor. 'In fact, this is the first ball I've ever attended.'

At that moment, Viktoria decided she liked Benno, for at least he was honest. 'I don't know how to dance either, but it was so boring listening to them talking politics.'

Benno put his arm round her waist, then bravely launched them out among the other dancers. 'It's all Papa and Ernst ever talk about.'

After that, the evening livened up considerably so far as Viktoria was concerned. While the grown-ups talked, danced and drank champagne, she and Benno sat together and she told him all about the Hotel Quadriga, in which, to her great delight, he seemed fascinated. Suddenly, she became aware of a figure standing beside her and looked up into a pair of smiling brown eyes. 'Viktoria, would you permit me the honour of this dance?' Peter von Biederstein asked.

Instantly, she forgot all about Benno. 'Why, Peter, that would be so nice.'

He held out his hand and she took it and again, as earlier in the evening, she felt suddenly shy. She wanted to be with him, but at the same time, she was scared of him. He seemed to be a much better dancer than Benno, however, for he did not tread on her toes nearly so often. And, although he was younger than Benno, he somehow seemed more adult. Perhaps, she thought, this was why he made her feel shy. With Benno, she felt as though they were both children together, while Peter almost seemed to be laughing at her, rather in the way Uncle Ewald teased her.

It was while she was still dancing with Peter that the orchestra suddenly stopped playing and her father stepped onto the podium. 'My most gracious ladies and gentlemen, it is midnight. On behalf of the Hotel Quadriga, I wish you all a very happy and prosperous New Year and ask you to stand to drink to His Majesty. The Kaiser!'

The dance floor emptied as couples hurried back to their tables, while waiters scurried to and fro through the room, popping corks and filling empty glasses, then everyone stood and answered the toast, '*Sein Majestaet*, the Kaiser!' 'A happy New Year!' 'All the best!' '*Prost Neu Jahr!*' Husbands embraced wives and shook

170

hands with old friends. A frenzy of kissing and hugging broke out, as everyone congratulated each other on the new century.

Streamers cascaded through the air and the sky outside was illuminated as the first of a magnificent firework display lit up the entire sky over Berlin, followed by trailing rockets, golden rain and gigantic catherine wheels. On Unter den Linden a roll of cannon fire saluted His Imperial Majesty, Emperor Wilhelm II, and throughout the city, church bells pealed in every tower and steeple.

But Viktoria remained unaware of all of this, for in the ballroom of the Hotel Quadriaga, seven-year-old Count Peter von Biederstein took her in his arms and kissed her.

There were further festivities a few months later on 5 May to celebrate the coming-of-age of the Crown Prince. Not only the Hotel Quadriga, but the whole of Unter den Linden was decked with flags and flowers and even the Brandenburg Gate was given a new look with an extra-dimensional coat of wood, hung with garlands of flowers, wreaths of pine and laurel, gaily-coloured bunting and yet more flags.

Viktoria and Elli Zimmer joined many of the guests from the hotel on the long balcony above the Hotel Quadriga's portico, cheering and waving as the long ceremonial procession passed beneath them, the gaily coloured uniforms of the foot regiments resplendent in the sunshine, the hooves of the cavalry horses echoing on the cobbles and the blaring of the trumpets, the rolling of the drums and the sound of the soldiers' voices lifted in old patriotic songs, lingering on the air long after they were gone.

When Crown Prince Wilhelm himself rode by, Viktoria thought she would burst with pride, for he looked up at the hotel and, she could have vowed, he smiled. 'Oh, Elli, why isn't Papa here?'

'Your father's busy.'

But when they returned to the apartment, they found Papa and Dr Blattner clapping each other on the back and drinking champagne. 'Papa, the Crown Prince smiled at me!'

For once, however, her father wasn't interested in the royal family. 'Come with me,' he smiled, putting down his glass and leading her into the nursery. 'Come and see your new sister.'

Viktoria stared into the cradle and saw a red-faced, wrinkled little object with screwed-up eyes. So that was why her parents had not been with her and Elli Zimmer on the balcony, and why Nurse Bauer had suddenly returned to the hotel. The Nurse had brought a new baby. 'But she's not very pretty, Papa. Couldn't Nurse Bauer bring another one that looks nicer?'

Karl roared with laughter. 'That's exactly what I said when I first saw you, but I didn't send you back!'

'I didn't look like that, Papa. I couldn't have done. You'd never have loved me.'

'Well, I can assure you that you did, and I still loved you.'

Viktoria was thoughtful for a moment, then she asked, 'Papa, did you tell them to put up all the decorations because you knew my new sister was arriving?'

Karl laughed. 'That's right, my pet. How did you guess?'

Viktoria looked accusingly at Elli Zimmer. 'She told me they were for the Crown Prince, but I know better. Papa, no wonder he smiled at me. He must have known about my sister!' Then she frowned down at the baby. Since it was going to stay, she supposed it had better have a name. 'Papa, what are we going to call her?'

'What about Luise?'

She nodded approvingly. 'That's nice. Then we'll be Viktoria Luise, like the Princess.'

The years after Luise was born were sweet for Ricarda. Not only could Karl run the hotel without her help, but he found opportunities to take time off himself and, once Luise was old enough to be taken out in the perambulator, they made many family outings together.

During the summer months they travelled out to Heiligensee, often taking Opa with them, who was becoming sadly crippled with arthritis. While he and Ricarda sat on the fallen oak with Luise beside them on a rug, Karl taught his older daughter how to swim. Later, as the evening drew in, they cooked a simple meal, which they ate on the verandah overlooking the lake. 'We haven't done this since our honeymoon, have we?' Karl asked.

'Then you should have done,' his father-in-law reprimanded him.

Ricarda just smiled at them both. It didn't matter. The intervening years had been full and interesting. They had two beautiful daughters and they were happy. That was all that mattered.

Sometimes on Sundays, particularly during the winter months, their expeditions took them through the city of Berlin itself. Karl, in his best suit with a stiff bowler on his head, strode ahead, while Ricarda in a wide-brimmed hat elegantly furnished with ostrich

172

feathers, followed with Viktoria in white muslin over starched petticoats and a fur cape round her shoulders. Behind them came Nurse Bauer, pushing Luise's baby carriage, and Elli Zimmer.

Ricarda knew Karl loved these excursions, for he adored showing off 'his' city. He took them down the Kurfuerstendamm, now an impressive avenue lined with expensive apartments, shops and cafés. 'When I was your age,' he proudly told Viktoria, 'none of this existed. It was called the Pappelallee then, and was just meadows. But it was from those fields and these buildings that I made the money to build the Hotel Quadriga.'

On other occasions they visited the Siegesallee, the Victory Mall that ran through the Tiergarten, a row of huge white marble statues that the Emperor was having erected in memory of the glorious victories of his ancestors. It was seldom that Karl criticized anything His Majesty did, but on this occasion he permitted himself a chuckle. 'Everyone is calling it Sweetmakers' Alley, and they do look rather like huge sugar figures, don't they?'

'I don't like them,' Viktoria shivered. 'Look at that one. His head's all wrapped in bandages, he can't put his helmet on.'

'That's Otto with his arrow,' Ricarda told her. 'He had to live the last years of his life with an arrow embedded in his skull.'

She expected Viktoria to look sorry, but instead the little girl said vehemently, 'I expect it served him right.'

On another Sunday they all trooped along with the rest of Berlin to stare at the huge monument dedicated to the old Emperor, Wilhelm I. It was inscribed 'Wilhelm the Great, German Emperor, King of Prussia, 1861-1888. In gratitude and true affection — the German people.'

'Well, that's how much bronze you can buy for four million marks,' a man behind them sniffed disdainfully. Ricarda smiled for to her this irreverent remark typified the people of Berlin. In their thousands they would come out on the streets and cheer their Kaiser but they never allowed their enthusiasm to get the better of their common sense. Deep down inside them, they always retained a native scepticism and dry wit. They allowed His Majesty to take liberties with their money, but they reserved the right to comment cynically on what he did.

'Papa, will the Emperor build a monument to you one day?' Viktoria asked.

'Heaven forbid! I think Berlin has enough monuments to last for ever.' Around them, several people laughed.

173

'Herr Jochum has already built his own monument,' a man commented, raising his hat to Karl. 'And although it, too, may have cost a mint of money, at least the Hotel Quadriga serves a useful purpose!'

But Ricarda's richest moments were those spent watching her daughters grow and develop. In no time at all, it seemed, Luise had celebrated her fifth birthday and Viktoria was approaching her eleventh. Already the two girls were very different in both looks and character. Luise was thin and wiry, with her mother's vivid chestnut hair and green eyes, and gave early promise of her mother's artistic ability. She was very fond of music, but she was unable to concentrate on anything for very long and sometimes reminded Ricarda of a butterfly, flitting from flower to flower.

In Viktoria, the Jochum strain grew ever more defined, as she grew tall, with waving blonde hair and blue eyes above high cheekbones. Seldom provoked to anger, she was dogged, determined, and tenaciously loyal, sometimes to the point of obstinacy. They were laudable characteristics but during the summer of 1905 Ricarda had her first hint of how they might threaten her elder daughter's happiness.

That June, the marriage was due to take place between the Crown Prince and Princess Cecilie of Mecklenburg-Schwerin. Once again, the Hotel Quadriga was full, as people travelled from all over the country to watch the wedding procession or, in the case of a lucky few, actually to attend the ceremony. Among the invited guests were Count Johann and Countess Anna von Biederstein, while Count Ewald was with the Brandenburg Guards in attendance upon their Royal Highnesses.

It was the first time the Fuerstenmark von Biedersteins had visited Berlin since the New Century Ball and Viktoria awaited their arrival with increasing impatience. Ever since Peter had kissed her on the ballroom floor, she had dreamed about him, talked to him in her mind and even planned a kind of childish future with him. As the actual day of his arrival approached, however, she was assailed by strange fears. Perhaps he had forgotten that he had kissed her, perhaps he would not even remember her! Not having any brothers, she knew very little about boys. Indeed, the only boy with whom she had had any dealings was Otto Tobisch and since that dreadful experience in the Palm Garden Room, she had gone out of her way to avoid him.

To her great relief, however, Peter not only remembered her, he went out of his way to be extremely gallant to her, inviting her and Luise to join him and Trudi on the balcony overlooking Unter den Linden to watch the procession. He was twelve now and growing very handsome. 'Damn it all, that boy's the spitting image of Ewald,' her father said when he saw him. 'Should have been Ewald's son. He'll break some hearts before he's much older.'

From first light, people had been gathering on the streets, flags, flowers and handkerchiefs in their hands and, by the time the Princess was due to ride past, all that could be seen from the Quadriga's balcony was a dense forest of heads, perhaps twenty deep, reaching out from the walls of the hotel to the kerbside, where police had formed a human chain to keep them back from the road.

Once again decked with flags and garlands of flowers, the Quadriga's balconies, too, were packed, all the private ones belonging to rooms on the second, third and fourth floors, as well as the long one stretching out above the portico. It was on this that Viktoria and Luise stood with the von Biederstein children, not far from Baron Heinrich von Kraus and his family.

Although she had curtsied and said hello to them, the two Kraus boys made her feel shy now, for they were considerably older than she was. Ernst at nineteen, was very much a young gentleman and Benno, three years his junior, was already sixteen. The familiarity she had felt with Benno five years ago when they had both been children together seemed to have gone. In any case, Viktoria had time for only one person — Peter.

Suddenly, an excited cry went up from the crowd and Viktoria forgot everything else in her excitement. 'She's coming! The Princess is coming!' At this very moment, Luise suddenly wailed, 'I can't see ! Vicki, I can't see! Where's Papa?' Annoyed, Viktoria looked round to try to spot her parents, then saw them, standing on tiptoe right at the very back of the balcony. 'Papa's right at the back. I'll lift you up, then you can see.'

'I want to be with Papa,' Luise cried, tears forming in her eyes. Thrusting away Viktoria's hand, she started to force her way back through the crowd. Divided between her desire to stay with Peter at the front of the balcony and her concern for her little sister, Viktoria made a move to follow her, but Peter's hand grasped hers. 'She'll be all right. Stay here. Look, there's the Princess's carriage.'

Behind her, people were making way for the desperate small

figure with gleaming red hair and tragic green eyes, who was beating a path through them, calling, 'Papa, Papa.' Then a voice said, 'Why, Fraeulein Luise, couldn't you see where you were? Look, if you sit on my shoulder, you'll be able to see perfectly. Come on, now, let's lift you up.' As Luise looked into Franz Jankowski's kindly face her tears stopped and she smiled. After her Mama and Papa, she loved the elderly violinist more than anyone else on earth. When Viktoria next glanced behind her, she saw Luise perched on Franz Jankowski's shoulders, laughing happily.

The traditional bridal coach, pulled by gloriously decorated horses and driven by splendidly liveried coachmen, was almost beneath them now. To Viktoria, the seventeen-year-old Princess Cecilie seemed the most beautiful person on earth, dressed in a cloud of white lace. Forgetful of decorum, she cheered as loudly as any of the ordinary people on the street below, her hand gripping Peter's in her spellbound excitement. How wonderful to be a princess and to be going to be married. Impetuously, she turned to Peter. 'Do you think I'll ever be grown-up enough to get married, Peter?'

Also carried away by the moment, he smiled at her, 'Of course you will, Vicki. Princess Cecilie is only seventeen. In six years' time, you'll be her age, and then you'll fall in love and get married.'

But Viktoria knew she was already in love. When her mother came to kiss her good night that evening, she told her dreamily, 'When I'm seventeen, I'm going to get married too.'

'Possibly. Who do you think you're going to marry?'

'Why, Peter, of course!'

Ricarda opened her mouth to start to explain the difficulty of such a marriage, then stopped. The child was too young to understand class differences and the vast chasm that still divided her from the von Biedersteins. Anyway, she was only eleven and she couldn't be serious. 'Well, we shall see.' But, in her heart, she was troubled.

While Countess Julia and Benno returned to Essen after the royal wedding, Baron Heinrich and Ernst remained in Berlin. Any day now Ernst was due to be called up to do his military service and the Baron wanted him to absorb as much information as possible about Kraus Industries before he was lost to the company for the next two years.

176

Baron Heinrich had followed the progress of the Russian-Japanese War in 1904 with very great interest. Anything to do with war concerned Kraus Industries, of course, but the most startling fact to emerge from the hostilities in the East had been the vast superiority of the British-built Japanese battleships over the French-built Russian ones. From the very outset, it had been obvious that Russia must lose this disastrous war, and when she did, it would be due, once again, to British naval supremacy and shipbuilding ability.

In order for Kraus Marin to be considered for building one of the great battleships Admiral von Tirpitz was currently commissioning, Baron Heinrich knew he needed a naval architect with the abilities of England's Cuniberti, so he set about discovering a lesser-known, yet equally talented, designer and came up with Wilfried von Wetzlar. Wetzlar, it transpired, was a German who, lacking the opportunity to develop his career in Germany, had forsaken his native land to become a naval architect in England. Still loyally patriotic, he saw in the Kaiser's successive Navy bills an opportunity to return home again and, when he was approached by Kraus Industries, he immediately booked himself a ticket to Berlin.

Baron Heinrich and Ernst met Wilfried von Wetzlar in the drawing room of their suite at the Hotel Quadriga. Instinctively, the Baron liked the naval architect, who gave him straightforward answers about his work for the British. 'And what can you offer me?'

Wetzlar hesitated, then said, 'I have been involved in some of the plans for HMS *Dreadnought*.' As Baron Heinrich stared at him, he went on, 'It's going to weigh nearly eighteen thousand tons, it will carry ten 12-inch guns and will have a speed of twenty-one knots.'

Such a warship as Wetzlar was describing was almost beyond belief and certainly had no counterpart in Germany. 'Could you design such a ship?'

Wilfried von Wetzlar indicated the rolled-up blueprints he had brought with him. 'I not only could, but I have. What is more, it is far superior to the *Dreadnought*.'

Heinrich Kraus was enough of an engineer to understand the basics of Wetzlar's designs, the thoroughness and audacity of which almost took his breath away. With a sense of mounting excitement, he sent a message to the Palace, requesting an interview with the Kaiser. 'Be prepared,' he warned Wetzlar. 'His Majesty also considers himself a naval architect.'

'I know,' he said, for the Emperor's love of ships was renowned, 'and he could also have made a very good one.'

Delighted to have an opportunity to discuss naval matters, the Kaiser received them with alacrity. He delved into his desk drawer and pulled out a sheaf of papers. 'Look at these,' he cried to Wetzlar. 'What do you think of them?'

With great seriousness, Wetzlar admired them, while Baron Heinrich and Ernst sat impatiently by, totally excluded from the conversation. Then the Kaiser detailed at great length the difficulties of establishing a German fleet large enough to deter any rivals and Admiral von Tirpitz's programme as Minister of Marine. Eventually, the Baron could contain himself no longer. 'Your Majesty, may I be permitted to show you the plans for the battleship Herr von Wetzlar has designed?'

'Oh, I suppose so,' the Kaiser said wearily, obviously expecting little to come of them. But as the Baron unrolled the blueprints, his eyes widened.

'She will have a displacement of twenty-five thousand tons,' Wetzlar explained. 'Her armour plating will be twelve inches thick. And she will have twelve $15\frac{1}{2}$-inch guns.'

'*Donnerwetter*! She will be the largest, fastest all-gun battleship in the world!' the Emperor exclaimed with something approaching awe. 'This is not a blueprint, Wetzlar, this is a prophecy.' He stood up and gazed out of the Palace window. 'We'll show the British! We'll show them who rules the waves!'

Chapter Seven

It was a chill December afternoon in 1906 when Franz Jankowski arrived at his humble apartment in the old town after his shift at Ullstein to find a stranger standing on his landing, a very thin young man, dressed in rather shabby clothes, an old suitcase beside him. 'Can I help you?'

'You are Herr Jankowski?' the young man asked in Yiddish.

'Yes,' he replied, also in Yiddish, 'I am Franz Jankowski.'

The boy looked very nervous. 'I am Georg, your nephew.'

Yes, he had the same dark, cavernous eyes and black hair as himself and his brother. 'Then you are welcome, boy. Come in. It's only a poor flat, but it's all I have.' If he weren't so thin, he would be a good-looking boy, Franz thought, as he ushered him into his simple kitchen and put a saucepan on the black coke stove. 'So you are Hans's son. And how is Hans?' Many years ago, his brother Hans had moved from Berlin to East Prussia, married a local girl and settled in Koenigsberg. The last time he had seen Georg was as a baby, some sixteen or so years ago.

'My parents are both dead,' Georg said dully. 'We had an influenza epidemic and they both died. I caught it, too, but I survived. Uncle Franz, I don't know where to go. The landlord repossessed our house because the rent was not paid and now I have nowhere to live. So I came here. You see, you're my only relative now.'

Franz stared at him in horror, then put his arms around him and held him tight. 'Of course you must stay with me, my boy.' He shook his head in disbelief. Hans dead. Hans's boy here in Berlin. 'Let us have some tea.' He made it weak, straining water from the pan over the few precious leaves, then he took it into the room where he lived, ate and slept. He was very fortunate, for it was a large room, even big enough to house an upright piano, which, after his violin, was his most treasured possession.

His mind still confused, he said, 'I don't know where you will sleep, Georg.' His eyes moved round the room, over piles of books and newspapers, a table, a couple of chairs, his bed curtained off in a corner, and finally they lit upon his beloved piano. 'I suppose the piano will have to go.'

To his surprise, Georg's eyes lit up. 'Oh, no, you must keep the piano.'

'You can play?'

Georg lifted the lid and ran his fingers caressingly over the keyboard. 'We had a piano at Koenigsberg. I hated to sell it, but I had to — for the train fare.'

'Do you want to play for me?'

Without a word, Georg sat down on the piano stool and, after a moment's hesitation, began to play Beethoven's *Hammerclavier*. Stunned, Franz watched the boy's thin fingers dance over the keys, then gradually he sank back in his chair, closed his eyes and let the music waft over him. The first movement ended and he did not move. Then came the gay, tripping scherzo, followed by the sombre adagio, and finally, the great fugue, that lifted them both right out of the miserable apartment into some other world of incredible beauty, flooded with light and hope and certainty.

Finally, it was silent. Franz opened his eyes and stared at the miracle that had walked into his life. Compared to this genius, his meagre talent was nothing. The boy must be given the best training available, he must go to the Berlin *Hochschule*, he must be taught by the masters! 'The piano will stay,' was all he said, for he knew no other words to express his feelings.

Humbly, for he knew that he was nothing but a poor Jew, Franz Jankowski sought an interview for his nephew at the Berlin *Hochschule*, which was frequented by the great musical names of the day, by Strauss, Busoni, Bruch and Nikisch. And to his great joy and despite his lack of credentials, the boy was accepted.

Franz was just over sixty when he took on the responsibility of his nephew, but he was not a lazy man and he did not expect to get anything for nothing. From the moment of Georg's arrival, he worked harder than he had ever done in his life before, for he not only now had two mouths to feed, but also Georg's fees to pay at the music academy. Thankful that his nephew could be left alone, he put in overtime whenever possible at Ullstein and took on as many engagements as the Hotel Quadriga could offer him.

It was then that he started giving music lessons to Luise. She was six and a half, a vivacious little creature with a crop of auburn curls and wide green eyes, a gift for absorbing new ideas quickly, learning new skills and doing well at almost everything she put her mind to. She had a beautiful little singing voice and was showing an early talent for both the piano and the violin. She had always adored Franz, and her lessons quickly became the highlight of her life.

Needless to say, it did not take her long to discover all about Georg and, after he had heard her play her practice pieces and given her some more exercises, she always swung round on the piano stool and demanded, 'Now, Herr Jankowski, please tell me about Georg!'

At first, Franz demurred, 'No, Fraeulein Luise, I should go. If the Herr Direktor ...'

It did not take Luise long to realize that Franz protested, not because he didn't want to tell her about Georg, but because every minute he spent chatting to her was money he wasn't earning. She remedied this situation very simply by telling her father she wanted longer music lessons.

To Luise, whose little world was virtually confined to the four walls of the Hotel Quadriga, Georg Jankowski appeared as a creature from another planet. Although she had never met him, her vivid imagination conjured up an image of him, a tall, dark, almost godlike creature, like a hero from the Greek myths that Elli Zimmer drummed into her as part of her classical education. As the months went by, she followed his progress with rapt attention, so that she soon knew almost more about the Jankowskis than she did about her own family.

Georg also heard a lot about his uncle's small pupil and he was glad of their friendship, for, although he was elated at his acceptance by the *Hochschule*, he felt very guilty about the burden he was imposing upon his uncle. 'Please let me work, too,' he pleaded constantly, worried by the deep lines etched on Franz's face and the bags under his eyes.

But Franz was adamant. 'You are going to be one of the world's greatest pianists. You must work at your music.'

Sometimes, when his uncle was at work, Georg wandered through the streets of Berlin, standing outside the massive news-paper house in the Kochstrasse where his uncle worked, or the impressive façade of the Hotel Quadriga, with its elegant commis-sionaires. One day, he vowed, he would make his uncle proud of him. He would be no humble hotel musician but a fine composer and the hotel would open its doors to him as an honoured guest.

181

When Sophie Ascher married Theo Arendt in 1907, there was only one place to hold the Jewish society wedding of the year, although, for once, Maître Mesurier could not prepare the food, which was cooked in kosher kitchens by Jewish caterers. Seldom had the Hotel Quadriga witnessed such splendour as that displayed by the guests who thronged its rooms on the wedding day. From all over the city taxis, horse-drawn carriages and brand new automobiles drew up outside the entrance to reveal passengers clad in the most elegant gowns and morning suits, and wearing the costliest jewels that money could buy. Members of the banking family of Arendt had arrived from all over Europe to be greeted in the foyer by Isaak Arendt, a striking figure now with his white hair.

Spellbound, Viktoria and Luise stood by the reception desk, watching the guests pass. 'Look at the those diamond earrings,' Luise whispered. 'Vicki, what wouldn't you give for earrings like those?'

'And that tiara,' Viktoria gasped.

'And that dress. Vicki, look, isn't it heavenly? Do you think we'll ever be grown-up and able to wear gowns like that?' Then she gasped. 'Oh, Vicki, look there's Sophie Ascher, I mean Sophie Arendt. And there's Theo! And Pipsi! Vicki, look at her hair! It must reach her waist. Oh, why can't mine look like that?' She ran her fingers through her bushy red curls, making them stick up from her head like a halo. 'Oh, but don't they look beautiful?'

They were so beautiful, his two daughters, Professor Ascher thought, as he followed Sophie and Theo into the restaurant with Pipsi on his arm. They were so beautiful that just to look at them caused a lump to come into his throat. Sophie looked like an exotic flower in her white bridal dress, while Pipsi with her long dark hair and enticing eyes was like a sparkling jewel, far more alluring than any precious stone worn by any woman in the room.

Professor Ascher was a thick-set man, with wiry dark hair over a high forehead, a fleshy nose and heavy jowls. He knew he looked very Jewish, but here in Berlin that seldom mattered. Although there might still be very few Jews in the military, and certainly no more than a handful of officers, they were to be found in almost every other profession. He had been welcomed at the Friedrich-Wilhelm University, where he had obtained first his master's degree, then his professorship, and had gone on to become one of the country's leading physicists.

Yes, Germany had been very good to the Jews, for it was

impossible to think of a wedding like this one taking place in Tsarist Russia, for example, where his parents had lived, escaping from the vicious pogroms just before he had been born. How proud they would be now, if they could witness this splendid match! And how proud his wife would be, too, but she had died twelve years earlier, giving birth to their second daughter, Pipsi.

As the evening passed, it became evident that Professor Ascher was not the only one to find his younger daughter bewitching, although she was only twelve. Her feet scarcely seemed to touch the ground, as one man after another asked her to dance.

Indeed, Pipsi was in her element. She loved to be admired and she loved to be the centre of attention. As one partner after another congratulated her on her dancing, she longed to tell them that one day they would be able to come and watch her perform on the stage — and not just dancing, for Pipsi was determined to become an actress. Today, she was a star at her sister's wedding. One day, she would be a real star.

That evening, Franz Jankowski described the Ascher-Arendt wedding to Georg. 'Theo Arendt is such a handsome man and he will one day inherit his father's bank, one of the wealthiest private banks in Berlin, they say.

'And you should see those two girls, Georg, they are so beautiful! But there you are, Georg, we may all be Jews, but you and I are poor Jews. The Aschers and Arendts, they come from a different class and they belong to a different world.'

It was midnight before Eitel Tobisch left the hotel after the Arendt wedding. Once again, the last omnibus had gone and he was faced with a long walk home. He felt in his pocket and pulled out his purse, looking inside it to see how much money it contained. There were just over thirty marks, far too many to take home to Liese. In a sudden moment of decision, he turned off Unter den Linden up the Friedrichstrasse in the direction of a certain little club that he knew would still be open even at this hour of night.

It was one of Eitel's luckier evenings. Instead of leaving the club two hours later with an empty purse, he had fifty marks and a warm invitation from the proprietor to return whenever he chose. His winnings, however, posed a new problem, for he was more determined than ever that Liese shouldn't have them. Not only would she confiscate them, but the secret of his gambling would be out in the open. It was a scene Eitel could do without. Although

Liese never rose before ten, there was no certainty that she would not search his pockets while he slept, so he had to find somewhere to hide the money overnight.

With practised ease, he let himself noiselessly into the apartment, lit an oil lamp, and stood for a few moments in the kitchen, gloating over his unexpected fortune. The small apartment did not offer many hiding places, but he was reasonably sure his money would be safe in the flour bin. He lifted the lid and stowed it securely and, at that moment, he heard a sound behind him. Jumping guiltily, he found his son standing barefooted in the doorway. 'Why, Otto,' he stammered nervously, 'I thought you were in bed.'

Otto moved ominously towards him, at fourteen already nearly as tall as he was and much broader. There was an evil smirk on his face. 'Give it to me.'

'What?' Eitel prevaricated. 'I was just getting a biscuit.'

'Your poker winnings,' Otto said, coldly.

'Poker winnings?' He was damned if he was going to give anything to this monster he had somehow bred.

'I'll tell Mother you've started gambling again.'

'You wouldn't dare.'

'Furthermore,' Otto went on, 'when I leave school next month, I want a job at the Hotel Quadriga. You needn't think I'm going to work in a factory until I join the army.'

'But why the Quadriga?' Eitel gasped, stunned by the realization that his son was blackmailing him.

'That way I shall be able to watch everything you do. Wherever you go, whatever you say, I shall know. You put one foot out of line, Father, and I'll tell Mother. Now give me that money.'

Eitel reached down into the flour bin and handed over the coins.

Fifty marks the richer, Otto went back to bed smug in the knowledge that he now had total domination over both his parents. He held final proof that his father had taken up gambling again, while he knew that his mother pretended to be saving part of her housekeeping for their old age, but actually spent the money on schnapps, concealing the bottles at the back of her wardrobe. Her so-called illness was little more than acute alcoholism. He kept her in a state of fear by threatening to tell his father. All that remained was to get a job at the Hotel Quadriga, where he was absolutely positive he would very soon instigate a rule of terror as absolute as he had done at school and as he did at home.

With many misgivings, Eitel asked Karl the next day about a job for Otto. 'He leaves school in June and he's set his heart on a career in the army, but it will be at least three years before he's called up. In the meantime, he thinks he'd like to work here.'

'Well, I'll certainly see him,' Karl agreed, 'but if he is taken on, he'll have to start at the bottom as a page boy, and, of course, he'll be under the total jurisdiction of the hall porter.'

'Of course,' Eitel said hurriedly, hoping in fact that at work Otto might be subjected to the discipline that he didn't get at home. The hall porter was a former sergeant major who ruled his page boys with a rod of iron. He alone out of all the hotel staff was not an employee, but a concessionaire, which meant that he exercised absolute power within his realm.

A few days later, Karl interviewed Otto, whom he hadn't seen since the boy started school. Now, he was a strapping lad, easily strong enough to lift heavy suitcases and trunks across the foyer and up into guests' bedrooms. He answered all Karl's questions easily, and seemed to have all the qualifications for a good page boy. Karl summoned the hall porter and recommended that Otto be engaged.

Yet there were a couple of things about Otto that perturbed Karl. One was the rather sullen set of his mouth and the other was the icy coldness of his blue eyes, both quite extraordinary in a boy of his age. If he hadn't been Eitel's son, Karl wasn't certain that he would have employed him.

Otto swaggered into the hotel on his first day as if he owned it, determined that he was not only going to lord it over his father, but also make life absolute hell for that toffee-nosed Viktoria Jochum, for he still clearly remembered that day she had found him piddling in the Palm Garden Room.

However, he was in for a rude shock. Looking him up and down in a deprecating manner, the hall porter said, 'Well, Tobisch, let's get this straight from the beginning. Just because you're the General Manager's son doesn't entitle you to any special privileges. Not with me, or with the guests or your colleagues. Is that understood?' Otto nodded sulkily and the hall porter barked, 'I asked if you understood, you 'orrible little man! When I talk to you, you will stand to attention and call me sir. Is that understood?'

Otto stood to attention. 'Yes, sir!' he replied.

'Page boys are front-staff, Tobisch, which means they are like soldiers in the front line of battle, except that instead of the enemy they are facing the guests. And the guests are always right. I warn you now that I expect my staff to conduct themselves as if they are troops in the finest regiment. I demand first-class service and total obedience. From now on, boy, you are in the army!'

For the next half-hour he detailed Otto's duties, then he gave him a printed copy of a rule book. Finally, he ordered another page boy to take him to the laundry to be issued with his uniform. 'You know my father is the General Manager?' Otto asked. His colleague cast him a pitying look. Otto wondered what it meant.

He soon learned. That very first day, as he stood on hall service, he experienced the humiliation of being a servant, at the beck and call of everybody, under the hall porter's constant and eagle eye. And, as the day wore on, he realized his father's position was little better than his own. He apparently spent his whole time scurrying round the hotel, grovelling and kow-towing to one after another of the hotel guests — and to the Jochums. Eitel had been a lieutenant in the Guards, whereas Karl Jochum had only been a private. Yet now, his father seemed to accept their reversed roles without any question. And this was not the least of it. Ricarda Jochum, the supercilious Viktoria and her silly little sister Luise also seemed to regard his father as some kind of menial, ordering him about in an offhanded fashion.

It required only a few weeks in the employ of the Hotel Quadriga for Otto to feel total loathing for the Jochums and their guests, and total contempt for his father in giving in to them.

The first decade of the twentieth century was proving extremely profitable for Kraus Industries. The machine gun, which Kraus had been developing since the nineties, had now been formally adopted by the army, so that the vast gun shops in the Ruhr and Silesia were fully employed producing them, and Baron Heinrich had good reason to believe there would soon be an increased demand for heavy siege howitzers. Then, of course, there was the related demand for the explosives made at Kraus Village.

But as Baron Heinrich von Kraus zu Essen was driven by his chauffeur in his new six-cylinder Mercedes tourer towards Berlin one April afternoon in 1908, his mind was on Kraushaven and the mighty battleship he was building. In 1906 the British had launched their first Dreadnought and the Kaiser had responded with new Navy Laws and formed the Navy League, so that the Baron was exceedingly glad he had discovered Wilfried von Wetzlar at the time he did. What, he wondered gleefully, would the British say when they saw the *Prussia*?

When the black Mercedes drew up in front of the entrance to the Hotel Quadriga, the Baron went immediately to his suite where Ernst was waiting for him. His eldest son was twenty-two now, his two years in the military completed, while Benno had now just started on his national service. Heinrich thought of himself at their ages and the way he had taken over from his own father. Ernst was now undertaking his management training in Kraus Industries, working in all departments of the company until he was thoroughly familiar with every function and, although at the moment he seemed perfectly happy just to obey orders, the Baron couldn't help wondering whether he was going to prove a chip off the old block or whether he was always going to remain a good second-in-command. Then what about Benno, who had shown little aptitude for industry when he left for the army? Well, there was time, for the Baron was only fifty that year and expected to have many more years at the helm. 'You've been to Kraus Chemie?' he asked Ernst.

'Yes, Father. According to Herr Merten our turnover has increased by thirty per cent in the last year.' They settled down to an extremely positive business discussion.

That evening when he met Karl Jochum, the Baron was in an expansive frame of mind. Jochum had proved a good businessman as well as a profitable investment and he was now rather proud of his association with him. 'Going to launch my new battleship, the *Prussia*, next month, Herr Jochum. I hope you and your family will attend.'

'My congratulations. We should be greatly honoured, Herr Baron. May I ask you how long it has taken to build it?'

The Baron needed no encouragement to talk about his pet project. 'Designing her, building a new slipway and preparing the berth took a couple of years or so. Actually building the ship has only taken just over a year. If you're really interested, Herr Jochum, let's have a drink and I'll tell you all about it.'

By the time the Jochums set out for Kraushaven, Karl Jochum had become an expert on naval matters, spreading almost as much propaganda on the navy's behalf as Admiral Tirpitz's Navy League. 'The *Prussia* will outrange and outpace any Dreadnought,' he lectured his family. 'The launch is only the first stage of her life. After this, she will be towed to her berth and then work can be finalized. In about another year's time she'll be ready for her sea trials and in 1910 she'll be commissioned.'

'Why, Karl, you sound as if you've built her yourself,' Ricarda teased.

'This is no laughing matter. If war broke out, our country's future could depend on this warship and others like her.'

'Do you really think there could be a war?' Viktoria asked.

'I hope not, but it's possible. There's no love lost between His Majesty and his uncle, Edward VII of England. The Kaiser, very rightly, wants Germany to become a great world power and he believes King Edward is trying to stop him. Then there is Russia, which keeps interfering in the affairs of the Balkans. It could even be that we shall find ourselves at war simply in order to keep the peace.'

Looking out of the train window, Ricarda sighed. 'It's such a beautiful day, it seems a shame to have to talk about such dreadful possibilities.'

'We have to be realistic, my dear, but there's no need to be despondent. I believe His Majesty is acting in exactly the right way.'

'I think politics and war are boring,' Luise complained. 'Why couldn't the Baron have built a liner instead of a battleship?'

They all laughed, because Luise's plea was so poignant and her small, heart-shaped face so dejected. 'Maybe he will one day,' Ricarda comforted her.

When the Baron's chauffeur-driven Mercedes tourer met them at the station, Karl took his seat in the back in a proprietorial manner. 'This is a very proud moment for us all.'

Huge marquees had been set up to accommodate the guests. A social secretary greeted the Jochums, ticked their names off on a list and led them into one of the tents, where a white-gloved waiter offered them glasses of champagne. Already the place was milling with guests and Viktoria stared around her in awe. Keeping close to her mother's side, she sipped her wine and nibbled a small sandwich.

'There's the Baron,' Karl exclaimed in satisfaction, leading them across to where Heinrich Kraus was holding court, dressed, of course, in his resplendent Reserve Officer's uniform, surrounded by a number of journalists furiously scribbling notes.

'What is the displacement of the *Prussia*, Herr Baron?' one man asked.

'Twenty-five thousand tons,' the Baron promptly replied. 'The equivalent British vessel only has a displacement of eighteen thousand.'

'And her guns, Herr Baron?'

'Twelve 15½-inch guns in four turrets, with a range of over fifteen miles.'

'Are they Kraus guns, Herr Baron?'

'Naturally! We have adapted Kraus siege guns for the purpose.'

'How fast will she travel, Herr Baron?'

'Twenty-eight knots,' he answered proudly.

A journalist emitted a low whistle of admiration. 'But the British Dreadnought can only reach twenty-one knots.'

'Is she coal-fired, Herr Baron?' another called.

'She has oil-fired turbines to obviate refuelling problems in mid-ocean.'

'Fraeulein Jochum, Viktoria, how nice to see you!' a voice exclaimed and Vikloria turned to find Benno Kraus standing beside her, looking very smart in blue army uniform.

'Why, Benno!' She found herself blushing, for not only had he turned into a quite good-looking young man, but he also looked, at first glance, remarkably like his cousin, Peter von Biederstein.

'Have you seen the *Prussia* yet?'

'No, not yet.'

'You can't miss her,' Benno laughed. 'Come outside and I'll show you.' He took her arm and led her out of the marquee, pointing upwards.

Viktoria gasped. 'That's the *Prussia*?' Standing amidst looming gantries and vast cranes, the battleship towered above them. Little figures scurried about her decks putting the final touches to her in preparation for the launching ceremony. Garlands decorated her bow and strings of pennants danced in the breeze over her. 'But she's enormous.'

Benno smiled ruefully. 'My father always makes everything bigger and better than anyone else.'

'Do you know a lot about ships?' Viktoria asked.

He shook his head. 'The *Prussia* is impressive, but I can't find any enthusiasm for her. I'd much rather we'd built a passenger liner.'

'How extraordinary. That's what Luise said earlier.'

'Your sister and I evidently have something in common.'

Viktoria decided she liked Benno best of all the Krauses. The

Baron rather intimidated her and she scarely knew the Countess Julia, while Ernst — on the brief occasions they had met — seemed a very cold fish.

At that moment, a whistle blew and there was a sudden flurry of activity. Following shouted orders from a foreman, workmen lined up beside the ship, while others donned their caps and crowded behind barricades. Benno looked at his watch. 'Good heavens, it's nearly two. We'd better hurry.'

From all the marquees, people were emerging and, with a thrill of excitement, Viktoria watched a horse-drawn carriage enter the gates of Kraus Marin. In it, with Admiral Tirpitz beside her, sat Princess Viktoria Luise. Baron Heinrich approached her, bowed low and helped her down. Naval dignitaries closed in around them and they made their way majestically along the red carpet that had been spread over the dockyard floor to the launching platform. 'The Princess has been entertained at the naval base at Wilhelmshaven,' Benno whispered in Viktoria's ear.

Slowly, the Emperor's daughter walked up the steep ramp until she reached the platform built almost level with the Plimsoll Line. 'It is my great honour to be present on this very auspicious day.' She started her speech in a thin little voice that nevertheless carried clearly across the dockyard.

When she had finished, the Baron handed her a bottle of champagne, suspended from a long rope. 'I hereby name this ship the *Prussia*. God bless her and all who sail in her.' The bottle smashed against the prow of the ship and an almighty cheer went up. Workmen standing behind the barricades threw their caps in the air, waving their arms and shouting in excitement.

By the keel of the ship, workmen armed with sledgehammers knocked at the chocks that had been holding the *Prussia* on the long, sloping slipway. Gradually, she glided backwards and entered the water with a tremendous splash, creating swelling waves. For a moment or two she rocked, then she steadied herself.

A fleet of small tugs, attached to her by lines, trumpeted their congratulations. Then, from all around, even as far away as Wilhelmshaven, hooters boomed and sirens sounded in a strident cacophony of triumphant noise. The biggest, fastest, all-big-gun battleship in the world had been launched.

The following year, Edward VII of England came on a state visit to Berlin. Once again the streets were lined with dense crowds of

190

people waiting to see the spectacle. Once again the Hotel Quadriga was covered with flags and bunting, its foyer and reception rooms amass with flowers, its every room reserved for weeks in advance as, from all over Germany, people crowded into the capital to witness the historic meeting between uncle and nephew. After all, Edward VII had German blood through his father, Prince Albert of Saxe-Cobourg. He was really one of them. Now, finally, he was proving it by coming home!

The Kraus family arrived early; all, that was, except Benno who was at Doeberitz with his regiment preparing to take part in the ceremonial parades designed to demonstrate to the British King the impressive strength of the German army. On this occasion, as on every other of public significance, Baron Heinrich was wearing his Reserve Officer's uniform, although at his age his country no longer expected him to perform reservist duties.

'Splendid thing this visit, Herr Baron. It'll soon put paid to any ideas of war,' Viktoria heard one guest comment to him, as she walked through the foyer on the day of the English King's arrival.

'By far the best thing that's happened since Queen Victoria died,' the Baron agreed pompously.

But Viktoria was not in the slightest bit interested in the struggles between monarchs for world power at that moment. Excited though she was at the prospect of the royal visit, she was in an agony of anticipation about the arrival of the von Biedersteins, and particularly Peter, whom she had not seen since the Crown Prince's wedding four years earlier.

She was fifteen now, her hair the colour of ripe corn, loosely drawn back from her face in a knot at the back of her head and crowned with a wide-brimmed straw hat decorated with fresh rose-buds. Wearing a new, pink, sprigged muslin dress, which just revealed her dainty white boots, and with a wide pink belt, clasped by a huge silver buckle, encircling her slim waist, she made a delightful picture.

'Why, Vicki,' her father said, hurrying past her with Eitel Tobisch on his way to supervise the arrangements for the ball that was being held that evening, 'what are you doing here? I thought you were already on the balcony with Luise, watching the crowds.'

Viktoria merely smiled, wishing she were old enough to attend the ball and consoling herself with the thought that Peter would not be attending it either, for at seventeen he had still a year to go until he came of age. Then all thoughts of the ball disappeared

191

because through the wide revolving doors she saw the unmistak-able figures of the Count and Countess von Biederstein, followed by Trudi and Peter.

He looked so handsome, much taller than last time they had met, and with the beginnings of a small dark moustache. She rushed down the foyer. 'Peter!' she cried, impetuously, 'I thought you were never coming! You'll miss the procession.'

Then she became aware of Count Johann staring at her curiously while Countess Anna frowned, and she felt the blood rush to her cheeks. In her mind she heard her mother's voice saying sternly: *Viktoria, that is not the way for a young lady to behave.* 'Count, Countess, I beg your pardon,' she muttered awkwardly, biting her lip.

The Countess smiled, 'That's all right, child, you're over-excited, of course.' Then she looked over Viktoria's shoulder at two approaching figures. 'Why, Johann, there's Heinrich and he has dear Ernst with him. Now, Trudi, come along and say hello to your cousin.'

Viktoria watched them move regally across the foyer, then heard Peter say, 'Vicki, it's lovely to see you again, and you do look pretty. Shall we go up to the balcony now, while they're all still talking?' So Peter hadn't been embarrassed by her gauche behaviour — everything was all right.

It was only as he took her arm to lead her up the main staircase that she realized the whole spectacle had been witnessed by Otto Tobisch, standing statue-like in his blue page boy's uniform. Despite her joy at being reunited with Peter, she felt a shiver run up her spine.

The balcony was already crowded with onlookers, despite the fact that there was at least another half-hour to go before the car-riage bearing their two Majesties was due to pass down Unter den Linden. 'Let's stay back here,' Peter suggested. He glanced appreci-atively at Viktoria's dress, then at her face. 'It's good to be back in Berlin. Life can get jolly boring at Fuerstenmark, I can tell you. But that'll soon change. You know I join the Guards next year, don't you?'

'At Karlshorst?'

'I've no idea. My ambition is to be accepted for the War Academy and become a member of the General Staff. I don't want to be like Uncle Ewald and doomed to regimental life for ever.'

'But the War Academy's in Berlin. Oh, Peter, wouldn't that be marvellous ...'

'There's a lot of competition for places. It could be several years before I'm accepted. But, I'm looking forward to it, Vicki. Just think of it, actually being a soldier at long last!'

Suddenly, she realized they were talking about two different things. She was looking forward to having him near her in Berlin, while he was looking forward to a career in the army.

At that moment, there was the sound of rolling drums and marching feet. Tumultuous cheers arose from the street below. 'His Majesty!' 'The Kaiser!' Flags were waved and voices raised in clamorous hurrahs, as the first troops appeared in view. They were truly magnificent to behold as they marched past in perfect formation, foot guards, artillerymen, infantrymen, and, on horseback, the cavalry, the life guards and finally, the greatest spectacle of them all, sitting stiffly upright in their carriage, looking more like brothers than uncle and nephew, the King of England and the Emperor of Germany.

When the last soldier had passed and the crowds slowly started to disperse, Peter von Biederstein still stood, immobile, on the balcony, his lips slightly parted, his eyes glittering. 'We are the greatest nation on earth and we have the greatest army in the world. Even the King of England must realize that now. And soon I shall be part of it.' Viktoria stared at him and a finger of fear touched her heart.

From his position in the foyer Otto Tobisch saw little of the parade, but he heard the sound of the drums and the marching feet. In a year, two years at the outside, he would be called up and he, too, would be able to march with the soldiers, he, too, would be able to wear a proper uniform, not this silly page boy's outfit. Men would step aside for him, Otto Tobisch, when they saw him on the street, for he would be a member of the elite, of the Kaiser's army. On that day, he would be the equal of Benno Kraus and Count Peter von Biederstein and then Viktoria Jochum would gaze at him as she had gazed at the young Count earlier that day.

'Otto!' The Hall Porter's voice growled threateningly in his ear. 'Are you going to stand there dreaming all day, or are you going to fetch the Duke's luggage?'

Otto went to fetch the Duke's luggage and one of the other pages sniggered. Both boys came off-duty at the same time that evening and for a short distance their routes coincided. It was in a dark alley that Otto suddenly knocked Horst to the ground and kicked him viciously in the ribs and stomach, where he knew he could cause the greatest pain but where no bruises would show. 'Don't you ever dare snigger at me again!' Horst crouched against the wall, snivelling. Otto turned tail in disgust and left him.

When a subdued Horst limped to work next day with a torn uniform, claiming he had fallen over, the Hall Porter docked him half a day's pay and Otto took no pains to conceal his satisfaction.

Very little — including Horst's condition — missed Karl Jochum's notice, and he could not help but suspect that Otto was somehow involved. He was already very concerned about Eitel Tobisch, for rumours had reached him that Eitel was spending every minute of his spare time in a gambling club on the Witwenstrasse.

Now it appeared that Otto was starting to cause trouble as he had feared. For the time being, he decided to do nothing, but already the triumph of the previous day's procession and ball were fading into a distant memory.

Franz Jankowski also watched the royal procession, not from the balcony of the Hotel Quadriga on this occasion, but among the crowds on the street, with Georg beside him. Despite the cheerful atmosphere and the obvious jubilation of the people around him, Frank was unhappy. He felt threatened by the mob and intimidated by this extraordinary demonstration of German military strength.

The procession was supposed to be a welcome for the English King, but in Franz's view it was as if the Kaiser were saying to his uncle, 'Look at this. Look at all these soldiers. Look at how they march. Look at how they are equipped. And now you have seen, go away and don't try to tangle with me. Because if you do, you'll get what you deserve.' Yes, to Franz, this supposedly splendid parade meant only one thing — that Germany, for all its talk of keeping the peace, was preparing for war.

Franz was not fearful for his own sake, but for Georg, because the boy was just finishing his third year at the Berlin *Hochschule*, from where he was almost certain to graduate with flying colours. At twenty and as a German citizen, Georg was liable for military service although, being a Jew, he stood no hope of any kind of promotion to the officer class. The next intake of new recruits would be at the beginning of October and it seemed unlikely that Georg would escape conscription this time.

As soon as the procession had passed, Franz took his nephew's arm. 'Let's go home. My head is full of military marches. Play me some Chopin, or this new composer, Debussy. I need to hear a melody.'

The next day, as he made his way to the Hotel Quadriga, his heart was still heavy, for not even Georg's music had been able to dispel his forebodings.

As soon as Franz Jankowski entered the schoolroom for Luise's music lesson, she knew there was something wrong. 'Herr Jankowski, what's the matter?'

'Oh, it's nothing.'

'But there is something wrong, I know. Please tell me.'

He looked at her and opened his battered violin case. 'Come on, child, it's time for your lesson.'

It infuriated Luise to be called 'child'. 'No,' she said adamantly. 'I'm not going to play until you tell me what's happened. You're worried about Georg, aren't you?'

Franz sighed and put down his violin. 'Yes, I'm worried about Georg. I think he's going to be called up for his military service.'

Luise felt disappointed. While she considered war and politics to be extremely dreary subjects of conversation, she thought being a soldier — and particularly an officer — one of the most romantic things in the world. 'But if he is, you should be proud of him.'

'Don't misunderstand me, Fraeulein Luise, it isn't that I don't want him to do his duty for his country. It's his music I'm worried about. What will happen to him, if he has to spend two years without his music?'

That was different! Luise nodded. 'But, Herr Jankowski, two years isn't very long. He'd still be able to play when he came back. He wouldn't forget. And I'm sure he'd enjoy being a soldier.'

The old man gave a weak smile. 'Bless your heart, Fraeulein Luise, you're probably right. And I'm being selfish because I shall miss him if he goes away.'

'Well, you'll still have me.'

She had her music lesson then, but all the time she was conscious that Franz was not really concentrating. And when he left, she had the feeling he hadn't actually told her the whole truth.

In October, Franz's worst fears were confirmed. The State had kindly permitted Georg Jankowski to complete his studies, but now it required him to serve his country in a military capacity. It sent him to Schwerin as a private. For two years, the only music in his life was to be military marches and the music he made in his head. For Franz it was a period of great emptiness.

195

The year that followed was an uneasy one. Viktoria, sixteen now and starting to take an interest in events outside her personal experience and life within the Quadriga, became aware of occurrences that seemed to threaten her old easy-going existence. To begin with, there were demonstrations led by the Social Democrats against what they claimed to be the undemocratic electoral system in Prussia.

Karl grew extremely angry about them. 'Social Democrats!' he exclaimed one evening at dinner after a particularly vociferous procession had marched along Unter den Linden. 'If we're not careful we'll find we have the same trouble here as the Russians did a few years ago. It's Bolshevism, that's what it is. I remember that man, Gottfried, going on about it at his wedding! Well, as I said to him then, and I say to you now, there's nothing the matter with our political system.'

Viktoria, who had been secretly reading *Vorwaerts*, one of the Socialist newspapers, asked, 'But why shouldn't everybody be treated equally? Why shouldn't I, or Mama, as women, be allowed to vote, for instance?'

'Bah! You sound just like your Aunt Grete, when she was your age! The fact that you ask stupid questions like that is reason enough in itself for women not to be given the vote!'

Viktoria frowned. She had never met her Munich relatives, although she always received very nice letters and presents from her Aunt Grete every birthday and name day. Before she could respond, however, her mother said, 'Karl, you're unfair. There is no reason why women shouldn't be given the vote. We have as much right to a say in the way our country is run as men do. And if that is what your sister Grete wants, then I entirely agree with her and Vicki.'

Looking rather nonplussed that Ricarda, of all people, should disagree with him, Karl said, 'Well, votes for women is one thing, but Social Democrats in the cabinet is another, and that's what this mob is demanding. His Majesty rules over Germany by divine right, while the Junkers are his appointed servants — and our leaders. Look at me, Karl Jochum — I don't expect to be a cabinet minister, so why should any of that red rabble?'

Viktoria opened her mouth to argue, but Ricarda motioned to her to keep quiet. Later, she said, 'Darling, your Papa's been like this all his life, and he won't change now. For him, the Kaiser and the Junkers are gods. But I rather agree with you, and I must

confess I'm beginning to wonder if there isn't something in what
Grete and Gottfried have been saying all these years.'

'What are they like, Mama?'

'I actually rather liked them when I met them, although that was
a long time ago. Why, your cousin Olga must be nineteen now.'

'Do you think I could visit them one day?' Viktoria asked,
intrigued by the thought of these unknown relatives with such very
different ideas.

'Why not? When you're a bit older perhaps.'

There were other events, apart from the endless socialist
demonstrations, which contributed to the unease in Berlin. A year
after his visit to the city, King Edward VII died and his son,
George V, acceded to the English throne, while, on the other side
of Europe, Austria, Germany's ally in the alliances, annexed
Bosnia and Herzegovinia, threatening to provoke Russia into a
declaration of war. 'And if they do declare war,' Karl said grimly,
'then His Majesty will have to intervene to maintain European
peace.'

With her new awareness, Viktoria anxiously scanned the newspapers and listened to the grown-ups talking.

'I don't know why you bother,' Luise complained. 'It's all so
boring. What has Bosnia to do with us?'

The difference in their ages had never seemed more extreme.
Luise was only ten, still a child, whereas Viktoria considered
herself almost an adult. 'It could have a lot to do with us,' she said
ominously. And as tension mounted, the word 'war' was heard
increasingly on the lips of guests at the Hotel Quadriga. More
young men seemed to be appearing in military uniform on the
streets and constant emphasis was placed on the importance of the
army.

It was a fresh September morning when the event occurred
which she had been dreading. Dapper as ever, his swagger stick in
his hand, Count Ewald sauntered into the hotel. 'Splendid news,'
he announced, finding Viktoria and her father together at the
reception. 'My nephew Peter's joined the Death's Head Hussars.'

'The Kaiser's own regiment?' Karl asked in awe.

Viktoria stared at him, big-eyed. So much talk of war and now
Peter had joined the army ...

'So he's at Danzig,' Karl stated in satisfaction. 'Ewald, I congratulate you. You must be proud.'

Not only was Peter in the army and his life in danger, he was nowhere near Berlin. Viktoria turned away, trying not to let her disappointment show. It could be months until she saw him again. Or — dreadful thought — she might never see him. She had to escape from here, go away somewhere out of the public gaze. Blindly, she walked towards the staircase.

'Vicki,' her father called after her. 'Pop up to the fourth floor and have a look at room 401. Count Ems specially asked that a bouquet of red roses be arranged for the Frau Countess. Make sure Herr Tobisch has organized them.'

She nodded and stepped, unseeingly, into a waiting lift, so absorbed in her thoughts that she did not notice that the page boy driving her up to the fourth floor was Otto Tobisch.

A page in charge of a lift was not supposed to desert his post under any circumstances, but Otto conveniently chose to ignore this instruction when Viktoria got out at the fourth floor. It was the first opportunity he had ever had of being alone with her. Close on her heels, he silently followed her over the pile carpet into room 401, then closed the door behind them.

When she turned and saw him standing there, the look of dismay and revulsion on her face sent the blood surging through his body. 'Get out of here,' she said, in a cold, hard voice.

Otto remembered that other time in the Palm Garden Room, eleven years earlier, when she had uttered the same words. 'I've got as much right to be here as you have,' he snarled. 'Who are you to order me about?' She thought she was so superior, didn't she? Well, he'd show her. He strode across the room towards her and she cowered back, fear in her eyes. He seized her by the shoulders and forced his mouth onto hers. She tried to get away from him, pummelling at his chest with her hands, twisting her face away from his, and his resentment was fanned into fury. Brutally, he picked her up and, ignoring her kicking feet, threw her onto the bed, lying on top of her. She was frantic now in her attempts to escape. He could feel the entire length of her body against his, stirring him into frenzied excitement.

'Let me go! Let me go!' she shouted.

He put his hand over her mouth and stared triumphantly at her. 'Now I'm going to give it to you,' he growled.

Sharp little teeth bit his hand and he withdrew it quickly. 'You little bitch! All these years I've been putting up with you and your hoity-toity ways ...'

She was stronger than he had imagined her to be. Taking advantage of his talking, she managed, by a supreme effort, to roll away from under him, leaving him momentarily helpless on his side, then she stood up and raced for the door. He grabbed her dress, hearing the material rip. In the silence of the room, he could hear her heart pounding, her breasts rising and falling under her tight bodice. 'So you want to play games, do you?'

'One more move and I'll press this button,' her voice trembled, but the finger she held poised over the bellpush did not. Suddenly, he knew he was beaten. He let go her dress and she walked out of the room.

'I'll get even with you one day,' he muttered after she had gone. 'You wait, I'll get my own back on you for this.'

Like a frightened animal, Viktoria ran down the corridor which, for once, was miraculously empty. Where should she go? What should she do? She tore down the stairs, anxious only to put as much distance as possible between herself and Otto. At the foot of the stairs, somebody had left a suitcase and, in her blind haste, she fell over it, sprawling across the landing. She heard her dress rip further, then she picked herself up and stumbled on.

'Why, Vicki, what have you done?' her mother asked aghast, as she tumbled into the apartment.

Suddenly, Viktoria knew she couldn't tell her. Her mind was reeling from one shock after another. First Peter and now that horrible experience with Otto. She shuddered. 'I fell over,' she mumbled, tears running down her face.

'Come and lie down. I'll get you some tea.' She led her into the bedroom she shared with Luise, helped her out of the ripped dress and pulled back the bedclothes. Thankfully, Viktoria slipped between the sheets and closed her eyes, while her mother went out to the kitchen. She could still feel Otto's rough lips on hers, his hot breath, the animal way he had looked at her. She felt unclean and somehow contaminated by the incident, but even more than that, she was afraid.

She remembered Otto's arm round her neck all those years ago in the Palm Garden Room. 'If you tell your father, I'll break your neck,' he had said. She had been petrified then and now she was even more terrified. If she did tell anybody what had happened and Otto found out, she was certain that he would kill her.

For a month, she lived in fear, then the miraculous occurred. Otto Tobisch was called up. When she heard the news, Viktoria felt as if a mighty weight had been lifted from her shoulders and that, gradually, she could begin to live again.

For Otto Tobisch, it was the supreme moment of his life. He shed the blue and gold page boy's uniform to replace it with the blue and silver of the Berlin Fusiliers. His old life was over, the bitter humiliations suffered during it pushed to the back of his mind.

He made no effort to thank Karl Jochum for employing him over the past four years, nor did he waste any more time than necessary saying goodbye to his father and mother.

When the Kaiser greeted the newest recruits into the army with the words, 'And if, in the light of current social unrest, I order you to shoot down your own relatives, brothers, even parents, then you will do it,' Otto Tobisch knew he would experience no scruples.

Virtually every room in the Hotel Quadriga was full one early December evening, a few months after Otto joined the army. His office door slightly ajar, Karl heard raised voices coming from the reception. 'But I made the arrangement personally with Herr Tobisch,' a man's voice was exclaiming. 'He promised me I could have an apartment. He's the General Manager, isn't he? Well, where is he?'

Normally, Karl would not have interfered, but the man's question made him realize that he had not seen Eitel Tobisch since the late afternoon. Instead of improving since Otto had left, Eitel's behaviour had been becoming increasingly odd, as he arrived in the mornings with a white face and a perceptible trembling of the fingers. He had also become very taciturn, often locking himself in his office for hours on end. Karl walked across to the reception desk. 'I'm Karl Jochum, the hotel proprietor. Can I help you?'

'My name is Baron von Trischler. Herr Tobisch personally assured me that I could have an apartment tonight at the Quadriga, but this man tells me he has no reservation in my name.'

'Perhaps if you would come to my office?' While the Baron walked ahead, Karl turned and asked Herr Quitzow, 'Where is Herr Tobisch?'

'I'm sorry, Herr Direktor, I don't know.'

'Well, send someone to find him, and if we do need a room for the Baron, is there one free?' The Reception Manager nodded.

When they were both seated in his office, Karl asked the Baron smoothly, 'You said Herr Tobisch promised you a room yesterday evening?'

Away from an audience, Baron von Trischler lost some of his bombast. 'At the gaming tables,' he admitted. 'Tobisch owes me a lot of money. I told him I'd accept a room at the Quadriga as part payment of his debt. I can see now that the circumstances were rather odd, but at the time ...'

Karl had feared it was going to be something like that. When he saw Tobisch, he'd have to bring the whole matter out into the open, but in the meantime, the Baron had better have his room. 'We have no suites free, but we do have a room. If you'll sign the register at reception.' He led him back to the desk.

At that moment, a page boy approached Herr Quitzow and murmured something in a low voice. Leaving one of his clerks to deal with Baron von Trischler, the Reception Manager walked across to Karl. 'The door to Herr Tobisch's office is locked, Herr Direktor. Fritz has knocked and there's no answer.'

'Is there a spare key?' Karl asked, with a mounting sense of panic. Eitel had given his oath that he would never compromise the hotel by his gambling, but now, because he lacked the money to pay his debts, he had done just that. What else might he have done in his desperation?

'All the spare keys are in Herr Tobisch's safe.'

There was nothing else for it. 'We'll have to break down the door,' Karl said decisively.

It took the combined strength of the two men and the page boy to force open the door and, when they had, a ghastly sight met their eyes. Hurriedly, Karl pushed the page boy out of the room, then with a white face turned to look at the remains of Eitel Tobisch. The pistol with which he had shot himself was still clutched in the hand stretched out across the desk. A hand and a desk covered in blood and the spattered pulp of his brains. Karl felt his stomach heave and turned away to meet Quitzow's green face. 'Poor, stupid bastard.'

It was a long night. First Dr Blattner, then two policemen came to the hotel and eventually, at three in the morning, when the hotel was asleep, Eitel Tobisch's body was placed on a stretcher and wheeled out through the service exit to a waiting police ambulance. Unable to delegate the horrible job to anyone else, Karl then cleared up the General Manager's office. At six o'clock, he sat down to compose a letter to Otto.

The next day, Otto Tobisch threw open the door to Karl's private office and stared at him with a cynical snarl on his lips. 'My father's death must have come at a very convenient time for you, Herr Jochum.'

Karl leapt up from his chair. 'Otto, I can't tell you how sorry I am.' He offered his hand, but Otto rejected it.

'Don't be such a hypocrite, Herr Jochum. You got what you wanted from my father, didn't you? You took him on out of pity and patronized him from the moment he arrived. And me too! You've just exploited us and laughed at us behind our backs! No wonder my father cracked!'

Stunned, Karl stared at him. 'But ...'

'My father respected you, Herr Jochum. He never stopped telling me how good you'd been to him and how much I owed you. But I think differently!'

Speechless, Karl just shook his head.

'No, I don't consider I owe you anything and what's more, I promise you that one day, I'll be the one who gives the orders in this hotel. Then you'll see who's who!'

He turned, to find Viktoria standing, white-faced, in the doorway. 'And you too, Miss Goody-Two-Shoes. I'll get even with you yet!'

Chapter Eight

Georg Jankowski completed his two years' military service in 1911 with a profound sense of relief and also gratitude that war had not, after all, broken out while he was in the army. Two years of one's life were quite enough to waste.

The door was unlocked when he reached the flat in the old town and he let himself in quietly, going straight to the one living room. A shaft of light shone through the window, silhouetting the stooped figure of a man sitting on the piano stool, his hands loosely on his lap, the lid to the piano open, so that the weak sunshine danced dustily over the yellowing keys. 'Uncle Franz,' he said softly, scarcely daring to disturb him.

Franz turned his lined face and Georg realized with a sense of shock that his uncle had grown old in his absence. 'Why, Georg, my boy.' He stood up with his arms outstretched and Georg saw that his hands were gnarled, the fingers twisted. 'Oh, Georg, I have been waiting so long. Every day, I have sat here, with the piano, waiting for you to come.'

Gently, as he would a child, Georg embraced him. 'I'm home, now, Uncle,' he replied in Yiddish. 'I shan't go away again.'

The old man drew away from him and Georg saw tears glistening in his eyes. Then he said in the same language, 'Play for me, Georg. Play as you did that other time. Play the *Hammerclavier*.'

It was so strange to feel the familiar keys once again under his fingertips. The first few notes he played hesitantly, then the first movement of Beethoven's sonata consumed him, the music seeming to flow out of him, as if it came from some fingers which were not his own. He was alive again, his life lay ahead of him, a life full of strength and hope.

To his joy, he was accepted back at the *Hochschule* on a teaching fellowship, although, to his dismay, his duties included giving singing lessons to budding young actresses. 'But I can't sing.'

His principal laughed. 'Neither can most of them. Don't worry; teach them the tonic sol-fa and they'll be happy!'

It was in his first singing class that he encountered her. She was absolutely beautiful, with dark brown eyes set in a perfect oval face and jet-black hair piled under a wide-brimmed crimson hat. Her white dress trailed the ground when she stood, cinched at the waist with a matching crimson sash, showing off to perfection her hour-glass figure. Georg took one look at her and lost his heart.

He struck middle C on the piano and she started to sing. Disappointingly, she had a weak voice and, even worse, a tendency to sing out of key, but not even that mattered to Georg. At the end of the class, when the other pupils left, she lingered. 'You're much better than my last music teacher,' she informed him.

He shuffled awkwardly, not knowing how to talk with her, scared of losing her, unable to keep his eyes off her perfect face.

'Are you new here?'

'Yes, I suppose I am, in a sort of way.' He dreaded the thought that she would suddenly disappear, and anxiously fumbled in his mind for some way to hold her. In the end, he said, hesitantly, 'I'm just going to have a cup of coffee. May I invite you, too, and then we can talk in greater comfort?'

To his delight, she said, 'Oh, that would be nice.' Then she laughed. 'Do you realize, we haven't introduced ourselves? My name is Pipsi Ascher.'

'And I am Georg Jankowski.' They shook hands and then the terrible realization dawned. Ascher. Suddenly, Georg heard his uncle describing the wedding at the Hotel Quadriga. 'They are so beautiful those two girls. But the Aschers and the Arendts come from a different class of Jew.'

Georg took her down to the refreshment room, determined to leave it as long as possible until he told her more about himself, positive that, once she learned he was just a poor student, she would leave him. But she seemed delighted to talk about herself, describing, utterly unselfconsciously, the house in Dahlem in which she lived with her widowed father, Professor Bethel Ascher, and her sister Sophie, who now lived in a beautiful villa in the Grunewald with her husband, the banker, Theo Arendt. 'You see, I don't need to have a career, Herr Jankowski. In fact, I don't think my father altogether approves, but he wants me to be happy.'

Georg thought he could just sit forever, watching the expressions that flitted over her face. He had known few young women in his life and certainly met none during the past two years in the army. Quite simply, Pipsi Ascher, with her slightly slanting, luminous dark eyes, her provocative mouth and her hair the colour of the ebony keys on his piano keyboard, was to him the most desirable creature he had ever encountered.

Finally, however, the dreaded moment arrived. 'And you, Herr Jankowski, where do you live?'

Hesitantly, he told her the story of his life and, to his great amazement, instead of being frightened away by his mundane tale of hardship, she stared at him with wide-eyed interest. 'But, how romantic! And, one day, I'm sure, you'll compose a masterpiece. You'll be a second Beethoven.'

He realized that she was totally sincere. 'It doesn't matter to you that I don't have any money, that I don't live in a fine villa in the Grunewald?'

'Money is nothing. It is art that is important.'

Hardly daring to believe his luck, Georg asked, 'May I invite you out this evening? I should so like to go to the theatre or to a concert with you.'

When she smiled, she curled back her upper lip ever so slightly, to display a row of even, rather pointed teeth. It was a provocative gesture that made Georg want to kiss her. 'I should love to come out with you.'

His heart pounding, he asked, 'Where would you like to go?'

'To the cinema,' Pipsi Ascher told him promptly.

When she got home, she told her father all about Georg. 'Papa, he's so incredibly romantic. He lives all alone with his uncle in a single room in the old town. Imagine, such poverty and such talent.'

'Jankowski?' Professor Ascher raised his eyebrows. 'Why, that must be his uncle who plays at the Hotel Quadriga.'

Pipsi gave a slight frown. The idea of her loved one's uncle being little more than a hotel servant didn't appeal to her. Then, as always when an unpleasant thought crossed her mind, she banished it. She was already quite convinced that she was in love with Georg Jankowski and she didn't intend to let his uncle intrude into her dream.

She went upstairs to dress and thought about her lover, his thin, sensitive face, his romantic, shabby clothes. He was so different from all the other young men she had met — vain, rather pompous sons of bankers, lawyers and intellectuals. To her seventeen-year-old mind, he represented a fairy-tale world, one in which impoverished artists and musicians achieved overnight success. Already she saw herself living in a garret, preparing simple meals, while Georg played idyllic music on his piano. A passer-by heard him, went to the Kaiser and Georg was summoned to Court. Then, her own talent would be discovered. She would act on the stage of the Royal Theatre in an opera for which Georg had composed the music.

'I don't like you going out on your own with a stranger,' her father objected, when she came downstairs, deceptively simply dressed in ivory silk. 'But since he's Franz Jankowski's nephew, I suppose it's all right.'

They met outside the *Kinematographisches Theater* Oskar Messter on Unter den Linden, popularly known in Berlin as the Kinntopp. Her heart thumping with excitement, Pipsi followed Georg into its murky depths. The cinema was so new, even more thrilling than the stage. Perhaps, one day, she would become a film actress and become known to millions of people throughout the world, not just to a few hundreds in Berlin. Imagine, seeing her face on the posters, her name on the hoardings outside the Kinntopp, her face on the screen!

For the hour or so that the film lasted, Pipsi was unaware even of Georg sitting beside her, scarcely conscious of his hand seeking hers and holding it. She just gazed, covetously, at the celluloid images in front of her and when they emerged, she was still in a trance. 'One day, I'm going to be a film actress.'

Georg's hand was still in hers. 'You'd be much better than Henny Porten or Asta Nielsen.'

'Do you really think so?' Her cup of happiness brimmed over.

He took her to Aschinger for a snack and, although it wasn't what she was used to, it was right for her mood that evening. It did not occur to her that Georg took her there because it was cheap. For only thirty pfennigs one could buy a bowl of soup with as many bread rolls as one could eat, and Georg had not eaten all day. She saw only people standing round small tables, among them many in evening dress recently emerged from the theatre, others dressed like Georg, aspiring actors, artists and poets. Listening to the hum of their conversation around her, she felt she was finally living.

Later, they took the omnibus back to Dahlem and, outside her front gate, Pipsi tilted her face up towards Georg, so that the moonlight shone on it, as Asta Nielsen had done in the film they had just seen, then she closed her eyes. Surely, now, Georg would kiss her.

He put his arms around her shoulders, drawing her slowly to him, until his lips were on hers and he was kissing her, gently at first, then with rising ardour. After a long, long time, they pulled breathlessly apart. She opened her eyes and gazed at him. There was an awed expression on his face and she was suddenly sure that she was the first girl he had ever kissed. 'Pipsi, I love you,' he murmured.

'I love you, too, Georg.' If Asta Nielsen could have spoken in the film, that is what she would have said.

'When shall I see you again?'

'Tomorrow? I have an acting lesson in the afternoon in the Bergstrasse. We could meet after that.'

'I'll be waiting for you.'

Benno Kraus returned to Essen after his two years in the army and was immediately set to work by his father to learn the business of Kraus Industries. Before his first day was out, he knew that he had embarked upon a life for which he was totally unsuited. He had always found the smog of the Ruhr suffocating and claustrophobic, always hated the vast gun shops with their eternal din, the furnaces with their searing heat, the steel-casting plants with their huge gantries, throbbing machinery and pale-faced men. But above all, Benno disliked the sensation that he, himself, was little more than a cog in a mighty wheel that turned the great machinery that produced weapons, which would, at some time, be used to kill people.

There was nobody in whom he could confide these sentiments. His mother, whom he suspected sometimes of being very unhappy but who plainly enjoyed her husband's wealth and prestige, took absolutely no interest in the business, while his brother, Ernst, had taken to it like a duck to water. Ernst grew more and more to look like his father; at twenty-five he was already rather stout, with florid cheeks, and he had the same cold, calculating mind, although he lacked the Baron's domineering manner. Even as children Ernst and Benno had had little in common and now their sole point of contact was Kraus Industries. Ernst would have little sympathy with Benno's dislike of his job. It was certainly not a matter which Benno could discuss with his father, so it seemed he had no choice but to do what was expected of him and pray that, one day, he would find a means of escape.

After a year spent in Essen and a further year in Silesia, Baron

207

Kraus announced that he now considered Benno sufficiently knowledgeable to go to Berlin. 'You will work under the supervision of Klaus Merten, Kraus Chemie's General Manager. As you progress, your situation will be reviewed. While you are in Berlin, you will, of course, live at the Hotel Quadriga.'

So, at the beginning of 1912, the luxurious first-floor apartment reserved for the sole use of the Kraus family, received a permanent occupant. Karl greeted him warmly. 'I wish you every success in your new position and I hope you'll be very happy here with us at the Quadriga. If there's anything you need, please don't hesitate to let me know.'

'Thank you, Herr Jochum.' Benno instinctively liked Karl.

'And if you feel lonely, you're always welcome to join our family.'

'Boy won't have time to be lonely,' Baron Heinrich growled. 'He's got work to do.'

The following morning, they drove out to Wedding and, used as he was to the massive factories in the Ruhr, Benno experienced a sinking feeling in the pit of his stomach when he saw Kraus Village, surrounded by its high, sooty walls, the tall factory chimneys belching forth dense clouds of sulphurous, black smoke.

Klaus Merten was standing waiting to greet them under a large sign reading *Kraus Chemie*, and, after shaking hands, the three men set off on a tour of inspection, starting at the railway line where freight trains unloaded the heavy raw materials right in the middle of the refinery. 'That's sulphur,' Merten explained, as they watched a number of men heaving great rocks into trucks. 'It has to be crushed, separated and then refined. It will eventually form a constituent part of explosives.'

Knowing he would never remember anything unless he wrote it down, Benno took his notebook from his pocket. Merten shook his head. 'Don't worry, Herr Benno. You'll learn as you go along and in the meantime I'll always be here to answer any technical questions you have. Your job is going to be keeping the finances of the business straight. Leave the production worries to me.'

His mind in a whirl, Benno followed his father and Merten through enormous workshops, full of vast tanks, whirring motors, men reading gauges and adjusting valves, calling out to each other, jotting down figures and making hasty calculations. 'Depending on what they are, the chemicals have to be distilled, combined or refined,' Merten told him, going on to list chemicals and processes of which Benno had never heard before.

208

'The liquids are then put into vats, the powders into barrels, then they are transferred to our production plant. These glass vats of acid, for instance, are going to the arsenal.' They left one part of Kraus Village and walked down a short road, through another gate, past a bowing porter, and into another huge factory. Huge bales of cotton were being unloaded in the first depot they entered. 'This has been cleaned to a very high degree of purity and is now ready for the gun cotton process.'

By the end of his tour, Benno decided that the only aspect of Kraus Village that he liked was Klaus Merten.

'I'll take you up to your office now.' On their way, they passed a door marked in large letters: *PRIVATE. ENTRY TO UNAUTHORIZED PERSONS STRICTLY FORBIDDEN.* 'Those are our research laboratories.' Merten turned to Baron Heinrich. 'Do you wish your son to see this process, Herr Baron?'

'I don't think that's necessary. Our research work doesn't concern Benno.'

'What do you research?' Benno asked.

'New chemical processes,' his father said smoothly. 'The laboratories operate on a fixed budget approved by myself personally. You needn't worry about them.'

But, strangely, out of everything he had seen and learned that day, the closed doors of the research laboratories remained most firmly etched on Benno's mind. What new, diabolical method of killing people was being developed behind them? One day, he determined he would find out.

For the first few weeks, the Jochums saw little of Benno as he struggled to master his new job, then, gradually, as he fell into a routine, he spent a bit more time in the hotel and less at Kraus Village. Sometimes, he joined them at their family table for dinner, occasionally diffidently inviting Viktoria for a coffee later in the Palm Garden Room or the bar.

He always looked very tired, as if his day at Kraus Chemie exacted too heavy a toll. 'It must take tremendous skill to run such a huge business,' she commented admiringly one evening.

Benno shook his head wearily. 'I don't think I shall ever be able to do it.'

She looked at him in surprise, for it was not a statement she had ever expected to hear from a Kraus. 'Does your father know how you feel?'

'I think he guesses. That's why he sent me here. It's a kind of test to see how well I do.'

'Can't you say something to him? Can't you explain how you feel?' As Benno shook his head, she paused, then went on, 'Do you actually have to work for Kraus Industries? Couldn't you take another job?'

Benno gave a weak smile. 'My father would disown me if I did. Grandfather built the company up from nothing, and, in due course, Ernst and I will be expected to take over.'

Viktoria stared at him curiously, feeling rather flattered that he chose to confide in her. 'What would you really like to do, Benno?'

He twiddled with his cup, then said, 'It will sound strange to you, but I'd like to run an hotel like this.'

She tried to conceal her surprise. 'Why?'

'Because you're dealing with people, with living things, not the constituents of death. Kraus is nothing but a great war machine. I loathe it.'

They were both silent for a moment. How dreadful, Viktoria thought, to have to spend one's life doing something one hated, and she began to feel very sorry for him. 'I wish I could do something to help you.'

'Do you really?' Benno's hazel eyes gazed at her with an almost embarrassing intensity. 'Would you allow me to invite you out somewhere? I mean, I should be so honoured if you'd permit me to take you to the zoo or maybe to a concert.'

It seemed such a simple request and Benno's expression was pathetically eager. Viktoria was about to assent on the spot, when she remembered her parents. 'I'll have to ask Mama and Papa, but I'd like to very much.'

His eyes lit up and his whole face was transformed. 'Oh, thank you, Viktoria.'

'He's so lonely,' she explained to her parents that evening. 'I feel so sorry for him.'

'Where are you thinking of going?' Ricarda asked.

'Benno suggested the zoo. I thought we could go there first, if the weather is fine.'

'I think it's a lovely idea. I hope you both enjoy yourselves.'

When they were alone, Karl said, 'It would be an excellent match, Ricarda. What better husband could you wish for her?'

'But they scarcely know each other.'

'Rubbish, Benno has been coming to the hotel since he was a

210

baby. It would be excellent for the hotel if a Jochum married a Kraus!'

'Viktoria won't marry Benno just because it suits your business plans.'

'Why not? He's a nice-looking young man, he's got money and he obviously thinks a lot of her.'

'What about Viktoria's feelings?'

'She could do worse. Anyway, presumably she likes him or she wouldn't be gadding off to the zoo with him.'

Although she privately agreed with him, Ricarda was determined to allow her daughter a little more time to make up her own mind. 'She's only eighteen, Karl, I won't have her pushed into marriage against her will.'

It was only when they started on their Saturday afternoon and Sunday excursions around Berlin that Viktoria realized Benno hardly knew the city at all. Except for his brief visits, he had spent his entire life in the Ruhr, for Baron Heinrich did not believe in spending money on travel simply to broaden the mind.

They started, as promised, with the zoo. Like all Berliners, Viktoria was inordinately proud of it, with its enormous elephant houses, monkey cages and lion pens. 'When it was built, it was right on the outskirts of the city, but now it's almost in the city centre,' she explained. Her enthusiasm was infectious. Benno was soon giggling at a huge gorilla nibbling a banana, and gazing in admiration at a rare, one-legged stork.

The highlight of their afternoon, however, was the parrot. In vain, they tried to teach it to say, 'Vicki', 'Benno', 'Jochum' and 'Kraus'. The bird stared blankly back at them from hooded lids. 'Oh, brrp to you,' Benno blew it a raspberry. In perfect imitation, the parrot imitated the rude gesture. They both convulsed in laughter.

At the end of the day, when they sat eating ices on the terrace of the zoo café, he said, 'Thank you, Vicki, I don't know when I've enjoyed an afternoon more.'

'There's more to Berlin than the zoo.'

'So where shall we go next weekend?'

She cupped her chin on her hands. 'Let's go to the Luna Park.'

Benno was so easy to be with, so simple to please. They travelled out to the amusement park in an old-fashioned horse-drawn carriage, calling out mockingly at the automobiles rushing past them. 'It's much more fun in a Droschke, isn't it?' Benno asked. 'Papa's so proud of his automobiles, but I think I'll always prefer horses.'

That did not prevent him from enjoying the mechanical roundabouts, the mountain railway or insisting on going on the devil's wheel, even though Viktoria was petrified. The only thing he refused to do was try his luck at the shooting booths. 'I have enough to do with guns the rest of the week. Come on, Vicki, let's go on the ghost train!'

They entered the dark tunnel and a damp spider's web brushed Viktoria's face. She screamed. Benno clasped her hand. A huge skeleton loomed up at them and she ducked towards Benno. His arms went protectively round her shoulders. 'A-a-a-h!' Two huge eyes stared out at them, and he pulled her head down onto his shoulder. She did not see what was waiting for them next, because Benno's lips were on hers and he was kissing her, a soft, warm kiss that made her feel as if she were melting in his arms.

Then, suddenly, she heard the sound of applause. 'That's right, mister,' a boy's voice called. There was laughter and she opened her eyes, pulling hurriedly away from Benno. They were once again in broad daylight and a small group of youths was gathered round the tunnel exit waiting for the next courting couple to appear.

She didn't look at Benno as he helped her from the train. Her face was flushed and hot, and her heart was beating so furiously, she was sure he must be able to hear it. As they walked away, she was certain that his kiss was indelibly printed on her mouth and that people were staring at them, laughing and talking about them.

And yet, when she thought about it, it had been a rather wonderful experience. His lips had been so tender and his arms embracing her so gentle. In fact, she realized, as her racing pulse quietened and the blood started to leave her cheeks, that she had actually enjoyed the sensation, except for one thing. She did so wish that it had not been Benno who had kissed her, but Peter.

Walking diffidently beside her, Benno wondered what he should say. It was the first time he had ever kissed a girl and his immediate reaction was that he would like to do it again. As they had boarded the ghost train, he had entertained no notion of kissing her, but when she had screamed and moved towards him, he had automatically put his arm around her — then, almost before he had known what he was doing, his lips had found hers. It was the most exciting moment of his life.

But what about Viktoria? Suddenly, Benno was suffused with a sense of guilt. If they had not been in the dark tunnel, he would never have dared kiss her, for she would undoubtedly have smacked his face for insulting her in public. He glanced at her cautiously. She was looking straight ahead, her cheeks still flushed. Yes, he had evidently deeply offended her — and that, Benno realized, was the very last thing on earth that he wanted to do, because, at that moment, he knew that he was in love with her.

Looking back over the years, he thought maybe he had always loved her. He remembered dancing with her when she only a little girl of five at the ball to celebrate the new century. How sweet she had been even then in her pink taffeta dress and white boots! They had talked together, he recalled, until, suddenly, his cousin Peter had appeared and taken her on the dance floor. It was strange how all his memories of Viktoria seemed to be confused with meetings with his cousin. Perhaps it was just coincidence, for the Bieder-stains came to Berlin about as seldom as the Krauses did, and yet, whenever he remembered Viktoria in the past, Peter always seemed to be there.

However, Peter wasn't here now and Viktoria was, although if he didn't so something quickly, he might lose her for ever. Summoning up his courage, he said, 'Viktoria, I'm sorry, I shouldn't have done that. Please, please will you accept my apologies?'

To his great relief, she gave a weak smile and nodded. 'Yes, of course, Benno. But now, I think perhaps we'd better go home.'

The journey back to the city seemed to last for ever. Viktoria stared out at the fields and houses in silence, while Benno sat steeped in his miserable thoughts, convinced that she would never allow him to take her out again. Yet, when they reached the hotel, he knew he could not let her go just like that. 'Viktoria, can you forgive me enough to see me again? I promise I'll never again behave in such a dastardly fashion. Please give me another chance. I do so want to remain your friend.'

To his utter amazement, she said softly, 'Oh, I do understand, Benno. And, of course, we're still friends.'

Gradually, their relationship settled down into an easy-going friendship. Although Benno often longed to kiss her again, he controlled himself. He had so nearly lost her once, he wasn't going to take such a risk a second time.

So far as Viktoria was concerned, that ride in the ghost train and its consequences had clarified her mind about a lot of things, the most important of which was that while she liked Benno as a friend, she was in love with his cousin, Peter. And now that she knew she could trust Benno not to try to kiss her again, she was perfectly happy to keep him company until Peter eventually returned to Berlin.

Now she was sure Peter would return. The troubles in the Balkans were being averted by a series of peace conferences and Peter's life no longer seemed in danger. She even found she could enjoy the humour of the variety artist, Otto Reutter, whom Benno took her to see one evening at the Wintergarten Variété.

Reutter was a strange little man, who kept his audience convulsed with his daring couplets, using the unending peace conferences as a butt for his biting wit. So extreme were his sentiments on some subjects that the censors would not allow him to sing certain lines, so he coughed instead. An ecstatic audience coughed with him.

'I don't know that I like you going to see Otto Reutter,' Karl told her disapprovingly.

'What harm does he do?'

'The troubles in the Balkans are no laughing matter. If we're not careful, we could still find ourselves at war over them. Otto Reutter shouldn't poke fun at efforts to maintain the peace.'

'Benno thinks he's amusing.'

'Well, if Benno likes him, then I suppose it's all right.'

Benno could do no wrong in Karl's eyes. Delighted with his interest in the hotel, he took great pride in explaining everything to him and showing him round every part of it, even the cellars where few strangers were ever allowed to venture. 'I've built up this collection over nearly twenty years now.' With extreme care, he picked up a bottle, carefully wrapped in straw. 'Look, this one is from 1883. That's the year we opened Café Jochum. This one is 1889, when I married Frau Jochum. And this one 1894 — the year we opened the hotel, and Viktoria was born. And these here I laid down at the turn of the century to celebrate Luise's birthday.' He stared around the vast vaults. 'I could tell you the history of every bottle in this cellar, Benno. And, if I did, I'd be telling you the story of my life.'

Benno gazed round him in awe. 'Thank you for bringing me down here, Herr Jochum. I consider it a great privilege.'

'The more I see of young Benno, the more I like him,' Karl declared to Ricarda that evening. 'Boy's got a lot of sense.'

214

Ricarda, too, was becoming increasingly glad about Benno's presence in the hotel. To Karl, he was beginning to represent the son he had never had, a man with whom he could share his enthusiasms and talk business. Ricarda had little to do with the direct running of the hotel now, devoting most of her time to her children, charities and local organizations. Yet she couldn't ignore the fact that Karl was fifty-fiyr and the question was often in her mind as to what would happen to the Quadriga when he was too old to run it.

Viktoria had identified with and loved the hotel from the day she was born, but Ricarda knew love was not enough. No woman could run a hotel on her own — she needed a man to help her. Ricarda began to hope her eldest daughter was getting over her childish infatuation for Peter von Biederstein and that Benno might be the man.

For over a year, Professor Ascher had been watching the courtship between Pipsi and Georg with mixed feelings. The more he saw of the young musician, the more he liked him. Discreet enquiries at the Berlin *Hochschule* revealed that he was highly thought of and had a fine career ahead of him. He might be a penniless student at the moment, but one day he would undoubtedly be a great pianist. No, the Professor had no doubts as to whether Georg was good enough for Pipsi. To his private dismay, he was wondering whether his daughter was good enough for Georg.

Then the fateful day arrived when Georg asked his permission to marry Pipsi. The Professor sighed. 'Sit down, Georg, and listen to me carefully. Pipsi is a beautiful girl, but she lives in a fantasy world. It's my fault, I suppose, but I always tried to give my two daughters everything I never had in my own childhood, as if I wanted to make up to them for the hardships I suffered. I know I've spoiled them outrageously.'

'I should try to make sure that Pipsi never lacked for anything.'

'I know, but it isn't as simple as that. Take this wild idea of hers about becoming an actress. I've humoured her in it, I confess, and I've paid for lessons, but Georg, I can't give her talent. Perhaps, if she were married, she'd give up the idea. If she became an ordinary housewife ...'

'I don't want her to give up her profession because of me. I love her for herself, not because she might be a good housewife.'

The Professor had to laugh. 'She's never done a stroke of housework in her life! Since my wife died, we've always had a housekeeper.'

215

'Then I shall find some way of employing a servant.'

The Professor stared at him, then shook his head sadly. 'You really do love my daughter, don't you? Well, let's be realistic. You haven't got any money and neither has your Uncle Franz. So, I'll grant my permission for you to marry Pipsi on one condition — you allow me to subsidize you both for a while, until you find a job.'

'No, sir, I can't accept it.'

'Then at least permit me to rent an apartment for my daughter, for I won't have you both living in some old attic. It might seem romantic to start with, but the novelty would soon wear off and that, believe me, Georg, is where the trouble would start.'

'If Pipsi really loves me, she'll put up with anything.'

Damn the obstinate young fellow! Did he really see Pipsi as a romantic little doll? Had he really not seen that she was just a vain, spoiled, rather silly young girl? 'If you really love her, you'll do what's best for her,' the Professor insisted firmly.

To his relief, Georg acquiesced, although obviously unhappily. 'Thank you, sir, but believe me, I'll repay you as soon as I can.'

'Make my daughter happy, Georg. Be a good husband. That's all the payment I require.'

Georg reached out his hand. 'I love Pipsi, and I know I shall love her until the day I die.'

Franz Jankowski had also been watching the romance with deep misgiving. First he had lost his nephew to the army, now to Pipsi Ascher. And, on top of that, he knew that his crabbed fingers would soon no longer be able to play the violin. Suddenly, his world appeared very bleak.

As soon as she saw him, Luise knew something was the matter. Full of concern, she took his hand and led him to a chair, 'Herr Jankowski, what's happened?'

He rubbed his hand across his forehead. 'It's Georg, Fraeulein Luise. He's going to get married.'

Thunderstruck, Luise stared at him. Franz had told her nothing about Georg's courtship and it had never occurred to her that her hero might marry. 'Married? But who to?'

'Pipsi Ascher,' the old man sighed.

Pipsi Ascher! Luise tried to absorb this astonishing news. She did not know Pipsi at all except by sight and had still not met Georg. However, if Georg had to get married, then she was pleased to think he was marrying someone as beautiful — and rich

— as Pipsi. 'But surely it will be a very good match, won't it?'

'She comes from such a different background. She's never been poor and hungry. For a while, she may think it's romantic to be married to a poor musician, but after a while, she'll get tired of it, Fraeulein Luise. She's going to get bored and want to buy nice clothes and go to fine hotels like this one. Georg can't afford that. And what will happen then?'

Luise clasped his hand sympathetically, hating to see him distraught. 'But Georg's going to be one of the world's greatest musicians,' she reminded him. 'He'll earn lots of money then.'

Franz summoned up a little smile. 'God bless you, child. Yes, of course he will.' Then he was hit by a new worry. 'Do you think, if he's married to Pipsi Ascher — and he's so rich and famous — he will still come to see me?'

'But of course he will.' Suddenly, she realized that Franz was jealous of Pipsi and was afraid that she would steal Georg from him. She struggled to find the right words. 'I love my father and mother and Vicki — but I still love you as well. It is possible to love more than one person at the same time, you know.' But as Franz began to look happier, Luise felt a niggling sense of annoyance with Georg for hurting his uncle. And she decided she did not like Pipsi Ascher very much.

Pipsi loved the unconventional. If she could have had her way, she would have eloped with Georg, marrying him against her father's wishes in an obscure town hall, then returning to announce the fact to her flabbergasted family. Since this was impossible, she agreed to a compromise. She and Georg were married in a small synagogue, then held their wedding reception in the Professor's house in Dahlem. The mere fact that it was different from Sophie's wedding delighted her. When one of her old aunts asked her about her health, she was overjoyed. That night, when they were alone in the flat Professor Ascher had rented for them in Charlottenburg, she told Georg, 'They think we're marrying like this because I'm pregnant!'

Her new husband stared at her in horror. 'But that's terrible!'

'I think it's lovely, but then I love shocking people. Aren't they going to be disappointed when they discover that I'm not?'

'Would you like to have children?' Georg asked her shyly.

'No,' Pipsi told him quite definitely. 'Children are such a nuisance, particularly if one has a career.' She moved closer to him, nuzzling his neck. 'But I think I shall probably like the process of making children very much.' As Georg's hands ran over her naked body, she shivered with pleasure.

A few months later, Pipsi obtained her first real stage part as a soubrette in the operetta, *Hurra! Hussar!* Although she spoke only one line, she was delighted with her role, for her costume was wonderful, low cut and tightly laced to show off her breasts, and at one point in the play, when the handsome young hussar who was the hero of the show came home from the war, she had to lift her skirts and display her garters, thus giving the audience the full benefit of her shapely legs.

Georg was, of course, among the packed audience on the first night. At the best of times, he did not like operettas, and this one, he considered, was in ultimate bad taste, glorifying the military and war. He particularly disliked the actor who played the hussar and who seemed to study Pipsi's cleavage more than his role demanded, and he was utterly miserable when his wife lifted her skirts to display her legs to half Berlin.

When he went backstage after the performance, he found Pipsi surrounded by a dozen or so young men, all in officers' uniforms, laughing and flirting with her. She blew him a kiss, calling out, 'I should go home, darling. I'll be ages yet.'

Georg hesitated, uncertain what to do. Then, unwilling to make a scene, he left. Already, he was slowly realizing that Pipsi Ascher was not the girl with whom he had fallen in love. Perhaps, he thought miserably, that girl had never really existed.

In the spring of 1913, the whole of Berlin was thrown into a fever of excitement, for in May, Princess Viktoria Luise, the Emperor's twenty-year-old daughter, was to marry Prince Ernst Albert of Brunswick. For months in advance, the Hotel Quadriga was fully booked, with a long list of people asking to be advised if cancellations occurred and, as the great day approached, the activity increased, for this wedding represented a new pinnacle in the hotel's splendid and glittering lifetime. Work continued day and night, as the hotel prepared to receive guests from the most noble and important families of Europe.

In the restaurant and banqueting rooms, Max Patschke organized his staff, checking and rechecking the arrangements for an unending series of dinners, banquets, buffets and balls, while in the kitchen, Maître Mesurier, with his army of under-chefs and commis, embarked upon preparing a succession of menus, the fame of which would spread throughout the European continent, Russia and America. For Mesurier, too, the royal wedding represented the peak of his career, for after it was over he was going to retire to a small cottage he had bought in Périgord, there to spend the twilight of his life in the company of his grandchildren, eating the very finest of truffles. Assisting him in his final gala performance was a young chef he had long been training in the Quadriga kitchens.

As on every royal occasion, the hotel was throwing a magnificent ball to celebrate the princess's wedding, to which Benno was delighted to be able to invite Viktoria at his partner. Her eyes shining, she confessed, 'I thought you'd never ask me. Do you realize, Benno, I've always been too young in the past? Now, at last, I'm grown-up!'

So much was Benno looking forward to the ball that not even his father's arrival in Berlin dampened his spirits. Baron Heinrich had decided to combine the wedding with an extended visit to Kraus Village to inspect Benno's progress. They were arduous days for Benno, during which he was cross-examined on all aspects of the business, but as he answered most of the questions lucidly, he realized to his surprise, that he had picked up far more than he had imagined about the chemicals business and running a company. His father also appeared pleased for, although he offered no words of praise, he said, 'You may as well stay on here for a while. Oh, and I've decided to give you a raise in your salary.'

There were no special concessions made for family employees of Kraus Industries. Benno was paid a weekly wage the same as any other manager. However, both he and Ernst owned shares in the company as part of a complicated trust set up by the Baron to avoid death duties and inheritance taxes although, until they married, the dividends were held by the trust. So Benno's salary rise was very important to him.

It also meant that he could, at long last, afford to get married. He had been courting Viktoria for one and a half years now and, although she had never actually said that she loved him, he felt confident enough of her feelings to approach Karl Jochum.

Karl looked up with a frown as Benno entered his office, then smiled when he saw who it was. 'Benno, come in.'

'Herr Jochum, there's something I wish to ask you,' Benno said hesitantly, wondering if he should have chosen some other moment.

'Anything, Benno!'

'Well, you probably realize I admire Viktoria greatly. May I have your permission to ask for her hand in marriage?'

Karl beamed at him. 'Benno, I can think of no son-in-law I should welcome more. Of course you can ask her. And I hope she has the sense to say yes!'

'I think I shall wait until the royal wedding is over.'

'Why wait? It's the early bird that catches the worm.'

'No, sir, I'd rather wait. Viktoria's a woman, after all, and women get very emotional about royal weddings. I want her to reflect seriously about her decision, not make up her mind on the spur of the moment. After all, if we get married, it will be for the rest of our lives.'

While Benno, quite unknown to her, was having this conversation with her father, Viktoria was standing by the reception desk, her eyes skimming the guest list for the royal wedding. 'Biederstein, Count Johann and Countess Anna von, Biederstein, Countess Gertrud von,' she read, and on, the next line, 'Biederstein, Count Peter von.' Her heart pounded. Peter was coming to Berlin for the royal wedding! It seemed an eternity since she had last seen him. Indeed, it was three years since Count Ewald had given them the dreadful news that he had been posted to Danzig. What would he say when he saw her again? Would he find her beautiful? Or had he met some aristocratic young lady in Danzig, whom he would be bringing with him? Hurriedly, she dismissed the thought.

That evening, she asked her mother, 'May I have a new dress for the royal wedding?'

'I don't see why not. Do I take it that Benno has asked you to be his partner at the ball?'

'Yes,' she breathed happily, although she didn't tell her mother the real reason for her joy. 'And do you think I could have a new day dress as well as a ball gown? I've grown out of all of mine, and, anyway, they're old-fashioned now.'

The dress they finally decided upon was pale pink, in the new fashionable length that revealed her ankles.

'That frock is most unbecoming,' Karl roared, when she put it on to show him. 'It's improper, showing off your legs in that manner!'

'Karl,' Ricarda laid a placating hand on his. 'I think Vicki looks very pretty. And far from being improper, the dress is very fashionable. In fact, the dressmaker told us that the next skirts from Paris are going to be calf-length.'

'Calf-length,' Karl snorted in disgust, then shook his head in bewilderment. 'Well, if you say it's all right, my dear, then I suppose it must be. And where do you think you're going to wear it? To the ball, I suppose?'

'But, of course not, Papa, this is a day dress.'

'It looks more like a night dress to me.'

The morning of 21 May 1913 dawned with hardly a cloud in the sky. 'It's Kaiser weather!' Karl exclaimed jubilantly. Huge vases of flowers graced the entrance and reception rooms of the hotel, perfuming the air and adding splashes of vivid colour to the muted blue, gold and white of the decor. Smaller arrangements adorned each bedroom and suite, while buttonholes and tiny hand posies were on sale with the flower girl in the foyer. Garlands of fresh blossoms festooned the balconies overlooking Unter den Linden, where flags waved cheerfully in the spring breeze.

Once again, the streets were lined with people and the din of the traffic was drowned by the sound of the military tattoo sounded to welcome His Majesty's illustrious guests to Berlin. At eleven o'clock in the morning, the Emperor, with his escort from the Garde du Corps, greeted his English relatives, King George V and Queen Mary, at the Lehrter Station, and the train of carriages, drawn by high-stepping horses, accompanied by resplendent Guardsmen with gleaming daggers, shining cuirasses and bannered lances, conveyed their noble convoy through the central archway of the Brandenburg Gate, down Unter den Linden to the Imperial Palace on the Schlossplatz.

The following day, Tsar Nicholas II of Russia arrived, was welcomed with the same pomp and dazzling ceremony and, also entering Unter den Linden through the central arch of the Brandenburg Gate, was driven through the ecstatic crowds to arrive with full ritual honours at the Emperor's Palace.

Standing with Luise on the balcony above the hotel portico, Viktoria cheered and waved her handkerchief enthusiastically but the person she was really waiting for was Peter. Her eyes impatiently scanned the milling crowds, the arriving motor taxis and horse-drawn carriages. 'Did you know that the mad monk, Rasputin, wouldn't allow the Tsarina to accompany the Tsar to Berlin?' Luise asked.

Viktoria did not reply.

'And people are saying that His Majesty didn't really want the Tsar to come. Vicki, what's the matter with you? You aren't even listening to me. And why have you got your new dress on? Why are you so excited?'

But Viktoria did not hear her, for she saw a carriage had drawn up bearing the von Biederstein crest, from which the occupants were already descending. She flew down the stairs and into the foyer, just as the Biedersteins swept regally in. The Count was looking about him with a masterful air, while his wife nodded at acquaintances, the rigid brocade of her dress creaking slightly as she walked. With her arm through her mother's, a disdainful look on her plump face, walked seventeen-year-old Trudi. But, behind them, extremely elegant in the ornate braided uniform with the insignia of a skull and crossbones of the Death's Head Hussars, marched Peter von Biederstein. His dark hair and moustache had been fashionably trimmed, while his brown eyes surveyed the bustling scene around him with languid amusement.

Slowly, Viktoria approached them across the gleaming marble floor. Then he saw her. Smiling admiringly, he walked swiftly towards her and grasped her hand warmly in his. 'Viktoria, my dear, how nice to see you again.'

In her high-heeled boots, she was nearly as tall as he was, but so nervous did she feel that she could scarcely bring herself to look him in the face. Around her, as if from a vast distance, she heard the conversation continuing — Countess Anna congratulating her father on the hotel's appearance, Count Johann asking whether Lord Fitzjames had arrived yet, and Trudi enquiring whether Ernst Kraus was there. Then she heard her own voice, curiously high-pitched, saying, 'Peter, I'm so pleased you're back in Berlin.'

'It's splendid to be back. Why, Vicki, I do declare you've grown up since I've been away. You look positively enchanting.'

So, he had noticed her fashionable, pink dress! 'Thank you, Peter. And, you, you look so elegant.'

'Peter, come along, accompany us to our rooms,' his mother called.

'Will you be at the ball this evening?' Peter asked.

Her eyes shining, she nodded.

'Then I hope you will permit me the honour of dancing with you.'

She thought she would die from happiness.

That evening, she could hardly eat for excitement and it was with the greatest difficulty that Ricarda forced her to sip some bouillon and nibble a little bread. Luise watched her through narrowed eyes. 'You really are acting very strangely today, Vicki.'

'I'm excited about the ball,' she replied, aware of her mother's penetrating glance.

'Bah! It's not the ball you're excited about. It's the thought of dancing with Peter von Biederstein!'

'Luise, that's no way to talk to your sister,' Ricarda scolded.

'Well, it's true. You should have seen the silly way she looked at him when they met this morning!'

'You don't know what you're talking about,' Viktoria retorted, 'you weren't even there. You were on the balcony.'

'I wasn't! I wasn't going to stay there on my own. I was in Herr Quitzow's office. But you didn't notice me — you only had eyes for Count Peter!'

Ricarda stood up, looking with misgiving at both her daughters, Viktoria blushing and Luise's green eyes laughing mockingly. 'Luise, finish your supper, and Viktoria, come along and let me help you dress.'

When Benno knocked on the apartment door, Viktoria looked ravishing in a long, jade dress, that trailed the floor behind her, tightly sashed at the waist with wide green ribbons, and her blonde hair intricately curled and pleated into an elegant chignon. 'Viktoria, you look beautiful.'

'You don't look bad either,' Luise informed him, eyeing his immaculate dinner jacket, black tie and sharply creased trousers. Then she added longingly, 'Oh, I wish I were older, so that I could come too. Thirteen is such a dreadful age! Benno, are you sure Ernst isn't looking for a partner?'

Benno grinned at her. 'Even if you were old enough, Ernst already has a partner.'

Luise sniffed. 'Yes, Countess Gertrud von Biederstein, I suppose.' She stood up and gave an excellent imitation of Trudi walking across the foyer. 'Quite what the attraction of the Biedersteins is I don't understand.' She looked meaningfully at Viktoria. 'But it's been obvious for a long time that Ernst is going to marry Trudi one day. I must say, I find it a bit strange, first cousins marrying.'

'Luise!' her mother called icily. 'If you don't behave you are going straight to bed. What Benno's brother does is none of your

223

business!' Then she turned to Viktoria and Benno. 'Now run along and have a lovely time. I shall be down later myself with Karl.'

Viktoria allowed her arm to rest lightly on Benno's as the master of ceremonies announced their names, but while they made their way across the crowded room to their reserved table her eyes were sweeping the faces of the guests, searching, in vain, for Peter. Disappointed, she was just taking her seat when the master of ceremonies boomed: 'Count Johann and Countess Anna von Biederstein.' 'Colonel Ritter Emerich and Countess Maria von Schennig.' 'Countess Julia and Baron Heinrich von Kraus zu Essen.' 'Lieutenant Count Peter von Biederstein and the Honourable Ilse von Schennig.' 'Countess Gertrud von Biederstein and Herr Ernst Kraus.'

She stared at them as they made their way in stately procession across the cobalt carpet. She saw the Colonel in the full dress uniform of the Death's Head Hussars — and she saw his daughter, Ilse von Schennig, hanging possessively on Peter's arm, a girl of about her own age, dressed in the very latest of Paris fashions. She was much shorter than Viktoria, with a pert, round little face, framed with a halo of curling blonde hair, but by far the most startling thing about her were her piercingly blue eyes. While Viktoria watched, she raised them to Peter, said something, and he laughed. 'Good God, the whole family!' Benno exclaimed, but she hardly heard him. The only thing of which she was aware were those bluer-than-blue eyes looking at Peter.

From that moment, she saw and heard everything as from a great distance. Two orchestras alternated in playing an unceasing round of waltzes, polkas, galops and polonaises. Waiters in frock coat and white gloves wove their practised way between excited guests, opening bottles, pouring champagne. And the guests themselves were gorgeously arrayed — officers in the most magnificent dress uniforms, ladies in the most fashionable of evening gowns.

Woodenly, trying to conceal her disappointment, Viktoria allowed Benno to lead her onto the dance floor. She had been looking forward to this evening so much and before it had hardly started the glory had gone from it. She saw Peter ask Ilse von Schennig to dance. Oh, why had she been such a fool as to believe that he liked her?

The orchestra struck up a foxtrot, a new dance recently introduced from America and deemed a scandal in Berlin. 'Shall we try?' Benno asked. Apathetically, she nodded. What did it matter? She allowed Benno to lead her in the unknown steps. 'You realize that if Police President Traugott von Jagow could see us he'd have us in gaol?' Benno laughed. But Viktoria had no heart for humour.

The evening dragged by. As she and Benno danced, she noticed her parents dancing together, greeting people as they moved round the dance floor. Her mother smiled at her and she forced herself to smile back. She heard the sound of laughter from closely-packed tables, mingled with the music, the clink of glasses, and voices raised in excited conversation. Everyone was happy, it seemed, except her.

'Can we sit for a while?'

'Vicki, what's the matter? Don't you feel well?'

'I'm all right,' she said listlessly, resting her head in her hands. Then, suddenly, her heart seemed to stop beating, for a voice asked, 'Viktoria, would you permit me the honour of this dance?'

Slowly, she turned, a flush colouring her cheeks, a feeling of joy surging through her. She saw a pair of elegant black boots, the black uniform of a cavalry officer. Then she looked up into a pair of laughing brown eyes. 'Peter,' she heard herself say in an almost inaudible whisper. 'Why, Peter, that would be so nice.'

He took her hand and helped her to her feet, then led her gently on to the dance floor. 'I thought my turn was never going to come. Whenever I looked, you were dancing with Benno.'

'But, I ...'

'Vicki,' he laughed, 'it's only right that someone as beautiful as you should have admirers.'

It was as if all the chandeliers had just been lit. He hadn't been ignoring her. He had been waiting for her to be free. She looked up at him with a radiant smile on her face. 'Admirers? Oh, no, Peter ...'

'And my cousin?'

Without a qualm, she replied, 'Oh, Benno's just a friend. He's staying at the Quadriga while he's working at Kraus Village.'

'He gives the impression of being more than a friend. From the way he's been looking at you, I somehow had the impression that you were close, possibly even engaged to be married.'

'Oh, no, you're quite wrong.'

Peter smiled, for he was enjoying himself immensely. Ever since he had seen her that morning in the foyer in that saucy dress revealing her neat ankles he had been unable to banish her image from his mind. To think that little Viktoria had grown up into such a beautiful young filly!

He compared her momentarily with Ilse von Schennig. Both were blonde, both had blue eyes, but there the similarity ended. Ilse was the only daughter of his Commanding Officer at Danzig, last scion of one of Germany's oldest families, for Ritter von Schennig could trace his ancestors back even beyond the von Biedersteins to the Teutonic Knights. Their family seat was near Luebeck, now a rather impoverished estate, he believed, but the title was still beyond value. As soon as his Commanding Officer had introduced him to his daughter, Peter had known they would one day marry. Not only was she eminently socially acceptable, but, as an officer's daughter, she was ideally suited to be an officer's wife. Furthermore, her father would do everything in his power to further his son-in-law's career. As Ilse's husband, Peter saw a long and glorious future ahead of him.

However, he could not flirt with Ilse. Until they were married, he would not so much as kiss her, and, in the meantime, he was a healthy young man with a healthy young man's appetites. It was these appetites that Viktoria awoke in him. She was stunningly attractive, obviously liked him, and — what was more — she was only a hotelier's daughter. She could be excellent sport.

As if she were reading his thoughts, Viktoria asked, 'Are you going to stay much longer at Danzig? I thought maybe you'd be posted to Berlin.'

'Jolly bad luck, isn't it? But I have to obey orders, you know. Still, shouldn't be surprised if there aren't some changes soon. These troubles in the Balkans — the size of the army has been increased considerably.'

She frowned, not wanting to hear about the Balkans. 'Did you meet Ilse von Schennig in Danzig?' If he was engaged to her she would rather learn it from his lips than from any others.

'She's just the daughter of my Commanding Officer. Father insisted they joined our party, you know. Bit of a bore really.'

So he wasn't in love with Ilse von Schennig! There was still hope for her! She suddenly remembered standing on the balcony with him on the occasion of the Crown Prince's wedding. They met on such splendidly romantic occasions that it must augur well for them. 'Don't you think Princess Viktoria Luise's marriage is a wonderful thing? She must love the Prince so much.'

Peter looked at her curiously. 'I doubt very much that our little

Princess is marrying for love. Much more likely for politics.'

'You think Prince Ernst doesn't love her?'

'How can I tell? I hope so, for her sake, but I doubt it.'

'When I marry, it will be for love.'

'Then you'll be fortunate.'

What did he mean? Did he say that because he feared his parents would not allow him to marry her, or was he trying to tell her that he loved her? At that moment, the music speeded up to a crescendo and the dance was over. He led her back to Benno. 'Your partner is not only beautiful, cousin, but a talented dancer. I congratulate you.'

Benno could not get over the miraculous change that seemed to come over Viktoria the moment Peter asked her to dance. His mind went back again to that first occasion at the turn of the century, when an almost identical thing had happened, except that they had all been so much younger. He recalled his fears in the Luna Park. Were Peter and Viktoria in love with each other? Well, there was only one way to find out. He had to find the earliest possible opportunity to ask her to marry him.

Although the von Schennigs left to visit relatives immediately after the wedding and Benno returned to work, there was no opportunity for Viktoria and Peter to be alone together, for his mother kept him busy until their return to Fuerstenmark. 'I'll be back as soon as I can,' he assured her jauntily, as the Jochums bade their guests goodbye. 'Don't forget me in the meantime.'

When Benno learned his cousin had departed, he breathed a deep sigh of relief.

For a long time after Peter had gone, Viktoria felt as though she were walking on air, although no word arrived from him from Danzig. She hummed as she walked round the hotel, smiled as she helped her parents and sang loudly in her bath.

Luise viewed her darkly. 'You're mad. You don't really think he'll marry you, do you?'

'I don't know what you're talking about. Who's mentioned marriage?'

'Count Peter obviously hasn't.'

'Oh, go away and play.' If Luise had noticed, other people might realize she was in love and she preferred to wait until Peter actually declared his feelings for her before she made hers public.

A month after the royal wedding, Berlin was celebrating again, on this occasion, the Emperor's Silver Jubilee. 'We're closing the works for the day,' Benno told her. 'Some of our staff are taking part in the procession of the trade guilds. You will come with me and watch them, won't you?'

Viktoria hesitated for a moment, suddenly realizing Benno might think her happiness was because of him. Since she had danced with Peter, Benno seemed very ordinary and rather predictable, stuck in his routine of Kraus Village and the Hotel Quadriga. But Peter was in Danzig and Benno was here and it seemed unkind not to accept Benno's invitation. 'Of course I will.'

Again, it was Kaiser weather. The skies were gloriously blue and a hot June sun shone down on the crowds lining the streets to cheer their Emperor, dressed in the uniform of the Death's Head Hussars, as he rode down Unter den Linden with the Empress. He reminded her again of Peter and Viktoria waved enthusiastically, but Benno had a preoccupied look. Even when the Kraus guildsmen paraded past them, his thoughts seemed elsewhere.

His mood continued into the evening, when they attended a production at the Kroll Opera House, specially mounted by the officers of the Berlin militia of 'The People at Arms', at which the Emperor himself put in an appearance, accompanied by the Bavarian Prince Regent. Throughout the performance, Benno shifted restlessly on his seat, glancing anxiously at her from time to time, paying little attention to the music.

'Would you like a glass of wine before we go home?' he asked, when they came out of the opera house.

It was a mild evening. 'Why don't we sit on the terrace of Café Jochum for a while?' she suggested. It seemed the least she could do.

They found a small table at the back of the terrace and an Italian waiter took their order. From inside the café, the sound of the orchestra reached them faintly, playing strains of *The Emperor Waltz*. Benno leaned towards her and took her hand, gazing into her face intensely. 'You've come to mean so much to me over the past months, Vicki. I've never known anyone I've felt so close to, so much at ease with.'

She suddenly had a dreadful premonition of what was going to happen. She wanted to say something, to make him stop, but she could find no words. She could only wait.

'You're a very wonderful person. If it hadn't been for you, my time in Berlin would have been sheer hell. As it is, it's been pure heaven.'

'But, Benno, I'm ...'

Colour mounted to his cheeks. 'I know I'm not saying this very well, but I want you to know that I like everything about you.'

She had to say something. Tamely, she said, 'Thank you, Benno. You must know that I value your friendship too.'

'But what I feel for you is much more than friendship,' he said seriously, his hand grasping hers very tightly. 'I love you, Viktoria, and I want to marry you. Please, please say you love me too and that you'd like to marry me.'

Her first marriage proposal should have been the most romantic and exciting moment in her life, but, as it was, she just felt horribly confused. She liked Benno, but she was in love with Peter. She didn't want to hurt Benno, but she couldn't bear to lose Peter. Helplessly, she shook her head. 'Benno, I never realized, I mean, I've never thought ...'

He seized upon her words. 'It's all right, Vicki, you don't have to answer me immediately. But please tell me one thing.' He took a breath, then went on, 'There isn't anybody else, is there?'

She bit her lip. Benno could only be referring to Peter and, as Luise had so cuttingly pointed out, Peter had not proposed marriage. 'No, it isn't that. You are doing me a great honour, but ...'

'Please, Viktoria, don't say any more now, unless it is to tell me that you could never love me and never envisage me as your husband. But I'd be a good husband, I'd always love you — and our children. So, if you think there is a possibility that you could grow to love me as I love and respect you, then please at least think it over.'

She forced herself to keep her voice even. 'Benno, please try to understand. Obviously I've thought about marriage, for what girl doesn't? But I've never thought that I should marry so soon. You're five years older than me and you've lived so much more. I need more time — to think — and to find out what I want. You see, I'm just not sure that I'm ready yet for marriage.'

He smiled gratefully. 'Of course I understand, my dear, and your words give me hope. Thank you. I promise you that I'll wait as long as you want me to.'

Had she done the right thing? Wouldn't it have been more honest to tell him outright that she didn't love him? Viktoria didn't know. In her room, after he had left her at the door of the apartment with a gentle kiss on the lips, she sat down heavily on the bed, holding her head in her hands, trying to unravel her tangled emotions.

What was love? She had seen Peter on no more than possibly five occasions during her entire life and yet she was certain she loved him. She had spent nearly a year and a half in Benno's company and did not love him, although she felt a deep affection for him.

When she woke the next morning, she knew she had got into a situation beyond her control and that she had to talk to someone. She chose her mother. 'Benno's asked me to marry him, Mama.'

Ricarda looked up from the letter she was writing. 'That's wonderful, darling.'

Viktoria sat down beside her at the table, biting her lip. 'Mama, I don't know what to do.'

Her mother pushed aside her writing case and looked at her thoughtfully. 'Of course you'll make your father and myself very happy if you marry Benno, but the main thing is that you are happy.'

'I don't think I love Benno.'

Ricarda sighed deeply. 'You don't still think you're in love with Peter von Biederstein?' As Viktoria avoided her gaze, but nodded, she said sternly, 'Listen to me, Vicki. Peter is from one of Germany's oldest Junker families. It's quite likely that he will one day inherit the whole Fuerstenmark estate, and for that reason, if for no other, his parents will never allow him to marry you.'

'But what's wrong with me?' Viktoria asked, unhappily.

'There's nothing wrong with you, personally, darling, indeed you are so beautiful you could marry almost anyone you set your heart on, but not a Biederstein. Our family simply isn't good enough for them.'

'But the Krauses ...?'

'The Krauses are very, very rich.'

'But if Peter loved me?'

'Has he ever said he does?' Her mother's voice was still harsh.

'No, but I love him, Mama. I always have. I can't just stop loving him. It's not possible. Oh, what shall I do?' She buried her face in her hands.

Ricarda stroked her hair. 'Darling, I do sympathize with you and it's an almost impossible situation for you, with Benno living right here in the hotel. You need peace and quiet to think things through.' She was silent for a moment, then she went on, 'I think you should have a total change of scene. Why don't I write to your Aunt Grete in Munich and see if you can go and stay with her?

Your cousin Olga's only a little older than you are. Perhaps you could become friends.'

Anything was better than staying in Berlin. Viktoria welcomed the suggestion thankfully.

The ball given in celebration of the royal wedding had proved to Franz Jankowski that his gnarled fingers no longer possessed their old agility, nor had he any heart for playing since Georg had left him. Somehow the music seemed to have gone out of his soul. 'I'm nearly seventy, Herr Direktor,' he told Karl. 'I think it's time for me to retire. Herr Ullstein is willing for me to stay on at the newspaper on a part-time basis and that will give me enough money to live on.'

'I'm sorry, but I understand. We're none of us getting any younger, Franz. I'm fifty-five this year, and Max is nearly as old. Where have the years gone, eh?'

Luise was devastated when she heard Franz's news, throwing her arms round him and bursting into tears. 'But Herr Jankowski, you're my friend! You can't leave me!'

'You should have friends of your own age, Fraeulein Luise. You don't need an old man like me now you're a young lady,' he said, although he was deeply touched. Her companionship had been very valuable to him through the past, difficult years. He disengaged himself gently from her embrace and left quickly, fearful lest he, too, should start to weep.

Luise rushed into her mother's room to tell her the dreadful news. 'Mama, Mama, Herr Jankowski's leaving!' She was still sobbing bitterly and her hair was awry.

Ricarda looked up from the letter she had just received from Grete Fischer and held out her arms to Luise. 'Luischen, my pet, don't upset yourself so. You'll see him again.' Then, as Luise's sobs subsided, she said, 'You and Vicki have both been invited to Munich to stay with your cousin, Olga. Would you like to go?'

'To Munich?' Luise blew her nose. 'What, just Vicki and me?' When her mother nodded, she said, 'Oh, yes, please. Oh, Mama, when can we go?'

If only Viktoria could reconcile herself as swiftly to the loss of Peter von Biederstein as Luise to Franz's departure, life would be quite simple, Ricarda thought wryly.

Chapter Nine

The Fischers lived in an old, narrow house under the shadow of the Peterskirche in the centre of Munich. Professor Fischer was in his mid-fifties, his bushy eyebrows and his beard grey, his head almost bald, while Grete, who would soon be fifty, was a plump, comfortable person, looking very much as Klothilde had at that age. Viktoria and Luise immediately felt at home with them.

Olga was a different matter. Obviously instructed by her parents to make her cousins feel welcome, she accompanied them to their room on their arrival. Three years older than Viktoria, she was a thin girl, with a pale oval face dominated by large grey eyes, and fine hair drawn back in an inelegant bun at the nape of her neck. Luise, always eager to make friends, opened her suitcase. 'Would you like to see my new frock?' she asked Olga. It was a miniature version of one of her mother's, in vivid emerald to match her eyes.

Olga shrugged. 'Clothes are boring, just another example of bourgeois values.'

Luise bit her lip, unsure what bourgeois meant and rather hurt by her cousin's scornful tone.

'Munich seems a very beautiful city,' Viktoria said, hoping to fare better on a more neutral topic. 'You must have a lot of fun here.'

'Fun?' Olga raised an eyebrow. 'I enjoy my studies at the university, that's true, but I don't have much time for pleasure.'

'What are you studying?' Viktoria asked, politely.

'History, but my main interest is politics. I'm a communist.'

'Oh, I see. How interesting.' Viktoria's secret reading of *Vorwaerts* had vaguely familiarized her with socialist ideals and she had heard her father ranting against Bolsheviks and Mensheviks, but she was not at all sure what they were.

'I've met Lenin. After the revolution, my friend Reinhardt and I will go with him to Moscow.'

Viktoria took note of the names Reinhardt and Lenin, determined to learn more about them, but Luise asked aghast, 'Revolution? What revolution?'

'The world revolution, when the workers of the world unite against the capitalists. The time has nearly come. We almost succeeded in Russia in 1905 and in Warsaw a year later. Soon it will be Germany's turn.'

'*Donnerwetter!*' Luise exclaimed, when she had gone. 'She doesn't like clothes and she has no time for fun. Why did we come here, Vicki? I think Olga's boring.'

Viktoria was too stunned to reprimand her sister for swearing. 'I think Olga is very intelligent,' she said slowly, then she ruffled her sister's hair. 'And I'm sure we'll like Bavaria.'

She was right. Everything about it was different from Berlin. The warm, predominantly wooden architecture of the houses was intriguing. The mild, almost sultry, southern air first enervated, then invigorated the two girls, tanning their cheeks and giving them keen appetites. Never could they forget the tantalizing proximity of the Bavarian lakes and the rugged Alps, distant, white-capped sentinels, so enticingly unlike the flat Brandenburg landscape to which they were accustomed.

It was soon apparent that the people were also very different. To begin with, they had difficulty in understanding their soft, lilting dialect and had to adapt to a whole new vocabulary, but soon Luise, in particular, with her innate gift for mimicry was, to the delight of Uncle Gottfried and Aunt Grete, speaking fluent Bavarian.

They took the two girls on many excursions through Munich and, further afield, to the mountains and the Starnberg Lake, where King Ludwig II had been found drowned after living a mere 102 days in his fairy-tale castle of Neuschwanstein. Luise was thrilled by the tall turrets, soaring out of the pine trees high above the Forggen Lake. 'Imagine what it would be like to live here,' she breathed.

The girls' enthusiasm pleased their hosts. 'Marry nice Bavarian boys and settle in Munich,' Uncle Gottfried told them. 'Berlin is a terrible place. Its people have no humour, they never laugh. They don't know what living is about.'

'Uncle Gottfried,' Luise teased him, 'be fair; even Bavarians don't laugh all the time!'

He smiled. 'Ah, you mean Olga? She's very like I was at her age. Don't worry, she'll become more phlegmatic as she gets older.'

Luise looked at him doubtfully, sure that Olga would never

change, just as she knew they would never have anything in common.

Viktoria enjoyed their outings, but she was far more interested in her relatives' ideas. Every evening, new people turned up at the Fischer home, fellow students of Olga and pupils of her father, young men and women, who sat round discussing unorthodox political ideas into the small hours of the morning. Possibly because they conflicted so greatly with those she heard at home, she found herself fascinated by them — and became increasingly conscious of her own ignorance. What, she wondered, was the difference between socialism as practised by Uncle Gottfried and the communism advocated by Olga and her friends? In the end, she summoned up the courage to ask.

Her uncle answered her smilingly. 'I belong to the Social Democrat Party, which now holds over a third of the seats in the Reichstag. We represent over four million voters, nearly all of whom come from the working classes and we believe we are entitled to a government of the people by the people. But political and every other kind of power still lies almost exclusively in the hands of the landowning Junkers and the military who, answerable only to the Emperor, determine the way Germany is ruled. Our representatives are kept away from all positions of power.'

'Ach, socialism,' Olga snorted impatiently, 'that's not enough. What we need is a totally classless society, in which all conventional government is done away with and people give according to their means — and receive according to their needs. We must fight for a proletarian revolution, which will lead us to a communist society.'

Uncle Gottfried shook his head. 'I thought like you once, Olga, but I've had to change my mind. What you want is idealistic and incapable of achievement. You're assuming that all people are equal — and they're not. You cannot achieve equality overnight.'

Viktoria couldn't get used to Olga talking about a revolution as if she really believed it would happen. That, and everything else about Munich, was rather like being in a foreign country, where the landscape, language, buildings and all ideas were quite different from home. Mama was right in one thing, at least. She was certainly having a change of scene. But, despite all this, she could not forget Peter.

While a passionate debate continued to rage between father and daughter, she wondered how to phrase her next question. In a lull,

234

she asked, in what she hoped was a casual tone, 'If the socialists, or communists, gained power, would that put an end to class differences?'

'How do you mean?'

'Well, if power were taken away from the Junkers, as you're suggesting, and redistributed among the workers, would that make me a social equal of, say, a Count von Biederstein?'

Luise looked up from her book and smirked.

'Of course it would! After the proletarian revolution, there will be no more aristocracy,' Olga replied.

Uncle Gottfried shook his head. 'It wouldn't happen that easily. It might take many years.'

'Why shouldn't she be the equal of a von Biederstein?' Olga demanded.

'So far as I'm concerned, she is, but it's going to take his family very much longer to become convinced.'

Maybe Olga scented a potential convert to her cause, but certainly after this she took a greater interest in Viktoria and, as the days went by, a friendship began to develop between the two girls, despite their very different personalities and backgrounds. After about a week, she trusted her sufficiently to bring Reinhardt Meyer to the house and introduce him to her cousins. 'This is my friend, Reinhardt,' she said, proudly, holding his arm possessively, 'he's a journalist.'

Startled by a new note in her cousin's voice, Viktoria realized that this was more than just a friendship. She sensed that Olga was in love with Reinhardt, which pleased her, for it seemed to offer them a further point of contact, although no two men could have been more different than Peter and Reinhardt.

Reinhardt was tall and gangling, with thinning brown hair and glasses. His trousers did not seem to meet either his shirt or his boots, his hair stuck up on end and his spectacle lenses needed cleaning. However, he greeted both her and Luise in a friendly manner, then asked in delight, 'If you come from Berlin, you must know Rosa Luxemburg and Karl Liebknecht?'

'I think I've heard their names,' Viktoria said doubtfully.

'Liebknecht's father was the founder of the Social Democrat Party and editor of *Vorwaerts*,' Olga told her severely, 'while Rosa Luxemburg is a wonderful person. She led the revolutions in St Petersburg and Warsaw. She and Karl Liebknecht have given their lives for the cause.'

'Liebknecht is a pacifist,' Reinhardt added. 'He's violently anti-war.'

As a vigorous argument ensued on the merits and demerits of various politicians, Luise stared at him, wondering how anybody could be a violent pacifist. Reinhardt intrigued her, for he had a certain charm about him, if only that he had smiled at her when they met, while all Olga's other friends had virtually ignored her. Here was someone, she decided, of whom she could ask a question which was bothering her. 'Why do all socialists look so untidy? Isn't it possible to be attractive and still be a socialist?'

Reinhardt looked at her in astonishment. 'Appearances mean nothing. What matters is what goes on in people's hearts and minds.'

Luise grimaced. 'Well, I think it's possible to look beautiful and be clever, like I am.'

'Luise!' her sister exclaimed, shocked.

'I don't know how you put up with all that endless rubbish about socialism,' Luise yawned, as they changed into their night-clothes to get into bed. 'It just sends me to sleep.'

'You should listen. What they're doing could affect your life one day.'

'If only they'd do something, instead of just talking about it. Do you know what? I think you're going to become as boring as Olga if you stay here much longer. Peter von Biederstein's preferable to her!'

'What do you know about Peter?'

'Oh, I keep my eyes and ears open,' and before Viktoria could react, she blew out the candle.

On several occasions Viktoria was tempted to confide in Olga her true reasons for coming to Munich, but somehow the right moment never arose, and whenever Olga spoke of Reinhardt it was as her comrade, not as her lover. Viktoria suspected that Olga would be incapable of understanding her feelings for Peter, would disapprove of him anyway and would think very little of Benno as the son of a capitalist industrialist. In the end, it was easiest to say nothing.

As the train drew into Munich station to take them home, Olga told her, 'I hope to come soon to Berlin with Reinhardt. When I've passed my finals, I'm going to try to work with Rosa Luxemburg and Karl Liebknecht. I have to be at the centre of things.'

'Let us know when you're coming.'

236

'You'd better be careful what you say when you meet Papa,' Luise warned her, giggling.

Uncle Gottfried laughed. 'Yes, he's always been loyal to the Kaiser, hasn't he? Well, it takes all sorts to make a world.'

'Come the revolution,' Olga stated pompously, 'the Kaiser will be forced to abdicate.'

'That would be a shame,' Luise said. 'I'm rather fond of him.' Viktoria shot her an acid look.

'I hope my family hasn't bored you too much with their politics,' Aunt Grete said, while Gottfried requested the guard to keep an eye on the two unchaperoned girls during their long journey.

'On the contrary,' Viktoria assured her, 'I've learned a lot. Thank you so much for having us to stay.'

Luise was thankful just to be getting away at long last and, as the train eventually pulled out of Munich, she declared with a huge sigh, 'You can say what you like, Vicki, but nothing in this world will ever convince me that Olga Fischer isn't the most boring person on earth.'

As the powerful steam train sped through the countryside, Viktoria sat in a corner seat immersed in her thoughts, while Luise gazed out at the passing countryside, stifling an urge to do or say something outrageous, merely to celebrate her sense of freedom. Towards midday, as the train drew into Nuremberg, she also began to feel decidedly hungry, despite the large breakfast the Fischers had given them to see them through their journey. At that moment, their privacy was disturbed by two young men, who politely asked if they minded them joining their compartment.

The guard immediately appeared in the doorway. 'Excuse me, gentlemen, but this carriage is reserved. If you'll come with me.'

They were obviously brothers, the elder dressed in army uniform and probably a year or two older than Viktoria, while the younger one was somewhere between them in age, possibly sixteen, Luise decided, studying him with unconcealed interest. Both had olive skin, curly dark brown hair and slightly tilted brown eyes, which, in the case of the younger brother, glinted mischievously at Luise. 'Oh, we don't mind sharing our compartment,' she assured the guard.

'We shall protect the young ladies with our lives,' the younger brother grinned, nonchalantly giving a handful of change to the man.

The bribe was far more effective than Uncle Gottfried's prudish instructions. 'Thank you, sir. Well, the train is rather full,' the guard said, 'so, if the ladies don't object ...'

Delightedly, Luise watched them take their seats, then, as the train gained momentum again, the young man opened a small bag and asked his older brother, 'Do you want something to eat, Sepp?'

Sepp shook his head and pulled a book out of his pocket.

'Will it disturb you ladies if I eat?' the boy asked.

Viktoria said, 'No, of course not,' and returned to her dreaming.

Luise stared in amazement as he spread a napkin over his knees and undid various little packages to display a mouth-watering array of cold meats, cheese, bread and even a dish of pickled vegetables. Then he produced a corkscrew and opened a bottle of red wine, which he poured into a small glass and raised to Luise. 'To your health.'

'Surely you're not going to eat all that by yourself?'

'Don't you think I could?'

Reluctantly, she nodded.

'Or would you like to help me? If so, I think I could spare you a bit, since Sepp isn't hungry, though first you'll have to introduce yourself. I never share my food with strangers.' He grinned.

Luise glanced doubtfully at her sister, then told him, 'My name is Luise Jochum and this is my sister, Viktoria.'

Carefully, he put the plate and serviette on the seat beside him and stood up, then bent low over her hand and kissed it. 'Rudi Nowak, at your service, gracious lady.'

She laughed delightedly, as he repeated the same performance with Viktoria, who looked less pleased. 'Herr Nowak, pray don't let my sister trouble you.'

'Nor my brother trouble you,' Sepp's voice said from the opposite corner. 'Ladies, I am Josef Nowak, usually known as Sepp.' He bowed, a brief smile lighting his face, then returned to his reading.

'Now the formalities are over, let me offer you some food, Fraeulein Jochum.'

Without any further ado, Luise took the plate Rudi handed her and started eating. 'Where are you going?'

'Home, to Berlin. Sepp's been stationed at Nuremberg, but now he's been moved to Lichterfelde, just outside Berlin. And you?'

'To Berlin. We've just been to Munich to stay with relatives, but now we're going home. My father owns the Hotel Quadriga.'

Rudi Nowak looked suitably impressed. 'My father's a tailor. I'm supposed to be learning to be one, too, but I don't like it.' He pulled a face, 'It's boring.'

Sepp looked up from his book. 'Don't worry, it won't be long before they have you in the army! Later this year, when you're seventeen!'

Fascinated, Luise stared from one to the other of them. 'Are you in the cavalry?' she asked Sepp.

'No, I was in the artillery, but now I'm learning to fly.'

'Fly? What? Airships, like Count Zeppelin?'

'No,' Rudi interrupted scornfully, 'Sepp's going to fly fighter aeroplanes.'

'Oh,' Luise sighed wistfully, although she knew nothing about planes, 'I'd like to fly in an aeroplane.' She turned to Sepp. 'Would you take me for a flight in one?'

Sepp smiled at her, not at all as though she were only a child. 'Perhaps one day.'

'I'd like that.'

'As much as you'd like some apple tart?' Rudi asked.

'Well, about the same. You know, it's very kind of you to share your meal with me.'

'I hate to see a lady starve,' Rudi informed her seriously.

Luise was in seventh heaven. For the first time in her life, two young men were paying attention to her and not Viktoria. For once, she was the centre of attraction and that knowledge made her brave. 'You must come to the Hotel Quadriga sometime and have coffee and cakes with me.'

'Are you sure that will be allowed?'

Privately wondering what her father would say if the Nowak brothers suddenly appeared, she looked across to Viktoria for reassurance, but her sister's eyes were closed. 'Oh, yes, of course it will be all right.'

Rudi cleared away the empty plates and produced a pack of cards. 'Can you play Skat?' Luise shook her head. 'Then I'll teach you. Since it wouldn't be fair to play for money, we'll play for buttons.'

Luise won three games in a row hands down. 'I thought you said you'd never played before,' Rudi said plaintively.

'I'm just a quick learner.'

She could hardly believe it when Viktoria suddenly stood up

and reached her coat down from the rack. 'We're nearly there, Luise.' As the train drew into the Anhalter Station, she leaned out of the window. 'There's Papa!'

At the carriage door, while his brother looked on with an amused smile, Rudi shook hands with Luise, then said, 'Any time you need something to eat, you know where to find me.'

Sepp nudged his brother's elbow. 'I thought you were a gentleman,' he said, lifting the girls' cases down from the rack and placing them on the platform. Then, with his pack on his back and bowing quickly at Karl, he marched Rudi swiftly down the platform.

Karl frowned at their departing backs. 'Who are those men?'

'Their name is Nowak,' Luise said, watching them leave with obvious reluctance. 'Sepp is in the army and Rudi is learning to be a tailor like his father, although he's bored with it ... And he's coming to see me at the hotel,' she added defiantly.

'Luise, don't you realize it isn't done for a young lady to issue invitatations to strange men? Viktoria, what were you thinking of ...?' Then he put his arms round each of their shoulders. 'Girls, it's good to have you back. Did you enjoy yourselves in Munich?'

Luise noticed that Viktoria, very diplomatically, said nothing about the endless political arguments and concentrated on the Bavarian sights they had seen. Neither mentioned Reinhardt Meyer.

A couple of weeks later, Rudi Nowak turned up at the Hotel Quadriga, dressed in his best suit, a cheeky grin on his face. Smoothly, the Hall Porter intercepted him. 'Can I help you, sir?'

'I've come to see Fraeulein Luise Jochum.'

'You have an appointment, sir?'

Rudi was not a bit abashed. 'I'm a friend of the family.'

'I'll tell the Herr Direktor you're here. What's your name?'

Rudi stood his ground. 'Nowak, Rudolf Nowak.' But when he saw a stern-faced Karl Jochum approaching, he felt less sure of himself. 'I met Fraeulein Luise on the train, so I thought I would come to ask after her health.'

'My daughter is in excellent health, thank you, and she is far too young to have gentlemen friends. So, Herr Nowak, good day.'

That lunchtime, Luise was severely reprimanded. 'You're only thirteen,' her father admonished, 'and what's more, I think you said his father is only a tailor? I'm not having the sons of tradespeople running around after you, Luise.'

Afterwards, Luise asked her sister crossly, 'Why is it all right for you to have admirers and not me?'

Viktoria looked disapproving. 'You're only a child, Luischen. You're not old enough for admirers. And besides, I didn't like Rudi Nowak. I thought his attitude was very flippant, although his brother seemed a little better bred.'

'You're just jealous because they didn't take any notice of you,' Luise said spitefully. 'Anyway, it's all right for you, with Peter and Benno!'

Benno missed Viktoria dreadfully while she was in Munich. He had been saddened but not deterred by her refusal to marry him, for although many young women were married by the time they were nineteen, he accepted her view that she was too young to commit herself and he had no desire to force her will. At least she had not said she didn't love him.

His father was frequently in Berlin that autumn and winter, so that the two men were working closely together. 'The situation in the Balkans is beginning to look highly explosive,' Baron Heinrich said, one day, soberly. 'One false move and there will be war.'

'You believe the Russians are going to support Bosnia and Herzegovina in their claim to join Serbia?'

'Yes, and this time I doubt very much that the Kaiser will intervene for peace. He'll side with Austria. He and Emperor Franz Josef are just looking for a pretext to declare war on Russia.'

'Why? Economically and industrially, we're stronger than any other nation in Europe. Why do we need to show our military superiority when we're so much stronger in every other way?'

His father sighed. 'Benno, we're militarily stronger too. Why else do you think we've steadily been increasing the size of the army and building up our navy? Think of the *Prussia*. We didn't build her for show. She was built to fight.'

Benno thought of the huge battleship, which was currently touring the North Sea, receiving great admiration from the Germans and causing great consternation to the British, who were rumoured to be trying to copy her. The Navy League could have no better floating ambassador. 'But why do we have to fight?'

'The Emperor wants an empire,' Baron Heinrich said ponderously, fingering the decorations on his Reserve Officer's uniform, a uniform that Benno was also now entitled to wear, but chose not to. 'He wants an empire over which the sun never sets, like the

241

British. Even the Dutch and Portuguese have bigger empires than we Germans. But the only way he will obtain one is by war.'

'And do you believe we would win?'

'Against Russia, I don't see why not but, because of the alliances, war with Russia would also mean war with France, which would mean fighting on two fronts. That thought perturbs me greatly, because we are simply not strong enough.'

'If France were involved, would that mean England would also be drawn in?'

'First, they'd have to cross the Channel, but yes, ultimately, it could mean a full-scale European war.'

'We have the arms,' Benno said, thinking of all the vast Kraus gun-shops.

'And over the next months, we're going to be working even harder to produce even more, but that doesn't mean they have to be used, boy. We'll produce them and we'll sell them to the German Ordnance Department, but, at the same time, I'll be doing everything in my power to prevent war breaking out.'

Benno looked away from him, afraid that his face would betray his thoughts. At that moment, he hated his father almost as much as he hated Kraus Industries, for it seemed the Baron's sole objective was to exploit the dangerous situation in which his country found itself to his own maximum profit, appearing to support his Kaiser, while at the same time plotting against him. If war did not break out, Kraus would not lose. If it did, it would profit immensely.

During the next few months, Benno spent every minute of his waking day at Kraus Village, working — as his father had predicted — harder than he had ever done in his life before. No sooner did he drop exhaustedly into his bed at night than a page boy was knocking on his door telling him it was time to get up. As he shaved, snatched a quick breakfast and got into the chauffeur-driven car waiting to take him to Wedding, his thoughts were absorbed by the pile of orders for ammunition waiting for the company from the Ordnance Department. In the armaments factories in the Ruhr and Silesia, he knew his brother was coping with similar demands for siege guns, rifles, howitzers and torpedoes, while the vast steel mills were producing the armour plating for motor vehicles, battleships and submarines. Soon Benno had absolutely no doubt that, whatever his father might try to do to avert it, war was on the very near horizon.

During those days, he saw little of Viktoria, nor when he did manage to spend a few moments with her did he raise again the subject of marriage. He still loved her more than anybody else in the world, but, somehow, the threat of war put a very different complexion on everything, including marriage.

On 28 June 1914, the heir to the Austrian throne, Archduke Franz Ferdinand, and his wife, the Czech Countess Sophie Chotek, were assassinated by Gavrilo Princip, a schoolboy Serbian fanatic in the Bosnian capital of Sarajevo. The Kaiser, incensed at the murder of his personal friend, denounced Serbia without any reservations and insisted to Vienna that she must be punished. Then, to everyone's horror, he went cruising in Norway.

The atmosphere in Berlin grew tense. There were increasing numbers of soldiers on the streets, while hotel bars and cafés were full of handsome young lieutenants, dancing, flirting and taunting passers-by. The popular operetta *Hurra! Hussar!* enjoyed record audiences. A number of reservists were called up, although Benno and Ernst were not among them; being in charge of munitions factories, they were exempt. All over the country, troops were being moved from one place to another, among them a unit of the Hussars, transferred from Danzig to Karlshorst.

By this time, every room in the Hotel Quadriga was taken, not, on this occasion, with guests in festive mood to celebrate a wedding, but by men with long, serious faces, there to discuss and debate, some of them with the aim of trying to prevent a war, others glorying in the prospect.

Baron Heinrich was there, of course, and so, too, was Benno's uncle, Colonel Count Ewald von Biederstein. Benno attended one dinner at which they were both present. 'If Russia has any sense, she'll back down,' his father said. 'She'd be mad to provoke a war at this time.'

'But it is a war she can only lose,' his uncle declared confidently. 'No, damn it all, Heinrich, if Russia wants a war, let her have one!'

'I know the Emperor loves travelling,' the Baron fumed, 'but does he have to go now? Even the Chancellor seems unable to contact him!'

'We should mobilize and have done with it. The troops are ready. Damn it all, even my nephew Peter's been transferred to Karlshorst. He's just spoiling for a fight.'

Benno stared at them in silence, the news of Peter von Biederstein's presence in Berlin merely serving to increase his forebodings.

He felt as if they were all on the very edge of a precipice and, for some reason, Peter's arrival would cause them all to topple over. However, he had little time to brood, for he was quite simply too busy. During the days and weeks that followed he frequently even slept in his office at Kraus Village, lacking the time even to drive back to the Hotel Quadriga.

The murder of Archduke Franz Ferdinand had less impact on the Jochums than it would normally have had, because they had personal worries of their own. That spring, Ricarda's father had contracted bronchitis, from which he had never really recovered. Crippled with arthritis, he had been bedridden ever since and Ricarda, who had engaged a nurse for him, spent most of her days at his side in Charlottenburg, reading and talking to him.

Viktoria, who had always loved her grandfather dearly, desperately wished there was something she could do for him, but, as Ricarda told her, there was nothing. 'Don't be sad, darling. Dr Blattner assures me he isn't in any pain. And he is an old man now.' But, what with Opa's illness and the news from Sarajevo, Viktoria could find little to relieve her depression.

Then, one glorious day in early July, when Ricarda was with her father, a page boy knocked on the door and announced that Lieutenant Count Peter von Biederstein was waiting downstairs. Without more ado, Viktoria glanced at herself in the mirror, then flew down to the foyer.

He was leaning over the hall porter's desk, his helmet under his arm, tapping his cane against an elegantly booted leg, discussing the results of the latest horse race at the Hoppegarten. With a brief last comment to the hall porter, he moved swiftly towards her.

'Viktoria, my dear, how charming you look.' He bent low over her hand. 'Can you spare time to take coffee with a humble soldier?'

During the days that followed, Peter spent every free minute with Viktoria. She saw other girls gazing at him admiringly, but he never showed any interest in them, nor did he ever mention other girlfriends, although she constantly dreaded hearing the name of Ilse von Schennig. It was as if he assumed a relationship existed between them that did not need clarifying and Viktoria did not question it. It was sufficient for her to be with him, to hear his voice, to feel his hand in hers, to gaze into his eyes and to know that where he went, she went too.

There was a popular song heard everywhere that summer of 1914 in Berlin, sung in every café, played by every orchestra:
'It was a day of roses in August
When the Guards had to march out ...'
It was to this tune that Viktoria and Peter danced, along with thousands of other young lieutenants and their girlfriends, fiancées and wives, a gay, brightly-coloured company. They danced, they laughed and they sang, borne along by the tide of tension and excitement that surged through the city.

As the threat of war drew nearer, a subtle change in their relationship slowly seemed to occur, drawing them closer together, as if they both realized that the glorious summer days of roses weren't going to last for ever. The feeling of uncertainty around them increased and a sense of urgency permeated their relationship. Peter, particularly, became very gay, as though he knew time was running out and he needed to pack as much living as possible into every day.

One night in the dark of the Tiergarten he drew her to him, tipped her face towards him and kissed her on the lips for the first time with a fierce passion. Viktoria clung to him desperately. All over Berlin other young lieutenants were taking other young women in their arms and kissing them, but none of them were experiencing the yearning, the longing and desire of herself and Peter. What they had was unique and it included the certainty that if anybody found out about them, their love affair would be doomed.

But nobody had any time to notice them. Karl's whole attention was on the hotel and the political situation. Ricarda's mind was on her father. Benno was engrossed with Kraus Chemie. Peter's parents were in Fuerstenmark, while Count Ewald was preparing for war. And Luise — well, Luise was only a child.

'I want to be alone with you,' Peter mumured.

'So do I,' Viktoria whispered back.

The next day they drove out to Heiligensee. Their conversation was stilted during the journey, Viktoria's mood alternating between acute nervousness and elated anticipation. When they arrived, Peter paid the taxi driver, took the key from Viktoria's hand and unlocked the door. Then he locked it again behind them.

One dim table lamp illuminated the room, the open windows onto the verandah allowing the mild summer air to penetrate the thick handwoven curtains. Peter threw his jacket over the back of a chair and drew Viktoria to him. It was the first time they had ever been alone together, yet as he took her in his arms, she felt as if this were the most natural moment of her life, one for which she had been born and one which had to arrive almost inevitably. Through the thin silk of his shirt, she could feel his warm body, the beating of his heart against her chest. His hands ran gently over the bodice of her fine lawn dress, cupping her tiny breasts, stroking her flat stomach, feeling her hips, while all the time he pulled her closer to him, moulding their bodies together.

A sensation of liquid heat consumed her, frightening in its intensity. Shaken, she tried to move away, trembling with closed eyes. 'Viktoria,' Peter's voice said, gruff and low, 'Viktoria, I need you.' He took her hand and led her to the couch where, with his arm around her shoulder, his fingers digging into the bare flesh below her collarbone, he forced her round to look at him. His face was pale, his eyes deep pools beneath his fine dark brows, his lips slightly parted under the soft brown moustache.

Wide-eyed now, she gazed at him hungrily, filled with an almost unbearable longing to feel and be felt, to touch and be touched, to hold and be held, to have and to be had, to possess and to be possessed. 'I love you, Peter. I shall always love you.' Wonderingly, she put her fingers up to touch his face, trace the skin under his eyes, touch the corners of his lips, smooth his cheeks, know the curve of his chin and the hollows of his temples.

With great tenderness, he undid the little buttons of her dress, slipping it off her shoulders, kissing the white skin of her neck and her upper arms. Then he stood, holding his hands out to her, raising her, so that the dress fell to the ground. Next, he took off her thin chemise, running his hands lightly over her body. One by one, savouring each moment, he peeled off her petticoat, her stockings, her shoes and her lacy pantaloons, then, putting one arm round her shoulders and the other under her knees, he lifted her up, carried her upstairs into a bedroom and laid her on the bed.

In the dim light, she saw him take off his own clothes, a white shadow, almost a phantom shape, thin and firm and strong, beautiful in his masculinity. He lay down on top of her.

Finally, he was in her and they were whole, a complete person at last, rolling and tumbling, limbs intertwined, laughing, crying, learning, knowing, then rising, soaring upwards and outwards and onwards towards a fine, high, distant peak of glorious oneness. It hurt, but it was such a delicious pain. She buried her face in his shoulder, her teeth biting into his flesh, to stifle her cries. Then the journey continued, so that the here and now ceased to exist, giving way to a mighty, world-shattering explosion within her, after which she knew nothing could ever, ever be the same again.

Very much later, when the sky outside was dark and their bodies were faintly luminous outlines against the bedclothes, very much later, when the earth had stilled itself and breathing was quiet and even, and the silence was no longer so fragile that it could be shattered by unnatural sound, Viktoria said hesitantly. 'Peter, I love you so much.'

There was no answer. She sat up, leaning on one elbow, to gaze at him. His eyes were closed, his eyelashes long and dark on his cheeks. His breathing was slow. Peter von Biederstein was asleep. For a moment, she wanted to burst into tears. She had just experienced one of the most exquisite moments of her life, but now it was gone, she felt a sudden need for reassurance. Already within her there were twinges of doubt, as to whether she had done the wrong thing, if, having given herself to him, he was now going to despise her. She wanted words of love, comforting arms around her, acknowledgement that he treasured the greatest gift any woman could give a man. But, instead of that, Peter was sleeping.

Gently, she shook his shoulder. His eyes opened immediately and he instinctively reached for the gold half-hunter beside the bed. Then he turned and stared at her, as if he had forgotten her presence. 'Vicki, look at the time! We must get dressed. I must get back to Karlshorst.'

Biting back her tears, she watched him jump out of bed and, with a haste she assumed he had learned in the army, pull on his clothes. 'Peter,' she asked timidly, 'did I make you happy?'

She got out of bed and, turning her back on him, so that he shouldn't see her, dressed herself. It all suddenly seemed so sad and sordid, such a terrible end to a wonderful evening.

Before he unlocked the door to let them out, Peter kissed her lightly on the forehead. 'Yes, Vicki, you were wonderful.'

The taxi driver they discovered in Heiligensee's village square had amazing news for them. 'His Majesty's back. Came back by a special train, he did. The Chancellor met him at the railway station.'

'Jolly good!' Peter exclaimed. 'That means the end to all the indecision. We'll mobilize now!'

Viktoria sank silently back into the padded leather seat, wishing she were already home. Never had the fifteen miles from Heiligensee to Berlin seemed so far. Her legs were trembling and there was a sick feeling in her stomach. 'Why, Vicki, old girl, what's the matter?' asked Peter.

'Frightened for the Lieutenant, are you, Miss?' the cabby asked, swivelling round in his seat to study her face. She turned and stared out of the window. 'Now, don't you worry about him. Before you know what's happened the war will be over and he'll be back, a row of medals on his chest. Isn't that right, Lieutenant?'

'That's right. In six weeks we'll have taken Paris and St Petersburg. I'll be back by Christmas, more's the pity!'

It was more than she could bear. Tears welled in her eyes and she buried her face in her hands.

'Bah, women!' the taxi driver grumbled. 'Most glorious moment in a man's life and they burst into tears.' He turned his attention to the roadway, as Peter put his arm round Viktoria's shoulders.

'Peter, I can't bear the thought of you going to war.'

'I'll come back.'

'And then what, Peter? What will we do then?'

'Why, we'll see each other again, no doubt. Damn it all, Vicki, don't say you regret this afternoon?'

'No-o-o.' But already the ecstasy of their time together had been replaced by anxiety. 'Peter, what happens if I have a child?'

He gazed at her in horror, then said confidently, 'I'm sure you won't. No, it's not possible.'

'But if you are away ...'

He looked rather abashed. 'Must say I hadn't thought of that. But, if it did happen, I'd make sure you never lacked for anything.'

She waited for his assurance that he would marry her, but the words did not come.

When they reached the hotel, he told the cabby to wait and take him on to Karlshorst. As he helped Viktoria out of the cab, he said, 'Wish me luck in battle.'

'Good luck. And goodbye.' She gazed at him from huge, tragic eyes.

'To the confusion of our enemies!' he cried gaily, then he was gone with not a single word of love.

In the Reichstag, parliament — including the Social Democrats — voted unanimously for war. Delightedly, the Kaiser declared, 'I see

248

no parties any more, only Germans!' On the first day of August, Germany declared war on Russia, and two days later on France. The long months of waiting were over.

As from a great distance, Viktoria watched the troops march through the Brandenburg Gate, their arms raised in confident salute, their wives, children, sisters and sweethearts walking beside them, way beyond the city boundaries. As from another world, she heard their voices chanting:

'Gloria, Viktoria,
With heart and hand
For the Fatherland — for the Fa-ther-land!'

For them, war seemed a glorious thing. As the Prussians had returned in triumphant procession through the Gate in 1871, now they marched confidently westwards under the statue of the Quadriga, the Goddess of Victory.

But for Viktoria, life seemed to have drawn to a blinding halt. Peter had given her his arms, his lips and his body, but he had not given her his heart. No, he had not given her that single, most vital thing. He had given her everything except love. And now, he was gone.

Others went too. The family went *en masse* to the Anhalter Station to see Count Ewald leave for the front. Karl walked stiffly upright, Ricarda's arm in his, gazing around him with pride at the seething mass of troops. 'Makes me wish I could go too.' When they found the Count, he shook hands fervently with his old friend. 'Ewald, you give those Frenchmen what they deserve, eh?'

The Count slapped his thigh. 'Been looking forward to this for years! Damn it all, one of the few things I ever wanted was to have a good skirmish with the French! Now I've got my opportunity!'

Viktoria stared miserably at the long train with its plushly upholstered, first class compartments reserved for officers, the ranks on hard wooden seats or packed, standing, in the corridors, and behind them, the horses, their forage, the huge cannon they would have to pull and the ammunition they would fire.

'Wonderful thing, the railway, eh?' Count Ewald said. 'In the old days, we should have had to ride to the front, now the railway takes us, our men and our horses right into Belgium. Luise, come over here, young lady, and I'll introduce you to Elvira, my favourite mare. Your father will remember her great-granddam, who was also called Elvira.'

Luise's face was aglow, her eyes shining, as the Count showed

249

her the horse which was standing obediently in a truck. Viktoria wondered how her sister could look so happy, when the Count, of whom they were all so fond, was leaving for battle, possibly never to come back. Could none of them see what a dreadful thing this war was — and how it was already tearing her apart?

'Well, if it isn't the two charming Miss Jochums!' a voice suddenly exclaimed.

Luise spun on her heel and stared at the young man dressed in private's uniform, his beady eyes smiling slightly slantingly from beneath his spiked helmet. 'Herr Nowak!' she cried.

Rudi Nowak saluted Count Ewald, bowed to Karl, then took each of the ladies' hands in turn, bowing over them and kissing their gloves.

Karl, apparently forgetting he had once turned Rudi Nowak out of his hotel, now eyed his uniform approvingly. 'Ah, yes, Herr Nowak. So you, too, are going to fight for the Fatherland?'

'Yes, sir, albeit only as a humble private, sir.'

'Are you also with the cavalry?'

'With the infantry, sir. My skills on a rocking horse failed to impress the generals, so they decided I had better stick to my own two feet.' Rudi grinned mischievously. 'Not that I intend to remain a foot soldier for long. If my brother is considered safe in an aeroplane, I think they should entrust me with a motor car.'

'Your brother is a pilot, Private Nowak?'

'Yes, sir. He's already with his flight division as an observer, but he'll soon be promoted and then he'll actually be able to fly. Flying is all he lives for.'

Luise shook her head wistfully. 'I think it's all so romantic. Oh, I wish I were a man, so that I could go to war.'

Noticing Karl's attention momentarily distracted, Rudi took Luise's arm and led her a short way up the platform. 'I'll try to bring you some delicacies back from Belgium. I'd hate you to starve while I'm away!'

At that moment, a voice bellowed in his ear. 'Nowak!'

His smile was wiped from his face, as he turned to find his sergeant standing there. He clicked his heels and stood to attention. 'Sergeant?'

'What do you think you're doing? Where's your rifle, you horrible little man? Get back to your unit. You're on a charge!'

Rudi Nowak sighed and winked at Luise.

'*At the double!*'

Forgetting his pride, Rudi ran back through the amused bystanders towards his unit on platform eight.

'Maybe I don't want to be a soldier after all,' Luise said thoughtfully, watching him as he ran.

'Cheeky young blighter!' Count Ewald laughed. 'Reminds me a bit of myself at his age. I always had an eye for the ladies too, if you remember, Karl? Well, it's time to say goodbye. Until we meet again, Karl, Ricarda, Viktoria and Luise.' He shook hands with them all, then impulsively picked Luise up and kissed her on each cheek. 'Be a good girl in Uncle Ewald's absence.'

He entered the train which started to move off almost immediately. On an impulse, Luise lifted her skirts and ran along beside it. 'Goodbye! Good luck!' Soldiers of all ranks, tall in their new field-grey uniforms, spiked helments gleaming, packs neat on their backs, stopped in their disciplined march down the platform to smile at the lovely young girl in blue, with her vivid green eyes. From the full length of the train, soldiers waved, called and laughed back at her, until she was standing at the end of the platform, a mere speck in a blue dress, waving a cornflower blue hat.

Georg Jankowski's farewell with his wife was of a very different nature. Pipsi was furious that he had been called up and even more angry that, despite his two years' national service and his reservist duties since, he was still only a private. She continued to voice her feelings on the platform, until finally he said, 'Look, dear, there's no point in you waiting round here.'

'Yes, it could be hours before your train leaves.'

They kissed each other with an almost formal coldness; then Georg watched her slim figure move up the platform, before entering the cramped third class compartment. Perhaps things would become clearer at the front. At least there wouldn't be any women there to confuse the issue. But his music, what would happen to his music? Would he ever be able to return to the Berlin *Hochschule*, to his teaching post and to his compositions?

And his uncle, what would happen to him? Would he ever see him again? Franz had aged so dreadfully in the last few years; it seemed almost impossible that he would still be alive when he returned.

Georg shook his head and looked out of the window. The train was slowly beginning to leave. A girl in blue was running beside it.

251

Her hat had come off and she was waving it high above her head. With the other soldiers, he waved back and as he gazed at her auburn hair and green eyes, a melody started to form in his mind, a dance tune, yes, a valse. The train carried them out through the suburbs of Berlin and he translated the melody in his head into crotchets and quavers. Unlike most of his compositions, Georg Jankowski's *Cornflower Waltz* was in a major key.

Another soldier left Berlin that day for the western front. Lost in a sea of field-grey uniforms, he had nobody to bid him farewell and good luck. As he stepped smartly onto the train, he felt no regret at leaving Berlin, only pleasure at a war that represented the culmination of his hard work for the past four years. He believed it would bring trophies rightfully belonging to Germany, colonies, natural resources and territories over which she would rule.

And for himself, it would bring promotion to higher ranks, a coveted Iron Cross presented by the Kaiser himself and — who knew? — perhaps even an administrative job in one of the new military outposts.

Then, suddenly, across the platform, he noticed the Jochum family. He saw his hated former employer shaking hands with Count Ewald von Biederstein. So that old buffer was still going strong! And there was Ricarda, frowning at Luise, who seemed to be making eyes at an unknown private. Yes, and there was prim little Miss Viktoria, still looking as if butter wouldn't melt in her mouth. What a bad-tempered bitch!

He watched the Count's train move out of the station, with Luise running alongside it, waving her hat in the air and calling to the soldiers. She wouldn't wave to him, if she saw him. No, she'd turn her supercilious little nose in the air and look the other way. Well, one day, he'd get even with them once and for all. When he came back from the war, he'd make them dance to *his* tune, all right!

Those were the thoughts in the mind of Second Lieutenant Otto Tobisch, as he left Berlin in August 1914.

The war had an immediate effect on the Hotel Quadriga, for all male personnel who were still reservists were promptly called up, while foreigners, among them the French chef, returned to their native countries. While the remaining staff were so far free from conscription, the threat of it still hung over them. After taking on some new waiters, Karl brought Fritzi Messner to the hotel from

Café Jochum and appointed a new manager for the Café, a man called Oskar Braun, who had suffered from tuberculosis in his youth and was therefore exempt from military service. After a few brief visits to the café, Karl declared himself satisfied with Braun's capabilities and left him to run the place in his own way, for he himself had long ago lost interest in it.

There was also a dramatic change in the guests, for although there were few people on pleasure visits to the city, every room was soon filled as, one after another, administrative authorities set up headquarters in Berlin, the heads and senior officials of which all booked rooms at the hotel, which were reserved for the duration of the war, however long that might be. With the presence of such important personages in the Quadriga, Karl soon believed himself to be at the very centre of the war operations.

It was about a week after war was declared, while the Jochums were having a quiet supper in their apartment, that a page boy knocked on the door and told them that Olga Fischer and Reinhardt Meyer were in reception.

For the first time since Peter had gone, Viktoria experienced a tremor of excitement. If Olga were in Berlin, it would mean she had someone to confide in, although as Olga entered the room, she experienced a moment of doubt, for her cousin's clothes were still plain and drab, her fine hair drawn back in a knot and her oval eyes full of a burning intensity that betokened not love but politics.

'How are your father and mother?' Karl asked, having kissed Olga and shaken hands awkwardly with Reinhardt, looking askance at the young man's untidy, civilian suit.

'They're very well and send their love.'

Karl nodded, but his eyes kept turning to Reinhardt. In the end, he asked, 'What? Not in the army yet?'

'Reinhardt's been given a job on the *Vorwaerts* newspaper.'

Viktoria tensed, waiting for her father's reaction. '*Vorwaerts*, that red rag!' he cried, horrified. 'God almighty, man, why aren't you volunteering for the army?'

'I'm a pacifist,' Reinhardt replied quietly. 'I don't believe in the rightfulness of this war.'

Karl scrutinized him narrowly. 'Don't believe in the rightfulness of this war. Do you realize what you're saying?'

Reinhardt nodded. 'It's the very worst thing that could have happened to Germany.'

Viktoria could see her father struggling to keep his temper.

253

Ricarda laid a restraining hand on his. 'What are you going to do in Berlin, Olga?' she asked.

'I've been given a teaching job in Wedding.'

'In Wedding? But Wedding isn't a very nice area, Olga, dear. It's a very poor district, full of working-class people. Couldn't you find a better post, maybe in Dahlem or even Charlottenburg?'

Viktoria cringed. Her mother couldn't have said a worse thing if she'd tried.

Olga's chin jutted obstinately in a curiously Jochum manner. 'The future of the world belongs to the working classes. Come the proletarian revolution, there will be no other class.'

Scandalized, Karl stared from one to the other of them. 'And I suppose you agree with this young man's views on war, too?'

'Oh, yes, I agree with him, Uncle Karl. He will be much better fighting with words than with fists or a sword.'

'Fighting what?'

'The system. A political system that forces the elected representatives of the people to vote against their inner convictions.'

'I suppose you're referring to that rascal, Liebknecht. Well, even he voted for war in the Reichstag.'

'Because he was forced to,' Reinhardt said. 'It's something I suspect he'll regret to the end of his days.'

'Bah!' Karl exclaimed, his face red. 'You young poppycocks think you know it all. You do realize that even *Vorwaerts* has had to acknowledge that Germany had no alternative but to go to war? We have to defend the peace!'

'With all due respect, Uncle Karl, that is a lie,' Olga said. Viktoria held her breath. How could the visit be turning out so disastrously? Why couldn't Olga keep her political ideas to herself?

'What? You mean you agree with everything this scoundrel is saying?'

'I believe Germany has just been looking for an excuse to go to war for a long time. It isn't being fought to defend the peace against the Russian Tsar's barbarities or for any other benefit to the German people — it's being fought for the Kaiser's own imperialistic aims.'

'Olga! Do you realize what you're saying?' her uncle thundered. 'Those are words of treason! I will not have them uttered in my house! If you wish to spend the night here, which I presume is the reason you've turned up, then you will retract them and apologize.'

'I wouldn't stay in a capitalist prison like this if I were paid to. No, thank you, Herr Jochum, we have taken lodgings for the night — in Wedding. Tomorrow we shall be looking for a flat of our own.'

This was too much for Karl. 'You mean you are going to live in sin with this peacemonger? Does Grete know about this?'

She shrugged. 'I've no idea. I've never talked about my sexual relationships with my mother, but she knows I don't agree with marriage as an institution.'

Viktoria covered her eyes, awaiting her father's next outburst. When he spoke, his voice was dangerously calm. 'I'm sure that not even she agrees with you, though. And I, for one, think you are talking the most unmitigated nonsense. Marriage, like the monarchy, is a sacred institution. I will not have either of them blasphemed in this household, in front of these children.'

'Sir, I object, you have no right to talk like that to Olga,' Reinhardt's face was white.

'And you have no right to publicize your foul thoughts. Not only are you too chicken-hearted, too cowardly, too selfish to fight for your country in its hour of need, but you persist in trying to poison the minds of innocent people with your vile treacherous ravings.'

Never had Viktoria known her father so angry. 'But, Papa ...'

'Viktoria, you came to the station to see Colonel Count Ewald von Biederstein off to the front. Do you know how old the Count is? Well, I'll tell you. The Count is fifty-eight, an age when most men are thinking of retiring, of putting their feet up and resting after a busy life in the service of their country. I know that the Count could have applied for and been given a staff job, but no, he saw his duty as being among his men, fighting in the field. County Ewald comes from one of the greatest, oldest, most influential German families, but does he flinch from his duty, does he question his Emperor's orders? No,' Karl roared, 'he does what every good, loyal German should do: he goes out and fights!'

'Then the Count is a fool,' Reinhardt retorted.

'And you, sir, are a traitor! Get out of here! I will not have the good names of my best friends besmirched by lily-livered milksops, who do not undersand the meaning of words like patriotism, loyalty and fidelity!'

Olga stood up and took Reinhardt's arm. 'Come on, let's go.' Her face was very pale and her eyes were glittering with tears of shame and anger.

255

Red with embarrassment, Viktoria accompanied them to the door. 'Olga, please let me know where you are, so that I can come and see you,' she whispered.

Olga smiled wanly, then the door shut on them.

Karl's voice was still raised in fury. 'Viktoria! Luise! I forbid you absolutely to speak to your cousin again. Her name is never to be mentioned in this house. As from today, I recognize nobody by the name of Olga Fischer. She is no longer my niece, no longer a member of this family. And the same applies to you, if I ever hear you have disobeyed my orders. Understood?'

The two girls looked at him, then nodded. 'No hardship for me,' Luise muttered to her sister. 'Olga's just as boring as she ever was.'

Viktoria just said, 'Yes, Papa, I understand.'

On the outskirts of a small Belgian village, Colonel Count Ewald von Biederstein assembled his troops in the early morning of 12 August. As he did so, he experienced a supreme moment of satisfaction. It was a fine morning, the field of golden corn ahead of them moving gently in the breeze. But above all, it was a morning which seemed to vindicate his lifetime's service to his country. With an army such as hers, with generals such as hers, Germany would win this war — and win it very soon.

General Alfred von Schlieffen had been a clever old bastard, the Count reflected irreverently, for the former Chief of General Staff had been dead eight years now, but his war plan was still strategically as sound as the day it had been adopted by the army in 1894. Its basics were mobility and surprise and its success depended upon the German army funnelling its way through Belgium at high speed, then encircling the French army before either the Russians or the British could intervene. And the Schlieffen Plan was working! Just as they had anticipated, they were receiving little opposition from the virtually negligible Belgian army. There was no reason at all why they shouldn't reach Paris in six weeks.

Ewald peered over the high corn at the unsuspecting village. His scouts had already reported that the enemy comprised only one cavalry division, which meant they were vastly outnumbered by his troops. 'Fire!' he shouted. The air reverberated to the sound of German artillery.

There was no answering Belgian gunfire.

'Charge!' Four thousand German cavalrymen, lances to the

fore, charged towards the village, their horses' hooves flattening the ripe corn as they went. Still the Belgian village remained quiet. Ewald's spirits soared. Another victory! Another conquest on the road to Paris!

Only when they were on the very edge of the village, did the Belgian horsemen make their presence felt. And by then it was too late. To the front of his troops, Ewald felt Elvira rear. He saw the oncoming cavalrymen, he was distinctly aware of the bayonet plunging into his heart. In brief succession, images flickered through his mind, of Fuerstenmark, of his mistresses, of his long-dead wife, of Karlshorst, of a little girl in cornflower blue on a railway platform — then Elvira fell and he plummeted to the earth.

At the end of that day, three thousand German cavalrymen lay dead in a Belgian cornfield, having been responsible for the deaths of a mere three hundred enemy soldiers. One of the first to die was Count Ewald von Biederstein.

In the middle of August, the first lists of names of those wounded or killed in action arrived, among them that of Count Ewald von Biederstein, Colonel, First Brandenburg Guards. Karl could not believe the news. 'The First Brandenburg is the finest regiment in the country. Somebody's got it wrong. It's socialist propaganda.'

When a memorial service was held for the Count at the garrison chapel at Karlshorst, he was forced to accept the truth. Countess Julia attended, dressed in black silk, wearing a black veil, gloves and jewellery, her hair pinned up with black combs. The men all wore black bands round their left sleeves.

'Earth to earth, ashes to ashes, dust to dust ...' Karl listened bleakly to the chaplain's voice intoning the words of the funeral service. He saw Ewald, elegant and dapper as he had first known him at Karlshorst. He heard his voice, with that languid drawl: *Damn it all, Karl, you amuse me. Let's see if we can't make a gentleman of sorts out of you. It would be good sport, if nothing else.*

Karl looked across to Heinrich Kraus, remembering how they had carried the heavy trunk containing the red-headed lady down the stairs at Karlshorst after the passing-out parade. Kraus had been a sergeant then, now he was a baron. Karl had been a private, now he was the proprietor of Berlin's finest hotel. And Ewald, who had helped them both to achieve their ambitions, was dead.

'Thirty-eight years,' Karl thought in bewilderment, 'thirty-eight years I've known Ewald. How can the cavalry have met such a terrible defeat so soon? Six weeks to reach Paris, they said. And already Ewald's dead. Before he ever reached Paris. Before he ever had his skirmish with the French. No, I just can't believe it.'

When the service was over, he stumbled out of the church and felt Ricarda take his arm. For the first time, he felt himself an old man, in need of a woman's hand to help him along. He could not face the strong sunlight, but kept his eyes on the ground. Ewald, his oldest friend, his guide, his mentor, the man he had respected above all others, Ewald was dead.

Viktoria was also shocked by Count Ewald's death, but she had something even more worrying on her mind. Previously always as regular as clockwork, she was now a week overdue on her menstrual period. Every morning, she woke up feeling sick and it was not until lunchtime that she felt able to swallow even a little food. Maybe, she thought, there was a perfectly logical reason for her condition. It could be caused by shock over Peter's abrupt departure, the outbreak of war, or even the Count's death. But she had every reason to fear it could be because she was pregnant.

Benno noticed the change in Viktoria when the family gathered together for supper after the Count's memorial service. It was the first time he had sat at the same table with her since Archduke Franz Ferdinand's murder at the end of June and the first evening he had spent away from Kraus Chemie for literally months.

What could have happened in his absence? Her grandfather, he knew, was seriously ill and she could, understandably, be upset by the outbreak of war and Count Ewald's death, but none of these really accounted for her extreme pallor, her gaunt face and the weight she had undoubtedly lost. Benno remembered the evening when his Uncle Ewald had proudly announced that Peter had arrived at Karlshorst and the sensation he had then had of being on the edge of a precipice. Although he had not seen his cousin, he knew he had visited the hotel.

Benno stared across the table at his father with a sudden burst of loathing. By what right did he drive his family with the same ruthless intensity as he did himself? There were other things in life besides work and war. Why had Benno been such a fool as to blindly obey his father's orders and let the one person he loved slip out of his clutches?

What harm had been done to Viktoria during that time? He

258

watched her picking at her food, he studied the dark bags under her eyes and felt a moment of great pity. Was Peter von Biederstein at the root of all this?'

There was only one way to find out. After dinner, he took her arm, leading her into a quiet conservatory off the Palm Garden Room. 'Vicki, you look so pale, are you all right?'

She did not draw away from him as he had feared. 'Oh, yes, I'm fine.'

It was strange and wonderful to be alone with her again, even though they were separated by a vast distance of time, for it was over a year since he had proposed to her and during those intervening months he felt he had aged beyond belief. He was no longer the naïve boy who had kissed Viktoria on the ghost train, but a man, responsible for the lives and deaths of millions of other people.

During their time apart, he had never ceased loving her, but his love had become less selfish. Now, as he watched her fingers nervously fidgeting with her hair, he knew he cared for her as a person in her own right, loved her as he might a child, as an individual who needed looking after. 'Vicki, you know I am still your friend?' Hopelessly inadequate words to express the depth of his feeling.

She looked at him from big eyes that contained a hint of tears. 'Yes, thank you, Benno.'

How could he get at the truth without forcing it out of her? 'Something is the matter. I know it is, but I don't want to know what, unless you want to tell me. However, I am going to say this, Vicki. I still love you and I shall always love you. You will always be the only woman in my life. And I should still like to marry you.'

She looked away and his worst suspicions were confirmed. She was in love and it was not with him.

But he could not leave it like that. He had to know the worst. 'Has anybody else asked you to marry them, Vicki?'

She gazed away from him into the darkening night; then, slowly, she shook her head. 'No, Benno, nobody else has asked me to marry them.'

There was a tremor in her voice and at that moment it was almost as if he could see into her mind and watch with her the visions racing through it. He saw armies crossing the Belgian plains, the clashing of arms, the gunfire, the smoke, and he saw the slaughter, as soldiers — the gallant lieutenants, who had left Berlin

259

so gaily less than a month ago — fell to their death, even as Count Ewald had done. But, instead of Count Ewald, they were both seeing the body of Peter von Biederstein.

'If you should ever change your mind, Vicki, I want you to remember that nothing has changed mine. I love you and I want to marry you. And I am also your friend. If ever you need anything, remember that.' Then he walked away into the bustle of the hotel.

For a long time after Benno was gone, Viktoria remained in the conservatory. Count Ewald's death had filled her with fear for Peter's safety, but Benno's words had pushed even that fear to the back of her mind, as she realized the full horror of the dreadful mistake she had made. Peter had never loved her, he had merely made use of her, whereas Benno truly loved her.

At that moment, she suddenly felt only a consuming hatred for Peter, and a deep tenderness for Benno. If she had only had the sense to marry him a year ago, none of this would ever have happened. But she had persisted in believing in a Peter von Biederstein who had never existed except in her imagination, and now it was too late.

Over the next few days, Viktoria realized how desperately she needed a friend. Since Ewald's death, her father had grown older and slightly frail, as if his confidence had been undermined. Her mother, too, was pale and tired, deeply concerned about Opa, now very seriously ill but maintaining a tenuous hold on life to the bitter end. Ricarda was the last person to whom she could unburden her troubles.

So, since Benno had again extended the hand of friendship, she grasped it tentatively, unwilling to abuse it, but also terrified of losing it. They started to take their coffee together in the evenings, sitting in the Palm Garden Room until it was time for bed, taking care never to let the conversation become too personal, but gradually rediscovering things they had in common.

Every morning at breakfast, Karl informed his family of the latest news from the front. 'Ludendorff has captured Liège. His howitzers have battered the city to pieces.' Another day, he told them, 'We've reached Mons.' Then, 'The British have reached Mons, too. We'll show them!' Anxiously, he watched the armies under Kluck and von Buelow's commands as they approached Paris.

On 5 September 1914, the German armies crossed the River Marne in France. By the time this news was reported in the newspapers, Viktoria was certain she was pregnant.

Chapter Ten

The streets of Wedding were narrow and dark, banked on either side by tall, squalid blocks of flats, grey washing hanging damply on dank balconies. Viktoria hurried through them, her head lowered, trying not to see, as well as not to be seen. The air around her was yellowish and smelt acrid. Already her white gloves were grimed and her eyes felt dry and gritty. How could anything grow in a district like this? How did people exist in rooms where sunlight never entered? Small, barefooted children, with runny noses, grubby faces and ragged, ill-fitting clothes, stared at her from doorsteps, alleyways and gutters, some following her for a short way, shouting out in an almost incomprehensible dialect. Their mothers, vast, slatternly women, followed her with their eyes, calling out to their neighbours.

Despite her attempts to be inconspicuous, there were so many giveaway signs which drew attention to her class. The old coat cast off by a hotel maid, which she had surreptitiously borrowed, had once been bought at Wertheim's department store. Her shoes, her handbag and, of course, her accent — none of these belonged to Wedding.

The secretary at the first school she found stared at her curiously. 'No, we have no Fraeulein Fischer here.' Why, Viktoria wondered, had she come on this fool's errand? Even if she found Olga, she had no certainty that her cousin would help her, particularly after the way Karl had treated her; but she knew no one else whom she could trust.

Then, softening at the desperate look on Viktoria's face, the woman suggested, 'Perhaps you'll find her at the school in the Wiesenstrasse.'

Wiesenstrasse — Meadow Street. How could there be a Meadow Street in Wedding?

The secretary at the Wiesenstrasse school also raised a doubtful eyebrow at Viktoria's appearance. 'We have no Fraeulein Olga Fischer here.' Then she looked thoughtful. 'Are you sure you don't mean Frau Meyer? I believe her first name is Olga.'

The last thing Viktoria had expected was that Olga might have married. 'Yes, that must be her.'

'She's in class at the moment, but if you'd like to wait school will be over in half an hour. You can sit in my office if you like.'

As she watched the school emptying, Viktoria felt curiously moved. Although they wore the same patched clothes as their younger brothers and sisters, these children were well-scrubbed and well-behaved. For the first time she saw what Olga was trying to do — and the hopeless task she had. If the streets of Wedding represented the living conditions of the working classes, they surely deserved all the help they could get. For a moment, she forgot her own misery and sympathized deeply with the plight of others.

'Why, Viktoria!' Olga's voice said. 'I heard I had a visitor, but I didn't expect you.'

Now she had found her, Viktoria felt even more nervous. In her drab clothes and with her colourless features, Olga seemed to merge into her background. 'I wondered if we could talk. I need help, I'm afraid.'

Olga studied her, then nodded. 'You'd better come to our flat.'

'Will Reinhardt be there?' Viktoria dreaded the thought of confiding her problem to masculine ears.

Olga shook her head, walking across the school courtyard and into the street. 'No, he's working.' Then she explained, 'We had to get married so that I could keep my job. The headmaster wouldn't have one of his teachers living with a man. Thought it would set the pupils a bad example. As if a five-minute ceremony with a registrar makes any difference!'

But it could make a lot of difference, Viktoria thought, if one were pregnant. 'I hope you're happy,' she said, not knowing what else to say.

'Reinhardt's my comrade. If the only way I can be with him is to submit to conventional morality, then I'll do so. But I did it for the right reasons — for the sake of the people of Wedding, not for men like your father,' she added contemptuously. They reached the entrance to a blackened block of flats which looked identical to all others in the area. 'I hope your legs are good. We live on the top floor.'

The flat consisted of three cramped rooms, a living room, a bedroom and a kitchen, each seemingly stacked floor to ceiling with books and newspapers. Viktoria stood at the small window

262

and gazed down into a small courtyard, across which lines of washing were strung above huge black dustbins. Blocks of flats, similar to Olga's, formed the other three sides of the square, completely blocking off any light which might have reached the children playing in the yard below. The smoke from tall, belching, factory chimneys hung like a pall over the whole neighbourhood. 'Welcome to the courtyard culture,' Olga laughed bitterly. 'Well, you'd better tell me what's happened. Has your father turned you out of the Quadriga as well?'

Viktoria bit her lip. 'No, but he would if he found out. You see, Olga, I think I'm pregnant.'

'Pregnant! Are you sure?'

'No, but I've missed my period.'

Olga opened a cupboard door, took out a bottle of schnapps and filled two small tumblers. Then, with genuine concern, she asked, 'Have you been to your doctor?'

'That's just it. Our doctor not only looks after the hotel, but all our family. I can't see Dr Blattner. I wondered if you knew a doctor round here, someone who wouldn't ask too many questions.'

'There's Dr Katz. He has a good reputation. Would you like me to come with you?'

Now that she knew she was no longer alone, Viktoria felt better. She took a large gulp of schnapps, wincing as it hit the back of her throat. 'Yes, please, Olga.'

'And the man? Where's he? At the front, I suppose. One of our glorious soldiers.'

Viktoria nodded. 'But if I am pregnant, and even if he knew, he wouldn't marry me. You see, I'm not good enough for him and, anyway, I don't think he really loved me.'

Olga stared at her. 'But, why on earth ...?' Then she shrugged. 'What difference does it make? Come on, let's find out if you are pregnant first. Then we'll decide what to do.'

Even with Olga sitting beside her in the doctor's waiting room, Viktoria felt very small and fearful. She thought all the people around her must know why she was there, for her shame must surely be written on her face. Could this room, these fat, crude women, with the snivelling children and their soot-grimed menfolk, really be the end of that one evening spent with Peter von Biederstein, those few hours of consummate oneness, of something more than love?

The doctor's face was tired. He nodded, when she introduced herself as Frau Schmidt, whose husband was fighting in France. 'Take off your lower garments,' he instructed, pointing to a screen on the far side of the room. 'I'll have to examine you. Have you brought a urine sample with you?'

She handed him the small bottle that Olga, surprisingly knowledgeable, had made her bring, then lay back on the gynaecological couch. The room was clean, but in need of a coat of paint. She gazed at the flaking ceiling, as the doctor poked and prodded inside her. 'It's too early to be certain, Frau Schmidt, but I'd say you're probably pregnant. The test will be conclusive. If you'll get dressed again now, then come back in two days' time.'

The next two days seemed interminable. Viktoria tried to immerse herself in a book, but she could not concentrate. She went for walks, looking at the shops on Unter den Linden and the Alexanderplatz, but found no consolation. Ricarda was seldom at home these days, for Dr Blattner had given Emil Graber only a few weeks to live, so more out of desperation than anything else, she started to help her father in the hotel. It was interesting, and it helped the time to pass.

She returned to the doctor's surgery in Wedding on her own. Again the waiting room was full and the doctor looked tired. 'Ah, yes, Frau Schmidt, I have the results here. I'm pleased to tell you, you are pregnant. My congratulations.'

'But, Doctor, it can't be true.' The room seemed to spin round her. She closed her eyes and took a deep breath. Then, numbly, she took her bill from his outstretched hand and left the room.

Outside on the street, she looked blindly at the grey ranks of barrack-like blocks of flats, then down the dusty street. She felt someone take her arm. 'I've been watching for you,' Olga said, surprisingly gently. 'Come on, I've made some tea.'

'What do I do?'

Olga opened the flat door and let them in. 'If you've got any sense, you'll get married.'

'And the baby? How would I explain the baby?'

'There are such things as premature births.'

The two girls sat sipping tea, each immersed in their own thoughts. Gradually, Viktoria stopped trembling and started to feel braver. 'You've been very kind to me, Olga. I don't know how I can ever repay you.'

Olga waved a deprecating hand. 'I haven't done anything.'

'But you have, you've been a friend when I needed one most. And what's more, you haven't told me that I have been a fool.'

'Perhaps that's because I understand you better than you think. You see, I believe you were in love with the father of this baby, and, although I would never admit this to anybody else, I do understand what it means to be in love. I always say that Reinhardt is my comrade, but he's much more than that — he's the most wonderful person I have ever known. I can't imagine life without him. If anything happened to him, I'd be utterly lost.'

She paused. 'I was a socialist long before I met Reinhardt, of course, but he somehow strengthened and gave purpose to my belief. It sounds silly, but everything I do is for the good of the people, but also for Reinhardt.' She looked embarrassed, but went on, 'That's why I married him, really. Because I love him.'

Impulsively, Viktoria took her hand, for her cousin's admission moved her deeply. 'Thank you for telling me that. And now, more than ever, you have to promise me that if you ever need anything, you will come to me. Despite everything Papa said to you.'

'All right. I hope I never need to, but I'll remember.'

Viktoria stood up and walked over to the window, staring down on the courtyard below. If her father discovered she were pregnant, he would almost undoubtedly disown her, throw her out of the hotel and she would end up somewhere like this. Was this was she wanted for her unborn child? No, a thousand times no. If the war ended and Peter came home, he might give her financial support, but he would never marry her. And if the war didn't end? Or if Peter were killed?

It was already becoming apparent that more than six weeks were going to be required for the German armies to reach Paris and, after the retreat from the Marne, there was not room to list all the names of the dead and wounded on the public notice boards. Now, the orchestras in the cafés no longer played the *Watch on the Rhine* and women did not laugh and wave when their sons and husbands went off to war; increasing numbers of them were dressed in mourning black.

Six weeks to take Paris and St Petersburg, Peter had gaily declared, as they had driven away from Heiligensee after that fateful visit. Instead, it had taken her six weeks to discover she was pregnant. She could afford no longer to find a father for her unborn child. Firmly, she banished Peter to the back of her mind. She had made one mistake, but she was not going to make another one.

She thought of Benno, of whom Olga's words had reminded her so strongly. Benno might lack the superficial charm of Peter, but he was a very good, kind person. Much too good, in fact, to be deceived. Indeed, if she had one ounce of decency in her, she would simply confess to him that she was pregnant by his cousin and await his reaction. But that was a risk she could not afford to take, for if he knew she was pregnant, there was every likelihood that he would not want to marry her any more. After all, what man would knowingly take on the responsibility of another man's child? No, she decided again, no more mistakes. It was sad that she had to lie to Benno, but that was the only way it could be.

'What are you going to do?' Olga asked.

Viktoria took one last, lingering look at the courtyard below, where children were playing amidst tall dustbins. 'I'm going to follow your advice. I'm going to get married.'

As soon as Benno saw her walking towards him across the hotel bar, he knew something had happened to change her mind. She was still thin and drawn, but her hair was newly washed and dressed and she was wearing his favourite cerise frock. Above all, however, it was her look of quiet dignity that impressed him, a confidence in her manner that had been lacking before. Instinctively, Benno knew that the little girl, Vicki, was gone, and the woman, Viktoria, had taken over.

He walked to meet her, took her arm, and led her to the corner table reserved for the Jochum family and their close friends. A waiter followed with Benno's drink and took Viktoria's order. When they were alone, she said, 'Benno, I don't think I have been very kind to you over the last year and I want to apologize.'

He opened his mouth to stop her, but she leaned forward earnestly, 'Please, Benno, don't say anything yet. Let me finish first. You see, I have behaved rather stupidly and I'm now ashamed of myself.' She hesitated, staring down at the table and he offered her a cigarette. To his surprise, she took it, coughing slightly as she inhaled the smoke. Then she went on, 'I don't know if you ever guessed, but for a long time, ever since I was a very little girl, I thought I was in love with your cousin, Peter.'

Extraordinarily, now that his rival had been named, Benno felt better. The fact that he was Peter came as no surprise.

'I can see now that I took him far more seriously than he did me, but when you asked me to marry you, Benno, I didn't know that. I thought that, one day, he would ask me to marry him.'

Benno watched her with a strange feeling of compassion. Poor little Vicki, believing that a von Biederstein would stoop to marry a Jochum. 'And now?'

'Something happened, and then war broke out, and I knew he would never marry me. Please, Benno, I would rather not talk about what happened, but, as a result, I went to see my cousin Olga and I realized what a fool I'd been.' She ground out her cigarette in the ashtray. 'She was talking about the reason why she'd married Reinhardt and she said that although she always told people he was her comrade, in fact he was much more than that, that he was the most wonderful person she had ever known. She said she couldn't imagine life without him and that if anything happened to him, she'd be utterly lost. And suddenly, I knew what you had meant when you had said you were my friend.'

He took her hand. 'I meant it, Viktoria, I shall always be your friend.' Yet as he spoke, he wondered what had happened between her and his cousin. He thought of Peter, so charming and debonair, so like his Uncle Ewald, who had reputedly had many mistresses during his life. Had Peter left her with a few callous words when he departed for the front or had there been something deeper? Part of Benno wanted to know the answer, while the other part did not.

'Benno, are you angry with me? Can you forgive me?'

The past did not matter. What did matter was that, even if she did not love him as she had loved Peter, she liked him and needed him as her friend. 'Of course I'm not angry with you. I'm proud that you feel able to confide in me. You see, Viktoria, I love you and when I say that, I mean that I love everything about you. It sounds trite, but it's true.'

'Thank you, Benno,' her voice was very small.

He lifted her hand to his lips and kissed it. 'Viktoria, will you marry me?'

'Yes, Benno, I will.'

'Soon?'

'It's all right, Benno, I shan't change my mind. But, yes, we'll get married tomorrow if you like.'

A feeling of warmth flooded over him. He had loved her so deeply for so long and with so little hope, it didn't seem possible that his dreams were finally coming true.

They went up to the apartment together to tell her parents.

Karl's face lit up when he heard their news. 'I always told you that I couldn't hope for a better son-in-law. Congratulations.' Suddenly, he looked like his old self again. 'We'll have a huge party.'

Viktoria shook her head. 'Papa, I'd rather not, if you don't mind. Under the circumstances, what with Count Ewald and the war and everything, it wouldn't seem very tactful. If you're agreed, Benno, we'll just have a small wedding breakfast, with our two families.'

'The most important thing is that you're marrying me and that we get married as quickly as possible.'

Viktoria saw her mother shoot her a troubled look. 'Now we've made up our minds, we'd like to get married soon,' she explained. 'After all, with a war on, who can tell what will happen?'

After Benno had left, Ricarda followed Viktoria to her room. She sat down on the bed and drew Viktoria to her. 'I know I haven't seen much of you since Opa has been ill, but, Vicki, this seems very sudden. You didn't tell me you had decided to marry Benno.'

'He asked me a long time ago, Mama.'

Ricarda looked ill at ease. 'In my experience, people who get married in haste usually have a reason for doing so. I don't like to ask you this, Vicki, but has Benno got you into trouble? Do you have to marry him?'

With a sense of relief that she wasn't really lying, Viktoria said, 'No, Mama, Benno hasn't got me into trouble.'

Obviously relieved, Ricarda put her arm round her and kissed her. 'I'm glad. I like Benno. And I do hope you will both be very happy together.'

When she broke her news to Luise, her sister looked at her sceptically. 'Does this mean I can't be a bridesmaid?'

'I'm sorry, Luischen, but I don't want a church wedding.'

Luise sniffed. 'It would have been different if you were marrying Peter von Biederstein, wouldn't it? Then you'd be having a huge ceremony in the Cathedral.'

Viktoria looked at her sharply. 'Well, I'm not marrying Peter and I'd be grateful to you, miss, if you could stop talking about him. I'm marrying Benno, and that's that.'

There remained only one other person to tell. Once again, Viktoria made her way to Wedding and, looking out towards the tall chimneys of Kraus Village, confessed to her cousin that she was going to marry Benno Kraus.

Olga stared at her disbelievingly. 'You're going to marry a Kraus? One of those capitalist swine? Well, don't expect me to come to your wedding.'

'Benno is a good, kind person.'

'There's no such thing as a good, kind Kraus.'

'One day you'll meet him and then you'll see,' But when she left, shortly afterwards, she knew their brief intimacy had been destroyed. Olga would never tolerate Benno and all he stood for.

On the morning of her wedding day, Viktoria was very sick. As she stood retching in the bathroom, she felt her mother put her arm round her. 'Vicki, darling, you poor child. There's no need for you to be nervous. I know Benno will be a wonderful husband to you.'

When she had finished, she allowed Ricarda to lead her back to her room and she lay wanly on the bed while her mother made some weak camomile tea. Reassured by Viktoria's words two weeks earlier, she, at least, believed her state to be caused by nerves. But, what if this should happen again tomorrow, the first day of her married life? Viktoria was woefully ignorant of the symptoms of pregnancy and was sure that Benno knew even less, but even he must have heard of the morning sickness?

Viktoria went through that day in a kind of trance. By noon, when they drove to the town hall for the short civil ceremony, she felt physically extremely well, but her mind was still in turmoil. Dimly, she heard Benno vowing to love and honour her in sickness and in health. Distantly, she was aware of her own voice responding. He placed the gold band on the third finger of her right hand and, instead of feeling that this was the happiest day of her life, she was convinced it was the most miserable.

Their wedding breakfast was held in the private dining room looking onto Unter den Linden in which Karl had entertained the Kaiser on the day Viktoria had been born, twenty years earlier. It was a small and intimate gathering. Sitting opposite her was her father, openly delighted that she had married a Kraus, his old enmity for Baron Heinrich and his youthful love for Countess Julia equally forgotten. Now he could claim them as relatives by marriage! Luise was seated between the Baron and her father, concentrating on her food and paying little attention to the conversation, while Ernst Kraus sat between his mother and Ricarda.

'The French and British are forcing our armies back,' he was saying. 'This war isn't going to be over for a long time.' He adjusted his spectacles, looking at them all gravely. 'I just wonder if Moltke is the right man to be in command.'

'He's a fine general,' Karl said.

'Bah! Moltke's an idiot,' Baron Heinrich contradicted him. 'He doesn't know what he's doing. The Kaiser should replace him. I was against this war from the beginning and made no secret of it. But now we're in it, we should fight to win. Bring back someone like Hindenburg, I say, someone who knows what they're doing.'

'Hindenburg's an old man,' Karl said doubtfully. 'He must be at least ten years older than I am and I'm fifty-six.'

'But he's got experience! You and I may be getting on a bit, Karl, but we've learned something along the way. I always say to my two boys, you can't put an old head on young shoulders.'

It all seemed so unreal — her marriage, the war, the Kaiser. All Viktoria could think of was her sickness that morning and the baby that was growing inside her.

Countess Julia sighed, 'The war, the war, always the war. Let's talk about something more pleasant. Viktoria, dear, where are you and Benno spending your honeymoon?'

She meant to be kind, but her words only made matters worse. 'We're going to Heiligensee,' Viktoria replied.

'It's a family tradition,' Ricarda explained. 'My grandparents, parents, and Karl and I spent our honeymoon there. It's a beautiful cottage, set right on the edge of the lake.'

Viktoria could not bring herself to look at Benno. What a dreadful thing she was doing in taking him, for his honeymoon of all things, to the scene of her love affair with Peter. In a state of rising panic, she wondered if she should confess the whole truth now, admit that she was already pregnant and that Peter was the father. But, as she listened to their complacent voices, she knew it was already too late. Either she should have told Benno before she married him or she must never tell him at all.

At that moment, Baron Heinrich cleared his throat and stood up, looking at Karl. 'A lot of water has passed under the bridge since you and I first met, Jochum. Little did we know, when we were a couple of young soldiers in the First Brandenburg Guards, that our lives were going to become so interwoven. But I'd like to say now, sir, that it's been a privilege knowing you.' Karl inclined his head. 'You've got a very lovely daughter and I'm absolutely delighted to be able to welcome her to the Kraus family.' He turned to Benno and Viktoria. 'I wish you both many years of happiness.'

When toasts had been drunk to the bride and groom and to their respective parents, the Baron reached in his pocket and pulled out an envelope. 'Benno, now you're married, you are entitled to the shares left to you in your grandfather's will. Here are the certificates.'

Karl was not to be outdone. 'Children, come with me. I want to show you my wedding present.'

Outside was an Opel car in the same blue and gold coachwork as the house colours of the Quadriga. With tears in her eyes, Viktoria stared from it to her father and Benno. 'Papa, you shouldn't . . .'

'This marriage has made me very happy,' Karl said gruffly, drawing her to him and kissing her on the forehead.

Obviously very moved, Benno shook his hand warmly. 'Thank you, Herr Jochum.'

An hour later, they were driving away from the hotel in the new automobile, while the two families and most of the hotel staff stood under the portico to wave them goodbye. As the wind rushed through her hair, Viktoria felt the full burden of her guilty secret. Suddenly, she was no longer Viktoria Jochum, but Frau Jochum-Kraus, a married woman, Benno's wife. But, even on this, the very first day of their married life, she was deceiving him. She had never felt so despicable.

It was one of the worst moments of her life when Benno led her upstairs to the bedroom at Heiligensee. She almost expected to see Peter sitting on the edge of the bed waiting for them. But the room was fresh and aired where the maid had come in from the village to prepare the cottage for them, and there was no vestige of Peter's presence.

'I'll leave you for a few moments,' Benno said and she was grateful for his tact. On this occasion she wanted to undress in privacy. She put on a new night-dress and slipped between the sheets, growing increasingly fearful. Would Benno be able to tell that she wasn't a virgin? Would she do something that would give her away?

But when he entered the room in his dressing gown, she realized that he was as nervous as she was, if for different reasons. He turned out the light, then got into bed beside her. Gently, with

271

trembling fingers, he drew her towards him. She felt his hands on her bare shoulders, tenderly stroking her.

He was very, very different from Peter. Benno was infinitely caring and considerate, so very intent on not hurting her, on giving her pleasure as well as taking it for himself. Despite her worries, she found herself responding, wanting to love him as much as he loved her.

Later, as they lay under the tangled bedclothes, he whispered, 'Oh, Vicki, I love you so much.'

She burst into tears. Those were the words she had waited for Peter to say, but, instead, he had rolled over and gone to sleep. Now, dear, dear Benno was saying them. How could she have been such a fool as to believe what she had experienced with Peter was love?

'Vicki, darling, please don't cry,' Benno's voice pleaded anxiously. 'Vicki, it's all right. Everything's all right.' He bent over her, drawing her head to his chest, holding her as if she were a little girl. 'Hush, my darling, hush.'

'Oh, Benno, please don't leave me. Please, never leave me.'

'Of course I'll never leave you, my love. I shall always love you. For ever and ever and ever.' He was still holding her tightly to him, when she drifted into sleep.

The next morning, when the sick feeling started, she lay very still, not daring to move even to sip a glass of water. Eventually, Benno got up and brought her a light breakfast in bed. Miraculously, it settled her stomach. Perhaps it really had been nerves that had caused her wretchedness the previous day. And, as the days went by, with no further recurrence of the sickness, Viktoria began to feel more optimistic about the future.

The weather was kind to them in their lakeside retreat that September. Early morning frosts carpeted the grass with white, then the sun came up and in soft golden light flickered on the water and danced on the myriad falling leaves. Often, by day, they walked through the fields or sat on the fallen tree trunk, holding hands and saying little. Then, in the evening, they cooked simple meals, and sat by a log fire, talking or just gazing into the flames.

His honeymoon was a wonderful time for Benno. He never tired of being with Viktoria, of watching the changing patterns of her face, of listening to her voice, of holding her body in his arms, of looking at her while she slept, seemingly so young and vulnerable like a child. On their first night together, he had been very

272

nervous, scared that he would hurt her, frightened that when they shared that most intimate of human relationships, she would draw away from him. But she had not. And, strangely enough, her tears had moved him deeply. More than any words, they had shown him that she trusted him.

Sometimes, although neither of them ever mentioned his name, he found himself wondering about her relationship with Peter, for his cousin's behaviour had obviously hurt her badly. Often it was on the tip of his tongue to ask, for he knew it would make her feel better if she could share her trouble, but each time he bit back the words. One day, she would have sufficient faith to confide her secret and then, he knew, he would be really certain that she loved him. In the meantime, it was sufficient for him to be near her.

He also experienced a tremendous sense of relief at escaping from the real, outside world of newspapers, great battles, lists of wounded people and Kraus Village. As the halcyon days drew to their close and the time approached for their return to Berlin, he confessed to Viktoria his reluctance to return to his work.

She smiled at him sympathetically. 'Even honeymoons have to come to an end some day, but we can come back here whenever we want.'

He nodded gratefully, but already his mind was back in Kraus Chemie, watching thousands of men making the equipment of war. And, above all, it was thinking of a door marked, *PRIVATE. ENTRY TO UNAUTHORIZED PERSONS STRICTLY FORBIDDEN.* Although he had a far greater knowledge of chemistry now than when he had first arrived in Berlin, he was still no chemist. That door was no longer closed to him, but he was little wiser for having entered it. All he knew was that the research chemists were making some kind of gas. The ramifications filled him with fear.

On their last evening, he took her hand and walked beside the lake. 'So long as I stay in the family business, I shall one day be a very wealthy man. You realize that, don't you?'

'But that's not why I married you.'

'Hush, I never thought you did. No, Vicki, what I want to warn you is that, one day, I may be forced to disagree with my father over a matter of policy, and, if that happened, I could well lose and be thrown out of the company. In such a case, would you back me and be prepared to take the consequences?'

'You mean you'd be disinherited?'

'I might be and so might our children, if we have any.' Viktoria was silent and Benno glanced at her. There was a slight flush on her cheeks. 'You realize that after this honeymoon it's quite possible that we'll have children?' When she nodded, he continued, 'So we have to think of them as well as ourselves.'

'You've never really liked working at Kraus Chemie, have you?' You've always said you'd prefer to work with people. Well, there is always the Quadriga. Ever since Count Ewald died, Papa seems to have aged. I've been helping him a bit and I'll help more once we're home again. I know the hotel is very small compared to Kraus Industries, but you'll always have a home there. Marriage is a partnership. You've helped me, so of course I would help you.'

'Helped you? What do you mean?'

She reddened. 'Nothing. I just mean that you've been so kind to me, that already you've proved such a wonderful husband, I want to be a good wife to you.'

He had 'helped' her. It was a strange thing to say. But Benno had already decided to bide his time. 'You're the most wonderful wife in the world,' he assured her, putting his arm round her shoulders and drawing her close to him. He, at least, was telling the truth.

The day they arrived home from Heiligensee, Emil Graber passed away in his sleep. Although he had been ill for such a long time, the old diplomat's death affected Karl deeply, for not only had he been fond of Ricarda's father, he also knew that the success of Café Jochum and the Hotel Quadriga had been due in no small measure to him.

'He introduced me to the new cuisine and to Mesurier,' he said sadly to Ricarda after the funeral. 'If it hadn't been for him the British trade delegation would never have come to Café Jochum and the Kaiser would never have dined in my restaurant. And, as a result of that dinner, of course, we built the Quadriga. First Ewald and now your father. All our old friends are dying.'

Viktoria, walking between her sister and Benno, following her parents through the small churchyard at Charlottenburg, thought how they had both aged. Ricarda's auburn head was now heavily streaked with grey, while Karl's hair and moustache were almost white. Before her marriage, she hadn't noticed these changes; now they hit her with force.

That evening, she asked Benno, 'Do you mind if I help my parents more in the hotel?'

'If it makes you happy, my dearest.'

So, every morning, she accompanied her father down to his private office and started to learn the intricacies of running the hotel. To her surprise, Karl not only did not object to her presence, but seemed pleased, increasingly leaving the administration to her while he talked to guests in the bar or the Empire Room. Soon, indeed, she began to believe she was running the hotel, for increasingly the staff came to her and not her father with their problems and even guests referred to her with their requests.

She felt so well those days that she found it hard to believe that she was pregnant. Her tummy was still quite flat and the morning sickness had passed. Sometimes she looked at herself and wondered if she really were pregnant, for other than Dr Katz's confirmation and the fact that she had not bled for over three months, there was no sign of a new human being growing inside her.

She realized, however, that some time she had to break the news to Benno and to her family, and that in this, yet again, the timing was of ultimate importance. But once that hurdle was passed, she reflected thankfully, most of her problems would be behind her.

In the middle of November she went to see Dr Blattner, whose plush surgery on the Kurfuerstendamm was very different from the squalid conditions of Wedding. 'You were married in September, I believe, Frau Jochum-Kraus?' he asked gravely, after he had examined her. 'But I presume you would prefer nobody to know that you celebrated your marriage in advance?'

Embarrassed, she nodded. 'My husband, our parents ...'

'I understand. There's nothing so unusual about the situation. We shall just tell everyone that the child is premature. You're fortunate that it isn't showing yet. But it will soon.'

That evening she summoned up her courage to tell Benno. 'We're going to have a baby?' he said. 'But, Vicki, what wonderful news!'

'Dr Blattner says it's due about the end of June.' She held her breath, as Benno calculated back nine months.

'So you conceived at Heiligensee. Isn't that a lovely thought?' Then he looked at her anxiously. 'You must take great care of yourself from now on and not work too hard in the hotel. It would be dreadful if anything went wrong. In fact, Vicki, maybe you should stop working and just rest.'

'Oh, don't be silly! I feel better than I've ever felt in my life.' It was true. She felt as if a great weight had been lifted from her shoulders.

When she told her parents, Karl immediately insisted upon opening a bottle of champagne, his spirits lifting at the first good news he had received for many months. Ricarda kissed her tenderly, remembering her own long, childless years. 'I'm so pleased for you, my darling.'

Only Luise looked at her in a strange fashion and, when they were alone, said to her, 'Wasn't that a bit quick, Vicki? Why on earth do you want to have a baby?'

Just fifteen, Luise was already quite tall, more delicately built than Viktoria, with thin hands and a long, lean body. Her mane of copper-coloured hair and her vivid green eyes enhanced the rather Slavic bone structure that she had inherited from her mother. She was attending Fraeulein Luetzow's Academy for Young Ladies, but had no idea what she wanted to do with her life. Although she loved the hotel, she did not see it in the same way Viktoria did. To her it was a background or a stage upon which she performed to the admiration of staff and guests — but it was not a place of work. Work, like so many other things in Luise's vocabulary, was boring.

Now, she thought it very strange that, having become so involved in the hotel, Viktoria should decide to have a baby. But then, Viktoria had changed such a lot since the beginning of the war. Why, she wondered, had her sister suddenly decided to marry Benno for a start? He was a nice enough person, but why hadn't she at least waited for Peter von Biederstein to come home on leave? Something very odd had happened and Luise was now certain it was to do with the baby. She might only be fifteen, but she was not totally ignorant. Who, she couldn't help wondering, was the father — Peter or Benno? Since she had never much liked Peter, and never understood what Viktoria saw in him, she rather hoped it was Benno.

Benno carried the thought of his wife and his unborn child with him wherever he went, for they gave his life a purpose it had never had before. It seemed simple, at Heiligensee, to talk about leaving Kraus Chemie but now that he had these additional responsibilities he knew that he must see his job through to the bitter end, which meant to the end of the war.

The greatest source of information about the state of the war were wounded soldiers who were now starting to return home in depressingly large numbers. So far as Benno could ascertain, the war had reached a deadlock on both the eastern and the western fronts. After the failure of the Schlieffen Plan, General von Moltke had been sacked and replaced by General Falkenhayn, while General Hindenburg had been duly brought out of retirement. After seizing Antwerp, German armies had come up against the British at Ypres, where the battle still continued. In the east, since the victorious battle of Tannenberg in August, fighting was no longer taking place on German soil, but had moved to the Austrian-Hungarian-Russian borders.

Even Baron Heinrich seemed little more informed when he and Ernst visited Berlin in December. 'There's a deadlock on land and a deadlock at sea, although the deadlock at sea is because no major engagements have been made. Much against Admiral von Tirpitz's better judgement, nearly all our battleships are simply sitting in harbour. A flagship like the *Prussia* should be knocking hell out of the British.'

'I believe the Kaiser is reserving her for a special role in the war,' Ernst ventured.

'Thank you, Ernst, no doubt His Majesty knows what he's doing.' However, a puzzled frown creased the Baron's brow. 'I can't help feeling that we should be building more submarines.' He was silent for a moment, then he shuffled his papers decisively. 'Well, Benno, suppose you give us the quarter's results for Kraus Chemie.'

For the next half-hour they discussed the chemical plant's turnover and profits, which were, needless to say, excellent like the rest of the Kraus Group. If the war continued as it was doing, the Kraus family would be one of the richest in Germany. 'Well, I think that's all,' the Baron said in satisfaction.

'There is one other thing,' Benno said. 'I want to know about the gas that we're making here. I have every reason to believe it's poison gas, and, if that's so, it was banned by the Hague Convention in 1899. I'm responsible for this factory, Father, and I think I've a right to know what's going on.'

His father shook his head impatiently. 'It's only experimental, but if you really want to know, it's tear gas. It isn't poisonous; it merely causes temporary blindness, that's all. In battle, it reduces the effectiveness of the infantry, allowing our troops to gain territory while creating havoc on the other side.'

Benno shook his head. 'I don't like it.'

'War is a nasty business, Benno, but it's where we make our money.' He stood up. 'Ernst and I are going to Breslau now, and then we're travelling to Fuerstenmark for the weekend. Have you told your brother your news?' he asked Ernst.

'I'm engaged to Trudi von Biederstein,' Ernst said proudly. 'We're getting married at Fuerstenmark in February. You and your wife will be invited, of course.'

'My congratulations.' Benno shook his brother's hand. As the elder son, Ernst was, and always had been, the most important figure in his father's eyes, for he was the heir apparent to the empire. His engagement was not unexpected, but somehow it seemed to push his own news into insignificance. 'You'll be pleased to hear that Viktoria is expecting our first child in June,' he said.

The Baron was already halfway through the door. 'Good, good, another Kraus,' he commented matter-of-factly. Benno knew he was much more interested in Ernst allying the family closer with the Biedersteins than in anything his second son did.

Their visit left Benno feeling depressed. He had done nothing to halt the production of the tear gas, although he at least now knew what it was. His father's reception of his news about his coming baby had been casual to say the least, and on top of that he and Viktoria were expected to go to Fuerstenmark in February for Ernst's wedding.

Before he left his office, he decided to try to find out whether Peter von Biederstein would be present before he told Viktoria the news.

Ernst volunteered the information in a brief letter enclosed with their invitation. 'We are very sorry to tell you that Cousin Peter is unable to obtain leave, so will not attend. However, all the rest of the family will be present.'

Viktoria did not look forward to the wedding. She scarcely knew Ernst and had never liked Trudi, who had always treated her contemptuously. Their marriage, she supposed, was a good thing for both families and, to her father's joy, would link the Jochums with the von Biedersteins, albeit tenuously. However, Ernst and Trudi would probably be happy together, and, while Ernst continued to expand Kraus Industries, Trudi would become a good wife and mother, never deceiving her husband in the way Viktoria was deceiving his brother.

By the time she and Benno went to Fuerstenmark, she was already big with Peter's child. Sitting for the first time in the small church where, twenty-six years earlier, her parents had met, she stared at the stiff von Biederstein backs in front of her, wondering what they would do if they knew her secret. She could imagine their righteous indignation, the scandalized gasps, the horrified cries. Well, they will never know, she thought. I shall never give them the satisfaction.

As the pastor's address echoed down the nave, she glanced at the couple standing by the altar. Once she had been foolish enough to think that she would be standing there as the bride to the heir of Fuerstenmark. Involuntarily, tears rose to her eyes.

At length, the service was over and they made their way, through a guard of honour made up from village children, across the courtyard into the castle, where the bride and groom were waiting to receive their guests. With all the dignity she could muster, Viktoria shook hands with them, with Count Johann and Countess Anna, with Baron Heinrich and Countess Julia, the feudal lords and ladies of Fuerstenmark, to whose ranks she had once, naïvely, aspired to belong.

The huge, vaulted room was crowded with people from the aristocracy, from ministries and diplomatic circles; the same kind, in fact, whom they welcomed to the Hotel Quadriga. But that was the difference. Whatever she and her parents believed themselves to be, they were still the servants of these people. They were no different from the waiters handing out glasses of champagne. Viktoria's mistake had been to believe herself their equal. Suddenly, she shivered and grasped Benno's hand.

'Come and sit down,' he said, leading her to a seat in a quiet corner. 'Do you know that this is the first place I was brought after I was born?'

She smiled, grateful for his tacit understanding. 'Yes, Papa's often told me. Apparently you saw him and yelled.'

'I'm sure it wasn't because of him. I think it was because all these Biedersteins intimidated me even then!'

Slowly, the day dragged past. As Viktoria watched the assembled guests in the draughty hall, she couldn't help feeling that, instead of attending a wedding, she was participating in a wake, the ghostly celebration of the end of her life with Peter.

They did not stay the night, but travelled back by train that evening. All day long, neither of them had mentioned Peter, but each was aware of his presence in the other's thoughts and both knew that the other was relieved the wedding was over.

As the last weeks of her pregnancy approached, Viktoria felt a sudden surge of excitement. At long last she was going to see the child she had carried within her for so long. Already she and Benno had decided that if it was a boy they would call him Stefan and if it was a girl, Monika. But whatever it was, boy or girl, she knew it was going to be a very special baby. By April, she was huge. She waddled about the hotel in an ungainly manner, continuing to help Karl with his paperwork. 'Mama worked until the last minute,' she told Benno, 'and my baby isn't due for ages yet.'

He looked at her worriedly. 'I think we should call in Dr Blattner.'

After the doctor had examined her, he told them, 'It looks as if it may be a premature birth. You must rest and not exert yourself too much, Frau Jochum-Kraus. With a first pregnancy, one can't be too careful. Try not to worry her, Herr Kraus.' Viktoria smiled at him, grateful that he had remembered his promise.

'You've been doing too much,' Benno scolded her. 'Now, for once, you're going to do what you're told and rest. This is my child we're talking about, remember?'

Benno went around with a drawn, preoccupied look those days, although when Viktoria asked him if she could share his problems, he always forced a smile, saying, 'It's only work, darling. This damned war is going on too long. The sooner it's over the better.'

Ricarda spent as much time with her as possible, for, in Viktoria's absence, she had started helping Karl again. Often in the late afternoon, when Viktoria had taken her afternoon nap, they sat companionably together, Ricarda working at her embroidery, Viktoria restlessly watching her. Sometimes she wondered if her mother suspected the truth now about her sudden decision to marry Benno, but if she did, she never said anything. Possibly her anxieties about Opa and Karl at that time had clouded her memory.

Her labour started in the early hours of 28 April. Throughout the long, agonizing hours that followed, Ricarda sat beside her, wiping her forehead with a damp towel, holding her hand and murmuring calm words of comfort, while outside Benno and Karl anxiously paced the hall, watched with slight amusement by Dr Blattner. 'Let's hope it's a boy this time,' Karl said. 'Always wanted a boy myself, and I got two daughters.'

'Two very charming daughters,' Benno said politely, but his mind was on Viktoria, filled with dread that something might go wrong, that the terrible tales he had heard of women dying in childbirth might prove true in her case.

'Ricarda took a long time, too,' Karl told him. 'She had Viktoria the day the hotel was opened, you know.'

'Was it like this for you, too, Mama?' Viktoria asked, her hair hanging moistly around her temples, fighting the urge to scream at the pain.

'It's worth it,' Ricarda assured her.

When Dr Blattner finally placed the wrinkled little bundle that was her son in her arms, Viktoria stared at him in awe. This was her child, she thought fiercely, holding him to her protectively. 'You're mine, and nobody is ever going to take you away.'

Dr Blattner smiled. 'Well, I'm afraid I'm going to take him away now, Frau Jochum-Kraus. You must rest.'

'Just a few minutes more,' she pleaded. She felt very tired, but this was her moment of glory, something she had worked towards for nine months. The doctor nodded, and Viktoria held Stefan tightly to her. It was as if, for the first time in her life, she had something that belonged totally to her. She was overwhelmed by a sense of love, greater than any she had ever experienced before. 'I love you,' she told her baby, 'oh, I love you so much. I loved you before you were born, but now you're here, I'm going to spend my whole life proving how much I love you.'

While she slept, Benno stood in the nursery, gazing down at Stefan. He was so perfectly formed, it did not seem possible that he was premature. Gently, Benno lifted his tiny hands, with their minute fingernails, then smiled as they bunched into a fist around his finger. He looked at the soft, brown down on his head, the button nose, the tightly closed eyes. Was this really his son, he wondered, or was this, in fact, the secret that Viktoria had been keeping from him? 'Something happened,' she had said, 'and then war broke out and Peter went away.'

Who was his father — himself, or Peter von Biederstein? Then Stefan opened his eyes and stared back at him, looking more like a very wise old man than a helpless infant. For a long time, they stared at each other and suddenly Benno had the sensation that the child was trying to tell him something. He was gazing at him intently, as if he wanted to get to know Benno as much as Benno wanted to know him. Then he yawned, as if to say, 'You'll do.'

'Hello, son,' Benno said.

At that moment, Nurse Bauer, now in her sixties and back to look after another generation of Jochums, bustled into the room. Stefan looked again at Benno, then started to cry. 'Bless his little heart, he's telling us he's hungry.'

But Benno knew differently. Stefan had just assured him that he considered him his father.

The first months of Stefan's life flew by with almost frightening speed, so far as Viktoria was concerned. As soon as she could, she started helping her father again in the hotel, leaving Nurse Bauer to look after Stefan's basic needs. The nurse found herself with the almost impossible task of keeping Benno out of the nursery. 'Herr Kraus,' she scolded, 'it's not good for the baby for you to keep picking him up! He needs to sleep!'

Often, Viktoria awoke in the night to find the bed beside her empty and Benno sitting by Stefan's cradle. 'I thought I heard him cry. I came to make sure he was all right.'

'I've never known a household like it,' Nurse Bauer complained. 'Anyone would think he doesn't trust me to do my job. It's not natural, a father interfering like this all the time. Why, most men can hardly be bothered to come into the nursery.'

'Why, I think that's rather sad, Nurse Bauer,' Viktoria commented. 'Poor children, growing up without a father's love.'

'Yes, I seem to remember your father was rather soft about you and Miss Luise, too. Must be something funny about the air in this hotel.'

It was then that Viktoria finally decided never to reveal to Benno the truth of Stefan's parentage. It did not matter, she convinced herself, so long as he and Stefan believed they were father and son.

'It's amazing,' Benno said, 'even his hair and eyes are like mine. And look at the way he curls his fingers. Just like I do.'

'From the way you talk, Benno,' Luise remarked, 'anyone would think that Viktoria had nothing to do with this baby at all.'

'Well, perhaps his mouth is like his mother's. But, of course, he's a boy, so it's natural that he should look like his father. Come on, Stefan, say hello to Papa.'

The baby gurgled and Benno cried. 'Did you hear that? He said Papa.'

'Nonsense,' Luise said, 'he's just hungry again. Nurse Bauer starves him.'

282

'Do you think so?'

'Oh, Benno, you really are amazing. Of course she doesn't starve him. Just look at the size of him. He's enormous!'

'You don't think he's too fat?'

Did Benno suspect the truth, Viktoria wondered. Was that why he constantly sought to assure himself and others that the baby took after him? Was this his way of begging her for reassurance? Was Nurse Bauer right when she said that his behaviour was unnatural? Or had her pregnancy and confinement tired her more than she thought, making her imagination over-active, so that she read double meanings into the most innocent words and acts? 'It's time for Nurse Bauer to change his napkins. Do you intend to stay here arguing all night over my son?'

'Your son?' Benno asked. 'My son, please.'

Lieutenant Count Peter von Biederstein's battalion was holding the front line trench some twenty miles from Ypres. So far as his eye could see the Belgian landscape stretched ahead of him, bleak and bare, empty of any tree, for those that had not been blasted out of the earth had been felled to make supports for the trenches. Fifty or sixty yards away, beyond the great fence of rolled barbed wire, was the ruined farmhouse that marked the enemy's front line trench.

It seemed to Peter that he had been looking at those blackened ruins for half a lifetime. Every day, they went through what had almost become a routine. Ever since they had encountered the British, neither side seemed capable of making the other give way. They had settled into the deep trenches dug by the infantry, vast ditches that cut through the Belgian countryside in a sharp line, north to south, and there they stayed.

At first light their huge siege guns thundered their shells into the British lines, in an attempt to blast the enemy to smithereens by the sheer velocity of their bombardment. And from the enemy's back lines came the returning barrage of the enemy's big guns, the howling of shells, the crash and rending explosions as they landed, the earth spouting up and shattering in huge clods. Deep in their dug-outs, Peter and his men waited as the ground shook around them.

At last there came that moment of eerie silence, so familiar to them now, when the big guns were quiet, and they waited for a voice to roar the order to attack. Then, from mile upon mile of trenches, grey-uniformed men poured up from the bowels of the earth towards that stretch of no-man's-land that separated them from the enemy, determined that by the end of the day it would be captured.

Peter never unbuttoned his Luger from its leather holster as he charged up and over the protective sandbags in front of his men without thinking of his Uncle Ewald, visualizing how splendid he must have looked as he led his cavalry charge, lance at the ready, through the cornfield towards that small Belgian village the previous August. Ever since he had learned of Ewald's death, he had sworn revenge. One Biederstein might have fallen, but another was still living to avenge him and German honour!

That morning, as the ranks of khaki British uniforms came cautiously through the mist towards him, he fired his Luger wildly into their ranks, with no certainty of making a kill from such a short-range weapon, yet strangely positive that he was immune from death. From all around him, there was the cracking of rifle fire, of muzzles crashing and recoiling, of breechlocks whirling home, the shrieking of bullets, the screaming of men as they twisted and fell in the dust, an intoxicating cacophony of strident sound. Then the gas mortars were fired, releasing greenish, yellow clouds of tear gas over the enemy lines, immobilizing the British troops more effectively than any Luger could hope to do.

At the end of the day, hundreds had been killed, while others, horribly mutilated, lay wounded on the soil of Flanders — Germans and Englishmen, often side by side, until the stretcher bearers came to carry them away. Peter von Biederstein led his depleted troops back to their dug-out. They had gained no ground and they had lost many valuable men. But they were still alive.

Waiting for him was a letter from Trudi. After rhapsodizing about life in the 'Fortress' she mentioned that Benno and Viktoria had had a baby son. Peter paid the news as much heed as he had that of their marriage. Viktoria had been amusing, but she meant nothing to him any more. After supper, he dutifully started a letter to Ilse von Schennig.

But not even to Ilse, the daughter of his commanding officer, could he tell the truth about the war. Sometimes he secretly feared they would still be in the same trench in a year's time. The only way they could hope to win was by pouring in an ever greater bombardment of artillery and even larger numbers of men. It was a discouraging prospect.

That August, Georg Jankowski was suddenly given his first week's leave. As the train slowly drew into the Anhalter Station, there were none of the cheering crowds who had seen the mobilized troops off so gaily a year earlier, no auburn-haired girl waving a cornflower blue hat, only echoing halls and grey faces. Georg shouldered his pack wearily, said goodbye to his travelling companions, and took a tram to Charlottenburg.

The flat was empty when he arrived and, although he was disappointed at the lack of welcome, he was not surprised to find Pipsi out, nor was he altogether sorry, for a short while alone would give him time to readjust to civilian life and, above all, to freedom. He unpacked his kit, made himself a cup of coffee and took a bath; then, unsure what to do next, he walked round the rooms. The once so familiar furniture and pictures seemed alien to him and he felt like a stranger in his own home. Within an hour, the silence of the apartment grated on his nerves and his very inactivity grew oppressive. Desperately he began to wish that Pipsi would return, but there came no sound of a key in a lock. In the end, he lay down on the bed and went to sleep.

He was woken by somebody shaking him roughly and, for a moment, he thought he was still in his billet in Belgium; then he heard Pipsi's voice saying peevishly, 'Really, Georg, you might have warned me that you were coming home. You gave me the shock of my life, when I came in here and found you lying on the bed. And you could have taken off your boots. Look at my white bedspread ...'

Instead, he looked at her. She was even more beautiful than he remembered, dressed in a tight-fitting cream costume with a yellow hat and long yellow gloves that accentuated the darkness of her features. But there was a petulant scowl on her face and no smile of welcome in her eyes. She did not kiss him, but turned abruptly away, throwing her hat and gloves on a chair. 'Well, you'll have to look after yourself, because I'm very busy this week. I have a part in a play at the German Theatre.'

He stood up and took her in his arms. 'Pipsi, I'm sorry I gave you a shock, but there was no way of letting you know.'

She allowed him to kiss her, then drew away and went into the kitchen. 'Well, since you're here, we may as well have something to eat. There isn't much. I eat out most evenings.'

As they ate she told him a little about her life during his absence. 'The theatres closed very soon after you went, but now they're open again, although the plays that are being staged are pretty dreadful,' she complained. For about half an hour she continued to talk about the theatre, then she looked at the clock. 'Well, darling, I'm sorry, but I must go. Don't bother to wait up for me. I'm sure to be very late.'

Unable to bear the loneliness of his own company and the desolation of his thoughts, Georg put on his jacket and took a tram to Uncle Franz's flat. There, at least, he knew, he would find a different kind of reception.

When he opened the door the old man looked at him as though he were a ghost, and then he took Georg in his arms. 'My boy, my boy, so you've come back safe! Every night, I have prayed for you. And now, my prayers have been answered. Come in and talk to me.'

Even now that he had an audience, however, Georg found it hard to speak of the misery of the war. 'Week after week, the front line hardly moves. Every day, we wake to the sight of the same desolate piece of no-man's-land and the knowledge that, by the time that day is over, hundreds more men will have been slaughtered. Uncle Franz, why are we fighting this war?'

His uncle shook his head.

'I don't hate the tommies,' Georg went on, 'and I don't believe they hate us. In fact, I sometimes believe that if the generals and politicians left it to us, we would cut through those barbed wire fences and embrace each other, just to call a halt to the whole, senseless business.'

Franz laid a gnarled hand on his. 'I am sorry, Georg, I am so sorry.' He paused for a moment, then he went on, 'But you must be careful not to talk like this to anyone else. Here, at home, everyone believes in the war and that Germany will win it.'

Georg rubbed his hand across his eyes. 'Win, lose, what does it matter? All I know is that to live on the battlefields of Belgium is to know hell on earth.'

'That isn't what we are told here. I believe you, Georg, because at Ullstein, I see the reports that are filed by the few journalists who are permitted at the front. I also know that other things, like our U-boats sinking the British passenger liner *Lusitania* in May, are dreadful matters, although they are hailed as mighty victories. But all journalists' reports are censored and every defeat is turned into a victory. The public want to believe that we are winning. They don't want to know about hell on earth.'

286

'Why don't the newspapers print the truth?'

'The editors aren't allowed to. Any paper that defies the censorship laws is closed down. Already many editors have lost their jobs. Now most of them simply comply with the rules.'

Although he was pleased to see Uncle Franz, Georg felt very depressed when he left him late that evening. The flat was in darkness still and it was one o'clock before he heard Pipsi come in. Rather than face an argument, he pretended to be asleep.

The only evening of his leave that he really enjoyed was the last one, which they spent with Theo, Sophie and their two boys in Grunewald. At thirty-five, Theo looked very much as his father had done at the same age, his dark hair turning silver at the temples, his elegant suit made by Knize, the city's best tailor. He now ran the Arendt Bank, for Isaak had suffered a stroke some years earlier and lived an invalid's existence in a wing of Theo's villa.

Both Theo and Sophie made Georg feel very welcome, serving a fine dinner with excellent wine and, when the meal was over, Theo invited Georg into his study to ask him many pertinent questions about the progress of the war. When he had finished his hesitant account of his experiences, Georg added, 'Of course, I'm not a general, I'm just an infantryman, but, from the depths of my heart, I wish it could be over soon.'

Theo nodded, a worried frown creasing his forehead. 'You're not alone, although few people are brave enough to admit it. Apart from the loss of lives, Georg, we can't afford for this war to go on much longer. You probably haven't been home long enough to realize it, but war is already starting to prove very expensive. Food prices are rising sharply and, if there is a bad harvest this autumn, there are going to be drastic food shortages. I don't know what army rations are like.'

'The food isn't very good and the men complain all the time that there isn't enough, but that's the army.'

Theo sighed deeply. 'British ships are blockading our ports, although they can't prevent home-grown supplies reaching us from the east. But, as more men are conscripted, our agricultural land is being neglected. I believe we're in for very troubled times if the war goes on much longer.'

That night, possibly because they had both drunk too much wine, Pipsi allowed him to make love to her for the only time. To his great mortification, it was over within seconds, and Pipsi was rolling away from him, muttering sulkily, 'Well, if that's all you can do, after being away from me for so long ... And you didn't take any precautions. Let's just hope I don't get pregnant.'

Very early next morning, he left again for the front. It felt almost as if he were going home.

In order to finance the war, the Reichstag had approved a series of war loans already amounting to four and a half milliard marks, with another ten milliard loan just being approved. To augment these loans, parliament also asked for donations from the public.

A giant wooden figure of Field Marshal Hindenburg was erected in front of the Reichstag, into which people were invited to hammer nails. It was this huge statue that the Jochums approached one autumn afternoon in a stately procession, Karl and Ricarda leading, Luise and Viktoria behind and, in the rear, Nurse Bauer pushing six-month-old Stefan in his perambulator. Solemnly, Karl reached into his purse and handed the attendant in military uniform a handful of gold coins. 'Thank you, sir,' the man reverently counted the money, then gave Karl five gold nails and a hammer. With great ceremony, Karl knocked his gold nail into Hindenburg, then passed Ricarda her nail and the hammer. Nurse Bauer paid her own contribution to the War Loan. Unlike the Jochums, she could not afford a hundred marks for a gold nail, so she gave five marks and received a silver one.

When they were all finished, Karl announced with satisfaction, 'Our brave lads are doing their duty on the battlefield. Now we have done ours. Tonight we can sleep with easy minds.'

As they returned to the Hotel Quadriga, they passed many wounded men, hobbling along on crutches, with bandaged heads and arms in slings, but Karl ignored them, for they were a result of the war upon which he preferred not to dwell. There had to be casualties, but it was only pessimists who spoke about them.

That evening, after supper, he reached for his newspaper. 'We shall win at Loos. The French have stopped their attack. The British can't last now. We shall have won by Christmas.' They looked at him doubtfully, and he knew they were thinking that this time last year he had been saying the same thing. 'I'm going to the bar,' he declared, picking up his paper. 'There will be somebody there who agrees with me.'

To his joy, he discovered Benno and Theo Arendt deep in conversation and made his way towards them. 'Listen to this,' he announced triumphantly. 'It says here that the French can't last out much longer. They're losing their coal fields, their industrial plants and their iron mines. All behind German lines! The English are keeping them going for the moment, but they can't do that for much longer.'

Theo brushed Karl's newspaper aside. 'Herr Jochum, you shouldn't believe everything you read in the newspapers. Most of it is just propaganda. Any newspaper that tries to tell the truth about the war is suppressed, particularly any which supports the peace effort.'

Karl stared at him belligerently. He didn't want peace — he wanted victory. 'I should think so, too! To talk of peace is defeatist, it's what the socialists want.'

'Not just the socialists. You and I are all right, we have our fine houses and a comfortable bed to sleep in at night. But think of the ordinary people, Herr Jochum, think of the infantryman, plodding through the mud without enough to eat, and the factory worker here at home trying to produce arms enough to keep the war machine going and wondering where his next meal is coming from. Rising food prices may not affect us — yet — but they do affect the workers.'

'Rubbish, it's not as bad as that.'

'But it will be, you mark my words, it will be. Take the War Loans, for instance — and this is something I do know something about. The money for those loans has to come from somewhere. And what happens when there is no more money? What is the government going to do then? That's why I believe the people who disagree with them should be allowed to voice their opinions publicly — politicians like Karl Liebknecht and journalists like Reinhardt Meyer.'

With a great effort, Karl forced himself to control his anger. 'Men like that are traitors and cowards. I've met Meyer and I know his sole aim is to overthrow the government and the Kaiser. He is using the war for his own, vile political purposes.'

'But he's a competent journalist with a good brain, Herr Jochum, and I believe he has as much right to be heard as you or I. Censorship is a bad thing.'

'No! If the truth is detrimental to the public good, it must be suppressed. There has to be censorship. We are constantly being warned to be on our watch for spies, but if we allowed our newspapers to print every defeatist thought uttered, the enemy wouldn't need spies. No, Herr Arendt, we must show a brave face, confident of victory, both to ourselves and to the outside world.'

'And are you so confident of victory, Herr Jochum?'

Karl stared at him astounded. 'But, of course I am. Germany has the greatest army in the world. We are winning on both fronts. The war will be over by Christmas. Look, it says so in the paper!'

Theo looked at his watch. 'I'm sorry to have to interrupt this discussion, but I ought to be leaving. Sophie will be wondering what's happened to me.'

'Jews!' Karl exclaimed after the banker had left. 'You'd think they didn't stand to make a pfennig out of this war!'

Benno, who hadn't said a word until now, looked at his father-in-law thoughtfully. 'I'm afraid I agree with much of what Theo said, sir.'

'Bah, don't tell me you're becoming a socialist too. What do you think I do all day here at the Quadriga? Live on caviar and champagne? Yes, I know the hotel is full, but do you think I'm making any money out of any of these people, all these officials who are staying here? Of course I'm not. But I still have outstanding mortgages that have to be paid off, wages, salaries, supplies and services to pay for. All of which puts me in a slightly different situation from the Arendt Bank and Kraus Industries.' He held up a warning finger. 'Now, hear me out, Benno, for this concerns you too.

'Who organizes the War Loans? And who finances industrial companies like yours? The Jews, of course! And who finances the Russian, British and French armies? The Jews, Benno. And who finances their armaments and shipbuilding industries? The Jews. So, who's going to win this war? In the long run, the Jews are! But who are now saying that the war should end? The Jews!'

Benno looked at him doubtfully. 'Theo is also a German.'

'So why hasn't he volunteered for active service?'

'Like myself, he has a business to run and he's a family man.'

But Karl was not prepared to listen to reason. 'He's a socialist. Jews and socialists — they're the bane of our lives. They all ought to be locked up or shot!'

That winter Viktoria found her load of the hotel administration increasing. All able men between the ages of eighteen and forty-five were called up and, for the first time, women were employed in the kitchens. It seemed as if the whole character of the hotel was being remoulded in front of her very eyes. Every care was taken that its standards did not suffer, but that in itself required time, money and constant attention.

She saw her task as a tremendous challenge, rising to it with verve and decisiveness. The government officials who lived at the hotel did not require the seven-course meals for which the Quadriga had gained a reputation, and for them the kitchens had to provide the good quality, conventional German meals for which Fritzi Messner was famous. But, at the same time, huge banquets were still held by wealthy industrialists, often in support of the war effort. Food had to be bought for all these functions and, gradually, Viktoria found herself meeting with suppliers, haggling over prices, sometimes buying in bulk; her father simply let her get on with it.

'Do you know, Benno,' she said one evening, in the privacy of their room, 'I think Papa is more interested in the war than he is the hotel.'

Benno laughed wearily. 'Well, it looks as if you're doing a splendid job. Let's just hope your father discovers a way of winning the war quickly.'

He had deep worries of his own, which he did not confide in Viktoria. He knew now that the chlorine gas made at Kraus Chemie had been used by the German armies at Ypres in April, just before Stefan was born, and that research was continuing into more lethal gases. Whenever he passed the door to the laboratory at Kraus Village, he visualized to himself the ghastly sensation that must be experienced by British soldiers when that greenish yellow cloud appeared in front of them. Those days he was not proud to be a Kraus.

His constant source of joy and consolation was his son, whom he loved more with every day that passed, spending at least a few minutes with the baby every day, even if it was late at night and Stefan was asleep. On his first birthday, he even took the afternoon off work so that he could join in the birthday celebrations.

To mark the event, Karl personally made a cake with one large candle, while Viktoria, Ricarda, Luise and Nurse Bauer decorated the nursery with flowers and paper chains. Stefan's presents were piled high on a special birthday table. 'So where's the birthday boy?' Benno asked, as he entered a room tense with excitement.

Viktoria lifted him off his grandmother's lap and put him gently down on the floor. Instead of tumbling to his knees, Stefan's face took on a look of grim concentration, then, unaided by anyone, he crossed the room with tottering steps. 'Papi, Papi!' he gurgled.

Benno picked him up and swung him round in the air. 'He can walk and talk! Only one year old and he can walk and talk! Aren't you the cleverest little man in the world, Stefi?'

For a few hours, that April afternoon in 1916, he forgot about the war.

Chapter Eleven

Baron Heinrich was at Kraushaven in May 1916 when news reached him that Admiral Tirpitz, the head of the Navy League, had resigned. To the Baron, this could mean only one thing, namely that the Admiral had lost his long fight with the Kaiser over unrestricted submarine warfare and had been forced out of office.

For a long time, a battle had been raging between army and navy chiefs and political party leaders about submarine warfare, with von Tirpitz, supported by the Junkers, advocating unrestricted submarine warfare on all enemy shipping including unarmed merchant ships. The Chancellor and the Kaiser insisted that their battle fleet would prove the only decisive weapon in the war. Privately, the Baron was convinced Tirpitz was right and the Emperor wrong. Ever since they had sunk the *Lusitania*, events had proved that Germany could rule the waves, not with the huge warships so favoured by His Majesty, but with U-boats, sneaking underwater, sinking unsuspecting surface shipping with their deadly torpedoes.

Like Tirpitz, he believed that the war could be won most effectively and swiftly by using U-boats to blockade and mine British ports, thus swiftly starving the island into submission, before America could intervene.

The view was supported by the fact that, alongside the Kaiser's other dreadnoughts in Wilhelmshaven and Kiel, the *Prussia* had now lain idle for nearly two years awaiting her long-promised moment of glory in battle. Regularly, Baron Heinrich had written to and met with the Admiral Tirpitz and other navy chiefs, seeking a commission to build another *Prussia*, but each time he had been refused, although his shipyard had been kept busy with orders for small battle cruisers.

The Admiral's resignation, however, put a different complexion on matters. For a long while, Baron Heinrich sat at his desk, thinking over the ramifications and wondering how best to profit from the situation, then he sent for Kraus Marin's general manager and ordered him to prepare for an intensified construction of submarines. Tirpitz might be gone, but his supporters remained, as did the brutal reality of the war. Before long, there was going to be a demand for more submarines and when it came, the Baron was going to be ready for it. Next he summoned his secretary and dictated a carefully worded letter to the Navy League repeating his desire to serve his country by building another warship.

He soon had reason to be glad of that letter, for towards the end of the month he received confidential word from a friend in the Admiralty that the High Seas Fleet, under its Commander-in-Chief Admiral Scheer, was about to lure the British Grand Fleet out into the open seas off Jutland with the intention of destroying it by sheer overwhelming force. At long last, it appeared, the *Prussia* was preparing for battle. However, although from his vantage point at Kraushaven, he saw other great battleships leave Wilhelmshaven, the Baron did not see the *Prussia*.

Then, in the very early morning of 30 May, he was rewarded by the sight of two escort destroyers moving out to sea, followed by the unmistakable silhouette of the *Prussia*. He watched her with a critical eye, for he knew all her virtues and shortcomings. Fatter and with less draught than British dreadnoughts she had, like all flatter-bottomed boats, a propensity to roll in high seas. But, unlike British warships, the Baron knew that the *Prussia* was unsinkable, for her thick armour plating would protect her from British shells.

As if in confirmation of his thoughts, the *Prussia* hooted and clouds of smoke issued from her four distinctive funnels set in tandem. The *Prussia* was going to war. The Baron wished her luck.

Lieutenant Commander Roger Hicks gently raised the periscope of his E-series submarine. As in earlier observations, the sea was still dangerously calm. His field of vision swept towards Wilhelmshaven and he now saw a heavy pall of smoke clearly apparent in the dawn light. Could this be the *Prussia*? As the E26 had crept stealthily into the German Bight the previous night, Hicks had received coded radio orders from Commander Keys to watch out for and destroy the huge flagship. The Battle of Jutland was not going well for either side and if the *Prussia*, with her huge firepower, joined the fray, then Jellicoe's Grand Fleet could well lose what was, so far, the most decisive naval battle of the war.

So intent was he that he almost failed to notice the sinister shape of a German high-speed patrol boat near the periphery of his vision. He slammed down the periscope. 'Dive! Dive! Dive!'

Bells jangled as the submarine adopted a precarious angle. Loose crockery and cutlery crashed onto the deck as the coxswain stolidly called out the depth readings. Calmly, Hicks ordered, 'Hold her steady at ten fathoms and check the charts, Navigator.'

'Steady at ten fathoms, Captain.'

'Full ahead both. Hard a-starboard.' Coming towards them, they could hear the steady *thrum, thrum, thrum* of the patrol boat's propellers. 'Stop motors!'

The submarine gently creaked, a tin mug rolled from a table. The crew looked at each other from haunted eyes. Hicks concentrated on his watch. If they had been spotted, the depth charges would soon follow. He counted off the seconds — one, two, three ... twelve, thirteen. The sounds of the enemy's engines gradually receded. There were no explosions. 'Musta bin one of them Huns wiv fick specs,' a cockney voice said. There was a ripple of relieved laughter.

Half an hour later, Hicks brought his submarine up once more to periscope depth. With a flat sea, he knew he was taking a chance, but this time he did a slow 360° sweep with the periscope before concentrating again on Wilhelmshaven. 'My God,' he exclaimed, as the unmistakable silhouette of the *Prussia* emerged from behind the headland, 'the old man was right!' He counted the escort destroyers preceding her. Only two? 'Down periscope!' 'Bearing starboard twenty. Both ahead.' 'Load tubes one to six.'

'Tubes one to six ready, sir.'

Hicks's number one tapped him on the shoulder. 'Charts show a probable minefield ahead, sir.' Then he added quietly. 'Navigator suggests a passage to the North-West.'

'At her speed, we have only one chance of a hit, Number One. Maintain course.' He raised his periscope. The *Prussia* was now heading at full speed towards Heligoland. 'Fire! One to six!' he ordered. He felt the submarine judder as the torpedoes left her and sped through the water towards the German flagship.

The watchkeeper high in the *Prussia* saw the six white torpedo trails speeding through the water ahead of the massive battleship, with the obvious hope of intercepting her. He yelled down the phone to the bridge.

Admiral von Mecklenburg reacted swiftly. 'Hard to starboard,' he ordered, then waited anxiously as the ship started to change course. One torpedo after another passed harmlessly in front of her, as she manoueuvred awkwardly in the water. Four torpedo trails led out to sea.

The fifth torpedo exploded against the ship's torpedo net. The sixth hit her rudders and propellers. At a speed of twenty knots, the flagship went out of control, continuing to turn at an angle of 240°. 'Stop engines!' the Admiral shouted in panic, but even as he gave the order, he knew it was too late. The velocity of the *Prussia* was simply too great to stop her on her careering course towards destruction.

Aboard the British submarine, Hicks stared in awed horror as he saw the mighty flagship turn in the water and head towards the minefield. One moment she was there in the sight of his periscope and the next he could see only a sheet of flame as her magazines exploded. Her huge guns were tipped up at an awkward angle and then they disappeared as she was enveloped in a furnace of burning oil. There was a huge pall of black smoke and the *Prussia* sank.

'She's gone, Number One,' Hicks called and a cheer rang out from the crew of the submarine. He turned and grinned at them.

When he looked back through his periscope seconds later, however, he ceased to smile. The *Prussia*'s escort destroyers were heading towards the E26 at full speed. 'Dive! Dive! Dive!'

In his haste, he forgot about the mines that had sealed the *Prussia*'s fate. As the submarine tilted towards the ocean bed there was an ominous rasping sound against her side, followed by a massive explosion. Her lights went out and, as water poured into her, she lurched at a crazy angle, then plummeted to the bottom of the sea.

For a long time, the Baron stood on the quayside at Kraushaven staring at the pall of black smoke that hung on the distant horizon, unwilling to believe that his *Prussia* had been sunk. Not until twenty-four hours later were his fears confirmed. The *Prussia* was gone, only ten men surviving out of a crew of nearly thirteen hundred.

The newspapers described the disaster as a cowardly attack by a horde of British submarines and deplored the loss of Germany's mightiest flagship. They also hailed the Battle of Jutland as the country's greatest naval victory. But Baron Heinrich knew there had been no real victory and that they could not afford another such battle. Nor was he alone, for once again lobbying set up in the

Reichstag for unlimited submarine warfare to beat the British at their own game.

Very soon orders were pouring in to Kraus Marin for submarines, which, because of the Baron's farsightedness, the shipyard was able to fulfil promptly. Yet in the vicious political battle that continued to rage for and against unlimited submarine warfare, no decision was reached. With his devious mind, the Baron could see that many issues were at stake, for some factions hoped to force the Chancellor to resign, while others were fearful of American reprisals if the submarine lobby had its way.

Baron Heinrich did not openly take sides with either group. With his production at Kraushaven now totally committed to submarine production, his mind was already ranging far ahead to the days when the war would be over and there would be no more demand for either dreadnoughts or submarines.

Strangely enough, his plans for the future were based on something Benno had said when they had first visited Kraushaven. 'I thought you might build a transatlantic liner,' the boy had said, 'one even bigger and faster and more luxurious than the *Wilhelm der Grosse*, so that Kraus could win the Blue Riband for Germany.'

The *Wilhelm der Grosse* had been sunk in active war service in 1914 off West Africa, while the shares the Baron held in Ballin's Hamburg-Amerika Line had risen enormously since the beginning of the war. The demand for passenger liners was going to increase immediately the war was over — whichever side won.

Without telling anybody, Baron Heinrich von Kraus made a journey to see Jan van der Jong, an old friend in Rotterdam in neutral Holland, with whom he had dealt before the war. His company was a small one, engaged mainly in the building of flat-bottomed barges and tugs.

'Despite everything the politicians, the military and the papers say, I'm not at all certain that Germany is going to win the war,' the Baron explained. 'We're in stalemate on all our fronts and the Kaiser refuses to listen to reason about unrestricted submarine warfare. Now, whatever happens, I intend that Kraus won't lose. However, it may be that we shall need friends in neutral countries. Would your company be interested in a joint venture with Kraus Marin?'

'I'd be very interested.'

'We still have Wetzlar and we shall always have access to raw materials and components. And we shall still have Kraushaven, with its long slipway. My intention is to build a transatlantic liner. Are you willing to help?'

Van der Jong nodded enthusiastically.

'In the meantime, of course,' Baron Heinrich said smoothly, 'our discussion here today remains purely confidential.'

Nothing was further from Benno's mind than transatlantic liners. What had been a murmur of discontent among the workers in his factory was now rising to almost open rebellion. 'The people are becoming disillusioned and want peace,' he told Viktoria one evening, after a particularly tiring day. 'Agitators like your cousin, Olga, and journalists like her husband, Reinhardt, have a very real following among my workforce. Prices are going up and wages simply aren't keeping up with them. I think that unless something is done, there's going to be very real trouble soon.'

'But what can be done?'

'Personally, I believe we should allow President Wilson of America to mediate, as he's offering. We should at least consider his proposals seriously, even if they do mean a peace without victory. Anything is better than involving ourselves in a war against America, which we could only lose. And then, we should sort out our internal affairs, because if we're not careful, we're going to find ourselves not only involved in a world war, but in a civil war.'

'Are you serious?'

Benno nodded. 'Olga waits outside the gates of Kraus Chemie every evening to harangue the workers as they leave the factory. Her speeches are backed up by her husband's articles, which, very occasionally, escape the censors. One day, however, she will be inciting our workers to strike, as a show of solidarity against the government. Of course, strikes are forbidden, but they are the workers' strongest weapon.'

'You mean Olga has become that important?'

'Not here in the city centre. But in Wedding she has become a figure-head. She makes no secret of her hatred for capitalists like myself and for the profits Kraus is making from the war. And she is demanding peace. Both are very potent attractions for the down-trodden working classes.'

'Surely you don't agree with her, Benno?'

'No, I don't like the way she works, and I don't agree with her politics, but strangely enough, I do have a certain sympathy with her. You see, I, too, would like the war to be over.'

On May Day, a huge demonstration was staged by Karl Liebknecht, Rosa Luxemburg and Olga Meyer on the Potsdamer Platz,
as a result of which Liebknecht was arrested and thrown into
prison. Benno hoped that would be the end of the matter, but he
soon realized he was underestimating the strength of the people's
feelings.

When Liebknecht's trial started, workers all over the city,
including many from Kraus Village, marched through the streets to
demonstrate their support for him; and when Liebknecht was
sentenced to two and a half years' hard labour, these same men
went on strike. Reluctantly, for he knew they and their families
would suffer great hardship as a result, Benno had no choice but to
sack his striking workers and later he learned that many of them
had been arrested and sentenced to hard labour or conscripted as
punishment. As a result of these political strikes, which threatened
the war effort at its very heart, a military court increased Liebknecht's sentence to four years' hard labour.

When Rosa Luxemburg was also arrested in July, Benno waited
with bated breath to hear that Olga Meyer had suffered the same
fate. However, it seemed that she had escaped the net for the time
being, although she no longer waited for his men outside the gates.
Gradually, for want of leadership, the unrest was quieted and
Kraus Village returned to normal working. When Baron Heinrich
came to Berlin to review the half-year's figures, Benno was able to
report that no production had been lost during the disturbances.

Olga was shocked to the marrow when first Karl and then Rosa
were arrested. Not only were they her friends, they were also the
leaders and founders of the Spartacus League, the left-wing party
named after the man who had led the slave revolt against Rome in
73BC. The Spartacus League was Olga's natural political home,
for she had never had any sympathy with the wishy-washy policies
of the Social Democrats. But what would happen to Spartacus now
that its leaders were in prison?

Her first instinct was to urge the workers to yet more violent
opposition, but in the end Reinhardt's common sense prevailed. 'I
do understand, Olga, but what good can you do anyone in prison?
You are needed here in Wedding. The wives of the men who have
been arrested need money, their children need food. Now is the
time for practical help, not political action.'

Stifling her impatience, Olga did as he suggested. The price of war was digging deep into the pockets of the people of Wedding and gnawing at their stomachs. For them there was no butter, no lard and no flour. Potatoes had been restricted to ten pounds a head for a fortnight since the spring, while bread and meat were severely rationed. Over the next few months, she helped set up soup kitchens where the poor could buy a bowl of thick carrot or turnip soup for a few pfennigs. This opened her eyes even wider to the iniquitous gap between poor and rich.

More than ever now she bitterly regretted having helped Viktoria, particularly since she had married, of all people, a Kraus. Compared to his father, Benno was a moderate, who did everything he could to help his workforce, but for all that, he was a war profiteer and a capitalist, the deadliest enemy of the proletariat. When Olga learned that Baron Heinrich was giving a 'War Dinner' at the Hotel Quadriga in December, she could contain herself no longer. Such ostentatious displays of so-called patriotism where wealthy industrialists and bankers gorged themselves on Lucullan feasts while raising money for the war effort, lashed her fury to a peak.

Regardless of Reinhardt's pleas and the knowledge that she faced certain arrest if the police discovered her, she gathered a contingent of her supporters and went to Unter den Linden. There she stood on a box not far from the hotel.

'While Baron Kraus gives his patriotic dinners, German soldiers and German people are starving!' Her thin voice rang out across the wide avenue. Her hair was greasy, her clothes old and worn. 'Baron Kraus drinks champagne and calls it patriotism while men die on the battlefields from the weapons he has created!' Attracted by her words, strangers started to join the small crowd.

'You are paying for this war. You have no food in your bellies! Your brothers are dying in their thousands on the Somme and the Ardennes. You did not ask for this war! You did not vote for it! Demonstrate your dissent! Strike, comrades, strike!'

'Kraus gives us work!' a voice yelled.

Olga ignored it. 'Take the fate of the working class out of the hands of the profiteers and the capitalists. Fight for your industrial freedom! Fight against the war, which is the root of all our troubles! These two fights, comrades, are one and the same!' A couple of men cheered and the crowd increased in size. 'This war is no accident, but a capitalist war of aggression fought to defend capitalist values.' There were several hundred people listening to her now and her confidence grew. 'Can you only do what the Kaiser asks? Have you no minds of your own? You will no longer be exploited! Down your tools and show your support against this war of aggression! Strike for freedom! Strike for the proletarian revolution! Strike to free the waiting workers of the world!'

'Frau Meyer,' a voice said heavily beside her, 'are you going to get down off that soapbox of yours of your own accord or do I have to help you?'

She looked disgustedly at the policeman in his spiked helmet. 'Are you arresting me?'

'Yes, for inciting the people to act against the Kaiser.'

She was taken to the cells under the Berlin Police Headquarters in the Alexanderplatz, where she was soon filled with an even greater hatred for the imperialist system and for their police. Her cell was small, a filthy, stinking, verminous, windowless hole, with no artificial light and no facilities of any kind. All day and all night it vibrated to the rumbling of the trains overhead and when she tried to rest she was disturbed by the sound of her gaolers' boots in the corridor. Rats ran across her mattress and her diet consisted of watery soup supplemented by an occasional rotten turnip.

Close to despair, she was forced to acknowledge that Reinhardt might have been right. She could only believe her gesture had been in vain.

There was little sympathy for Olga at the Hotel Quadriga and Karl was openly delighted at her fate. 'They should have done it years ago, when she first came to Berlin. Damned Bolsheviks, they should all be locked up!'

Ricarda was perplexed. 'I don't understand why she had to become so involved in politics in the first place. Oh, I do wish she had listened to me and taken a teaching job in some nice place like Dahlem or Charlottenburg. Then this would never have happened. Poor girl.'

Luise shrugged. 'I always thought Olga was boring. Obviously the police do, too. Let's hope they put her in solitary confinement, so that she can bore herself for two years.'

Viktoria alone was disturbed. 'I wish I could do something for her,' she told Benno.

'She's a silly little fool,' he replied. 'She was doing a lot of good in Wedding with her soup kitchens. But no, she had to become a martyr for her cause! Well, let's hope she comes to her senses soon.'

Her arrest was briefly mentioned by the businessmen who attended his father's War Dinner. 'She can't achieve anything in prison,' was their unanimous opinion, as, well-dressed and prosperous, they sipped aperitifs in the Empire Room. 'Maybe now the workers will stop demonstrating and get on with their jobs.'

The hotel provided a superb meal that evening. It commenced with assorted hors d'oeuvres, then a consommé from fresh chicken stock with whipped egg, followed by young doves stuffed with a salpicon of mixed vegetables. The fish course was sea perch baked in the oven, and the main meat dish was roast rump of beef with madeira sauce, accompanied by a salad. To follow, there was a choice of preserved fruits, cheeses and ice creams. Needless to say, the banquet was accompanied by exquisite wines from Karl Jochum's extensive cellars.

At the end of the excellent six course dinner, Baron Heinrich called for silence and invited Theo Arendt as the guest speaker for the evening to address them. There was brief applause, then, as they sipped their brandies and lit up cigars, Theo began his speech.

It was evident from his expression that the banker was worried and, after a brief resumé of the military and political situation, he gave them a detailed assessment of the country's financial situation, ending with the words, 'To summarize, gentlemen, if the wars ends now and suitable peace terms can be arranged, I see no danger for Germany. I, therefore, personally believe we should accept President Wilson's invitation to state our aims and allow him to mediate.'

'We don't need the American president,' one of his audience interrupted angrily. 'All we want is for the Americans to stay out of this war.'

Theo ignored him. 'The fact quite simply is that our country's money supply is running out. Paper money is being printed now, with the result that our currency is already becoming devalued. No attempt has been made by the government to pay for the war out of taxation. On the contrary, taxation has actually been reduced. None of you gentlemen need me to explain what is going to follow. The German currency — and the currencies of other participating nations in this war — are going to become inflated. We have the prospect of very great hardship on the horizon.'

302

'When we win the war, we can simply repudiate our war loans,' someone suggested. 'The British and the French can pay.'

'If we win the war,' Theo corrected him, 'but whoever wins, somebody will have to pay for the blood that has been spilt and the damage done.'

'We were attacked by France and Russia in 1914,' a belligerent voice spoke out. 'We have to make sure we are never attacked again.'

Backwards and forwards across the table the argument raged. Eventually Baron Heinrich spoke for the first time and Benno suddenly noticed that his father was no longer wearing his Reserve Officer's uniform. 'I believe we should pay attention to the policies of General Hindenburg and General Ludendorff. Somehow we must try to get the Russians onto our side or out of the war. Then we'll only be fighting on one front. At that point, we shall be able to demand our own terms of the western allies. We want the French iron ore fields, control of Belgium, the Belgian Congo and Poland. We should settle for nothing less.'

'What makes you so sure we'll succeed?' one of his colleagues asked.

'The Russians are in a mess. In my opinion, they are on the verge of revolution. We should help the revolutionaries and thus divert the Tsar's armies away from us. And, so far as the British are concerned, the answer quite simply is unrestricted submarine warfare.' He stared down the long table, at which they had just eaten such a copious meal. 'We shall starve the British into submission, as they are currently trying to starve us.'

Theo Arendt gazed at him, then said quietly, 'Gentlemen, at the risk of making myself extremely unpopular, I have to reiterate my point. I trust and hope that Germany will win the war and that there will be no price for us to pay to the Allies. However, our country is already facing — and I cannot stress this too strongly — an extremely serious financial crisis. I repeat, Germany has run out of money. As a country, gentlemen, we are bankrupt.'

When the dinner was over, the Baron invited Benno up to his suite for a night-cap. 'I've always had great respect for the Arendts,' he said ponderously, pouring two large brandies from a decanter, 'and if the country really is in the parlous financial situation that Theo describes, it's time to place Kraus's money elsewhere. I'm certain that the policy of unlimited submarine warfare I myself am advocating will certainly bring America into the war, not because their security will be threatened, but because their prosperity will be. You see, Benno, America is booming at the moment, its order books are full and a huge proportion of its production is going to England and France. If we stop that, America will be in huge trouble, so she will go to war.'

Not for the first time, Benno was staggered by his father's cynical view of things.

'Now, you know, Benno, just as we have licensing deals set up in England, South Africa and the Far East, we also have similar extremely lucrative arrangements in America, as well as shares in a number of American companies. So, what affects American prosperity, boy, also affects Kraus.'

To Benno, it was one of the many great anomalies of the war that both sides were shooting at each other with guns manufactured under Kraus patents. And now, it appeared, the Americans were going to join the fray.

'So, what we have to do, Benno, is think ahead and keep all our options open. We've made a lot of money out of Germany during this war. Now's the time to make some out of America.'

'You mean you're going to invest money in America? You're going to finance America in war against Germany?'

'Why not? The important thing in this life is to be on the winning side.'

'But it's immoral!'

His father snorted in disgust. 'The only immorality I recognize is losing money.'

When Benno left the Kraus apartment a little later, his dislike of his father had never been greater. As soon as the war was over, he determined, he was going to leave the company.

Baron Heinrich also gave Benno a passing thought. Boy was doing a reasonable job here in Berlin, but he was too soft. Immoral, indeed! Perhaps he thought Kraus was a charity!

Then he pulled out a sheet of paper and started to write instructions to his agent in Switzerland, for transmission to America. He wrote in an agreed code, so that the censors would let it through.

In January 1917, the government announced that all shipping, including that of neutral countries, would be shot at sight in the war zone of the eastern Atlantic. The policy of unrestricted submarine warfare had been implemented. When he received the news in the 'Fortress' above Essen, the Baron permitted himself a moment of self-congratulation.

In Berlin, Karl Jochum greeted the news with delight. 'It's only the Americans who've been keeping the British going,' he explained to Ricarda. 'The British have been blockading our supply ships — now we'll sink theirs. They'll have no more arms, food or raw materials. We'll fight them in the air, we'll fight them on land, we'll fight them at sea, and we'll starve their civilians to death. Yes, in six weeks we'll have England starved into submission.'

'I seem to remember we were going to take Paris in six weeks.'

'That was Moltke's fault. The man was an idiot. But now Ludendorff's in control, we'll take Paris yet.' His finger stabbed at his newspaper. 'The new ground attack against Arras will be successful. And in the air, pilots like the Red Battle Flier and the Yellow Peril are wiping out the Royal Flying Corps. These are men to be proud of. They are heroes!'

'Why can't we simply compromise? We're all so tired of war. Everybody wants peace.'

'Compromise peace?' Karl turned scandalized eyes on her. 'Why should we settle for a compromise peace when victory is in sight? Belgium is ours and I see no reason to give it up, which is what the Allies want. We were provoked into this war and we shall win. *Gott strafe England!*'

Ricarda winced, hating the phrase 'God punish England!' which was heard more and more as the war continued. Although she had long since lost all her connections with England, she still maintained an affection for it and it saddened her to hear her husband abuse the country where she had spent much of her youth.

Nor was this the only thing that saddened her about Karl these days. Since the deaths of Ewald and her father, he had seemed to lose all interest in the hotel, apparently content to leave its running in Viktoria's hands, while he took up station in the bar or the Empire Room pontificating on the war. She might not have minded this so much had his attitude to the war been less belligerent, but, as it was, his support of the Kaiser and the Junkers seemed to grow in proportion to Germany's defeats. It was almost as if he believed that his bombast and bellicosity in themselves would ensure his country's victory.

'No, Karl,' she said quietly, 'I just want an end to all the senseless bloodshed.'

'You'll be sticking up for the Americans next!'

'Well, what will happen if America does enter the war?'

'Huh! They won't. Wilson wants peace. Like all Americans, he wants to grow rich on other people's misfortunes.'

From that point on, however, his hatred for the Americans grew positively vindictive. He refused to allow American newspaper correspondents and even the American Ambassador to set foot in the hotel. For the first time, Ricarda confided her worries in Viktoria. 'I know it's a dreadful thing to say, Vicki, but sometimes I think he's slightly deranged. I hate to think what will happen if we lose the war.'

Viktoria nodded anxiously. 'It's as if he takes the whole thing personally. But I don't see what we can do, except hope and pray.'

On 6 April, Karl was proved wrong and Baron Heinrich right, for America declared war on Germany. Karl studied the editorials in the newspapers carefully, then announced confidently, 'It will make little difference. They have no army yet, so first they'll have to conscript and train their men. Furthermore, because they're going to need all their military equipment themselves, they won't be able to supply the British and the French. If anything, the Americans are helping us.'

At Douai in France, Lieutenant Sepp Nowak knew nothing of the rumours circulating in Berlin about a compromise peace, nor did he know that the Army General Staff, the politicians and even the Kaiser himself were pinning their hopes upon unrestricted submarine warfare as a last resort to win the war. He knew that the Kaiser's fleet of battleships had proved ineffective at Jutland and he knew that the armies had suffered terrible losses at Verdun and on the Somme. From the air he could not help but see that the troops were slowly retreating day by day, nor, when he returned to base, could he ignore the low morale of the soldiers. But Sepp had little to do with the ground troops. His war took place in the sky, one that despite all the efforts of Allied aircraft, he was certain could be won.

He was twenty-five that year, recently transferred to the fighting section led by Baron Manfred von Richthofen. As soon as he had started flying combat patrols, he had known there would never be any other life for him than flying. He revelled in the sheer exhilaration of it, loving the sensation of wind flying through the open cockpit of his biplane, pulling back the skin on his face, the smell of the exhaust, the rattle of the struts. He loved the dizzy feeling as his machine fell through the air, spinning and rolling, in a long, deep dive, then the spectacular moment of power as he pulled up her nose and went soaring up again into the clouds.

Then there was the sport of making a kill. He felt no personal enmity for the Allied pilot he was hunting, for to him the enemy aircraft was merely a target. Since he never saw the bodies of the fallen pilots, they had no personal significance for him other than adding to his prestige as a flier. And prestige came quickly to daredevils like Sepp Nowak. Within two months he had shot down forty planes, and won the coveted Blue Max — the *Pour le Mérite*, the blue and gold enamelled cross, the highest award for individual gallantry — and was now determined to beat von Richtofen's record.

That April morning, Sepp's spirits were high, as he pulled on his helmet and climbed into the Albatros D III fighter, to which he had become almost passionately attached, and went through the routine of starting. Like all others in the squadron, Sepp's plane had a name. Yellow, with a green undercarriage, she was christened *Pipsi* after an actress he had seen perform before the war in a review, *Hurra! Hussar!* Sepp, himself, had been nicknamed the 'Yellow Peril'.

The propeller turned, the plane moved off down the runway and he lowered his goggles. The wind tore at his jacket and rattled the struts and wings of his plane above even the noise of his engine. The plane ahead of him was in the air. Three minutes later, Sepp was airborne too, then soon, he levelled out and the Jasta settled into formation, flying west towards the enemy. It was going to be another good day. In the air, at least, the Germans were winning the war.

Towards Arras, two ancient RE8s, Australian observation planes, were trying to get near enough to the ground to take photographs. Sepp and three other planes swooped joyfully down to get them, their Spandaus trained on their prey. The rest of the Jasta dived to assist, ignoring the British anti-aircraft fire from the ground. Sepp's face broke into a grin.

Behind him, seven Sopwith Strutters dropped from above, pulling out of their dive close over the Albatroses. Sepp laughed. The REs dived and moved out of the fight and the real battle commenced. Sepp picked out a cherry-nosed Strutter and banked towards it, squinting through his gunsight, then, lining the plane up between his two Spandaus, pressed the firing button. Black smoke gushed from the British plane's engine and it spiralled earthwards. Another kill! Eyes shining behind his goggles, Sepp shot over it, then pulled on his joystick to lift *Pipsi* up.

The first he knew of the BE2 behind him was when the bullets peppered his wings. Instinctively, he threw a half loop, trying to prevent the Englishman getting on his tail. The other pilot knew exactly what he was doing, for he rolled to his right. Sepp smiled, then jerked the stick back hard and climbed. The BE2 was still there. He put *Pipsi* into a spiral dive. The BE2 followed him.

For possibly ten minutes the two planes jousted with each other in the open sky, twisting and turning, rolling and diving, like two great birds, equally matched in skill and strength. They were the supreme moments of Sepp's life, during which his respect so grew for his combatant that he forgot they were fighting a duel to the death, and it was with an unnerving sense of shock that he felt *Pipsi* shudder and lurch, as his antagonist sent a hailstorm of bullets into her side.

Suddenly, his gaiety vanished and the sour taste of fear rose in his throat. There was something the matter with *Pipsi*'s balance. She was being relentlessly dragged towards the ground. He jabbed at the trigger of his machine-guns and realized to his horror that it had jammed. Any minute now, the BE2 would hammer home her advantage and he would plummet to his death.

Then an extraordinary thing happened. The BE2 looped and flew across Sepp's head, the pilot lying almost on his back. Sepp tried to push *Pipsi*'s nose up toward him, so that his machine-guns were directed towards his enemy. He could see the British pilot's face now, blackened like his own, beneath his helmet, the first British pilot he had ever seen at close proximity. Grinning, the other man waved his hand, as if in salute and thanks for a gentlemanly fight.

Thunderstruck, Sepp waggled his wings in gratitude at this unexpected reprieve. Then, to his horror, he noticed another Albatros swooping down on the unsuspecting BE2 from behind, its Spandaus aimed on the Englishman's tail. Within minutes, it was over. A sheet of fire, with black oil smoke gushing behind it, the unknown Englishman's plane plummeted earthwards, scattering its debris through the air as it fell.

Her airframe tattered, her engine spluttering, *Pipsi* limped home towards Douai, but Sepp knew something had changed in his life that day. He genuinely regretted the death of the English pilot, who had so chivalrously spared his life. As Jasta II celebrated its victories that evening, he drank more than usual, unwilling to admit, even to himself, that for a moment he had felt more in common with an enemy pilot than with his own colleagues. As he fell into bed that evening, he suddenly realized that he was tired, mortally tired. It was as if, within the space of twenty-four hours, nearly three years of fighting, of daily challenging death, had caught up with him.

The mood of depression passed but the tiredness did not. Now, instead of facing the coming day's foray with excitement, he felt only a great weariness. When he was sent on leave at the end of May, he was actually thankful, for he feared he was losing his touch and if he flew any more he would make a fateful mistake.

Leaving *Pipsi* at Douai, he was flown in a utility plane first to General Staff Headquarters for de-briefing, and then in the same machine to Berlin. For the first time, he wondered what he would do with himself when he got home. His brother, Rudi, was somewhere on the eastern front, and his father had been killed on service during the first year of the war. His leave, to which he had been looking forward, now seemed less attractive as it grew nearer to reality.

Even from the air, the waiting crowds at the Berlin airfield were clearly visible, but it was only when he stepped out of the plane that he realized they were waiting for him. There were cheers and shouts of 'Nowak! Nowak! The Yellow Peril! Welcome home!' A city official came forward to seize his hand and a small girl, bearing an enormous bouquet of flowers, was pushed towards him. Sepp Nowak suddenly realized he had become a hero.

Wherever he went during the following weeks, a crowd of small boys accompanied him, trying to touch his coat, pounding him with questions, gazing at him with worshippping eyes, pleading for his autograph. If he called in at a café for a drink, women stopped their chatter and stared at him adoringly, many even approaching him and introducing themselves without any sign of embarrassment. There were, he discovered, even postcards on sale with his portrait on them. Fame was a new, but gratifying, experience — and one that, without any hesitation, he decided to enjoy.

It was not just the youth and ladies of Berlin, however, who were interested in Sepp Nowak. Baron Heinrich von Kraus had been following the war in the skies with increasing admiration. At the beginning of the war, the aeroplane had been treated with derision by the military, but now it had really come into its own. Of course, there was no chance that the aviators could win the war by themselves, but they had definitely proved that their machines were here to stay. Look at the distance a plane could cover in such a short space of time, far more quickly than a train or a car!

These days, the Baron's thoughts were increasingly centred on what was going to happen after the war and how Kraus Industries was going to make its money. Aviation, he decided, was the transport of the future. He registered the name of a new company, 'Kraus Aviation', then he sent an invitation to Sepp Nowak inviting him to a dinner at the Hotel Quadriga. When the war was over, he was going to need pilots for his new civilian airline, and a prior acquaintance with the fighter ace could be very useful. In accordance with his personal philosophy, he was keeping all his options strictly open.

The high point of Sepp's leave came when he received the Baron's invitation to dinner at Berlin's grandest hotel. Who had heard of him when he left Berlin back in 1914? Now, his company was sought by one of Germany's wealthiest industrialists.

The Baron even sent a limousine to convey him to the hotel and it was as the car drew up in front of the Quadriga's impressive portico that Sepp recalled a train journey from Nuremberg four years earlier. There had been two sisters, one blonde, and the younger one, whom Rudi had fancied, with ravishing red hair. He had been reading, but he remembered her saying, 'My father owns the Hotel Quadriga.' What was her name? Sepp searched his memory and then it came to him — Luise Jochum.

Standing in the hotel foyer, waiting in a frenzy of excitement for the guest of honour to arrive at Baron Heinrich's dinner, Luise asked Viktoria wistfully, 'Do you think he'll remember me?'

'Why on earth should he?' Viktoria snapped. She was busy and very tired. All day long, she had been coping with the increasing problems of running an hotel during a war. The housekeeper had complained that they needed new sheets; Max Patschke had demanded new table linen; and Fritzi Messner was insisting on serving sauerkraut at the dinner that evening, because he claimed there were no fresh vegetables available in the entire city. She ran her hand through her limp hair. There was nothing she could do. Everything the country produced went to the war effort.

At that moment, Benno walked across the foyer. Like Viktoria, he looked tired, with deep lines etched across his forehead and bags under his eyes. It was how people looked these days. Berlin was peopled with men and women with anxious faces. Or with wounded soldiers, hobbling on crutches, with broken or amputated limbs, bandaged, crippled, maimed and blinded. Benno ruffled Luise's hair. 'Hello, little sister. Waiting to greet the Yellow Peril?'

'Do you think he'll remember me, Benno? I met him once on a train.'

'So you keep telling us,' Benno laughed. 'Well, you'll soon find out. That looks like my father's Mercedes outside the door now.'

There was a flurry of movement as the commissionaires ushered Sepp Nowak into the hotel, page boys casting adoring eyes at him, and a bustle among the many people who had been waiting, like Luise, to catch a glimpse of the fighter ace. Karl himself hurried forward to shake the Lieutenant's hand and welcome him to the Hotel Quadriga, then personally escorted him towards the Empire Room where Baron Heinrich and his guests were waiting.

Among the milling crowd in the foyer, however, there was one figure that stood out above all others. To Karl's astonishment, Sepp left him and walked across to Luise, young and vibrant, her face aglow with excitement. Taking her hand in his, he bent low over it. 'Fraeulein Jochum? I don't expect you remember, but we met on a train several years ago ...'

'Oh, but I do!' Luise assured him breathlessly.

Close to, Sepp's face showed the strain of the war. It was scarred from a plane crash, the nose slightly bent, the eyes aged beyond his years. But his smile was sincere. 'I believe I offered to take you in an aeroplane. Well, I should just like to tell you that I haven't forgotten. One day, I shall.'

'Oh, thank you, Lieutenant Nowak.'

Two days later, Sepp Nowak left Berlin again for Douai, but for a long time after he was gone, Luise continued to dance on air. She pinned photographs of him up on her bedroom wall, gazing at them in adoration. 'Isn't he wonderful?' she demanded of everyone she saw.

'He's very brave,' Viktoria said. 'God knows how he lives that kind of life and keeps on smiling.'

'He lives for his flying,' explained Benno, who had attended the dinner. 'It's the only thing he could talk about all evening. Just aeroplanes. He even told us about one incident when his machine-gun jammed and a British pilot let him go. A most extraordinary fellow. But I liked him and so, apparently, did my father.'

Luise wasn't interested in the Baron's thoughts. Nor was she interested in aeroplanes. It was Sepp himself who fascinated her.

In April, Olga Meyer was moved from the temporary police cells under the Alexanderplatz to the Barnimstrasse Military Women's Prison. She had still not been tried and was under 'protective custody', meaning that she was re-arrested every three months, a process that could apparently continue for ever. However, conditions were very much better in the Barnimstrasse. With access to daylight, better food and hygiene, her health slowly recovered from her dreadful incarceration under the Police Headquarters. She was allowed books, she could write and receive letters, although these were obviously censored, and she was even permitted to see an 'approved' visitor once a month.

When she saw Reinhardt for the first time in nearly six months, she felt almost delirious with happiness. In order to pass the military guards, he had made a great effort with his appearance, looking almost respectable, and was pretending to be her cousin, knowing that as her husband he would never be allowed to see her. Their conversation was odd and very stilted, for they had so much to communicate to each other and had to be very careful of the listening ears of the warder.

The news that Reinhardt brought Olga from the outside world was almost as overwhelming to her as the sight of himself. It was contained in a letter he had carefully concealed in the spine of a book he left with her and, back in the privacy of her room, she read it with disbelieving eyes.

There had been a revolution in Russia, led by the liberal Alexander Kerensky, and the Tsar had abdicated! Immediately, the Bolsheviks had started re-establishing the workers', peasants' and soldiers' soviets they had set up in 1905, and were now attempting to seize power from Kerensky's provisional government.

The next part of Reinhardt's letter was even more astounding. Lenin was back in Russia! 'He returned from Switzerland, through Germany, in a sealed train,' Reinhardt wrote. 'He travelled with full permission of General Ludendorff, who has his own reasons for wanting to further the cause of the Bolshevik revolution in Russia. The General believes that, since the Russian people are already starving, they will welcome Lenin, who will persuade them that the war against Germany should end. At that point, of course, Germany will only be fighting on one front and therefore, in Ludendorff's misguided eyes, stands a chance of victory.

'So far as I can ascertain, Lenin is virtually in hiding in Russia, for now that the Tsar has gone there are many others seeking control. I fear many bloody battles will ensue before Lenin achieves his aim, but, Olga, he will succeed! One day, our old friend from Munich will be Head of the Soviet of People's Commissars.

'Now, we must watch and learn from everything that happens in Russia. Here, in Germany, the people are also ready for the revolution, but we lack the leadership, we lack cohesive policies. Liebknecht, Luxemburg, yourself and so many others are in prison. I can write articles, pamphlets and letters, but I am a journalist, not a politician. Please use your time in prison to think coherently, Olga, for when you are released, I fear we shall have little time to think. Your loving husband and comrade, Reinhardt.'

From that moment on, Olga's hopes did not falter. What was being achieved in Russia could also be achieved in Germany. Lenin had not given up, so neither would she. Over the next few months, the circle of her correspondence increased. She received news from Rosa Luxemburg in Wronke prison in faraway Posen, and of Karl Liebknecht in Luckau gaol. Not only Reinhardt, but she too, contributed articles to their newspapers, *Spartacus* and the *Red Flag*, in which they promised the workers of Germany an immediate peace, control of their factories, food and equality.

Over the next months, these newspapers were printed and distributed in increasing numbers, coming into the hands of thousands of discontented factory workers throughout the country. Nor were they limited to the workers. Through the hard work and commitment of Reinhardt Meyer and his friends, they reached sailors in the great ports of Kiel, Hamburg, Bremen and Wilhelmshaven, men who had been waiting since the Battle of Jutland for another decisive sea victory. They found their way to soldiers at the front, men weary and disillusioned with a war that seemed to have no end.

Olga Meyer might be in prison but her voice was heard throughout the German empire. 'We must all extend our hands in brotherhood and peace. Only then will there be an end to this hell on earth which we are all enduring. Become soldiers of the revolution, comrades! Let your battle-cry from now on be, "Workers of the world, unite!"' This was her message from gaol that reached into the hearts of many thousands of people.

There were others, too, who rejoiced at the abdication of the Russian Tsar. From the London Branch of the Arendt Bank, run by Theo's cousin, Hugo, a note was received, bearing only the cryptic message, 'Debt repaid'.

313

Theo looked at it for a long time, feeling an immense satisfaction. He wished his father could still be alive to see it, but Isaak had passed away earlier that year after a second, fatal stroke. Theo took the note into the long conference room, in which his portrait had been added to the gallery of Arendt ancestors and looked at the one of old Abel.

In 1846 a Russian Tsar had refused his grandfather permission to set up a bank in St Petersburg. Now, there was no longer a Tsar of Russia and the London branch had sent a loan to the Russian revolutionaries in support of their cause. The Jews had many enemies and they never forgot them. Today's small victory over the Tsar was a story that Theo would tell his two boys, Felix and Caspar, when they were older. They would remember and, in their turn, tell their children and their children's children.

Theo was also aware, however, that the revolution in Russia could have many serious, long-term effects on Germany. Inspired by their example, German workers were rebelling against the war and there were many strikes and demonstrations for peace, although few of them were reported in the newspapers. At Kiel, a mutiny was quashed. Among politicians, there was a complete loss of faith in the Chancellor, who finally resigned in July.

Chancellor Michaelis, who replaced him, was totally under the domination of Hindenburg and Ludendorff, so that Germany virtually became a military dictatorship. The first thing the new Chancellor did was to accept a resolution for peace without annexations or indemnities, which could only mean that the generals were finally tacitly admitting the possibility that Germany might not win the war.

It still appeared, however, that nobody in Germany believed they were going to have to pay the full price for war. Well, Theo had tried to warn them. If they would not listen, they could blame nobody but themselves for what must eventually happen.

There were moments during those last two years of the war when Benno thought he would collapse under the weight of his worries. The previous autumn's bad harvest had worsened the food situation dramatically. Boulette had become the staple dish of many households. A dish of meatballs, it had been known for decades, but now it really came into its own. 'Boulette,' Berliners said with their own, derisive wit; 'nobody knows what's in it, so nobody can denounce us for enjoying forbidden pleasures.' But for many, there was not even boulette. For the workers of Kraus Village, turnip coffee had become the norm, accompanying dreadful meals of turnip bread, spread with turnip jam.

Even the Hotel Quadriga was beginning to experience difficulties and Viktoria greeted Benno not with a sunny smile when he came home, but with worried reports of drastic shortages of food and other vital supplies. He admired her more at that time than at any other during their married life. Not only was she trying to bring up Stefan and look after her parents and sister, she was also shouldering virtually the whole responsibility of the hotel. He could not help comparing her to his brother's wife, Trudi, who had just given birth to her first son, Werner, and never done a stroke of work since the day she married Ernst.

The question of food worried Benno greatly, for without it the hotel would be unable to function. For the moment they could still buy from neutral Holland, Switzerland and Scandinavia, although prices were steadily rising, due both to demand and to the steadily devaluing German mark. However, so long as there were guests in the hotel who could afford to pay its prices, there was no problem. It was while thinking of Karl's magnificent cellar of wine that Benno lit upon a solution. 'We should buy in as much canned food as possible,' he told Viktoria, 'and keep it as an emergency supply in the cellar.'

'But the Quadriga has never served tinned food.'

'It may have to,' Benno replied grimly. 'Vicki, look at the facts. We simply cannot produce enough food for ourselves now. Our farms are being neglected while their workers are away. Even when they return, they won't be able to grow crops overnight. It will be at least a year, if not two, before we see a decent harvest. Then, what will happen when the war ends and the troops return? The army will no longer be feeding them, so the country's food supply is going to be halved. We're facing an extremely serious situation.'

She gave him a strange look. 'You know, Benno, you're very like your father, sometimes, aren't you? Hoarding tins of food against a future disaster is just the sort of thing he'd do.'

The accusation stung him to the quick. Then, ruefully, he had to admit it was partly justified. 'The difference between myself and my father, however, is that he would then sell those tins to the highest bidder, whereas I am genuinely concerned about our future.'

315

'I'm sorry, Benno. We'll start buying tins.'

Over the next few months, the storerooms in the cellar slowly filled with a wide range of cans. They were expensive, but the Hotel Quadriga could afford them. Benno viewed them, like the wine, as a kind of insurance against the future.

In November, Lenin led a Bolshevik revolt against Kerensky's government and the first thing he did after setting up administrations in most major Russian cities was to agree a cease-fire with Germany. This was the moment the German workers had been waiting for. Incited and inspired by the Spartacist leaders still in prison, they, too, demanded, 'Peace, land and bread!'

Once again, the workers of Wedding rose up in arms and marched through the streets of Berlin demanding their rights. And on this occasion, they knew they were not alone, for their action was reported in the newspaper for the first time. Four hundred thousand men, *Vorwaerts* claimed, participated in the strike the first day, with another hundred thousand joining them the second.

'I'll give them strike!' Karl roared, lying in wait for Benno, when he arrived home that evening. 'Germany has a war to fight! These traitors are just helping the enemy by going on strike. Benno, what are you going to do about it?'

Benno shook his head wearily. 'They've starving. They deserve to be heard.'

'They deserve to be shot!'

'God knows, this damned war can't go on much longer.'

Karl's bombast suddenly evaporated. 'We'll win, Benno. Now Russia's out of it, we'll have a great victory.' But his tone was that of a small child, seeking reassurance.

The strikes ended and an uneasy peace settled once again on Kraus Village. Benno's troubles, however, were nowhere near their end, for at the beginning of January, he made a discovery that chilled him to the marrow. Arriving at the plant earlier than usual, he parked his car and then, instead of going immediately to his office, made his way — for some reason or the other which he never recalled — to the back of the building.

Here, a very strange sight met his eyes, for, instead of the yard being empty, as it should have been, two men were clambering down the fire escape from the research laboratories, struggling with a large, unwieldy sack. At the bottom of the iron staircase stood an open van, already loaded with several similar sacks. His first thought was that the building was being burgled and he shouted, 'Here, you, what are you doing?'

The two men hesitated for a moment and stared at him; then Benno recognized them as janitors. He marched across the yard to them. 'What's in there?'

The research laboratories were still his father's province, staffed and financed by the Baron from a separate account. Although the work that went on in them had continued to trouble Benno ever since that terrible day in 1915 when he had discovered that the gas produced by them was being used in Belgium, he had never again discussed the subject with his father. Rumours had reached him of experimental work using rabbits and rats, but he had deliberately not inquired into the details. Apart from anything else, he had quite simply been too busy running the rest of the massive plant.

Now, looking at the ominously shaped bags, he knew he could remain ignorant no longer. 'Open that sack!'

'No, Guv'nor,' the janitor shifted uneasily. 'Leave it be.'

'Open the sack.' Hesitantly, the man complied, and Benno peered inside, then hurriedly turned away as bile rose in his throat. The sack contained a dead pig, a pig that had obviously died a terrible death, its features horribly distended and discoloured, and exuding the most noisome odour. Benno pointed with a trembling hand to the other sacks. 'Are those all dead pigs?' The man nodded.

Sickened, Benno made his way to his office, smoking two cigarettes in swift succession as he tried to banish the dreadful image from his mind. Then he sent a message for the scientist in charge of the research laboratory to come to his office.

To begin with the man prevaricated, claiming that Benno had no jurisdiction over what took place in his laboratories. 'I only take orders from the Herr Baron.'

'I'm not giving you orders,' Benno said coldly, 'I am asking you a question, Herr Doktor. How long have these experiments on pigs been going on and what is the chemical you are using?'

Interpreting his question as professional interest, the chemist opened up. It was, he informed Benno, the latest kind of gas. 'The chlorine gas used at Ypres in 1915 was nothing compared to the mustard and phosgene gases we are preparing now. These poison, blind and burn through contact with the skin.'

Struggling to conceal his disgust, Benno asked, 'And do they also kill?'

'Oh, yes, Herr Kraus,' the scientist replied eagerly. 'Our

experiments show that these gases can cause death in a most unpleasant manner. When the English encounter these, our latest, most secret weapons, they are going to wish they had never declared war on us.

When he had gone, Benno opened the window to rid the room of his presence, then he lit another cigarette. He had to do something to stop production of this lethal gas, but what? There seemed only one solution and that was to write to his father.

His father's reply was brief and to the point. 'We are fighting a war,' he scrawled across Benno's memorandum. 'The English and the French are using gas, too.'

Thick mist shrouded the countryside near Arras that early April morning in 1918. Second Lieutenant Georg Jankowski had been leaning over the edge of the trench for the last two hours, peering into the murky gloom through his field glasses, his ears alert to the slightest noise. Somewhere out there were the British, but the fog muffled all sound.

He took the glasses away from his eyes. What did it matter if the British did come upon them unheard through the mist? For nearly four years they had been fighting over the same muddy swathe of land, constantly being told they were pushing forward to Paris and, each time, they were relentlessly pushed back again. Nobody believed any more that Germany was going to win the war. She couldn't, not with the shortages of soldiers, of food, of armaments, of ammunition. Every day, men disappeared and it was no longer certain that they were dead. Some in desperation, surrendered to the enemy. Others simply deserted. Everyone was filled with a sense of utter desolation and hopelessness.

Georg was tired. He almost envied the men now who fell to the enemy shells, for death itself was preferable to this. There was a chill in his lungs and in his heart, while the hunger that gnawed at his stomach had become so habitual he scarcely noticed it any more. He lived in a kind of dream, in which he obeyed and gave orders, slept where and when he could, and watched men die. Of all the men who had left Berlin with him in 1914 not a single one was still alive. Now they were sending out boys, scarcely out of short trousers, and old men who could hardly lift a rifle. And he had been made an officer, albeit only a second lieutenant, an incredible thought considering he was a Jew.

Berlin seemed so far away these days. They talked about home in the trenches, wistfully, like some figment of their imagination. The raw young recruits spoke of their parents and girlfriends, the older men of their wives and children. Sometimes, Georg thought of Pipsi, but somehow he could not visualize her features any more. After the battle of Verdun in 1916, the April following his leave, a curt letter from her had informed him that he was the father of a baby girl. Minna, she was called, after Lessing's heroine. He wondered what she was like, this little girl, the result of a moment's loveless union.

He had received more frequent letters from his Uncle Franz, but these told him little, for the censor's thick pen obliterated any titbits of information the old man obtained from the Ullstein newspapers. Franz never saw Pipsi. He had visited her once after Minna's birth, he had written, and she had discouraged him from returning. Most of Franz's letters contained the plea that Georg should return home soon and continue with his music. 'I long to hear the *Hammerclavier*.'

Music, Georg thought, staring at the fingers holding the binoculars. Would these hands, which had helped dig so many trenches, so many front lines, so much of the Hindenburg Line, and which had been responsible for the death of so many foreign soldiers, ever play the piano again? He flexed them bitterly. There was still music, sometimes, in his head, melodies that sprang up from nowhere, melodies he never wrote down, bittersweet tunes that taunted him with their dancing memories of other, long-gone, braver days.

And there was the *Cornflower Waltz*, the valse inspired by the red-haired girl on the Anhalter Station back in 1914. So often during the past four years, whenever he wondered what he was doing in some godforsaken muddy corner of Europe, fighting this pointless battle, her face had come back to haunt him, more real in many ways than Pipsi's. What had happened to his cornflower girl?

Then it started, the familiar barrage of the enemy's siege guns from the back lines, the howling of shells, the crash and the rending explosions as they landed, followed by that familiar moment of eerie silence, as the huge cannon stopped. Georg cautiously lifted his head above the sandbags. Further along the line, he saw men rush forward, their rifles cracking. He noticed shapes in the slowly-clearing mist, he saw horses rear as a shell descended among them. He saw bodies lying inert and bloodstained, their limbs sprawled out at ungainly angles, dead in the deep, rutted mud of Flanders.

The trench telephone rang and a boy answered it, then scurried along the trench. Suddenly Georg heard a voice roar, 'Action!' All around him, men tensed. 'Fire!' roared the voice again. Down the line, triggers were pulled and the voice was lost in the thunder of gunfire.

Dimly above the din of their own guns, Georg became aware of the drone of planes and when he looked up through the acrid smoke, he could see a formation of three Fokker DrI triplanes. Throughout the war, these brave fighter aces had been a source of consolation to the men in the trenches. Georg stared up at them. How did this desolate, miry landscape look from the sky?

There were figures ahead of them now, creeping through the trees — tommies, with guns in their hands and gas masks to their faces. 'Gas mortars, fire!'

At that moment, he heard it, the low whine of an enemy shell, that became a high-pitched shriek, screaming through the air towards him, hanging for a second, then falling, faster and faster until, with a deafening crash it exploded in the trench, pitching earth, gas cylinders, rifles, sandbags, helmets and bits of men high into the sky.

For an indefinite period of time, Georg lay stunned on his back, then slowly, he became aware of an excruciating pain in his abdomen and his left leg. He opened his eyes and tried to lift his head to look at it, but it seemed he was pinned to the earth. He stared upwards and then he saw it, the yellowish cloud of gas released from their own gas mortars, just before the shell had landed. He felt it claw at his nostrils, burning at his skin. Vomit rising in his throat, he turned his head away, trying to bury his face in the earth. The foul vapour caressed him, swirled around him, then, at a slight breeze, eddied away towards another victim. Georg's body lay motionless.

Once, he opened his eyes, when a medical orderly cut off his boots, then ripped his trousers. He saw a soldier handing him bandages, sensed them being wrapped around his leg. The pain was unbearable. He opened his lips to scream, but there was no sound. Vaguely, he heard the medical orderly say, 'If only we had some morphia.' He slipped once more into unconsciousness.

The medical orderly stared down at the bloody mess of the lieutenant's thigh and his burned face and shook his head. 'Poor bastard. Doesn't stand a hope in hell.' Then he shouted,

'Stretcher!' As shells continued to burst black around them, stretcher-bearers carried Georg's body back behind the lines towards the dressing station.

From the dressing station he was taken by ambulance to a field hospital outside Mons, where for several days he lay in a deep coma, hovering between life and death. Then, just when the medical staff had almost given up hope, he opened his eyes.

He awoke to a drugged subconsciousness of pain followed by sweet injections that sent him back to his dreams. For several more days he lay like this, dimly aware of bandages around his face, his hands and his legs. Then a doctor, a thin, tired-looking man, with a grey face and grey hands, pushed through the screens around his bed. Dully, Georg listened as he described his injuries — severe burning from the gas on the hands and face, and his left thigh and foot were shattered. 'Besides the burns, which will hopefully slowly heal, you have a bad chest infection from the gas. We thought for a while that we might have to amputate your leg, but now you've regained consciousness, I hope we'll be able to save it.' He looked away. 'Are you a married man, Lieutenant?'

'Yes,' Georg replied through his bandages. 'I have one daughter.'

The doctor sighed. 'Fragments of shrapnel have penetrated your groin. I can't tell you yet what damage they may have done. But I have to warn you, Lieutenant, that you may never be able to father any more children.'

'You mean I'll be impotent?'

'It's possible.'

Georg closed his eyes, wishing he had died at Arras.

Chapter Twelve

Karl Jochum did not know what to make of the world, that spring of 1918. Although he still believed that, somehow, Germany would win the war, even he could see that matters were going desperately wrong. Of course, it was not the army's fault, but the fault of the socialists who were trying to undermine the people's confidence and who were responsible for the strikes that kept breaking out. Why, there was even talk of a revolution in Germany, like that which had taken place in Russia. His heart filled with fear at such a thought, particularly since it was now rumoured that the Tsar and his entire family had been assassinated.

Yet Berlin was undoubtedly in a sorry state. Gradually, the shortages of food and other vital supplies were starting to hit the Hotel Quadriga. The guests were fewer and of a very different kind than its pre-war clientele. There were none of the gay young lieutenants who had crowded the bars in 1914, but some elderly, often wounded, military men, a few worried businessmen and the anxious bureaucrats who had been there since the beginning of the war. Many landowners simply did not come to the city any more, as they were able to live better from their own estates. Fresh meat, fish and vegetables were almost impossible to buy, while real coffee was becoming an almost unheard-of luxury. To his disgust, the hotel was now forced to serve ersatz coffee, made from chicory and ground acorns and flavoured by just one or two real coffee beans.

Thanks to Benno's foresight, they had ample stocks of tinned foods in the cellar, but the hotel was rapidly running out of soap, linen, towels and other necessities. And there was also the question of clothes. Luise, in particular, kept pestering him for new dresses, claiming she was tired of wearing Viktoria's old ones.

Of course, it was possible to obtain all these items, but chiefly from black market traders and with these men he refused to deal. Not only were their prices exorbitant, but they were traitors because they were profiting from the country's misfortunes.

Then there was the shortage of trained personnel. Such staff as returned from the front were seriously wounded, many with amputated limbs, all too sick for active work. And the stories they brought back with them were horrific. They told of overcrowded field hospitals that were running out of medicines and soldiers' messes where there was no food. Not only the civilians were starving, but Germany's armies were too.

Then, at the end of April, Max Patschke announced that he had received his call-up papers. 'You, Max? But that's ridiculous. Why, they'll be recruiting me next.'

Max smiled resignedly. 'No, Herr Direktor, they'll keep you in Berlin to direct the war.'

'But what about your rheumatism, Max?' Ricarda asked anxiously, when she heard his news. 'Won't they exempt you on medical grounds?'

'We're going to break through the Flanders Line, Frau Jochum. His Majesty and General Ludendorff need my help, so I shall go. But all I can say is that if they expect me, with my flat feet, to march all the way to Paris, then they'd better reconsider.'

'Perhaps if Baron Kraus put in a word on your behalf?'

Max shook his head. 'If His Majesty needs me to go and fight for him, I'll go. But I tell you, Herr Direktor and Frau Jochum, as I'd tell him if he were here, it's grave news for Germany.'

Karl watched his old friend go with a heavy heart. He himself was sixty that year. Max was only a year or so younger. It just didn't seem right.

Rudi Nowak made a striking figure that May morning, as he walked sprightly up the steps of the Hotel Quadriga, allowed the ancient commissionaire to open the glass doors for him, accepted the crippled hall porter's bow, then strode across the foyer to the reception desk. His dark brown hair gleamed with brilliantine, his small moustache was neatly trimmed, and over his extremely fashionable suit — made by Berlin's best tailor — he wore a brown leather coat. His neat shoes were highly polished.

'I'd like to see Herr Jochum, please,' he told the clerk, reaching in his pocket to pull out a soft lizardskin wallet, from which he handed him a card.

The clerk looked at it respectfully. 'Certainly, Herr Nowak. If you'll take a seat, please.'

Rudi placed himself elegantly on a deep settee and looked around him. Here, at least, despite the restraints of the war, a sense of affluence still prevailed, but there were unmistakable signs of hardship. No, this time, old Jochum wouldn't turn him away with a flea in his ear as he had four years earlier. Then, after he had dealt with Karl Jochum, he'd have another look at Luise, who, according to Sepp, had grown into a pretty little wench.

Poor old Sepp, he was still somewhere in France, fighting the battle of the skies, but a battle that couldn't go on much longer by the sound of it. Baron von Richthofen, the Red Battle Flier, had been killed as had, by the sound of Sepp's latest letter, most of the rest of the squadron. A man called Hermann Goering was his commander now. Rudi would not have changed places with his brother for anything in the world. Rudi's war might have been less spectacular, but it had been infinitely more profitable; witness the fact that he was at that moment sitting in the Hotel Quadriga, twenty-one years old, well-dressed, well-fed and in the process of making a lot of money.

Of course, luck had played a hand in his good fortune. Realizing very quickly that an infantryman's life was sheer unadulterated hell, Rudi had inveigled himself a position in the quartermaster's office and from then on, it had been plain sailing. In the army, as everywhere else in the world, there were men who could be bribed, and as food, clothes and supplies became increasingly scarce, so their value had risen both among soldiers and civilians. By the middle of 1917, Rudi had had a very nice little racket going, as well as a tidy store of valuables which he had taken in exchange for coffee, potatoes, tins of food and other army property.

He was on the eastern front then, where it was not difficult to guess the outcome of the war. Russia was in the throes of a revolution and a cease-fire seemed imminent, meaning that the war would soon be over, in which case it was time for him to disassociate himself from it. A suitable bribe to a medical officer obtained him a discharge certificate on the grounds of trench fever and he came home.

As soon as he returned to Berlin, he knew his timing was absolutely right. One of his old army contacts supplied him with a lorryload of tins. He rented an old stable, patched up a handcart and was in business. Now, almost a year later, he had a fine warehouse in the Neue Friedrich-Strasse, an apartment in Charlottenburg and a second-hand automobile. He made weekly trips to

Switzerland and Holland to buy fresh food and had contracts to supply most of the city's hotels and restaurants, including several private arrangements with managers like Oskar Braun at Café Jochum. Deliberately, for it was likely to become his largest customer, he had left the Hotel Quadriga till last.

He watched the hotel's guests walking through the foyer, then his eyes lit up, for walking towards him was a slim figure with a mane of auburn hair. Sepp was right. She was beautiful, but, his observant mind registered, her clothes were old and out of fashion, probably her sister's cast-offs. Well, that was something he would be able to remedy. He stood up with alacrity. 'Fraeulein Jochum?'

Her vivid green eyes took in his elegant appearance with a glance, she blushed slightly, then a look of incredulous surprise spread over her face. 'Herr Nowak?'

He took her hand and, bowing deeply, allowed his lips to stroke her skin. 'Rudi Nowak, at your service, most gracious lady.'

'Herr Nowak, how wonderful. But what are you doing here?'

'I've come to see your father. However, when we've conducted our business, perhaps you'll permit me to invite you for a coffee?'

At that moment, the reception clerk hurried up. 'I am so sorry to have kept you waiting, Herr Nowak. Herr Jochum will see you now in his private office.'

'I'll wait here for you,' Luise told him.

Rudi's first sight of Karl Jochum shocked him. His face was aged and lined, and his body seemed to have shrunk, but Rudi sensed his eyes taking him all in, his clothes, his age, his manner. 'Well, young man, what can I do for you?'

'I was invalided out of the army last year, sir, and started up my own wholesale business. I hope that my company may be able to supply the Hotel Quadriga.'

'Huh, what do you supply?'

Rudi listed the contents of his warehouse. 'Soap, salt, pepper, salami, canned goods, cognac, whisky, flour, chocolate and so on. Then I also I have lengths of material, silk stockings, French perfumes, and other luxury items. In addition to this, I can regularly supply you with fresh meat, fish, fruit and vegetables ...'

'Yes, Herr Nowak, I understand. In other words, you are a black marketeer.' He glared. 'Why were you invalided out of the army?'

'Trench fever, sir.'

Karl shook his head angrily. 'Herr Nowak, I have men working here who had trench fever. They can hardly hobble about the place. They were sick men then and they are still sick men. I watched you walk in here. You've never had trench fever. In fact, I doubt you were ever near a trench!'

This was not the way the interview was supposed to go, but Rudi was not easily defeated. 'As you like, sir,' he said politely.

'Well, I don't like liars, Herr Nowak, and I don't like black marketeers.' Karl's expression darkened. 'I don't like anybody who tries to profit from the war and from other people's misfortunes. The Hotel Quadriga has always dealt honestly and it will continue to do so. Now, get out before I lose my temper!'

'But, sir . . .'

'I think you should be ashamed of yourself! Your brother is risking his life for his country and you are peddling your tawdry little wares. Why, only the other day, my head waiter, a man of my own age, was called up. And you, you have the nerve . . .'

For the second time, Rudi knew he was beaten by Karl. 'I'm sorry to have wasted your time, sir,' he said smoothly, then, leaving him in full throat, he left the office.

Luise was waiting in the foyer. He took her arm and propelled her as quickly as possible out of the hotel, before Karl followed him. 'Let's go to Café Jochum.'

She looked at him quizzically. 'You didn't get on too well with Papa?'

He grinned ruefully. 'He seemed upset that I was out of uniform when his head waiter had just been called up.'

'Don't worry, Papa's angry with everyone these days,' Luise told him blithely. 'But don't let's talk about him. Herr Nowak, you don't know how wonderful it is to see you again. I've thought about you and your brother so often.'

As Rudi linked his arm through hers, she glowed with joy. Newly released from Fraeulein Luetzow's very respectable Academy for Young Ladies, she was impatient to experience real life and could think of nobody better than Rudi to experience it with.

They sat down on the terrace and, when the waiter asked them for their order, Rudi said, 'Tell Herr Braun Rudi Nowak is here and we'd like a pot of his special coffee, please. Oh, and some fruit flan with whipped cream for the lady.' He turned to Luise, 'I take it you still have a good appetite?'

Luise hesitated. Didn't he realize there was no fruit flan, no whipped cream? 'But, Herr Nowak . . .'

He grinned at her. 'Please call me Rudi and let me call you Luise.' He let his hand brush hers. 'When Sepp wrote and told me he'd seen you, I was green with envy. Every day I've been away from you, I've thought of you, every night my dreams were filled with your eyes, your face, your mouth. I wondered, in the heat of battle, if we should ever meet again, and every time death threatened me, I thought of you — and death spared me.'

She knew he was teasing her, but she didn't mind. Sepp seemed distant now that Rudi was beside her. She had never really known him, whereas she had felt at ease with Rudi ever since he had shared his lunch with her on the train. And he was actually very much more handsome than Sepp. His features were more even, his nose was straight and his eyes showed less strain.

At that moment the waiter approached, carrying a tray high above his head, from which the wonderful aroma of fresh coffee emanated, causing other customers to stare enviously at them. With a flourish, he placed a copious helping of flan heaped with whipped cream before Luise.

'But how on earth ...?'

'Oskar Braun and I have a special arrangement,' Rudi smiled, 'about which your Herr Papa knows nothing.'

He was by far the most exciting thing ever to happen to her. 'Rudi, tell me what you're doing in Berlin.'

'I call myself a wholesaler, although your Herr Papa prefers to label me a black marketeer.'

She opened her eyes wide. 'And what do you wholesale?'

'Coffee and cream,' he smiled, looking at her plate. 'Then, almost anything you care to name. What is Madame's fancy today? Some fine Scottish tweed, French champagne, some silk stockings?'

'Do you really have all those things, Rudi?'

'A whole warehouse full for your pleasure. Tell me what you'd like more than anything else in the world.'

'I'd like a new dress,' she said promptly.

'I think that might be arranged. Let me see, I have some emerald green crêpe de chine that would match your eyes to perfection. And I might even have leather shoes in the same colour.' As she gazed at him with unconcealed delight, he took her hand in his and asked, 'Has anybody ever told you that you are beautiful, Luise?'

A tremor ran up her spine. She thought she might be falling in love.

All that evening, Karl ranted against black marketeers and Rudi in particular, but by the following morning, he had forgotten the episode. Luise had not. A few days later, she came home with a length of crêpe de chine, some new shoes and a graphic description of Rudi's warehouse. 'You just can't imagine it,' she told Viktoria, as she spread her treasures on the bed. 'It's like an oriental bazaar. It's stacked floor to ceiling with just about everything you can think of. He's got material, Vicki, satin, taffeta, silk, wool, organdie, tulle, lace, damask, brocade, velvet, chintz, muslin, of every single colour and shade. Oh, and his shoes and gloves ...'

'It sounds a bit like Wertheim's department store,' Viktoria commented drily.

'Yes, it is, but like Wertheim was before the war.'

'But where does it all come from?'

'Goodness knows. I didn't ask. I just said thank you prettily and accepted my presents with good grace.'

Viktoria looked at her in horror. 'Rudi gave you that material? Luise, didn't you pay for it?'

'Well, not with money anyway.' Luise smiled impishly. 'I gave him a little kiss. He seemed very happy with that.' She wound the fine silk around her like a sari and swirled round the room, her eyes shining.

Viktoria bit her lip. It would be easy for Luise to get into trouble with someone like Rudi. 'Luise, you should be careful. Men like Rudi Nowak can be dangerous and I'd hate to see you hurt.'

Poised on one foot, Luise smiled at her confidently. 'Oh, rubbish, Vicki. Don't be so boring. It's such a long time since I had any fun — and Rudi's fun.'

'Maybe, but you're only eighteen; you're awfully young, don't forget.'

It was the wrong thing to say. Luise's eyes narrowed. 'I'm older than you were when you fell in love with Peter. And I'm certainly not going to make a fool of myself over Rudi like you did over him.'

Viktoria stared at her, at a loss for words.

Quick to press home her advantage, Luise added triumphantly, 'And if you think you're going to spoil my fun by telling Mama and Papa that I'm seeing Rudi, you shouldn't forget that there are some quite interesting things I could tell Benno, if I chose to!'

What exactly did that mean? Was she referring to Viktoria's childhood love for Peter or was there a deeper significance to her words? Did Luise suspect that Stefan was Peter's son? Viktoria stood up. 'I was only offering you advice,' she said stiffly.

Immediately contrite, Luise rushed across the room, throwing her arms round her sister's neck. 'Oh, Vicki, I'm sorry. I didn't mean to be hateful. It's just that it's so lovely to have someone to give me nice presents and spoil me, — oh, and make me feel important. Please don't let's quarrel, not about Rudi.'

Viktoria nodded ruefully. 'All right,' she conceded, 'but do be careful, won't you?'

That scene in Luise's bedroom continued to haunt her for the rest of the day. She wished she could have explained to Luise that it was because Peter had flattered her and made her feel important that she herself had got into such trouble and that she dreaded the thought of Luise finding herself in the same situation.

Peter seemed a very shadowy figure now. Nearly four years of living with Benno had pushed him to the back of her mind, although as thousands of men had died on the battlefield, she had often wondered if he were among them. But now, as the war was obviously reaching its end, she knew she had to face the possibility of his return. She no longer loved him, but that did not alter the fact that as a result of their brief affair she had borne a child and, although Stefan did not look unlike Benno, he looked even more like Peter.

As Viktoria went about her duties that evening, conferring with the new reception manager, the temporary head waiter, the bad-tempered chef and the fraught housekeeper, she wished, once again, from the bottom of her heart that she had never met Peter von Biederstein. But, when she went up to say good night to Stefan, and saw his dark head on the pillow, she knew she could never totally regret the affair. She hugged him close to her. 'Stefi, Stefi, darling, you're all mine, aren't you?'

'And you're mine,' he replied kissing her on the lips. Then he stared at her anxiously. 'Mama, why are you crying?'

She brushed the tears away. 'It's nothing, darling. It's just that I love you so much. Grown-ups are silly people, Stefi, they cry when they're happy. Now, go to sleep, darling.'

Quietly, the nursery door opened and Benno was standing beside her. 'He's a splendid little man, isn't he?' He bent over and kissed Stefan good night. 'Sleep well, son. Sweet dreams.'

'Good night, Papa.'

The dim image of Peter receded.

Unaware of the worries she had revived in her sister's mind, Luise found herself swept by Rudi into a new world. Because of its central situation, he chose Café Jochum as his centre of operations. With Oskar Braun's blessing, but without Karl's knowledge, for Karl seldom left the hotel those days, Rudi had his *Stammtisch* where people always knew they could find him at certain times of the day. Many of them were artists, poets and writers, asking him to accept a painting or a play in exchange for some tins of food or the price of a room for the night.

Oskar Braun did a similar trade, exchanging antique books for a bottle of wine, a Meissen figurine for a veal cutlet, leather gloves for a slice of chocolate gateau, paintings by Berlin's increasing colony of artists, unknown names like Otto Dix, George Grosz, Wassily Kandinsky, in exchange for two eggs in a glass. These valuables he bartered with Rudi Nowak for sacks of coffee, bars of chocolate and crates of fruit.

Luise watched the transactions wide-eyed. 'This is what your father should be doing at the Hotel Quadriga,' Rudi told her. 'Before very long it's going to be the only way to do business.'

'But why?'

'There's little food available and there's less and less money to pay for it. War is an expensive business, my treasure.'

That summer, Luise realized Berlin was changing before her eyes. The steady influx of artists, musicians and writers continued, many of them converging on Café Jochum, which reverberated to an excited babble of voices. The café's clientele and the subjects they discussed were very different from those elite figures who had thronged its terraces over thirty years earlier, when Karl had first opened it. To Luise, they were infinitely more appealing.

'Where do they all come from?' she asked Rudi.

'Some were invalided out of the army. Others escaped military service by fleeing to Switzerland when war broke out. Now, they're coming back. Others were here all the time, but kept out of sight.'

'Why?'

'Because they are socialists or communists,' he said indifferently. 'Many of them are pacifists, my treasure.'

He called her his treasure, he kissed her hand, he paid her compliments and he gave her presents, but for the first couple of months of their relationship, he made no attempt to seduce her. Since they always met at Café Jochum, they were, in fact, never alone together. As the novelty of just being seen with him began to wear off, Luise began to wonder whether there was something the matter with her. She dreamed of him at night, incredible, erotic fancies, from which she woke excited and dissatisfied. Rudi never did anything without a reason, so why did he give her presents if he did not want to make love to her?

Then, one afternoon, after he returned from his weekly visit to Switzerland, he invited her to his warehouse. 'I've just bought some silk. Come and choose yourself another dress length.'

As they stood close together in the shadowy storeroom, piled high with bales of cloth, sacks of provisions and crates of supplies, she asked, 'Why do you give me presents, Rudi?'

'Profit, my treasure, profit.' He pointed to an oil painting leaning against the wall. 'Like that, you are an investment. Your value increases with time.' He put his arm round her and drew her to him, kissing her for the first time on the lips.

Her mouth yielded to him, and a strange feeling of warmth surged through her. Her arms went round his neck and she clung closely to him, her excitement mounting as she felt his firm body hard against her own.

After a long time, he gently released her. 'Not here, my treasure. I have work to do. Come to my apartment this evening.'

Mumbling excuses to her parents about seeing an old school friend and ignoring Viktoria's sceptical glances, Luise took a taxi to Charlottenburg that evening. She believed she knew exactly what was going to happen, although she had no idea what it would be like.

Rudi opened the door to his apartment, marvellously clad in a scarlet silk kimono, emblazoned with golden and orange dragons. On his feet were golden Turkish slippers that curled up and over at the toe. He held a glass flute of champagne in one hand and a cigarette in a long, ebony holder in the other. 'Welcome to my humble abode,' he grinned, bowing elaborately.

He looked so different from the Rudi she was used to and, dressed in her conventional costume, she felt paled into insignificance beside him. 'Rudi, you look amazing!'

He took her jacket and led her into his living room which was lit only by a table lamp, and when she was seated, he handed her a glass of champagne and offered her a cigarette. As she took them, she found, to her dismay, that her hands were trembling. Rudi appeared not to notice. 'Do you realize, my treasure, that we have never pledged friendship? Don't you think it's time we did?' He slipped his arm through hers, so that their right arms were linked as they drank. Then, lingeringly, his lips brushed hers. There was a sweet taste to his mouth, of wine, of cigarettes and of something else, tantalizingly, indefinably masculine. The sweet taste of desire. His tongue probed inside her mouth, caressing her teeth, her tongue, her palate. Her whole body was trembling now.

His hand slid down her shoulder to her breasts, stroking them, arousing a tumult of strange new emotions. She put out her own hand and encountered his bare knee, where his dressing gown had parted.

Then he lifted her up and carried her from the room, across the hall and into a bedroom flooded by soft, pink light and dominated by a huge, four-poster bed, hung with peach-coloured curtains.

Luise felt as if she were moving in a dream. Rudi's fingers were undoing her clothes, removing her blouse and letting her skirt fall to the ground, until she stood before him clad only in her chemise and stockings. Then he picked her up and laid her on the satin sheets. Poised over her, he opened his arms and his kimono fell open to reveal his naked body. 'Was this worth waiting for?' he asked huskily.

She gazed at him and felt a responding, mounting urgency in her own body. Involuntarily her legs parted, and he smiled. Casting his kimono away, he lay down beside her and began to peel off her stockings, tracing her body with minute kisses until she was writhing.

'Kiss me, too,' he muttered and obediently she allowed her mouth to travel over his hirsute chest and arms. Then he pushed her head down and down, until it reached his erect phallus. Half-longing, half-frightened, she took it in her mouth. Above her, Rudi let out a deep, ecstatic sigh. She felt him shudder and, suddenly, her mouth was full of sticky liquid, choking her and making her feel rather sick. Uncertainly, wishing she had a handkerchief, she moved her face away and let it dribble out onto the satin sheets.

This was not how she had imagined it would be. She did not understand exactly what had happened, but she knew Rudi had been satisfied, while she remained disappointed. Tears came to her eyes and she forced them back. For a long time, they lay like that, until Rudi's hand found hers and guided it to his groin. 'I'm ready again.'

But Luise was not. Her body was tense and when Rudi turned her onto her back, wrenching her legs apart so that he could enter

332

her, she was dry. Far from being the sublime moment she had anticipated for so long, it was agonizing. She buried her face in his
chest to stifle her screams of pain.

Rudi, however, apparently believed her cries to be a natural
reaction. When eventually he drew away from her, he gazed at her
in satisfaction. 'Let's have some more champagne,' he exclaimed,
leaping off the bed. 'Then we'll do it again.'

Numbly, she gathered the sheet round her to cover her naked-
ness and wished she had never come here. Her glance fell on a
small ormolu clock beside the bed and she saw, to her horror, that
it already read ten o'clock. While Rudi was still fetching the champagne, she staggered towards her clothes and started to pull them
on.

'What on earth are you doing?' he asked from the doorway.

'I have to go. My parents will be worried.'

He shrugged. 'Yes, I forgot you're so young. Well, you don't
mind if I stay here, do you? I feel rather tired now.' He lay down
on the stained, rumpled bedclothes, watching her as she dressed.
'Do you know this bed is supposed to have once belonged to Marie
Antoinette? I got it in return for a lorryload of potatoes. Not a bad
bargain, eh?'

Still naked, he came with her to the door of the apartment. 'I'll
be at the café tomorrow afternoon. I expect I'll see you there?'

Her hand on the doorknob, she nodded.

'Here, my treasure, what's the matter?' He cupped her chin
under his hand and forced her to look at him. 'You enjoyed yourself, didn't you? You sounded as if you did.'

'Yes,' she mumbled.

'Well, look a bit happier about it then. It's not such a tragic
thing to lose your virginity, you know. Thousands of women do
every day. Go home and have a good sleep. And dream of Rudi.'

She did dream of Rudi, but they were not pleasant dreams. All
too clearly she saw that she had paid for his presents by giving him
her body. To her horror, she realized it made her little better than
a common prostitute.

The following morning, she roamed restlessly around the hotel,
not knowing whether to go to Café Jochum that afternoon or not,
frightened that Rudi would crow over his success with her to all his
friends. Finally, she knew she had to see him again, if only to put
her mind at rest.

When she got to the café, he was at his normal table, chatting with Oskar Braun. Gallantly, he rose and kissed her hand. 'Luise, my treasure, how lovely to see you.' She breathed a sigh of relief. Outwardly, at least, nothing had changed.

During the next few days, her self-confidence gradually returned. When Rudi again invited her to his apartment, she refused and, instead of being angry as she had feared, he smiled tolerantly. 'We haven't signed a marriage contract, treasure. You can please yourself what you do, but any time you change your mind, just let me know.'

Lothar Lorenz arrived in Berlin from Zurich in July. He was a short, rather plump man, with a round, smiling face and wearing the most outrageous clothes Luise had yet seen. The day he burst in upon Café Jochum, he was dressed in yellow and black checked knickerbockers, a yellow bow tie, a flowing black cape, and sporting a flat, working-man's cap on his head. A monocle dangled from his eye. 'Rudi, dear boy, they said I'd find you here.'

'Lothar!' Rudi shook his hand. He introduced Luise, then asked, 'And what brings you to Berlin?'

'I couldn't stand Switzerland any more!' Lothar Lorenz exclaimed dramatically, throwing himself down on a chair. 'Four years is enough! I was stifling, suffocating, I was going mad.'

'Lothar's father owns a sausage factory in St Gallen, Luise,' Rudi explained with a grin. 'I buy a lot of my preserved meats from him. However, Lothar here considers himself above such banal items as sausages. He describes himself as an art dealer and collector. He's bought a lot of the pictures I've acquired. He seems to think they're going to be valuable one day!'

'You may laugh, Rudi, but don't forget that I was one of the first to discover the Impressionists. Ach, Renoir, Cézanne, Monet! Your Kaiser calls them French dirt, but one day they will be worth a fortune! But enough of that! Let me tell you my latest enthusiasm. Rudi, Luise, Lothar Lorenz has discovered Dada. Yes, I am a Dadaist!'

'What's Dada?' Luise asked. She felt herself immensely attracted by the small man's bubbling personality.

'Dada is the cultural revolution. Dada seeks to destroy all recognized art forms, it insults conventional ideas, it despises the authoritarian precepts upon which society has been run for so long. We Dadaists hate the war, the Kaiser, the capitalists — and we laugh at them! We are anti-everything and in order to expose the pointlessness of existence, we ridicule it! That is Dada!'

Rudi regarded him cynically. 'And what do you do, Lothar?'

'Me?' He puffed out his chest. 'I subsidize the poor poets, I buy pictures from the struggling artists, I finance Dada events. Here, in Berlin, I shall help stage theatre productions. I am part of the revolutionary cause!'

After Rudi left the café that afternoon, Luise remained with Lothar, who was soon telling her the story of his life. 'I loathed both the sausage factory and St Gallen from the day I was born,' he admitted candidly. 'When I was still a student, I inherited some money from my maternal grandfather and immediately broke loose and went to Paris. Ach, Paris was wonderful then.' He shook his head reminiscently. 'It was there I met my wife. Yvette was a beautiful girl, a cabaret dancer at the Folies Bergères with the most superb legs. We married and within a year she had left me. She was enticed away to join the Ziegfeld Follies in America.'

He paused and Luise felt some comment was expected of her. 'How sad.'

'No, Luise, it taught me a lesson. I had believed I owned my wife, but it wasn't true. Since then, I have realized that beautiful objects can never become everyday possessions. Beautiful women, like beautiful pictures, should be admired, revered — and kept in a safe place. If you cannot look after them properly, you should not have them at all. Love, like art, should give pleasure, it should stimulate, amuse and sometimes make one sad, but it should never be a cause of worry.'

Then, abruptly, he changed the subject. 'Do I understand from your name that your family owns this café?'

'Yes, and the Hotel Quadriga on Unter den Linden.'

He clasped her hands in his. 'What a remarkable coincidence! That's where I'm staying! Let us return together.'

Viktoria, who saw them enter the hotel, asked Luise later, 'Who is that extraordinary little man?'

Luise found herself rising to his defence. 'I think he's fascinating. Vicki, he's a Dadaist. He's a cultural revolutionary.'

Viktoria rubbed her hand wearily across her forehead. 'Oh, when are you ever going to grow up?'

Luise thought of Lothar Lorenz, who must be at least thirty but was still young at heart. 'I don't think I ever want to grow up.' Certainly not, she added mentally, if it meant becoming tired and bad-tempered like her sister.

Lothar was a happy person and his gaiety was infectious. Within a very short time, Luise felt closer to him than she had ever been to anyone in her life before, with the exception of Franz Jankowski. Perhaps the great age gap between them helped, but instinctively, she knew that Lothar liked but was not in love with her, that he wanted her companionship but not her body. And, because of this unspoken understanding they were able to enjoy one of those very rarest of human relationships — true friendship between a man and a woman.

Now that she had Lothar, she was able to distance herself from Rudi. Of course, they still met at the café, but he no longer offered her presents from his warehouse, although he intermittently invited her back to his apartment. To her relief, she found she could refuse his propositions laughingly.

Word spread like wildfire among Berlin's artist community that Lothar Lorenz was a sponsor of the arts. The mere fact that he was staying at the Hotel Quadriga gave him financial status, and a former acquaintance in Zurich with Dadaists like Richard Huelsenbeck and Tristan Tzara lent him cultural respectability. Arrayed in his exotic fashions, Lothar was soon holding court at Café Jochum, expounding the anarchic theories of the Dadaist revolution.

'You two have a lot in common,' Rudi said mockingly, one day. 'Has Luise confessed that Olga Meyer is her cousin?'

Luise pulled a face, but Lothar gazed at her with respect. 'That's a very brave woman. It's absolutely wicked that she's locked up because of her beliefs.'

Huge crowds, demonstrating on the streets for the release of Karl Liebknecht, Rosa Luxemburg and Olga Meyer from prison, confirmed his opinion. 'You see,' Lothar declared, 'they know, even if your generals don't, that the war is over.'

Most of Lothar's disciples agreed with him, declaring themselves to be fervent revolutionaries and believers in the Spartacist cause. Despite her lack of interest in politics, Luise found herself fascinated by the people he attracted to him. Like Rudi's supplicants, these too wanted something, be it a publisher for their latest book, a gallery in which to hang their paintings or a stage and a producer for their most recent play. In turn, they acquired their own acolytes: journalists, singers, dancers, variety artistes, actors and actresses, all hoping for work.

One of the actresses was Pipsi Ascher. Although she was twenty-three that summer, Pipsi looked little older than when

336

Luise had last seen her at Theo Arendt's wedding to her sister Sophie, over ten years earlier. Her black hair, loosely drawn back from her face with a ribbon, still hung to her waist, and only her figure had grown rather more voluptuous. With her dark oval eyes set in her pointed face, she was incredibly beautiful, while her blatant sexuality was almost overpowering.

Remembering her childhood dreams of Georg Jankowski and Franz's misgivings when Georg had married Pipsi, Luise could not help but be intrigued by her. Finding herself alone with her one afternoon, she summoned up the courage to ask about Georg.

Pipsi shrugged her beautiful shoulders. 'He's in hospital somewhere in Belgium. Apparently he's been gassed and half his leg has been blown off.'

'But Pipsi, that's terrible. Can you go to see him?'

'No, of course not. Anyway, what could I do? I can't stand the sight of blood. I don't know how to cope with invalids.'

Luise's heart leapt out towards the young man she had never met.

Ignoring her silence, Pipsi continued, 'Never get married, Luise, dear. People make it out to be such a wonderful institution, but they don't tell you the bad bits. Even before the war, I hardly saw Georg, he was working all the time, for he was determined to pay Papa back as soon as possible for our apartment. Then, when I got my part in *Hurra! Hussar!* he was so jealous he became quite unbearable. Of course, not long after that, he was called up and I've only seen him once since war broke out.

'It was when he came home on leave that I got pregnant.' She sighed. 'I was twenty-one when I had Minna and at the time I believed I might just as well be dead. Fortunately, Papa engaged a nanny for her, so that I could continue with my career.'

Luise frowned, thinking how much attention Viktoria and Benno devoted to Stefan. 'Don't you mind leaving her alone with her nurse?'

'I'm sure Nanny looks after her much better than I ever could,' Pipsi replied indifferently.

The clientele of Café Jochum, many starved for years of the company of attractive women, welcomed Pipsi with open arms, and it took Luise little time to realize that Lothar Lorenz had fallen heavily for her charms. He bought her flowers, plied her with invitations to dinner, and gazed soulfully at her whenever she appeared in Café Jochum. Pipsi did not respond until one day he said,

Fraeulein Ascher, as soon as I find a suitable production, I shall make sure you play the starring role.'

'Herr Lorenz, I love you,' she said, kissing him on the cheek.

A blush spread all over Lothar's plump face. 'What a wonderful girl,' he told Luise ecstatically later. 'I'm sure she's a very talented actress.'

'You realize she's married, don't you?'

He looked pained. 'My intentions are strictly honourable.'

Very soon, however, it was apparent that he had a rival in Rudi, whose intentions were far from honourable. When Luise saw him employing the same tactics on Pipsi as he had used on her, she felt decidedly uneasy. As a single girl, she had, she supposed, been fair game, but Pipsi, she could never forget, was married. Nor were Rudi's gifts to her restricted to dress lengths. She turned up at Café Jochum flashing a diamond ring and draped in a new ermine stole, making no secret that they were gifts from Rudi and openly insinuating what she gave him in return. Their affair became public knowledge.

Lothar apparently accepted his defeat with resignation, seeking mute solace in Luise's company and devoting all his energies once again to Dada and the cultural revolution.

At the beginning of October the newspapers announced that the High Command had decreed Germany should become a democracy. Karl read this news aloud to his family while they were having breakfast, his white face vividly depicting his bewilderment. 'Prince Max of Baden has been appointed Chancellor and Social Democrats have joined the government. There's to be no more censorship, *Vorwaerts* and other left-wing papers are to be published again and some political prisoners are to be released. All, apparently, with the blessing of Ludendorff and Hindenburg. Now, why should they do that?'

'I believe Ludendorff knows we've lost the war,' Benno said quietly. 'I think it's because he wants a civilian government to negotiate the basis for peace.'

'Lost the war? Who says we've lost the war? We haven't finished fighting yet. We've still got our fleet, haven't we?'

'Do you really think the war is over?' Ricarda asked Benno.

'Yes. Our factories are almost idle because the country simply can't afford to pay for any more arms. As Theo Arendt forecast a long time ago in this very hotel, the coffers are empty. My father, as you know, has close contact with the generals and, according to him, very harsh terms will be imposed by the Allies on a militaristic Germany, but they may be prepared to deal more leniently with us if they think we've voted the military out of power. You see, it's the Kaiser and the generals who are hated abroad — not the German people.'

'I haven't voted the generals out of power,' Karl blustered. 'They've just foisted this democracy on me.'

Ricarda ignored him. 'What do you think will happen now, Benno?'

'I don't know, but I fear that, now the Social Democrats finally have a legitimate political voice, they're going to make it felt.'

As the October days went by, Karl grew very quiet as many of his worst fears seemed to be coming true and Benno's prophecies were proved right. The newspapers were now able to report many of the government's actions to a people who were demanding the right to know and to participate. Prince Max requested an armistice, not from the Allied Commander-in-Chief but from President Wilson, and accepted the American President's fourteen-point peace programme.

'Seems harmless enough,' Karl grunted when he read through them, 'but they're just idealistic nonsense. A League of Nations! Reconciliation among all peoples. Who does this American think he is? God Almighty? America declared war on us, remember, not we on them! And now the Americans think they can dictate the terms of peace!'

He was far more angry when he learned that Prince Max had overruled the generals and admirals and agreed that unlimited submarine warfare should be stopped. 'We're still at war, damn it all! Who does that liberal think he is to dictate to the Admirals? Has he forgotten the Kaiser? He rules this country and nobody should forget it.'

'No,' Benno told him, 'in a democracy, government holds the power, not the Kaiser. He's only a constitutional monarch.'

But Karl could not be bothered with such trivial details. 'He's still King and Kaiser as far as I'm concerned!

'The people blame him for the war. They want his head.'

Karl's fury knew no bounds when, on 23 October, Karl Liebknecht and Olga Meyer were released from prison. An excited, shouting mass of people marched their heroes in triumphant procession down Unter den Linden. The hotel guests, who seemed to be dwindling in number every day, stood on the balcony and stared gloomily down at them.

Lothar was with Luise. 'Isn't that a wonderful sight? Now the people have their leaders back, the revolution can become a reality. It's as if the sun has suddenly come out after years of darkness.'

She was not so certain. Lothar's was the only happy face on the balcony — all the others were drawn and etched with worry. If the sun had come out, she could nevertheless sense a chill of fear in the air.

'Why don't they send in the army?' Karl shook his fist at the elated crowds. 'If Ludendorff were here, he'd see this mob off the streets in minutes.' He stood glowering at the cheering workers then, muttering wrathfully, went back into the hotel, slamming the door behind him.

'He's wrong,' Benno said. 'He's a lone voice, persisting in a worn-out belief in bygone days. Only Karl Jochum and the Kaiser believe they still have the army behind them, and even they, in their heart of hearts, can't really believe it.'

As Olga was borne in triumph down Unter den Linden, she was scarcely aware of her surroundings. Her eyes were dazed by the bright light after nearly two years spent in a dark prison cell. Her ears were deafened by the tumultuous cheers of the crowds following long months of silence. But her heart was jubilant. From behind her prison walls she had helped to overthrow the monarchy. The time for revolution had arrived!

Back again in Wedding that evening, she wasted no time in reliving the glories of the day. Reunited again with Reinhardt, secure in the knowledge that Karl Liebknecht was released and that Rosa Luxemburg would soon join them again, she threw herself into her work. In her absence, Reinhardt and the other comrades had not been idle. As in Russia, the organization was prepared and the people waiting to set up soldiers' and workers' soviets in all of Germany's major cities. Now it only remained to overthrow the coalition government and to declare a soviet republic under the leadership of Karl Liebknecht.

Yet, strangely, Reinhardt seemed doubtful. 'You're moving too fast. You've been away so long, you don't realize what life is actually like now, here in Germany. I think we should seek some kind of alliance with the Social Democrats.'

She stared at him in horror. 'The Spartacists should ally themselves with men like Friedrich Ebert and Philip Scheidemann? Reinhardt, are you mad?'

'No, I'm realistic. We are simply not strong enough to rule the country on our own. We have no programme and no proper organization. We need a real newspaper of our own in order to publicize our aims and win the people to our side. We need ...'

But Olga had heard enough. 'Throughout their lifetime, the people have had no say in the way their country is run. Now they have an opportunity to show their true feelings. We, Reinhardt, will lead them in their right to strike against the government and the Kaiser. When the whole country grinds to a halt, we shall know we have the people on our side.'

That night, as they lay together for the first time in almost two years, Reinhardt held his wife closely to him, caressing her emaciated body. 'I've missed you,' he said tenderly.

But Olga heard him only dimly. Now they were together again, she forgot how dreadfully she had missed him and accepted his lovemaking almost mechanically. Her mind was racing feverishly ahead, writing articles for their new newspaper, setting up the administration that would be needed for their new government, and agitating on street corners for a general strike. There would be time later for love.

During the days following the release of the Spartacist leaders from prison, Benno watched events with increasing despair. The Spartacists wasted no time in stirring up an already disillusioned population and public demonstrations and rallies reached an ever more fervent pitch. They soon had their own newspaper, for they seized the offices of the *Berliner Lokaleranzeiger*, from which they issued the *Rote Fahne* — the Red Flag. In strident terms it stated the party's programme: the abolition of capitalist rule and transfer of power into the hands of the workers, confiscation of private wealth, the formation of a workers' militia ...

Benno could see that if the Spartacists succeeded, they would spell death to Kraus Industries. On Baron Heinrich's orders, the chemical plant at Kraus Village discontinued the production of explosives and reverted to its original purpose of making paints, dyes, glues and polishes, products with a peacetime application. Benno spent long hours in consultation with Social Democrat trade union leaders, trying with them to prevent the more militant of his workforce from occupying the factory.

As he did so, he suddenly realized that he did not very much care what happened to Kraus Village. He was weary to the very marrow of his bones and totally disgusted with his father's hypocrisy. The war was all but over now and he considered he had more than done his duty, both to his country and to his family. Let them seize control of the factory, so long as they left him alone, in peace, to spend the rest of his life the way he wanted to live it.

In the meantime, one after another, Germany's neighbouring countries were succumbing to revolutions, all faithfully reported in the newspapers, all on a much smaller scale than the Russian one, but nevertheless terrifying in their proximity. With President Wilson's blessing, they withdrew from the war and were declared independent republics. Soon, Germany was going to stand all alone, open to invasion from the Allies.

At this point, the Kaiser took the law into his own hands. He peremptorily sacked General Ludendorff and left Berlin for army headquarters at Spa in Belgium. 'You see, the Kaiser believes we can still win the war!' Karl announced triumphantly. 'Ludendorff was just a defeatist!'

Benno did not bother to contradict him. The hotel was virtually empty now, for the bureaucrats who had occupied its rooms for so many years were all quietly disappearing, like rats leaving a sinking ship. Let the old man keep his illusions as long as possible, Benno thought.

It was on 3 November that news reached Berlin of the Kaiser's final attempt to win the war. A few days earlier, his pride and joy, the High Seas Fleet, had been ordered to put to sea. But it never departed from Kiel, for the sailors, who had not left land for almost two years, were as sick of the war as their counterparts in the factories. In an unprecedented moment in German naval history, they mutinied, and the mutiny spread like wildfire to other parts and naval bases. They were joined by striking civilians and deserting soldiers and, united in their cause, they stormed through the streets. 'Long live the Revolution!' was their battle cry now.

Benno knew then that there would be no need for the Allies to invade Germany. The workers of Germany had brought the country to its knees. The government now had no option but to ask for an armistice, unless it wanted civil war at home. Reinhardt Meyer wrote triumphantly in the *Rote Fahne*, 'The Revolution is spreading. Nobody is left to defend the monarchy. Soldiers are leaving their barracks, sailors are leaving their ships and factories are standing empty. This is the beginning of the German Revolution. Long live the German workers' republic!'

Next day, when Benno approached Kraus Village, he found an angry, gesticulating mob gathered outside the gates. Two huge banners had been slung across the walls. One read *Peace and Freedom!*, the other *Death to Capitalism!* When they saw his car, the crowd started to surge towards him and he felt a moment of very real fear. Within seconds they could tear him to pieces. Then, to his relief, he heard a voice shout an order and they parted ranks to allow two figures through: one, an armed man, still in army uniform, but with the cockade torn from his cap; the other, one of his trade union leaders.

The trade union man spoke authoritatively, so that the striking men could hear him. 'We don't want no trouble, Herr Kraus. But we run this factory now. Go home!'

The soldier's rifle was poised on him, but Benno needed no persuasion. He nodded, then reversed his car. He knew he would never again return to Kraus Village.

Back at the hotel, he telephoned his father to tell him what had occurred. The Baron raved at him down the telephone, but Benno quietly replied, 'My family needs me here, Father. There is nothing more I can do at Kraus Chemie.'

'What will your father do?' Viktoria asked in concern.

Benno shrugged. 'There's nothing he can do at the moment. His hands are going to be more than filled with similar problems in Essen. But one day, we shall have to meet and decide what my future is going to be.' He hoped it would not be until the current troubles and the war were over, for, although he wanted to get out of Kraus Industries, he would like the parting to be amicable. Apart from anything else, a head-on collision with his father would probably mean he would lose his considerable shareholding in Kraus Industries and he hadn't devoted so much of his life to the company just to lose everything in a fit of the Baron's pique.

On the morning of 9 November 1918, they rose to the sight of great crowds marching up Unter den Linden, many with rifles over their shoulders, some carrying huge red flags and wearing red armbands, and all with red badges in their buttonholes or pinned to their jackets. From all the side streets, more striking workers were marching to join the procession.

Inside the hotel they were a pitifully small group, the staff far outnumbering the guests, for it was only socialists or eccentrics like Lothar Lorenz who cared to stay in Berlin at such a time. But during the morning, their numbers were slowly augmented by Berliners who were either afraid to stay alone in their own homes or who wanted to be at the centre of things. These people brought with them incredible stories of silent streets, where every window was locked and barred, and of government offices, newspaper buildings and railway stations in the possession of the revolutionaries.

Throughout the morning, Karl stood at the window of the hotel bar, a sad and shrunken man, staring at the demonstrators, shaking his head in disbelief. 'I'll give them general strike. They should all be at the front.'

It was a morning of tension and wild rumours. People sat in quiet groups in the bar, starting each time anybody entered the revolving glass doors. 'They've taken the Imperial Palace,' one new arrival announced. 'Imagine revolutionary guards outside His Majesty's palace!'

A spasm of anguish flickered across Karl's face and Ricarda left her family to stand beside him. Occasionally others joined them at the window, shook their heads dolefully, then returned to their seats. Silently, the hotel staff moved between them, obeying unspoken orders to refill a coffee cup, serve a fresh glass of claret or pour a tankard of beer. It was as if they were all waiting for something to happen, but none of them knew what the event would be.

Regardless of the protesters, Ullstein tricycles wove their way through the crowds, delivering one newspaper edition after another to the hotel. Silently, the papers were handed from one guest to another. There was nothing new to be read. Even *Vorwaerts* only announced the general strike.

While the shouted slogans and cheers of the mob penetrated the dim quietness of the hotel, they continued to wait, all absorbed in their own fearful thoughts. Benno, Viktoria and Stefan sat close together, Luise and Lothar opposite them, even the garrulous Swiss silenced for once. Like statues, Karl and Ricarda stood silhouetted against the window.

Then, suddenly, the sepulchral stillness was shattered by a man hurrying in from the street, his face flushed. 'Scheidemann's declared a republic at the Chancellery! Prince Max has handed over power to Ebert! Ebert's going to be Chancellor! Long live the

344

German Republic!' There was a hiss of released breath, as people gasped, getting to their feet.

Seconds later, another stranger rushed in, yelling excitedly, 'Liebknecht has declared a soviet republic from the Imperial Palace! Long live the Republic! Long live the Revolution!'

They stared at each other. Two republics? The excitement on the streets reached an even more frenzied pitch and more people dashed into the Quadriga, shouting their news to anxious ears.

'Prince Max of Baden has resigned as Chancellor! The Kaiser ...'

'Liebknecht's Chancellor!'

'Long live the free Socialist republic!'

'Prince Max has left for Belgium to be with the Kaiser ...'

'The Kaiser has ...'

'Ebert's Chancellor!'

Over and above the pandemonium, a voice shouted, 'The Kaiser has abdicated!'

'No,' Karl cried in anguish, 'no, it can't be!'

Then, as they gazed fearfully at each other, the strident cry of the Ullstein newsvendor was heard. 'Read the *BZ am Mittag! BZ, BZ, BZ am Mittag!* The Kaiser's abdication! Read all about it in the *BZ!*' Benno pushed his way roughly through the mob to obtain a copy of the newspaper. Karl snatched it from his hand.

They stood back as he scanned the paper's leading article, his face slowly draining of colour until it turned an ashen grey. 'I don't believe it. Ullstein's made it up. It's a lie! A fabrication!' He let the newspaper fall to the ground. 'But how can it be?' he asked the sea of faces around him. 'How did it happen? An Emperor and King, appointed by divine right, but now no longer an Emperor ...' He turned to Ricarda. 'His Majesty will return, won't he?'

By tacit agreement, they all stayed together, guests, family and staff, united in their fear of what was going to happen next. Outside, the streets still seethed with people. Spasmodically, above the cheering and chanting, they could hear the sound of gunfire. Karl sat huddled in a corner, his face lined with pain, his eyes staring unseeingly into space. Stiffly upright, Ricarda sat beside him, still clasping his hand. Viktoria held Stefan on her knee, his head cradled against her chest, talking to him in a low voice, trying to reassure him at the same time as herself. The little boy said nothing, but his eyes were large with fear. Luise and Lothar sat at the bar, drinking brandy and smoking cigarettes. Although Lothar kept quietly insisting that the revolution was exciting, they both knew they were actually frightened.

Benno kept up an anxious pacing between the kitchens, the foyer and the bar. His own experience at Kraus Village had taught him what to expect next. He had locked and barred the service entrance and the doors to the cellars and, once the kitchen staff had prepared a simple snack, he made them join the others in the bar. Then he waited for a visitation of revolutionary troops to that last bastion of monarchy, the Hotel Quadriga.

They came at about eight o'clock, bursting through the glass doors, their guns pointing wildly at the assembled guests and staff, whom they then forced roughly into the foyer. A young sailor leapt onto a chair and, with blazing eyes, cried, 'When I give the signal you will all shout three times, "Long live the Revolution!"'

There was an awkward shuffling, but nobody said a word. Benno glanced at Viktoria and saw her eyes glaring defiantly. He looked swiftly behind him and found the same expression on nearly all the other faces. The soldiers raised their rifles and, at a nod from their leader, aimed them at the sullen group of people. God, he thought, this is no moment for principles. These men are desperate enough — and stupid enough — actually to open fire.

Then, ringing loudly through the foyer of the Hotel Quadriga, a Swiss voice cried with conviction, 'Long live the Revolution!' It was followed by Luise's softer, but also clear, 'Long live the Revolution!' In a desultory, ragged refrain, the others, including Benno, joined in. 'Long live the Revolution!'

The soldiers lowered their rifles. Benno relaxed. Then he stiffened again, as the sailor got down off the chair and exclaimed, 'Good! Now my men will search the building for any officers and capitalists you're concealing here.'

How much did they know? Did they know Benno Kraus of Kraus Village was Karl Jochum's son-in-law? He glanced at the rifles. It was better to give himself up now than risk all their lives. But before he could move, he was pushed roughly aside as an infuriated Karl burst past him. He marched up to the sailor and, disregarding the twitching rifles, demanded, 'Who the hell do you think you are?' He caught hold of the man's lapels and shook him. 'This is a private hotel and I am the owner. It's my business who stays here and who doesn't!'

'Listen to him,' one of the soldiers jeered. 'Private hotel! Ah, shut your mouth, you old fool, or do you want me to shut it for you?'

Ricarda moved forward, but a revolutionary pushed her rudely back. Incensed with rage, Karl turned on him with outstretched fists, whereupon the soldier hit him round the head with the butt end of his rifle. Karl staggered, then fell to the ground with a crash. Ricarda and Viktoria rushed to his side, while Benno, all fears for his own safety suddenly forgotten, moved angrily towards the revolutionaries, followed by the staff and guests.

'Enough!' the sailor shouted. 'We just want to make sure you're hiding no traitors here.' Benno looked away from him down to his father-in-law's inert body. 'You' — the sailor jabbed him with his rifle bore — 'take him in there and look after him. And you' — he pointed to Lothar — 'you go with him.' Then he signalled a soldier. 'And you, too. And I warn the rest of you that if we find anything, one single weapon or one person that is against our revolutionary cause, we will shoot all three men!'

It was a long hour while they waited beside Karl's unconscious body in the bar as the hotel was searched. With the soldier's rifle trained unerringly upon them, Benno did not dare move. As the only capitalist in the whole building, he was aware that he put them all at risk, but he was even more conscious of the debt he owed Lothar and Karl. Out of whatever misguided notion Lothar supported the revolution, his courage in speaking out had saved all their lives once, while Karl's outburst had stopped him from giving himself up.

Finally, the sailor reappeared at the door of the bar and signalled the soldier to release his hostages. Karl stirred and opened his eyes. 'No officers? No capitalists?' he asked bitterly.

The sailor eyed him narrowly. 'We'll catch the traitors yet.' Then he turned on his heel and left the hotel.

Dr Blattner came and examined the large lump on the side of Karl's head, but Karl seemed to be suffering no other side effects from the assault. 'You should stay in bed and refrain from such useless gestures in future.'

'He was accusing me of treachery. How can it be treacherous to be loyal to the Kaiser? If it weren't for the Kaiser, the Hotel Quadriga wouldn't be here.'

'Hush, Karl, you were very brave, if foolhardy,' Ricarda said.

'Thank you, sir,' Benno said, but Karl just stared at him blankly. He didn't realize that Benno had anything to thank him for.

Two days after the announcement in the Ullstein newspaper, the Kaiser actually signed his formal abdication as King of Prussia and Emperor of Germany and took up residence in Holland. 'It was a trick,' Karl muttered hollowly. 'The newspapers announced his abdication before it had really happened. They forced him to abdicate.'

That same day, in a railway carriage at Compiègne in France, Matthias Erzberger, a Centre Party politician, signed the armistice on Germany's behalf. Under its terms, German soldiers were to withdraw from all occupied territories in the west, including Alsace-Lorraine. Allied armies were to occupy the left bank of the Rhine and bridgeheads fifty miles beyond it. Germany was to hand over large stocks of war materials and much of her fleet. The war was over.

The massive exodus from the occupied territories commenced immediately. Trains that had taken cheering, confident regiments out to Belgium over four years earlier now brought them back again, dejected troops of men, their numbers sorely depleted, their field-grey uniforms hanging loosely from their bodies, their minds unable to understand what had gone wrong.

They had not understood why they were fighting, but they had known that victory was their aim. They had fought in blind obedience for the Kaiser and the Fatherland. Through no fault of their own, they had lost. Gradually, they came to see that the Social Democrats had sold them out to the enemy.

The army had no further need for the thousands of volunteers and conscripts among them. Upon their arrival at their home railway stations, they were disarmed and left to mix with the frenzied, rebellious crowds already roaming the streets. It took them little time to realize that they no longer had any jobs — that, having given years of their lives to their country, their country no longer had any need for them. But the revolutionaries could use them, for these demobbed soldiers were practised in using firearms. They gave them back their weapons and urged them to join them in their fight for freedom.

Major Count Peter von Biederstein and his men arrived back in Germany towards the end of the month. As the lorries bringing them home passed through cities and villages on their long journey to Danzig, nobody cheered them. On the contrary, they were subjected to jeers and insults, to shaking fists and obscene gestures. Armed men, deserters, who had torn the cockades from their hats and wore red armbands denoting their membership of soldiers' councils, raised their rifles threateningly, then hurriedly lowered them again, signalling them to continue on their way.

The hard-faced major stared back at them contemptuously. Scum, that's what they were, the dregs of humanity. Socialist scum. It was incomprehensible to him that the Kaiser should have abdicated, and that Matthias Erzberger, a politician from the wretched coalition government could have been tricked into signing the armistice agreement. But, by the time they reached Danzig, he understood. It was not the army which had surrendered, it was the politicians, who had wanted power out of the hands of the military into their own. The rumour that was going round was correct. Germany had been stabbed in the back by an enemy, only that enemy was not invisible, its form was social democracy.

The professional soldiers and officers of the Death's Head Hussars were not demobilized. They were ordered to stay at the garrison for regrouping, checking their arms and ammunition, and counting the roll call of the dead from the war. Out of their still quite considerable regimental funds, new uniforms were ordered for the men. Once the current troubles were over, they were promised leave.

The first thing Peter intended to do was travel to Luebeck and propose marriage to Ilse von Schennig, in which plan he was totally supported by Major-General Ritter von Schennig. The marriage, he was determined, would take place within the next year. In the meantime, he and his men remained at Danzig, still the elite of the German army, the force upon which Germany had been founded.

Not all the German army returned home. After Russia had withdrawn from the war and the treaty of Brest Litovsk was agreed, some troops had remained on the Eastern Front, for the generals did not trust the Bolsheviks and were fearful of a resurgent Red Army. Even after the armistice had been signed, men remained to guard the Russian border. Among these was Captain Otto Tobisch.

He and his men were among the toughest and fittest in Germany. They had seen their comrades die in their thousands, but they had survived. They had survived because they knew no fear, because of a native, brutal instinct in them that fought the enemy to the death, permitting no mercy, allowing no leniency. This was particularly true on Germany's north-eastern frontiers, where they were dealing with White Russians fleeing the communist regime, escaped German prisoners of war from Russian camps, and communist agitators disguised as German soldiers, trying to reach Berlin and the Spartacist revolutionaries. Single-handedly, Otto had shot, strangled or beaten to death hundreds of these migrants, regardless of their reason for trying to cross his territory. He had been awarded no *Pour le Mérite* for his courage, but his intrepid barbarism had earned him the respect of his comrades — and his commanding officers.

When he learned of the ignominious terms of the armistice, he was bitterly angry, especially as his future and that of his men now became ambivalent. Theoretically, as soon as they were released from their border duties, they would be demobilized. Such a thought was an anathema to Otto, because there was no place in civilian life for a man like him. He felt a gloating satisfaction when he learned that others, too, shared his resentment. Not just the soldiers, but many aristocrats and generals were furious at the humiliating peace agreement and refused to allow the German armies to be disbanded and scattered to the four winds of heaven. Revolution threatened on the streets of Germany's cities and civil war seemed imminent. Experienced soldiers of Otto's calibre were going to be needed to put down this red rabble. Funds were raised and Otto's men were told that they were now part of a new fighting body of mercenaries — the Free Corps.

They were given a new name — the Tobisch Brigade. And, on their helmets, they wore the insignia of a swastika, the hooked cross that they had discovered during their campaign in the Baltic. What its origin was, Otto neither knew nor cared, but it seemed to have a potent symbolism.

Under the command of General Luettwitz, the Tobisch Brigade continued their ruthless onslaught against the Poles, Russians and Slavs within their border territory. But, all the time, they awaited the order for them to return to Germany, to declare war upon the enemy at home.

From his room in the Hotel Quadriga, Karl saw the dispirited soldiers trudging through the streets, joining forces with the revolutionary rabble, listening to agitators like his niece, Olga Meyer,

350

and Karl Liebknecht, as they harangued them from street corners. He simply could not understand what had happened.

He was still confined to bed, a spectre of the man he had once been, when Max Patschke returned from the front. Suffering badly from trench foot, Max hobbled into the room and sat down beside Karl's bed. 'Wouldn't you have thought they'd have given me a job in the catering corps, Herr Direktor?' he grumbled. 'Oh, no, they put me in the infantry. I thought all that rain and mud was going to be the end of me.'

Karl gave his old friend a pitiful look. 'Surely we were winning, Max? Surely we didn't have to surrender?'

'It was the socialists' fault, Herr Direktor. Like everybody's saying, we were stabbed in the back by our own people.'

'Where are the Guards, Max? I've heard they're at Karlshorst. Why don't they march into the city? Why don't the young lieutenants come and celebrate their return at my hotel?'

Max stared at him. Didn't his old friend realize that the military no longer had any power? The socialists were in charge now. Until the army's role in this new Germany was determined, the Guards could do nothing but wait in their barracks.

'I didn't think it was going to be like this,' Karl said, and Max was horrified to see there were tears in his eyes. 'I thought we were going to have a victory like that of 1871. I could see the conquering troops marching through the Brandenburg Gate under the statue of the Quadriga, garlanded with flowers, with their standards raised triumphantly above them, and, in their lead, the Kaiser.'

Chapter Thirteen

Sepp Nowak fought his last battle on 5 November 1918. A few days later, the squadron's commander, Hermann Goering, called his men together and told them an armistice had been agreed and they had been ordered to demobilize. In order to avoid capture by the French, they were first to fly to Darmstadt and then find their own way home. There were angry mutterings, but nobody questioned his instructions, for despite the near impossibility of taking over command of Jagdgeschwader 1 after the Red Battle Flier's death, Goering had proved a sound leader.

Goering's was the first plane to land at Darmstadt and, as Sepp still circled above him, he saw armed men rush out of the hangars, rifles pointed towards the pilot. They were German soldiers, but they wore red armbands. So this was the revolutionary rabble of which word had already reached them. Unerringly, Sepp trained the machine-guns of his Fokker D VII on them. He saw Goering gesticulate and faces peer up in horror. The soldiers disbanded and Sepp came in to land.

'I told them you'd attack,' Goering said that evening, as they made their way through Darmstadt, staring about them in disgust at the mobs who roamed the streets. 'Now I wish I'd given the order.'

In an automatic gesture, Sepp's hand reached for his *Pour le Mérite*. What was going to happen to him now? Until a few days ago, he had been a hero, with sixty kills to his credit. Now, suddenly, he was a civilian, with no money and no job. On this chill, damp evening in Darmstadt, the future looked very bleak.

At that moment, a man barred their way, a soldier, clad in a grey army coat, with a red armband, and a rifle in his hand. He knocked Sepp's hand away from his *Pour le Mérite* and seized hold of his prized medal. 'Just a bit of old tin,' he jeered. 'Why don't you take it off?'

Sepp's instinctive reaction was to raise his fists, but Goering seized his arm. 'Not here. We'll get our own back one day.'

Reluctantly, Sepp allowed himself to be led away. A few yards down the street, another soldier barred their way. 'Just returned to Darmstadt, comrades?' He thrust a leaflet into their hands. 'You should go to the officers' meeting. It's just started.'

The two pilots looked at each other, then Goering shrugged. 'Why not?'

The huge hall was crowded when they entered, the attention of all the uniformed men on the speaker, some kind of official. 'The war is over,' he was shouting. 'From now on there will be no more elites. The Corps of Officers will cease to exist. All men will be equal and work together for the glory of the Republic. Lay down your badges of rank as symbols of conquered tyranny and become comrades among comrades!'

The deep anger rising in Sepp was echoed in the threatening mutters around him. He stood up to shout a protest, but as he did so, Goering pushed passed him, through the dense ranks of men and on to the platform. At the sight of him, the speaker moved to one side and the audience grew quiet.

'We are not comrades,' Goering declared authoritatively. 'I am the last commander of the Richthofen Wing and this coat that I am wearing is considered as a coat of honour. Should I throw it in the dirt and trample on it?'

Sepp stared at him, as it suddenly occurred to him that Goering was not only a natural leader, but a gifted orator, capable of putting his own incoherent thoughts into words. 'My comrades,' Goering's voice continued, dangerously low, then rising to a crescendo, 'we have fought for the Fatherland, suffered, bled, and many of us have died for the Fatherland. Should the dead also lay down their badges of rank?' There was tumultuous applause from some parts of the hall, while hissing and booing broke out in other areas.

'We do not ask for a reward,' Goering's voice carried above the noise, 'but neither have we earned your scorn. And to those of you who mock us today I say, we shall send you to the devil. That day will come!'

With a last baleful glance at the auditorium, he stepped off the platform and shouldered his way back towards Sepp, his eyes glittering with anger. 'Let's go.' They made their way out of the building, followed by the cheers of their fellow officers and the angry taunts of the revolutionaries. Outside on the pavement, as the rain fell heavily around them, Sepp asked, 'What are you going to do now?'

'Keep on flying and see this lot to hell. And you?'

'I suppose I shall go home, but I've got to find another flying job. The only life for me is in the air.'

Goering held out his hand. 'If I hear of anything, I'll let you know.'

The collars of their leather coats hunched high, their peaked caps shielding their faces against the pouring rain, the two parted, Goering in the direction of Munich, Sepp north to Berlin.

Even in the civilian suit Rudi had given him, Sepp looked very out of place in Café Jochum. His scarred, drawn face belied his twenty-six years and although he was much younger than many others of the café's clientele, he seemed a generation older. Although he no longer wore his *Pour le Mérite*, for it had nearly got him into more fights than he could count, his hand still went instinctively to his throat and his eyes betrayed his bewilderment when he found it gone.

Luise, remembering his triumphant visit to Berlin a year and a half earlier, felt deeply sorry for him. Rudi introduced him to his friends, not as one of Germany's greatest living aces, but as his older brother, 'just back from the war, poor bastard.' In a sudden moment of perspicacity, Luise saw them all as Sepp must see them, a chattering colony of intellectuals, pacifists, artists, empty-headed women and fervent radicals, with nothing else on their minds but to celebrate the abolition of censorship by overturning that very world which Sepp, for over four years, had been trying to save.

'What are you going to do?' Luise asked him.

'Try to find a job with a civilian airline.'

'Oh, forget about flying,' Rudi said scornfully. 'There's no money in it. Pilots are two a penny nowadays. Come into business with me.'

Sepp gave him a weak smile. 'Thanks for the offer, Rudi, but I'll never make a businessman. As for all the superfluous pilots around, you're quite right, but the situation will change.'

Luise looked at him thoughtfully, thinking of Benno's father, vaguely remembering hearing that the Baron was setting up his own aviation company. 'You met Baron Heinrich von Kraus, didn't you? Why don't you talk to him?'

'Apart from the fact that he must now have a waiting list of pilots a kilometre long, I don't think Baron von Kraus would be very interested in seeing me at this moment. He must be having 'problems of his own with all his factories,' Sepp told her drily.

'Maybe my sister or Benno could talk to him on your behalf.'

'Well, obviously, if you think they can do anything, I'd be very grateful. I'm beginning to realize that it's not what you know but who you know that counts in this world.'

At that moment, Pipsi arrived at their table. Laying her hand possessively on Rudi's shoulder, she smiled at Sepp. 'You must be Rudi's brother. I'm Pipsi Ascher.'

To Luise's surprise, a faint flush coloured Sepp's cheeks. He jumped up, took Pipsi's hand in his and kissed it. 'Fraeulein Ascher, I'm most honoured. I've long been an admirer of yours.'

'I know,' she said flirtatiously. 'I'm told you even named your plane after me. I hope I brought you luck.'

Rudi laughed coarsely. 'A flight in Pipsi is something nobody can forget.'

She narrowed her eyes. 'Rudi, dear, you may be rich, but sometimes you're so common.'

Luise frowned. With Lothar and Rudi already dancing to her tune, surely she couldn't want Sepp as well? 'Pipsi,' she asked pointedly, 'have you any news about Georg?'

'Oh, I gather he's coming back some time, but I've no idea when. In the meantime, I'm sure he's in good hands.'

Later, when Rudi and Pipsi had left, Sepp remained with Luise. 'Who's Georg?'

'Her husband, Georg Jankowski. He's wounded, in hospital somewhere.'

'You mean she's married? Does Rudi know that?' When Luise nodded, he said, 'And yet she's still sleeping with my brother? Well, what a cow! To think I named my plane after her!'

Luise felt extreme satisfaction in knowing that one man at least had evaded Pipsi's clutches.

The better she got to know Sepp, the more she liked him. He was very old-fashioned compared to her other acquaintances — like her parents, Viktoria and Benno, he seemed a relic of a different generation. Yet strangely, possibly because they had met before and he therefore found her trustworthy, Sepp appeared drawn to her. His fingers tapping the table top nervously, smoking one cigarette after another and drinking incessant cups of Rudi's coffee, he sat silently with her and Lothar, half-listening to the conversations going on around him, gazing longingly out of the café window at the grey, late November sky.

He was not living with his brother, but had taken a room in a small guest-house in Wilmersdorf. 'After all, I don't intend to stay here long. As soon as I get a job, I'll be gone. I can't stand this place.' He made no secret of his dislike of the mobs that roamed the streets, and the revolutionaries, both cultural and political.

One evening, she took him back with her to the hotel and introduced him to Benno and Viktoria. As she had suspected, they all got on very well together, but when Luise explained that she hoped Baron Heinrich would help Sepp, Benno looked sceptical. 'I'm not exactly in my father's best books at the moment, but I'll do my best.'

Later, when they were alone, Viktoria told her sister, 'I like Sepp much better than I like Rudi. I hope you'll bring him here more often. It was nice for Benno to have somebody to talk to, too.'

Luise smiled, but said nothing. Viktoria was already hearing wedding bells, she was certain, but she had no intention of getting married for a long time. And neither, she was sure, had Sepp.

Germany's industrial heart, the Ruhr, had ceased to beat. As everywhere else, armed mobs roamed its streets, while workers' councils tried to seize control of its factories. For weeks, Baron Heinrich and Ernst had been negotiating with the trade unions in Essen, so that Kraus factories and mills could remain open. The concessions they had to make were incredible, but anything was better than having them occupied by revolutionary workers' councils, and in due course, when order was restored, the Baron was determined he would renege on these agreements, claiming they had been made under duress.

He had also held a couple of secret meetings with officers of the French troops who had been sent in to occupy the Rhine. Many French industrial areas had been totally devastated by the war and he saw an immediate possibility of keeping his own factories going by supplying his country's former enemy.

But, in Berlin, to the Baron's disgust, Benno had made no attempt to salvage production facilities at Kraus Village. So, despite the fact that he was his son, he knew the boy had to be sacked. In the first week of December, after instructing his wife and daughter-in-law not to leave the Fortress under any circumstances and Ernst to continue his bargaining with the unions, the Baron left for Berlin. He was stopped many times along the way but each time he managed to find a plausible reason for his journey. He omitted to mention his title, describing himself as a salesman, and always greeted his interrogators with the words, 'Long live the Revolution!'

The closer he was to Berlin, the greater he knew his danger to be, for the capital's police headquarters were now occupied by the Spartacists, who had installed their own police president, an evil man called Emil Eichhorn who was rumoured to torture and even execute anybody whom he considered to be an enemy to the Spartacist cause. When the Baron's car was halted on the Charlottenburger Chaussee, the armed guards reacted suspiciously to the name Kraus, but, to his relief, after demanding to know his destination, they let him pass.

He was tired and extremely irritated when he reached the Hotel Quadriga. Huge crowds jostled on Unter den Linden, but they were not particularly threatening and it seemed to him that they were just waiting aimlessly for something to happen. These were the men who should be at work at Kraus Chemie, he thought belligerently.

There were no commissionaires waiting to greet him at the hotel's doors and, when he marched into the foyer, he discovered it almost empty except for a couple of page boys, who stared at him in amazement, and the hall porter, who lurched on his crutches from behind his desk, exclaiming, 'But, Herr Baron!'

'Where is Herr Benno? Fetch him immediately!'

Benno, sitting with Viktoria in her father's office, trying to calculate how long the hotel's food supplies were likely to last, heard his father's voice and rose slowly to his feet. 'It looks as if the moment of truth has finally arrived.' He strode into the foyer, trying to show a confidence he did not altogether feel. Nervously, Viktoria followed him.

The Baron was in a towering rage. 'What the devil do you think you're doing here, boy? Why aren't you at the chemical plant?'

At that moment, the revolutionary soldiers burst in, a dozen of them, their rifles aimed uncompromisingly at the Baron and his son. 'Get moving!' one shouted. 'Come on, Kraus, into the van!'

'Benno!' Viktoria screamed, rushing towards him, but a soldier pushed her roughly aside, so that she stumbled and fell. 'Keep out of this, woman.' As she struggled to her feet, she saw the two men bundled unceremoniously through the glass doors into a waiting police van. Terrified, she limped across the foyer in time to see them drive off towards the Alexanderplatz. Numb with shock, she buried her face in her hands. 'Benno, Benno ...' she whispered. Tears streamed down her face. The hall porter gazed at her anxiously, then ordered a page boy to fetch Frau Ricarda quickly.

At police headquarters, Benno and his father were herded immediately into Eichhorn's presence, who informed them coldly. 'You are accused of treason and anti-revolutionary activities. You are enemies of the people and have asked for the intervention of French troops in order to prevent the socialist revolution.'

Benno stared at him blankly. 'But I've been nowhere near the French. I haven't left Berlin for weeks. I've got witnesses to prove it. My wife can tell you. My father-in-law, the owner of the ...'

Abruptly, Eichhorn cut him off. 'Those witnesses are all bourgeois. Their statements have no value.' Then he turned to the Baron, prodding him with his rifle. 'You, you've been negotiating with the French. You went to Dortmund, you've been collaborating with French officers.'

Benno stared at his father, fearing him quite capable of such an act. He would do anything to save his business, he would lie, swindle and commit any form of treason, caring nothing about whom he hurt in the process. 'Rubbish!' the Baron snorted. 'Haven't left Essen in ages.'

'Why are you in Berlin?' Eichhorn asked ominously.

'To look at my works in Wedding,' the Baron growled.

Eichhorn stared at him in disgust, then ordered their guards, 'Take them to Moabit.'

Once again, they were roughly pushed into the back of the police van and driven to the Moabit prison. By this time, Benno was starting to feel extremely frightened. He was innocent of any crime, except that of being a capitalist in revolutionary Berlin, yet now he was threatened with incarceration and possibly even execution because of his father's greed. He thought of Viktoria and little Stefan, Karl, Ricarda and Luise, people who had grown to mean more to him than any others in the world. He could not bear the thought that he might never see them again.

The van screamed to a halt inside the prison gates and their guards ushered them out at gunpoint, then handed them over to prison officials, men who wore no revolutionary armbands. 'My name is Kraus, Baron Kraus,' the Baron said importantly. 'I'm sure there must have been a mistake. I demand to see the prison director.'

To Benno's amazement, the gaoler appeared impressed. 'Stay there, I'll go and get my instructions.'

A few moments later, he returned with the prison director, who bowed to them both and apologized abjectly, 'I just don't understand what's going on. They keep sending me people such as yourself, Herr Baron, landowners and industrialists, who have not been tried and who can be guilty of no crime. Men who are the very pillar of society. Well, I can't release you, but I'll put you in the investigation cells and do my best to see you're well looked after.'

'He's answerable to the Prussian state, not the Police President,' the Baron mumured to Benno, as they were led to their cell, the prison director hovering anxiously, almost as if they were royalty. 'He'll see where his duty lies. We shan't be here long.'

Now the immediate threat of execution had passed, anger was replacing fear in Benno's heart. The showdown between father and son was at last taking place, but not in the way either had anticipated, and Benno was determined to twist the circumstances to his own advantage. He was going to leave Kraus Industries, but it was going to be on his own terms.

'Now, Benno,' the Baron said glacially when they were settled in their uncomfortable cell, 'why have you not been doing your job at Kraus Chemie?'

'I want to resign my position,' Benno said curtly.

'You're not resigning, you're dismissed. What's more, you'll have no further financial interest in the company.'

It was the reaction he had expected. 'It can be proved that not only have I not been involved in negotiations with the French, but I have also handed Kraus Village over to the workers,' Benno said deliberately. 'Therefore, if what you say about the prison director is correct, I don't believe I shall be kept here very long. You, however, are in a slightly different position. Even if you are released, it would not be difficult to arrange for your re-arrest. You shouldn't forget that my wife's cousin is Olga Meyer — who now wields considerable power in Berlin — and she has hated you all her life.'

His father stared at him open-mouthed. 'But that's blackmail.'

'Maybe, but I shall carry out my threat unless you agree to my terms. I want no further executive participation in the company, but I retain my directorship and my shareholding.'

An expression of grudging admiration flickered across the Baron's face and Benno could almost see him thinking, 'Boy's showing the Kraus spirit at last!' He hammered home his advantage. 'I'm sick to death of guns, explosives, poison gas and battleships. From now on, I'm going to try to give pleasure to people, instead of killing them. I shall help the Jochums run the Hotel Quadriga.'

He waited for his father's scornful reaction, but none came. Instead, a look of cunning crept into his eyes. 'I don't want to lose you, Benno. We may still be able to work together, boy. You see, for a long time now, I've been moving Kraus Industries away from the armaments business into other areas. I've set up a civilian airline company and I've started a new division within Kraus Marin. Do you remember when you were a little boy, you wanted me to build a transatlantic liner? Well, that's what I intend to do next.'

'What's that got to do with the Quadriga?'

'As the Quadriga is the most luxurious hotel in Germany, so my ship will be the most luxurious passenger liner. If I allow you to keep your directorship and shareholding, will you help me with it?'

It was Benno's turn to stare. Germany was just defeated in a world war and his father was talking about transatlantic passenger liners! Was there no situation the old man was not able to twist to his own benefit? 'All right,' he said, with the feeling that his father had somehow emerged the victor from their confrontation. But the old man's mention of his aviation company sparked off another thought. Determined the gain maximum advantage from this encounter, he asked, 'Can you find a job for Sepp Nowak in your airline?'

'Nowak? Oh, I remember. Yes, he must be having a hard time at the moment. Well, I suppose I can find him something. Not as a pilot, of course, because the airline isn't flying yet, but perhaps as a salesman. Tell him to come and see me in Essen.'

It wasn't much, but Benno hoped Sepp would think it was better than nothing.

'Good,' Baron Heinrich said, pulling a fat cigar out of his breast pocket and lighting it. 'And now we must hope that somebody will get us out of here as quickly as possible. Do you think that wife of yours will be able to use her influence on this Meyer woman?'

The grim reality of their situation suddenly returned to Benno.

With a shock, he realized that his father was not totally convinced that the prison director would be able to effect their release. At the final count, they were dependent upon the Spartacists.

Viktoria was still standing helplessly at the hotel's entrance when she felt an arm round her shoulder and heard her mother's voice. 'He hasn't done anything wrong, Vicki, he'll be all right.'

'He's a Kraus,' Viktoria said bleakly. 'They'll murder him. Mama, what can I do?'

'Is it worth trying to see Olga?'

'Olga hates the Krauses. No, I think all I can do is go to the Alexanderplatz and plead for his release. God, Mama, I don't even know why they've arrested him, although it must be something to do with Baron Heinrich.'

'I'll come with you.'

'No, it's better I go alone. I'll wear an old coat, so I don't look conspicuous. Oh, I do hope he's all right.'

Not even when she had found herself pregnant had she felt as despairing as she did that day. As she pushed her way through the crowds, she suddenly realized just how much Benno had come to mean to her over the last four years. Looking back, she supposed that she had always loved him, but, because of her romantic idealization of Peter von Biederstein, she had never been able to see his value. Now, when he was lost from her, she saw with a dreadful clarity his stalwart values, his dependability, his common sense, his concern, not only for herself, but for Stefan and the rest of her family. Without Benno, she realized, she would be nothing. Oh, could she really have learned this lesson just as she was about to lose him?

Armed guards stood round the police headquarters, making it appear like a fortress, and, as the revolutionary soldiers pointed their rifles in her direction, she was momentarily tempted to turn and run. Then, with her head bravely held high and her hands clenched to stop them trembling, she walked forward. 'I wish to see the Police President.'

The inside of the building was seething with people, most of them on the same hopeless task as herself. Some four hours later, she succeeded in seeing a policeman, who told her Benno and his father were accused of conspiring with the French in Dortmund and had been taken to Moabit.

'But that's ridiculous. My husband hasn't left Berlin.'

361

'He wouldn't be arrested if he wasn't guilty.'

'But what will happen to him?'

'He'll probably be shot,' the policeman replied laconically. 'Most traitors are.'

It seemed Olga was her only solution. 'Where can I find Olga Meyer?'

'Why do you want her?'

'She's my cousin.'

The policeman regarded her doubtfully, then he said, 'I think she's at the *Vorwaerts* building.'

To her surprise, there were no armed guards outside the newspaper building. A caretaker conducted her up to Olga's office, where, surrounded by piles of papers, her cousin's thin face stared up at her bleakly. 'Yes, Viktoria?'

It was as if their friendship had never been. From the bottom of her heart, Viktoria wished that she did not have to ask this second favour of her, but with Benno's life at risk, she had no choice. 'Your people have arrested Benno. Please, Olga, I beg you to have them release him.'

Olga ran her fingers through her lank hair. 'At a time like this, you're worried because one greedy capitalist has been arrested?'

'Olga! He's my husband.'

'Then all I can say is that you should have thought more carefully when you got married. The Krauses and their kind deserve everything they get.'

At that moment, Viktoria saw Reinhardt approaching them across the room. Absolutely desperate now, she rushed up to him, tears pouring down her face. 'Reinhardt, please help my husband. He's done nothing wrong, but they've put him in Moabit. Reinhardt, please!' Curious faces stared at them, but Viktoria was past caring.

'Do you know anything about this?' Reinhardt asked Olga.

'For heaven's sake, I've got more to worry about than Benno Kraus! Don't any of you realize that most of Berlin is starving, that there is no medicine, that people are dying ...?'

Surprisingly gently, Reinhardt took Viktoria's hand. 'I'll telephone the police headquarters. Don't worry, he'll be released.'

'Don't waste your time, Reinhardt,' Olga said bitterly. 'What has Benno Kraus ever done for you?'

Reinhardt ignored her. It took a long while, but eventually he got through to Eichhorn's office, giving his personal word that

362

Baron Heinrich and his son were not guilty of any crimes. When the conversation was over, he said to Viktoria, 'Now you should go home and wait. He'll be all right.'

She took his hand. 'How can I ever thank you? Particularly after everything my father said to you?'

'Ours is not a corrupt party. We want to help people, not to frighten them away.' He stared towards Olga and sighed. 'She will never understand that there has been too much bloodshed, too many people dying. Ours should be a peaceful revolution.'

Viktoria was waiting in the foyer when Benno arrived back at the hotel. She rushed to him, throwing her arms round his neck, laughing and crying simultaneously. 'Oh, Benno, I was so frightened. I thought I was never going to see you again.'

He pulled her close to him, holding her so tightly she could scarcely breathe. When they finally drew apart, he said, 'I'll never leave you again.' In a few brief sentences, he described his conversation with his father. 'He's gone straight back to Essen,' he said cynically. Then he waved a hand round the empty hotel foyer. 'This is my home now.'

By tacit agreement, Benno assumed overall charge of the Hotel Quadriga. Viktoria continued to take care of the hotel's administration, such as it was during those bleak days, while Ricarda seldom left her husband's side. Luise and Lothar, seemingly impervious to the battle that was raging around them, continued to go nearly every day to Café Jochum.

As soon as Benno told him that his father could find him a job, Sepp Nowak followed hard on the Baron's heels to Essen. Luise missed him briefly, then, because there was so much else happening, pushed him to the back of her mind.

Lothar's round face radiated joy those days, for the revolution was the most exciting event he had ever experienced. He fervently believed that the workers had a cause but, since armed combat was hardly his forte, he directed his efforts into fighting the cultural revolution. That December, he and a young playwright conceived a stage show aimed at ridiculing the conventional theatre.

In a moment of genius, hearing about the huge success of the review in which Pipsi Ascher had played to packed pre-war audiences, Lothar hit upon the title *Hurra! Dada!* Whereas *Hurra! Hussar!* had glorified the army and the war, *Hurra! Dada!* was a superb skit on the military, Junkers, conservatives, capitalists and profiteers. He also saw in it a marvellous opportunity to win Pipsi away from Rudi Nowak. The part he proposed for her was a parody on the role she had played in *Hurra! Hussar!* Provocatively dressed, she would heap scorn on the arrogant young lieutenants and red-faced generals who sought her favours, choosing a penniless poet as her lover.

Pipsi was in seventh heaven. She described Lothar as 'her dearest friend, the theatre producer', bestowing little kisses on him whenever she saw him, while Rudi looked on with an amused air. As soon as Lothar had rented a theatre, she made a tremendous commotion about learning her lines and left for rehearsals with a very self-important air. At long last, she was an actress again.

This new, post-war Berlin seemed a wonderful place to Luise, too. She did not really understand her father's decline during the war years, nor his collapse at the Kaiser's abdication. Never a political person, she cared neither for the Social Democrats nor for the Spartacists, yet on the other hand, apart from a childhood affection for the Kaiser because of the role he had played in the lives of the Jochums, she had no particular sympathy with the Conservatives. Vaguely aware of the problems her family was facing with a virtually empty hotel, she gave them scant thought as she passed her days in a crowded Café Jochum.

Karl had left the confines of his bedroom now, spending his days at the bar window, a shadow of his previous self, peering out at Unter den Linden through the archways of the portico. As the Socialist leader, Friedrich Ebert, refused to accede to any of the political demands made by the breakaway Spartacist Group, the revolutionaries proceeded to take Berlin by force. Ebert was powerless to do much, for he had only a few troops at his command, housed mainly in the Reichstag building itself.

To his horror Karl saw the revolutionaries gain possession of the Brandenburg Gate, their snipers crouched beside the statue of the Quadriga, their machine guns erected beside its giant doric columns, flanking the central archway through which only the Emperor was allowed to pass. 'Why don't the Guards ride in from Karlshorst?' he asked Benno pitifully.

'You wouldn't expect the First Brandenburg Guards to take orders from a Social Democrat, would you? Field Marshal von Hindenburg isn't going to compromise the honour of his troops for nothing. Ebert is going to have to find his own way of beating the Spartacists.'

Yet during the days that followed, Benno frequently wished the Guards would march in from Karlshorst, Potsdam or Doeberitz, for as the revolutionaries advanced towards the Imperial Palace, Unter den Linden itself suddenly became a battlefield, with the Hotel Quadriga situated at its very centre.

Not even Luise and Lothar left the hotel then, for the only people on the street were soldiers — the desperate, half-starved revolutionaries, and Ebert's Regular Army troops from the Reichstag. Instead of the shouting of demonstrating crowds, the wide avenue now reverberated to the sound of gunfire. Benno looked over his own sparse contingent of men and picked the fittest to stay on the hotel's ground floor. Everybody else he sent to upstairs rooms at the back of the building, with strict instructions to lock themselves in and not leave under any circumstances. Only Karl refused to move. 'This is my hotel,' he said stubbornly. Benno knew it was useless to argue.

That day, the Hotel Quadriga became a battleground, as first revolutionary, then government troops tore through its corridors, taking possession of rooms and firing through open or smashed windows onto the street below. Standing helplessly in Karl's office doorway, Benno watched them charge through the white marble foyer, rifles and grenades in their hands.

In the evening, there was a lull. 'Did they fight them off?' Karl asked.

'No, they've moved further east, towards the Palace.' Then a new fear entered his mind. 'We're in their territory now, Herr Jochum. They know we're a hotel. They'll be back, looking for food.'

'They can starve!' Karl growled.

'No, they'll rip the place apart.' His heart sank as he thought of his precious store of tins in the cellar. Then, with sudden horror, he remembered Karl's wine, nearly a million bottles carefully packed in straw on racks stretching out right beneath Unter den Linden — bottles marking all the anniversaries of his life, the history of the hotel itself. The cellar door was locked, but these desperadoes could easily knock it down. 'The wine!'

With one accord, both men rushed into the kitchens and started to pile chairs, tables, crates, everything they could find against the door. Next Benno proceeded to throw utensils, saucepans and crockery around the kitchen. 'It must look as if we've already been raided.'

365

At that moment, the glass doors of the hotel burst open again and they could hear voices shouting in the foyer. Benno took a deep breath, then went out to face them. There were about twenty of them, again brandishing their rifles in his face. 'Give us your supplies!'

'We have very little,' Benno prevaricated, his heart thumping.

'This is a hotel, isn't it?' The man pushed past him towards the kitchen.

It looked very realistic, Benno thought, as he entered hard on their heels. Karl was standing in the middle of the chaotic room, bewilderment and contempt clearly etched on his face, as he surveyed the tumult Benno had created. The soldiers, however, ignored him, for on the shelves, where Benno had deliberately left them, they could see cans of precious food. Greedily, they snatched them, filling their pockets. 'And drink?' the leader demanded.

With a calmness he didn't feel, Benno faced him. 'There's been a war on. Supplies to Berlin have been blockaded. No wine has been delivered from France for a long time. We've run out.'

The man stared suspiciously round the kitchen, then he walked deliberately towards the crates piled in front of the cellar door. He kicked one of them and it echoed hollowly. To Benno's relief, he nodded. His men moved impatiently, for they were hungry. After glaring again at Benno and Karl, the leader said, 'Let's go.' Their arms full of food, they left the hotel.

The two men stood in the foyer, watching them depart, then Karl said quietly, 'Thank you, Benno. You know, I'd rather have died than let those reds have my wine. Yes, I'd rather have given my life.'

Benno stared at him wonderingly. He would give his life for his family — or even his country. But to die for a cellar full of wine?

By Christmas, the government troops had been ousted from the Reichstag and had to make their headquarters in the Hotel Kaiserhof. Revolutionary soldiers had entered the Chancellery and not even a detachment of troops sent in by Hindenburg could dislodge the People's Marine from the stables of the Imperial Palace.

At last, Ebert was forced to act and he appointed a man called Gustav Noske as his Minister of Defence. Even Benno viewed the appointment with dismay, for Noske's reputation had gone before him. A master butcher by trade, the Social Democrats considered him an expert on military affairs. When he announced to the press that 'Somebody has to be a bloodhound,' Benno knew that the city's troubles were far from over and that Noske's butchery had yet to begin.

'Will Noske bring in the Guards now?' Karl asked hopefully.

'No, Herr Jochum, he might want them, but they won't obey his orders. Hindenburg will stay out of this war. The Kaiser's army won't fight on the side of the socialists, not even against communists.'

'Then what will happen?'

They all looked at Benno, but even he did not know the answer to that question.

New Year's Eve at the hotel was a far from festive occasion. An armistice was declared, but still they sat with one ear cocked, listening for shots. Although there were very few residents, some local people came in to celebrate the first New Year since the war and for them a makeshift orchestra played in the Palm Garden Room. Crackers were pulled, confetti and paper streamers flew through the air, but the atmosphere remained muted and not long after midnight people started to disperse.

Karl's eyes were deeply sunk in his face, staring forebodingly around the room. 'It's the last New Year I shall ever see in.' Nothing any of them said could cheer him up.

Two days later, fighting was being waged as fiercely as ever on the streets. Another general strike was called and this time, to Karl's horror, even waiters from his hotel participated in it. Armed pickets positioned themselves outside, preventing outside staff from entering. Karl went out to remonstrate with them and returned, his face suffused with rage. 'Not only will they not allow our personnel in,' he stormed, 'they won't let us out. They say we're in no-man's-land here and it would be unsafe to allow us on the streets. Imagine that, now we're made prisoners in our own home!'

The strike hit every section of the city. All transport ground to a halt. Electricity and gas supplies were cut off. Shops, restaurants, factories and offices were closed. In the centre of the confused, chaotic cityscape, the Hotel Quadriga remained a sheltered refuge. With its own electricity and water supplies, it could still function. Running on a skeleton staff, meals could still be cooked. Its lights shone out brightly into the fog that blanketed the city.

At Doeberitz, outside Berlin, Gustav Noske was gathering

together his troops, preparatory to entering Berlin. From the Russian border came Captain Otto Tobisch, marching his battle-scarred mercenaries in helmets that bore the insignia of a swastika. They carried their sparse packs on their backs. Their armoured trucks were loaded with machine guns and ammunition. They greeted each other monosyllabically, for they had grown unused to social niceties in the barbaric existences they had been leading on the frontiers. At the slightest unusual sound, their automatic reaction was to reach for their guns. Shoot first was the motto of the Tobisch Brigade.

They were joined by the troops of Captain Arthur Ehrhardt from the Baltic. From the east came Captain Waldemar Pabst. They converged on Doeberitz and waited there for their orders to march on Berlin and put an end to the red revolution.

Otto observed these men with grim satisfaction, for he knew them to be the fittest and toughest in the country. It was on them that General Luettwitz and Defence Minister Noske had called, not on Field Marshal Hindenburg's elite troops, resting at Danzig, Karlshorst and Potsdam. Otto was certain that Germany's salvation depended upon the men of the Free Corps.

Olga looked out of the window of the Spartacist headquarters at the crowds gathering in the foggy street. This, she knew, was the moment towards which she had been striving for so many years. This was the day of the German Revolution!

Workers armed with rifles occupied newspaper buildings and railway stations. They stood outside government offices and ministries. Their snipers were crouched beside that symbol of Germany, the statue of the Quadriga above the Brandenburg Gate. The city belonged to them. And so, too, did its people.

All morning, the striking workers marched into the city centre. From the furthest outlying districts, they set out at dawn to demonstrate their loyalty to the Spartacists. They came from Lichtenberg, Friedrichsfelde and Wartenberg. They walked from Reinickendorf, Pankow and Wedding. They marched from Weissensee, Kreuzberg and Schoeneberg. Thousands and thousands and thousands of them. Then they stood, shoulder to shoulder in the fog, patiently waiting for the word. The fog slowly lifted and still they waited. They waited to be told what to do.

And Olga knew that they would do anything, give anything, even their lives, but they needed to be given the word for action.

Until that word was given, they could do nothing, except wait.

She turned in exasperation to stare at her comrades in that smoke-filled office, arguing, as they had been for days, as to what course of action they should take. They were, she realized, already divided between themselves, with two very clear factions emerging. One, to which she and Karl Liebknecht belonged, wanted to seize power at any cost, regardless of the number of lives that would be lost in the process. The other, led by Reinhardt and Rosa Luxemburg, was advocating caution, winning power gradually, not seizing it by force.

'The people don't want the Social Democrats, they don't want Ebert and Scheidemann, any more than they want the Kaiser to return,' she cried passionately. 'They want a soviet republic. They want the people's revolution. They want power for the people!'

'No, Olga,' Reinhardt said quietly, 'if we are to be leaders, we must prove ourselves good leaders. We need a programme of government. We're not just talking about Berlin, Olga, we're talking about the whole of Germany. To rule Germany requires a thought-out plan and somebody with the personal authority to run a country, not a committee of squabbling idealists, who don't know what to do next.'

'But Karl has already proclaimed a republic.'

'So has Ebert. And what's more, don't forget that he now has Noske, who is doubtless already gathering his troops.'

'We have the people behind us, Reinhardt. What can Noske do against so many people?'

'Don't underestimate him.'

'Noske's troops aren't here yet,' she said defiantly. 'We've taken control of the city. We have the people on our side. Now, we should hound the Social Democrats out of Berlin.'

'No,' Rosa Luxemburg's voice interrupted them, 'no, Olga, that should be the very last act of our drama. It's too soon. We must go gently, step by step.'

'We're not prepared,' Reinhardt agreed. 'Everything's happened too soon. The timing is wrong. I'm sorry and I agree that it's a shame.'

'A shame?' Karl Liebknecht cried. 'It's a scandal! There must be over two hundred thousand people out there. They want action! They must have it!'

'No,' Reinhardt said adamantly, 'it will only lead to bloodshed. Ours must be a peaceful revolution.'

369

The interminable discussion continued. Olga clenched her teeth, trying to see Reinhardt's point of view, remembering the past occasions when he had been proved right. They seemed to have spent their entire lives arguing, but, as she looked at him, the calmest person in the room, she knew that — even if she did not agree with him — she still loved him. And now, she was certain, although she had not yet told him, that she was carrying their child.

At the end of that day, the people went home, but next morning they were back on the streets again in their hundreds of thousands, still waiting patiently for their leaders to give them their orders. The few government troops stationed within the city rode out, trying to disperse them. They shot into the crowds, they kicked and pummelled the demonstrators, but there was little so few could do against so many. They desperately needed reinforcements.

The Spartacist leaders had not slept. Thirty-six hours after the strike had commenced, they were still arguing. Their faces were tense and weary, the air stale with cigarette smoke. Olga watched the people reassembling on the streets. 'This is crazy. We hold nearly every government building, we have the people, and what do we do? We just sit and argue! You can be sure that Ebert and Noske aren't just sitting and talking. No. They're getting ready to attack, to cause that bloodshed you are so frightened of. Reinhardt, we must act!'

But Reinhardt shook his tousled head obdurately, his eyes glinting through his thick spectacle lenses. 'No,' he repeated, 'no, Olga, I'm sorry, but the timing is wrong. We must fight our revolution not with guns, but with words.'

In the wake of the dispersing crowds that evening, they made their way to the *Vorwaerts* building. As she and Reinhardt struggled over the next day's editorial, Olga had a dreadful feeling that the revolution was over. They had had their opportunity and they had let it go.

When the new day dawned, it was obvious that through lack of direction the strike had petered out. Through the window, she saw people going to work, scurrying quickly into offices with fearful looks on their faces. Then a strange silence fell over the city, into which entered a fresh sound, that of marching men, of machine-gun fire, of armoured trucks riding over cobbled streets. She grasped Reinhardt's hand in fear. 'Noske's men.'

He looked up from his article. 'Then we must surrender, Olga.'

'No, Reinhardt, we won't give in.'

He kissed her on the forehead. 'The timing is wrong, Olga. But, one day, I promise you, our revolution will succeed. One day, the Communist Party will rule in Berlin.'

General Luettwitz's orders to the men of the Tobisch Brigade were explicit. Each unit had specific Spartacist strongholds to attack, then they were to report to Free Corps headquarters set up at the Hotel Eden for their next directive. Within twenty-four hours, peace was to be restored to the city. Preferably, not a single Spartacist or communist supporter was to be left alive.

There were few civilians in sight as Otto's car bore him through Berlin for the first time in over four years. From everywhere came the sound of gunfire and already bodies were heaping up on the pavements and in the gutters, as Free Corps troops broke open revolutionary fortresses.

His car drew to a screeching halt in front of the *Vorwaerts* building, swiftly followed by army lorries carrying the rest of the soldiers in his division. Under their captain's shouted directions, the men surrounded the building quickly and efficiently.

'Come out and surrender your arms,' Otto called through his megaphone, but he had no intention of allowing his enemy to escape so easily. He waited only a minute then he shouted, 'Fire!' A barrage of trench mortar and machine-gun fire pounded the windows, followed by a rain of hand grenades, lobbed through broken glass. At the back of the building, his men were using flame-throwers to burn out the revolutionaries. This would put paid to the lily-livered, pacifist scribblers, whose biting criticisms of the war had caused so many of his men to desert in the last weeks before the armistice.

Some figures emerged through the door and Otto regarded their white flag of surrender bleakly. As he had thought, they were too frightened even to defend the wretched little newspaper they had taken over. One of them, a tall, thin man, wearing thick spectacles, seemed familiar and Otto identified him as Reinhardt Meyer, one of the most persuasive of the journalists.

His troops were hesitating at the sight of the white flag, awaiting Otto's next order. There was no doubt in his mind. His orders had been to destroy the revolution. 'Fire!' he roared, and the peace delegation was flattened by a burst of machine-gun fire. He watched the journalist's figure as the bullets hit him, knocking him

371

this way and that, until he was only a bloody silhouette against the wall. Slowly, he sank to the ground, one leg bent crazily under him, the other outstretched. The thick lenses of his spectacles shattered into myriad pieces.

Olga ran through the dark city night like a wounded animal looking for a hole in which to take refuge. Every street corner threatened danger as more Free Corps detachments marched into Berlin. Her breath came in short, sharp gasps and tears streamed down her face. Once, she was almost caught. 'There's one!' a soldier shouted and aimed his rifle down the alleyway through which she was running. She pulled back into an open doorway and heard the bullet ricochet from the archway above her head. She waited for the pounding of army boots on the cobbled street and wondered if she might not be wise to give herself up, until she remembered Reinhardt, and by then, the soldiers had gone away.

She could not run for ever. Sometime, she had to stop. Where to go? She had to ensure that Reinhardt's death was not in vain, that she continued to serve the cause for which he had given his life, and there was only one way in which she knew how to do this. She herself was never going to be a great leader — she lacked the abilities that had marked Reinhardt out as one of the great political thinkers of the future — but within her, she was certain, she carried the means to make certain that Reinhardt lived on.

'One day the Communist Party will rule in Berlin,' he had said to her that morning. Reinhardt's son, she determined, would be there when it did.

Wearily, she turned into Unter den Linden, towards her last hope, a person who had many years before promised to help her if ever she were in need. In front of the revolving doors of the Hotel Quadriga, however, she stopped, memories crowding to her mind. She recalled Karl Jochum turning her and Reinhardt away. She remembered her own callous words to Viktoria when Benno had been put in Moabit. Why should they help her now?

But as she stood, she knew she had no choice, for she was simply too tired to go any further. She had been for two nights almost without sleep, had scarcely eaten for three days and that morning she had seen her husband killed. The hotel's façade swayed before her and a clammy coldness broke out all over her. She clung onto a column of the portico and waited for the dizzy spell to pass. Then, slowly, she mounted the steps.

Perhaps it was the look of total desperation in Olga's eyes which persuaded the hall porter to wake Viktoria, even though it was three in the morning. Leaving her collapsed on a chair in the foyer, he returned with Viktoria and Benno, who stared down at her in consternation.

'You promised to help me once, Vicki,' Olga mumbled. 'Now, I need your help. The Free Corps are looking for me. They've killed Reinhardt and they'll kill me if they find me. Please hide me.'

She could see the doubt in her cousin's face. She knew she, too, was remembering the occasion on which she had begged for Benno's life. So, as Viktoria had turned to Reinhardt on that occasion, Olga stared pleadingly at Benno.

'For God's sake,' Benno said, 'what are you waiting for? Hans, help us get her upstairs. And for heaven's sake, don't tell anybody she's here!'

They laid her on the spare bed in Benno's dressing room and before Viktoria had even laid the blankets over her, she was asleep. Back in their own room, they discussed what should be done with her. 'We can't hand her over to the Free Corps, that's certain,' Benno said. 'But neither can we keep her here. Well, let's try and get some sleep ourselves, and perhaps we'll think of something in the morning.'

Karl was furious when he heard Olga was in the hotel. 'I told you I never wanted to see her here again. I won't have Bolsheviks in this house!'

'Karl, the poor child is desperate,' Ricarda said. 'They could kill her if they find her.'

'Then she should have had more sense than to get mixed up with this communist rubbish. I always knew she'd be nothing but trouble.'

'She is your niece,' Ricarda pointed out quietly. 'Surely you wouldn't turn your sister's child out on the streets in her hour of need — just because you disagree with her politics?'

'I'm not having her here,' Karl repeated. 'It's the first place they'll look for her and I've had enough of soldiers marching through my hotel as though they own it. I tell you, I've had enough.'

'I agree with you, Herr Jochum, and I've had an idea,' Benno said. 'Why don't we take her to Heiligensee? They won't think of looking for her there.'

'Why, that's an excellent idea, Benno,' Ricarda said.

Karl turned on her suspiciously. 'Are you really saying we should help her?'

Ricarda smiled at him tenderly. 'Yes, Karl, I think we should. And so, my dearest, in your heart of hearts, do you.'

He sighed, all his bombast evaporated. 'All right, she can go to Heiligensee, but once this fighting's over, back to Munich she goes.'

Benno and Viktoria drove Olga out to Heiligensee. Already the city seemed to be getting back to normal, with people walking on the streets of the suburbs, shops and cafés open again, only the occasional armoured truck betraying the presence of the Free Corps. Olga said little on the way and mutely acquiesced to their instructions not to leave the cottage. But when they had left her, Viktoria wished she could have gone straight to Munich.

Now that Noske's troops occupied the city, a semblance of normal life started to return to it. Luise went back to Café Jochum, Lothar recommenced his rehearsals for *Hurra! Dada!* and gradually, new guests booked in at the Hotel Quadriga. The hotel now bore scant resemblance to the elegant establishment that had housed the illustrious guests attending the royal wedding in 1913. Many of its windows were smashed from marauding troops and its kitchens were denuded of food. Only the bar, one of the best stocked in the city, remained constantly busy, as people sought to drown their troubles in alcohol.

The hotel's clientele was also very different. Mostly businessmen, they fell into two categories. There were some who, after four years at war, now returned to the city to try to pick up the thread of their broken lives, to attempt to obtain orders for empty factories, to meet with former customers or simply to look for a job. Most of the hotel's guests, however, were people whose businesses had dramatically prospered as a result of the war. Small companies making boots, shoes, clothing, satchels, saddlery and optical instruments had suddenly been inundated with orders to equip an army of several million men. Their profits had been immense and now they looked forward to even better times, for the long-neglected civilian population was crying out for whatever they could produce and was willing to pay whatever price they demanded.

Karl looked at them in disgust. 'I didn't build the Hotel Quadriga for these jumped-up nouveaux riches. Look at their table manners, watch the way they treat our waiters. Germany's never going to recover from all this, nor will the Quadriga. This is the beginning of the end.'

Benno alone understood the true reason for Karl's dismay. These new guests came from the same background as himself. The aristocrats had gone, and the Quadriga had become the home of the bourgeois middle class.

In the elections that were held on 19 January for the new National Assembly, women were allowed to vote for the first time, but Karl was so distraught by the results that he was scarcely aware of this final proof of female emancipation. Not only did the Social Democrats win the largest number of seats, although it was not quite enough to give them a majority, but it was announced that the new Assembly would take place, not in Berlin, but in Weimar. 'What's the matter with Berlin?' Karl demanded.

Benno was also troubled. 'They say Berlin is too unsafe. But I agree with you, Herr Jochum, the new Republic should start as it means to continue, from a position of strength. Moving to Weimar means the politicians have no faith in themselves.'

'Berlin is the capital of Germany,' Karl stated dolefully. 'I've never liked this business of a republic. The Kaiser would never have moved to Weimar!'

'Is there a future for us?' Ricarda asked quietly, that evening after Karl had gone to bed. 'Things have changed so much since the Kaiser's abdication. How does a hotel like ours fit into a republic?'

Benno reached across and took her hand. 'Yes, I'm sure it has a future. The guests will change but they will still come to the Hotel Quadriga, because it will remain one of the most exclusive hotels in Europe. Faces may change, but human nature won't. There will always be the rich who want the best, no matter what their class or social background.'

Ricarda was silent for a moment, then she said, 'You realize that Karl can't cope any more? I haven't said anything to him yet, but I think, this summer, we should maybe spend a long time at Heiligensee and leave you two to run the hotel. After all, you've virtually been running it for years.'

Viktoria put her arm round her. 'Mama, I'm so sorry, but I think you're right. You and Papa are both tired, aren't you?'

Ricarda leaned back in her chair, her face pale and drawn beneath her white hair. 'Yes, I'm tired. I'd like to get away from here, to do some water colour painting, some embroidery, spend some time in the country — and with Stefan.' Then she patted Viktoria's knee. 'At least Karl won't have to worry about the hotel. He'll know you and Benno will look after it well.'

'When are you going to make your suggestion?'

'Not yet. Let's wait until things have settled down, until we have a proper government. Once everything's back to normal, then, maybe Karl will see what I mean.'

It was two weeks before men of the Tobisch Brigade found Rosa Luxemburg and Karl Liebknecht hiding in a flat in the Wilmersdorfer Strasse and took them to the Hotel Eden where Otto and Waldemar Pabst were waiting to interrogate then. The hour that followed was one of the most satisfying in Otto's life, as he put into practice all the finer methods of torture he had learned when operating against the partisan forces on the Russian border. Neither of the Spartacist leaders, however, would tell him where Olga Meyer was hidden.

Eventually, he snarled, 'We'll find her, don't worry.' He signalled to the guards to take the almost unconscious couple away. Outside the Hotel Eden, they were put in two separate cars, Otto and a couple of his men accompanying Karl Liebknecht, Pabst taking Rosa Luxemburg.

In the Tiergarten, Otto ordered his driver to stop, then he told one of his men to open the car door. 'Go on, Liebknecht,' he sneered. 'There's freedom. You can run away now.'

Liebknecht stared at him in dazed bewilderment, then, assisted by the blunt end of a rifle, he staggered from the car. Otto watched him fall, pick himself up and fall again. 'Communist scum,' he growled. Then he pulled his Luger from its holster and shot the Spartacist leader in the back.

The newspapers, now firmly back in the hands of the Social Democrats, reported that Liebknecht had tried to escape and had been shot while running through the Tiergarten. Rosa Luxemburg, they said, had been seized by an angry crowd, who had killed her. Otto knew that she had been shot through the head and her body thrown into the Landwehr Canal.

However, he cared no longer about Liebknecht and Luxemburg, for his sole aim now was to find Olga Meyer. His mind went back to the days when he had been a page boy at the Hotel Quadriga. He had never met the Jochums' Munich relations, but like every other piece of potentially useful information, he had stored the knowledge of their existence in the back of his mind. Where else could Olga go, except to them?

The next day, he and his men drove to the Hotel Quadriga. Armed with rifles, they burst in through the glass doors. 'Bring me the General Director!' Otto demanded, as his men covered the hotel employees with their guns. Now, at long last, Karl Jochum was going to pay the price for all the humiliations he had inflicted upon him in the past. Then Otto started, for it was not Karl who stepped out of the office, but Viktoria.

As soon as she heard the commotion in the foyer, she knew who their latest unwelcome visitors were. Thankful that her father was upstairs, but wishing Benno weren't with him, Viktoria forced herself to appear calm. 'What's the matter?' she asked the Free Corps captain coldly. Then she paused, seeing something familiar in his chill blue eyes, his narrow lips and fair hair. 'Otto Tobisch.'

'*Captain* Tobisch.'

For a long time, they stared at each other, then Otto said, 'It would be much better if you just told us where she is, so that my men don't have to ransack the place looking for her.'

'Looking for whom?' Viktoria asked deliberately.

'Your cousin. Where is Olga Meyer?'

'She isn't here.'

Otto's men tensed, their guns aimed at her. Viktoria stood unflinching, remembering how neither her father nor Benno had shown fear when placed in similar situations. She was certainly not going to allow Otto Tobisch, of all people, to believe she was afraid.

'Take her away!' Otto ordered his men. 'Hold her at gunpoint and don't let her move. The rest of you search the hotel.'

'I refuse to allow you ...'

'Shut up,' Otto snarled, 'or it will be the end of you.'

Rough hands seized her arms and bundled her into the office, two men remaining guard over her, while Otto led the others on their search. At that moment, Karl and Benno appeared at the top of the stairs. 'What the hell's going on here now?' Karl roared.

Otto did not bother to reply. 'Put them in with the bitch,' he told his men. Before the two men could react, they were seized and dragged into the room with Viktoria.

Otto knew the hotel, of course, like the palm of his hand. Like a tornado, he passed through the restaurant, the private dining rooms, the ballroom, the Palm Garden Room, the ladies' salon, the bar and the kitchens. He overturned tables, he turned out cupboards full of table linen, he ripped down curtains. It was an orgy of wanton destruction, for he knew that if Olga were in the hotel, she would be concealed in one of the upper rooms, in a wardrobe or a blanket chest.

So having wreaked his fury on the ground floor, he ordered his troops upstairs. He stationed an armed guard outside the Jochums' apartment, for he was sure Olga was not there, then the men went systematically through every other room, forcing any occupants out at gunpoint, ripping sheets off beds, digging their bayonets deep into wardrobes, strewing the contents of chests of drawers over bedroom carpets, turning out the linen and laundry rooms on each floor, scattering the feathers from eiderdown quilts down the corridors. But they did not find Olga Meyer.

Two hours later, they returned to the office. Otto dug his pistol into Karl's ribs. 'Where is she?'

Karl merely stared at him in utter contempt.

Otto looked from one to the other of them, convinced they knew where she was. But without proof there was nothing even he could do. 'You'll pay for this,' he vowed. Then he turned on his heels and marched his men out of the hotel.

Karl was shaking with anger. 'I've had enough. That's the last time anyone comes into this hotel telling me what I can or can't do. I refuse to be intimidated any more.'

Ricarda came flying down the stairs. 'What's been happening? I've been imprisoned in our apartment! Are you all right?'

Viktoria sank down on a chair. Now the ordeal was over and Otto was gone, she felt very weak. 'Otto Tobisch was here. He's a captain in the Free Corps now and he's looking for Olga.'

'To hell with Olga!' Karl roared. 'To hell with Otto Tobisch! To hell with all communists, socialists, to hell with everybody! I've put up with this long enough! This is *my* hotel! *I* built it and nobody else is going to tell me what I can or can't do in it. Now I'm going to tell them!'

They all stared, frightened by the sudden change in him. No longer was he a rather pitiful old man, but an almost macabre replica of his old self. 'Karl, what are you going to do?' Ricarda asked, clutching his arm.

He shook her away, pulling on his top coat and cramming his hat on his head. 'I'm going to find Ebert and I'm going to tell him what I think of his lousy government!'

'But Karl . . .'

'You stay here,' he said roughly, 'this is man's work.'

'Papa!' Viktoria pleaded, then she turned to Benno. 'Benno, stop him.'

But Karl had gone. He stormed out of the hotel, then marched belligerently towards the Brandenburg Gate. As Ricarda, Viktoria and Benno crowded to the hotel entrance, they saw him halt at the top of Unter den Linden and look angrily up at the Free Corps soldiers now in possession of the vantage point beside the statue of the Quadriga. They saw him look instinctively to the left as he started to cross the wide road junction. When he reached the central arch of the Brandenburg Gate, however, he looked neither to right nor left.

All three started forward in horror as gunfire broke out, then started to run down the street, shouting and waving their arms as they saw an armoured car, followed by lorries and tanks filled with Free Corps soldiers approaching the Gate. 'Karl!' 'Herr Jochum!' 'Papa!'

Karl Jochum stood beneath the central arch of the Brandenburg Gate. He heard, but ignored, the shouted warnings from the soldiers above him. 'Gloria Viktoria,' he muttered under his breath, as a rain of shots was fired from the window of a building overlooking the Pariser Platz, to be answered by a hail of machine-gun fire from the gateway over him. Mesmerized, he stood still, a solitary figure in the middle of a battlefield.

Suddenly, he was aware of a car horn blaring, the thunder of truck engines and the screeching of rubber tyres on the cobbled roadway. He turned and saw the approaching army vehicles driving straight towards him. Furiously, he waved his fist. Didn't they know that this archway was reserved for the use of the Kaiser alone? What was the world coming to when armed brigands could force their way into your private property, threaten your life and — the final insult — drive through the Emperor's archway?

But the motor procession did not stop. Momentarily, Karl saw the face of the driver of the leading car, panic-stricken as he stood on the brake and tried to slew the vehicle away from him. Then, he was tossed high in the air, slammed up and sideways into the pathway of the army truck following. An excruciating pain shot through his body, as if his legs had somehow been severed from the rest of him.

On and on they roared past him as, from the windows of nearby

379

buildings, bullets from revolutionary snipers tried to pick out their Free Corps enemy. Then they were gone and Karl was left alone on the roadway. Slowly, he moved his head, trying to look towards the hotel.

From a great distance, he heard the sound of Ricarda's voice. He wanted to hold out his hand to her and tell her something. Where once the familiar Unter den Linden had been was only blackness and a great thundering roar in his temples, pressing in on him, as if the whole world were collapsing around him. Where the Hotel Quadriga should stand, flames were roaring up amidst its crumbling brickwork.

'Karli, darling . . .' It was Ricarda's anguished voice.

'Save the Quadriga,' Karl muttered.

'The Quadriga's all right,' Ricarda wept, cradling his head in her arms, staring in horror at his battered body. But Karl heard nothing any more. Death had taken him from his nightmare.

In a way, the activity of the next few days kept the pain at bay for all of them. There were meetings with Dr Duschek and depositions to be made with the police concerning the cause of Karl's death. Details had been taken from eye witnesses of the accident but, failing any positive identification of the driver of the armoured car, the reason for Karl's death was attributed to misadventure in time of civil war. Viktoria was positive that Otto Tobisch had been in the cavalcade, but she had no proof.

Viktoria attributed Karl's death to Otto, but she also held Olga to blame. Seeking to vent her grief in anger, she rushed out to Heiligensee. 'Get out of here,' she screamed. 'If it hadn't been for you, my father would still be alive. Get out!'

'Your father got what he had coming to him,' Olga retaliated. 'He always thought he was the Kaiser, with your bloody hotel as his palace. But he wasn't. He was just a nobody.'

Stupefied, Viktoria gazed at her, suddenly seeing her as she really was. For all these years, she had felt grateful to her for helping her out when she had first found herself pregnant. Now, she suspected that episode had merely provided her cousin with another weapon to strike back at the capitalists. 'Don't you have any feelings? Doesn't my father's death and my mother's grief mean anything to you?'

'I've lost my husband, too, don't forget!' Olga spat back. 'But, finally, we none of us matter compared to the cause. Viktoria, the

Revolution is for the sake of all people, it's for everybody in the world. Reinhardt knew that.'

'And how many more people have got to die before you achieve your aim?' Viktoria demanded bitterly. She looked at Olga's stomach, at the tell-tale bulge, where the child she was carrying was already beginning to show. 'And your child, is that what you're going to teach your child?'

'Yes, I shall bring up my child as a true communist, to take the place that Reinhardt should have occupied. The future of Germany depends upon children like the one I am bearing, for they will be the children of the Revolution.'

Viktoria's anger started to be replaced by pity for this baby. 'Then I feel sorry for your child.'

'And I am sorry for yours, for he is growing up under a lie. One day, your son and mine will meet and then we'll see which of them has turned out best.' Olga's eyes glittered.

Her pity evaporated. Nobody in the world was allowed to attack Stefan! 'Get out!' she said coldly, 'get out, and never let me see you again.'

'After everything you've said, nothing would persuade me to stay. I'm only sorry I ever came to you for help.'

'So am I,' Viktoria replied, with meaning.

A thin carpet of snow lay over the frozen earth and the horses drawing the funeral hearse slid on the icy roads leading out to the cemetery where Karl Jochum was to be buried. A biting east wind that had traversed the Russian Steppes all the way from Siberia pierced the bodies of the mourners as they stepped from their cars and carriages and grouped themselves around the deep hole dug to receive Karl's coffin.

Viktoria and Luise stood to either side of their mother and each threw a sprig of flowers onto the coffin, poor, wretched flowers, the merest apology for love, but flowers, like everything else, were hard to find those winter days in Berlin. The pastor's voice intoned, 'Forasmuch as it hath pleased Almighty God of His great mercy to take unto Himself the soul of our dear brother here departed, we therefore commit his body to the ground; earth to earth, ashes to ashes, dust to dust ...'

Around them, people were moving, shifting their feet surreptitiously inside their boots, huddling their hands against their bodies in an attempt to retain some heat in freezing limbs. Despite the weather, they had come from all over Germany to mourn Karl. Grete and Gottfried had managed the difficult journey from Munich, while the Kraus family had travelled up from Essen. Then there were old professional friends of Karl — the Arendts, the Duscheks and Dr Blattner. Leaning heavily on a stick, Max Patschke's face was awash with tears, as he bade farewell to the man with whom he had worked for nearly thirty-six years. Near him were Arno Halbe and Franz Jankowski. Beside the grave lay a wreath sent from France by Maurice Mesurier, a silent token of how love between men could overcome all international barriers.

Nor were these all. Countless patrons of the Hotel Quadriga had come to the cemetery to pay their last respects to a great man and an old friend. Looking around them in silent, wondering gratitude, Ricarda thought how proud Karl would have been to know they were all there. And she realized yet again, with a terrible pang, that she was going to miss him more than she could bear.

The newspapers that evening devoted considerable space to Karl Jochum. They described in great detail the history of the hotel and many mentioned the symbolism in his death. 'The true end of the Wilhelmine era,' ran one headline. To those who had loved him, it meant infinitely more.

PART THREE
1919–1933

Chapter Fourteen

Karl's death cast a deep shadow over the Hotel Quadriga. Ricarda, elegantly dressed in black, the sombreness of her attire offset by a fichu of ivory lace around her throat and frilled lace cuffs, moved with quiet dignity through its sedate apartments, lingering to touch a piece of furniture here or look at a picture there, never for a minute forgetting her loss but giving way to no ostentatious display of grief.

Viktoria, who had always been her father's daughter, missed him dreadfully. She said little, but Luise would frequently find her standing, gazing into space, a wistful expression on her face. She spent a lot of time with her mother and it seemed to Luise that the two of them had suddenly grown closer together, as though united by a pain she could not share.

When Viktoria was not with Ricarda, she was helping Benno, who was fully occupied in repairing the damages inflicted by successive invasions of revolutionary and Free Corps soldiers and in trying to restore the hotel to its former glory. There was no shortage of manpower now and he had soon engaged a new general manager, Fritz Brandt, a reception manager, Hubert Fromm, and an Italian chef called Vittorio Mazzoni. After this, he negotiated a contract with Rudi, so that the restaurant could once again serve the fresh meat and vegetables upon which it had always prided itself.

There seemed to be nothing for Luise to do. Her assistance was not needed in the hotel and she felt excluded from her mother's and sister's grief. It was not that she had not loved her father — it was simply that she felt she had never really known him. And there was something else. On the day he had been killed she had been at Café Jochum. She had not seen his mangled corpse and so, somehow, there was something unreal about his death.

So, she sought refuge again in Café Jochum, but her loneliness followed her even there, for Lothar was immersed in rehearsals and Pipsi, and she suddenly realized that although she had a lot of acquaintances, other than him she had no real friends. So, when Sepp Nowak returned at the end of January, she greeted him with joy. He seemed to understand her ambivalent emotions about her father's death and to sympathize with her feeling that she was excluded from her family's life.

In return, he talked to her about his present job with Kraus Aviation, and confided in her his frustrations and ambitions. Now that Germany had a properly elected government, Baron Heinrich finally felt confident enough to start his airline, which would fly between Berlin, Hamburg and Duesseldorf, later possibly taking in Munich as well. Sepp was to be one of the company's first pilots.

'I'm so pleased for you, Sepp.'

'Well, it's better than nothing, but it's not what I want to do. I'm going to be little better than a glorified taxi driver, shunting passengers and freight around the country. That isn't flying!'

'But what else can you do?'

'I don't know.' Then he smiled. 'Well, at least I have one consolation. Whenever I'm in Berlin, I'll be able to see you.'

Luise took this statement in the spirit it was meant. She and Sepp quite simply enjoyed each other's company. In fact, she thought, as she got to know him better, Sepp was very much the brother she would have liked to have.

One person, however, simply refused to see their friendship in this innocent light. Rudi missed no opportunity for making snide comments, describing them as 'a couple of lovebirds' and making elaborate excuses at interrupting them when they sat talking together. Now, more than ever, Luise regretted the occasion she had gone to bed with him, unable to understand how she had been taken in by him and dreading the thought that he might brag about her to Sepp.

Sepp was puzzled by his brother's behaviour, which seemed boorish and unintelligible. Finally, positive that Luise must once have refused Rudi's advances, he decided Rudi was quite simply jealous of him. The more he got to know her, the more he liked Luise. Unlike so many girls in this new Berlin, she seemed to have a rather quaint, old-fashioned morality about her. And Sepp was at heart an old-fashioned person. If a man wanted to go to bed with any girl other than a prostitute, he should do the decent thing and propose to her.

For the moment, however, he was in no position to propose to anybody, and so, content to enjoy Luise's company and proud to be seen with her, he let their friendship drift along. She was stimulating, she was fun and, whatever Rudi might insinuate, his conscience remained clear.

Much against his will, Luise persuaded him to accompany her to the première of *Hurra! Dada!* that was held at the beginning of February. 'I don't like Dada and I don't like Pipsi Ascher,' Sepp complained, 'but for your sake alone, I'll come.'

The old variety playhouse Lothar Lorenz had rented just off the Nollendorf Platz had been renamed The Expressionist Theatre of the Proletariat. An incredible figure in an authentic cowboy's outfit, but with his monocle still clamped in his eye, Lothar himself greeted them as they arrived that Saturday evening. In his holster he carried a water pistol, telling everybody that this was his personal protest against the brutality of war.

The shabby interior of the theatre was devoted to an exhibition of the most evocative and controversial of Dada art. Pictures by artists with whom Luise was now quite familiar hung round its walls — caricatures and horrific scenes from the war by George Grosz; works by John Heartfield and Raoul Hausmann; collages by Hannah Hoech; and countless Dada posters and leaflets. But pride of place was taken by the stuffed figure of a German general, with pig's features, suspended by a noose from the ceiling and carrying across its chest a banner reading, *Hurra! Dada!*

There were many angry mutterings from the milling crowd and Sepp looked around him in distaste. 'Are you sure you want to go through with this?'

Privately, Luise was rather shocked, but she wasn't going to admit it. 'It's only harmless fun.'

The actual play, when it commenced, was the most extraordinary event she had ever witnessed. Much of it was spoken in phonetic verse, which had a compelling rhythm but was totally unintelligible. The actors' costumes were all grostesque parodies of military and civilian dress. Pipsi, the only woman in the show, was exaggeratedly made-up and dressed like an angel, complete with wings and a halo, which she flapped whenever a character came on stage. Her black hair hung loose to her waist.

The audience tolerated five minutes, then some began to boo and others to laugh. Luise felt sorry for Lothar, until she realized this was what he wanted. Leaping on to the stage, he pulled his water pistol from its holster and began to fire it into the auditorium. Then, he stood there silently, just gazing at them, a solemn, tubby, rather ridiculous little creature, inviting them to poke fun at him.

For the next hour and a half, incredible figures moved about the stage and the audience grew more and more incensed. From all around her, Luise heard people muttering, 'This isn't theatre.' 'It certainly isn't art.' 'It's sacrilege.' Yet few people actually walked out. Some loved it. Most didn't understand what Lothar was trying to do. All of them wanted to be shocked.

Backstage, later, as corks popped in champagne bottles, Lothar explained excitedly, 'Dada is anti-everything. It's anti-war, anti-authoritarian and it's anti-art!'

'He's mad,' Sepp murmured to Luise, but he was smiling for, like most other people, he found it impossible to dislike him.

Everybody, it seemed, except Pipsi. She had discarded her halo and wings and was standing, loosely draped in white, surrounded by an admiring male audience. When the champagne was finished, Lothar shooed them away, then put his arm round her shoulders. 'You were absolutely magnificent.'

'Thank you Lothar, darling,' she purred.

'Now, to celebrate, I'm taking you out to dinner. You shall go wherever you desire, for tonight you are the toast of the town.'

She narrowed her eyes and looked disdainfully at him. 'Oh, Lothar, darling, you really are a tiresome little man. Rudi's throwing a party for me. Now, run along, dear, while I get changed.'

Luise and Sepp did not hear their actual words but it was not difficult to guess what had passed between them. After a quick look at Sepp, who nodded, Luise hurried across the room, slipped her arm through Lothar's and said, 'Lothar, will you come out to dinner with Sepp and me this evening to celebrate your success?'

With a last, pathetic look at Pipsi, he nodded. Later that night, after they had all drunk far too much, he announced, 'Pipsi Ascher is a cow! I don't know why I gave her a part in my play!'

They all solemnly raised their glasses.

Georg Jankowski arrived at the Rosa Leviné Meyer Hospital in Berlin the following day. By that time he knew his illness was not just physical but mental. Four years in the trenches, facing constant bombardment and living daily with death, had taken their eventual toll. Now he was using his coughing attacks to cover up the deep, nervous confusion that racked him, knowing that if the doctors decided to diagnose a mental complaint, he would be removed from his ward, banished to a lunatic asylum and probably never see the outside world again.

A nurse bustled into the ward. 'Doctor will examine you shortly, Lieutenant, and then I believe your wife is coming to see you.' She felt his pulse and stuck a thermometer in his mouth.

So the moment had finally arrived for him to see Pipsi again. Georg stared blindly at the nurse's white apron, unwilling to admit even to himself how much he was dreading this first meeting in over three years. Even if she had wanted to, it would have been impossible for her to visit him in the field hospital at Mons, where he had first been taken last April after his leg had been shattered and the German gas had poisoned him. But she could, conceivably, have made the journey to Pasewalk, where he had been taken next. She had written just one letter, that was all, full of her own news, asking nothing about him, except that he be sure to let her know well in advance if he was coming home.

The doctor came in then and examined his leg. 'You're a lucky man, Lieutenant Jankowski. They made an excellent job of this at Mons. Does it cause you any pain?'

'Not really.' It didn't. Now, there was only the mental anguish, the fear of what those pieces of shrapnel had done when they had pierced his groin.

'Turn over onto your chest, please, Lieutenant.' The doctor pushed and thumped his back so hard that he started to cough again. Would these attacks never end, Georg wondered tiredly. Although the doctors said their medicine would soothe the inflamed lungs, there seemed to be no improvement. Sometimes he could not only feel, but hear, the liquid that filled them, gurgling inside him, threatening to complete what the war had never achieved, suffocating him to death. 'You'll live,' the doctor told him in a satisfied tone.

He was still coughing when Pipsi came through the door. She had a long sable coat slung across her shoulders and her magnificent black hair was piled high on her head under a Cossack fur hat. She looked so beautiful, Georg momentarily forgot all the doubts and suspicions that had clouded his mind for so long. She walked across to the window and looked out on the wintry day. When the coughing was over and he lay weakly back against the pillows, she turned and said unfeelingly, 'You look terrible.'

So, nothing had changed after all. Her beauty was still just an illusion. 'How are you,' he asked, 'and how's Minna?'

She shrugged. 'There isn't enough to eat. The bread is abominable and most of the time we're sold horse meat and told it's beef. But, if you know the right people, you can get most things you need.'

'And you know the right people?'

'I seem to. I must be lucky.'

'What does Minna look like now?' There had been no photographs.

'Oh, Minna,' Pipsi answered vaguely. 'People say she looks very like me.'

'Will you bring her with you next time you come?'

'What? To this place? Why, she might catch anything. No, darling, you must see that's impossible. You've waited three years to see her, you can wait a bit longer. It wouldn't be fair on the child. She'd be frightened to death if she saw you looking like that.'

'But I am her father.'

'Then you won't want her upset, will you?' She tapped her long, polished nails on the end of his bed. 'Well, I have to be going, darling. You see, I'm a working girl now. I have the starring part in a new play.'

The distance between them had never seemed so vast. 'New play?'

'It's great fun. You remember *Hurra! Hussar!*? Well this is a parody on it, called *Hurra! Dada!* It ridicules the war, the military, the officers, you know, all that sort of thing. We gave the première last night. The audience thought it was hilarious. In fact, I think I shall have quite a future as a comedy actress.'

Georg stared at her, unable to find any words to say.

'Well, goodbye, darling, I'll come and see you again soon.' With a brittle smile and a toss of her head, she was gone.

She hadn't kissed him, she hadn't even touched his hand. She hadn't asked him how he felt, or when he was going to be allowed home. She hadn't asked him about his war. But she was acting in some farce that ridiculed all he had been doing for the past four years . . .

'That your wife, sir?' the man in the next bed asked.

'Yes,' Georg said heavily, 'that's my wife.'

'Don't some people have all the luck?'

His uncle came to see him the next morning. A small, bent figure in a shabby suit, Franz Jankowski embraced Georg as if he were a baby and kissed him on both cheeks. 'Georg, Georg, I've missed you so much. And you are looking well, my boy, much better than I thought you would. Now, tell me, can you walk again? This leg, is it healed? And your chest? Ach, that was a dreadful thing. Imagine it, our own gas poisoning our own men.'

His uncle's hand clasped in his, Georg answered his questions as best he could, feeling his warmth flow into him, gradually melting the ice that had formed around his heart since his reunion with Pipsi.

Eventually, Franz asked, 'Has your wife been to see you?' When Georg nodded, he said, 'I've heard ...' Then he shook his head. 'Ach, it doesn't matter. People always say such terrible things and usually they aren't true.'

'She told me she's acting in a play.'

'Oh, I didn't know that, but you see, Georg, I know nothing about the theatre.' They were both silent for a moment, then he asked, 'When you come out of hospital, you will come and play my piano?'

Georg squeezed the gnarled hand that lay in his. 'Yes, of course I will.' But he knew he was lying. He would never play the piano again.

For the next three weeks, Franz was a constant visitor at Georg's bedside, and every day Georg grew stronger, as if the old man's stubborn vitality was infectious. Soon, the doctor was talking of sending him home and Georg now knew, that with his uncle's help, he would be all right. His fears of the outside world were disappearing, for gradually Franz told him what had been happening in Berlin, describing the Spartacist revolution, the arrival of Noske's Free Corps and the death of his old patron, Karl Jochum. 'And the troubles go on, Georg. Now, it isn't only the Spartacists who are causing the trouble, but Noske himself. They've given him and his bloodhounds too much power. Men like the Tobisch Brigade have instituted a reign of terror over the city.'

Georg struggled to understand this complicated story of revolutionaries, soldiers' soviets, Social Democrats and Free Corps, then gave up. He gathered, however, that Noske's excessive brutality had swung his uncle firmly in favour of the revolutionaries.

In early March, Franz arrived at the hospital with an angry glint in his eye. 'There's going to be another general strike. As from tomorrow, the entire city will grind to a halt and this time, Noske won't be able to break it.'

With the story of Karl Jochum still in his mind, Georg took the old man's hand fearfully. 'Uncle Franz, do be careful. If anything happened to you, I couldn't bear it.'

'I shan't be fighting, but I shall be at the Ullstein building to show my support for the strikers. And I'll still be there when the papers print the news of the "master butcher's" defeat.'

'No, Uncle, please don't go. Please stay at home.'

But his uncle was adamant. 'Herr Ullstein helped me when you arrived in Berlin and he kept me on long past my retirement throughout the war. The least I can do is support him now.'

When he had gone, Georg lay back with closed eyes, filled with an unholy fear.

Franz arrived at the Ullstein building early next morning, shook hands with old colleagues, then sat staring out of the windows onto the crowds gathering in the street below. Around him, journalists, printers, typesetters, secretaries, talked in low, excited tones. It was very strange to see the inactivity after the normal bustle of the newspaper offices. Every now and again, a telephone rang and, from the news they received from outside, it was obvious that this strike was going to reach proportions never previously experienced.

Some trams were running to bring in demonstrators from outlying districts, but other than those there was no transport. During the morning, the telephone went dead and the lights went out. Then, outside, in the distance, the sound of shooting was heard.

There was movement in the Kochstrasse and Franz saw a lorry disgorge a detachment of the People's Marine, who rushed to the front of the building and stood, peering down the street, their rifles at the ready. They yelled warnings to the demonstrators, who started to disperse. The gunfire came nearer and with it, the heavy rumbling of tanks over cobblestones, the shrieking of car tyres, the sound of stentorian voices shouting through loud-hailers.

A journalist, armed with a rifle, pushed Franz aside, crouching by the window, his weapon aimed into the street. Suddenly, Franz thought of Georg. In his hospital bed he, too, must be in the middle of the battle. What was he doing here in the Ullstein building, when he should be with Georg? He had thought he was helping Herr Ullstein, but he was merely an old man, getting in the way.

An armoured lorry rounded the corner, Free Corps soldiers standing on the open trailer, the swastika insignia on their helmets clearly distinguishable. As Franz stood up, the People's Marine loosed a hail of bullets towards them and the men of the Tobisch Brigade fired wildly back. A bullet smashed through the window, splintering glass onto the floor.

'Get down!' the journalist screamed, taking aim at the lorry.

But it was too late. Franz Jankowski's body lay slewed on the ground. Blood gushed from the hole in his head, where the Free Corps' bullet had entered. He was already dead.

That evening, the Expressionist Theatre of the Proletariat was sparsely populated. The foyer and the stage were lit by oil lamps and candles, which cast long, macabre shadows over the bare auditorium, for most people had chosen to remain safely at home behind shuttered windows and barred doors. Some of the actors too had stayed away either out of sympathy to the revolutionaries or from fear. Surprisingly, Pipsi had turned up, although she refused to put on her halo and wings.

When the cue came for Lothar to rush onto the stage with his water pistol, he simply hadn't the energy. To tell the truth, he was already losing faith in Dada. It had seemed such fun at the time, but since his rebuff by Pipsi and the increasing brutality exercised by Noske's troops against the Spartacists, revolution had lost its allure. As he hovered in the wings, he heard an uproar in the foyer.

As soon as they heard the noise, the actors became silent, glancing at one another in fear, then, with one accord, they left the stage. 'Free Corps!' they cried, discarding their outlandish costumes as they ran. Lothar peered round the curtains and saw the few spectators scurrying towards the exits, where they came face to face with grey-uniformed men bearing rifles.

He waited to see no more. Grabbing Pipsi by the arm, he dragged her through the stage door, down the street and into his parked car. With trembling hands, he cranked the starting handle, peering nervously over his shoulder to see if the soldiers were following them, until, to his great relief, the engine fired. He leapt into the car, put it in gear, then roared down the road. Suddenly, a soldier barred his way, his rifle aimed deliberately at the car's wheels. 'Drive on!' Pipsi screamed. Lothar needed no second bidding. He heard the bang as the bullet shattered the tyre and beneath his hands the steering wheel pulled violently to the left. With a strength he didn't know he possessed, he straightened it, then, of its own velocity, the car skidded into the Motzstrasse.

Lothar tried to collect his scattered wits. To drive into the city centre seemed to be asking for trouble, so he continued south until he was certain nobody was following him, then pulled up to the kerb. Pipsi, by now, was in floods of tears. 'Take me home,' she wailed.

Half an hour later, he had changed the tyre and was driving cautiously towards Charlottenburg. As Pipsi continued to howl beside him, his mind was working furiously. It would take the Free Corps little time to discover who rented the theatre and even less to discover his address at the Hotel Quadriga. Almost certainly a warrant was already out for his arrest. After he had got rid of Pipsi, his best plan seemed to be to drive straight on out of Berlin. He drew to a halt in front of Pipsi's apartment and decided it was, perhaps, time to pay a visit to Switzerland.

Just as they reached her door, it opened and a man appeared, a candle in his hand illuminating his shock of grey hair, his rugged jowls and deepset eyes. 'Pipsi?'

'Papa? Oh, Papa!' She flew into his arms.

Although he longed to get away, Lothar felt some explanation was due. 'My name is Lothar Lorenz, sir. I run, or rather I ran, the Expressionist Theatre. Unfortunately, we had some trouble this evening ...'

Professor Ascher nodded sombrely. 'There's been trouble everywhere today. That's why I'm here. Pipsi, are you all right?'

'She's just frightened, sir. We weren't hurt.'

Pipsi looked up at her father from tearstained eyes. 'Free Corps soldiers broke into the theatre, they shot at our car ...'

'They've done worse than that,' Professor Ascher told her. 'They attacked the Ullstein newspaper building and killed several people, including Franz Jankowski. Pipsi, think of what that news is going to do to Georg!'

Lothar knew neither Georg nor his uncle. He bowed his head and turned to leave. As he went, he heard Pipsi's petulant voice crying, 'To hell with Georg, what about me? I might have been killed!'

Suddenly, Lothar felt very sorry for Georg Jankowski.

Since Pipsi refused to break the news to Georg about his uncle, Professor Ascher undertook the sad task. Georg stared at him dully. 'I heard the shooting. I was afraid. When Uncle Franz didn't come here ...' He was silent for a long time, then a tear trickled down his cheek. 'He was all I had,' he whispered, 'he was the only friend I had in the world. Oh, why did he have to die?'

Professor Ascher offered no trite words of comfort, but his heart went out to him. From the depths of his soul, he prayed that once he and Pipsi were reunited, his daughter would improve her ways and become the wife this brave young man deserved.

Despite all his outside commitments, the Professor made time to visit his son-in-law every day, taking over the role that Franz had played until his death, and, to a great extent, it was he who gave Georg back his will to live. Pipsi, to his disgust, was given another acting role, this time at Jessner's State Theatre, and used this as an excuse not to visit her husband. So it was due to Professor Ascher that the confusion in Georg's mind slowly retreated, until he could once again face the thought of picking up the broken strands of his life.

'When you get home, you'll find a surprise waiting for you,' the Professor told him one day smilingly.

In April, Georg was discharged and, accompanied by Professor Ascher, finally returned home. As the taxi drove them towards Charlottenburg, the Professor reflected how difficult it was now to imagine the battles that had raged in these very streets, for the government, frightened by the carnage committed by Noske's Free Corps, had ordered them to leave Berlin and deal with other trouble-spots in the Ruhr and in Bavaria. He was thankful, not least because he hoped this new peace would give Georg a final chance of recovery.

At the apartment he stayed only a few minutes to witness Georg's reception. What he saw did not encourage him. Pipsi gave her husband a frigid peck on the cheek, while Minna stared at him from frightened eyes. 'Who are you?' she asked.

Georg knelt down in front of her. She was a very pretty child, with a marked resemblance to himself. 'I'm your Papa.'

'You're not my Papa. I've never seen you before in my life.' She ran out of the room, calling, 'Nanny, Nanny, where are you?'

'You've frightened her,' Pipsi said coldly. 'What else do you expect? You look like some kind of ghost — thin and white.'

Professor Ascher sighed and took his leave.

That night, lying in the double bed, Georg put out a tentative hand towards his wife. It had been so long since he had felt her body and he longed to touch her. Pipsi did not repulse him, even if she did little to encourage him. Then, as he stroked and caressed her, he felt her body react and knew a sudden burst of confidence. Pipsi was such a sensual person — if only he could make love to her, the past might be forgotten and they could take up again where they had left off in the very first months of their marriage. He moved against her, praying that the doctor in Mons had been wrong.

Her tongue probed his mouth and he could taste the perfume of her desire. He wanted her so badly and he wanted so much to make her happy. She writhed beneath his fingers, moaning, 'Take me, Georg, take me.' And, at that moment, he recognized bleakly that the doctor in Mons had been right.

Her hand ran down his body and discovered his secret. For a few moments, she fondled him, but there was no reaction. In utter misery, Georg lay there, knowing that in this most important of all matters, he had failed her. She withdrew her hand. 'What the hell's the matter with you, Georg? You haven't slept with me for years, but now you can't even get an erection.' She moved away from him. 'You're impotent.'

The next morning, after announcing that from now on they would sleep in separate rooms, she told him that she was not going to allow his homecoming to change her routine. 'I have rehearsals every afternoon and performances every evening. I'm seldom home before midnight. I don't expect you to wait up for me.' Georg nodded resignedly. Nothing seemed to matter any more.

After she had gone, he entered his old study and there it was that he discovered the Professor's surprise. Under the window stood Uncle Franz's ancient piano. It conjured up such a host of memories that for a long time, Georg just stared at it. Then, slowly, he walked across the room, sat down on the piano stool and lifted the lid, allowing his fingers to drift silently across the old keys.

It was there that Minna found him. Shyly, she stepped into the room and stood beside him, gazing up at his face. Then she asked hesitantly. 'Is that your piano?'

'Yes, it's my piano now.'

'Will you play me a tune?'

He shook his head. 'Not now, but one day, maybe.'

'I'd like that,' she said, and then she added, 'Papa.'

It was the beginning of a friendship between a tired, bewildered man and a lonely little girl.

Nanny Simon, delighted that her charge finally had at least one parent to love her, did everything she could to encourage them. Soon, they were taking all their meals together, going for walks every afternoon and Georg had the sole responsibility for tucking his daughter up in bed and reading her to sleep each night. In no time at all, they had become inseparable.

When Professor Ascher asked Georg to meet him at the Hotel Quadriga one April afternoon for a drink, it was only natural that Minna went with him. On the steps of the hotel, he hesitated, remembering suddenly how he had stood here in his student days, vowing that one day he would enter it as a famous pianist. How hard Uncle Franz had worked to pay for his studies at the Berlin *Hochschule* — how desperately he had wanted to make the old man proud of him. And now ...

'Papa, have you ever been here before?' Minna asked.

'No, sweetheart, but my Uncle Franz used to work here.'

A top-hatted commissionaire bowed them in and a page boy hurried up to them to ask if he could assist them. 'We're just going to the bar,' Georg told him, and although he had never seen it, he knew exactly where it was.

'It's awfully grand, isn't it?' Minna whispered, as the page boy led them through the foyer.

'Uncle Franz used to tell me it was the finest hotel in Europe.'

'I think it's beautiful.'

So, in a strange way, did Georg. From Franz's descriptions, he could imagine the Kaiser striding through this very hall, Karl Jochum's elegant figure hovering beside him. From the bar came the sound of a piano playing Viennese waltzes. It all seemed rather like the relic of a more elegant, bygone age.

The Professor rose to greet them, ordered their drinks, then started to talk about a student of his at the university. 'His name is Einstein and I'm positive he'll be awarded the Nobel Prize for work he is currently involved in on the relativity theory ...'

But Georg did not hear him. Towards the back of the room, the bar itself protruded somewhat, and between it and the rear wall a secluded corner contained a largish table with several chairs round it, obviously the homing place for regulars. She was sitting at this table, a slim girl with auburn hair and dancing emerald eyes. Georg's mind went back to that day at the Anhalter Station, when he and hundreds of other soldiers had leant out of a train window calling goodbye to a girl in a bright blue dress, who, soon a mere speck in the distance, was waving her blue hat.

Suddenly, the memory of the melody he had composed started to return to him. He closed his eyes and the notes danced in his mind. A happy tune. A valse. In a major key. He opened his eyes and stared at her again and a thrill of excitement shuddered through him. This was it! This was what he had been waiting for!

He jumped up from the table and rushed across the room towards the pianist playing quietly on the Bechstein in the corner. 'Excuse me, but there's something I must try out.' There were words in his head, too, but they were not yet clear.

The pianist looked at him in surprise but relinquished his seat without any protest. Suddenly, as Georg's fingers spanned the keys, the years since he had played contracted into minutes and it was as if he were back again in August 1914, when hope was everything and youth a magic that would last for ever.

Tenderly, his fingers caressed the ivory and ebony keys and yieldingly they delivered their enchanted message. To start with, there was only the tune tripping lightly through the room, laughing, dancing, singing. People stopped their conversations and listened, but he was unaware of the hush. Then the words came, isolated phrases, disjointed, but right, oh, so right!

'You are the dream that I clung to, in blue, cornflower blue,' and 'When I thought there was no hope to hope, I found you again in my dreams.'

But this note was wrong, it should be more emphatic, and that one should be a tone higher, so Georg started again and this time he was satisfied. Only when he had finished and stood up to thank the pianist for giving up his piano, was Georg aware of a room full of people staring at him open-mouthed. Then, to his utter surprise and embarrassment, they were standing, clapping and cheering, shouting, 'More, more!' 'Bravo!' 'Encore!'

Smiling diffidently, he returned to his table. Professor Ascher clapped him on the shoulder. 'Well done, Georg, well done!'

Minna clasped his hand. 'Papa, you're wonderful.'

On the other side of the room, Luise forgot the conversation she had been having with Sepp and gazed, mesmerized, at the dark-haired young man bent over the piano keys. When he finished, she stood up, clapping louder than everyone else. 'Who is he?'

'Go and ask him,' Sepp suggested, grinning. 'It's not like you to be shy, Luise.'

'That's exactly what I'm going to do.' She marched across the room to where the pianist was sitting down with Professor Ascher and a little girl. 'That was absolutely incredible.'

The Professor beamed at her. 'He's a talented young man, isn't he?'

'But who are you?'

'Luise!' Professor Ascher exclaimed. 'You mean to say you two have never met? You don't know my son-in-law, Georg Jankowski? Georg, this is Luise Jochum.'

As he put his hand in hers, she examined his gaunt face, with its cavernous, hooded eyes and thin, sensitive lips, and felt suddenly diffident. So this was Georg, whose life she had shared as a child through his Uncle Franz. This was Georg, whom Pipsi betrayed. And this was Georg, who was, she intuitively knew, the greatest pianist she had ever heard. 'You're Georg?' It was as if they were the only people in the room. 'You wrote that music?'

'I wrote it for you. I wrote it when I first saw you, nearly five years ago. You were standing on the platform of the Anhalter Station, waving your blue hat. I had no idea who you were, but I christened you the "cornflower girl".'

'For me?' She shook her head in bewilderment. 'You wrote it for me? But that's ...'

Professor Ascher's voice brought them back to reality. 'Why don't you sit down, Luise? And let's call your friend over. He must be feeling lonely, left on his own.'

Reluctantly, she loosened her hand from Georg's, then beckoned to Sepp to join them. 'This is an old friend of mine, Sepp Nowak. Professor Ascher — Georg Jankowski.' For the first time, she became aware of the little girl. 'And you must be Minna.'

Minna looked up shyly at her father and Luise was immediately aware of the bond that existed between them. Contrasting so strongly to Pipsi's casual rejection of her daughter, it made Luise like Georg even more.

'Are you a musician?' Sepp was asking him. 'I don't know the first thing about music, but you sounded pretty good to me.'

'He's brilliant,' Luise said.

'And are you working now?'

Georg shook his head helplessly. 'What can I do?'

'Take a job,' Sepp told him, 'any job, but take it. In these days, we can't afford to be choosy.'

It was then Luise had her brilliant idea. The news of Franz Jankowski's death had upset her almost more than her own father's, for in many ways theirs had been a closer relationship. Now she saw a very simple way of helping the nephew he had loved so much. 'Georg, why don't you come and play here at the Quadriga, like your Uncle Franz did?'

'Well ...'

'I think that's an absolutely splendid idea, Luise,' Professor Ascher declared.

'Er, shouldn't you talk to Benno and Viktoria first?' Sepp asked drily.

Luise smiled at him confidently. 'Oh, they'll be delighted that I'm taking an interest in the hotel. I'll go and find Vicki now.'

Watching her cross the room, Georg found himself prey to a welter of conflicting emotions. He was still shaken by the impulse that had so unexpectedly driven him to the piano and somehow shocked by his own and Luise's reactions. Although she had haunted his thoughts for years, their actual encounter left him feeling disturbed. Within the space of half an hour, his whole life seemed to have changed, leaving him no longer in control. Luise, Sepp, Professor Ascher were all so self-assured, they couldn't possibly understand that he quite simply lacked the confidence to take over his Uncle Franz's job. He sensed Sepp gazing at him thoughtfully and gave him a troubled look.

'I'm sure you're much too good to be a hotel musician,' the pilot said consolingly, misinterpreting Georg's hesitation. 'Look at me, I was an ace during the war and now I fly a miserable little transport plane for Kraus Aviation. I'd much rather be attempting to cross the Atlantic, but at least I'm flying. So, you'd like to conduct the Philharmonic. And one day, I'm sure you will. In the meantime ...'

Luise's voice interrupted them. 'Georg, meet my sister, Viktoria Jochum-Kraus. Vicki, this is Franz Jankowski's nephew.'

Still in a daze, Georg shook hands with Viktoria, seeing a tall, slim woman dressed in a severe costume, her blonde braids framing a strong, squarish face. As she greeted the Professor, then bent down to say hello to Minna, he instinctively liked her.

'Herr Jankowski, my sister tells me you might like to play here at the hotel.' She had a firm, low voice, as controlled as Luise's was excited. 'We should, of course, be very pleased to have a Jankowski back with us again. Your uncle was a dear friend of the hotel — and of my father. We were very sorry to hear of his death.'

'And, although I never met him, I was very sad to hear of Herr Jochum's death,' Georg replied. 'My uncle told me a lot about him.'

Viktoria's face clouded. 'Yes, we live in sad times.' Then she shook her head. 'Well, we must all be brave. Now, Herr

Jankowski, when would you be able to start?'

'You mean you don't want to hear me play?'

Her smile made her appear much younger and Georg realized she was probably only a few years older than her sister. 'No, I'll accept Luise's word. She's the artistic person in our family.'

'Well, I suppose I could start today.'

'Good,' Viktoria said decisively. 'Now you'd better come and meet my husband and we can settle all the formalities.'

'Papa,' Minna asked tremulously, 'what about me?'

Viktoria smiled at her. 'How old are you, Minna?'

'I'm nearly four.'

'My little boy, Stefan, is nearly five. Why don't you come here and play with him sometimes?'

To Viktoria's joy, Stefan and Minna, after an initial shyness, got on well together and they made a pretty couple, both with brown, serious eyes and dark hair, that faintly luminous bloom to their skin that marked above all else to Viktoria the fragility and the transience of childhood. And, in Stefan's case, his babyhood seemed to have passed so quickly.

'It's nice that he has company of his own age at last,' Ricarda commented, when she heard of the arrangement. 'I've always thought it's rather sad to be an only child.'

Soon, the nursery echoed to their laughter and a new generation discovered the jungle-like plants in the Palm Garden Room, the joys of the hotel kitchen and the fact that old Max Patschke could be twisted round their little fingers.

Her mother's words, however, sparked off another thought in Viktoria's mind. Now the country seemed to be growing calmer, possibly the time had come to consider having another child. It would, as her mother pointed out, be company for Stefan, but it would also — in a strange way — help repay the debt that she felt she owed Benno.

That April, Benno, Luise and her mother started to act very strangely. Frequently, she discovered them closeted together in her father's old office, piles of paper on the desk, which they hastily shuffled out of sight when she appeared. She found herself growing used to the fact that their conversation stopped as soon as she drew near. Obviously, they shared a secret to which she was not going to be privy.

Then Benno announced that the Empire Room was going to be

shut for redecoration. 'Germany is no longer an empire, but a republic, so we should keep up with the times.'

'But what about Mama? That was Papa's favourite room.'

'Not one I ever liked,' Ricarda said firmly. 'No, Benno and I are entirely agreed about what we're going to do with the Empire Room.'

They did not, however, tell her, and Viktoria was wise enough not to ask. She was pleased to see her mother involved again in the hotel, a smile in her eyes and the shock of Karl's death apparently behind her. She hoped, if ever she found herself in the same situation, that she would behave as sensibly.

There was constant activity during the weeks that followed as a small army of carpenters, painters and decorators worked behind the Empire Room's closed doors. Luise went round with a secretive look and Stefan was obviously bursting with importance at being a party to their plans. Gradually, Viktoria sensed that the rest of the hotel's staff was becoming involved, as she discovered her husband in low-voiced consultations with Max Patschke, Arno Halbe and Georg Jankowski. For the first time in years, an atmosphere of cheerful optimism permeated the establishment.

At the beginning of May 1919, two unconnected events shattered this happy mood. The first was a letter from Grete in Munich telling them of Gottfried's death from influenza. Viktoria, in particular, was sorry, for much as she disliked Olga, she had been fond of her uncle. In an attempt at cheerfulness, Grete's letter ended, 'But we are eagerly awaiting the birth of poor Olga's baby in July.' Luise sighed. 'I don't think I can stand the thought of another Olga.'

The second event manifested itself in the person of Benno's father, who arrived a couple of days later. 'I'm waiting for news from Paris,' he told them, his face worried. 'Theo Arendt has promised to telephone me as soon as he hears the terms of the Peace Conference.'

Viktoria paid little attention to him. She was vaguely aware that representatives from America, Britain, France and Italy had been meeting in Paris since January to determine Europe's future now the war was over, but so far as she was concerned, this convention had no significance. Germany had signed the armistice and had withdrawn its troops from the countries it had occupied. 'What is this peace conference?' she asked Benno that evening.

'There are still a number of matters to be resolved. For instance, French troops are still occupying the Rhine, while other parts of Germany go on being disrupted by the revolutionaries. Our factories in Essen are still closed, for instance. I think the Allies want to try to effect a stable Germany. I suspect they will forbid us from producing arms for a while longer, but apart from that, they're going to want to get rid of the communists, who threaten us and, therefore, all of Europe.'

'Then why is your father so anxious?'

'You know Father. Only one thing worries him and that's Kraus Industries. An arms embargo means the end to a very substantial part of Kraus business.'

'Why has Theo gone to Paris?'

'Germany hasn't been allowed to participate in any of these discussions,' Benno explained patiently. 'But Theo, as a banker, has apparently been selected as one of the German peace delegation. I'm sure my father would dearly love to have gone, but being a munitions manufacturer, he is obviously excluded.'

Dismissing the whole business as something that concerned only Baron Heinrich, Viktoria forgot about it, until the evening of 7 May. They were sitting in the Palm Garden Room after dinner, listening to Georg's piano, when Baron Heinrich burst into the room. He pushed brusquely past a waiter, causing the startled man to drop a tray of glasses onto the polished parquet floor with a resounding crash.

In the silence that followed, everybody in the room turned to stare at him. Only Georg's piano continued its muted playing. Benno leapt up, 'Father, what's happened?'

'I've just had news from Paris,' the Baron stuttered. 'It's absolutely dreadful. They're going to cripple us, pull us apart limb by limb. They won't be content until Germany is destroyed.' Unseeingly, he picked up a glass from the table and swallowed its contents in one gulp. 'Germany is to admit total guilt and total responsibility for the outbreak of war. Not only are we to lose all our colonies, but much of our territory here in Europe. Alsace and Lorraine are to be returned permanently to French rule. The Saar is to be occupied by the French, and the Rhineland by Allied troops for fifteen years.'

There was a horrified gasp.

'Poland is to become an independent republic, including Upper Silesia and West Prussia,' the Baron went on grimly, 'and Danzig is

to become a Free City, belonging to neither Germany nor Poland.'
He took off his glasses and rubbed his hand over his eyes. With a
sense of shock, Viktoria realized how old he had become. 'But
that's not all! The size of the German army is to be limited to one
hundred thousand men and we must build no more tanks, planes,
airships or submarines. Nothing of a military nature. For companies like mine, that news is, of course, disastrous.'

He was surrounded by a sea of shocked faces. 'The Allies have
also decided that, because we are considered to have started the
war, we must pay war reparations for the damage we have inflicted
on other countries and people. The exact sum has yet to be
decided, but payment will have to be made in the form of industrial goods and in gold marks.'

Even Georg had stopped playing now. Nobody moved. The
room was perfectly silent. Then a voice muttered, 'God Almighty,
what kind of idiots are they in Paris? Our principal mining and
industrial areas are the very ones that they are proposing to seize,
and yet they expect us to pay in manufactured goods?'

The Baron nodded heavily. 'Yes, you're right. Because of the
very limitations the Allies are imposing, we shall never be able to
fulfil those obligations.'

'But don't they realize that?'

'Apparently not. Herr Arendt tells me that he and his
colleagues have been trying to tell them that Germany is already
bankrupt, but they won't listen.'

'Then we simply won't sign,' somebody announced.

'I don't think we're being given any choice,' the Baron said
drily. 'Unfortunately, gentlemen, we lost the war.'

For long into the night, people sat on in the hotel's rooms,
discussing this disastrous news. Once the immediate shock had
passed, their attitudes grew more belligerent. Almost without
exception, the hotel's guests blamed the Social Democrats for signing the armistice in November. For the first time, Viktoria heard
the phrase, 'November criminals'. Next to blame were the
communists who had instigated the revolution, thus giving
Germany the 'invisible stab in the back' that had caused them to
lose the war. By signing the Peace Treaty, some claimed, the
government would be playing straight into communist hands, for
the people would not tolerate its terms, but would rise up again in
revolt against the government.

Then Baron Heinrich's voice cut through them. As everybody

around him grew more excited, he became calmer. 'I don't see that our government is going to have any alternative but to sign. Let's look at the facts. The French already occupy the Rhine and American and British troops could quickly be assembled to invade us. We are simply not strong enough to fight another war.' Then he paused meaningfully. 'Not yet, anyway.'

Viktoria, still unable to understand the full implications of the proposed Peace Treaty, left Benno and his father still talking and went upstairs with Ricarda. Slipping her arm through hers, she sighed, 'They make it all sound so dreadful, Mama. I thought the war was over and now they're already talking about the next one.'

Ricarda patted her hand. 'Don't worry about it, dear. I'm sure the men know what they're doing.'

Very soon, Viktoria all but forgot the Peace Treaty, as the hotel filled with businessmen, politicians, army officers and journalists from all over the country meeting in Berlin to discuss its ramifications. So busy was she that she even forgot the work that continued to go on in the Empire Room, only reminded of it by Stefan's bubbling excitement and when she saw the old heavy, Wilhelmine furniture removed and huge packing cases arrive.

It came almost as a shock to her when Benno announced at supper in the middle of June, 'It's your birthday tomorrow. I thought we might have a small celebration, you know, something to cheer us all up and take our minds off this wretched Peace Settlement. Why don't you take the afternoon off — go and have your hair done and buy a new dress?'

She raised her eyebrows. 'New dress?' Although the shops were slowly filling with goods, there were still tremendous shortages and men like Rudi Nowak were prospering more than ever.

'I'm sure Luise can find you one,' Benno grinned.

'But the hotel's so busy, I don't like to take time off.'

'Oh, Vicki, don't be boring,' Luise said.

'Yes, dear,' Ricarda urged, 'you and Luise go off for the afternoon. Benno can look after the hotel perfectly well.'

Viktoria looked at them all suspiciously, more convinced than ever that they were all involved in a plot of which only she knew nothing. 'All right, since it's my birthday.'

When she and Luise arrived back the following evening, tired after a successful afternoon at the hairdresser and with a delightful evening gown that, by some coincidence almost too good to be true, fitted her perfectly, she was rushed through the foyer and straight up to her apartment. There, Luise proceeded almost to stand guard over her. 'Promise you won't move until you're told.'

'What is going on?'

'You'll find out soon. Now, Vicki, promise!'

'All right,' she laughed.

When Benno came up, she was standing in front of the mirror staring at her reflection. The dress was white, covered with thousands of silver sequins that shone blue in the light. Around her shoulders she had draped a white ermine stole of Ricarda's. It was almost as if she were looking at a stranger.

'Vicki, you look beautiful,' Benno murmured. He came and stood behind her, putting his arms round her. 'Are you pleased with it?'

She spun round. 'Benno? You don't mean to say you ordered this dress?'

He smiled. 'Well, Luise and I organized it between us.'

'But how did you know ...?'

'Oh, Luise sorted out all the measurements and things.'

'Well, I never. And I thought it was a coincidence.' Tenderly she put her hands to his face and kissed him. 'Oh, Benno, thank you. It's beautiful. Why, I hardly recognize myself.'

'Well, just admire yourself for a few more moments while I change, then we'll go downstairs.'

Arm in arm, they left the apartment, walked down the main staircase and across the white foyer towards the old Empire Room. 'Is the room finished?' Viktoria asked in surprise. 'You didn't tell me, Benno.'

He put his fingers to his lips and a page boy, grinning broadly, opened the door. The room was in darkness except for a host of shimmering candles, forming the number twenty-five. Then the silence was broken by the tinkling of a piano, playing a familiar tune. Suddenly, voices were raised: 'Happy birthday to you, happy birthday to you, happy birthday, Quadriga, happy birthday to you.'

Slowly, lights came on and she saw a room packed with people, each carrying a candle in a silver holder. But what a room! Gone were the forbidding dark oak panels and in their place was heavy white wallpaper, that glittered with silver flecks very like the sequins on her dress. From the ceiling hung silver chandeliers, while the chairs that stood against the walls were also inlaid with silver. To her dismay, she found tears rolling down her cheeks. 'The Quadriga's Silver Jubilee. Oh, Benno, what a lovely idea!'

He reached in his pocket. 'And this is a little present for you. Happy birthday, darling.'

She took the box and carefully opened it. Inside, on a bed of cotton wool, intricately carved in silver, lay a model of the hotel, suspended from a chain.

Gently, Benno removed her stole and hung the pendant round her neck. Then, standing back to admire her, he suddenly smiled. 'You and the Hotel Quadriga are both a quarter of a century old. I doubt very much that I shall live to see it, but I hope from the bottom of my heart, Viktoria dear, that you live to see a full century.'

His words relieved the tension. Everybody cheered and people started to move towards her. Stefan gazed at her with adoring eyes. 'Mama, you look so beautiful. You didn't suspect, did you? You didn't know about your surprise party?'

Deeply touched, she shook her head. 'Stefi, I had no idea. Why, did you know?'

'Yes,' he said proudly, 'we all knew. Papa, Grandmama, Aunt Luise and I planned it. Then, of course, we had to tell everybody else.' He bit his lip. 'I nearly told you so many times.'

She put her arm around him. 'I'm very proud of you, Stefi. Now, I'd better say hello to everyone else.'

There were so many of them, so many dear friends of the hotel and of herself. Baron Heinrich was still there, but had been joined by Countess Julia, Ernst, Trudi and their two-year-old son, Werner. In an unexpected moment of confidence, Trudi told Viktoria that she was expecting another child early next year. Theo Arendt, back from Paris, had brought Sophie and his two boys, Felix and Caspar, who were in charge of Minna Jankowski for the evening, while Georg played the piano. With them, also, was Professor Ascher, but, Viktoria noticed, not Pipsi.

Luise, she was pleased to see, was with Sepp Nowak, who seemed to have become her closest friend since Lothar Lorenz's precipitate departure for Switzerland in March. Looking radiant in the green crêpe de chine dress that had so nearly caused an argument between them the previous summer, Luise was introducing Sepp to many other hotel guests and friends from Berlin who had been specially invited to the celebration. In all, Viktoria decided, there were probably a hundred people in the room.

Then, for the first time, she noticed the magnificent buffet Chef Mazzoni had prepared. Despite the shortages, the tables, decked in

407

blue and white linen cloths, were almost groaning under the weight of the food. There was lobster, caviar, prime fillet of beef cooked in the English fashion, fresh asparagus and artichokes, finely sliced smoked salmon, pink shrimps in aspic, roast crowns of lamb, jugged hare and venison and, as the most fantastic centre-piece, a whole spitted boar. Turbot, carp and sole lay glassy-eyed on beds of chopped lettuce, garnished with red paprikas, olives and parsley. There were flans, tarts and cakes, made from fresh apricots, peaches, strawberries and raspberries, accompanied by jugs of stiff whipped cream. Huge dishes of ice cream lay in big bowls of crushed ice.

If only, she thought, her father could still be alive, the evening would be truly perfect. As if reading her thoughts, Ricarda came and stood beside her. 'We planned it a long time ago, Vicki. After all, you and the hotel were born on the same day. Karl could never forget that.'

At that moment, Benno asked for silence. Reverently, Arno Halbe came forward with some decanted bottles of wine. Picking one up very carefully, Benno poured it into glasses, handing them to Ricarda, Viktoria and Luise. 'Karl Jochum laid these bottles of wine down in 1894 to celebrate the opening of his hotel. I propose we all drink his toast. To Karl Jochum!'

'To Karl Jochum!' Their voices reverberated through the room.

Supper eaten, the dancing over and the guests departed, Viktoria and Benno made their way up to bed. After hanging her lovely dress up in the wardrobe, Viktoria put her arms round Benno. 'I don't know how to thank you. It was a wonderful evening.'

'I love you, Vicki. I'm glad I made you happy.' Gently, he led her over to to the bed, and drew her down beside him. 'You looked so beautiful tonight, it hurt me to look at you, but, although it seems impossible, you look even more beautiful without any clothes at all.'

He turned out the light and made love to her with a tender passion. As she responded to his caresses, Viktoria knew with absolute certainty that this night she was going to conceive their first child.

Although the other birthday guests left, Baron Heinrich remained at the Hotel Quadriga, conducting many meetings and awaiting the final confirmation of the Versailles Peace Treaty. In an extraordinary manner, it was this Treaty that effected a major change in the relationship between the Baron and his younger son.

On 28 June 1919, with a dramatic black border round its front page, the *Deutsche Zeitung* proclaimed the news: 'Vengeance! German nation! Today in the Hall of Mirrors at Versailles, a disgraceful treaty is being signed. Never forget it! On that spot where, in the glorious year of 1871, the German Empire in all its glory began, today German honour is dragged to the grave. Never forget it! The German people with unceasing labour, will push forward to reconquer that place among nations of the world to which they are entitled. There will be vengeance for the shame of 1919!'

The Baron read the article and pushed the newspaper to one side. 'It is a black day, but it's not entirely unexpected. As soon as the Allies refused to negotiate with the army, we should have known what was going to happen. I actually feel sorry for Erzberger, who had to sign the Treaty. He's going to be blamed — and he is, in fact, a good man.' There was genuine regret in his voice.

Benno suddenly looked at him in a new light. Was it possible that there was a human side to the man whom he had always regarded as a tyrant? 'What will happen to us, Father?' As Benno asked his question, he realized that his country's situation bound them all closer than they had ever been.

The Baron, too, seemed to sense this. His tone, when he replied, was moderate, with none of his former hectoring belligerency. For the first time he spoke to Benno as an equal. 'So far as Kraus Industries are concerned, we shall survive. The troubles in the Ruhr will go on for a long time, I suspect. I doubt if the French are still really happy with the Treaty and I have a feeling they will march into the Ruhr on the slightest provocation. Certainly, so long as the Rhine is demilitarized and the French are guarding it, we're going to have labour problems in Essen, because the workers simply aren't going to tolerate the situation. So, for the time being, I shall leave Ernst in charge there and concentrate my energies in other areas.'

'You're surely not still considering building a passenger liner?' Benno asked incredulously.

His father looked cautiously round to make sure nobody was in the vicinity, then with a familiar, crafty expression in his eyes, replied, 'Let me take you into my confidence, son. Benno, we're going to establish the Kraus-Amerika Line. America is the wealthiest country in the world at the moment, for it lost least and gained most from the war. Furthermore, most of our steel is at Kraushaven and any more that we need we can import from Sweden. I don't know if I told you, but before the war ended, I negotiated a contract with Jan van der Jong in Rotterdam against just such a contingency. We may not be permitted to build ships in Germany, but there's nothing to stop us doing so in Holland.'

Benno nodded in reluctant admiration. His father had just turned sixty but his brain was more agile than many a younger man's.

'We may not be able to manufacture arms here, but we still own the patents,' the Baron continued. 'Many Kraus arms are already being manufactured under licence abroad and we can expand our sales still further, to South America, the Far East and South Africa. We made considerable developments during the war — those rights can be sold, as can the stocks we still hold. There's always a war going on somewhere.

'And now I come to the final point, which will actually even affect you here in your hotel, Benno. I firmly believe that Germany is going to experience a very bad financial depression from now on. Kraus Industries will be moving considerable sums of money out of Germany, to Switzerland and America. You should do the same.'

Benno gave a hollow laugh. 'Father, the Hotel Quadriga doesn't have any surplus funds to move.' He hesitated for a moment, wondering whether to trust him with information that he hadn't even discussed with Viktoria. But why not? 'The mortgages that Karl Jochum took out in 1893 become due in 1923.'

'Yes, I was instrumental in arranging them for Jochum.'

'Well, I've been spending a lot of time since Herr Jochum's death going through the hotel books. So far as I can see, the Hotel Quadriga has been operating at a loss since 1914. The last few months, needless to say, have been almost disastrous, what with the damage we incurred during the Revolution and due to the fact that, for so long, we had no guests. Now, although the hotel is filling up again, prices are rising so quickly, we are scarcely breaking even.'

'That spread you put on the other evening must have cost a pretty penny, eh?' the Baron asked shrewdly.

Benno nodded ruefully. Rudi Nowak had obtained all that he wanted for him, but his charge had been exorbitant.

'I'm going to give you some advice, Benno, and I'd urge you to listen to it. Do you remember attending a dinner I gave here in 1916, when Theo Arendt spoke to us about the War Loans? Well, he was right in everything he said, although nobody wanted to heed him, they were all so certain we were going to win the war. What has happened is that when the money supply of the country ran out, the government simply printed paper money to repay its loans, causing inflation. Now, on top of that, we're going to be faced with paying war reparations. Where is that money going to come from? I'll tell you, we shall just go on printing more — until the point when it won't even be worth the paper it's printed on.'

'You really think it's going to become as serious as that?'

'I very much fear so. The only currency to retain its value will be the American dollar, so, if you take my advice, Benno, you'll start buying dollars. Forget about your mortgages for the time being. Forget about German marks and any other European currencies, for that matter. Buy dollars.' He reached into his pocket and pulled out a notebook, filled with tightly-written figures. 'I've been keeping a record. At the beginning of the war, there were about four marks to the dollar. In January this year, the exchange rate was about nine to the dollar. Now, just six months later, there are fourteen to the dollar.'

Benno raised his eyebrows thoughtfully. Sometimes it did seem that being a Kraus had its uses. 'Thank you, Father.'

The Baron shook his head irritably. 'It's common sense, son, common sense. I'm just doing what I've done all my life, looking the situation in the face and seeing how I can use it to my best advantage. The trouble with most people is that they waste so much time grumbling about things, they never get anything done. Germany may have been defeated in the war, but that doesn't mean that we, as Germans, have to lose.'

Chapter Fifteen

That autumn, after the signing of the Treaty of Versailles, Major Count Peter von Biederstein and his men, still under the command of Major-General Ritter Emerich von Schennig, were moved from what was now the Free City of Danzig to Stuttgart. No longer known as the Death's Head Hussars, they were distinguished only by a number, a regiment of one of the three cavalry divisions stipulated by the ignominious peace treaty for Germany's armed forces, now called the Reichswehr.

Unable to accept the terms of Versailles, Field Marshal von Hindenburg had resigned, leaving General Groener to negotiate with the government. Then Groener, too, had resigned, leaving General Hans von Seeckt, the head of the new Troop Office, effectively in command. There was nothing Seeckt could do but comply with the Treaty and, gradually, the ranks were thinned to the regulation hundred thousand men and the number of officers to four thousand, a mere shadow of the Kaiser's glorious army which had been able to mobilize nearly four million men in August 1914. Many of Peter's fellow officers were dismissed and left to find civilian work in a country where the first ravages of unemployment were being felt.

What were the prospects for Peter? This was the question he was determined to have answered when he dined with his future father-in-law in his new quarters at the Stuttgart garrison, one evening in September 1919. The marriage between himself and Ilse von Schennig was due to take place at Osterfelde, their estate outside Luebeck, in the middle of October and, at a time when he most needed to be confident of his future, he knew only a sense of seething discontent and insecurity. Ilse, with her blonde hair and bluer-than-blue eyes, was an attractive woman, but that had never been his reason for proposing to her. No, the marriage was taking place because she would make an ideal officer's wife and because, through her father, he intended that his army career would be assured. But did he still have a career?

At the end of an excellent meal, von Schennig himself introduced the subject. 'I believe it's time you and I had a man-to-man discussion, Biederstein.' He leaned back in his chair and lit a fat cigar, gazing at him impassively through a haze of blue smoke. 'Perhaps you should realize that it isn't just because you are engaged to Ilse that I have used my influence to keep you in my regiment, but because you fit absolutely into Seeckt's officer corps. Very rightly, he is suspicious of wartime officers, for too many of them, like the ones we see commanding the Free Corps now, are successful in war but cannot stand the boredom of peacetime discipline. Like myself and Seeckt, you come from a Junker family with a military tradition and you gained your commission before the war. It is on men like you that the future army of Germany depends.'

While Peter listened intently, he went on to explain that, although, under the terms of the Treaty, the General Staff, the War Academy and all officer cadet schools had been abolished, the Troop Office had already covertly begun to take over the role of the General Staff and would soon form the new Reichswehr into an even finer version of the Kaiser's army. 'There is nothing the Allies can do about it. They cannot expect Germany to remain defenceless.'

For the first time since the end of the war, Peter began to believe that all was not lost. Far from mutely accepting its defeat, the army was already finding ways to circumvent the terms of the Versailles Treaty. In a sudden burst of enlightenment, he asked, 'And the Free Corps? Are they also part of General von Seeckt's plan?'

Major-General von Schennig permitted himself a thin smile. 'Yes. And not just the Free Corps, but all the other private armies that exist throughout the country. The Stahlhelm, the biggest of the ex-servicemen's associations, has thousands of members, all men, like those of the Free Corps, hardened by war and disillusioned by the peace. All these organizations are being unofficially supported by the Troop Office.'

Peter nodded. 'So the strength of the army may be limited officially to a hundred thousand men but already, if one includes the Free Corps and the Stahlhelm, it numbers nearer a million?' Then he frowned, as he was struck by a sudden worry. 'But, sir, these private armies are vastly bigger than the Reichswehr. What if they challenge our power at any time? We'd be powerless to resist.'

'I don't think that's likely. Like ourselves, most of the Free Corps brigades are essentially pro-monarchist and right-wing organizations. Their strength — and the purpose for which they are currently being used — is in putting down the communist uprisings. They have no more reason to challenge the Reichswehr than we have to seek their abolition. And, one day, of course, they will be amalgamated into the Reichswehr.'

Peter marvelled at General von Seeckt's cunning, until he recalled another concern. 'Under the terms of the new constitution, sir, President Ebert has been made Supreme Head of the armed forces and we have all had to take an oath of allegiance to the constitution. Does this mean that the army is answerable to the Social Democrats?'

Major-General von Schennig ground out his cigar butt contemptuously. 'The Prussian army has always prided itself on standing above politics, Biederstein. Our duty has always been, and always will be, to the German nation, not to the individual politicians who govern it. In my opinion, the socialists and the communists are responsible for Germany's current situation. They are dangerous people and we owe them no allegiance.'

Satisfied, Peter cupped his glass of Ansbach in his hands, savouring its mellow aroma. All his doubts were allayed and he could, finally, view his future with equanimity. It might not be for a very long while, but, one day, the aristocratic officers of the Reichswehr would prove themselves in their former glory as the elite of Germany.

Von Schennig walked across to his writing bureau and returned with a sheaf of papers. 'Received the guest list for the wedding from Osterfelde this morning,' he said, much as he would comment on a deployment of battle troops. 'Looks like there are going to be some couple of hundred guests, what?'

Peter glanced quickly down it, noticing with approval names from most of Germany's noble families, including his uncle, Baron Heinrich von Kraus and his cousin Ernst, with their families. Then he raised an eyebrow and permitted himself a rare smile, for under their names appeared those of Benno, Viktoria and Stefan.

For the first time in years, Peter thought of Viktoria, hazily recalling those few weeks they had spent together before war broke out. She had been an amusing little thing then — and excellent sport — but what was she like now? A crashing bore, no doubt, like all married women, particularly if they were commoners.

414

Suddenly, he wondered what sort of wife Ilse would prove in the conjugal bed. It wasn't actually an aspect of his marriage to which he had given much consideration.

The country might still be in turmoil over the Peace Treaty, armed communist insurrections might continue in the Ruhr and other parts of Germany, but Viktoria, personally, was happier those days than she had ever been in her life before. She was nearly four months pregnant and, free from all the guilt that had attached itself to Stefan's birth, felt almost smug about her condition.

That late September evening, as she sat in the nursery, reading Stefan his good-night story, her mind kept wandering to the next summer, when she would have two children. Would this one be a boy or a girl, she wondered, and rather hoped it would be the daughter Benno wanted, a sister for Stefan whom they could call Monika. She glanced fondly at her son. His long dark eyelashes were curled against his cheeks in sleep and his breathing was even, so she laid the book to one side, kissed him gently on the forehead and left the room.

'Frau Viktoria, late post for you,' Herr Fromm said importantly, as she crossed the foyer to Benno's office. She took it, glanced at the Luebeck postmark, then entered the room, where Benno was frowning over the hotel's accounts. Casually, she slid her finger under the flap of the envelope and pulled out a stiff card. 'Why, it looks like an invitation,' she exclaimed then, as she stared at the names on it, the blood drained from her face. It was an invitation — to the wedding of Peter von Biederstein and Ilse von Schennig.

'What's that?' Benno asked, engrossed in his figures.

She did not reply, just gazed blindly at the words dancing before her.

'Vicki, what's the matter?' Benno leaned across the desk and took the invitation from her hand. 'Ilse von Schennig? Wasn't she with him at the royal wedding in 1913? Pretty little thing, as I recall, with big, blue eyes?'

As if it were yesterday, she recalled their conversation at the ball. 'She's just the daughter of my commanding officer. It's a policeness.' But Peter had been lying to her. From the very beginning, he had used her, quite simply used her. 'Benno, we don't have to go, do we?'

'Of course we must, darling,' he replied brightly. 'It would never do to upset my Biederstein relatives. Now, let me finish these accounts.'

Mutely, she nodded and, still very pale, walked slowly out of the office. When she had gone, however, Benno pushed his ledgers to one side and buried his face in his hands. He had been so happy when he had learned that Viktoria was pregnant again, for on this occasion he was absolutely certain that he was the father. Without any doubt, this baby had been conceived on the night of the hotel's silver jubilee!

But now the spectre of Peter had once again raised its head. Neither he nor Viktoria had mentioned his name since their marriage and after that private agreement with Stefan on the day of his birth, he had tried to push all doubts about the boy's real parentage to the back of his mind. It was sufficient that, as the years passed, the love between them deepened and Stefan grew to resemble him more. Now, he realized this was not sufficient and that he should have insisted, right from the start, that Viktoria be honest with him, for so long as this cloud hung over them, they were all three living under a lie.

He lit a cigarette. This was not the time to raise the subject. They must go through with the wedding and let events take their course.

On many occasions during the weeks leading up to Peter's wedding, Viktoria tried to think of excuses that would prevent her attending but could think of none which would not alert Benno's suspicions. There seemed to be only one thing for it. She must put on a brave face and see the whole thing through unflinchingly, as befitted a true Jochum. After all, Peter meant nothing to her any more. She really did not have anything to be frightened of.

Yet, when she found herself actually standing in the crowded church at Osterfelde, with Stefan's hand clutched tightly in hers, her resolution all but failed her. There, walking up the aisle in a cloud of white lace, was the girl Peter had chosen in preference to her, and, a few pews ahead of her, elegant in his dress uniform, was Peter himself.

As from a great distance, she heard them take their vows, then, with Benno and Stefan to either side of her, she followed the large congregation out of the church into the train of waiting cars and was driven to the Schennigs' home. Soon, she consoled herself, as they entered the ancient manor house, this trial must be over and they could return to the safety of Berlin.

As their turn approached to greet the newly-married couple,

Benno took her arm. She glanced up at his face, but his expression was impassive. If he had any qualms about this reunion with his cousin, he was not revealing them. When he shook hands with Peter, he congratulated him heartily on his good fortune and smiled pleasantly at Ilse as they were introduced. Then he moved on to pay his respects to Peter's parents.

For the first time in five years, Viktoria felt Peter's hand in hers and sensed his eyes flickering over her in what seemed to be amusement. So he does remember, she thought miserably. Why else should he look at her in that sardonic manner, if he were not recalling their brief affair? 'Why, Viktoria,' he drawled, 'how nice to see you again. I trust you're well.' He turned to his wife. 'Ilse, my dear, this is Viktoria Kraus.'

Dazed, Viktoria found herself shaking hands with her. Never, she decided, had she disliked anybody as much as this little blonde with her innocent big blue eyes, who looked as if butter wouldn't melt in her mouth. She said coldly, 'My name is Jochum-Kraus.'

She heard Peter laugh and experienced a sudden, rising anger. How dare he come back into her life after all this time and laugh at her? How dare he parade his wife so callously in front of the girl he had deserted at the outbreak of war? Then, shocked, she realized how childish her thoughts were. 'Excuse me. I'm pleased to make your acquaintance. And I hope you will both be very happy.' With a curt little bow, she turned to look for Benno.

Her ordeal, however, was far from over, for she suddenly heard Ilse exclaim, 'Oh, what a handsome little boy! Is he your son?'

Stefan was staring up in open admiration at Ilse, then politely held out his hand as his father had taught him. 'My name is Stefan Jochum-Kraus.'

Laughing, Ilse shook hands with him. 'I'm very pleased to meet you, Stefan.' Then she turned to Viktoria. 'It's quite incredible, I feel I've met him before — but I can't have done, can I? He reminds me awfully of somebody I know. Don't you think so too, Peter?'

Viktoria held her breath. She forced herself not to look at Peter, dreading that he should notice the similarity between himself and her son. But before any of them could say a word, Benno returned and ruffled Stefan's hair. 'Come along, son.'

Ilse gazed at him, then shook her head ruefully. 'Of course, how silly of me. I had forgotten you and Peter are cousins. He is remarkably like you, Herr Kraus.'

Stefan nodded importantly. 'Yes, Papa and I are very similar.'

Trembling now in every limb, Viktoria took Stefan's hand again and allowed Benno to lead them over to where his father, Ernst and the rest of his family were standing, sipping champagne. She was appalled at her own behaviour, wishing she had not displayed her agitation so openly in front of Ilse. After all, what had happened between Peter and herself had not been the girl's fault.

Under any other circumstances, she would have enjoyed the wedding, for many of the guests were old friends of the Hotel Quadriga, who had stayed there before the war and enquired kindly after her mother, expressing their sincere condolences about her father's death. Still disturbed by Peter's mocking laugh and Ilse's remark about Stefan's appearance, however, Viktoria left Benno to converse with them, frequently looking at her watch and wondering how time could pass so slowly.

Much of the talk, particularly with so many army officers present, was about the Treaty of Versailles and it was after Baron Heinrich had been holding forth at some length on its iniquities, that Peter joined their group. 'I don't think any German will ever forgive the Allies the terms of Versailles, particularly not the loss of Danzig. Do you realize that nearly two million German subjects are now going to be subject to Polish rule? West Prussia and Upper Silesia have been German for nearly six hundred years, but now, Poland claims prior right to them. I tell you, we won't put up with it. Those lands are rightfully German. One day, we'll get them back.'

'Had to move out of Danzig, eh, boy?' the Baron asked. 'Where are you now?'

'Stuttgart,' Ilse told him. 'Peter and my father went there last month. Now I shall join them.'

Dreading that they were going to be posted to Berlin, Viktoria gave a small sigh of relief. If they were in Stuttgart, deep in the south of Germany, it was possible that they wouldn't see them again for years.

'Papa's recommending Peter for a position on the General Staff,' Ilse chattered on.

But I thought the General Staff and the War Office had been abolished?' Benno frowned.

'In name only,' Peter replied drily.

'And then,' Ilse continued excitedly, 'we hope that with his family connections and with Papa's influence, he may even be sent abroad, possible as a military attaché to one of our embassies. After all, one of his uncles is in the diplomatic service in Argentina.'

'Would you like to go abroad?' Benno asked.

She lifted her happy, round little face to his, her blue eyes shining. 'I'd like to do anything that helps Peter in his career.'

Viktoria hoped the Biedersteins went to Argentina and never returned.

'Pretty little thing, isn't she?' the Baron commented, as Ilse, her arm linked through Peter's, went off to mingle with other guests.

At long last, it was time for the couple to depart on their honeymoon and everyone crowded to the doors to wave them goodbye as they left amidst a shower of rice and flower petals in a chauffeur-driven limousine. To Viktoria's horror, Stefan let go her hand and rushed over to Ilse. 'Please come and see us at our hotel,' he implored.

Ilse bent down and kissed him. 'One day I'm sure we shall.'

As Stefan watched their car drive away, he turned to his mother. 'I hope she comes to see us. I like the way she laughs.'

'Oh, for heaven's sake, Stefi, I don't expect we'll ever see her again.'

He looked at her, puzzled, then he whispered, 'I love you most of all, Mama. And I like Papa much more than Uncle Peter.'

She swept him up in her arms, covering his face with kisses, her irritation vanished. 'Oh, Stefi, my little Stefi, I love you so much. Promise me you'll always love me.'

He smiled back at her. 'Of course I'll always love you, Mama.'

Watching them, Benno suddenly smiled too. He could not avoid seeing the similarity between Stefan and Peter, which even Ilse had noticed, but suddenly it did not disturb him. If Peter really were the boy's father, he was obviously not aware of it, for his offhand, arrogant attitude towards Viktoria clearly showed that he had forgotten his brief affair with her. Benno found that, rather than being intimidated by his cousin, he actually rather despised him for this. Strangely, this wedding had put his mind at rest, for Peter, now he was married, no longer posed any threat to them. Now, more than ever, Benno was determined that Stefan should have every possible advantage in life that money and influence could obtain him. Whoever's son he might be, Benno was going to lay the world at his feet.

Since the Jubilee party that summer, Luise had grown much closer to her family. It was almost as if, now they had shed their mourning for Karl, the invisible barrier had been swept away and she was, once again, included in their lives. She still spent a lot of time at Café Jochum, but since Lothar was gone it had changed. Many of the writers and artists whose company she so enjoyed had forsaken it for the cheaper and more fashionable Romanisches Café on the corner of Tauentzienstrasse. So, to Luise's relief, had Pipsi. So far as Luise knew, the affair between her and Rudi still continued, but Rudi had become an important businessman, with an office of his own in his vastly enlarged premises on the Neue Friedrich-Strasse and Luise's only contact with him was through Sepp.

Luise's problem was that she was bored. She missed Lothar and Sepp's time was fully occupied by Kraus Aviation's rapidly growing schedule of flights around the country. As she complained to him one evening, 'Everyone has a proper job except me.'

He looked round Café Jochum. 'I confess I didn't particularly like some of your bohemian friends, but they added colour to the place and I actually miss old Lothar. If he ever comes back, perhaps you should talk seriously to him about making Café Jochum into a sort of high-class Romanisches Café. After all, he has the connections and you enjoy mixing with that kind of people.'

'But goodness only knows where Lothar is and in the meantime, Sepp, I'm bored.'

'Keep your eyes open like I am and look for an opportunity. One day, when you're least expecting it, it will turn up.'

Luise smiled at him ruefully. 'Poor Sepp, are you dreadfully fed up with working for Kraus?'

He patted her hand affectionately. 'It's better than nothing and one day I still intend to fly a proper plane again.'

As always, when they met, they talked easily and at length about their problems and their plans. Eventually, Sepp looked at his watch and said, 'Well, it's time for me to go. I should be back on Wednesday. See you then?' He bent down and pecked her affectionately on the cheek, then with his jacket thrown over his shoulder, made his way jauntily out of the café.

How different he was from Rudi, Luise thought not for the first time, and how very much nicer. He had never once made an improper advance towards her, never once given her more than a brotherly kiss. In fact, she almost wished she were in love with him, simply because he was such a nice, kind person.

As the weeks went past, she followed his advice, keeping her eyes open for opportunities and it was just before Christmas that she hit upon her first idea. Walking through the silent rooms of the hotel, she noticed groups of ladies sitting chatting dispiritedly among themselves, while recently-demobilized lieutenants tried to make a glass of beer last several hours. In the afternoon, the Hotel Quadriga was not a very welcoming place. About six o'clock, as the bulk of the guests returned from their business, it took on new life. The bar filled, the restaurant grew busy, and a little later, the orchestra started to play.

When she commented on this to her mother, Ricarda said dreamily, 'The English have a very different life-style. After a cooked breakfast, they have coffee at about eleven o'clock, luncheon at about one, tea at five o'clock, then...

'Tea at five o'clock? What does that consist of?'

'Tea, served in bone china of course. Cucumber sandwiches and dainty cakes.'

'If the men are working, it must be the ladies who take five o'clock tea?'

'You could say that. Certainly, a lady can be invited out to tea on her own. She doesn't need a male companion.'

'Mama, has it occurred to you that there are now far more women than men in Berlin, many of them with time on their hands, not knowing what to do with themselves? Why shouldn't we serve five o'clock tea for them at the Quadriga?'

'What a lovely idea.'

Benno seized upon it with alacrity, when Luise approached him with it that evening over supper. 'Why on earth haven't we thought of it before?'

'Because the problem wasn't there before,' Viktoria pointed out, a trifle acidly. She was now six months pregnant and starting to become rather ungainly. 'All these women are a post-war phenomenon. Well, I haven't the time or the energy to organize five o'clock teas.'

'But I have,' Luise told her gently. Poor old Vicki seemed to be suffering far more with this baby than she had with Stefan.

'What do you know about it?' she snapped.

'Not much,' Luise admitted, 'so maybe it's about time I started to learn.'

Benno looked at her thoughtfully. 'Well why not? It is her idea after all. Why don't you talk to Georg, Luise?'

Since that memorable afternoon, when Georg had played his *Cornflower Waltz* in the bar, she had barely spoken to him, for he spent all his free time with Minna. When she explained her idea to him in the Palm Garden Room the following evening, he looked rather disappointed and, for the first time, she wondered if he were happy in his work. 'What sort of music do you want me to play?'

'Something light and cheerful, like you play in the evenings. Just background music in other words.'

'Of course.'

It was not until a few days later, when the notice outside the hotel reading, *FIVE O'CLOCK TEA IS NOW BEING SERVED*, had attracted a chattering crowd of women, that Luise wondered why it had to be just background music. Some of these ladies stopped by after visiting the hairdressing salon, others had been shopping, but most had left their homes with the specific purpose of taking five o'clock tea at the hotel. And their main attraction were the handsome young lieutenants who now congregated in the Palm Garden Room.

'What I'd give to dance with one of them,' the wife of one of Berlin's wealthiest stockbrokers sighed to Luise. Her ample figure was dripping with diamonds and a mink stole hung casually from her plump shoulders. 'The proprieties have to be observed, I suppose, but they must all be terribly hard up and I can't help thinking that if I paid them twenty marks, they'd be pleased to give an old lady a thrill.'

Luise stared at her in astonishment. 'You'd pay to dance with one of those young men?'

'Why not? I pay for my tea. Why shouldn't I pay for a dancing partner?' As she was speaking, two women got up from another table and started dancing together.

Luise smiled weakly, but her mind was whirling. 'Women can't ask strange men to dance with them and the officers can't afford to invite them,' she explained later to Benno. 'But if we employed them as dancing partners, everyone would profit. After all, the lieutenants come from very good families.'

'Well, I'll certainly broach the subject with them.'

The former army officers agreed with alacrity. As one of them confided bitterly to Luise, 'It wasn't what I expected when I joined the Guards, but then it's better than starvation.'

When Benno offered him extra money for his additional afternoon duties, Georg had a suggestion of his own. 'I have an old piano at home, of which I am fond, but it has nowhere near the quality of your Bechstein. I wondered if, instead of paying me a fee, you would mind if I practised here sometimes, when the hotel isn't busy.'

'Of course not. Why not come early in the afternoon or stay after five o'clock tea?'

These hours became Georg's salvation. Scornful of his position at the hotel, Pipsi took no interest in his life nor did she ever volunteer any information about her own activities. Berlin being the place it was, however, it had not taken him long to learn about Rudi Nowak and any last hopes he entertained about their marriage had been destroyed. Sadly, he was forced to acknowledge that the only reason he stayed with her was for the sake of Minna.

But during those hours alone in the Palm Garden Room, he forgot Pipsi, just as he forgot the dreadful tea-dances and the lieutenants who were now little more than paid gigolos, for since his return to Berlin, he had found a new kind of music. Prevented by the war and then by his illness from keeping abreast with developments in modern music, he had only just discovered ragtime and Dixieland's cheerful melodies. They burst upon his famished spirit like a breath of fresh air and he haunted the music shops until he had bought every available piece of sheet music in Berlin. Within weeks, he had fallen in love. Georg Jankowski had discovered jazz.

He experimented with new rhythms, making his own ingenious improvisations. Totally engrossed, he often forgot the time, emerging from his music only when waiters came to arrange the room. Then, regretfully, he put the treasured sheets back in the battered old music case that had once belonged to Uncle Franz and devoted his attention once more to Franz Lehár and Johann Strauss.

One early evening in February, however, he was disturbed, not by a waiter but by Luise. 'What's that music?' she asked, coming to stand beside him.

He smiled at her. 'Do you like it?'

'It's wonderful. Did you compose it?'

'No it's by an American composer called Scott Joplin.' Surprised by her obvious enthusiasm, he asked curiously, 'Did you really like it?'

'I've never heard anything like it before, but I think it's marvellous.'

There was no doubt that she was telling the truth and, when he went on to tell her more about the origins of ragtime and jazz, she listened attentively. When he stopped, she said regretfully, 'What a shame you can't play music like that here, but I don't think our guests would appreciate it.'

So used had he become to having nobody to share his interests and amazed at finding encouragement from such an unexpected quarter, Georg suddenly wished he could get to know Luise better. Until now, he had seen her only as the inspiration for his *Cornflower Waltz*, which by some fortuitous chance had obtained him this job. Since then, apart from their brief conversation before the tea-dances began, he had hardly spoken to her. Like her sister and brother-in-law, she belonged to the upper echelon of the hotel's hierarchy, with whom lesser mortals, like himself, seldom came in contact.

Now, he suddenly saw her as a beautiful girl, who loved music as much as he did. Without thinking what he was doing, he grasped her hand. 'I could play some pieces for you, sometime, if you'd like to hear them.'

She did not pull her hand away. Instead, she replied, softly, 'I'd like that very much.'

At that moment, the doors burst open and a bevy of waiters surged into the room. Confused, Georg released her hand and started to pack away his music. 'Well, back to Strauss,' he said, trying to appear casual.

All evening his thoughts kept returning to Luise, hoping she would return the following afternoon. Their meeting filled him with an unexpected warmth, that lasted long after he had reached home and even survived Pipsi's iciness. It even prompted him to wonder again if he and Pipsi might not get divorced.

But when he went in to look at Minna's sleeping figure, he knew the answer. Somehow or another, they would stay together for the child's sake, for he loved her more than anybody else in the world and was not going to have her life ruined by the scandal of a divorce. The mere thought filled him with horror, particularly since Pipsi would undoubtedly be given custody of her. But, as he gazed down at her, he couldn't help wondering what life would be like with Luise.

Luise's mind, also, was on Georg that evening. His music, heard by chance through the closed door, had excited her and drawn her into the room, so different was it from anything she had ever heard

424

before. She had felt that music in her soul, and had not needed Georg's explanations about syncopation and polyrhythmic innovations, but she had still hung breathlessly on his words for they had revealed him as a person, no longer just a pianist, no longer just Franz's nephew and Pipsi's husband — but a person in his own right.

Before she went to bed, she stood quietly at the back of the Palm Garden Room, listening to him playing light music for a disinterested audience and felt a moment of deep sympathy. It seemed wrong that his ability should be stifled and his vast talent not allowed free rein. She looked at his slim figure, elegant in a black frock coat, and recalled that moment when his hand had grasped hers.

Something momentous had happened to her that afternoon, but what it was she wasn't sure. She went to sleep still thinking of him and his was the name on her lips when she awoke next morning. She could not wait to see him again. Startled, she wondered if she were falling in love with him, if, possibly, she had always been in love with him, even before they had met.

Then, as she washed and dressed, she soberly reflected how dangerous the ground was that she was proposing to cross. However much she might like to listen to more of his music, she would be seeking his company for the wrong reasons. It was the musician not the music that had the greater attraction for her — and that musician was a married man.

To embark on any kind of love affair with him could only lead to great pain and unhappiness. With a strength of mind she hadn't known she possessed, Luise made sure she left the hotel as soon as the five o'clock teas were over. She was sorry if Georg was disappointed, but it seemed the most sensible course of action.

It was a long winter for Viktoria. Seeing Peter again had disturbed her equilibrium, dispelling the happiness she had felt about her coming baby. The baby made her big and cumbersome and, as March approached, instead of sleeping soundly, she found herself tossing restlessly in the double bed she shared with Benno, unable to get comfortable, waking in the middle of the night from racking nightmares.

'I wish there was something I could do,' Benno said helplessly.

'Make sure I don't get pregnant again,' she snapped.

'But I thought you were pleased about the baby.' Benno was

also tired, spending his days running the hotel and having his nights disturbed by Viktoria.

'I don't know, Benno. I just wish it would hurry up and be born.'

'It's a shame it couldn't be premature, like Stefan,' Benno said drily, and Viktoria stared at him, her heart suddenly thumping. What did he mean? Did he suspect about Stefan? But he said nothing more.

She held out her hand contritely. 'I'm sorry, Benno. I don't seem to be being a very good wife to you at the moment, do I? I'll try and improve once the baby's born.'

'I'm sorry, too. I think we're all rather overwrought. We must try and get some holiday this summer.'

The baby was due at the end of March, but during the second week of that month, dreadful rumours circulated through the city. Under the terms of Versailles, the government had called on the Free Corps to disband their troops. The most notorious, the Tobisch and Ehrhardt Brigades, were furious with this order and were, apparently — with the support of General Luettwitz and General Ludendorff — proposing to march on Berlin and install their own regime.

Viktoria was horrified at the thought of Otto returning to Berlin. 'Benno, I hate that man. I have terrible nightmares about him taking over the hotel. What's going to happen now?'

So real was her terror that Benno insisted upon calling Dr Blattner, who examined her, then said, 'It will be several weeks before your baby is born, Frau Jochum-Kraus. But you must rest. We don't want any last-minute complications, do we?'

Viktoria, however, found it impossible to rest. She had no appetite, her back ached and her mind was in turmoil. Not even Ricarda could persuade her to remain in her room and all day she blundered round the hotel, peering out of the windows onto Unter den Linden, starting at any sudden noise, saying very little, but thinking to herself, 'I don't like this baby. She's going to bring bad luck.'

The next morning, she was awake long before the rest of the hotel, dreadfully aware of the silence in the streets. Unable to stand it any longer, she dressed and went downstairs. As she reached the foyer, she heard the sound of marching boots on cobble-stones, followed by the distant roar of trucks.

Standing by the revolving doors, peering through the granite

426

portico, she saw the first troops march through the Brandenburg Gate, carrying — not the black-red-gold flags of the republic — but the black-red-white standard of the Kaiser's imperial Germany. Painted starkly on the helmets of these men was the emblem of the swastika. On and on, they marched towards the Alexanderplatz.

She was no longer alone. Benno, Ricarda and Luise were standing beside her now and behind them, all the hotel guests and staff. 'They want to restore the monarchy,' one man murmured. 'They want the Kaiser back.'

'They'll never succeed,' another vowed. 'The Kaiser can't return now.'

'Ebert will turn the army on them.'

'The army won't shoot on the Free Corps.'

'The socialists can't allow them to win. They'll have to do something.'

'The Free Corps are only demanding what we all believe to be right, They're expressing their rejection of the Versailles Treaty. Why should they be disbanded?'

But although Viktoria heard their words, her eyes were on the road, for there, passing in front of her in an armoured car, was the unmistakable figure of Otto Tobisch. He did not so much as glance in their direction as he drove past, but she was certain he knew they were standing there. A cold sweat broke out all over her and a feeling of nausea rose in her throat. Then the world went black, and with a resounding crash, she collapsed to the floor.

When she came to, she was lying on her bed, with Benno and Ricarda staring anxiously down at her. 'I've telephoned Dr Blattner,' Benno said.

She reached out a tired hand. 'I'm sorry, Benno. It was the sight of Otto, but I'm all right now.' Her body hurt from her fall and she still felt sick, but above all it was the marching boots and the swastika on Otto's helmet that haunted her mind.

After his examination, the doctor smiled at her sympathetically. 'I'm sorry, but there is nothing I can give you. All I can suggest is that you take some herb tea and just try to keep calm.'

'What's happening out there?'

'Don't worry about it.'

'But, don't you see, I have to know.' Incoherently, she babbled out the story of Otto, of how she had hated him as a child, how he had tried to rape her and then, how he had threatened them after Eitel's suicide. 'Dr Blattner, Otto Tobisch was here in the hotel just before my father died. I'm sure he caused my father's death.'

The doctor sat down and took her hand. 'I'm sorry, my dear, I didn't understand. Well, I'll tell you what I know. So far as I can gather, Defence Minister Noske fled from Berlin early this morning, so he had gone before the Free Corps even arrived. Tobisch and his men went straight to the police headquarters on the Alexanderplatz and now have, if not the support of the police, at least no active opposition from them. I believe their troops are occupying most of the ministry buildings and they have installed a man called Dr Wolfgang Kapp in the Chancellery building.'

'Have they killed anybody yet?'

'Not that I know of. So far, it all seems very peaceful.'

'But what's going to happen?'

He patted her hand. 'I don't know, my dear, but as soon as I hear anything, I promise I'll let you know. And I'll come back and see you again later today. Now, please, will you do as I ask and try to sleep?'

Intermittently, she slept. Sometimes, when she woke, she found Ricarda beside her bed. On other occasions, Benno or Luise were keeping vigil over her. All of them assured her that the city was quiet. That evening, true to his word, Dr Blattner returned. By then, Viktoria felt so wretched she cared nothing for what was happening in the city. Numbly, she allowed him to examine her and wearily accepted his prognosis that it might be days before her baby was born.

In the living room, the doctor reassured Benno about Viktoria's condition, then gratefully accepted a drink. 'It looks as if we have trouble ahead,' he said, worriedly. 'Apparently General von Seeckt has refused to allow the Reichswehr to participate in what he considers to be a purely political matter and since he considers the Free Corps to be part of the Reichswehr, he will not allow his soldiers to fire on other soldiers.'

'So the socialists are going to do nothing?' Benno asked.

'They're calling a general strike,' he replied drily. 'For once, it appears that the socialists and communists are united. I gather their theory is that if they can cripple the country, this putsch cannot succeed.'

Benno nodded wearily, 'What a way to run a country.'

Tired though he was, Benno tried to stay awake that night, as Viktoria dozed fitfully. He was worried about her and the unborn baby, and he was also worried about the hotel, the city and the whole country. He sympathized with the nationalists who wanted a return of the monarchy, but he dreaded the thought of the Free Corps gaining more power. During the long, dark hours of the night, he stared out on the city over which the republican government ought to be ruling from a position of strength, but which it had been unable to control from the very first day of its inauguration. How much longer could Berliners live in fear?

The next day, they felt the first impact of the strike, when many of their staff stayed away and no newspapers were delivered. There were no trams on the streets. During the morning, Fritz Brandt told him that the electricity had been cut off and he had switched power over to the hotel's emergency generator. A few moments later, Chef Mazzoni informed him that there was no gas and that he could, therefore, only prepare meals on the standby electric hobs. Nobody left the hotel that day, for the strike affected every part of Berlin. No civil servants reported for work, most shops were closed and there was no transport. And, that evening, as dusk drew in, no street lamps were lit. A pall of darkness settled over the city, with only the Hotel Quadriga blazing forth a beacon of light.

In the early hours of the morning, Viktoria's labour pains began. For the second night running, Benno kept a vigil beside her, his eyes red and sore from lack of sleep, all thoughts of the Kapp putsch banished from his mind, his sole concern Viktoria.

In vain, Ricarda and Nurse Bauer tried to persuade him to leave the room. But as Viktoria screamed with pain and sweat poured down her face, Benno insisted, 'We must call Dr Blattner.'

'The doctor will come if he's able to, but if he can't, I've delivered many babies in my time,' Nurse Bauer assured him.

'Benno, dear, please try and get some rest,' Ricarda urged. 'Can't you see you're upsetting Vicki? We'll call you if there's any change.'

Reluctantly, Benno gave in, sitting upright on a chair in the living room, his ears alert for any sound from the bedroom. But at six that morning, the baby had still not been born. Pale with exhaustion, Viktoria lay limply under the sheets, scarcely able to open her eyelids. 'There's something the matter. I'm going to fetch Dr Blattner,' Benno told Nurse Bauer, With no telephones working, the only way to reach the doctor was in person. But what if something happened while he was gone?

'The doctor knows how she is. He'll come as soon as he is able to. Why don't you have some breakfast first with Stefan,' she suggested, but he could see she was also worried.

Stefan seemed to be the only person immune to all the excitement. His appetite as healthy as ever, he asked, 'Papa, when is Nurse Bauer going to go and fetch the new baby?'

'Later,' Benno told him, but that morning he could not find the heart to talk, not even to Stefan. He sipped some coffee and lit a cigarette, feeling very relieved when Luise volunteered to play with Stefan in her room.

It was ten o'clock before the doctor arrived, by which time Benno's ashtray was full. 'She's been in labour for eight hours.'

With maddening slowness, the doctor took off his coat and then ushered them all, except the nurse, out of the room. After what seemed an eternity, he returned. Benno scanned his face, dreading the news that Viktoria was going to die. 'It will be a while yet,' he said, as if what was happening was the most normal thing in the world. He pulled his pipe from his pocket and lit it ponderously, billowing clouds of blue smoke into the room. 'I don't think the Kapp regime will last much longer. A lot of the Free Corps soldiers are apparently already defecting. Interesting, eh, the thought of soldiers mutinying against mutineers?'

'To hell with the bloody Free Corps!' Benno shouted. 'What about Viktoria?'

Dr Blattner stared at him, as if he was aware for the first time of his agitation. 'Herr Kraus, do you have any brandy in this hotel?'

'Bottles of it.'

'Then I'm going to prescribe a glass for your nerves. Listen, your wife's a strong woman. And there's nothing to worry about the baby being a couple of weeks premature.'

'Stefan was premature, too. She didn't have any of these complications then.'

'Was he? I don't remember that. Funny, I always thought he was a perfectly normal nine-month baby. Well, you may be right. I've delivered so many in my time, I can't remember them all.'

At that moment, Nurse Bauer put her head round the door. 'Dr Blattner, I think it's starting.'

The hour that followed was agony for Benno. He realized that the doctor had all but confirmed his worst thoughts about Stefan, but even that mattered little now. Whatever had happened in the past was nothing compared to the drama that was being enacted now in the next room. At one point, he even put his hands

430

together and prayed out loud, 'Dear God, I love Viktoria, please don't let her die.'

Then, suddenly, silence descended on the rooms, which was broken a few moments later by the wailing of a baby. A broad smile on his face, Dr Blattner came into the living room, wiping his hands on a towel. 'A daughter, Herr Kraus. My congratulations.'

Benno burst past him into the bedroom. Viktoria was lying deathly white against the sheets, their baby cradled in her arms, but Benno ignored the child. Kneeling down beside the bed, he clasped his wife's hand in his and burst into tears. 'Oh, Vicki, Vicki, thank God you're alive.'

Quietly, Nurse Bauer took baby Monika away. She could not have said why, but she was certain neither parent was going to interfere this time in her upbringing of their daughter.

Bitter, contemptuous fury surged through Otto Tobisch, as he stared out through the windows of the Viktoriastrasse headquarters of the Free Corps onto the darkened city of Berlin. Candles flickered on window sills and only here and there, in establishments like the Quadriga, did light blaze forth. The hopelessness of his situation welled up in him. It was as if Germany did not want to be saved, as if it were hell-bent on its own destruction.

His anger was aimed at the socialists who had called this crippling strike, which left Dr Kapp and the men of the Free Corps bereft of any means of publicity for their new regime and also without transportation for their troops. The socialists had deployed the only weapon left to them and it was working brilliantly in their favour. Kapp could not survive long with the country at a standstill.

Otto, however, was astute enough to realize that the socialists would not have been forced to adopt these drastic measures if they had had the Reichswehr on their side. For the first glorious day of the Kapp Putsch, when the Reichswehr had disobeyed President Ebert and Noske's orders and refused to shoot on the Free Corps, he had believed General von Seeckt was on their side, but his disillusionment had been swift. General von Seeckt might not be prepared to side with the socialists, but neither was he going to commit himself on behalf of the Free Corps. In this struggle for power, he was going to remain aloof.

He was not surprised when, next morning, General Ludendorff told him and his men, 'Kapp has fled. Word has come through from Weimar that if we move quickly, no action will be taken against us and the Reichswehr will give us protection. A new nationalist government has been installed in Munich. We shall, therefore, go to Bavaria.'

So within days, the Kapp Putsch had failed. Even with General Luettwitz and General Ludendorff in command, the Free Corps were not strong enough to defeat a nation of striking workers. Yet, with the power of the Reichswehr on their side, they would have been. Why had the Reichswehr not given their support? Even in this black hour of disappointment, Otto knew the answer. In many ways they had committed the same mistake as the Spartacists a year earlier. They had wanted to seize power too quickly and the Chancellor they had installed was a weak, unknown quantity. Kapp had not been a leader.

Surely there must be one man at least out there who was prepared to do something to save Germany in her hour of need? One day, Otto determined, he would find him — a leader who would make Germany great again.

As the men of the Tobisch Brigade marched out of Berlin, its streets were no longer empty, hung with a cloak of fear. Now, silent crowds lined Unter den Linden, watching them depart. Still very weak, Viktoria stood at her bedroom window, baby Monika in her arms, Stefan by her side. 'Why are the soldiers leaving, Mama?'

'Because we don't want them here,' she replied bitterly.

A small boy of about Stefan's age ran out from the crowd, calling something to the men, laughing. To her horror, two of the soldiers broke ranks, seized him, knocked him brutally down, then started to kick him. Instinctively, she pulled Stefan to her, trying to hide his face in her dressing gown and at that moment she saw Otto, staring up at the windows of the hotel, a look of icy hatred in his eyes.

Through the window, she heard his voice shout an order and suddenly, guns were pointed towards the portico. She screamed and threw herself, Monika still in her arms, and Stefan, down to the floor, out of range. Outside, she heard shrieks from the crowd and the staccato rattle of machine-gun fire. Then, all was silent, except for the tramping of boots on cobble-stones, as the Tobisch Brigade resumed its march through the Brandenburg Gate.

As soon as he and his men entered Munich, Otto knew he was among friends. Not only were they not jeered on the streets, but they were personally welcomed by Captain Ernst Roehm, a staff officer from the Reichswehr's District Command VII. Immediately Roehm started to speak denigratingly about the Weimar Republic and of his hatred for the November criminals who had signed the Versailles Treaty, Otto knew the Tobisch Brigade had found a home. Not for this scarred, bullnecked Captain the elitist attitude of the Prussian Reichswehr, but a burning conviction that the lower and middle classes — from which he and Otto both originated — could build a new nationalist Germany.

Captain Roehm was a founder member of the National Socialist German Workers' Party, the NSDAP as it was called for short, and already he had loosely organized other Free Corps and Stahlhelm units to silence hecklers at political meetings and to break up the meetings of other political parties. Here, the expertise of the notorious Tobisch Brigade was made more than welcome and in no time at all Otto and his men were creating brawls in beer halls throughout the city, fighting not only with their bare hands, but also with guns provided through Captain Roehm by the Reichswehr.

It was at one of these meetings that Otto first met Adolf Hitler. Propaganda chief of the NSDAP, Hitler's background was not impressive, for he came from a poor Austrian family and had only been a corporal at the end of the war. But he was still the holder of an Iron Cross won for valour in the war — and there was something immensely compelling about his blue eyes, that seemed to see straight into people's minds, and something even more hypnotic about his way of speaking.

When Otto heard Hitler address a meeting before the June elections that summer, ranting against the Versailles Treaty and the humiliating shame it had brought to the country, the weak Weimar government, socialists, communists and Jews, he knew he had finally found a politician after his own heart. Without any doubt, they wanted the same things — and, even more importantly, it appeared that Hitler was prepared to fight for them.

Otto's proudest moment came when Hitler designed a flag for the NSDAP. It was red, with a white disc in its centre containing the black swastika that the men of the Tobisch Brigade wore on their helmets. 'In red we see the social idea of the movement,' Hitler explained, 'in white the nationalist idea, in the swastika the mission of the struggle for the victory of the Aryan man.' Otto only knew that the insignia he and his men had adopted in the Baltic was the emblem that heralded the birth of a new, strong Germany.

Under Captain Roehm's unofficial command, the various Free Corps brigades and fighting groups were formed into an organization called the *Sturmabteilung* — the SA — a large private army, wearing the swastika armband over their distinctive brown shirts, that marched through the streets of Munich, instilling fear into the hearts of its citizens. But, as the months passed and nothing more happened, Otto felt an increasing sense of disappointment. It seemed that Hitler was, finally, just like every other politician — a fine orator, but not a man of action. Creating havoc in Munich was all right, but it was not enough. What was needed was to kill Germany's enemies — the enemy within.

He soon discovered he was not alone in his thinking. Other Free Corps officers, too, were impatient with the politicians of Bavaria and had already determined to dispense summary justice to all enemies of the state. They drew up a list of many hundreds of names — communists, socialists, Jews — men like Erzberger, the politician who had signed away Germany's right in the Treaty of Versailles; of Philip Scheidemann, the former Chancellor; of Walther Rathenau, the Jewish Foreign Minister, who even now was discussing the methods in which the country could honourably fulfil the terms of the Treaty and pay the bill for war reparations that the Allies had just presented, totalling 132 billion gold marks; of Theo Arendt, the private banker who was supporting him.

Every week, members of the Free Corps were given assignments — their task to seek these men out and assassinate them. Otto joined their ranks without a second thought.

Within weeks of Monika's birth, Viktoria was back behind her desk, feeling no compunction about leaving Monika in Nurse Bauer's care. She knew it was wrong, but she would never love her daughter in the same way that she loved Stefan. Apart from anything else, she would always associate the little girl's birth with the Free Corps and Otto Tobisch. Although the Free Corps had fled to Bavaria, they had constant reminders of their existence, for nearly every week the newspapers reported political murders in one part or other of the country, laying the blame for these firmly on the mercenaries. When the assassins were caught, they were given very lenient sentences, seeming to demonstrate a growing disillusionment, even in the courts, with the Weimar government.

This was reflected in the June elections, when votes swung sharply away from the Social Democrats in favour of parties to the extreme right and to the extreme left, giving the country a hung parliament. 'What we need is a strong leader,' Benno said worriedly. 'Ebert is a nonentity. And now he has no real control at all.'

But as the weeks passed, life at the hotel again resumed a pattern of normality and memories of Otto were replaced by other events of more personal impact. In September, Benno engaged Fraeulein Hilde Metz as Stefan's governess. Tall and thin, soberly dressed in grey and with a pince-nez perched on her sharp nose, Fraeulein Metz had received her training before the war in England. She filled Viktoria with foreboding, telling her, 'Oxford University is the only place for young gentlemen to be educated. We must groom him for Oxford.' Discovering another Anglophile in Ricarda, she asked, 'Don't you agree, Frau Jochum?'

'I think it's a wonderful idea,' Ricarda agreed.

'But he's only five,' Viktoria cried in dismay, unable to bear the thought of Stefan ever leaving her.

Even Fraeulein Metz and her grandiose plans for Stefan's future, however, were eclipsed by Baron Heinrich's news a month later. Those days, the Baron saw himself as the patriarch of the Kraus dynasty, which embraced at one end of the social scale the Jochums and at the other the Biedersteins. Every new addition to the family acquired for him the significance of a new subsidiary company, although it was evident that their value varied tremendously. Monika, for example, was far less important than Ernst and Trudi's second son, Norbert, born that summer. But anything to do with the Biedersteins was of such great consequence that he could not resist telephoning Benno. 'Peter and Ilse have just had a baby daughter. Her name is Christa.'

'Please convey our congratulations,' Benno said drily, while Viktoria gazed at him quizzically.

'And that's not all,' the Baron's voice boomed down the earpiece. 'They're being sent to Argentina, as they hoped. Excellent news for Kraus, because it should mean that we shall be able to fix up some armaments deals with Irogoyen's government, as well as renewing our connections with the Argentine Biedersteins.'

When the conversation was eventually ended, Benno turned to Viktoria. 'Apparently Peter has become a father for the first time.'

To her chagrin, she blushed but, as Benno went on to tell her that they were leaving Germany, she forgot her discomfiture. That terrible mistake she had made and the lie she had told Benno no longer mattered, for there was every probability she and Peter would never meet again.

Chapter Sixteen

Rudi opened his first bar, 'Hades', on the Kurfuerstendamm in January 1921 and, overnight, it became Berlin's most fashionable and controversial night club. Despite her dislike of Rudi, Luise yearned to visit it, but although she pleaded with Sepp to take her, he refused. 'I've heard a lot of nasty things about it and I'm sure it's not a suitable place for you,' he said adamantly. Luise argued for a while, then gave in, convinced he would one day change his mind.

Now Viktoria was working again, there was little for Luise to do at the hotel, but she did not really mind, for the novelty of the tea-dances had already palled on her and she much preferred the atmosphere of Café Jochum to the hotel's old-fashioned elegance. Her brief infatuation with Georg almost forgotten, her constant companion was still Sepp, who organized his flight schedule so that he stopped over in Berlin as often as possible. He was still unhappy with his job and complained of the low wages Kraus paid.

Sepp was not mean, but he was starting to feel the effects of inflation and steadily rising prices. 'You remember me talking about Goering, the last commander of the Richthofen Squadron?' he asked Luise one summer evening, sitting on Café Jochum's terrace. 'He went to Sweden after the war. Well, apparently now he's married a wealthy Swedish Countess and has gone back to Munich with her. Got mixed up with some political party down there. He promised me that if he ever heard of a job for me, he'd let me know. Well, obviously nothing will come of that now. Maybe I should go to Sweden.'

'Sepp, you know, I'd miss you dreadfully if you went.'

'You could always come with me.'

'But what would I do?'

'As my wife you wouldn't need to do anything.'

'As your wife?' Luise stared at him, open-mouthed. Then, assuming he was joking, she burst out laughing. 'Oh, Sepp, don't be silly!'

He smiled ruefully. 'I was actually being serious. Luise, we've been going out together for so long, why don't we get married? If I do decide to go abroad, you might as well come with me.'

They knew each other so well, Luise didn't wait to think through her answer. 'But I don't love you, Sepp. I like you, but I'm not in love with you.'

He didn't appear at all upset. 'Well, that's honest enough, but I think you're making a mistake. However, you never know, I might ask you again. In the meantime, you mustn't be upset if I do decide to take myself off somewhere.'

However casually his proposal had been made and cheerfully though he accepted her refusal, Luise hated the thought of having hurt him. It would, she reassured herself, have been a betrayal of their friendship to have given him any hope, but she did wish afterwards that she hadn't laughed and, in an attempt to make up, she tried to be particularly nice to him after that.

Sepp, himself, was almost relieved at her response. He knew that he couldn't afford a wife, but each time he saw Luise she seemed to grow more desirable and since he was convinced she was not the sort of girl to indulge in an extramarital affair, the simplest solution had been to propose to her. Frequently, during those next few weeks, he wished he had said nothing, for her deliberate cheerfulness and obvious determination to make amends introduced an awkwardness into their relationship. It strengthened his resolve to leave Germany, but did not solve the problem of where to go.

He seldom saw Rudi those days, but it so chanced they met shortly after this and, foolishly, Sepp mentioned his decision to him. Rudi had changed a lot since Sepp's return — his face was very pale and he had blue pouches under his eyes, as if he seldom went into the fresh air. But he was still an attractive young man — and an extremely wealthy one. 'Bored with Luise?' he asked triumphantly.

'No, I've just got the wanderlust. Been in one place too long.'

Rudi shook his head sceptically. 'You don't know how to get on with women, that's your trouble. All you and Luise do is sit around Café Jochum. Bring her to "Hades" to see my new cabaret act — it's spectacular.'

'No, thanks.'

'Sepp, I do believe you're getting middle-aged. Well, if you won't ask her, I'll invite Luise myself.'

Sepp stared at him, filled with the terrible certainty that Rudi would carry out his threat just to score off him. Pushing his reservations to the back of his mind, he conceded grudgingly, 'All right, we'll come this evening.'

So, to her surprise, Luise got her own way. Arriving on the Kurfuerstendamm, she wondered for a moment if they had come to the right place, for no sign lit up its unprepossessing entrance, only a notice advising them to ring the bell. Inside, however, a uniformed commissionaire took their coats and led them into a large, smoke-filled room, where a small man with a pointed nose and beady eyes materialized out of nowhere. 'Herr Nowak,' he said ingratiatingly, when Sepp told him his name, 'but, of course, Herr Rudi told me to expect you.' He smirked at Luise. 'I'm glad to see you've brought a lovely friend with you.'

He minced ahead of them through the room, his pungent eau de toilette wafting behind him. 'God,' Sepp muttered in disgust, 'a homosexual.'

The man showed them to a table, asking, 'Champagne for Monsieur et Madame? With Herr Rudi's compliments, of course.' Then he leered at Sepp, 'My name is Guenther Vogel, but my friends call me Little Bird. I hope you'll enjoy your evening.'

After the champagne had been served, Sepp took a deep breath. 'Well, now we're here, I suppose we may as well drink Rudi's champagne, but God, what a place.'

Luise was staring round her in fascination, determined to ignore Sepp's ill humour and enjoy herself. At first glance, it seemed little different from any other cabaret. In a corner, a band was playing and some couples were dancing closely embraced. Then, as she watched, a man slipped his hand inside the loose bodice of his partner's dress and fondled her breast. Startled, she blinked, then turned away.

It was at that moment that she noticed Pipsi, sitting by the bar, but just as she was turning to point her out to Sepp, a voice asked, 'Would you like to dance?' She looked up to see a man smiling encouragingly at her, immaculately dressed in a black dinner jacket. Sepp shrugged non-committally, so Luise took the stranger's arm. Even if Sepp didn't want to enjoy himself, she was determined to.

'Is this the first time you've been to "Hades"?' Her partner asked, drawing Luise closer to him, his face brushing her hair.

'Yes, it is.' There was something strange about his voice. Luise glanced up at his face, delicately featured and smooth, like a young boy's. Perhaps he was another like Guenther Vogel, she thought, although the way he was holding her felt anything other than disinterested. His hand crept down her hips, fondling her bottom. She moved it, returning it to her waist. A few seconds later, it returned, its intentions now obvious. Certainly not a homosexual. 'Don't be boring, dear. You feel so nice.' Then the hand changed direction, moving up towards her chest.

She snatched it away. 'No.'

'If you don't want fun, dear, why are you here?'

'Would you mind taking me back to my table?' It was only when he helped her to her seat that she noticed his hands. They were slim and graceful, like a girl's. She took a large gulp of champagne.

'Not your type, Luise, darling?' Rudi asked, startling her. Perching himself on the edge of their table, he grinned at her mockingly. 'But, of course, you like your men to be masculine, don't you, darling?'

Instead of replying, she looked away from him around the room. Long-legged, slim-hipped, with curvaceous bosoms and shoulder-length hair, two figures at the bar looked entirely feminine to her eyes. One of them nudged the other and they smiled towards their table, ignoring her, but fluttering their eyelashes invitingly at Rudi and Sepp. 'Transvestites,' Sepp said, distastefully.

Rudi laughed. 'Wait until you see Anita Berber. I can assure you she's a real woman.' Then he stood up. 'Well, darlings, have fun. I'll see you later.'

'You mean those aren't really girls?' Luise asked Sepp incredulously.

'No more than your partner was a man.'

Suddenly, she wished they hadn't come. There was something nasty about the place. The 'man' who had just danced with her. Rudi. All the other people in the room. Scantily-clad waitresses were flittering among guests who were becoming ever more intoxicated. A portly, florid-faced gentleman was drinking champagne from his partner's slipper. A girl — or was it a boy? — danced on the table, collapsed at the end of its solo act in a dead faint and had to be carried out to recover. Men took off their jackets. Women removed their stoles. Shoulder straps slipped to reveal semi-naked breasts. 'Let's go,' she whispered to Sepp.

He nodded and started to stand. 'Surely you're not leaving

now?' a voice asked and they looked round to find Pipsi standing beside them, her long black hair streaming over her bare shoulders. She held a tiny paper sachet in one hand. 'Look what Rudi's just given me.' She pulled a chair up to the table. 'Do you know what this is?' She smiled dreamily, 'It's cocaine.'

With a groan, Sepp sat down again. 'Pipsi, have you ever taken cocaine before?'

'No, but Rudi tells me it's going to change my life.'

He reached out to snatch it from her. 'Don't do it. Please, Pipsi!'

'Oh, Sepp, you're such a spoilsport. Everyone takes cocaine nowadays.' She tipped a little of the powder onto the palm of her hand and sniffed delicately.

'Have you been drinking too?'

'At least a bottle of champagne.'

At that moment, the lights dimmed and a single spotlight shone on the stage. While the band played a haunting kind of eastern music, six girls came into view, swathed from head to toe in flimsy, transparent material, their figures silhouetted through their robes. While five of them danced, the sixth took her place on a kind of throne, perched high above them like a buddha. Voices around Luise murmured, 'Anita Berber.' Despite herself, Luise could not take her eyes from the spectacle. One by one, as they danced, the girls shed their trailing garments, until they were naked except for a kind of loincloth, concealing their most private parts, and a star over each nipple. They lay on the stage, propped on one elbow, their bent legs pointing towards the central figure on whom the spotlight now uniquely focused.

With sinuous movements, Anita Berber stood up in time to the music, unwrapping the fine layers of material. Her hair fell forward, concealing her upper body, as she bent to unpin a brooch at her waist, then tantalizingly unwound her skirt. Pipsi's hand seized Luise's. Her lips were parted, her tongue slightly protruding. The final piece of material fell to the floor and Anita threw back her head, so that she was revealed in her nudity to her audience. From all around Luise, there was a sharp intake of breath.

The girl was dancing now, but Luise was no longer looking at her, for Pipsi had loosened her grasp on her hand and, in an almost trancelike state, a beatific smile on her face, was standing up and gradually removing her own clothes. 'Pipsi,' Luise whispered urgently, grabbing at her wrist, but Pipsi shook her away. Stepping

441

out of her dress, she moved across the room to the stage and joined in the dance.

Suddenly, Luise could take no more. She looked at Sepp and he nodded. Quietly, they made their way through the room and into the street. 'I'm sorry,' Sepp said quietly, 'I should have realized it was going to be like that.'

'It doesn't matter,' she told him, but she knew it did. The people in the bar, Anita Berber's performance and Pipsi's behaviour had all shocked her, but above all, Rudi's words had filled her with fear. Sepp believed her to be pure and innocent — what would he do if he ever discovered she had been to bed with his perverted brother? From the bottom of her heart, she wished she had never insisted on going to the nightclub.

A couple of days later, however, she even forgot 'Hades' in her excitement at the return of Lothar Lorenz. He burst into the Hotel Quadriga amidst a flurry of trunks, suitcases, page boys and commissionaires, plumper and more ebullient than ever, his monocle still firmly clamped in his eye, but dressed in a garishly-checked golfing outfit. 'Hi, folks!' he exclaimed with an American accent. 'How's life in little old Berlin?'

That evening in Café Jochum, it seemed almost like the old days again, as he sat between Luise and Sepp and plied them with wine. Almost, but not quite, for as Lothar pointed out in shock, Café Jochum's prices had changed dramatically since they had last sat there. 'Everything's so cheap here.'

'Cheap?' Sepp cried. 'You call this cheap? This bottle of wine cost about eight marks when you were last here, now it's over a hundred!'

'But that's only about an American dollar. You couldn't buy a bottle of wine, not of this quality, in America for a dollar. What's happening here?'

'Inflation,' Sepp told him grimly. 'Lothar, you'd do better not to exchange your American dollars. They're becoming worth more than gold dust.'

Luise shifted impatiently on her seat. 'Oh, stop being so boring and talking about money. Lothar, have you really been to America?'

'Yes, ma'am', he drawled, 'I've been to California. Sepp, if you ever grow tired of Berlin, that's the place for you. I met a fellow out there, a German, except that he's a naturalized American now, called Erich Grossmarck. Can you imagine what he's doing? In

442

some tin hangars, stuck in the middle of the desert, he's making movies! I tell you, people, films are the thing of the future.'

Luise grinned. So Dada was a thing of the past — Lothar's latest enthusiasm was moving pictures. 'What kind of films?'

'That's just the point! He's making aviation pictures. Seems this guy helped make training films for the army during the war and was so excited by aviation, he now makes commercial films about flying. Apparently, there's quite a demand for them.'

'You mean he's actually got planes in those hangars?' Sepp demanded, excitedly.

'And real pilots, from all over the world, flying them! You should see them, Sepp, looping the loop, gunning each other down — every kind of stunt you can imagine.'

'They weren't stunts during the war, they were real then.'

'Well, the way Grossmarck makes those films, they look real now. He doesn't pay all that well, of course, about fifty dollars a stunt, I believe. Though I suppose by German standards now, that's quite a lot of money.'

'What kind of man is Grossmarck?'

'He looks a bit like Baron Kraus, but shorter, and he goes round everywhere in a Prussian general's uniform, you know, jackboots, monocle, medals and the rest. He always acts the part of the enemy general in his war films. But his ambitions don't stop there. These movies are just a means for him to make money until he can make the sort of movie he really wants to. Yes, I'm sure that, one day, Grossmarck will be famous. He's not just talented — he's a genius.'

Sepp wasn't listening to him any more. He was staring out of the café windows up into the sky, remembering the feel of an open cockpit, the wind in his face, the rattle of the struts and the sweet smell of a plane's exhaust.

He was still thinking of Erich Grossmarck, when he bumped into Rudi a few days later on the Kurfuerstendamm, near 'Hades'. As memories of that dreadful evening flooded back to him, his brother's words brought him quickly down to earth. 'You and Luise left very early,' Rudi jeered. 'Don't tell me Luise pretended to be shocked?'

'Pretended? She *was* shocked. After all, it wasn't exactly the kind of performance you'd expect to appeal to an innocent young girl from her sort of background,' Sepp replied indignantly.

'Oh, Sepp, you really are naïve, aren't you? Innocent young

girl.' He stared at him incredulously. 'Don't tell me you've never been to bed with Luise? I don't believe it! God, I had her when she was still almost a schoolgirl!'

Seized with a blinding rage, Sepp had to clench his fists in his pockets to stop himself striking at his brother. 'If you were half a man, I'd hit you!' Rudi laughed and Sepp looked at him unhappily, suddenly sensing that he was telling the truth. 'Did you really go to bed with her?' he asked reluctantly.

'Of course, I did. What's more, she was a virgin. But, I don't think you've missed much, brother dear. She wasn't very exciting.'

Sepp stared at him for a long time, disappointment welling up inside him. In this confused, post-war world, Luise had seemed to him the only person on whom he could depend — and now, it seemed, she too had let him down. No wonder she had laughed at his proposal, for she must have been laughing at him throughout their relationship, perhaps even mocking him, with Rudi, behind his back. He let his eyes linger contemptuously on his brother, then he said, quietly, 'Goodbye, Rudi. I doubt we shall ever meet again.'

'But, Sepp ...'

He was already gone, walking briskly towards the Post Office, where he put through a telephone call to the Hotel Quadriga. 'Please may I speak to Herr Lorenz?'

That evening, he did not meet Luise, but, in a quiet bar off the Leipzigerstrasse, he and Lothar came to an agreement. The Swiss gave him a letter of introduction to Erich Grossmarck and lent him his fare to California, which Sepp promised to pay back into Lothar's American account. 'Thank you, Lothar, you've no idea what this means to me.'

With unexpected understanding, Lothar replied, 'I think I have. Aeroplanes have always been the first love of your life, Sepp, just as art has always been mine. If I thought you and Luise would make a success of marriage, I wouldn't encourage you in this, but you're wrong for each other, just as my wife and I were wrong for each other. Go and make a new start. Maybe, in ten years' time, you'll come back and things will be different.'

As soon as she saw him the following day, Luise knew Sepp had made his decision. 'You're going to America to work for this man, Grossmarck, aren't you?'

Sepp nodded. He wanted to ask her if Rudi had told the truth, but he also knew the question was superfluous. Lothar was right —

his real love was flying. It always had been and always would be. 'What will you do?'

She was silent for a moment, then she gave a bright smile. 'Now that Lothar's back, I may talk to him about making Café Jochum into the sort of place we talked about before — you know, an upper-class café for artists.'

He made excuses to leave her early, kissing her quickly on the cheek and walking away with a jaunty, 'Good luck, Luischen, and see you again soon.'

Yet as he walked out of the café, she had a dreadful premonition that he was walking out of her life. For a moment, she was tempted to run after him and plead, 'Take me with you, Sepp!' But she stopped herself, for, deep inside, she knew it was too late.

The first thing Luise did after Sepp left was to have her hair shingled. To her regret, it was too curly to be cut into a pageboy style, but losing her heavy ringlets gave her a luxurious sense of freedom. For a week or two, she wandered aimlessly around, then, when a letter arrived from California telling her that Sepp had been engaged by Grossmarck, she decided to keep her promise and start work.

She said little to her family about Sepp's departure, so that it was impossible for them to know her true feelings. One result became, however, immediately visible, for she threw herself into the life of the hotel and Café Jochum with a determination she had never shown before. She demanded that Viktoria explain the intricacies of the hotel's reservations system, the kitchen, the bar and the restaurants, and the administration that was needed to make the hotel run smoothly.

Benno, delighted by her interest, described pricing structures, purchasing budgets, the difference between profit and loss, and utterly confused her by putting all these items into balance sheet form. Then, he lectured her at length on the problems the hotel was encountering through inflation. 'Prices are changing from one day to the next now,' he explained, 'which means neither the hotel nor Café Jochum can maintain a stable price tariff.'

'I don't think I actually understand what inflation means.'

Benno smiled at her sympathetically, trying to find a simple answer. 'It means that the mark is becoming worth less and less. In some ways, it's not a bad thing, for it means Germany can sell goods abroad at prices much lower than those of our foreign

445

competitors — and it means an increase in foreign visitors to Germany, because they can buy much more with their money than they could before.'

'Like Lothar? He says how cheap everything is here.'

'That's right. Lothar's dollars are useful to him — and to us. In fact, we're asking people to pay their bills in dollars, if they can. Marks lose their value almost overnight, but dollars don't.'

Luise's first inkling of how inflation was affecting other people came from Max Patschke. Max was sixty-one now, approaching retirement age, and he confided in Luise his dreams for a small cottage in the country. 'I know just the place, Miss Luise. It's outside Potsdam, right near a lake. But now, I don't know I'll ever be able to afford it. You see, it costs me more and more just to live every day, even in my modest way. Already, I'm being forced to spend my capital.'

'Max, that's dreadful. Isn't there anything you can do about it?'

'No, Miss Luise. You see, I'm paid from a percentage of the restaurant takings. Now, Herr Benno is putting up the prices every day, but by the time I've been paid my share and put it in the bank, it doesn't seem to be even half its original value.'

Then, a few days later, he took her confidentially to one side and told her, excitedly, 'I shall be all right now, Miss Luise. Don't you worry about me any more. Listen to this.' He pulled a piece of paper from his pocket and explained, 'I've become a partner in a consortium with a man called Max Klante. Since he's another Max, he must be a good sort, don't you think? Well, he's devised an excellent scheme. What he's doing is asking for business partners to invest in his horse-racing business, and, what's more, he's promising us all three hundred per cent interest!'

Even to Luise this seemed high. 'Isn't that rather a lot?'

'I thought so, too, but I've had my first interest payment and that's what he's sent me. Three hundred per cent. If he goes on like this, I'll be able to buy two cottages in Potsdam!'

As the weeks went by, Max continued to treat her to snippets of news about Max Klante. 'That man's a genius, Miss Luise. He's got his own newspaper, now. Look at it. *The Riding News.* I've just reinvested my last interest payment in him.'

'Max, are you sure that was wise?'

'Look here, Miss Luise. If I leave my money in the bank, it's just going to disappear. So why not give it to Max Klante to gamble on the horses? He knows what he's doing.'

In return for his confidences, she admitted to Max her ambitions for transforming Café Jochum. He nodded sagely. 'I think you're right. I've always had a fondness for Café Jochum, but after he built the Hotel Quadriga, the Herr Direktor seemed to lose interest in it. It's just become another café, hasn't it? Of course, what he should have done was move it to the Kurfuerstendamm. Well, perhaps if he'd lived, that's what would have happened.'

Encouraged by his support, Luise ventured to mention her ideas to Lothar, who grasped them with enthusiasm. 'Oh, I can see it now, Luise darling. You need one of the Bauhaus architects, Gropius, Mies van der Rohe — or, even better, Erich Mendelsohn. He designed the Einstein Observatory Tower at Neubabelsberg.'

'Why, if we built something like that, we'd have the most controversial building in Berlin. Do you know Erich Mendelsohn?'

'I know everybody, my sweet. And what's more, these architects and artists are nearly penniless at the moment. I'm sure he'd work just for his keep. Imagine, we could hang the most beautiful pictures on the walls — all the latest works by Kandinsky, Klee, Kokoschka. What a challenge!'

'There's only one problem. We don't have a site to build it on.'

Lothar looked glum. 'No, not even I can afford a building on the Kurfuerstendamm. However, maybe if we talked to Benno?'

'We could try, I suppose, but from the way he's talking at the moment, I don't think the hotel is doing that well.'

To their surprise, he took them seriously. 'So that's why you've suddenly started to take such an interest in business, is it, Luise?'

'Benno, imagine a new, modern building on the Kurfuerstendamm, something really striking, in concrete, chrome and glass.'

'Lothar's introduced you to Bauhaus, has he?' Benno asked drily.

'You know about Bauhaus?'

'I keep my eyes and ears open. You see, I think your idea has quite a lot to commend it. I don't honestly see how we can afford to make any changes at the moment, but I'll certainly bear it in mind.'

'Perhaps if we sold the Potsdamer Platz?'

'That would have to be your mother's decision, of course, but even if we did, I doubt we could afford a new café of the type you're describing. Don't forget the hotel mortgages become repayable in 1923 and that's in just over a year's time.'

Benno himself introduced the subject casually over supper one evening. Ricarda listened thoughtfully, then said, 'I rather agree with Luise. It is a shame that Café Jochum has been neglected and I don't see any reason why we shouldn't move it to a new site, so long as there is still one Café Jochum in Berlin.'

'But surely you don't expect to run the café on your own, Luise?' Viktoria demanded.

'Good heavens, no, Vicki. It's the building I'm interested in — and the people. Oskar Braun would still have to manage it. I just know the sort of atmosphere I'd like to create.'

'It doesn't sound as if it's going to fit our conventional image at all. Café Jochum has always been very traditional.'

Luise tossed her auburn curls. 'Vicki, look at you, with your hair still in braids, you really do still belong to the nineteenth century! But I'm a child of the twentieth century. I know my ideas are right for my time.'

As Viktoria looked indignant, Ricarda smiled. 'Benno, why don't we bear Luise's ideas in mind, at least? Maybe you could discuss them with Theo Arendt and Dr Duschek and see what they say? Then, depending upon what happens with the country's economy, maybe we should consider a change of direction.'

'But, Mama ...' Viktoria exclaimed.

'Many people said we were mad to build the Hotel Quadriga,' Ricarda reminded her. 'Once, it too was ahead of its time.'

During the months that followed, Viktoria had scant opportunity to pay attention to Luise's plans for a new café, for the hotel absorbed almost every minute of her day and it was only with difficulty that she managed to steal time to spend with Stefan and Monika. Now, more than ever, she appreciated the advantages of being married to Benno, for he seemed actually to enjoy coping with the grave financial conditions that were starting to prevail.

When she commented on this, he laughed. 'You should be thanking my father and Theo Arendt, because they warned us what was going to happen — and advised us what to do about it — though I don't think even they thought things were going to become this extreme. Look, this morning's exchange rate was four hundred marks to the dollar.'

'I don't really understand how the exchange rate helps us.'

'It's quite simple really — we take out credits in marks, buy dollars with them, then repay the credits with devalued marks. In other words, we're quite simply speculating against the dollar.'

448

'And what about our marks?'

'They just become worth less and less. You realize that we're extremely lucky — both to have been given good advice — and also with the business we're in. At least our sort of guests also have dollar accounts. No, the hotel won't come to any harm from inflation, but I fear a lot of other people are going to suffer badly.'

To Viktoria's horror, she learned that Max Patschke was one of these. It was the Head Waiter's pride to serve personally all members of the family when they ate in the restaurant and he was pouring her coffee one summer morning, while she opened her newspaper to catch up on the day's news. There, the stark headline hit her: *BOOKIE MAKES OFF WITH HOUSEWIVES' SAVINGS.*

Beside her, Max's tray fell from his hands with a shattering crash. Shocked, she looked up to find him staring at the paper, white-faced and open-mouthed, shaking his head in disbelieving horror. 'Max, what on earth's the matter?'

'It does say Max Klante, doesn't it?' he whispered.

Quickly, she scanned the news item, which told the story of a bookmaker, who had taken peoples' savings with the promise of giving them three hundred per cent interest on their investment. Now, of course, unable to fulfil his promises, he had been bankrupted. 'Max, you didn't invest in him?'

Numbly, Max nodded. 'To begin with, he paid, but recently, there was nothing. I wrote to him, but I didn't get any reply. I didn't know what to think ...'

She got up from the table, signalled a waiter to clear away the debris and led Max into her office. 'Oh, Max, why did you do it?'

He sank into a chair, a bent, weary old man. 'I suppose I was a fool, but I so wanted my little cottage in Potsdam.'

She poured him a brandy, putting her arm round him as she would a child, while he drank. 'Did you invest all your savings in Klante?'

'Nearly everything,' he replied, almost inaudibly.

'Max, I'm sorry. I'll talk to Herr Benno. Maybe he can help.'

'No, Frau Viktoria, I don't want charity. At least I've still got a job. I'll be all right.'

She tried to persuade him to take the rest of the day off, but he wouldn't hear of it. 'I'll be all right,' he kept saying.

For weeks afterwards, however, he still looked like a pale ghost of his former self. His hands shook and his limp from the trench foot he had suffered at the end of the war grew more pronounced. 'He really ought to retire,' Benno told Viktoria worriedly. 'We can't have him hobbling round the restaurant like that. He looks dreadful.' But he said nothing to Max and gradually, to their relief, the old man seemed to recover.

Nobody could fail, those days, to be aware of the growing unrest among the ordinary people. Like Max Patschke, they were watching their savings diminish and were once again reduced to a diet of turnip coffee and turnip cutlets. Many small companies, unable to keep up with rising costs, were going bankrupt and, every day, more and more unemployed people joined in demonstrations that marched along Unter den Linden demanding that the government do something to help them.

Nor was there any abatement in the political murders that continued to make front-page headlines in the newspapers. In August of the previous year Matthias Erzberger, the politician who signed the Versailles Treaty, had been assassinated. In June 1922, rumours circulated that an attempt had been made on the life of the former Chancellor Philip Scheidemann and, only days later, the Foreign Minister, Walther Rathenau, was gunned down in Berlin itself — because he said Germany should fulfil the terms of the Versailles Treaty, but also, without any shadow of doubt, because he was a Jew. Benno was horrified, for he admired Rathenau greatly. 'He was one of our most capable politicians. What do these madmen hope to achieve by murdering him?'

Shortly after this, Baron Heinrich paid one of his infrequent business visits to Berlin for a meeting with Theo Arendt. Looking grosser and more affluent than ever, he was in expansive mood, dispensing advice with a free hand. 'You should do what I'm doing,' he told Benno and Viktoria over dinner on his first evening. 'A lot of small companies simply can't stand rising costs and are going to the wall. Kraus Industries are buying them up for next to nothing. Maybe you should consider buying up some small hotels.'

'We are thinking of opening another café,' Benno admitted.

The Baron rubbed his hands. 'Excellent! I believe if you wait just a bit longer, you'll be able to buy property extremely cheaply. People just aren't going to be able to survive, you know.'

Viktoria frowned, thinking of Max. 'It seems wrong, somehow, that we are profiting from inflation, while others are suffering such fearful hardships.'

Her father-in-law waved her objections aside. 'Nonsense, my dear Viktoria. We all have the same opportunities, but some of us know how to use them and others don't. By taking over these small companies, for instance, Kraus Industries are doing the workers a favour, because if it weren't for us, they would be unemployed. Here, at the Quadriga, you are keeping people in employment that they wouldn't otherwise have. No, my dear, we represent stability for the country.'

He also told them about some of his other projects. 'Work will soon start on my new transatlantic liner. Think we'll call her the *Countess Julia*, Benno, in honour of your mother. It's good to think that long slipway up at Kraushaven will be in use again and it will be useful to have our own links with America because we're going to be doing a lot of business there in the future. The Arendt Bank has already opened a branch in New York and I want to talk to Theo about my quite considerable shareholdings in American companies.'

After his meeting, the Baron invited Theo back to the hotel for dinner and it was while the two men were walking through the foyer towards the restaurant that Viktoria heard one of the porters mutter to a colleague, 'Look, that's Arendt, another of those bloody Jews who were at Versailles.'

She found it impossible to remain still that evening for, since Theo's arrival, a strange tension pervaded the atmosphere. At about nine, Luise arrived back early from Café Jochum, her face white. 'Vicki, someone just came into the café and said they've seen Otto Tobisch in Berlin.'

Up and down the foyer Viktoria paced until, at last, Baron Heinrich and Theo emerged from dinner, then, trying to appear calm, she approached them. 'We've just heard Otto Tobisch is in Berlin.'

The Baron shrugged nonchalantly, but Theo paled. 'Who are they after this time?' He turned to the Hall Porter. 'Have my chauffeur bring my car round immediately.'

They stood on the steps to watch him drive away and at that moment a hail of bullets rained into his limousine, shattering glass and tyres, so that the car skidded uncontrollably towards the central avenue of lime trees. 'Theo!' Viktoria cried, racing across the road. As she went, she saw the sturdy figure of a man, clutching a rifle in his arms, run from the shelter of the trees towards the Brandenburg Gate. 'That's him! Catch him!'

451

While people chased in pursuit, Viktoria wrenched open the door of the car. 'Theo?' There was a stifled groan, then slowly Theo's bent body righted itself. A cut gashed his forehead and blood was pouring down his face, but otherwise neither he nor his chauffeur seemed hurt. Already a crowd was gathering, shouting and gesticulating in horror and relief.

'Did they catch him?' Theo asked.

'It was Otto, I know it was Otto. I'd recognize him anywhere.' She helped Theo back into the hotel, where Herr Brandt was already telephoning for a doctor and the police. After Dr Blattner had examined Theo and a policeman had taken statements, she asked, 'Why did he want to kill you, Theo?'

'Because I'm a Jew. Because they believe I'm to blame for the trouble Germany is in and am profiting from it.'

'But aren't we as well? From everything Benno tells me, we're profiting from inflation. So, for that matter, is Baron Heinrich. Why didn't Otto try to murder him?'

'There's a difference,' Theo told her quietly. 'You see, Vicki, you and the Krauses are Germans.'

'But so are you.'

'Not in the eyes of men like Otto Tobisch, Vicki. To them, I am first and foremost a Jew.'

Otto was arrested later that night, rifle in hand, waiting for a train at the Anhalter Station. He did not even attempt to deny the charge of attempted murder. 'Arendt is a Jew,' he declared. 'He's an enemy of the state.'

Shaken to the marrow by the whole event, Viktoria said, 'He's a madman. He tried to murder Theo. Surely they must hang him?'

Otto, however, was not hanged, but merely sentenced to one year's imprisonment in a Brandenburg penitentiary. Viktoria was appalled, but at least she knew that for the next year she would be able to sleep in peace.

Ever since Olga Meyer had fled from Berlin after the failed January Revolution in 1919, she had remained quietly in Munich, conscious of her danger should Otto Tobisch discover her whereabouts. They had been dreadful years, for Kurt Eisner's socialist republic had been toppled shortly after her return, with Kurt himself assassinated, and the soviet that had then been established had lasted scarcely a month. Shortly after that, her father had died, leaving her mother a pale ghost of her former self. Olga was sorry for her, but also impatient with her grief, for since Reinhardt's death people did not seem to matter to her very much.

In July, however, she gave birth to Reinhardt's son and everything changed. Once again, her life had a purpose, for she was determined that through Basilius her husband's dreams of a communist Germany would be realized. By then, the government of Bavaria was becoming increasingly right-wing, providing a refuge for the Free Corps, Patriot Leagues and other nationalist sympathizers. Even without the danger of Otto, to admit to being a communist was tantamount to signing one's own death warrant. So for the first three years of Basili's life, other than maintaining a discreet correspondence with old comrades, Olga took no active political role.

Then, Otto was arrested and, weeks later, her mother, who had long been ailing, finally died. At last, she was free to escape with Basili to Berlin. Here, as a hero of the Revolution, she was greeted with fervour and immediately found a job writing articles for the *Rote Fahne* and incendiary leaflets to be handed out among the city's workers. As before, she made her home in the tenement blocks of Wedding, where a pall of sulphurous smoke from Kraus Chemie still hung over grey washing hanging in courtyards where the sun never penetrated. But with horror, she soon realized conditions were even worse than during those dreadful last months of 1918. Many labourers had no work and those who were employed were earning scarcely enough to live on, let alone feed their large families. Many were being forced to pawn even their meagre sticks of furniture just to buy their next meal. The marks they were given decreased in value as they went from the pawnshop to the market stall.

For them, Olga's message had more meaning than ever. 'Workers of the world, we must unite against the capitalist oppressors!' she cried in the hall in Wedding, where hundreds had crowded to hear her speak. 'The Russian Revolution was the first step in the great world Revolution. We are no longer talking about dreams, comrades, but about reality. Now is the time to take action and that action is to strike. Down your tools and show your support against the industrialists who are exploiting you!

'Is Baron Heinrich von Kraus starving? No, comrades, the Baron is richer than ever before. In the last two years, he has bought over two hundred — two hundred, I repeat — small companies, which have been crippled by inflation. But do his profits find a way into your pockets? Has he increased your wages? Has he provided food for your families? I say to you, comrades, lay down your tools and strike for better rights.'

After one such meeting, a small, grey-haired, defeated-looking woman hesitantly plucked her sleeve. 'Frau Meyer, everything you tell us is all very well, but it just won't work. You see, all we care about is how to live from one day to the next. If my husband went on strike, we'd starve even worse than we are now.'

It was then Olga remembered the soup kitchen she had run during the war. What better way to help the people of Wedding, to gain votes for her party and to show up the Baron's rapacity than by opening a co-operative for her people? It could not be financed by the Party, for their funds were in no way large enough, but it could be paid for by the people themselves.

Soon, money had little meaning in Wedding. Plumbers, carpenters, dressmakers, artisans of all kinds paid for their keep by their services, provided with the basic necessities of life by people who, from one source or another had access to vegetables, soap, flour and salt. They did not live well, but as least they did not starve.

Before long, Olga knew all the people in her block, but the couple who intrigued her most lived in the dingy apartment beneath her own. They were a former Kraus labourer and his daughter, both with wiry black hair and eyes and coffee-coloured skin hinting at negro ancestry, but whereas Adam Anders was tall and spare, his daughter, Emmy, aged no more than fourteen, was very short and composed of little more than skin and bones. One day, meeting her on the stairs, Adam Anders pushed her forward. 'Here, Emmy, you tell Frau Meyer what you been telling me.'

Emmy stared at him from huge, frightened eyes. 'No, it isn't right. I won't do it.'

Adam Anders shook his head in exasperation. 'My Emmy's just got a job,' he told Olga. 'She's a kitchen maid in a posh hotel on Unter den Linden and she says the food they've got there is beyond belief. She says just the waste they throw out would feed half of Wedding.'

With a surge of excitement, Olga asked, 'What hotel is this, Emmy?'

'The Hotel Quadriga,' the girl whispered.

'While we're trying to make do on turnips and old potatoes, they're guzzling themselves stupid. I say she should bring home whatever she can lay her hands on,' Adam Anders said belligerently.

'But I couldn't take it. That would be stealing.'

Olga shook her head. 'Emmy, you can't steal what is rightfully yours and we have as much right to that food as anyone in the hotel.'

'See,' Adam Anders told her roughly, 'it's our right. Now, you see that you bring something home every day, or I'll throw you out on the street. You got a duty to us now.'

From then on, when Emmy returned home her pockets were weighted down with sausages, fruit, coffee, chocolate and soap, all rifled from the hotel's shelves. Soon, her father had organized a gang of men to meet her near the service exit, so that she could return for more. If anybody noticed the disappearing food, they said nothing.

Soon, he had wheedled out of her the exact layout and time-table of the Quadriga's kitchens, including the fact that the key to the main storeroom was often left in the door. 'You borrow that key, so I can get a duplicate made. One day, we'll have the lot.'

'No, Father, I can't.'

'You do what I say or I'll beat you black and blue and throw you in the gutter,' he threatened, raising his fist.

So, one terrifying day, when Chef Mazzoni's back was turned, she borrowed the key. Nobody noticed.

'You're a credit to the Party,' Olga Meyer told her, but Emmy herself just grew thinner, her small face with its halo of black hair even more pinched, and blue bags under her eyes.

Of course Viktoria and Benno heard of Olga's return, but the first they knew of Grete's death was when Ricarda's Christmas letter to her was returned with a note from a neighbour giving the news. Olga's lack of family feeling increased their distrust of her. But since Benno had no involvement in Kraus except for the receipt of his ever increasing dividends on his shareholding, her activities did not affect them.

They had far more important matters on their minds. By January 1923, menus at the Hotel Quadriga and Café Jochum were no longer produced with prices on them, but Benno provided the staff with tables to calculate the new daily tariffs. There were now about seven thousand marks to the dollar and a cup of coffee that had cost a mark eighteen months earlier now cost a thousand marks.

Then, in the middle of the month, an event occurred which paled all their past troubles into insignificance, for French troops marched over the border, invaded and occupied the Ruhr. The newspapers were full of bloody battles being fought between factory workers and French soldiers, with many people killed. As soon as he read the news, Benno telephoned Essen, concerned about the safety of his mother and his brother's two small boys. 'Are you all right?' he asked his father anxiously.

'Of course we're all right,' the Baron's voice boomed down the telephone.

'But why have the French invaded?'

'Because we can't make these damned reparations payments. Even before inflation, they were ridiculous, now they're just impossible. But the French won't see reason.' Despite the telephone line, Benno caught a note of satisfaction in his voice that made him wonder whether he and his fellow industrialists might not have deliberately made it impossible for the reparations payments to be effected.

'But why should they do that?' Viktoria asked later, when Benno expounded his theory to her.

'Father's profiting all ways. Because of inflation, he's buying up defunct companies all round — and now he isn't having to supply the coal and manufactured goods that formed part of the reparations payments. I shouldn't be a bit surprised, however, if he isn't still selling those same items to the French — for a profit.'

Certainly, whenever they spoke on the telephone, the Baron did not seem unhappy, even when the entire workforce in the Ruhr went on strike. 'We're calling it passive resistance. The French will soon get tired of it and, in the meantime, the government is, of course, paying us compensation for our lost production.'

By this time, however, Benno had scant time to pay attention to the troubles in the Ruhr, for life in Berlin was taking on a totally unreal aspect. The value of the mark plummeted daily, dropping to eighteen thousand to the dollar upon the occupation of the Ruhr, then losing tens of thousands overnight. Not just the working classes, but the middle classes, trying to live on fixed incomes, were being driven to the wall, forced to sell not just their jewellery and family heirlooms to survive, but frequently their very houses, thankful to receive even a few dollars in compensation to enable them to live from day to day.

With his shrewd Kraus mind, Benno was not slow to see the advantages to the Hotel Quadriga. The outstanding mortgages of five million marks were rapidly becoming worth little more than the paper they were written on and he had little worry now about being able to repay his father-in-law's debts. In July, when there were an incredible one million marks to the dollar, Benno paid off the mortgages for the equivalent of six cups of coffee and bought a deserted premises on the Kurfuerstendamm for four hundred dollars. 'There you are,' he told Luise, 'the site for the new Café Jochum.'

Luise stared at it for a long time, then announced, 'Benno, it's hopeless, we'll have to pull it down and start again.'

He shrugged. 'Why not? Labour's cheap enough. What I'd like to see is a three or four storey building with the café on the ground floor and offices above it. That way, we'll be able to start recouping some of our costs in rents right from the beginning. Well, talk to your architect friends and let me know what they think.'

She flung her arms round his neck. 'Oh, Benno, you're wonderful! I didn't think you'd allow me to do it.'

Rather embarrassed, he said gruffly, 'Just make sure you do it right, Luise.'

'Oh, I shall.' From that moment on, her feet scarcely touched the ground. As her mother had done thirty years earlier, she spent her every hour on the site, discussing plans with Lothar Lorenz and Erich Mendelsohn, then watching as the old building was demolished, waiting impatiently until reconstruction could commence.

Viktoria listened to her sister's vivid descriptions of her plans for the new café, but her mind was no more on the project than it was on the troubles in the Ruhr. Those days, her every waking minute was spent trying to cope with the problems of the hotel. Inflation was of little concern to those of their guests with dollars, but for others it was disastrous, because these people could find that the price of a meal one evening bought them only a cup of coffee the following morning. The tariff for a first-floor apartment one night paid for a small attic room the next. The administration of the hotel had become a nightmare.

Retired printers and their families were recalled to Ullstein and other printing houses to help print banknotes with which the Mint could no longer cope and these notes took on ever huger denominations. Viktoria gave up even trying to work out what they were, actually worth, for although everyone in the country appeared to have become millionaires — if not billionaires — they all knew their millions were just so many worthless scraps of paper.

They paid their staff daily now, Herr Brandt and the page boys going to the Reichsbank with laundry baskets loaded on porters' trolleys to carry the notes back to the hotel. But as the millions became insignificant and nobody even mentioned them, the most effective method of payment was in food. As in Wedding, barter became the medium of exchange.

It was early one August morning that Chef Mazzoni called Viktoria to the kitchen and showed her the empty storeroom. 'This is where we keep all our cooked and preserved meats.'

Viktoria stared round the room, past the staff all quietly engaged in their duties, to the doors and windows. 'There doesn't seem to be any sign of a break-in.'

The chef led her into his office. 'It was an inside job,' he said heavily. 'I've been aware of pilfering going on for some time, but I've ignored it. After all, these people have families to keep and when you see some of the waste coming back from the restaurant you can understand how frustrated they feel. But this is outright robbery.'

She understood exactly what he meant. Petty pilfering, whether by staff or guests, was an accepted fact of hotel life. Stealing the entire contents of a storeroom was another matter. 'Have you any idea who's responsible?'

'The first person in the kitchen every morning is Emmy Anders,' Chef Mazzoni said, pointing through the window to a small girl, enveloped in a huge white apron. 'Her job is to scrub the floors and tables and have the kitchen clean by the time the rest of the staff arrive. It would have been easy enough for her to hand food out to someone waiting by the window.'

As if she sensed they were talking about her, Emmy turned and stared at them, huge black eyes filled with guilty fear in a pathetically thin little face. Now that Viktoria saw her again, she remembered remarking on her foreign appearance, although she had never spoken to her, for the chef engaged all his own staff. 'But surely Emmy Anders doesn't have a key to the storeroom?'

'I'm afraid it would have been simple enough for her to borrow it and get one cut. In the early days, I wasn't always as careful as I should have been. But, then, I thought I could trust my staff.'

'It sounds as if we'd better talk to Emmy, but not in front of the others. You'd better send her along to my office.'

As soon as the girl entered Viktoria's presence, she collapsed into tears. 'I didn't want to do it, ma'am, but they made me. You

458

see, when Kraus laid my dad off, we didn't have any other way of getting food. They said it wasn't really stealing.'

She was only a child, Viktoria realized in horror. 'Who are they?' she asked gently.

Incoherently, Emmy babbled out the whole ghastly story of how her dad had told the communist lady about her job and how the lady had said it was all right for her to take the food. 'My dad said he'd beat me up if I didn't take it, and Frau Meyer said it was our right.'

Viktoria pursed her lips grimly. 'I do so wish you'd told someone before.'

'Oh, ma'am, what's going to happen to me now?'

'You're not going back there,' Viktoria told her firmly. 'From now on, Emmy, you'll live here at the hotel.'

Emmy stared at her incredulously. 'You mean you aren't going to have me arrested?'

'So long as you never take anything again. And I don't think you will, will you, Emmy?'

'Ma'am, I never wanted to steal from you. Oh, if you'll let me stay here, I'll do anything for you, I'll work so hard, I'll ...' Words failed her. In her relief, Emmy threw herself across the room, burying her head in Viktoria's lap and burst into a fresh paroxysm of tears.

Emmy was soon installed in a small room with two other maids and Viktoria virtually forgot about her, as other events of national and international significance took precedence. In August, a new Chancellor was appointed, a right-wing politician called Gustav Stresemann, whose first action was to end the passive resistance and who immediately announced his intention of trying to gain the respect of other nations by honouring the peace treaties and fulfilling Germany's obligations.

'He's putting his head on a block,' Benno told Viktoria, 'but he's right. Somebody must have the courage to take the responsibility upon himself. Stresemann's got guts. He's going to make a lot of enemies, but I think he's doing the right thing.'

There were outbreaks of violence and angry demonstrations throughout the country. In Saxony and Thuringia, communists seized control, setting up their own regimes, while in Bavaria, Gustav von Kahr declared a right-wing dictatorship.

Opinion regarding Stresemann was as strongly divided in the hotel as it was in the country. Viktoria heard people muttering angrily, 'He's just giving in to the French.'

459

Others responded equally irately, 'Fat lot of good passive resistance has done. Stresemann's right, we'll do better to talk to the French than to fight them.'

In one thing, however, they were all agreed. Inflation had to be stopped. Most of the country was now starving, many being driven to suicide as the sole solution to their problems. A pound of potatoes cost fifty thousand million marks, a loaf of bread two hundred and sixty thousand million and just a single match nine hundred million.

In November, there were over four billion marks to the dollar and a cup of coffee at the Hotel Quadriga cost six hundred thousand million. Benno did not even bother to bank the notes any more. He gave them to his children and suggested they used them to redecorate the nursery.

Otto Tobisch returned to Munich after this year in prison to a very different atmosphere from the one he had left. Not only was Hitler openly denouncing Stresemann as a traitor, he was determined to overthrow Gustav von Kahr's government and, having established himself as dictator in Bavaria, follow Mussolini's example in Italy and march on Berlin.

The SA now numbered some fifteen thousand men and was daily being augmented by members of the Stahlhelm and other private armies, drawn by the promise of a fascist putsch. Still unofficially supported by Captain Roehm and the Bavarian Reichswehr, and fronted by General Ludendorff, the SA was certainly strong enough to stage a revolution. It had also, during Otto's absence, acquired a new commander. He was Hermann Goering.

After the fiasco of the Kapp Putsch, Otto had scant patience with General Ludendorff, but his admiration for Goering grew by leaps and bounds. He might be a politician, but he had proved his courage during the war. He was brash and bombastic, but he also knew how to inspire his men. At a meeting of SA leaders called in October to discuss the putsch, he told them, 'Anyone who makes the least difficulty must be shot.' This was language Otto understood.

Yet, time and again, the putsch and the march upon Berlin were postponed. Goering explained to them that the problems facing Hitler were manifold. Although he and Gustav von Kahr ostensibly had the same aims, they both wanted ultimate power for themselves, so before Hitler could march on Berlin, he had to gain control from Kahr. If possible, he wanted to do this peacefully, for he wanted no repetition of the Kapp Putsch.

Otto cared little for the political implications: all he knew was that he and his men were spoiling for a fight and that if they didn't hurry, they would be too late.

Eventually, the great day arrived. On 8 November, Goering ordered Otto to assemble his troops outside the Buergerbraeu House, a huge beer hall on the outskirts of Munich, where Gustav von Kahr was holding a political meeting. There was too little notice, they had too few troops immediately at hand, but — at last — the long-awaited moment had arrived. First, they would over-throw the Kahr regime, then, with the Reichswehr on their side, the SA — with Hitler at its head — would march on Berlin.

Crouched outside in the dark, his machine-gun at the ready, Otto could hear the drone of Kahr's voice, then, suddenly, Goer-ing gave the signal. With one accord, they flung open the doors to the beer hall and burst in. For a moment, Otto blinked in the bright, smoky atmosphere, then, pushing against objecting men and knocking over tables, he ran to his allotted corner of the room, where he trained his machine-gun on the occupants. His twenty-four colleagues were all doing the same thing, as Hitler, a pistol in his hand, elbowed his way through Kahr's surprised audience and leapt onto the platform. There was an outraged uproar.

'The National Revolution has begun!' Hitler cried, brandishing his pistol wildly. 'This building is occupied by six hundred heavily armed men. No one may leave the hall. Unless there is immediate quiet, I shall have a machine-gun posted in the gallery. The Bavar-ian and Reich governments have been removed and a provisional national government formed. The barracks of the army and the police are occupied. The army and the police are marching on the city under the swastika banner.'

Crouched beside his machine-gun, Otto wondered at Hitler's confidence, for he knew his words were pure bluff. Still, obeying his orders, he aimed his weapon at the three men sitting on the platform, signalling some of his company to surround them and accompany them off the stage. Muttering resentfully and obviously being moved against their will, Kahr and his two colleagues followed Hitler at gunpoint into a small room, out of sight, behind the stage.

There was a swelling, angry murmur from the audience, as the bullnecked Bavarians started to protest against Hitler's private

461

army. Lining the walls, to protect the politicians from just such an invasion as this, were security policemen. One Bavarian near Otto shouted to the police, 'Don't just stand there! Shoot the bastards!' His blue eyes glinting coldly, Otto trained his gun on the policeman, who moved helplessly, but did nothing.

Amidst this tense, threatening atmosphere, Goering stepped onto the stage. 'There's nothing to worry about,' he assured them, his red face beaming confidently as he explained that Hitler, von Kahr and the other politicians were at that very moment discussing the formation of a new government. It was not Goering's words, but the stormtroopers' rifles and machine-guns that kept Kahr's indignant audience in their seats. They knew Kahr, they agreed with his programme — Hitler was nothing but an upstart revolutionary, bent on trouble. As the men shifted irritably in their seats, Otto grew tense. What if Hitler did not convince Kahr? What if they were betrayed by the Reichswehr or the police? His finger twitched on the trigger of his gun.

Then, suddenly, his face wreathed in smiles, Hitler returned to the stage. 'The Bavarian Ministry is removed,' he announced excitedly. 'A new national government will be named this very day here in Munich.' Although they were not on the stage with him, it sounded as if Kahr and his colleagues had agreed to collaborate with Hitler, and Otto sensed a gradual change in the mood of the audience. 'A German National Army will be formed immediately,' Hitler continued, 'of which Ludendorff will take control.' Now there was a slow murmur of approval, for Ludendorff was greatly admired. 'The task of the provisional German National Government is to organize the march on that sinful Babel, Berlin, and save the German people,' Hitler screamed. 'Tomorrow will find either a National Government in Germany or us dead!'

At that moment, General Ludendorff himself appeared, escorted by one of Hitler's aides, and the temper of the crowd changed completely. Although Otto could see that the old General was completely taken by surprise by events, the audience did not. To them, his sudden appearance simply gave the seal of approval to Hitler's actions that they needed. They cheered and thumped their fists on the table. Now the politicians and the military were united, they could march on — and overthrow — Berlin!

As Ludendorff joined the other politicians in the small room, the audience left them in no doubt as to what they wanted. Hitler alone had been one thing — Hitler alongside Ludendorff and Kahr

462

was a totally different matter. They swigged their beer confidently, they shouted and cheered, and very soon all five men returned to the stage. How changed the atmosphere was now from when they had made their first dramatic entry. General Ludendorff made a brief speech, then each of them swore allegiance to each other and to the new regime.

The three thousand Munich citizens crammed into the immense beer hall knew no bounds to their enthusiasm. As Hitler stepped forward again to address them, he had to wave a calming hand to quieten them. Finally, Otto's fingers relaxed.

'I want now to fulfil the vow which I made to myelf five years ago, when I was a blind cripple in military hospital,' Hitler said, an almost beatific expression on his face. 'Then I resolved to know neither rest nor peace until the November criminals had been overthrown, until on the ruins of the wretched Germany of today there should have arisen once more a Germany of power and greatness, of freedom and splendour.'

The honest burghers of Munich could no longer be restrained. Beer steins were lifted as voices were raised in thunderous applause. Beefy, Bavarian hands thumped each other on the back, shouted, whistled and roared their approval. Otto Tobisch, his machine gun redundant, stood and bellowed his own unreserved enthusiasm for his leader, and, as he cheered, he felt tears rise to his eyes.

By the next morning, however, everything had changed dramatically. Once they had left the beer hall the previous night, Kahr and his colleagues had swiftly gone back on their word and had turned the Bavarian army, which had promised allegiance to Hitler, against the stormtroopers. Only General Ludendorff remained faithful to them. While Roehm had seized the War Ministry on behalf of the new government, no other ministries or government buildings had been occupied and, furthermore, Roehm was now apparently surrounded by government troops.

As the stormtroopers reassembled at the beer hall gardens, the atmosphere was muted, charged with a new tension. Carrying a carbine with fixed bayonet over his shoulder, Otto was at the head of the column that followed Hitler, Goering and other NSDAP leaders towards the city centre. At the head of the procession, the swastika flag of the NSDAP was proudly carried. Behind them, a truck carried machine-guns and gunners.

Their first aim was to release the beleaguered Roehm in the War Ministry and, to reach him, they had to pass through the narrow Residenzstrasse, leading eventually into the wide Odeonsplatz. There were halts along the way, as armed police tried to break up the column of men, while others tried to join it. The mood was ugly.

At the entrance to the Residenzstrasse they found their way barred by a detachment of armed police. Assuming that the police, like the army, was unlikely to fire on a general, Hitler's personal bodyguard, stepped forward. 'Don't shoot!' he cried. 'His Excellency Ludendorff is approaching!' Behind him, Hitler shouted, 'Surrender! Surrender!' But to the policeman, Ludendorff's name meant nothing. He was not a soldier.

Otto did not know who shot first, but suddenly gunfire rang out, a hail of bullets echoing across the narrow alley. Then, almost immediately, there was silence and the shooting was over. He stared around him and saw Hitler, Goering and about twenty other National Socialists and policemen lying on the ground, dead or wounded. Only General Ludendorff continued to march past the barrels of the police rifles until he reached the Odeonsplatz, where he stood stiffly to attention, a solitary figure, waiting and watching as not one of the National Socialist leaders followed.

Otto had not reached the age of thirty without acquiring a very strong sense of survival. One further glance told him what he needed to know. General Ludendorff was being arrested. Hitler was being helped hurriedly into a waiting car, without waiting to see how his friends were faring. Clutching his groin, Goering was being pulled into a nearby building. The dead lay motionless in the roadway. 'Company, disperse!' Otto shouted, and ran back into the narrow streets of Munich.

It took him several days to reach the safety of Austria, where he eventually found work on a farm overlooking the Traunsee in the Salzkammergut. The Feldmanns, who owned the small farmstead, were thankful to have work from this strong young man. Old man Feldmann was gnarled and bent from rheumatism and his only daughter, Anna, though she worked like a horse, still could not do a man's job.

Anna acted like a drug on Otto. The scent of gunpowder still in his nostrils and his blood still surging from the revolution, he followed her wherever she went, watching her as she fed the chickens and gave milk to the baby goats. She smelled of the farmyard,

464

the clean, honest scent of straw and manure. He felt a heat in his loins and a stiffening under his trousers. It was a long time since he'd had a woman. He looked at her full breasts under her tight white blouse and brushed his arm against them.

A week after his arrival, they met in the cowshed. Her thick blonde plaits swinging over her shoulders, her sturdy arms were carrying two heavy pails of milk into the dairy for cheesemaking. She turned and smiled at him, her cheeks ruddy from the north wind that was bearing snow to Traunsee. 'Here,' he said, gruffly, 'give me one of those.' Their fingers touched. Clear blue eyes looked into his.

Then she put down the buckets, took his hand and led him towards a pile of hay at the far end of the barn. She bent to move a bale, so that they could lie down, but Otto had no time for such preliminaries. He unbuttoned his trousers, then lifted her skirts to reveal a pair of thick white thighs and plump buttocks. Gripping her firmly round the waist, he entered her from behind, thrusting into her savagely, as the Feldmann bull served the cows when they were on heat. Under him, Anna moaned with pleasure.

When he had done, they sank down into the hay, Anna's legs inelegantly parted to reveal a thick bush of blonde hair. 'More,' she groaned.

'As much as you want, pretty one.' He ripped open the buttons of her blouse and a heavy, blue-veined breast flopped towards his greedy mouth. God, it had been a long time. Already he could feel himself stirring. In five or ten minutes, he would take her again, this time from on top. He chewed her large, pink nipple, enjoying her cries of pain. He felt her hands between his legs, urging him back into life. Then he was inside her again, her capacious thighs encircling him, as they rolled over and over on the hay.

Yes, Otto thought, one day he would return to Germany but, in the meantime, Traunsee would suit him fine.

Chapter Seventeen

If Baron Heinrich had not brought Hitler's failed coup and his subsequent arrest to Benno's attention, he would have taken little note of it, for it aroused scant interest in faraway Berlin. As it was, the Baron, at the Quadriga on his way to Paris, commented, 'The Kapp Putsch all over again, and again failure. If this man Hitler had been serious about his counter-revolution, he should have collaborated with Kahr and his right-wing colleagues, not fought against them.' He shook his head. 'But, of course, he wanted power for himself. Well, maybe he'll see the error of his ways now he's in prison.'

Benno looked at him in surprise. 'You know Adolf Hitler?'

'I've never met him, but I make it my business to know about everyone who may influence German politics — and, therefore, Kraus.' He paused for a moment, then added, 'I don't believe we've heard the last of Hitler, boy. If Stresemann's efforts don't succeed for any reason, Hitler will make another attempt to seize power.'

In Paris that December, Baron Heinrich was among the German delegates included in the international committee of financiers and businessmen who met under the chairmanship of an American called Charles Dawes. One of their first achievements was the creation of the Rentenmark, worth one billion old marks. A foreign credit of eight hundred million gold marks was opened for the country as a new gold basis for the Reichsbank and fresh terms were agreed upon for the war reparations payments. Once the terms of the Dawes Plan were accepted by the Reichstag in 1924, loans started to pour in from abroad, particularly from America.

Forgetting all about Hitler, Benno felt happier than he had for a long time. Thanks to Stresemann, there finally seemed a chance of stability and prosperity for Germany. At last, they were on the road to recovery and they could start to consolidate and build. He gave orders for reconstruction work to begin on the new Café

Jochum in the Kurfuerstendamm and for Dr Duschek to start looking for a purchaser for the building on the Potsdamer Platz.

In February, the Baron was once more at the hotel. 'Now the Dawes Plan has been accepted, I've instructed Kraus Marin to start work on the *Countess Julia*,' he announced. 'The keel plates should be laid within the next year. Benno, we have a splendid time ahead of us.'

In the kitchens of the Hotel Quadriga, Emmy Anders knew little about Stresemann and it is doubtful if she ever heard of the Dawes Plan, but she did know that, suddenly, everything had changed for the better. They had real marks and pfennigs now, not silly billion notes that weren't even worth the paper they were printed on. Soon, she might even be able to save enough to buy some new clothes. Despite all her fears, Frau Viktoria had kept her on at the hotel and, what was more, Chef Mazzoni was promising that if she worked hard, he would teach her how to prepare vegetables and even to weigh ingredients. Her hands deep in a sink of soapy water, Emmy Anders started to sing.

'Eh, you are happy?' the chef asked. Embarrassed, Emmy stopped, but he smiled at her and in his funny Italian-German said, 'I like to hear people sing. In Italia, we sing all the time. Go on, Signorina Emmy, you sing to your heart's content.'

Since most of the kitchen staff were at supper, there was nobody to complain, so Emmy opened her mouth and sang. It made washing dishes much less of a chore.

In the Palm Garden Room, Georg Jankowski was playing his latest discovery — George Gershwin's *Rhapsody in Blue*. As his fingers danced over the piano keys, he imagined the jazz orchestra accompaniment and vowed that, one day, he would have the real thing. Then, after an hour's sheer pleasure, he put Gershwin away and pulled out some handwritten sheets of music — his own latest composition. He sang his own lyrics, although his voice did them scant justice. Not only did he want a jazz orchestra, he reflected ruefully, he needed a jazz vocalist — all in all, a pretty impossible wish. And even if he found them, where was he going to play? His kind of music certainly didn't fit the Hotel Quadriga, with its sedate clientele.

When waiters came in to prepare the room for the evening, Georg put his music away and thought, as so often, of the occasion they had disturbed him with Luise. Although their paths occasionally crossed in the hotel, he saw little of her and had heard from Max Patschke that she was deeply involved in the new Café Jochum that was being built on the Kurfuerstendamm. For a moment he wondered hopefully whether his music would suit her new establishment, then he pushed the idea away. Luise had made her feelings about him very clear.

In the foyer he pondered how to spend the next hour. At times like this he felt his loneliness most, for now that Minna was seven she went to the same small school in Grunewald as her cousins, usually returning to the Arendts' house with Nurse Simon for tea. As for Pipsi, she was possibly in some café somewhere, more probably in some other man's bed. So long as she left Minna alone and himself in peace, Georg neither knew nor cared.

He walked down the passage towards the service exit, then stopped still in amazement. What on earth? Somebody was singing — but what singing! What a voice! He pushed open the doors and stared round the deserted kitchen. 'Eh, Signor Georg, you like our little prima donna, eh?' Chef Mazzoni grinned at him from under his towering white hat.

Georg ignored him, staring at the small figure standing on a duckboard to reach into the sink. Her white overall reached down to her ankles and her face was almost hidden by a huge white cap. All he could see was a pair of big brown eyes and a wide open mouth.

'You hungry, Signor Georg?' the chef called. 'You like I prepare you a nice Wiener Schnitzel, eh?' Georg didn't even hear him. He walked over to the little kitchen maid and tapped her on the shoulder. Startled, she stopped singing and gazed at him nervously.

'Have you ever sung to a piano?'

She shook her head. 'We've never had a piano at home,' she replied in a thick Wedding dialect.

'When do you stop work?'

'I'm a good girl. I go straight to my room when I finish work.'

Georg turned to the chef. 'Does the girl get any free time during the day?'

Chef Mazzoni smiled at him, then wagged his finger. 'From three till four, but don't you go stealing my little kitchen maid.'

'God in heaven, Herr Maître, there are kitchen girls by the thousand in Berlin, but nobody else who can sing like this one.'

468

The next afternoon, after Chef Mazzoni personally brought Emmy to the Palm Garden Room, Georg locked the door firmly, then handed her the lyrics he had written. First he told her to read them while he played, then he asked her to sing. At the end of the hour, he knew she was going to take a lot of teaching but that he had found the vocalist of his dreams.

At four o'clock, her head reeling, Emmy returned to the kitchen and, while she washed the dishes, she practised Georg's song. Chef Mazzoni listened to her, then shook his head. 'That is terrible. Why you not sing nice Italian song, eh? Signor Georg, he is lovely man, but he has no musical appreciation.'

Emmy just gave him an urchin grin. She could not possibly have explained it, but she felt Georg's music somewhere deep inside her.

Gradually, she started to lose her nervousness in Georg's presence and asked him about jazz. 'It isn't German music. Where does it come from?'

He stared at her for a long time, then said gently, 'From the same place as you probably did, originally, Emmy. From Africa.'

She was silent while she thought this over. There was foreign blood in her family, she knew, for her grandmother had been much darker than her father and herself and at school she had sometimes been teased about her looks. Then she looked at Georg, whose colouring seemed very similar, only his features quite different from her own, the shape of his nose, the set of his eyes. 'Does it matter?'

He shook his head. 'It makes us different, that's all. And it gives us talents other people don't have. Your African blood enables you to sing like you do. My Jewish blood is, partly, responsible for my music.'

Soon Emmy's whole life centred on the hour she spent every day with Georg. For the first time in her life, she had somebody who saw her as more than a drudge, who was trying to give her something, rather than just take away. In her mind, Georg gradually became more like her father than Adam Anders had ever been.

With astonishing speed, the new Café Jochum started to take shape. It was very different from any other building in Berlin, a vast, concrete, avant-garde edifice, with a flat roof, rounded balconies on each storey and a central motif over the entrance to the building like graduated organ pipes, over which the words 'Café Jochum' soon flashed in dazzling neon lights. As conspicuous as the sign to the Hotel Quadriga was small, Café Jochum announced itself again in giant art deco letters high on the roof itself, from which rivulets of orange lighting cascaded over the fourth floor exterior to swirl round the building's circumference, illuminating each of those curved terraces.

Whenever he was in Berlin, Lothar Lorenz went with Luise to mark its progress, his round face beaming with enthusiasm, making suggestions for improvements here, applauding and approving there. He brought her pictures, sculptures and catalogues full of the latest designs. 'Look, this is what they're doing in Paris, in London, in New York,' he would cry. But most of their talent was found in Berlin itself, for under the Weimar government, arts were encouraged and the city was, more than ever, a cultural melting pot.

By August 1924, the offices were completed and let to various Berlin businessmen, including Duschek and Duschek. Now, at long last, the fitting out of the actual café began, the furniture was ordered and all the artistic treasures that Luise and Lothar had been hoarding for so long, brought out to view, arranged and re-arranged. 'The only thing that's missing is the music,' Lothar said one day.

'Oh, we'll find somebody,' Luise replied casually.

'It's not going to be that easy,' he warned.

Leaving Lothar at the café, Luise returned to fetch some papers from the hotel, lingering for a few moments on the Kurfuerstendamm as she always did to admire her creation.

'Looks like a bleeding battleship,' a man behind her muttered.

'If it were a battleship, it would sink,' another man said.

'If old man Jochum could see that monstrosity, he'd turn in his grave.'

Luise grinned and walked on. She had been determined to build something so controversial it couldn't be ignored, and it appeared she had succeeded.

Back at the hotel, the foyer was almost empty and silent, except for a very faint sound of music emanating from the Palm Garden Room. It was a long time since she had heard Georg play and she had almost forgotten the afternoon he had introduced her to jazz. Suddenly, the whole scene flashed across her mind: her joy at the new kind of music — the wonder of his hand grasping hers. She hesitated for a moment, then quietly pushed open the doors and let herself into the room.

An incredible sight met her eyes. Georg was seated at the grand piano and by his side stood the most extraordinary little figure. Scarcely reaching Luise's shoulder, she was draped in long white overalls that reached right down to her ankles and on her head was a kitchen maid's cap. Her shoulders back, her forehead creased in a frown of concentration, her mouth was wide open, from it pouring an amazing sound.

Approaching them silently, Luise listened with mounting excitement. What a fool she had been not to remember Georg, when Lothar had spoken to her about music for the new café! So involved had she been in her own affairs, she had all but forgotten that Georg composed his own songs, and she had certainly been totally unaware of this small contralto. When the song finished, she said softly, 'That was wonderful.'

Startled, Georg spun round on his piano stool, his face lighting up when he saw her. For an instant their eyes met and instinctively she knew he was remembering their last meeting in this same room. The girl shuffled awkwardly. 'Shall I go now, Herr Jankowski?'

Georg looked startled. 'No, Emmy, it's all right.' Then he told Luise, 'This is Emmy Anders. She works in the kitchens.'

Luise gazed at Emmy's pointed little face, dominated by huge eyes, then removed her white cap, so that her wiry black hair sprang loose. If it were styled and the girl wore proper clothes, she would be beautiful. 'Do you have any more songs like that one?'

He pointed ruefully to a pile of handwritten scores. 'I've never stopped writing — and since I've found Emmy ...'

'Can Emmy sing them for me?' He looked at her to assess whether she was serious on this occasion, then turned back to the piano and began to play.

Never had Luise felt more moved, for, as the music and words flooded over her, she knew that this was not just a performance, but a part of Georg's soul that was being revealed to her. The songs told of hunger, loneliness and love in a cold, comfortless world — the story, she realized, of Georg's own life. She stole a glance at his rapt face, noticing the lines etched round his mouth and the corners of his eyes, and had to stifle an impulse to reach across and touch them. Suddenly, she realized that when she had run away from him before, she had been running away from her own emotions.

Eventually, he put his hands on his lap. 'That's all.'

She forced herself back to reality. 'I've never heard anything like them before in my life,' she told him sincerely. 'Would you be willing to play at the new Café Jochum when it opens, Georg?'

'Be willing? But I'd love to. Do you mean it?'

'Oh, yes, I mean it,' she assured him, but she knew that, once again, it was as much the musician as his music that she wanted.

'And Emmy?'

'Emmy's part of your music, isn't she?' Once again, their eyes met and Luise was certain her feelings were reciprocated.

'You mean I'm going to sing at Café Jochum?' Emmy's voice asked aghast. 'Me? At Café Jochum?'

Luise forced her attention away from Georg and looked down at the little girl. 'Yes,' she promised, 'by the time Georg and I have finished with you, you'll never have to wash another dish in your life!'

That very evening, Benno announced, 'I had thought we would hold a gala New Year's Eve ball here at the Quadriga this year, but the more I think about it, the better it would seem that we open the new Café Jochum on New Year's Eve. What do you think?'

'Oh, Benno, that would be wonderful!' Luise cried. 'Will it be all right if Georg plays the music?'

'I shouldn't have thought Strauss and Lehár were right for Café Jochum.'

She saw that she was going to have to confide in him and Viktoria at least, so breathlessly she described the music Georg had played that afternoon and Emmy's singing.

When she had finished, Viktoria said, wonderingly, 'Well, to think that little Emmy has all that talent. I'm so pleased I kept her on — and I am glad Georg found her. Can we come and listen to her?'

But Luise was jealous of her discovery. 'No, please trust me. I want them to be a surprise for everyone.'

Not even to Lothar did she reveal her secret. Indeed, when he left for London, promising to be back in time for the New Year, she was almost relieved.

During their rehearsals, she became ever more convinced of Georg's genius and Emmy's incomparable natural ability. Yet, during the weeks that the three of them worked together, another, indefinable element entered their relationship. As Emmy looked devotedly to both her and Georg for guidance, Luise sometimes felt that they had taken over the role of Emmy's parents. It drew her and Georg ever closer together, creating a bond of responsibility and affection between them that she suspected had never existed between Georg and Pipsi.

Frequently, he came with her to the new café, where work continued apace. Soon, the kitchens were fitted out, the furniture installed and the walls decorated. The interior was black and chrome. Long, black, leather benches and angular chairs surrounded tubular steel, glass-topped tables. Lamps, supported by brackets and stands sculpted in extraordinary geometric designs, illuminated the rooms and on the walls hung pictures by Bauhaus and Blaue Reiter artists. Along the length of an entire wall was a mural by Otto Dix, Berlin's present-day Toulouse-Lautrec. The other three walls were of glass.

Then Oskar Braun started to move equipment and staff from the Potsdamer Platz, while Luise turned her attention towards the first night. 'I'm absolutely determined to have a star-studded audience,' she told Georg. 'I'm going to invite everybody that's anybody in Berlin. And I'm going to try and get the evening broadcast live on the radio. Georg, you're going to be famous!'

It seemed quite natural that he should sit with her in the new office, helping her address the embossed cards. 'Do you really think all these people will turn up?' he asked.

'Most of them. After all, we're offering them the greatest New Year celebrations since the war.' Impulsively, she seized his hand. 'It's going to be a night to remember. Georg, our Café Jochum is going to be the most exciting place in Berlin.' Then, realizing what she had said, she smiled, 'Well, it seems to have become our Café Jochum now, doesn't it?'

This time, no waiters burst in on them. Georg stared down at her fingers lying in his, then he said, 'I have a lot to thank you for, Luise. I don't know why you've done so much for me, but I want you to know that I'm very grateful.'

Before she had time to reflect on them, the words left her mouth, 'But I love you, Georg.'

The room was silent. A shadow passed over his face, then, still not looking at her, he murmured, 'And I love you, too, Luise. God knows, I've tried not to, but I can't help it.'

'Is it such a very dreadful thing?'

'In our case, yes. You see, I'm a married man, Luise. I don't love my wife but I do love my daughter and I won't do anything

473

that might hurt Minna. Nor will I do anything to hurt you.'

'But why should we be hurt?'

'We could never get married.'

She stared at him. It was love that was important to her, not marriage. It was being close to Georg, sharing his thoughts, his music, his life. 'But surely we can be friends? That's all I want.'

He nodded, but a look of pain still haunted his eyes. 'Yes, of course we can be friends. Just, please, never ask any more of me. Promise me that.'

He was so intense, Luise couldn't help wondering what dark secrets were concealed in his heart, but she gave her promise.

The people who flocked to the café's opening that New Year's Eve far exceeded Luise's wildest dreams. From all corners of Berlin, they converged on the Kurfuerstendamm. From the theatre, there were the directors Erwin Piscator, Leopold Jessner and Max Reinhardt, and from the stage, Alexander Moissi, Fritz Kortner, Oskar Homolka, Werner Krauss, Tilla Durieux, Fritzi Massary, Max Pallenberg, Elisabeth Bergner, Richard Tauber and countless others. There were Bertholt Brecht and Arnolt Bronnen; the poets Klabund and Gottfried Benn; Max Slevogt, the painter, and Roda Roda, writer of comic chansons. Nobel Prize winner, Albert Einstein, was there with Professor Ascher. The theatre critic, Alfred Kerr, was sitting with Lothar Lorenz. Anita Berber, Rudi Nowak, Pipsi Ascher, Theo and Sophie Arendt — all Berlin was there!

The opening was, as Luise had hoped, being broadcast live on the Berlin radio by the reporter Arthur Funck, whose cumbersome box microphone was set up near the stage and from which a spaghetti of thick wires and cables coiled out of the room, through the streets to Broadcasting House, to enable him to make a very rare live programme, commenting on the well-known names and faces at Café Jochum to an audience listening on earphones attached to crude crystal sets in their homes.

As waiters wove their practised way between the guests and a new quartet accompanied the dancing with a repertoire of light, modern music, Luise, her green eyes sparkling and her auburn hair falling in a thick, heavy bob, greeted her guests, chatted for a few moments to each of them, then circulated further. Everyone had something to say about Café Jochum. Some loved everything about it on first sight. Others hated it. Nobody in the room was indifferent. Lothar grabbed her arm, as she danced past him. 'Happy?'

'Lothar! I've done it,' she cried exultantly. 'Oh, but wait until you hear my surprise!'

'It's nearly quarter past eleven on the evening of 31 December 1924,' Arthur Funck was telling his invisible listeners, 'and here at the Café Jochum on the Kurfuerstendamm, the tango is ending and the lights are dimming as we prepare to watch the cabaret.' The lights dimmed over the podium and the quartet removed themselves and their instruments.

'This must be her surprise,' Lothar murmured to Alfred Kerr, but frowned as Georg Jankowski settled himself at the Bechstein.

'Jankowski?' Kerr raised an eyebrow. 'Nothing very surprising about him.'

The pianist sounded a few, foot-tapping notes, with a strong rhythm. Lothar glanced across to Luise, standing near the piano, a look of tense expectation on her face. Georg's melody was lithe and compelling. It was music to dance to — but, suddenly, nobody was dancing. They were all staring at the stage.

Into the circle of light cast by a single spotlight, a girl stepped. Lothar gasped. Emmy Anders was quite simply beautiful. Even in her high-heeled slippers, she was not tall, and at a time when thinness was commonplace, either through the exigencies of fashion or bare necessity, her extreme slenderness was exceptional, giving her a look of almost frightening fragility. Yet, despite this, she was perfectly proportioned. As she stood facing her audience, her slim arms to her sides, her delicate hands loosely clasping her skirt and the slight buds of her breasts gently rising and falling under the clinging material of her dress, she gave the impression of brittle strength. She was dressed in a sheath of flame red, that fell from a halter round her neck, over her narrow hips to her pointed gold sandals and swirled in a train behind her.

Even in the stark spotlight, her skin shone faintly olive, its texture smooth and firm. Her hair was black, flaring round her small, pointed, urchin face like a halo, each strand seemingly vibrant with its own individual life, crackling with the electricity of its owner's personality, emphasizing the hugeness of her black eyes and the wideness of her mouth. Her lips were generous, but not overfull. Her nose was neat, but quite distinctive. Her eyes were so enormous, they seemed to leave no space for any other features.

Emmy glanced at Georg and he nodded imperceptibly. Then

she raised her shoulders, threw back her head, closed her eyes and opened her mouth, displaying sharp, white, even teeth. Her voice seemed to come from the depth of her stomach, surprisingly low for one so small in stature. 'Hungry, so hungry,' she growled, her thin hands clasping her flat stomach, 'hungry and starved, Lonely in a city where hunger was carved, In bare leafless treetops and grey dirty streets ...'

Nobody was standing on the dance floor any more. They had all crept noiselessly back to their seats to watch this phenomenon in rapt silence.

Abruptly, the rhythm changed, the tempo speeded up and Emmy's voice jumped two octaves, making the hair rise on the back of Lothar's neck. 'Until I found you!'

She could be no more than sixteen, yet her voice conveyed the pathos and experience of one many years older. It soared effortlessly to the high notes, plunged remorselessly to bottomless depths, moving her audience through a welter of experiences, skimming over tears, jolting them into laughter, then returning them skilfully from the brink of emotional turmoil to smooth, elegant reality. She crooned to them, she serenaded them, she wooed them and she frightened them. She lifted them up and she flung them relentlessly down. She enchanted them and then she disillusioned them. At one with her music, she ended one song and started on another, until she came to her final number.

'Feeling,' she cried, 'I am only a feeling,' and her statement was a vast accusation hurled at her audience, who momentarily believed themselves to be as insubstantial as Emmy Anders. 'My feeling for you-ou.' The song ended on a high, triumphant note, echoing backwards and forwards between the paper streamers and the confetti and, as Emmy bowed low to them, preparing to walk off the stage, every single person in the room was quiet for a second, then rose to their feet in silent homage of the almost unearthly magic they had witnessed.

Then, with a great roar, they burst into thunderous applause, clapping with their hands high above their heads, beating on the tables, standing on chairs, screaming, shouting, many with tears pouring down their cheeks, 'More! More! More!'

But the spotlight dimmed and the lights came on again. Instead of Emmy Anders, Benno stood on the stage. 'My ladies and gentlemen, it is midnight! On behalf of Café Jochum, I should like to wish you all a very happy, healthy and prosperous New Year!'

476

An almighty cheer went up and, still in the throes of the emotions aroused by Georg and Emmy, the Berliners, stolid burghers, staid businessmen, earnest professors, unkempt artists, unorthodox actors and all the other outlandish guests, threw their arms round each other, hugging and kissing in an orgy of goodwill. Outside, the church bells rang, fireworks lit up the frosty sky and rifles fired.

Dazed, Lothar found his hand being pumped by the normally impassive Kerr. 'Lorenz, who is she?' the theatre critic was demanding. All around him, voices were asking the same thing.

He shook his head. Emmy was incredible, but he recognized that, without Georg, she was nothing. To think that, for all those years, Georg's talent had laid dormant and it had taken Luise to uncover it. Now, however, everything would change, for Lothar himself would see to that. He would give him everything he needed: money, time, pianos, introductions ... The name of Georg Jankowski would become famous throughout the world.

He hurried across towards Georg and was reaching out his hand to congratulate him, when he was pushed aside by Luise. She threw her arms round Georg's neck, kissed him warmly and said, 'That was the most wonderful music I've ever heard. Thank you, my dear. A very happy New Year to you.'

The words in themselves were innocuous, but there was a note in her voice which Lothar immediately recognized. His little friend Luise had finally fallen in love. Diplomatically, he stepped back and, as he did so, a movement caught his eye. On the other side of the room, Pipsi was standing up, her mouth in a hard, thin line. Contemptuously, she glanced across at Georg, Luise and himself, then, as quickly as her tight black dress would allow, she walked towards the exit. Why was she leaving? Surely, tonight of all nights, she should be proud of her husband, must want to bask in his glory? Or did she already know that Georg and Luise were in love? Then, as he heard all around him voices muttering the name, 'Emmy Anders', Lothar understood. Pipsi, who had always wanted to be a star, was jealous of Emmy.

That realization strengthened his resolve to help Georg. Nothing in the world would give him greater satisfaction than to see Pipsi Ascher discomfited, especially if he could bring happiness to Luise at the same time.

Pipsi Ascher's eyes were narrowed in fury. She looked round the table at her father, openly wiping his eyes and not attempting to hide his emotion. Theo and Sophie had their hands clasped and were still gazing mesmerized at the stage. Nearby, Rudi was talking excitedly to Anita Berber. Beside the stage, Luise Jochum was kissing Georg, with Lothar Lorenz looking on. A mob, headed by Alfred Kerr, was almost swamping Emmy Anders. Abruptly, she got up and marched defiantly across the room.

Nobody tried to stop her. Nobody asked her why she was leaving. Nobody seemed even to notice her departure. They only had eyes for Georg and that little guttersnipe, Emmy Anders.

Never had Pipsi felt so humiliated. Why hadn't Georg told her he was composing music and, more importantly, why had he not asked her to sing it? All the way home in the taxi, she fumed and, when he eventually walked through the door, she threw herself at him in an avalanche of fury. 'How could you do that to me? How could you ask that hussy to sing?'

He stared at her for a long time, then asked slowly, 'Surely you didn't expect to sing, did you, Pipsi?'

She was beyond restraint. 'Of course I did. I'm your wife, aren't I? And I'm a singer.'

The last thing he wanted was a row with Pipsi. The evening had been so fantastic: the audience's reception of his music and Emmy's singing; the way Luise had thrown her arms round his neck and kissed him; and, finally, Lothar Lorenz's incredible proposal to manage him while he wrote the music for a show. Why did Pipsi now have to spoil everything? 'Pipsi,' he said, quietly, 'it isn't your kind of music. Your voice hasn't got the range. You just couldn't cope with it.'

'Then write something I can sing, for God's sake. You did it deliberately, just to humiliate me in front of all my friends. All these years I've stood by you, waiting for you while you were away during the war, putting up with you playing at the damned Hotel Quadriga. Now you've written your first good piece of music — and you give it to someone else to perform!'

'I'm sorry you see it like that.'

'I'll make you sorrier. I'll make you very sorry for putting that little tart before me. You've got a sick mind, Georg, that's your problem. You're perverted.'

'What do you mean?' His voice was cold.

'Anyone can see it a mile off!' Pipsi spat. 'She's not German! God knows what she is, but she's not German.'

'Of course she's German. As German as you are.'

'She's got African blood in her. Look at her hair and eyes. She's not even European, she's a half-caste of some kind. We had pictures of people like her in our geography books at school.'

George bit back a stream of angry words. 'Pipsi, I think it's time you went to bed.'

'Well, you needn't think I'm sleeping with you, letting your dirty hands maul me, after they've been touching that filth!' As she paused, Georg realized with relief that she did not suspect any kind of relationship between himself and Luise. All her hatred was directed towards Emmy. 'Though when she finds out you're impotent she'll leave you soon enough.'

Furious, he raised his hand and Pipsi cowered. 'Get out!'

'I'll get my own back on you for this,' she screamed, rushing through the door and slamming it as hard as she could behind her.

Georg sank down in the nearest chair, burying his face in his hands. One more scene like that and he would simply walk out, taking Minna with him. And he would fight tooth and nail in the divorce court for custody of the child. But even as he made his decision, he knew he would never see it through, for, as she had just reminded him, Pipsi still held the ultimate weapon. She would not hesitate to flaunt his impotence in the courts, or throughout Berlin, if she found it served her cause. He would lose Minna. And he would lose, not Emmy, but Luise.

Luise, who said she loved him, who believed she could make him happy. Luise, who did not know a shell falling on a battlefield in France had inflicted a wound not even she could cure. She, just like Pipsi, would flee from him in disgust, when she learned he was only half a man. No, he realized with despair, he was caught in a tangled web from which he could never escape, unless a miracle occurred. And miracles did not happen to people like him ...

He slept little that night, yet when he awoke he was curiously refreshed and his first memory was not of his fight with Pipsi, but of his musical triumph the previous evening. That, and the consciousness that this was the first day of a new year, heralding a fresh page in his life. This positive mood was heightened during the champagne lunch he had with Luise and Lothar.

'From now on, I'm going to be your manager,' Lothar declared. 'And the first thing I say is, no more tea-dances at the Hotel Quadriga. Georg, you are going to write the music for a show.'

'But I have to earn my living.'

Lothar waved an airy hand. 'Luise and I have just been discussing this and we're both agreed. We understand that you have your pride and that you don't want to be beholden to anybody, so we have decided you and Emmy may make guest appearances at Café Jochum, but the most important thing is for you to gain exposure throughout the country. You must both tour Germany and then the rest of Europe.'

It was a heady thought. They were offering him an escape from all his troubles, with the additional bonus of possible glory at the end of it. After all, he was thirty-five and if he didn't move now, he probably never would. There seemed to be only one drawback — in this new life, he would see even less of Luise. 'What do you think?'

'I shall miss you,' she admitted, 'but I think Lothar's right. You've been wasting your time at the hotel.'

'What about Viktoria and Benno? I don't like to let them down.'

'I've already spoken to them. They're sorry to lose you, but they quite understand. They'll soon find somebody else.'

'And this is only the beginning,' Lothar promised him. 'I believe in you, Georg. I know you're going to become one of this century's most famous composers.'

'It's what your Uncle Franz always wanted,' Luise added.

Georg looked at their smiling, enthusiastic faces. 'Thank you. I'm lucky to have two such good friends.'

A week later, Lothar telephoned him to say he had arranged the first booking for him and Emmy in Hamburg in a fortnight's time. Georg suddenly found he was looking forward to it tremendously.

The opening of the new Café Jochum wrought many changes in Luise's life. She had achieved what she had set out to do — overnight the café had become Berlin's most fashionable venue, filled constantly with the people she loved best. Soon, as the story of Georg and Emmy's success sped through the city, she was overwhelmed with applications from musicians and cabaret artistes begging to play both there and at the Hotel Quadriga. She had found her niche in life.

Benno, after congratulating her, took her into his office at the hotel and said, 'Your mother, Vicki and I have been talking things over and wonder if you would like to take this on as a full-time job, since you obviously have a flair for artistic matters. We were thinking of a title along the lines of Director of Entertainments.'

'You mean at Café Jochum and at the Quadriga?' Luise asked incredulously.

'I don't see why not. Watching people's reactions last night made me realize that we could have charged them an entry fee. The ballroom here is often empty — if we rearranged it, we could book artistes to perform in front of a paying audience.'

Her eyes shone. 'We could provide a whole evening's entertainment. Guests could buy tickets for dinner, dancing and a show. In the Palm Garden Room, we could still have the quartet and just a pianist in the bar. At Café Jochum, we could try out unknown artists and if they're good they could be invited to the Quadriga ... Oh, Benno, it's a wonderful idea!'

'You're going to be kept very busy.'

'I can't think of any way I'd rather spend my time.'

'Well, the first thing you can do is look for a replacement for Georg. Chef Mazzoni has already found a new kitchen maid.'

Luise found a replacement for Georg, then embarked on long discussions with Herr Brandt and Max Patschke about combining dinners, dances and cabaret acts. Everyone was unanimous that Georg and Emmy should give the inaugural performance.

Lothar greeted Luise's news ecstatically. 'I feel my life finally has a real purpose, so much so that I've decided to take a flat here in Berlin. I've flirted with Dada, Expressionism, Bauhaus and motion pictures, but, now that I'm nearly forty, I've finally discovered that music is the true love of my life.'

'You've forgotten your Impressionists,' she smiled.

'Like the sausage factory, I'm saving them for my old age. When I've exhausted all the other wonderful things that life has in store, they'll still be waiting for me. In the meantime, my dear, we're going to have fun.'

His enthusiasm was, as always, contagious, and for all his flippancy, he took his commitment as seriously as she did. He transformed one room of his new flat into an office and installed a middle-aged secretary called Heidi Wendel, among whose tasks was looking after Georg and Emmy's bookings. Soon, Heidi was also stemming the flow of artists and musicians who flooded to his door in the hope of being discovered, for Lothar's short, flamboyant figure had become almost synonymous with Berlin's artistic scene, commanding affection and respect.

So far as Luise was concerned, he became invaluable, not only as a sorting house for talent, but also as a confidant. After all, they had known each other for seven years now and he was familiar with almost every aspect of her life. One day, when they were sitting in Café Jochum, their usual meeting place, he asked her outright about her relationship with Georg.

She replied candidly, 'I love him and he loves me. The trouble is, Lothar, I think it's going to be another of my "spiritual" affairs.'

When he raised an enquiring eyebrow, she explained about Sepp. 'Although he never once made love to me, he asked me to marry him. But I didn't love Sepp and I do love Georg.'

Lothar delicately raised an eyebrow. 'Georg is already married.'

'You call that a marriage?'

'I'm sure he is also a gentleman.' Then he grinned. 'However, I shouldn't be surprised if Pipsi doesn't force the issue soon.'

It was common knowledge that Pipsi and Rudi had drifted apart, and that Rudi was having an affair with the beautiful Anita Berber. He was now more prosperous than ever, driving round the city in an Isotto-Fraschini Tipo 8A sports car, one of the most luxurious and expensive models on the road. After inflation had reached its peak, he had sold his thriving wholesale business and, with the proceeds, bought two more cabaret bars. His 'Utopia' bar on the Motzstrasse now catered exclusively for transvestites and here 'Little Bird' was in his element, while 'Rudi's Casino' in the Putzkamerstrasse sold champagne only by the magnum and provided hostesses for every customer, dressed in little more than a pair of brief pants and a feather boa round their necks. He owned half the prostitutes on the Kurfuerstendamm and a very lucrative concession in drugs. All his businesses were under the protection of one of the Ring Associations, headed by Dr Dr Erich Frey, the lawyer king of the underworld.

Pipsi haunted Café Jochum those days. Dressed in an expensive fur, her dark hair hanging to her waist, she made an almost tragic figure as she sat alone over interminable cups of coffee. She was nearly thirty now and starting to look her age, although if she had ever had any acting ability this would not have told against her, but Pipsi's sole talent had always been her body. In the reactionary theatre of Berlin in the twenties, there were no roles for a second-rate actress like Pipsi Ascher.

So, outwardly very elegant and self-composed, she sat alone waiting for someone to notice her. Then, one day, her luck seemed about to change, for, totally unexpectedly and uninvited, Bertholt

Brecht sat down at her table. 'All alone?'

'I was just waiting for a friend,' she lied.

'I'll wait with you. Incidentally, you haven't got the price of a cup of coffee on you? I seem to have left all my money at home.'

'Of course.' As he signalled to a waiter, she looked at him thoughtfully. 'Haven't you just returned from Munich? I was reading the reviews of *Drums in the Night*. They were excellent, Bert.'

'Yes, they weren't bad, were they?' His manner was offhand but he looked pleased.

Pipsi continued her flattery. 'I've heard Piscator is about to produce *Edward II* at the Proletarian Theatre. I'm looking forward to that tremendously.'

'It's going to be even better than *Drums*,' Brecht told her with no attempt at modesty. Then he leaned on the table, his flat cap still on his head and a cigarette dangling from his lips, staring at her through his steel-rimmed spectacles. 'So what are you doing these days, Pipsi?'

'Oh, I keep busy, you know.'

'Do you now?' Brecht looked at her assessingly. 'Not so busy you couldn't find a moment or two for me sometime?'

Pipsi gazed at him from beneath lowered lids. His very coarseness attracted her. An affair with Brecht would be a new experience in her life and certainly an excellent way of getting her revenge on Georg. 'Maybe,' she said archly.

'Has anyone ever told you that you have a very beautiful face, Pipsi Ascher? Is the rest of you as good, baby?'

'I think so.' They were talking the same language now.

'One day, I'll write a song about you.' He started to hum, then shook his head. 'It's no good, I need my guitar. Why don't you come back with me now to my apartment?'

They took a taxi to his flat, for which she paid, then he pushed her into a small, very untidy and rather dirty room, while he ambled off, muttering about fetching his guitar. She sat down on the edge of an ancient sofa and waited. It hardly seemed an auspicious beginning to an affair.

Eventually, Brecht returned, wearing a grubby woollen dressing gown. 'I can't write that song. First, I've got to go to bed with you.'

It was the sheer bluntness of his approach that decided her. 'I think I'd rather like it.'

'Good.' He lay down on the settee, kicking off his shoes and leaving his socks on. An unpleasant odour assailed her nostrils, but she tried to ignore it. He pulled her towards him. 'Want to leave your clothes on? Well, I don't mind.' His hand reached up her skirt, pushing it around her thighs.

Hurriedly, she undressed and Brecht gave a whistle of appreciation. 'You're certainly something,' he exclaimed, letting his dressing gown part to show her his erection.

Before she knew what had happened, he had pulled her on top of him, forcing himself painfully into her. 'You feel good, baby,' he muttered, squeezing her breasts. With a sense of disgust, she saw his fingernails were dirty and even from where she sat above him, she could smell his armpits, as if he hadn't washed for a long time.

Beneath her, he moaned. 'Move, baby. Squeeze me.'

With a sense of desperation, she did what he asked, then, to her great relief, he gave a shout and it was over. Thankfully, she rolled off him.

'Feel better now?' he asked, scratching his groin. As she didn't answer, he shrugged. 'Well, don't look so happy about it. Or are you one of those women who suffers from post-coital *tristesse*? Oh, well, I've got to go to the toilet. Sex always makes me want to pee.'

She pulled on her clothes, trying not to listen to the sound of his urine streaming into the lavatory bowl through the open door. He didn't flush the toilet, nor did he wash his hands. 'I don't know about you,' he said, when he returned fully dressed, 'but I feel hungry now. Have you got any money with you? I've run out.'

Miserably, Pipsi nodded. But on their return to Café Jochum, her spirits rose. As they passed Luise and Lothar on their way across the room to join a group of Brecht's friends, Pipsi smiled possessively at Brecht, laying her hand on his arm. Word would soon get back to Georg now that she had become Brecht's mistress.

It quickly became apparent, however, that her and Brecht's ideas on an affair — and on almost everything else — were poles apart. For a start, she did not begin to understand his particular commitment to Marxism. She was used enough to the views of communists, like Piscator, Jessner and the Herzfelde brothers, who gathered in Café Jochum and the Romanisches Café, their work often funded from Moscow, and who believed that the Russian Revolution was a wonder that would slowly take over all Europe.

But Brecht took communism a step further, so that it permeated not only his writing but every other aspect of his life. He frequently claimed that his work should be socially useful, but she soon saw that this meant he cold-bloodedly used society for what he could suck out of it. To her horror, Pipsi realized that she was just one in a long succession of women whom he used equally mercilessly. There was no such word as love in his vocabulary. She and the other women in his life were part of his 'sexual collective'.

The Pipsi-Brecht affair was over almost as soon as it began, causing few ripples in Berlin society, and if Georg heard of it, he never mentioned it. It succeeded, however, in further hardening Luise's heart against Pipsi and in making even her conscious of the growing strength of the Communist Party. Merely the sound of the word 'communism' had made her yawn ever since her first meeting with Olga, but now she found herself involved ever more frequently in the political debates that seemed to rage continuously in Café Jochum.

'These people all seem so different from Olga,' she commented one evening over supper to Viktoria and Benno. 'They almost seem to have two different concepts of communism.'

'They do,' Benno replied drily, 'and neither has any bearing on reality. Your customers in Café Jochum are, almost without exception, idealists, dreamers. None of them have ever been to Russia and they know absolutely nothing about Stalin. In my opinion, they're playing a very dangerous game.'

'And Olga?' Viktoria asked. 'Whatever one thinks of her, one has to admit that she means well for the working classes. Apart from getting poor Emmy to steal from us, she did try to help the people of Wedding during inflation.'

'Yes, Olga isn't an intellectual communist, like Brecht, the Herzfeldes and Jung. But the German Communist Party still lacks real leaders and seems to have no proper organization. Its prime attraction for people is that it's against the Weimar government. However, I don't think you need worry too much, Luise,' he added, laughingly, 'Olga and her friends have lost two opportunities to seize power and I doubt they'll be given a third one. Thanks to Stresemann, we're at the beginning of a long period of peace and stability. There won't be any more revolutions.'

Yet within a few days, Benno's prophecy of peace threatened to be short-lived, when President Ebert died unexpectedly during a routine operation in hospital. As so often in the past, the occupants of the Hotel Quadriga lined the balcony to watch the sombre funeral procession wind its way down Unter den Linden. 'After all, he was the first President of the Republic,' Benno commented, lifting his hat as the cortège passed, 'and, for all his sins, he wasn't a bad man.' Then he voiced the thoughts of everyone present. 'The real question is: who is going to succeed him?'

The weeks that followed disrupted the brief months of tranquillity to which they had so recently become accustomed, as the presidential election campaign commenced. Ebert seemed to have no natural successor and when Field Marshal Hindenburg was called out of retirement and announced his willingness, albeit reluctantly, to stand for election, most people at the Hotel Quadriga greeted his re-emergence with relief. Hindenburg was the Grand Old Man of Germany. Called from retirement before, in 1914, he had done everything within his power to lead Germany to victory. Now, once again, at the age of seventy-eight, he was prepared to help his country towards national unity and strength.

Not everybody saw him as Germany's saviour. Once again, the voice of Olga Meyer was heard in Berlin, deploring Hindenburg as a monarchist and claiming he would lead the people back into another capitalist war. As his right-wing supporters roared through the streets in trucks, waving flags and standards, dour-faced socialists and communists marched through the city, shouting anti-militaristic slogans. All too frequently, these processions deteriorated into bloody brawls.

Although, when the election was held at the end of April, the margin of votes by which Hindenburg won against his closest contender — a Centre Party moderate — was narrow, there was never any real doubt that he would win. Strangely enough, however, it was Benno who said soberly, 'I voted for Hindenburg because there was no real choice, but I don't think he's the right man. For one thing, he's too old and, for another, he'll never be be able to forget he's a soldier. He's not a leader and he knows it. So long as we have Stresemann, we'll be all right, but if anything ever happens to him, I can see we're going to be in serious trouble.'

Luise shook her head impatiently. 'I don't actually see that it makes any difference who's President. I just thank God we can all get back to normal again.'

Certainly, in the months that followed, it appeared that Hindenburg's appointment was going to make little difference to anybody, for Stresemann, now Foreign Minister, continued to lead the country from strength to strength. Already industry was recovering from the devastations of war, revolution and inflation. Unemployment was going down and workers once again had money in their pockets. Furthermore, Stresemann was working towards guaranteeing peace in Europe through the Treaty of Locarno and endeavouring to have Germany admitted to the League of Nations.

Although Benno followed all these developments with keen interest, Luise had more important matters on her mind. After triumphant appearances in Hamburg, Frankfurt and Munich, Georg and Emmy returned to Berlin that summer to give their first performance at the Quadriga. To Luise's delight, seats were sold out weeks in advance and people even queued outside the doors in the hope of cancellations. 'Isn't it incredible?' she cried, linking her arm through Georg's.

'To think that I played here all those years and yet now people are actually paying to hear my compositions, yes, that's incredible.'

'It's wonderful to see you again. Oh, Georg, are you happy? Are you enjoying your new life?'

He pulled a wry face. 'Emmy certainly is, but, for myself, I'm not so sure. Oh, of course it's nice to be appreciated, but it isn't what I actually want to do. I want to write music, Luise, not play the same old tunes night after night.'

Whatever Georg thought about his engagements, he played as professionally as ever, but Luise suffered from a strange sense of disappointment. During his absence, she had missed him dreadfully, yet, now they were together again, he seemed, if anything, even more distant than he had been when he was playing in Munich. He obviously enjoyed her company — he confided as much in her — but other than occasionally holding her hand, he gave no demonstration of love.

Georg and Emmy's success at the Quadriga, coming on top of her disillusionment with Brecht, increased Pipsi's fury. Dressed in a fashionable cloche hat that almost concealed her eyes, a clinging cocktail dress that accentuated her new, straight silhouette, and swinging her vanity bag casually from her wrist, she went to 'Hades'.

Rudi himself was by the bar and, to her relief, he greeted her as a long-lost friend, crying, 'Pipsi, darling, how ravishing you look. Try one of my new cocktails. I've called it The Virgin's Dream.' With a deft hand he poured several ingredients into a shaker, shook the container vigorously, then poured the frothy drink into a glass.

Pipsi downed her cocktail in a couple of gulps, held out her glass for a refill and looked round the crowded, smoky night club. So many new faces — and so young. Then her glance fell on the seductive figure of Anita Berber, so slim, so beautiful, that it was no wonder Rudi was attracted by her. 'You remember Anita, don't you?' he asked.

The tip of Pipsi's tongue moistened her lips. 'Yes, I remember.'

Rudi looked at her thoughtfully, then reached down behind the bar. 'Like a cigarette?'

Pipsi stared in astonishment, for the cigarettes were made from five-mark notes. 'What's in them?'

'Good heavens, Pipsi, it's not like you to be out of fashion. Everybody smokes cocaine in notes these days.'

Her eyes glittered, as she remembered the last time she had tried the drug, also at 'Hades', also in Anita Berber's presence. Rudi put the cigarette between her lips and lit the tip. She inhaled deeply and choked.

'Gently,' Rudi laughed. 'It's supposed to relax you.'

Very soon she had forgotten all about Brecht, Georg and Emmy, as the tension seeped out of her. She felt herself to be young and desirable again, amusing and witty, like all the others around her. Total strangers came up and asked her to dance, invited her to drink more cocktails, told her how beautiful she was. And all the time, she was aware of Rudi's eyes following her, until it was suddenly three in the morning and there was only herself and Anita left, sitting to either side of Rudi, talking as if they were old friends. 'Come on,' he said, 'let's go somewhere private and have a last glass of champagne together.'

He led them through a door behind the bar into a dimly-lit room, dominated by a deep divan, a tiger skin spread over satin sheets. It reminded Pipsi of Marie-Antoinette's four-poster in his flat in Charlottenburg and, giggling, she threw herself on the bed. 'Anita, isn't this beautiful?'

Rudi pulled the cork in a bottle of champagne, poured three glasses, then drew the girls to either side of him. 'Don't you think you've got too many clothes on?'

They needed no second bidding. As she undressed, Pipsi became aware of Anita staring greedily at her body and found her own gaze travelling hungrily over Anita's small breasts and flat stomach. Rudi watched them with detached amusement, then removed his own clothes. Never in her life had Pipsi felt as free and elated as she did during the hour that followed, because all the time she and Anita were tantalizing Rudi with their movements, she knew they both really desired not him, but each other. When Rudi drew her down on top of him and reached his climax, Anita's lips kissing her breasts excited her more.

After that, they were seldom out of each other's company, lunching together, strolling arm in arm through the city to go shopping, giggling like a couple of schoolgirls as they tried on each other's clothes, drinking cocktails and smoking cocaine at 'Hades', then finally tumbling, happily, into Anita's bed.

Anita was like a child or a kitten, indolent, luxury-loving, delighting, above all, in being pampered — and Pipsi spoiled her with all the attentions she had never given anyone else before. Strangely, she found she enjoyed this feeling of being needed and being the stronger partner. Where she had gone wrong in her life, she decided, was devoting herself to men, when a relationship between two women was infinitely more satisfying.

Since meeting Anita, she no longer smoked her cocaine in banknotes, but bought it by the gramme, eking the precious powder out sparingly, for it was very expensive. It was so wonderful, however, that she ignored the expense. Not only did it give her a sense of incredible sexual euphoria, but, for the first time in her life, she felt supremely self-confident, and she was slim, almost as slim as Anita, for cocaine had ruined her appetite.

Although she usually went home sometime during the night, she seldom saw Minna or Georg those days. Nanny Simon took Minna to school before she got up in the morning and they often spent the rest of the day and all weekend at Sophie's villa in the Grunewald. As for Georg, he was either on tour or shut in his study, writing music. Neither of them meant anything to her now. They were part of another existence and she only stayed with them because, finally, it was easier to stay than to leave. Somehow, she did not have any energy these days for difficult decisions.

Yet she found herself confronted with one, that autumn, when Theo dropped her a private note, informing her that her bank account was overdrawn. Her first reaction was anxiety, then she sniffed a little cocaine and eventually decided the only solution was to ask Georg for some more housekeeping. Somewhat to her surprise, he just looked at her coldly, then asked how much she wanted. Even when she doubled the figure she had first thought of, he didn't so much as blink, but wrote out the cheque. Suddenly, she realized she meant as little to him as he did to her.

When, a few weeks later, her account again became overdrawn, she approached her father, but obtaining money from him proved less easy. 'What's the matter with you, Pipsi? You're very skinny. Aren't you eating these days?'

'Fuller figures are out of fashion. That's why I need some new clothes, Papa.'

Professor Ascher's keen eyes stared penetratingly at her. 'Georg should be earning well enough now. What do you spend all your money on?' Then, as she just shrugged, he said, 'Oh, well, I suppose if you need it, you'd better have it.' He wrote her quite a substantial cheque. Pipsi, of course, didn't spend it on clothes. She gave it to Rudi in exchange for more of the wonderful powder, which she naturally shared with Anita.

But, despite everything Pipsi did, she couldn't help seeing that Anita was already getting bored. She complained that 'Hades' was becoming tedious, she was tired of champagne, she announced vaguely that she wanted to do something different. So, one evening, Pipsi suggested that they returned to her apartment for a change.

Just the different surroundings made everything seem exciting. Putting her fingers to her lips in an exaggerated gesture, she led Anita down the hall, past the room where Minna and Nanny were sleeping, into the living room. Added to the euphoria caused by cocaine and the never-ending stimulation of seeing Anita's naked body, was now added the spice of danger. She had no idea where Georg was, but what if he should suddenly arrive home? Poor impotent little man, what would he think if he saw how well another woman was satisfying his wife?

That evening, Pipsi reached a fresh peak in her relationship with Anita. When they were both, finally, exhausted, they curled up together on the rug in front of the fire and went to sleep.

Georg very nearly spent that night in Magdeburg, where he and Emmy had just given their final performance, but Emmy vowed she wasn't a bit tired, so he drove back through the night, dropping her off first at the Hotel Quadriga and arriving at his own home at about three in the morning. As always, he let himself in quietly, for fear of disturbing Minna and Nanny, then decided to pour himself a nightcap before going to bed.

As soon as he opened the living room door he saw them, two

naked women, their limbs intertwined, asleep in front of the fire. For a long time, he stood and stared at them in disgust, battling against the desire to beat the living daylights out of Pipsi. How dare she sleep with another woman in his house, with Minna in the next room? He took a deep breath and left the room. Before he did anything else, he must get Minna away from here, then he would decide, once and for all, what to do about Pipsi.

Resolutely, he made his preparations, laying Minna's and Nanny's coats out in the hall, then he went into their bedroom and shook Minna awake. 'Minna, wake up, darling.' She stirred, then opened her eyes sleepily. 'Minna, wake up. We're going out.'

Then he knocked on the adjoining door where Nanny slept. 'Nanny Simon, wake up!'

The nurse was immediately awake, appearing at the doorway in a long, white night-dress, her hair hanging in braids over her shoulders. 'Herr Jankowski, what's the matter?'

'Get Minna ready. We must leave the house. I'll explain later.'

Obviously, his appearance was sufficient to satisfy her. In a couple of minutes, she reappeared fully dressed, a small travelling bag in her hand, and started to pack some of Minna's belongings. 'Quickly,' Georg urged her, helping his daughter to dress.

'Where are we going, Papa?' Minna asked.

'To Uncle Theo's.'

Only when they were both seated in the car, did he go back to the apartment for the last time, where he filled a bucket with cold water. The two women were still fast asleep. 'Whores!' he yelled, and hurled the contents over them. As the icy water hit her, Pipsi leapt up from the rug, shrieking. But Georg did not wait. He strode out of the flat, slamming the door behind him, got into the car and drove his two passengers to Theo Arendt's villa in Grunewald.

Vaguely, Pipsi heard the door slam and the car drive off, but for a moment she was so disorientated, she had no idea where she was. Then, Anita's voice said, 'What was that?'

'That was water,' Pipsi replied, bewildered. It seemed to have gone mainly over her, for Anita's hair was dry, while hers was soaking. Then, gradually, as she stared wildly about her, she recognized things. They were in her living room, so whoever had thrown the water must have been Georg. Suddenly seized with panic, she screamed, 'That was Georg!'

'Oh, please don't shout,' Anita said. 'It jars my nerves.'

'Don't you understand, you silly cow, that was my husband!'

The pupils of Anita's eyes were still dilated. Slowly, she uncoiled her slim body from the rug and stood up, a beatific smile on her face. 'Oh, Pipsi, darling, you're such a bore. I think I'll leave now. You look ugly when you're in a bad temper, and I can only love beautiful people.'

Pipsi watched her dress with a sick feeling in her stomach. 'Please don't leave me, Anita. I can't live without you.'

'Where's the telephone, darling? I have to call a taxi.'

'In the hall,' Pipsi fought back tears. 'Oh, please don't go.'

But Anita was dressed and all she could do was pull a blanket round her wet body and follow her helplessly. 'I love you so much, Anita. Promise me you'll come back.'

Anita merely smiled at her obliquely. 'Darling, I can't stand scenes.'

It was only after the taxi had carried her friend away into the night that Pipsi thought of Minna. When she entered her daughter's room, she found her bed empty and the door to Nanny's room swinging open, the lights full on. So, they had all left her. What should she do now?

Suddenly, she knew exactly what to do. Finally, she was free — and, far from feeling depressed, she should be feeling happy. In her handbag, she found a twist of paper containing a few grains of cocaine. Carefully, she tipped them on to the palm of her hand and sniffed them. Immediately, she started to feel better. Within thirty minutes, she felt on top of the world. So Anita had gone, had she? Well, what did that matter? She still had her cocaine, hadn't she? She threw herself onto her bed and fell into a dreamless sleep.

In Grunewald, Theo opened the door to his villa, elegantly clad in a silk dressing gown. Although they had obviously aroused him from deep sleep, he did not seem particularly surprised to see them. Nor, once Nanny had tucked Minna safely up in bed in a spare room, did he or Sophie appear astonished by Georg's story. 'Georg, dear, I'm so sorry,' Sophie said, 'but I know Theo and Papa have been worried about her for a long time.'

'Her bank account's overdrawn,' Theo said.

'And she's borrowed money from Papa,' Sophie added. 'She's so thin, I think she must be on drugs. Certainly Anita Berber is a cocaine addict.'

Suddenly, the night's revelations caught up on Georg. Wearily he buried his head in his hands. 'I had no idea,' he groaned. 'What on earth shall I do?'

Theo poured him a large tumbler of brandy. 'First you'll drink this, then you'll get some sleep. You look absolutely exhausted and I'm not surprised.'

'But Minna, she's not going back to Pipsi.'

Sophie took his hand. 'She can stay with us. She and Nanny Simon spend so much of their time here already, it's almost become their second home. Now, do what Theo says, get some sleep and we'll talk again in the morning.'

'Why couldn't Pipsi be like you?' he asked sadly.

The following evening, Luise and Lothar were sitting at their *Stammtisch* in Café Jochum, listening to Guenther Franzke sing, 'I am so homesick for Kurfuerstendamm ...', when Pipsi wafted past them almost ethereally, quite oblivious to their presence.

'God, look at her,' Lothar murmured, 'she's high as a kite. But where's Anita?'

He was not the only one to be curious, for the Pipsi-Anita relationship was notorious, and soon Pipsi was surrounded by an inquisitive crowd all wanting to be the first to learn the latest hot gossip. Word soon seeped back to Luise and Lothar. 'Pipsi's left Anita Berber. She's given up women.' Then, a little later, 'She's had a row with her husband. She's finished with marriage.'

Cold fingers of fear stabbing at her heart, Luise stared at Lothar. 'Where's Georg?'

Lothar also looked worried. 'He was in Magdeburg. I think he was due home today. Is Emmy back, do you know?'

'I haven't been at the hotel all day. Lothar, what do you think has happened?'

'I don't know, but I think we'd better find Georg. Let's go to your office and try the telephone first.'

There was no answer from Georg's apartment in Charlottenburg, nor had anybody at the Quadriga seen him, although Herr Fromm confirmed Emmy had returned. Already, Luise's imagination was running riot, visualizing terrible scenes in which Pipsi battered Georg over the head or he, in desperation, threw himself off a bridge into the Spree.

'Calm down,' Lothar said, 'I'm sure he's all right. After all, it's not just Georg who's missing, but Minna and her Nanny.'

'Theo's! Minna will be at Theo's.'

It seemed an eternity until the operator connected Lothar to the Arendts' house and Theo confirmed that Georg was with them.

Then, after Lothar had briefly explained about seeing Pipsi, he listened, giving only the occasional grunt, while Theo talked. Eventually, he said, 'We'll drive straight over.' Then he turned to Luise, 'Let's go.'

The drive out to Grunewald seemed interminable. 'What did Theo say?' Luise kept demanding. 'Is Georg all right?'

'I think so. Apparently, he came home last night and found Pipsi in bed with Anita. God, what a cow that woman is! Poor old Georg.'

Yet it wasn't until Georg was standing before her that she actually believed her fears had been unfounded. He looked very tired, but his eyes immediately lit up when he saw her. 'Luise, Theo said you were coming. I'm sorry to have worried you.'

'Georg, thank God you're safe. We didn't know what had happened to you.' Only Theo's presence stopped her from throwing her arms round his neck and kissing him.

'I should have let you know, but so much has happened.' Then he turned to Lothar. 'I gather Theo's told you the story?'

Lothar nodded. 'Georg, I'm truly sorry.'

'No, don't be sorry. Something like this had to happen sometime. I admit it was a shock last night when I found them, but I was angry for Minna's sake as much as anything.'

'Come and make yourselves comfortable.' Theo suggested, leading them into a spacious lounge. 'Let me get you a drink, then I'll leave you in peace to talk among yourselves.' He poured them all whiskies, then discreetly withdrew.

Lothar asked Georg all the questions Luise wanted to ask but didn't dare and, for the first time, she heard from Georg's own lips the truth of his dreadful marriage.

'Good God, man,' Lothar exclaimed, 'why on earth didn't you divorce her years ago?' He voiced Luise's own thoughts exactly.

'I kept hoping everything would get better and I didn't want to hurt Minna. After all, she's so young and the scandal would be dreadful. Then, there was something else, but ...' He suddenly stared at Luise and she caught a glimpse of sheer agony in his eyes. 'It's no good,' he whispered, 'I can't tell you.'

'It doesn't matter,' she said softly, but she knew it did.

Lothar coughed. 'Well, let's forget the past, eh? What are you going to do now, old boy?'

'I'm never going back to Pipsi. Theo and Sophie say Minna can stay here, so my first job is to find somewhere to live myself.'

'That's simple! My apartment's huge. You can stay with me!' And, as Georg stared at him blankly, he stated, 'Good, that's settled. We'll arrange for a van tomorrow to move all your things. Don't worry, Georg, there's plenty of room for you and your piano. Why, things couldn't be better — we'll be able to work on the music for your show together.'

'Well, if you're sure. It would only be for a short time, until I found a place of my own.'

'We'll see.' Lothar looked at his watch. 'Good God, look at the time. I'll just have a quick work with Theo, then we should leave.'

Finally alone with Georg, Luise took his hands in hers. 'Georg, I wish I could do something for you, too.'

'You have, just by coming here tonight, you've helped me.' They were both silent for a while, then he asked, 'Do you remember telling me you loved me?'

'Nothing's changed, Georg.'

'I'm free now,' he murmured, as if he were speaking to himself, 'I can do whatever I like. She can't hurt me any more than she has done already, but ... Luise, can you accept me and love me just as I am? I can't bear the thought of disappointing you. Not you, of all people.'

'You could never disappoint me,' she assured him, confidently.

As they heard Lothar and Theo's voices in the hall, he tipped up her chin and kissed her lightly on the lips. 'Dear Luise, you're such a dauntless little person, aren't you? I don't know what I'd do without you.'

'You don't ever have to be without me now. There's nothing to keep us apart any more, is there?'

As she drove home with Lothar, it hardly seemed possible that so much could have changed in such a short space of time. Her earlier fears totally forgotten, she said dreamily, 'Isn't it strange how things work out for the best in the end? Oh, Lothar, Georg and I are going to be so happy.'

'I hope so,' he replied, but there was doubt in his voice.

Georg's and Minna's belongings were soon moved out of the apartment and almost before he knew what had happened, Georg was installed in Lothar's flat, with Uncle Franz's piano in pride of place. He walked around in a dazed manner and kept asking, 'Where did I go wrong? Why did this happen?'

The following day, Professor Ascher arrived. 'We must talk about Pipsi,' he announced.

'Would you rather I left?' Lothar asked.

'No, she's been a stranger to me for a long time, Herr Lorenz,' he admitted sadly. 'You probably know her better than I do.' He turned to Georg. 'I went to see her yesterday, but I couldn't get any sense out of her. She basically told me to mind my own business, then asked me for some money. Which I gave her, of course.'

'Professor, I can't say how sorry I am.'

'Georg, I don't blame you. In fact, I'll admit now that when you asked me for her hand all those years ago, I had my misgivings about your marriage but I never imagined anything as bad as this happening.'

'I only wish I knew where I went wrong. I tried so hard to make her happy and give her everything she wanted.'

'Nobody could have given her more. Perhaps that's where we've all gone wrong. We've all spoiled her. I suppose there's no chance of your getting back together?' As Georg shook his head, he asked, 'What are you going to do? Petition for a divorce?'

'I've discussed it briefly with Theo, and he suggests I talk to Dr Duschek about getting a legal separation.'

'Theo says she's taking cocaine,' the Professor said. 'Do you know where she gets it?'

'From Rudi Nowak, I imagine,' Lothar told him.

'I could report him to the police, I suppose,' the Professor said doubtfully.

The next day he went to the police and asked them outright about Rudi Nowak. The police inspector sighed, admitting bluntly, 'We'd love to get our hands on Herr Nowak, but it's damned difficult. You see, Herr Professor, he's protected by the King of the Underworld, Dr Dr Frey, and unless we can make a cast-iron case against him, he and his lawyers will run circles round us.'

'I'm sure he's supplying my daughter with cocaine.'

'How old's your daughter, Herr Professor? Thirty? No, I'm afraid it's going to take more than that to put him behind bars. Something like selling drugs to a minor, who then takes an overdose. However, you can rest assured that we're watching him very closely.'

With that, Professor Ascher had to be content.

Gradually, during the weeks that followed, Georg started to relax. Lothar was a generous but unobtrusive host, leaving him free to come and go as he wanted, yet always there to stimulate and encourage. Thoughtfully, he rearranged Georg's schedule so that he had no more engagements until New Year's Eve at Café Jochum, giving him time to collect himself.

He neither saw nor heard anything of Pipsi and the letter Dr Duschek wrote to her about their separation remained unanswered. He did notice, however, that the weekly cheques he sent to cover the rent on the apartment and all her other expenses were promptly cashed, and it made him a little bitter to realize just how much she was costing him. But it did not really matter. For the moment, it was sufficient that he was relieved of the tension of sharing the same house as her.

Nor did he have to worry about Minna, whom he visited frequently. She seemed totally at home with the Arendts, accepted by them as one of the family, and remarkably unperturbed by the fact that her parents were no longer living together. 'Of course I'm all right, Papa. I've still got Nanny Simon.'

The happiest hours, however, were the ones Georg spent with Luise, sometimes quietly by the piano in Lothar's flat, at other times going to concerts and films, or, best of all, driving out through the frosty December countryside to the Havel lakes or the Jochums' cottage on the Heiligensee. She was so very different from Pipsi, with such an outgoing, generous, happy personality, that he soon came to realize the love he had professed for her before, which had stemmed more from a lonely desire to be loved than to love, was in fact rooted in something far deeper.

Every day increased the depth of his feeling for her and sometimes he felt a physical desire for her lithe, vibrant body so intense that it hurt. But when he tried to visualize a scene where he was making love to her, he was confronted by the fear of his impotence and shrank away from the image. What if Luise reacted the same way as Pipsi? He could not bear the thought of her scorn.

The ice was thick on the lakes that winter, so when Luise suggested one Sunday shortly before Christmas that they go skating, Georg leapt at the idea. Under its mantle of snow beneath an almost Alpine blue sky, the cottage at Heiligensee looked more beautiful than ever, but the atmosphere inside was raw, so before doing anything else they lit a wood fire in the grate and put a kettle over a trivet.

Their spirits soared as they fitted their skates, then made their first tentative steps over the ice, and the air was exhilarating, whipping colour into their cheeks, as they skated hand in hand near the shore. 'Let's go further out,' Luise cried impulsively.

Since she was a far better skater than him, Georg released her hand and watched her smilingly as she glided effortlessly away from him, humming an excerpt from *Les Patineurs*, moving with small, skipping steps, turning, pirouetting, forming figures of eight, then, as she grew more daring, jumping, turning in mid-air, landing on one foot and moving further and further out towards the middle of the lake. Motionless, he stood admiring her gracefulness, the richness of her auburn hair against the pure white of the snow and ice.

Then the silence was broken as beneath him he felt a tremor and, with a dry, rasping sound, the ice suddenly cracked. 'Luise!' he shouted, racing towards her, but she was already submerged in the freezing water, only her head and hands floundering helplessly above the surface. The ice moved and creaked threateningly under his weight and, after a last, few, tentative steps he was forced to stop. 'It's no good. I can't reach you. Is there a ladder at the cottage?'

'In the boathouse,' she stuttered, her teeth chattering.

Cautiously, Georg turned, moving gently over the ice until he felt it firm beneath him again. Then he skated as never before in his life, running over the packed snow on his skates into the boathouse, finding the ladder, carrying it effortlessly over his shoulder and hurrying back across the ice towards Luise.

He lay down, pushing the ladder in front of him, inching his way forward as the ice creaked and groaned around them. How desperately thin it was here, away from the shore. All the time, he talked to her, his breath steaming white in the air. 'You'll be all right, it's going to reach. Gently, now. I'll soon have you out, Luischen.'

When the end of the ladder was within her grasp, he slid away from her, lying full-length on the wooden treads. 'Pull yourself up by your arms.'

'I can't. Georg, I'm too cold.'

He knew a very real moment of fear. Any longer and it would be too late. 'Please, Luise,' he begged, 'try, for me. Bring your elbow up. Now, try and climb up sideways.' As she obediently did what he said, a great chunk of ice broke off. 'Darling, try again. A superhuman effort. Imagine you're in the swimming baths.'

He saw her take a deep breath, then, incredibly, she pulled herself up with her arms onto the end of the ladder. Again, the ice

498

moved, but the ladder, with Georg's weight on it, prevented it shattering. 'Now, move forward, crawl along it on your stomach.' To his relief, she managed it until she was finally lying full-length well away from the hole she had created by her fall. 'Stay there.' He slid backwards, until he was on the ice and able to drag the ladder and Luise's body towards the shore. Only when the ice ceased to creak did he dare stand up, drawing the ladder over the slippery surface until she was beside him. Then he picked her up as if she were a child and skated landwards.

Now, the winter air was truly bitter, cutting right through them. When they reached the shore Georg, wobbling on his skates, ran as quickly as he could over the snowy ground and into the house, where he set her down in front of the fire. Her fingers were much too cold to undo the buttons on her sodden clothes and, without a moment's hesitation, he took off her coat, dress, boots, then her underclothes and, staring wildly round the room for something to wrap her in, seized the hearthrug and enveloped her in it. He drew the settee up in front of the fire and sat Luise on it. 'Stay there, while I get some blankets.'

She shook her head, still too numbed to talk. Quickly, he removed his skates, rushed upstairs and returned with a vast eiderdown from one of the beds with which he replaced the hearthrug, then, with vigorous movements, rubbed his hands over her body to start her circulation. Gradually, the ghastly blue left her lips and tinges of pink entered her cheeks, but her entire body was shaking convulsively, while tears coursed down her face. To his relief, he saw a decanter of brandy left on top of the sideboard. Leaving Luise for a moment, he grabbed it, wrenched out the stopper and forced some of its contents down her throat.

His arms around her, he felt the trembling slowly subside to be replaced with racking sobs, as shock set in. 'Hush, Luischen, hush, my darling. Everything's all right now. You're safe.' She took a deep, shuddering breath, then, with a scream, buried her face against him. He held her tight, brushing his lips against her damp hair, stroking her, whispering reassurances and endearments, until she had spent all her tears.

Gently, he lifted her face. 'Have another sip of brandy.' Her skin was scalding to the touch, her cheeks flaming and her eyes red-rimmed from weeping, yet never had she appeared more beautiful to him. Tenderly, he kissed her salty mouth. 'Oh, Luise, darling, thank God you're safe.'

She grasped hold of his hand and spoke for the first time in a weak voice, 'Georg, you're so cold. You must change, too.'

Until that moment, he hadn't thought about himself, but now he realized that his own clothes were soaking wet from his long contact with the ice. Carefully, he laid her on the settee and went back upstairs to return a few moments later wrapped, like she was, Red Indian fashion in an eiderdown, with his damp clothes over his arm. Already she looked much better, her colour more normal and no longer shivering, but small and somehow pathetic with her wide green eyes staring out of her heart-shaped face above the bulk of the quilt. 'How do you feel now?'

She smiled tremulously. 'Georg, how can I ever thank you? If it hadn't been for you, I would have drowned.'

He longed to take her again in his arms but instead, he turned to the fire, threw a couple of logs onto it, pushed them with a poker and stared into the flames as a shower of sparks flew up the chimney. The kettle hissed, then released a cloud of steam. 'I'll make some tea.'

Luise watched him, willing him to come back to her, then, momentarily forgetting that her legs were still weak from their immersion in the lake, she stood up. She stumbled and her eiderdown became unwrapped, revealing the front of her naked body in the firelight.

Like a flash, Georg moved across and caught her, then he stared down at her. Slowly, he raised his eyes and, for a long moment, his arm on hers, the room around them silent except for crackling of the wood in the grate, they gazed at each other. Then he drew her to him, kissing her, his arms strong around her, pressing her body against him, until gradually they sank back onto the settee, lying full-length on it, their naked bodies touching.

She had always known this was going to be one of the richest experiences of her life, but Georg's tenderness and his almost humble excitement took her breath away. Never had she imagined such warmth, such delight in the discovery of another person's body, the wonderment of touch of finger and lip, the magic of skin against skin, of leg against leg, such fluidity, such joy in giving and yielding and surrendering and losing one's identity in the ultimate, frantic, delirious consummation. Until that moment, she knew she had been nothing. Now, through Georg, she had reached a new wholeness. She lifted her face to his to kiss him and, as she did so, realized his cheeks were wet with tears.

'Luise, I love you so much,' he whispered.

'And I love you, Georg. Oh, my darling, please don't be unhappy.'

He gazed at her wonderingly. 'Luise, don't you realize what you've done? Don't you understand how happy you've made me?' He drew her head onto his shoulder, clasping her fiercely to him. 'Luise, I thought there was something the matter with me. I thought I was incapable of being like any other man. They told me I was impotent. But, Luise, I'm not! Oh, my darling, thank you, thank you, thank you ...'

Chapter Eighteen

Luise made no attempt to conceal her happiness from the outside world. It showed in her vivacious laughter, in the vitality of her walk, the exuberant strength of her hair, and the clarity of her skin. No longer would Georg suffer, as he had done in the past, in the company of a woman who sought only to destroy him, for Luise was determined to give him everything Pipsi had refused him.

That she was succeeding was reflected in the joy that already permeated Georg's music, in the vigour with which he was throwing himself back into his work, in the positive notes that now rang out from his keyboard and transformed themselves into black crochets, quavers and semi-quavers over pages of scribbled scores.

Far from being jealous of his work, Luise encouraged him in it, for it represented another bond between them. Because she understood what he was doing, she did not feel excluded when he sat for hours alone in his room, leaving her to chat with Lothar, but proud that she had made his genius possible. That her faith in him was justified was plainly manifested at the first anniversary performance he and Emmy gave at Café Jochum on New Year's Eve.

On this occasion there was no need to send out invitations, for people applied far in advance for seats and many even stood throughout the evening. Emmy, no longer quite as thin and very much more confident than she had been a year earlier, looked even lovelier and her voice seemed to have acquired even greater strength. Georg's songs surpassed themselves. No longer did they tell of hunger and unrequited love, but spoke of hope and courage and joy.

When Emmy had bowed her way off the stage and the sound of bells rang out all over the city welcoming in 1926, Luise pushed through the crowded café to wish Georg a happy New Year. 'You were wonderful. When did you write those songs?'

'Since I've known you. You seem to have brought a new positive element into my life.'

She couldn't have asked for a better start to the New Year.

502

'Thank you,' she breathed, kissing him on the cheek. And when they eventually had to part for the night, even if he couldn't come with her, she at least had the satisfaction of knowing he wasn't going home to Pipsi.

The following day, it became apparent that her new relationship with Georg was not escaping Viktoria's eagle eyes. 'Luischen, you seem to be seeing an awful lot of Georg,' she said, when they had finished breakfast.

'Why not? We've always been good friends.'

'I think you're rather more than friends. Look, I don't want you to think I'm interfering, but I should hate you to be hurt.'

'Vicki, I don't think what Georg and I do is any of your business,' Luise retorted hotly. 'In case you've forgotten, we're both grown-up people. I've never interfered in your life or tried to pass judgement on your actions in any way, so may I suggest you just get on with looking after your children, your husband and your hotel and leave me to lead my own life?'

Stung to the quick, Viktoria said angrily, 'But I've never had an affair with a married man, Luise, and certainly not with a Jew!'

Luise stared at her, then stood up, pushing her chair backwards onto the ground. 'At least I hope I shall have the sense not to get pregnant,' she commented coldly and walked out of the room.

She soon forgot her anger with Viktoria, but her sister's remark about Georg being a married man lingered in her mind. Finally, she asked Lothar, who was the only divorced person she knew. 'It's Pipsi's fault the marriage went wrong. Why doesn't he divorce her?'

'I don't think it's that easy. He'd have to prove her infidelity and, of course, he'd run the risk that Pipsi would still be given custody of Minna, which is what he's always been afraid of.'

Luise bit her lip. 'So that means that, although he doesn't live with her, Georg may never get divorced?'

'It's possible,' Lothar admitted. Then he put her arm around her. 'Luise believe me, marriage isn't that important. Why don't you and Georg just enjoy yourselves? Be happy — and let the future take care of itself.'

As the weeks went by, she decided he was probably right. Although Georg was frequently on tour again, he returned to her as quickly as possible, and she spent all her free time in his company. Whenever her job allowed her, they spent long, ecstatic afternoons making love, followed by deep conversations about music, songs and the meaning of life. It seemed there was nothing upon which they were not agreed and every day seemed to bring them even closer together.

Before she knew it, the winter was over and spring was upon them, the lime trees along Unter den Linden bursting into tiny leaf and the lawns at Heiligensee a riot of golden daffodils. It was there, one glorious April day, as they wandered hand in hand beside the lake, that Georg announced, 'I'm going to start work seriously on the music for the show Lothar and I have been discussing.'

She turned to him excitedly, 'Oh, I'm so pleased. What's it going to be about, Georg?'

He grinned at her, 'The first love of my life — after you, of course. It's going to be about jazz.' He hugged her to him. 'You realize that it's going to take up a lot of my time. Do you mind seeing a little less of me?'

'So long as you're happy, I don't mind what you do,' she assured him. It was true. His happiness had become the sole purpose of her life.

That April Pipsi learned her husband was having an affair with Luise. When she arrived at 'Hades' one evening, Rudi told her gleefully, 'I saw them walking hand in hand through the Tiergarten, darling. They looked so sweet I nearly forgot where I was driving. But I'm sure you already know all about it and have instructed your lawyer.'

She stared at him blankly. Georg having an affair with Luise Jochum! It couldn't be true. Georg couldn't get an erection. He was impotent. He couldn't be having an affair. She felt her heart pounding and her fingers trembling, as panic rose in her. Then she noticed the look of satisfaction in Rudi's eyes. Forcing her voice to remain calm, she asked, 'May I have my cocaine, Rudi?'

He reached into the little drawer behind the bar, but before he gave her the small packet, he said, 'Oh, and darling, your account is getting rather high. Let me have some money sometime, won't you? After all, poor Rudi has to make a living somehow.'

Already on the way to the ladies' cloakroom, she hardly heard him. Whereas the effects of a small dose of the drug had lasted for several hours when she had first started taking it, now she seemed to need to take it more frequently. Shaking, she sank down in a chair and sniffed at the vital powder. Then she stared at herself in the mirror. The hollows in her cheeks made her eyes appear very big, while she could almost span her waist with her own hands. But, as they had been for some while now, her nostrils were inflamed and her sinuses hurt. She didn't seem to be able to smell anything any more. She fluffed a little powder over her nose.

Slowly, her palpitations began to subside and she thought about Rudi's news and his comment about her lawyer. If Georg were having an affair, she ought to be able to twist it somehow to her own advantage, at least get some money out of him to pay Rudi's account.

When she emerged into the bar again, she felt quite confident. There was a stranger sitting alone and she made her way towards him, fluttering her eyelashes encouragingly. 'Hello, I'm Pipsi.'

The man grinned at her knowingly, putting his arm round her bare shoulder and hugging her to him. 'Hello, Pipsi, I'm sure you like champagne.' He signalled a waiter and led her over to a dark corner. But when it was time to go, despite the fact that she had allowed him to put his hand up her skirt, he ignored her invitation to accompany her home and, for the seventh night in a row, she had to pay for her own taxi and sleep alone. That decided her. The following afternoon, she went to see her lawyer.

Making copious notes, he listened sympathetically to her account of her marriage with Georg, his impotence and the fact that he had left her without a word but, to all appearances, because he was having an affair with another woman. 'Leaving aside the technical question of whether an impotent man can have an affair, Frau Jankowski,' he said, when she had finished, 'may I ask you whether you would like to try and effect a reconciliation or if you want to petition for a judicial separation or a divorce?'

Pipsi stared at him. The last thing she wanted was to have Georg back again, but she was damned if she was going to give him the satisfaction of a divorce, so that he could marry Luise Jochum. 'What I really need, is some more money.'

'Have you seen your husband since he left you?'

She showed him Dr Duschek's letter. 'This is all I've heard.'

The lawyer studied it, then said, 'I suggest I contact Dr Duschek on your behalf and discuss a petition for a separation. In the meantime, if you let me have details of all your expenses, I'll try and obtain an increase in your allowance.'

Pipsi knew then it was hopeless, for the weekly cheque Georg sent her more than covered all her domestic needs and no judge was ever going to decree that her husband should finance her cocaine.

From that moment on, things grew progressively worse. Soon, Rudi would allow her no more credit and the bank refused to increase her overdraft, none of her impassioned pleas to Theo having any effect. 'Give up drugs, Pipsi, and we'll discuss the matter,' was all he said.

Then her father visited her again. Hoping that Theo would have said nothing to him, she asked, 'Papa, please lend me some money.'

'To buy drugs?' he snorted. 'No, Pipsi, you're not having another penny from me until you stop this dreadful habit.'

Her lip curled. 'I'm your daughter ...'

The Professor was having none of that. 'Pipsi, I'm not putting up with this any more. You've tried to wreck the lives of Georg and Minna and now you're ruining your own. For God's sake, girl, haven't you any sense?'

Pipsi turned on him, hissing like an angry cat. 'It's none of your damned business,' she screamed. 'It's my life and I shall do what I want with it. Why won't you all let me live in peace?'

He held out a placating hand. 'Pipsi, it's because we care. We hate to see you making yourself ill.'

'I'm not ill,' she yelled. 'I'm happier than I've been in my life before.'

'Pipsi, drug addiction is an illness. You're sick.'

'I'm not sick. It's all of you who are sick.'

'Pipsi, see a doctor, please. Give up cocaine.'

His words gave her an idea. She went to a fashionable doctor in the Kurfuerstendamm of whom she had often heard people speak at 'Hades', and told him a convincing story of sleepless nights and lack of appetite. Unquestioningly, he gave her a large bottle of sleeping tablets. 'Just one a night,' he instructed.

The combination of cocaine, sleeping tables and champagne was exquisite. Never in her life had she enjoyed such beautiful dreams. And soon she discovered that if she took two sleeping pills, she did not wake until midday.

Unable to raise money any other way, she started to pawn her bracelets, rings and necklaces until, one dreadful summer day, her jewellery casket was empty. She stared at it in disbelief, then looked around the apartment. It seemed there was nothing else for it. She would have to sell its contents.

Fortified by a couple of grammes of cocaine, Pipsi grandiosely authorized a house clearance company to take away all her furniture and pictures except for the bed and, although the sum they gave her in return was less than she had expected, it still represented enough money to keep her in cocaine for another month. When the lorry was loaded, one of the men grinned, 'You could throw a wonderful party here now.'

Pipsi was on a high that day. What a beautiful idea! She'd go to 'Hades' and invite everyone back to the apartment afterwards. Dressing carefully, she spent some of her new wealth on a taxi to the night club, but as they drew up to the entrance, the driver pointed to a police car parked outside and said, 'Looks like there's trouble here. Do you want me to drive on?'

The police car meant nothing to her. 'No,' she said haughtily, 'I want to get out.'

Just as she was paying him, however, Rudi emerged from the club, his wrists in handcuffs, his figure firmly wedged between two policemen. A small crowd was gathering, calling out ribald comments, to which the policemen snarled replies. Rudi, suave and elegant as always, smiled benignly, as if the policemen were doing him a great honour. When he saw Pipsi, he winked.

'Rudi!' she cried, but a policeman brushed her away, pushing Rudi into the waiting Black Maria. Bewildered, she watched them drive off towards the Alexanderplatz, then rang the bell to 'Hades'. The commissionaire who opened it stared at her coldly. 'The night club's been shut down until further notice. And there's nothing here for you. The police have taken it all.'

In a matter of seconds, her earlier excited mood changed to depression. She sagged against the wall, gazing piteously at him. 'Why have they arrested Rudi?'

'They say he's been supplying drugs to an under-aged girl, and she's died. They're accusing him of murder, Miss.'

'Murder?' The commissionaire's face swam hazily in front of her eyes. 'Rudi? Murder? But what about my cocaine?'

'You get out of here. They're coming back here any minute to search the place from top to bottom. If they find you, you'll be arrested too. Now, get moving.' He shoved her into the street and slammed the door behind her.

Tears sprang to her eyes. The couple of grammes of cocaine in her purse were all that remained to her and now Rudi was gone she did not know where to buy more. Suddenly, she felt utterly bereft. A taxi drew up to the kerb and almost in a dream, she asked the cabby to take her home.

It was only when she saw the empty flat again that she remembered she had been going to throw a party, although she was no longer sure who the guests were going to be, for she had no real friends any more and certainly none of her family gave a damn whether she lived or died. Indeed, so far as they were concerned, she might just as well be dead. She thought of Anita, the only person she had ever loved. How had Anita repaid her love? By walking out on her, by leaving her, just as everybody else had left her.

She took a sniff of cocaine, then pulled out the half bottle of whisky concealed under her bed and swallowed a couple of her sleeping pills. She had eaten nothing for two days and their effect was immediate. Swiftly, her depression started to lift, making her feel more confident. Suddenly, she thought of Georg. Georg had always loved her. This silly nonsense about him having an affair with Luise was all a ploy to get her back again. If he really wanted Luise, he would have asked for a divorce by now, but he hadn't — which must mean he still loved her.

It seemed so simple now she thought of it. Why not invite Georg to come and see her? The two of them could have a wonderful party together. She reached down to the telephone on the bare floorboards beside the bed, shuffling through her address book to find Lothar's number and, as she listened to it ringing, she began to feel quite exhilarated. If Georg came back, she need never be lonely again.

He answered the telephone himself and she thrilled at the sound of his voice. 'Georg, it's Pipsi.'

He was silent for a moment, then he asked, 'Yes, Pipsi, what do you want?' He sounded irritated.

'Come and see me, Georg. I'm so lonely. I want someone to talk to.'

'What do you want to talk about?'

'I want to talk about you and me,' Pipsi said and her voice seemed to come from a long way away. The pills, she thought hazily, were working well. 'I want you, Georg. I'm lonely.'

'Perhaps you should have thought of that before. Pipsi, I'm very busy. If you want to see me, make an appointment through your solicitor. Now, leave me in peace.' The phone went dead in her ear.

So, not even Georg wanted her. Mechanically, she swallowed three more pills and washed them down with more whisky. What kind of husband was that? As tears rose to her eyes, she lay back on the bed, staring at the ceiling. Why had everything gone so wrong in her life? She hadn't done anything to deserve such unhappiness. All she had wanted was to have some fun, to love and to be loved.

Her hand reached out to the sachet of cocaine and she sniffed some more. Soon it would all be gone and there would be no more, for Rudi was in prison. Poor Rudi. Poor Georg. But, most of all, poor Pipsi. Well, she might as well enjoy it while it was there. And the pills. And the whisky. She lifted the bottle. She swallowed some more pills. Soon, there was nothing more in any of the bottles and the scrap of white paper that had contained cocaine fluttered emptily to the floor. Her eyelids drooped and, sprawled awkwardly across the bed, she fell into a deep slumber.

She dreamed she was having a party, the greatest party of her life, but strangely, there wasn't any music, nor were there any guests. And, suddenly, there was nothing at all.

Pipsi Ascher was dead.

When Georg told Luise and Lothar about Pipsi's telephone call over supper that evening, he looked rather disturbed. 'We've been apart for over six months now and this is the first time she's contacted me. She said she was lonely and wanted someone to talk to. Do you think I ought to go and see her?'

Picking up the evening paper, Lothar gave a thin smile. 'I think I can explain it. Rudi's been arrested. "Hades" is shut until further notice.'

'Rudi?' Luise exclaimed, snatching the paper from his hand, but the news item told her very little. 'Well, I suppose that would explain why Pipsi was feeling lonely,' she said doubtfully.

'It will make it more difficult for her to get her cocaine.'

Georg looked worriedly at them both. 'You're probably right. Well, I think I'll get back to my work, if you'll excuse me.'

When he and Luise met the following afternoon, however, he was back to his usual good spirits. 'Lothar's out and his secretary's gone home, so we're all alone and we're going to spend the rest of the day in bed!'

Never had their bodies seemed in more perfect harmony than they were that afternoon and Luise, in her joyful abandonment, totally forgot about Pipsi until the telephone rang. 'Oh, let it ring,' Georg mumbled, his face pressed between her breasts. But, as it went on ringing, she felt him grow tense. 'I'd better answer it, I suppose, although heaven help her if it's Pipsi again.'

He was gone a very long time and when he returned his face was grey. Without a word, he started to dress. 'Georg, what's happened?' Luise asked, anxiously.

'Pipsi's dead,' he replied curtly. 'The Professor found her a couple of hours ago.'

'Dead?' Luise repeated, shocked, stumbling out of bed and starting to pull on her own clothes. 'But how?'

Georg stared at her blindly. 'It sounds as if she took an overdose.' He walked towards the door and opened it. 'I've got to meet the Professor at the mortuary.'

'Georg, wait, I'll come with you,' she cried, struggling with a stocking.

'No, this is my affair. I have to see it through on my own.'

'But, Georg ...'

'Luise, don't you understand? She telephoned me yesterday afternoon, pleading for me to go and see her. If I'd done what she asked this wouldn't have happened. But I didn't go — and now she's dead. I killed Pipsi, Luise. I've killed my wife.'

Before she could say anything, he was gone. Stunned, she sat back on the bed. She heard the engine of his car start, then a squeal of tyres as it pulled away. Automatically, she finished putting on her stockings, then made the bed, filled with a strange desire to suppress every sign of their lovemaking. But when that was done, she was at a loss to know what to do next.

The very silence of the flat was oppressive, but it seemed to offer her a link with Georg. While she stayed there, she was still a part of his life, but if she returned to the hotel, she had the feeling she might lose him for ever. She paced up and down the living room, trying to understand what had happened. Pipsi was dead. And Georg, because he hadn't gone to see her, believed he had killed her. It was nonsense, of course. Yet, the fact remained, Pipsi was dead.

She was still pacing the flat when Lothar returned. He took one look at her and, without saying a word, poured her a schnapps. 'Drink that, then tell me what's happened.'

She swallowed the neat spirit in a single gulp, then told him the little she knew. 'I had to stay here. I thought maybe Georg would phone. And I want to be here when he comes back!'

When they had heard nothing by midnight, Lothar said gently, 'I think I'd better take you home. He's probably staying with the Arendts or Professor Ascher. He'll want to be among his own family tonight.'

'Yes, I suppose you're right.' Then she voiced the thoughts that had been running through her mind all evening. 'Lothar, everything will be all right, won't it? After all, Georg hasn't loved her for years, so her death can't mean that much to him. And now he won't need a divorce. There won't be anything to stop us getting married.'

'I don't know,' Lothar said unhappily. 'Georg is a very sensitive person, Luise. If, as you said, he believes he killed Pipsi, it may take him a very long time to recover. I suggest you don't put him too hard.'

'Do you think I could try to telephone him at the Arendts' tomorrow?'

Lothar laid his hand on hers. 'This is his ordeal, Luise. He knows where you are. You must wait until he contacts you.'

She nodded, listlessly. 'I think you'd better take me home.'

Next day, the newspaper headlines read, *ACTRESS DIES FROM OVERDOSE*. There was a photograph of Pipsi at eighteen in *Hurra! Hussar!*, her long black hair streaming down her back and her full figure almost bursting out of her costume. The article alongside detailed her stage career, then went on to say, 'She was a well-known figure at Berlin's famous night club, "Hades", owned by Rudi Nowak, who was arrested two days ago for supplying cocaine to a minor. Herr Nowak is expected to appear soon in court.' It concluded, 'Miss Ascher's husband, the composer Georg Jankowski, is staying at the Grunewald villa of his brother-in-law, the banker, Theo Arendt, with his ten-year-old daughter, Minna. Said to be deeply shocked, he was unavailable for comment. The funeral will be taking place next Monday at the Grunewald Synagogue.'

Luise walked through life in a daze, never out of reach of a telephone, but although Lothar rang her every day to make sure she was all right, she heard nothing from Georg. Then a formal announcement, addressed to Benno, arrived at the hotel, inviting them all to the funeral. 'Poor girl,' Benno said, 'she can't have been very old.'

'She was a year younger than me,' Viktoria told him. 'Thirty-one, no age at all.'

'I don't remember seeing her since the opening of Café Jochum,' Benno went on, gravely, 'but she was certainly very beautiful then. Luise, you've been such friends with the Jankowskis, you'll certainly want to go, so I think we'd better all show our respect. I'm sorry for Georg and the Professor. They must be very upset.'

As soon as she could, Luise escaped, seeking refuge in her room. It was there that Viktoria found her. Sitting down on the bed beside her, she said, 'Luischen, you don't have to go to the funeral if you don't want to.'

'It isn't that. It's just that I feel so helpless. Vicki, there ought to be something I can do for Georg, but there's nothing.'

Viktoria could only say the same as Lothar. 'He knows where you are, Luischen. If he wants you, he'll get in touch.'

Luise saw Georg for the first time in a week at the synagogue and his appearance shocked her to the marrow. His face cadaverously thin and grey-tinged, he stood in the front row between Sophie and Minna, looking straight ahead of him from unseeing eyes. Even in the Jewish cemetery where Pipsi's body was laid to rest, he seemed to recognize and hear nobody and when the ceremony was finally over, he immediately left with his family.

'They all blame themselves for her death,' a portly Jewish matron beside Luise commented loudly to a friend. 'She and Jankowski weren't living together, you know, but I've heard she telephoned him the day she died. He was having an affair with some young flibbertigibbet, although I'm sure that's over now. Still, it's too late, isn't it? He should have thought before.'

'Poor Pipsi. What a pity she didn't marry someone like Theo Arendt, then she'd never have suffered like this,' her friend said.

Viktoria put her arm around Luise. 'Come home.'

In the car, Benno asked, 'Did you hear those women saying that Georg was having an affair? Did you know that, Luise?'

'Oh, for God's sake, Benno,' Viktoria snapped, 'why don't you shut up?'

Surprised, Benno looked from one to the other of them, then wisely said nothing more.

Luise allowed a few more days to pass then, when she could stand the tension no longer, she telephoned Georg. 'Please can I see you?'

With a reluctance obvious even to her, he agreed, suggesting one of the most innocuous — and most public — meeting places in the whole city. 'I'll wait for you at the entrance to the zoo at two tomorrow.'

The zoo was full of people that clear July afternoon. Their hands deep in their pockets, Luise and Georg made their way among them, two distinctly separate figures. Both their faces showed evidence of sleepless nights, their eyes were dulled with misery and their footsteps lagged. When Georg spoke, he did not look at her, but stared dully ahead at the animals in their barred cages. 'Luise, I'm sorry, I'm so confused, I just don't know what to think any more.'

'I love you, Georg. I so much want to help you.'

'There's nothing anyone can do. I feel so guilty. Nobody can take away that guilt.'

Numbly, she nodded. 'What are you going to do, Georg?'

'Work. It's the only thing I know how to do well. Luise, I'm sorry, but you deserve better than me. I shall never make you happy, any more than I made Pipsi happy.'

'But you have made me happy. Georg, don't you understand? I love you. I love everything about you, not just your body, not only your music, but you, Georg Jankowski. You are my life, Georg, you are all that I live for.' The words came out in a strangled sob.

It was as if he was unaware of her presence, as if he had already ceased to relate to her. He talked about Pipsi, explaining how he had promised Professor Ascher that he would love her until the day he died. 'But I failed her. When she needed me most, I wasn't there.'

'No, Georg, you did everything you could for her...'

He seemed not to hear her. 'I've failed Minna, too. She doesn't seem at all upset that her mother is dead. And she doesn't want to live with me, either. I've promised her that we will find another apartment, but she wants to stay with Theo and Sophie.'

Luise's eyes were huge in the whiteness of her face. 'Georg, she's confused, she's had a terrible shock. But you and I, we can start again. Perhaps, later, Minna will join us.'

'Don't you understand?' There was an almost savage bitterness in his voice. 'I can't just pick up where we left off. I need time to think things out, time to adjust, time to build myself a new life.'

'But one that doesn't include me,' Luise said bleakly. 'Georg, it wasn't my fault Pipsi died. What about me?'

For a long time, they stood in silence, the crowds jostling round them, children's laughter ringing in the sunshine. Then Georg said helplessly, 'I don't know, Luischen.' He leaned over and brushed his lips across her hair. 'I'm sorry, my dear, I just don't know anything any more.'

She scarcely heard him. She only knew that Pipsi, dead, had succeeded in coming between them as she never had alive.

For a long time, life lost all substance for Luise. Like an automaton, she continued to do her job, she wrote business letters, she smiled at guests, she picked at her meals and she smoked increasing numbers of cigarettes. But, whenever she had the opportunity, she haunted the forest at Grunewald, the cottage at Heiligensee, Café Jochum, the Palm Garden Room and the Jubilee Room, the Tiergarten and the Kurfuerstendamm. She stood outside Lothar's apartment, a dull ache where her heart had once been, waiting for Georg to appear. But Georg had gone away. Georg didn't live there any more.

Her friends were dreadfully kind. Kind, as people were to a small child, who had lost its favourite toy or found its pet kitten run over. Because she and Georg had not been married, but had merely been having an affair, they assumed her love for him had only been of a passing nature. 'I do understand, but you'll soon get over it,' Viktoria said. 'You'll soon find somebody else.'

Ricarda knew something was wrong, but she did not know what and Luise could not tell her. Sometimes, she desperately wished she could talk to her mother, but it was too late. First she would have to confess that she had been having an affair with a married man, even if his wife was now dead. Ricarda would never understand that.

And there was Lothar. Lothar, who told her that Georg had found a new apartment. Lothar, who let her know Georg and Emmy had gone on tour again. Lothar, who said, 'Luise, we've got to be very patient and understanding with him.' Lothar, who murmured, 'You still have me. I know I'm a poor substitute, but I'm very fond of you.'

They all spoke to her, but their words held no meaning. They reached out to her, but she could not feel their touch. Sometimes, she thought it was actually she who had died that summer and her ghost that moved among them. Sometimes, when the pain inside her grew almost unbearable, when she lay on her bed weeping dry, soundless tears, she wished she were dead.

Time and time again, she recalled her first meeting with Georg, the occasion their hands had touched in the Palm Garden Room, the opening of Café Jochum, the scene in Theo's drawing room, the day she had fallen through the ice at Heiligensee. And, always, she came back to that terrible moment when Georg had learned Pipsi was dead. Clearer than any others he had spoken, she heard his words, 'I killed Pipsi, Luise. I've killed my wife.'

Why? Why? Why? The questions hammered at her brain. Why had he not divorced Pipsi earlier? Why had he assumed the guilt for her death? Why did he persist in believing he had killed Pipsi, when in fact it was her, Luise, he had killed? Why, when they were now free to marry, had he deserted her? Why did he never contact her? And then came the final question, the hardest one of all to face. Had Georg ever loved her as much as she loved him?

Was it one of life's cruel ironies that in any partnership there was one who gave and one who took; one who wounded and one who was hurt; one who loved and one who was loved?

As the months went by and she heard nothing from him, Luise tried to accept the sober truth. They had enjoyed a brief interlude in life and they had been happy together, but it had been a love that could not last. Nothing lasted for ever. They had known a share of heaven, but that heaven had turned into hell. Georg had made her no promises. He had broken no vows. For the moment at least, their affair was over.

Perhaps, one future day, they could pick up the broken pieces and start again. Not from where they had left off, but from some fresh point. One day, when they had both had time to think things through, to adjust, to build new lives ... It was a slender hope, but it was the only one to which Luise could cling.

That December, after a mere six months in prison, Rudi Nowak was released. Berlin hummed with the news. Not only had Dr Dr Frey presented a brilliant defence for him, but during his imprisonment he had sold Rudi's three night clubs and his various other business concessions for, it was rumoured, a very considerable profit, of which Dr Dr Frey had undoubtedly taken a large percentage, and transferred the still substantial remaining proceeds to America. *NOWAK STARTS NEW LIFE* read the newspaper headlines, under which photographs showed Rudi, looking none the worse for his incarceration, boarding a train at the Anhalter Station on the first stage of his journey to California.

He meant nothing to her any more, but Luise felt an unexpected sadness at his departure. For all his sins, he had been a major influence on her life, one of the many people who had helped make her into the person she was. He had been her first lover. And he had been a link with Sepp, who had also gone to America to begin a new life. How long ago those days seemed now. As she gazed at Rudi's picture, she experienced a sudden nostalgia for a time that, in retrospect, seemed to have been full of hope and laughter.

Then she realized the futility of her thoughts. There was no going back. There was only the present — and the future. New life, new life ... The words echoed in her mind. If Rudi, Sepp and Georg could leave Berlin and build new lives, then so could she. If she could find work engrossing enough to absorb her every waking thought, there would be only the lonely nights to endure. If she were not reminded every day of Georg, she might be able to put him into perspective. Even if she could never forget him, she could, at least, come to terms with her loss.

Somehow, Luise survived the empty merriment of New Year's Eve without Georg. By then, the desire to escape had become the overwhelming impulse of her life. She did not care where she went or what she did, provided she could leave Berlin with all its memories behind her and — in a strange town, among strangers — go back to her beginnings and start afresh.

The sound of cannon and fireworks that had so resoundingly welcomed in 1927 had scarcely ceased reverberating, streamers and balloons lay where they had fallen in the ballroom, most of the hotel's guests were still recovering from their hangovers, but Baron Heinrich von Kraus had no time for such luxuries.

At nine that morning, a page boy knocked at the Jochum apartment door, bearing a note on a silver salver. Benno opened it and groaned. 'As always, Father chooses his times perfectly. Apparently, he has business to discuss. He requests the presence of all of us, including Mama, in his suite at ten. Well, we'd better obey.'

When they duly trooped into his rooms, the Baron greeted them abruptly, then addressed himself to Benno. 'The *Countess Julia* is reaching her final stages of preparation. It is my ambition to make her into a floating Hotel Quadriga and for this I need your expertise.'

'We don't know much about ships, Father,' Benno said, doubtfully.

'No, boy, but you know about passengers. I want the *Countess*

Julia to excel in opulence and luxury. She is going to have the finest cabins, the most excellent restaurants, the most superb entertainments, of any passenger liner in the world. Wetzlar has designed and Kraus have built the biggest and fastest liner in the world; now you are going to make her into the most luxurious.'

'It would certainly be a challenge,' Benno breathed, 'but exactly what would it involve?'

'The *Countess Julia* weighs over fifty thousand tons and is nine hundred and forty feet long. That's twice as big as the *Prussia* and some five times bigger than the Hotel Quadriga. She'll carry five hundred first-class passengers — no cabin or tourist passengers at all. What I want you to do is advise on and supervise the fitting of the cabins, the lounges, the dining saloons, the menus we should offer and the entertainment.'

'Not cabins, Heinrich,' Ricarda protested, 'they should be proper bedrooms for first-class passengers, with open fireplaces, deep pile carpets, silk curtains ...'

'Think, they'll have nothing to do all day, except amuse themselves,' Viktoria murmured. 'You could stage fashion shows, you could have shops and hairdressing salons, as well as cabaret acts, floor shows, fancy dress balls ...'

'And superb restaurants and bars,' Benno continued. 'The sea air is going to give the passengers an appetite. Yes, Father, we could certainly help you.' He paused. 'But with the best will in the world, I don't see where I'm going to find the time.'

Luise held her breath. Surely this must be the opportunity for which she had been waiting, an exacting and demanding job that also offered the chance to escape from her harrowing emotional dilemma? But would the Baron accept her? Wouldn't he think she was too young and inexperienced?

'Heinrich,' Ricarda suggested, 'why doesn't Luise administer the operation for you? She made an excellent job of Café Jochum.'

They were all silent for a moment, then they stared at Luise. 'That's not a bad idea,' Benno said slowly.

'I think it's wonderful,' exclaimed Viktoria. 'After all, Luise's inherited all Mama's artistic gifts and it was really Mama who was responsible for the design of the Quadriga.'

'And it's expense, if I remember correctly,' the Baron said drily.

Ricarda gave an indignant snort and Benno retorted quickly, 'I assume we'd be working to a budget.' He turned to Luise. 'Would you like to do it?'

'Oh, yes, I'd love to be involved.'

'Then I suggest, Father, that I supervise the whole operation, under your direction, of course, while Luise is our on-site manager.'

'You realize you'll have to spend a lot of your time at Kraushaven,' the Baron warned.

'I wouldn't mind that at all,' Luise assured him, then looked from one to the other of them. 'Do you trust me to do the job?'

Benno smiled at her. 'Don't worry, you won't be on your own. I'll be watching everything you do. And Father will be watching me!'

As they went on to discuss all the details of the job, Luise felt fresh hope stir within her. Of all people, it seemed Baron Heinrich had supplied the answer to her prayers.

The next month sped by at almost frightening speed. The Baron inundated her with blueprints, plans, sketches, photographs, piles of books and a daunting list of instructions. Her mother, Viktoria and Benno wasted no opportunity to impress upon her the salient features of the Hotel Quadriga, which they thought should be incorporated into the *Countess Julia,* for the advantages of a 'floating Quadriga', automatically bringing rich Americans to the hotel, promised to be immense. Hedwig Korb, the wife of Kraus Marin's General Manager, wrote to assure her that she would be most welcome to lodge with her family. Luise had not even started her new job, but already it was taking over her life.

At the end of January, Benno drove her to Kraushaven. She had been a little girl at the time of her only other visit, nineteen years earlier, to watch the launch of the *Prussia* and, in the meantime, the shipyard had grown beyond all recognition. At its centre there were now three building berths, surrounded by long sheds, vast engine-making shops and huge warehouses. Around them, a town had risen, a compact settlement of small shops and houses, every occupant of which was dependent, in some way, upon Kraus for its livelihood. And, lest anyone should ever forget to whom they owed their prosperity, there was marked in large letters on the towering cranes and gantries that dominated the shipyard, the name *KRAUS.*

Benno parked on the quayside and as they got out of the car, sleet slanted across the grey, choppy expanse of water, whipping their faces icily. Luise shivered and pulled up the collar of her coat. Benno grinned. 'It was like this the first time I came here.' Then he pointed at the massive hull of a ship looming high above them, almost concealed by building staging up which the tiny figures of Kraus workmen were scurrying.

'Is that the *Countess Julia*?' Luise asked in awe.

'That's the *Countess Julia*,' a voice laughed, and Luise turned to find herself confronted by a stocky, middle-aged man, in a seaman's jacket. Crinkled, grey eyes smiled at her from a weather-beaten face. 'And you must be Fraeulein Jochum. Permit me to introduce myself. I am Jurg Korb, the General Manager of Kraus Marin.' He took her hand in a firm grasp, then turned to Benno. 'Herr Benno, I'm pleased to see you again. Now, come inside out of this infernal weather.'

Benno did not stay long, because he wanted to get back to Berlin that night. When he had gone, Jurg Korb said, 'I'm sure you're tired and would welcome an opportunity to wash and change, Fraeulein Jochum. I'll take you home now. Tomorrow, I'll show you round the *Countess Julia* and you can start work.' Luise agreed gratefully. Suddenly, it was starting to seem a long day.

He piled her luggage into the back of his small car and drove for about five minutes, stopping outside a long, rambling house situated on a low headland looking up the mouth of the River Weser towards the North Sea. 'This is your new home,' he announced proudly. 'I hope you'll be happy here.'

The door opened and a woman hurried down the path, a small child clutching at her apron. 'You poor dear, you must be frozen,' she clucked, putting her arm round her, maternally. The house struck warm as they entered and smelt appetizingly of freshly-baked bread. Luise had an impression of spacious, rather untidy rooms, comfortable furniture and children's laughter. She looked at Hedwig Korb's plump, jolly face and was suddenly glad she was not staying at an impersonal hotel. Not only was she going to enjoy the challenge of her new job, but she was looking forward to becoming part of a cheerful family.

No, there was nothing at Kraushaven to remind her of her old existence. No café society, no modern music, nobody who had ever heard of Pipsi Ascher or Georg Jankowski. But there were the wild wastes of the estuary, the cries of the seagulls and the company of simple, happy people. Maybe, here, she could find herself again.

Luise spent sixteen months at Kraushaven, months that sped by so quickly for Viktoria that she was scarcely aware of their passing. This was, after all, the first period of real stability and prosperity Germany had known since before the war. Stresemann's magnificent efforts, first to effect the Dawes Plan, then the signing of the Treaty of Locarno and, finally, to gain Germany admission to the League of Nations, had made the country part of an integrated and peaceful Europe. There seemed not a cloud on the horizon.

To start with, Viktoria expected her sister to be homesick for Berlin, but if she was, she gave no sign of it. Her prolonged stay meant that they all took their turn at visiting her. Benno drove over once a week, leaving Berlin before first light and arriving back at midnight. Viktoria, Ricarda and the children made short holidays of their trips, Hedwig Korb somehow finding room for all of them in the rambling house on the promontory.

They were delightful days, particularly in the spring and summer, the clear, bracing, northern air bringing colour to their cheeks and stimulating their appetites. Ricarda, sixty now, her hair quite white, brought her easel and water colours with her, spending many happy hours painting the changing tints of sky, cloud and sea.

Stefan and Monika, too, benefited from a change in climate and made firm friends with the three Korb children. Stefan was twelve that year, a robust small boy, with dark, thoughtful eyes. He had now outgrown Fraeulein Metz and was attending the city's best grammar school, already proving himself a good all-rounder, top of his class in his studies and proficient at sports. Viktoria was inordinately proud of his achievements although, when Ricarda and Fraeulein Metz continued to talk about him going to Oxford University, she did sometimes wish he were less gifted. Blonde little Monika caused her no such heartache. Under Fraeulein Metz's tutelage, she was turning into a very ordinary seven-year-old, plodding obediently through her lessons, showing no sign of her brother's superior intelligence.

'They're lovely children, Frau Jochum-Kraus,' Hedwig Korb told her. It did not take Viktoria long to realize that the Korbs were playing a vital role in Luise's recovery. From the very beginning, Hedwig and Jurg appeared to have adopted her. 'She's such a thin little thing,' Hedwig confided to Viktoria. 'She needs looking after.' As for the three Korb children, they plainly adored their new Aunt Luise. For the first time, Viktoria realized that, given the right husband, Luise would be very good at running a home and caring for a family.

She was also, it appeared, taking her new job very seriously and, according to Jurg Korb, managing it extremely efficiently. Before very long, she had become so involved in the liner that she could talk about nothing else. It seemed to Viktoria that Luise talked and thought ships morning, noon and night. Even her letters to her in Berlin were full of her plans, demanding advice and information, and even suggesting innovations that could be adopted by the hotel. Benno laughed when Viktoria commented on this to him. 'Yes, I don't know what happened last year, but she certainly seems to have got over it now.'

Viktoria was not so sure, but it certainly seemed as if Luise had decided to start a new chapter of her life at the beginning of the new year. As the months flew by, her face filled out, becoming tanned by the sea air, and she seemed to have recovered all her old energy. One day that autumn, when they were strolling across the meadows near the Korb home, Stefan and Monika happily playing with the Korb children, Viktoria ventured to mention Georg for the first time. 'Are the old wounds healing?' she asked gently.

Luise was silent for a moment, then she said, 'I've thought lot about Georg since I came to Kraushaven and I've gradually started to understand why he acted like he did. Of course I'm sad that we've drifted apart but I hope that, one day, we shall be able to be friends again. Vicki, I'm twenty-seven now and I've only ever really loved one man in my life. But I'm beginning to see there's more to life than love. Like Georg, I'm finding both escape and satisfaction in my work.' Then she smiled. 'That's something you should understand. After all, you've done the same thing during your life.'

Ruefully, Viktoria admitted the truth of that remark. She linked her arm through Luise's. 'It's funny, I've always thought we were very different from each other, but in many ways we're quite similar, aren't we?'

Luise laid her head on Viktoria's shoulder. 'We're both rather lonely people. Perhaps it's time we became friends.'

Viktoria kissed her wiry, russet curls. 'Of course, we're friends, darling. I want nothing more than for you to be happy.'

By the time the fitting out of the *Countess Julia* was completed in the spring of 1928, Luise was scarcely recognizable as the pale ghost that had set out for Kraushaven. In recognition for her hard work, Baron Heinrich announced that he had decided to invite her and a companion to be the guests of himself and his family on the liner's maiden voyage.

Much as Viktoria would have loved to accompany her, she was delighted when Luise asked Ricarda. 'We promise to have an exciting cruise,' Luise laughed. 'Apparently the Baron has decided that the *Countess Julia* is going to win the Blue Riband back from the British *Mauretania*.'

To the unobservant eye, Luise was once more her old self. Back in Berlin again, she quietly resumed her old routines at the hotel and Café Jochum and her old friendship with Lothar Lorenz. But Viktoria was more perceptive. She saw tell-tale scars that marked the depth of Luise's suffering and the price she had paid for her recovery. Small lines creased her forehead and there was a new diffidence in her voice. Gone was the vivacious butterfly that had flitted giddily from dream to dream and love to love. Unexpectedly saddened by the transformation, Viktoria wondered if it would ever return.

Baron Heinrich was at the Hotel Quadriga that May when an ominous event occurred, a disturbing reminder of days they all believed had passed. With elections due to take place at the end of month, all the political parties were vigorously campaigning, although there was little doubt that, now the republic was so soundly established, the Social Democrats would finally gain the majority for which they had so long fought.

Viktoria and Luise were strolling down the Kurfuerstendamm one sunny afternoon, window-shopping for Luise's cruise, when they found their way blocked by grim-faced policemen. From a side street, they heard the sound of marching boots and shouted slogans and looked at each other in alarm. 'What now?' Viktoria muttered.

They didn't have to wait long to find out. Dressed in brown uniforms with knee-high black boots, a troop of men marched past them. Their standard bearer carried a red flag with a white disc, on which was emblazoned a black swastika. They wore the same emblem on their distinctive armbands. Fear gnawed at Viktoria's heart. 'The Tobisch Brigade,' she whispered, clutching Luise's arm.

'Fascists!' a man behind them shouted. 'Go back to Munich!'

A policeman stared warningly at him and he was quiet.

At that moment, from another side street, a band of working-class men appeared, flat caps on their heads and banners in their hands, chanting the communist *Internationale*. At a command from their leader, the brownshirts halted, despite shouted orders from the police to keep moving.

'Nazi pigs!' the man from the crowd yelled. It was as if this were a signal for which the two groups of men had been waiting. They surged through the police barrier and within seconds the street was transformed into a battlefield, as the two factions, unarmed except for their bare fists, started to beat each other to pieces. Viktoria and Luise did not wait to see the outcome. With most other pedestrians, shaken and frightened, they hurried back in the direction they had come.

'They wore the same symbol as Otto Tobisch wore during the Kapp Putsch,' Viktoria told Benno and his father fearfully when they returned to the Hotel Quadriga. 'I didn't see Otto, but they all looked like him somehow.'

The Baron nodded knowledgeably. 'They're the SA, the private protection squad of the NSDAP, or the Nazi Party, as it calls itself. It's a Bavarian party, led by a man called Adolf Hitler, who attempted a putsch in Munich five years ago. Hitler's having a certain amount of success in rural areas in the south of Germany, but I don't think he'll make much impression in Berlin.'

'Do you know what happened to Otto Tobisch?'

'The last I heard, he fled to Austria in 1923.'

'You see, you haven't got any reason to be afraid,' Benno said.

But Viktoria's fear remained, particularly when, following the election more closely in the newspapers, she discovered more about the Nazis. One of their candidates was Hermann Goering, the former fighter ace, and a founder Party member. Together with a Reichswehr captain called Ernst Roehm, he had formed the original SA in 1922, made up from Free Corps Brigades, including that of Otto Tobisch. Another of their members was Josef Goebbels, who was, apparently, the Gauleiter for Berlin. 'Is that an official title?' she asked.

Again, it was the Baron who explained. 'I have never met Adolf Hitler, but I have studied his party programme. I understand he's a great believer in organization. He has divided the country into *Gaue* or areas, each under the authority of a Gau leader. Should his party ever come to power, he will immediately be ready to assume control.'

Benno looked at him sharply. 'Do you think there's any likelihood of that?'

'Who can tell? My philosophy is to keep abreast of all developments, political, economic and commercial. At the moment, I can see no likelihood of the Nazis gaining any significant number of seats in parliament. But, in the future, who can tell?'

In the event, they won twelve seats, both Goering and Goebbels taking their place in the Reichstag for the first time. As had been anticipated, the Social Democrats won seats from both the communists and the right-wing nationalists and seemed set once more to hold the political power in Germany.

Although stormtroopers continued to march through Berlin, they contained their activities to poor suburbs, standing guard over meetings and rallies held by Dr Goebbels in beer halls and assembly rooms frequented by working class men. Gradually, Viktoria relaxed. The Nazis might trouble Olga, but they did not appear to threaten her. By the time Luise and Ricarda left for their cruise, she had virtually forgotten about them.

Viktoria and Benno drove to Hamburg to meet Ricarda and Luise on their return from their cruise. 'Oh, Vicki, we've had a wonderful time!' Luise cried, throwing her arms round her neck and kissing her on both cheeks. Almost non-stop, she chattered all the way home in the car. 'It was so exciting living in the ship that I helped create, to see it all working as I had imagined!'

Ricarda, looking years younger as a result of her holiday, laughed. 'She's done a wonderful job — and Benno, if you were responsible for the kitchens and restaurants, I congratulate you. The meals were absolutely superb.'

'Every morning, I had a swim or played deck tennis, while Mama went to the hairdresser or sat in a deckchair,' Luise explained, 'then it was time for lunch. After that, of course, it was teatime and then dinner.' She rolled her eyes. 'I think I must have put on pounds!'

'But the most thrilling part was the return voyage,' Ricarda broke in. 'On our outward journey, we averaged 26.75 knots, which was very fast, but not fast enough to put us ahead of the *Mauretania.* Coming back from New York, though, we were averaging nearly 28 knots and, as we came up the English Channel, we reached a speed of 29.8 knots!'

'Mama,' Viktoria exclaimed, 'it sounds as if you were on the bridge with the Captain.'

'I was part of the time and a very charming man he was. We sat at his table in the dining saloon. He was rather like Karl, broad, with blond hair and grey eyes. He even danced with me one evening.'

Benno coughed. 'All this is fascinating, but can either of you tell me whether the *Countess Julia* succeeded in beating the record of the *Mauretania*?'

Ricarda stared at him. 'But, of course, Benno dear. Surely you know by now that everything your father does is always bigger and better and faster than anybody else?'

Such a spectacular achievement could not go unmarked, particularly when it coincided with the Baron's seventieth birthday. At the beginning of October, Benno's brother Ernst made one of his very rare visits to Berlin to make arrangements for the celebrations.

Viktoria's first reaction when she saw Ernst again was how much like his father he was starting to look and how young Benno appeared beside him. There were only three years between them, for Ernst was forty-one to Benno's thirty-eight, but there could have been a decade or more. While Benno's hair was still dark and his figure spruce, Ernst's grey hair was receding rapidly and his body was becoming quite obese. The main surprise for both of them, however, was Ernst's pathetic pleasure at seeing his brother again. 'You did the right thing getting out of Kraus,' he told Benno gloomily after dinner on his first evening. 'You're your own master here, you can do what you want. I thought you were mad at the time, but now I almost envy you.'

'Good heavens, the hotel is nothing compared to Kraus.'

'But you haven't got Father,' Ernst muttered, darkly. 'Benno, he still treats me as a child, even after all these years. I have to report to him for every decision and, because Trudi and I live at the Fortress, I can't even escape from him at home. I'll admit to you, frankly, life is hell.'

'He can't go on for ever,' Benno tried to sound comforting. 'One day, he'll have to hand over the reins to you.'

Ernst shook his head. 'Not until he's on his death bed.'

'Can't you ask him to transer you somewhere else?' Viktoria suggested, surprised to find herself actually feeling sorry for him.

'Where? Essen is our head office.'

'What about America?' Benno said thoughtfully. 'Kraus already has considerable holdings in America and now the *Countess Julia* has established the Kraus-Amerika Line, Father will need an office over there. Why don't you volunteer?'

A glint of excitement shone in Ernst's watery eyes behind his thick spectacle lenses. 'Why not?'

It was an extravagant reception hosted by the Hotel Quadriga that October, as the cream of society thronged its rooms to celebrate the seventieth anniversary of Baron Heinrich's birth and the award to the *Countess Julia* of the Blue Riband. A huge model of the liner made out of flowers dominated the Jubilee Room, while the hotel staff were dressed in the ship's livery. Even the tables in the restaurant were arranged to resemble those of the liner's dining saloons, and the menus had a nautical flavour.

The Baron's guest of honour was Dr Alfred Hugenberg, a distinguished, silver-haired gentleman, the extremely influential leader of the German National People's Party, as well as a newspaper magnate and majority shareholder in Ufa, Germany's largest film company. Other prominent guests included Dr Hjalmar Schacht, President of the Reichsbank; Albert Vogler, Director General of The United Steel Works; Gustav Krupp von Bohlen, head of the massive Krupp empire; and Hermann Goering, one of the twelve Nazi Deputies.

Lothar Lorenz, representing the respectable side of the arts in Baron Heinrich's view, because of his family fortune and his involvement in Café Jochum, was also invited. Seated near Goering during dinner, he was delighted to discover they had an acquaintance in common in the form of Sepp Nowak. 'Last I heard of him, he was making aviation movies for Erich Grossmarck,' Goering said. 'That man was one of our greatest pilots. What a wicked waste of a life.'

'Erich Grossmarck?' Dr Hugenberg's voice interrupted them. 'Didn't he direct the award-winning, talking movie, *Mandate for Murder* in 1924?' Lothar nodded in surprise and Hugenberg explained, 'I own considerable interests in the Ufa film company and it is of great concern to me that in America they're already making talking films, but here in Germany, we're lagging far behind. Do either of you gentlemen know Erich Grossmarck?'

'I met him when I went to America in 1922, and we've corresponded ever since,' Lothar told him. 'Would you like me to approach him on your behalf?'

'I'll ask the studio head to contact you, Herr Lorenz, but, in principle, yes. Ufa is the only company with the resources to make that first, huge step from silent to talking films. I believe Grossmarck is the man to help us take that step.'

'You won't find him an easy man to work with,' Lothar warned.

Goering laughed, glancing from Dr Hugenberg to Baron Heinrich at the head of the table. 'Those who are truly great are never easy to work with.' It was difficult to know to whom he was referring. Lothar rather suspected it was to himself, for the former fighter ace, newcomer to politics though he was, did not seem lacking in self-confidence.

Later in the evening, he watched him deep in conversation with the Baron, the two men, apart from their difference in age, remarkably similar in appearance, both verging on obesity, both with florid faces, both displaying an outward bonhomie that belied, Lothar suspected, an inner ruthlessness.

Certainly, as Baron Heinrich stood to address his guests at the end of the magnificent banquet, he appeared a giant among giants. In a long and flowing speech, he boasted of his company's achievements since the war, enumerating its vast holdings throughout the world, its diverse business activities in steel, chemicals, electricity, aviation and now shipping. At this point, he informed them, 'I should like to take this opportunity to announce the imminent opening of the prestigious new office of Kraus-Amerika Incorporated in New York, to which I have decided to appoint my son Ernst as manager.'

As applause broke out, Benno turned and congratulated his brother. 'I'm pleased for you,' he said, sincerely.

Ernst's weak eyes peered at him sceptically. 'Father's sending me on my own, while Trudi and the two boys stay in Essen. He knows that way he's always got a hold over me.' Then he brightened. 'However, it promises to be an interesting assignment. The American stock market is booming and I think we stand to make a lot of money.'

The Baron's speech was reaching its finale. 'We are celebrating today an achievement that proves to the world that Germany is, once again, a force to be reckoned with. Many strangers may ask how this has come about. How a nation defeated so recently in war is now once again among the most prosperous in Europe. The answer is very simple. It is because we have never ceased to work. It is industry that has made Germany the country it is. And this is only the beginning. Ladies and gentlemen, I ask you to drink to our future!'

Hermann Goering stood up. '*I* ask you to drink to Baron Heinrich von Kraus!' he shouted. They all roared their approval, lifting their glasses and shouting his name. Baron Heinrich von Kraus zu Essen was seventy, his figure more gross than ever, but he had lost

527

neither his indomitable will nor his overweening lust for power and prestige.

That autumn, Luise met Georg again for the first time in just over two years. She was walking back up the Kurfuerstendamm, when he suddenly emerged from a shop, looking older than she remembered him, his dark hair streaked with grey, a slight stoop to his shoulders. Strangely, he reminded her more of Uncle Franz than her former lover.

As he recognized her, he looked embarrassed and she felt suddenly sorry for him. 'Georg, how are you?' she asked gently.

'I'm fine, Luise,' he mumbled. 'And you?'

'Are you in a hurry or will you come and have a coffee with me?' She was determined to see the interview through to the bitter end, prove to herself that she had fully recovered from the dreadful hurt he had done her.

They sat on the terrace at Café Jochum. Even less at ease than she was, he described the performances he and Emmy had given throughout Germany. 'But, no matter how hard Lothar tries and how much people say they like my music, that ultimate opportunity never seems to present itself. They all love Emmy, but no one seems to want to put money into my show or actually commission me to write music for them. It's terribly frustrating.'

No, she meant nothing to him. There was only music in his life now. It was almost as if they had gone the full circle and returned to their first fateful meeting in the Quadriga bar. She was silent for a while, wondering if she actually was as brave as she believed herself to be. Then she asked, 'You will play again at Café Jochum, won't you, Georg?'

He hesitated. 'Do you really want me to?'

Impulsively, she laid her hand on his. 'Georg, surely we can be friends? Despite everything that has happened to us, I still believe in you — and your music. I want to do everything I can to help you.'

Moved, he clasped her hand in both of his. 'Thank you, Luise. I don't deserve your friendship, but I'll always value it above all else. Of course I'll play at Café Jochum whenever you want me to.'

She looked down at his hands, then up at his face. It was rather like discovering somebody she had believed to be dead was, after all, alive. But her period of mourning was over and she had come to terms with her grief. Georg's hands no longer had any power to wound her.

Benno, who had never known of their affair, was delighted to hear Georg had agreed to play again at Café Jochum, although Viktoria looked rather surprised. Wisely, however, she said nothing. So, as a result of this chance meeting, Lothar arranged for Georg and Emmy to appear at the café during the week Erich Grossmarck was due to arrive.

Grossmarck travelled from New York on the *Countess Julia* to Hamburg, making the last stage of his journey by train, and Lothar accompanied the hotel limousine to meet him at the Anhalter Station, while Luise waited with Viktoria and Benno at the hotel, surrounded by a crowd of journalists. The film director made an extraordinary figure as he marched through the glass revolving doors followed by a procession of page boys carrying his trunks. A little taller than Lothar, he was even more rotund, with a florid complexion, small deepset eyes, thin lips and a bald, red head. Yet, despite his shape, he was impeccably dressed in an expensive dark suit, with a high collar that cut into his thick neck. He paused dramatically and, before Luise or the others could approach him, the journalists swarmed round him.

'This is the first time I have been in Berlin for twenty-one years,' Grossmarck declaimed, in an appalling American accent. 'I left here in 1908 as a young boy of fourteen, little thinking I would ever return. Yet now, I have been invited back, as a guest of the great Ufa film studios to direct their first talking motion picture.'

The reporters scribbled furiously. 'What is the film about, Herr Grossmarck?' one called.

He shook his head nonchalantly. 'You will learn in due course.'

Luise hurried up to him to introduce herself, but he brushed her aside. 'Another time, lady. I'm tired. I want to rest.'

They did not see him for the rest of the day, although he kept the hotel staff constantly on their toes, as his house telephone rang incessantly. Herr Grossmarck did not like the early morning sun in his room. Herr Grossmarck's bed was too hard. Herr Grossmarck did not want to be disturbed. Herr Grossmarck needed a beer. Herr Grossmarck needed a suit pressed. Herr Grossmarck wanted lunch. He wanted tea. He wanted dinner in his suite. 'If only he could be polite,' Herr Fromm muttered to Viktoria.

'He's our guest,' she replied sternly. But, during the next couple of days, it seemed that Erich Grossmarck was intent on disrupting and upsetting the entire hotel, as first Arno Halbe criticized his behaviour in the bar, then Max Patschke complained that he had offended other guests by having a shouting match with a contingent of Ufa representatives. Wherever she went, Grossmarck's loud, boorish voice seemed to follow her.

'Herr Grossmarck is going to be trouble,' she sighed that evening, as she and the family had supper in their apartment. 'Luise, can't you or Lothar calm him down?'

'I don't see what I can do,' Luise said in disgust. 'I might just as well not exist so far as he's concerned. God knows why Lothar made so much fuss about him. He's a pig!'

Benno looked thoughtful. 'Let's try another tack. Why don't we invite him to dinner tomorrow evening?'

Luise grimaced, 'Does it have to be tomorrow? It's Georg and Emmy's first night at the café.'

'Maybe we'll take him there after dinner.'

With an attentive audience, an excellent dinner and a bottle of claret inside him, Grossmarck certainly started to mellow, hardly stopping talking throughout the entire dinner. Impressed that Benno was the son of Baron Heinrich von Kraus zu Essen, he informed them, 'That was a damned good boat that I came across on. And Kraus Industries have just opened an office in New York. I know, because I have shares in some of their American companies. Grossmarck always picks the best,' he bragged. 'My financial adviser suggested I invest in Kraus. He emigrated from Berlin a couple of years or so ago. His name's Nowak, Rudi Nowak.'

'Rudi!' Luise gasped. 'Rudi's working for you?'

For the first time, Grossmarck appeared to notice her. 'You know him? Certainly likes the ladies. But an astute businessman all the same. I knew his brother a long time ago. He was a pilot, a restless guy, couldn't stay put in any one place longer than a few months. Left me to go to South America. Rudi tells me he was in Africa flying safaris last time he heard of him.'

It was so unexpected to hear of Sepp after all these years that Luise was assailed by a wave of nostalgia. Suddenly, she thought how nice it would be to see him again and how much she had missed him.

'America's in a funny state at the moment,' Grossmarck went on to tell Benno. 'The stock market's going up and up and Nowak has already introduced me to a few good tricks. He's advised me to buy on margin, then reinvest the shares. That way, you don't need much capital, but when we sell those shares, we're going to make a killing!'

Benno gave him a worried look. 'I know nothing about the American stock market, Herr Grossmarck, but I do know a certain amount about Rudi Nowak and I would advise you to be careful.'

Grossmarck laughed coarsely, 'Don't worry, Herr Kraus, I wasn't born yesterday.'

'Are you able to tell us something about your film, Herr Grossmarck?' Viktoria asked, as Max served their coffee and brandies.

He scowled. 'I want something that's European in flavour, but that can be played to audiences all over the world.'

'Don't you have a script?' Benno asked.

'Never work to script. I make the story up as I go along. People, places, actors, they all spark things off. The story evolves of its own accord. I thought Berlin would supply it. It's known as Athens on the Spree, the cultural melting pot of Europe. From the descriptions Rudi gave me, I was expecting to find sizzling night clubs, bars, cabarets and cafés, but now I'm here, it's no different from anywhere else.'

Luise glanced at Benno, who nodded. 'Would you like to come to Café Jochum? I think you'll find that's very different.'

'Place on the Kurfuerstendamm? I drove past it yesterday. I suppose it belongs to you people? OK, let's take a look at it.'

She bit back an angry response, then said, 'Well, if you'll excuse me, I'll just telephone them to expect us.'

Grossmarck continued to talk non-stop in the hotel limousine all the way to Café Jochum, but as they entered the vast, glassed-in room, with its Dix mural along the far wall and its gleaming black and chrome furniture, he actually stopped to take breath. A blue haze of cigarette smoke hung over the café and every table was packed with a noisy, colourful, gesticulating, cosmopolitan crowd, waiting to see Emmy Anders perform for the first time in over two years. On the stage, a small jazz band was entering its final number. 'Interesting decor,' Grossmarck commented, as a waiter led them to their table. 'Who designed it?'

'I did,' Luise said forcefully.

Not bothering to conceal his surprise, he admitted grudgingly, 'Not bad.' Then he returned to the subject of his film. 'But see what I mean — just the same faces that I could find almost anywhere else. Apart from the café itself, these people could be in New York, in Los Angeles, in Paris, Rome, London.'

Luise was no longer listening to him, for the jazz band had packed up their instruments and disappeared. Then there was an excited hum around her, as the lights dimmed and a single spot-light shone on the stage. She saw Georg sit down at the piano and heard him strum a few bars. The audience was silent now except for Grossmarck, who was still talking. 'Wherever you are, it's all the same. I tell you, Benno, there's nothing new —' His mouth stopped open as he stared towards the podium.

Emmy Anders was standing in the circle of light. She had sprinkled some kind of glitter on the black halo of her hair, so that it glowed like phosphorous in the darkened room. Her enormous eyes were ringed with black kohl and her lashes fluttered languidly from the smoke that circled up from the cigarette she held between her carmine lips. She was dressed in black satin that fell from one shoulder straight to the ground.

Georg started to play, a gentle, sighing melody. The atmosphere in the room was electric. Not a glass clinked, not a person coughed, not a waiter moved. Then, Emmy changed her stance, so that the black material of her dress fell away to expose a black-stockinged leg reaching almost to her navel. She raised her shoulders, opened her mouth and cried, 'You!'

Erich Grossmarck's mouth remained open.

'You!' Emmy cried again, moving, so that the folds of cloth fell back, concealing her leg. 'You are joy, you are fever, you are heaven!'

Erich Grossmarck stood up, staring at her through the dark, mesmerized. On and on, Emmy sang, her growling, husky voice sending shivers down the spine, then rising to a scream above their heads. At the end of the performance, she dropped her hands loosely in front of her and bowed deeply.

'You, dear God in heaven, and all Your children on earth,' Grossmarck muttered, as he joined in the thunderous applause. Then, as Emmy left the stage, the spotlight dimmed and all the lights came on, he turned to them all and shouted, 'I must have that girl!' His face was crimson with excitement.

Several heads turned, looked at him and some laughed.

'Benno! Viktoria! Luise! Do you understand, I want that girl. She's Berlin, I tell you. Clever, enticing, sexual, she's in a class of her own. You people, this café, the pianist and that girl — you're what I want to say in my film!'

'You mean you want to use us all?' Luise gasped.

'Yes, yes, yes,' he cried impatiently. 'It's all here. We'll film parts of it right here in this café. But who wrote the music that girl was singing?'

Luise's heart pounded. 'Georg, the pianist, Georg Jankowski.'

Grossmarck's drink stood untouched on the table. 'I've got to meet him. Bring him here! And that little doll. She has star quality. She's box office dynamite!'

Benno beckoned to a waiter. 'Ask Herr Jankowski and Fraeulein Anders to come to our table.'

'I tell you people we're going to make the greatest film in the history of the cinema!' Grossmarck raved. At that moment, Lothar crossed the room with Georg and Emmy on either side of him. Grossmarck rushed over to them. 'Emmy,' he cried, pumping her hand, 'I'm going to make you the greatest film star in the world. And you, Georg, are going to write the music.' Then he turned on Lothar. 'You know these people? Why the hell didn't you tell me about them?'

'Because you wouldn't listen,' Lothar replied quietly. Smiling at Georg and Emmy, who were looking totally bewildered, he explained, 'Meet Erich Grossmarck, here from Hollywood to make Ufa's first sound picture.'

'I think it might be a sensible idea if we adjourned to the office and discussed this whole matter quietly and in a little more detail,' Benno said soberly. Then, when they were settled, he asked, 'Now, Herr Grossmarck, what exactly do you want to do?'

'I want to base my film on your café,' Grossmarck explained, his face still flushed, 'and I hope to be able to shoot some of the scenes here on location. But most of it will have to be shot at the Ufa studios in Neubabelsberg, because there's no way that the sound recording equipment can be brought here.'

Benno rubbed his chin. 'I hope your filming won't disrupt the café too much?'

'You won't even know we're here and you'll be well paid for all your troubles, I can tell you.' He turned to Emmy. 'Have you ever had a screen test?'

She stared at him from big eyes. 'Never. But I'm sure I can act very well.'

'You just be yourself, baby,' he told her confidently.

'Herr Grossmarck,' Viktoria asked quietly, 'do you know now what your film is going to be about?'

'Yes,' he said triumphantly. 'It's going to tell the story of a little cabaret singer called Mimi during the twenties. And it's going to be called *Café Berlin*.'

533

It wasn't Café Jochum, however, but the Quadriga bar, which seemed to be in the centre of the heated discussions that raged during the next few days, as Erich Grossmarck attempted to convince Ufa that their first talking picture was going to be made his way.

'You have got to have a written scenario, Herr Grossmarck,' the producer kept saying. 'You cannot be this vague. Dr Hugenberg will not allow it.'

'This is the way I work in America and this is the way I'm going to work here,' Grossmarck stated adamantly.

'We have to know what the film is going to say. Please understand, as an American, you may do something that is detrimental to Germany. This we cannot allow.'

'I was born in Berlin,' Grossmarck shouted.

'Then you should understand that vagueness is forbidden,' the producer yelled back.

'Do you want to make a talking picture or don't you?' Grossmarck bellowed. In the end, he got his own way, and Ufa's legal department contacted Dr Duschek to draw up contracts for Georg, Emmy and Café Jochum. When she actually saw her contract and the — to her — vast sum of money she was being paid, Emmy was ecstatic. 'Imagine me, a little kitchen maid from Wedding becoming a film star! Fraeulein Luise, they'll show *Café Berlin* at the Ufa Palace, won't they? That means everyone will see my name across the hoardings!'

But Emmy still had a long way to go. So that it could be shown all over the world, the film was to be made simultaneously in German and English, which meant that she now had to struggle to learn her lines in both languages, a task in which Luise tried to help her as much as possible.

Georg, in the meantime, was shut in his apartment, battling with the score and the libretto. Grossmarck, who had only a very rudimentary knowledge of music, needed everything played to him and possessed the disconcerting habit of reading the words without the music. 'I want MAGIC!' he scrawled across Georg's first attempts.

'Sometimes I wish I'd never played in here that evening,' Georg commented ruefully one day, when the three of them met for supper at Café Jochum.

'Rubbish,' Lothar exclaimed, 'you look better than you have for years. Doesn't he, Luise?'

He was right. However much Georg might complain, it was

obvious that he was enjoying this new challenge.

'And I'm having a wonderful time,' Lothar continued. 'I think one day I might even try to make a film myself, although I admit some of the technical arrangements rather daunt me.'

Luise smiled. It seemed, suddenly, very like the old days, with the three of them once more together, all the awkwardness gone. And, she tried to convince herself, it didn't matter that she and Georg were no longer lovers.

The Baron Heinrich who arrived at the hotel in June was in a very different cast of mind from the triumphant mood in which he had celebrated the Blue Riband nine months earlier. When Benno, advised of his sudden arrival, hurried up to greet him, he found his father pacing up and down the suite, his mouth drawn in a tight line and an ominous glower in his pale eyes. 'I've just come back from Paris. It's all a bad business, boy, a very bad business. I warn you, now, Benno, we're in for bad times ahead, unless we're very, very careful.'

Benno stared at him in surprise, for everything in his life seemed to be going very well. The contract for *Café Berlin* was worth a lot of money, the ensuing publicity was going to be enormous and the hotel was full of extremely wealthy international guests. There seemed not to be a cloud on the horizon.

'It all goes back to the Versailles Treaty,' the Baron said heavily, staring unseeingly out of the wide windows overlooking Unter den Linden. 'If only we had been allowed to participate in the original conference, none of these troubles would have occurred. We should have been allowed a determining say in the amount of war reparations Germany could afford.'

'But, Father, that was ten years ago, surely the economy has recovered now? We seem to be prosperous as never before.'

'I suppose your mind is so full of film-making that you have no time to read the newspapers, Benno? If you did, you'd see that we have steadily rising unemployment, which is a sure sign that the economy is failing. We are now finding it extremely difficult to fulfil the terms of the Dawes Plan, which, with hindsight, was actually a very fair solution to our problems. In view of this, the government asked for more meetings with the Allies to re-examine the method of paying our war reparations. These have been going on in Paris for several months now, under the chairmanship of an American called Owen Young.'

'I had no idea . . .' Benno said, nonplussed.

'Neither have most people,' his father told him drily, 'but they're soon going to learn, because Young has just given us his ultimatum. The terms of the Dawes Plan are to be totally revised and now, instead of making the repayments in goods and money, they are to be made solely in money. The actual amounts have been reduced, I'll admit, but they are to be made for the next fifty-nine years. That means we'll still be paying for the war until 1988, Benno.' He paused dramatically, then added, 'And paying with money which we haven't actually got, because our entire economy and prosperity is based on loans, mainly from America.'

Stunned, Benno tried to absorb the implication of this news. 'But why do the Americans want the terms of the repayments altered?'

'Because they are in trouble. As you can imagine, since Ernst has been in New York, I've asked him to keep me as informed as possible about everything that happens there. Last year there was a dramatic fall in timber prices, this year there is a world glut of wheat. Suddenly, what America needs is money to keep her own economy stable. Now, if you need money, boy, where do you look? You look to people who owe it to you.'

Benno nodded, as the picture became clearer. 'What about the American loans to Germany? Do you think there is any possibility they may recall them?'

'If things continue as they are, there is a very real possibility, boy. All we can hope is that the Americans have the sense not to do it.'

'And is this new Young Plan final?'

'No, it still has to be agreed by the Reichstag, and I know Hugenberg, for one, will campaign against it. But with President Hindenburg and Foreign Minister Stresemann in its favour, it will probably be accepted.'

Both men were silent for a while, then Benno asked, 'Is there nothing Ernst can do in New York?'

'For Germany? Not a damned thing. But for Kraus, yes, he can and is doing quite a lot — on my instructions, of course. Shares on the Wall Street Stock Exchange in New York are changing hands at ever more fantastic prices and in our dealings there we are making a lot of money. But, simply because of what I've just been saying, it can't last for ever. Like a house of cards, it's going to collapse one day.' He gave a thin smile. 'However, Benno, before that day, we shall have sold all our holdings and started buying gold. Whatever happens, whatever trouble we find ourselves in, I am a survivor.'

In August, the terms of the Young Plan became general knowledge, when Stresemann accepted them at an international conference in The Hague. As Baron Heinrich had foretold, Dr Hugenberg led the strident opposition to them with a furious campaign in his newspapers, publishing many furious attacks on the government, not only by his own German Nationalist Party but also by Adolf Hitler, the Nazi Party leader. Because Benno agreed with his father that the terms of the Young Plan were catastrophic for Germany, he read all these articles with interest and found himself siding very much with Hugenberg and Hitler against the government.

Benno's concern passed unnoticed by the rest of the family for they were all totally engrossed in the filming of *Café Berlin*, with Luise, needless to say, at the centre of the activity. During August, Grossmarck shot all the exterior and interior shots he could of Café Jochum, armies of men marching through the building equipped with lights, cameras, measuring tapes, ladders, cables and rolls of film.

Luise was not the only one to be carried away by the excitement of the film, for it was rapidly turning into the most thrilling time of Stefan's life. He loved the frenzied bustle and the artificial sense of urgency and tension. He was ecstatic when he was allowed to peer through the camera viewfinder and almost beside himself when Erich Grossmarck allowed him to walk on as an extra. If he had had his own way, he would have spent all day at Grossmarck's side, but his mother had other ideas. 'Your schooling isn't going to stop just because of a film,' she told him. 'No homework, no film. So which way is it going to be, Stefi?'

'This is probably the only opportunity I'll have,' he groaned, 'and I want to know how a film is made. My schoolwork will wait.'

Viktoria found an unexpected ally in Grossmarck, who said, 'To become a film director, you have to pass your matriculation. Listen, young man, you do all your schoolwork and your mother can bring you and your sister out to the Ufa studios.'

Spurred on by this promise, Stefan worked harder at school than ever and to his great joy, they were invited to Neubabelsberg at the beginning of September when filming commenced on the

537

huge replica set of Café Jochum. 'It's incredible,' he breathed, 'it looks just like our café.'

The vast studio was crowded with people and Stefan's eyes grew ever wider as, at Grossmarck's roared commands, they all fell to their allotted jobs in a frantic bustle of activity. Mesmerized, they watched Emmy mount the stage to sing one of Georg's songs, but while Monika was mainly interested in her costumes, Stefan wanted to know everything about photography, cutting, editing and particularly how the sound and visual picture could be simultaneously recorded.

'You see those huge crates?' a technician asked him. 'Well, the cameramen are inside them, so that the camera noises aren't recorded.'

But the man hadn't time to answer all Stefan's questions, so that evening he plagued Erich Grossmarck who, with remarkable patience, explained everything that had been going on. 'Still thinking of becoming a film director when you leave school?'

Stefan rubbed his nose thoughtfully. 'No, I don't know. But it's fascinating, Herr Grossmarck. Imagine, when *Café Berlin* is released, it will be shown all over the world. Then, people who have never been here — in New York, London and Tokyo — will all know what Café Jochum looks like.'

'We'll all be famous,' Viktoria laughed, suddenly liking Grossmarck much more.

But Grossmarck turned suddenly serious. 'This is becoming the most important film in my career, because for the first time in my life I'm doing exactly what I want to do. But there's no guarantee that it's going to be a box office success. For a start, despite everything that Dr Hugenberg and his producers say, it's very German in flavour, and Germany is still not popular in the rest of the world.'

'You're not making a political film,' Viktoria objected. 'You're telling a story of Berlin, of people like ourselves and Emmy Anders.'

'Yes, and who, outside Berlin, has ever heard of Emmy Anders? Then there's another problem. Mimi, the character played by Emmy, has an extramarital affair. The American censors aren't going to like that very much.'

Despite all his fears, however, Grossmarck continued to throw himself with unflagging energy into his work, rising at six to be driven out to Neubabelsberg and returning late to the hotel, often

538

with people from Ufa with whom he held discussions into the early hours of the morning.

He was a month into filming when, on 3 October, the death was suddenly announced of Gustav Stresemann, plunging almost the entire nation into shocked mourning. Stunned by the loss of somebody who seemed more like a friend than a politician, people came from all over Germany and indeed from many other countries, to participate in the funeral, many crowding onto the hotel balcony to watch the long cortège, headed by the black, red and gold standards of the republic, process through the Brandenburg Gate towards the cemetery at the Hallescher Gate.

That evening, Baron Heinrich, who had attended the ceremony, said sombrely, 'He was one of the greatest statesmen any of us will ever know and he literally wore himself out with his efforts to save Germany. Whatever one thinks of the Young Plan, he always had our country's interests at heart. This is a sad, sad day.'

'It was strange,' Viktoria murmured, 'but as I watched the flags in the procession, it seemed to me almost as if it were the republic itself that were being buried.'

Startled, her father-in-law stared at her. 'Young lady, I think you may very well be right. What is absolutely certain is that, now Stresemann is gone, we are going to face extremely difficult times.'

Stresemann's death meant little to Erich Grossmarck, as he entered into the final week of filming *Café Berlin* and realized, to his great relief, that the film would be completed both within schedule and within budget. At the same time, he received a letter from Rudi Nowak, containing sensational news.

'I've sold your shares in Commercial Solvents and American Railway Express and bought Houston Oil and Studebaker, both blue chip companies. And still the market continues to go up. Erich, by the time you return at the end of the month, you and I will be able to sell our shares and buy up Paramount!'

Grossmarck wasted no time in telling all his friends at the Hotel Quadriga. 'Herr Baron, I hope your son is on the ball in New York. With your assets, you stand to make a killing!'

'Herr Grossmarck, I have very great respect for your abilities as a film director, but absolutely none for your or Herr Nowak's financial judgement. Two weeks ago I instructed Ernst to sell all our shares and start buying gold.'

'Sell?' Grossmarck gasped.

'Speculation fever is what I call the disease hitting America, which I suspect you and Herr Nowak have caught. You should be very careful — it may prove deadly.'

Worriedly, Grossmarck watched the financial pages of the newspapers as filming on *Café Berlin* reached completion, but still the Dow-Jones Index continued to rise. Then, in his joy at finishing the greatest film of his life, he dismissed Baron Heinrich's opinions as defeatist. 'We'll throw a huge party,' he told Benno, 'invite the entire cast and studio crew to a great celebration. Put it all down to my account. After all, thanks to Rudi, I'm rich.'

Grossmarck's party did not take place. On Thursday, 24 October, a radio news item announced unusual activity on the New York Stock Exchange, with what seemed like panic selling taking place. 'Do you think it's serious?' he asked Benno.

'My father is very seldom wrong on matters like that.'

All day long, Erich Grossmarck tried to telephone Hollywood, but the transatlantic telephone link was constantly engaged and all he could do was book a call for several days ahead. Newspapers soon advised the scale of the disaster. Thirteen million shares had been sold that Thursday, rising to a peak of sixteen million five days later, when he finally managed to speak to Rudi.

He took the call in Benno's office and emerged looking white and shaken. 'I've lost everything, my house, my automobile, everything. We used them all as securities against loans to buy shares. Now they're all gone.' He sank down heavily in a chair, his huge body suddenly deflated, like a burst balloon. 'Rudi says things are absolutely desperate over there. Banks are failing, businesses are folding and people are throwing themselves out of skyscraper windows. God, why didn't I listen to the Baron?'

Their own memories of the poverty and desperation that had followed the war only too clear in their minds, they listened to him sympathetically, the antipathy they had felt for him on his arrival in the city six months earlier totally forgotten.

'I'll return to America tomorrow, though not on the *Countess Julia*.' He turned to them pathetically. 'Thank God Ufa are paying me over here, so that I can, at least, afford my hotel bill and my fare home. And, so far as the future is concerned, well, that depends totally and utterly upon *Café Berlin*.'

Chapter Nineteen

In a very short space of time, the depression that was sweeping America in the wake of the Wall Street crash made its first effects felt throughout Europe. As Baron Heinrich had foretold, the Americans immediately started to recall their loans, and export orders began to dwindle, while ever fewer orders came to Kraus Industries from the home trade. By December, the Baron had been forced to lay off several hundred workers in Essen and two days before Christmas, he visited Berlin to instruct the manager of Kraus Village to discharge another couple of hundred.

'We'll have trouble with the unions and with the commies,' the manager said gloomily. 'You know that Meyer woman still lives in Wedding — and she's always held a grudge against you, Herr Baron. She'll bring the entire workforce out if she can.'

Sure enough, Olga was waiting outside Kraus Chemie the following morning, surrounded by the sacked workers, and with pickets stationed beside braziers, waving placards demanding, *Kraus 'raus! Kraus out!* As his chauffeur slowed down, the Baron stared in disgust at the woman's thin figure, wearing one of the same shapeless grey dresses she had worn fifteen years ago, when she had first come to Wedding to plague the Krauses, her hair still scragged back in a bun.

Even her words seemed not to have changed. 'Workers of Kraus Village, your future lies in your own hands! Strike now to show your solidarity with your unemployed comrades! Strike today to give Baron Kraus the same Christmas as he is giving you! You owe him no loyalty, no allegiance of any kind!'

There were cheers and fists waved at the Baron's Mercedes. *Kraus 'raus! Kraus 'raus! Kraus 'raus!* came a ragged refrain, but he noticed men were slipping past the pickets through the factory doors. No matter what Olga Meyer said, it was better to work than to starve.

'Comrades, it is your right to run your own factories, as it is your right to run your own country,' Olga continued. 'Discard the yokes that have bound you for so long! Pull down the walls of capitalism and free yourselves from bondage!'

Slowly the limousine inched its way through the crowd of flat-capped, angrily gesticulating men, but although they recognized him, nobody dared do more than shout abuse at him. As he emerged from his car, he heard Olga's voice still screaming, 'We shall avenge ourselves against the Herr Baron and his friends. Comrades, we shall take to the streets, and we shall fight, if necessary with our bare fists, against the industrialists and politicians who are determined to rob us of our basic rights as human beings. Fight for freedom, comrades! Fight for the proletarian revolution!'

That afternoon, when she returned home, she talked at length to her son. Basilius was ten now, a very serious boy, with a marked resemblance to Reinhardt, who shared all his mother's passionate dedication to his father's cause. Their dingy tenement flat was hung with pictures of Reinhardt, Rosa Luxemburg, Karl Lieb-knecht and Lenin, and Basilius had been brought up on stories of the October Russian Revolution and the January German Revolution in which his father had lost his life. The ambitions of his young life were to avenge the death of the father he had never known, but of whom his mother told such glowing stories, and to see Germany under communist rule.

Although it was the third time that Olga had seen a catastrophe of this kind hit Wedding, Basilius had been too young at the beginning of the decade to understand the effects of inflation, but now he was old enough to comprehend what unemployment meant to his schoolfriends, as the factories controlled by Baron Heinrich von Kraus suddenly had no further need of their fathers.

'Instant dismissal is all the thanks they get from Baron Kraus,' Olga said bitterly. 'They get no compensation, no relief, no food, nothing.'

'But somebody has to do something, don't they?' Basilius asked. 'Won't the government give them money?'

'The government? Basili, the Socialist Republic is built on a lie! The socialists seek to preserve capitalism and to keep the robber barons in luxury. But we shall destroy them.' She gave a thin smile. 'At long last, the German Communist Party is strong enough actively to oppose both the socialists and the right-wing conservatives. There has to be another election soon and then we shall demonstrate how powerful we have become. We shall overthrow the government yet and rid the country of parliamentary rule.'

542

Throughout the winter, Olga, frequently with Basilius at her side, addressed ever larger gatherings of the unemployed workers of Wedding, heaping scorn upon the socialists who were unable to look after them in their hour of need and promising vengeance against the robber barons.

In the meantime, however, where there was no work, there was no money, for the factory owners paid no relief and it soon became apparent that the unemployment relief fund controlled by the government was woefully inadequate. Communist deputies in the Reichstag sided with other enemies of the republic to condemn the Chancellor's policies and it was soon apparent that Olga would be proved right. In March, Chancellor Mueller resigned, to be replaced by Heinrich Bruening, leader of the Catholic Centre Party, who had scarcely outlined his financial programme before he had almost the entire Reichstag up in arms against him.

Olga's joy knew no bounds. 'We shall do everything we can to obstruct him,' she told Basilius. 'The day of the proletarian revolution is drawing closer.'

Baron Heinrich, too, was resolved that the days of the republic should be numbered. The time had finally arrived for direct intervention and action before all he had worked towards for so long was reduced to chaos. 'I am going to renew my acquaintanceship with Reichstag Deputy Goering,' he told Benno. 'If you would care to join us for a private dinner in my suite, I can promise you an interesting evening.'

In many ways, Benno thought, Goering could have been Baron Heinrich's son. Four years younger than Benno, he looked much more like the Baron than Benno ever would, while the similarities in their personalities became increasingly obvious as the evening wore on. Both were unabashedly greedy, working their way through gargantuan quantities of food and washing it down with copious glasses of wine. By the third course, neckties had been loosened, by the fourth, trouser belts eased out a notch or two.

Goering did most of the talking, proving himself a surprisingly good conversationalist, telling fascinating anecdotes of his experiences as a fighter ace and the hardships he had encountered trying to obtain work, until he had finally met the Swedish Countess who became his wife. Meeting her had opened up a whole new world to him, he admitted frankly, allowing him to rub shoulders with the upper crust of society. Benno smiled inwardly. Another point in common between his father and the politician. Goering then mentioned many aristocratic names familiar to them both. 'A lot of them have joined the Nazi Party and are giving us much-needed financial support. You see, Herr Baron, unlike traditional Junker parties, Dr Hugenberg's Nationalists, for example, we are not looking backwards to see how we can revive the past. We are radicals. Through our revolution we hope to build a new and better Germany than ever before.'

The Baron absorbed this piece of information silently, then, after a bevy of waiters under Max Patschke's supervision had cleared the table and they were sipping their brandies, he asked Goering bluntly, 'What does your party intend to do for us industrialists in our fight against the unions and the Bolsheviks?'

'When we are in power, all trade unions will be abolished and the Communist Party will be banned,' Goering replied blandly.

It was certainly a revolutionary solution to the difficulties that beset them, although Benno found it hard to believe Goering actually meant what he was saying. However, it was obviously the kind of positive response for which his father had been hoping. 'In my opinion,' the Baron said, 'we are experiencing the biggest trade slump the world has ever known. How do the Nazis propose to make Germany prosperous again and give the economy a stable basis?'

Goering explained that the Nazis would start huge public works schemes, such as the building of motorways, the construction of private homes and public buildings. Furthermore, his party was adamantly against the war reparations payments and would do everything within its power to free Germany from the restrictions of the Versailles Peace Treaty, including winning back the German territories forfeited in 1919.

After this, his arguments became less clear, as he rambled rather vaguely about Hitler's ideas, expressed in a book he had written in prison called *Mein Kampf,* in which he outlined a new Great Germany, which would spread out to the East giving the German people the *Lebensraum* — or living space — to which they were entitled by birthright. Germany must free itself not only of revolutionary Bolsheviks, but also of the Jews, who controlled private banking and finance and who, unlike industrialists such as the Herr Baron, merely squeezed the economy dry without contributing anything to it.

Benno listened sceptically to these theories, for he realized that private bankers like the Arendts had, in fact, taken very great risks on behalf of Germany. Jewish bankers had saved the economy after the war, again during inflation and were once again almost solely responsible for obtaining loan renewals now that the Americans and other countries were trying to extract their capital from Germany. Certainly, the Hotel Quadriga and Kraus Industries had profited very greatly from their associations with the Arendt Bank. Yet, on the other hand, the Jews had always been a race apart, never integrating fully into German society.

'Herr Goering,' the Baron asked, interrupting his thoughts, 'what about your private army, the SA?'

'It is the foundation of a people's army, to augment the Reichswehr,' Goering replied proudly, 'and it is growing in strength from day to day, currently numbering about a hundred thousand men, the same as the Reichswehr itself. Of course, as soon as we gain control, we shall authorize the expansion of all the armed forces, including the establishment of our own air force, a matter of vital importance to myself, of course.'

'And to Kraus Industries,' the Baron interjected.

Benno frowned. 'However, the SA is mainly formed from ex-Free Corps soldiers, men renowned for their violence.'

'My dear Herr Kraus,' Goering exclaimed, a reassuring smile on his round face, 'the task of the stormtroopers is not to attack innocent people, but to defend us from militarily educated reds who attack our meetings and terrorize our honest politicians and our supporters. You have nothing to fear from the stormtroopers. They are there to protect you. At this moment, Herr Hitler is trying to persuade our old friend, Captain Roehm, to return from Bolivia, and men like Captain Tobisch to come back from Austria. Their expertise is badly needed to give our troops discipline and leadership.'

At the mention of Otto's name, Benno experienced a frisson of apprehension, but before he could say anything, his father asked, 'Haven't I seen a few men in black uniforms? Are they part of the SA?'

'Ah, yes, Herr Baron, you must be referring to the *Schutzstaffel*, or the SS, as it is known. That is indeed a division of the SA, under the leadership of Deputy Reichsfuehrer-SS Heinrich Himmler.' It was evident from his tone that he had no affection for Herr Himmler.

'But who pays for the stormtroopers?' Benno asked. 'Where do they come from?'

545

'They are paid for out of party funds and many are recruited from the unemployed. You see, not only do we Nazis believe communism to be the greatest threat to mankind, we also have a social conscience. Of course, maintaining the SA is an extremely expensive business.'

The gentle hint was not lost on the Baron. When Goering rose to take his departure, he drew out his cheque book and wrote out a cheque for two hundred thousand marks. 'I hope this will help you, for I believe that your party and I want the same things.'

After thanking him profusely, Goering said, 'You are a man of many remarkable achievements, Herr Baron. And it is my firm belief that you have, today, added to them. Very soon, you will be able to congratulate yourself on being among the first to help the greatest leader in German history to come to power.' He shook both their hands, telling Benno, 'Excellent meal and an excellent hotel, Herr Kraus. I shall seek every opportunity to return here.'

When he had gone, Baron Heinrich said, 'An interesting evening, don't you agree, boy? No wishy-washy policies of appeasement, there. Get rid of the communists, trade unions and the Jews, all the people who are milking the country dry. Build up the armed forces, supplementing them by the stormtroopers, recover the eastern territories and make Germany great again.'

'It seems a rather ambitious programme,' Benno said doubtfully.

'But one that is tailor-made for Kraus,' his father replied.

That night, as they prepared for bed, Benno summarized the evening's events for Viktoria, omitting, however, to tell her about his father's contribution to Nazi Party funds. 'Finally, somebody is trying to do something positive for Germany. You know, Vicki, if Goering is typical, the Nazi Party may be the answer to our problems.'

'Really?' she asked bitterly, brushing her hair with unnecessary vigour.

'Vicki, what's the matter?'

She looked at his reflection in her dressing-table mirror, then sighed. 'I can't stand the thought of Otto returning.'

He understood her feelings, but at the same time he could not help thinking she was putting her personal antagonism towards Otto above her duty to her country. 'Be reasonable, Vicki. We shall probably never even see him and, if we do, he won't be a free agent but under orders from men like Goering. I told you what he said. The stormtroopers are a political force. They're not there to threaten people like us.'

Tightlipped, she spun round on her velvet stool. 'Benno, you're a fool if you believe that. Well, you can do what you like, but I'm not going to help Herr Hitler and Herr Goering, not if it means helping Otto Tobisch.'

'Aren't you making a mountain out of a molehill? Hitler's is going to be a peaceful revolution. Things have changed a lot since the Kapp coup d'état and the Munich putsch.'

'I'm sure Otto hasn't,' Viktoria said darkly.

Not a day had passed in the Alpine pastures above the Traunsee when Otto Tobisch had not railed against his confinement in that silent valley, with only Anna and the cattle for companions. When the call came for him to rejoin Hitler's stormtroopers, he accepted it with alacrity, feeling no compunction about leaving his wife and her ancient parents in charge of the bleak farmstead.

At the Nazi Party's impressive headquarters in Munich, Otto was fully briefed by Deputy Reichsfuehrer-SS Himmler on the party's organization and its intention to achieve power, not by force, but by entering the Reichstag legitimately by means of the votes of the German people. He learned all about the propaganda programme set up by Josef Goebbels, including the vast rallies through which they hoped to draw supporters. And he was informed what his special task was to be.

'Red Berlin is at the root of all our troubles,' Himmler told him, pale eyes glistening in his bloodless face. 'It is the heart of the Bolshevik conspiracy. Communists, Jews and other sub-humans, Herr Captain, are the source of all our misfortunes, and it is our sacred duty to rid Berlin and all Germany of these subversive elements. In this, you, as a Berliner, will be invaluable.'

From his tone, Otto was certain they were speaking the same language. Himmler had no more respect for the power of oratory than he did, not even that of Herr Hitler and Dr Goebbels. Tacitly, they were agreed that revolution could only be achieved through violence.

Two weeks later, Otto — now Sturmfuehrer Tobisch — returned to the city of his birth for the first time since his assassination attempt on Theo Arendt nearly eight years ago. Yes, he decided, as he marched purposefully through the streets in his black uniform with the swastika armband, Berlin was even worse than he had imagined. Fat, Jewish women, dripping with jewels, sat gorging

547

themselves with cream cakes on café terraces, while uncouth, degenerate artists painted lewd, formless pictures or played tuneless, decadent music.

He paused for a moment outside the Hotel Quadriga, memories rushing through his mind in quick succession of the humiliations he had suffered within its revolving doors. But not for much longer, he vowed. The communist rabble led by Olga Meyer, Jews like Theo Arendt and his father-in-law, Professor Ascher, would soon be forced to flee for the safety of their lives. And then, he would have Viktoria Jochum-Kraus abjectly licking the dust off his boots.

He also stopped outside the Ufa Palast am Zoo, Berlin's largest cinema, where advance posters were being pasted up, advertising the première of Germany's first talking motion picture. *Café Berlin*, it was called. In smaller letters, he read, *A portrait of our times.*

Noticing his interest, the bill sticker said conversationally, 'It's based on our Café Jochum in the Kurfuerstendamm. Some of it was even filmed there. You must know the star, Emmy Anders?'

Otto stepped forward to stare at the girl's portrait. Dark-haired and olive-skinned, she looked foreign, almost African, one of the very sub-human types against which Himmler had warned him. 'Films don't interest me,' he said coldly.

Two days later, when he heard Dr Goebbels speak for the first time, he changed his mind. It was at a massive rally in the Sports Palace, the most spectacular that Otto had ever envisaged, as rank upon rank of SA and SS men stood in strict formation holding aloft huge blood-red swastika banners. Soon, the vast stadium was packed with Berliners, some two hundred thousand of them, Otto surmised, all come to listen to the Gauleiter of Berlin.

Otto watched curiously as the small figure made his way onto the stage erected in the middle of the arena, finding it hard to believe that this dwarfish man, who walked with a limp, could hold any sway over a crowd of this size. Then, as Goebbels started to speak, he found that even he — who cared nothing for words — was listening to the vituperative hatred that issued from his lips.

'The theatre has degenerated into little better than a brothel,' Goebbels screamed, 'where every kind of debauchery and fornication can be viewed, where adultery is glorified and marriage is denigrated. Magazines show pictures of naked, lesbian dancers, who are paid vast sums of money by unscrupulous publishers to display themselves in a manner that brings dishonour onto the rest of fine, German womanhood. Cinemas show films about prostitutes and drug addicts and even ordinary housewives, who are willing to sell their bodies for a pair of silk stockings. This is not culture! This is pornography! This is filth!'

Otto's lip curled, as he thought about the film *Café Berlin* based on Café Jochum. When Goebbels came to the end of his speech, he raised his arm with everyone else in the stadium. '*Sieg Heil!*' he yelled, feelingly. '*Sieg Heil! Sieg Heil!*'

It came as no hardship to him to accept orders to take his men to disrupt the première of *Café Berlin*. Revenge seemed more imminent than he had dared hope.

Olga learned about Otto's return at the same time as she heard of the première of *Café Berlin*, both events lashing her into a fury. She hardly knew which she loathed most — the right-wing nationalism of the Nazis and their stormtroopers — or the wealthy, decadent society portrayed in this film based on Café Jochum. She hated Otto Tobisch, who had murdered her husband eleven years ago, and she hated Emmy Anders, who had defected from Wedding to join forces with the capitalist Jochums and Krauses at the Hotel Quadriga. Both equally epitomized to her everything that was fundamentally wrong with Germany.

Suddenly, however, it occurred to her that the première represented an excellent way of getting her revenge on both the Jochums and Otto. This film, with its Jewish, intellectual overtones, must be anathema to the Nazis, who would send their stormtroopers along to cause a disturbance outside the cinema. Well, when they arrived, they would find the communists waiting for them! The ensuing battle should ensure that the Jochums' evening would be ruined. In frenzied determination, Olga began to gather her troops.

The première of *Café Berlin* took place on Stefan's fifteenth birthday, 28 April 1930, and to his great joy his parents allowed him to attend it. It promised to be a truly magnificent occasion, attended by the cream of Berlin society, as well as many film enthusiasts who came from all over Europe, most of them staying at the Hotel Quadriga. Never had Stefan felt so proud as when he, his parents and his grandmother took their places in the front row of the Ufa Palast's vast auditorium.

A few seats along from them, Luise could not remember ever feeling so nervous. On her left, Georg was biting his nails while, to her right, Emmy kept demanding anxiously, 'It will be all right, won't it, Fraeulein Luise? It will be a success, won't it?'

Lothar, seated on Emmy's other side, was evidently experiencing none of their apprehension, for he was keeping up a running commentary on the audience. 'Theo and Sophie have just arrived, and Professor Ascher, Minna and the two boys are with them. They're sitting three rows behind us, Georg. Oh, and look, Emmy, what a tribute. The Buergermeister of Berlin is attending your première! Now, you can stop feeling nervous.' He was silent for a moment, as his eyes skimmed the crowd. 'Good heavens, there's Kurt Weill and Lotte Lenya, with Bert Brecht. Now here comes my old friend, Alfred Kerr. Emmy, I shall never forget the first time he saw you at Café Jochum . . .'

He continued to chatter happily until the lights dimmed, the curtains parted and a projector's beam lit the screen with the announcement of Ufa's production of *Café Berlin*. Luise tensed in her seat, feeling Emmy's damp hand slip into hers. Then, with a thrill of recognition, she heard the first notes of Georg's theme music flood the auditorium. The lettering faded, to be replaced with a vista of the Kurfuerstendamm, panning in to the unmistakable shape of Café Jochum, except that the lettering over its doors now read *Café Berlin*. At the bottom of the screen, they read the date *1923*.

On the pavement outside, Emmy's woebegone little figure searched in her purse for money, as people trundled handcarts of old Reichsmarks past her. The camera followed Emmy into the café and heard her plead to be allowed to sing in exchange for a meal. Then, as Emmy belted out the first of the glorious songs Georg had written for the film, Luise suddenly knew that everything was going to be all right. Grossmarck, Georg and Emmy had produced a masterpiece.

The story itself was simple. Mimi, the cabaret artiste portrayed by Emmy, was discovered in Café Berlin by a rich, older man, whom, in desperation, she married. Once the inflation was over, however, and the world returning to normal, she met and fell in love with a much younger and much more handsome man. Forgetting all about her husband, Mimi threw herself into a heady glittering existence, until her young lover grew bored and eventually left her. By that time, her husband, however, had tired of waiting and found a mistress of his own.

As the film progressed, Luise had the extraordinary sensation of seeing her life unroll in front of her, almost as if Grossmarck had lived it by her side, instead of coming in at the very end. Mimi, of course, was Emmy, but she was also Pipsi and even Luise herself. And those other figures, they were Rudi, Lothar and Georg ... All the glittering fun of the decade was reproduced here, its elegance, its sophistication.

As the film drew to its conclusion, they found Mimi once again in Café Berlin, splendidly made up to look old beyond her years, dressed in a dramatically revealing, black satin dress, which rode away to expose her beautiful legs. Putting a long cigarette holder in the side of her mouth, she stared at the café's clientele from beneath hooded lids, then sang the most haunting song yet:

'I was only sixteen and I was so alone,
But now the summer of our love has gone,
Oh, please come back, oh, please return to me,
I loved you so ...

Nobody in Café Berlin paid any attention to her, except her husband, a shadowy figure standing near the entrance, his face furrowed with sadness and longing. He listened to her, moved as if to approach her, but at the last moment, turned and went away.

As Georg's music faded and the lights went on in the cinema, the audience burst into wild applause, shouting Emmy's name. 'Come on, Emmy,' Lothar said, and, taking her by the hand, dragged her up onto the stage. With one accord, the audience rose to its feet, screaming and yelling its appreciation. With tears in her eyes, Emmy raised her arms, then bowed to them. 'Oh, thank you, thank you.'

Ecstatically, Luise turned to Georg, but as she did so, she heard a different kind of shouting, an angry din that rose even above the clamour of the audience. Suddenly, the doors burst open and armed policemen rushed in, addressing them through loud hailers. 'Ladies and gentlemen, this is the police. Take your seats please.' Hand in hand, Lothar and Emmy walked back to their places and, as a tense silence fell over the cinema, a policeman marched down the aisle and mounted the stage. 'Thank you. There is no need for alarm, but a violent demonstration is taking place outside. Our men have matters fully under control, but for your own safety, we should like you to leave by the stage doors.'

At that moment, the chain of policemen guarding the main exit was broken and the noise of the brawl taking place in the foyer burst thunderously upon the auditorium, as the rioters broke through their ranks. Truncheons waved, policemen shouted and a gun fired into the air. Panic-stricken, the audience surged towards the stage, screaming and yelling, tumbling over each other, in their haste to escape. The Jochums and Krauses, at the front of the theatre, found themselves propelled by the terrified mass of people behind them out into the street.

To her amazement, Luise found Georg still beside her. 'Are they fighting because of our film?' she asked in bewilderment.

'For God's sake,' Lothar exclaimed, pushing Emmy inelegantly into his car, 'hurry up, and let's get away from here.'

In the nearby hotel limousine, Stefan and Ricarda were already seated and the chauffeur had the engine ticking over. But Viktoria was rooted to the pavement, her mouth open, her eyes wide with fear, gazing towards the end of the side street. Silhouetted against the street lights was a woman's figure, her hair tied back in a bun, waving a red communist flag. 'God help us,' Benno muttered, 'it's bloody Olga! I should have known. Vicki, for heaven's sake, hurry up. Let's get away from here.'

But it wasn't at Olga that Viktoria was staring. It was at the man standing just behind her, straddle-legged, hands on hips, dressed in a black uniform. Even from that distance, she could see the arrogant smile twitching on his thin lips. Otto Tobisch. For what seemed an eternity, the three of them remained motionless, the old antagonists finally met together again.

Benno seized her arm and pushed her roughly into the car, jumping in after her. 'Drive back to the hotel, as quickly as possible,' he instructed the chauffeur.

When she turned to stare out of the windows, both Olga and Otto had disappeared, merging into the fighting mob struggling against each other and police outside the cinema. She shuddered. The film had been a moving account of the years they had all just lived through, but had those golden years really been as glittering as they had seemed? And what was going to happen after them? 'It was Otto,' she whispered, 'Benno, it was Otto . . .'

'Rubbish, my dear, you have Otto on the brain. But I certainly saw Olga. Perhaps we made a mistake in allowing Café Jochum to be portrayed in that film. It's not going to do us any good.'

'But Café Jochum is just like that,' Stefan pointed out.

'I know,' Benno said grimly. 'Perhaps that is also a mistake.'

Even the highly critical Alfred Kerr acclaimed Georg's music in his review of the film the following day, while nearly every other

552

newspaper, except those controlled by the Nazis and the communists, were ecstatic in their praise of *Café Berlin*. Inadvertently, the demonstrators also helped its success, because their pitched battle became front page news, causing many people to go to see the film who might not otherwise have gone.

A few weeks later, to Lothar's amazement, he received a cable from Erich Grossmarck in America. *CAFÉ BERLIN KNOCK-OUT IN NEW YORK AND LOS ANGELES*, he wrote. *AM AUTHORIZED BY PARAMOUNT TO OFFER IMMEDIATE CONTRACTS TO JANKOWSKI AND ANDERS. ADVISE ACCEPTANCE ASAP.*

Emmy stared in open-mouthed disbelief when Lothar showed her the telegram, then she said decisively, 'It sounds so exciting, but I don't really want to go to America, not even with Herr Jankowski. Herr Lorenz, I can hardly speak any English.' She hesitated, then added, 'And Berlin is my home.'

'You don't have to go. You wait and see, Emmy. After *Café Berlin* has been shown in Vienna, Paris and London, you'll have offers pouring in from all over Europe.'

Georg's reaction was very different. Wistfully, he said, 'Lothar, imagine what I could do in America. The home of Gershwin, Louis Armstrong, Duke Ellington, Bessie Smith, Cole Porter, Irving Berlin ... I shall never be truly recognized in Germany, but perhaps I could find my niche in America.' Then he shook his head. 'But, no, it's a dream.'

'Not any longer. This cable proves it. Not that I want you to go, Georg, but I would understand if you thought you had a greater future over there than here.'

'It isn't as simple as that. You forget I have a daughter.'

Lothar rubbed his hand thoughtfully across his chubby face. 'Perhaps you should ask her. You never know, maybe she, too, has always dreamed of going to America.'

Georg shook his head. 'Minna would never want to leave the Arendts. She's made her home with Theo and Sophie, but although they are more her parents than Pipsi and I ever were, I couldn't just leave her behind, not after everything else I've done to her.'

'I still think you owe it to her to give her the choice,' Lothar insisted. 'Georg, I'm not a total fool, I keep my eyes and ears open. I know what that demonstration was about the other night and I know what the Nazis are saying about the theatre and the Jews. I hope, I pray, that Hitler won't achieve any sort of power but, in the meantime, he and his brownshirts could make life very difficult for you. Perhaps it would be safer for both you and Minna in America.'

So Georg went out to Grunewald to talk to Minna. She was fourteen now, pretty, dark-haired, clever, and to his dismay, regarded him more in the way of a family friend than as her father. She listened to him politely, then said, 'Well, I think you should probably go to America. But, if you don't mind, I'll stay here.'

'Minna, darling,' he said, clasping her hand, 'please don't think I don't want you. It's just that I've had enough of war, revolution and demonstrations. I want to live out the rest of my life in peace, doing the one thing I do best — writing music. I beg you, come to California with me.'

'No, Papa, I do understand what you're trying to say, but I'd still rather stay here.'

Neither Theo nor Sophie attempted to discourage him. Theo, in fact, went so far as to say gravely, 'If the situation gets much worse here, we may even follow you. I know America is suffering badly from the slump, but at least its situation isn't exacerbated by the indecisiveness of our coalition government and the threat of the Nazi nationalists. Georg, I'm sure you're making the right decision.'

Even Professor Ascher, when Georg went to see him in Dahlem, encouraged him. 'Minna will be fine with Sophie and Theo, and much as I shall miss you, you deserve something better from life than the deal you've had so far. Go safely, my son, and write to me often.'

It seemed there was nobody and nothing to hold him. For the first time in his life, he realized he was actually free to do as he pleased. Before he had a chance to change his mind, he cabled his acceptance to Erich Grossmarck and was advised by return that a ticket was on its way to him for his passage to New York on the *Countess Julia*. Then he summoned up the courage to tell Luise of his decision.

He broke his news to her in the corner of the Quadriga bar where she had been sitting with Sepp on that first occasion he had visited the hotel eleven years before, the time when he had played the *Cornflower Waltz*. Suddenly, he found himself vividly remembering their years together. She had always been such fun, laughing, vivacious and generous, one of the greatest influences on his life. Why was he leaving her? Why could he not accept the happiness she offered him? What was it that would always keep them apart?

To his relief, she did not make a scene. 'I'm pleased for you, Georg. Of course I'm going to miss you, but I'm sure you're right. You'll find recognition in America you'll never get here.'

He took her hand in his. 'Dear Luise, I've treated you very badly. I've been very selfish and I don't know how to say I'm sorry. It's been a very one-way relationship, yours and mine, hasn't it? I seem to have done all the taking and you've done all the giving. Please forgive me.'

She stared down at their hands. 'There's nothing to forgive. I've always loved you, Georg, and I always shall. But I hope it's never been a selfish love. I wish you luck in America from the very bottom of my heart.'

'I'll write to you,' he promised, but he knew he wouldn't.

She smiled, as if she could read his thoughts. Then, decisively, she stood up. 'Thank you for coming to tell me. I should have hated it if you'd just left without saying goodbye.'

She accompanied him to the hotel steps, watching him as he walked towards the Brandenburg Gate. When he looked round, she was still standing there, a small figure in emerald green, her auburn hair gleaming in the sun. More than anything else, she reminded him of all he was leaving behind him and he very nearly changed his mind. Then, as he turned the corner, he encountered a gang of brownshirts. 'Filthy Jew!' one of them snarled, as they passed him.

Suddenly, he had the answer to his question. It was not Pipsi that had come between himself and Luise. Nor was it his music. At the final count, it was that they belonged to two different races. She was a Gentile and he was a Jew. And, rather than admit that he had failed, he chose to believe it was as simple as that.

Luise stood for a long time on the hotel steps, looking down the road where Georg had disappeared, scarcely able to believe she might never see him again. Yet, deep inside herself, she felt his departure put the final seal on something she had always known. It was not Pipsi or his music that had come between them. For some unknown reason, their love affair had been doomed from the beginning. Was it, quite simply, that she was a failure as a person, that, however deeply she loved, she was incapable of holding anybody to her?

The very next day, Lothar received a cable from Paris, offering Emmy a fantastic sum to give a solo performance at one of the city's major concert halls. She gazed at it in stunned amazement. 'I'm rich! I'm rich and famous. Oh, isn't it wonderful?' She threw her arms round Lothar's neck. 'Do you know what I'm going to do? I'm going to rent a flat of my own and I'm going to buy a little dog, a French poodle!'

Lothar grinned. 'Buy half a dozen, you can afford them, Emmy.'

A couple of days later, Emmy moved out of her attic room at the Hotel Quadriga into a flat in Wilmersdorf. Almost immediately, accompanied by her two new poodle puppies, she left Berlin for Paris.

Fortunately, Luise was so busy those days that she had little time to brood, for as the fame of *Café Berlin* spread, so, too, did that of Café Jochum and the Hotel Quadriga, and people travelled from all over the world to see them. Despite the depression, mounting unemployment, rising prices and an increasingly tense political situation, there were still many wealthy people to whom Berlin remained a cultural Mecca.

During the months that followed she learned from Lothar of the magnificent reception Emmy was given wherever she went in Europe. Particularly Paris, it seemed, had taken the little singer to its heart. Occasionally, Emmy sent postcards. 'I've got six poodles now,' one read, while another informed them, 'I've bought a white Rolls Royce Silver Ghost with a delicious chauffeur called Jean-Pierre.' From Georg in America, she heard nothing.

For company, she depended more and more on Lothar. Amusing, intelligent and easy-going, he made no emotional demands on her, yet always made her feel interesting and desirable. But, frequently, she found herself wondering when he, too, would desert her.

Although Viktoria did not see either Otto or Olga again after the première of *Café Berlin*, she could not help but be aware of their presence in the city for, as unemployment passed three million, demonstrations and street battles between the two factions grew ever more savage. The violence reached a new pitch when, failing to obtain a majority vote for his financial programme, Chancellor Bruening was forced to ask President Hindenburg to dissolve the Reichstag and it was announced that elections would take place on 14 September.

The entire city was swept by election fever, communists and socialists marching on foot through the streets, waving banners and shouting slogans, while Nazis and nationalists roared along its thoroughfares in trucks, blaring their message of salvation through loud hailers. On every street corner, in every beer garden, sports ground and assembly room, politicians harangued their supporters and detractors, their arguments faithfully reported by whichever newspaper supported them.

Not even the Hotel Quadriga remained immune, for its elegant bars, restaurants and reception rooms rang with their raised voices of people not only arguing the merits of their particular political party but, above all, blaming the socialists and the Weimar Republic for the parlous state in which the country now found itself. Whereas their more old-fashioned, aristocratic guests favoured Hugenberg's Nationalist Party or Bruening's Centre Party, Viktoria also noticed considerable support among the middle-class businessmen for Hitler and his Nazis.

The only people who seemed strongly opposed to Hitler were their Jewish guests. 'So the spectre of anti-Semitism once more raises its grisly head,' Theo Arendt commented sadly to Viktoria, one evening, when he stopped by for a drink on his way home. 'Well, I suppose it was only to be expected.'

'Surely you don't take all their talk about pure Aryans and a folk community seriously?' she demanded.

'It's in their party programme. If you read it, you'll find it categorically states, "No Jew may be a member of the nation." According to Hitler, I am an alien and a non-citizen.'

'But, Theo, you're as German as I am!'

'Perhaps even more so. My family has lived here longer than yours, but that still doesn't alter the fact that I am a Jew.'

'But what could they do to you?'

'Seize my bank, take away all my property, make life extremely uncomfortable for me.' Then he smiled. 'Well, don't worry, let's hope it doesn't happen.'

Still concerned, she accompanied him out to his car. Leaning arrogantly against the hotel portico were two brownshirts, calling out ribald comments at people passing by. When they saw Theo, one shouted, 'There's one! Jewish pig! Whore's son!' Suddenly, she was vividly reminded of that dreadful evening when Otto had made his assassination attempt.

'You'd better go in,' Theo told her gently.

557

But she didn't. Glaring haughtily at the two stormtroopers, she walked with him, taking his hand in hers, as his chauffeur opened the car door. One of the thugs spat, aiming at her shoe, and as Theo's car pulled away, he jeered, 'Are you a yid too, baby?'

The episode made her uneasy as no impassioned speech by Dr Goebbels could ever have done but, when she recounted it to Benno, he seemed more angry that the commissionaires were allowing brownshirts to hang around the hotel portico than that Theo had been singled out for his Jewishness. 'There's nothing new in anti-Semitism. Take your father as an example. He didn't like Jews very much.'

'Only because of Silberstein. He employed Franz Jankowski and he always banked with the Arendts.'

'But he was never close to them, as he was to my family, for instance. Vicki, you have to face up to it, the Jews are different from us. They have a different religion, celebrate different feast days, many of them look different — and, finally, it is true that most of them are a damned sight richer than most Germans.'

'So you agree with the Nazis?' Viktoria asked in dismay.

'To a great extent, yes. As Germans, our first obligation is to look after our own people.'

'I don't trust them. I don't like their methods, using stormtroopers to intimidate innocent people. I don't like their blatant propaganda. In fact, I don't like anything about them.'

'You don't know anything about them, and if you stopped to think, you'd realize you're being emotional instead of realistic. Vicki, this country needs a strong man to lead it. Bruening isn't the person, any more than Mueller was. And President Hindenburg is eighty-three; he's not only old, he's senile. In my opinion, Hitler is the only person to get us out of the severe economic trouble that we're in. He's offering jobs, an end to the reparations payments and an end to all corruption. He wants a great Germany — and I, for one, am becoming increasingly prepared to give him a chance.'

'He still doesn't actually tell us how he's going to achieve it.'

Benno turned on her impatiently. 'Exactly what other choice do you have? You have the socialists — and you can see for yourself what they've done. Or the communists. Do you really want Germany run by Olga and her friends? Or you have Hugenberg and his nationalists, who are still vaguely hoping for the return of the monarchy and the good old days. Then, of course, you've got any number of fringe parties, whose objectives are merely to disrupt and obstruct and who never have any hope of controlling parliament. Faced with those alternatives, Vicki, who are you going to vote for?'

She bit her lip and turned away. 'If voting for the Nazis means condoning Otto Tobisch and the stormtroopers, I won't do it.'

'For God's sake, Otto Tobisch isn't going to rule Germany!'

Unconvinced, Viktoria voted for the Nationalists, while Benno placed his vote firmly for the Nazis. Luise refused to vote at all. 'I've always found politics boring, and this election has all others beaten hollow. I don't care who gets in. I shall just be thankful when all the commotion is over.'

The results were staggering. Votes swung wildly to the extreme right and extreme left, so that although the Social Democrats remained the largest party, Hugenberg and Bruening's parties found themselves with virtually the same number of seats as the communists. The most sensational result, however, was that of the Nazi Party, which polled nearly six and a half million votes, increasing its seats from 12 to 107 to become the country's second largest party.

Benno was triumphant, as was his father, who telephoned from Essen to say, 'I think it might be expedient if we gave a celebration dinner at the Quadriga in Goering's honour.'

Now that it suddenly began to seem possible that Hitler might one day become Chancellor, Benno hastened to concur.

Viktoria was furious when she heard the Baron's proposal. 'So now we're going to start holding political rallies in the hotel, are we? Why can't your father hold his junket in Essen?'

'Viktoria,' Benno said warningly. 'you are starting to try my patience. Firstly, this will not be a political rally, but a dinner, like the many others we hold. And, secondly, it provides business for the hotel, that I do not propose turning away because of your half-baked prejudices. Now, can we stop all this stupid nonsense?'

Never had they bickered as much as they did that summer, and it seemed stupid that — of all things — politics were at the root of their quarrels. Biting back an angry retort, she said uneasily, 'I'm sorry you think I'm being stupid. I still don't like it, but if you want it, of course your father should hold his dinner here.'

Fearful of drawing the unwanted attention of the communists upon the Hotel Quadriga and causing a repercussion of the battle that had taken place outside the Ufa Palast, the name of Baron Heinrich's guest of honour was kept secret from the hotel staff. Troubled, Max Patschke cam to Viktoria and said, 'One of my waiters is a communist and has a real grudge against the Herr Baron. His father and brother have both been laid off from Kraus Village and Olga Meyer has been telling them it's all the Herr Baron's fault. For some reason, he thinks Herr Hitler is attending the banquet and he hates Herr Hitler almost as much as he hates the Herr Baron.'

Viktoria sighed. Poor old Max was nearly seventy now and it was obvious, even to her, that he just couldn't cope any more. They would seriously have to think about urging him to retire, especially since he must now have saved enough money to retire on. 'If you think that waiter is going to cause trouble, Max, then you'd better dismiss him.'

'Oh, I wouldn't want to do that, Frau Viktoria, not when he doesn't stand a hope of getting a job anywhere else,' Max said hurriedly. 'He isn't a bad boy. It's just that he's been hearing rumours, like everyone else. If we could tell them all who the Herr Baron's guest of honour is, then they'd quieten down.'

'That's no concern of anyone apart from the Herr Baron. Your waiters would be better advised to get on with their jobs.'

It was an exalted gathering which Baron Heinrich hosted that September evening, including many of his fellow industrialists from the Ruhr, the Bechsteins of piano fame, Max Amman who ran the Eher Verlag, which published the Nazi newspaper, influential directors from the Hamburg-Amerika shipping line, Norddeutscher-Lloyd and the Dresdner Bank. Gradually, they and many others assembled in the Jubilee Room, awaiting Goering's arrival.

Leaving Benno to mingle with them, Viktoria went into the private banqueting hall, where the dinner was to be held. Holding the seating plan in her hand, she looked down the horseshoe formation of tables, immaculately laid with white damask cloths, gleaming silver cutlery and sparkling crystal glasses. Then she frowned as she noticed that the tips of the knives down one side of the table were out of alignment. Another sign that Max was no longer up to his job. In the olden days, he would never have allowed such an oversight.

She put down the guest list and made her way up the table straightening the cutlery to her satisfaction. At the top, she looked back to survey her work and noticed one of the waiters bending over the seating plan, studying it in detail. When she approached him, he moved away with a last, shifty glance, as if committing it to memory. Hurriedly, she picked up the piece of paper and walked over to Max, who was busy giving his staff last minute instructions. 'Is that the waiter you told me about?' But when they turned to look at the room, the young man had disappeared.

Uneasily, she returned to the Jubilee Room just as Herr Brandt ushered in Hermann Goering. The Nazi politician greeted Baron Heinrich and Benno heartily, accepted an aperitif and, amidst a hubbub of conversation, proceeded to hold court. Unwanted and unnoticed, Viktoria slipped away, her mind still on that waiter. He had read her list and then disappeared. What if he had gone back to Wedding to inform Olga that Goering was going to be at the hotel that evening? What a catch for the communists if they could find this group of Nazi supporters all together! She walked into the foyer to ask the hall porter if he had seen the man leave.

It was then that she received the shock of her life. In front of the glass revolving doors a dozen brownshirted stormtroopers were standing to attention and, to one side of them, dressed in the black uniform of the SS, was Otto Tobisch. The blood drained from her cheeks and, to her horror, she felt her hands tremble. Then, as on the last occasion that he had invaded the privacy of the hotel, anger overcame her fear. 'What the devil are you doing here?'

Otto's lip curled in a sneer. 'We're here on Herr Goering's orders.'

'And, on my orders, you can leave again,' Viktoria told him bitterly. 'Get out of this hotel, Otto Tobisch!'

He stepped towards her, a menacing look in his blue eyes. 'Sturmfuehrer Tobisch,' he corrected her, coldly. Then he stared round the foyer. 'You still think you're so damned clever, don't you, Mrs Goody Two-Shoes? But you'll get your come-uppance, when we are the masters of this country. I know all about you and your friends, about Jews like Theo Arendt, Georg Jankowski and Professor Bethel Ascher.' He spat out their names. 'And I know about your sister, with all her pornographic artist friends at Café Jochum, socialists like Lothar Lorenz and African whores like Emmy Anders.'

Viktoria's fury knew no bounds. 'Get out of here immediately,' she hissed. 'Get out of here, or I shall call the police.'

For a long time, they stared at each other, then abruptly, Otto turned on his heel, barked an order to his men and they marched through the glass doors to take up their stations on the pavement.

'Frau Viktoria,' the hall porter called, 'are you all right?'

With an effort, she nodded, then she suddenly remembered her reason for coming into the foyer in the first place. 'Apart from the stormtroopers, have you noticed anything unusual this evening? One of the waiters acting in a strange fashion, for instance?'

'One left here in a hurry about half an hour ago. The communist one Herr Patschke's always complaining about. He looked so het-up, I assumed he'd been dismissed.'

It confirmed her worst fears. Beckoning a page boy, she told him, 'Go and find Herr Benno and ask him to come here immediately.' Then she turned to the hall porter. 'I think you'd better phone the police.'

The hall porter looked worried. 'But what shall I tell them?'

'I suspect we're about to have a riot on our hands.'

He was just picking up the telephone, when Benno arrived. 'Vicki, our guests are just going in to dinner. What on earth's the matter?'

'Otto Tobisch is on guard outside our hotel for one thing,' she said grimly, 'while I'm pretty certain that one of our waiters has left to alert his communist friends that Hermann Goering is here tonight. Any minute now, all hell is going to break loose. I've just asked Hans to ring the police.'

By now, they were surrounded by a circle of anxious faces. Benno wasted no time giving his orders. 'Bar those doors,' he told the commissionaires, 'and don't let anybody in at all!' Then, 'Herr Brandt, hurry our guests into their banqueting room and make sure they stay there.'

'Yes, Herr Benno, immediately!'

At that moment, they heard them. The sound came from the Brandenburg Gate and to start with appeared only a muffled shouting above the noise of the traffic. Then they clearly heard: '*Kraus 'raus! Kraus 'raus! Kraus 'raus!*' 'Down with Goering! Down with Goering!' 'We hate Nazis! We hate Nazis!'

Otto's stormtroopers were no longer staring into the hotel, but pressed flat against its doors, their bodies tense to beat off the expected onslaught. Into the arcs of light shed by the hotel's spotlights, the communist army suddenly surged, brandishing sticks, truncheons and waving banners. Threatening faces under flat caps shouted obscenities at the brownshirts, who kicked out at them, knocking them backwards down the hotel steps.

Suddenly, a brick hit one of the doors, splintering the glass and now the tumult in the streets could be clearly heard. 'Go upstairs,' Benno told Viktoria, but she couldn't move, standing rooted to the floor, as the portico was turned into a bloody battlefield. There seemed to be just a tangled mass of bodies, punching, kicking and pummelling one another, while beyond them the chanting chorus continued under red, waving banners. 'Down with Goering!' 'Power to the workers!' 'Long live the communist revolution!'

Again and again, the doors of the hotel moved under the force of the bodies thrust against them. It seemed impossible that Otto's small group of brownshirts could win against so many communists, but as Viktoria watched, she realized that more SA and SS men were arriving by the minute and the communists were faring worst. One after another, men in flat caps were knocked to the ground by brownshirts and blackshirts, kicked and trodden on where they lay.

Another stone hurtled through the splintered glass and, in a last desperate attempt to reach the security of the interior of the hotel, the communists launched a fresh attack on its doors. Shoulder to shoulder, like a human battering ram, they pitched their united strength against them. The cracked glass gave way and fell with a crash to the marble floor.

Viktoria screamed as men surged through the aperture, blood pouring down their faces and hands, their clothes torn from the fighting and the broken glass. Seizing her hand, Benno dragged her to the other side of the hall porter's desk into his office. As she went, she suddenly saw, lying on the floor, as the human tide flooded over him, the waiter who had caused all the trouble. Standing above him, savagely kicking in his face with a steel-capped jackboot, was Otto.

At that moment, the police arrived and, within minutes, the battle was over. The communists ran in one direction, the brown-shirts in the other. Inside the hotel, only Otto remained poised over the waiter's body, together with some half a dozen dazed communists. As the policemen clapped handcuffs on the commun-ists and charged them with disturbing the peace, Otto raised his hand to the officer in charge, said 'Heil Hitler!' and marched out of the hotel, throwing Viktoria a glance of mingled triumph and contempt.

'This one's dead,' a policeman called, pointing to the waiter. 'Must have got run over in the crush.' Roughly, he and a colleague picked him up and carried him out into the street.

Another police officer approached Benno. 'I understand Reichstag Deputy Goering is attending a function here tonight?' As Benno nodded, he said, 'Well, I'd appreciate it if you'd warn us in future, sir, then we can send an armed guard for your hotel. Stop anything like this happening again.'

'Thank you, Officer. We thought we'd taken adequate precautions...'

'Officer, the dead man,' Viktoria said, 'he was killed by the SS man, by Sturmfuehrer Tobisch.'

'No, I don't think so,' the policeman shook his head. 'Look here, you're very shaken, Miss, and understandably so. I'd recommend a brandy to steady your nerves.'

Benno was staring at the chaotic foyer, where the hall porter was already organizing some staff to clear up and effect makeshift repairs to the doors. He turned to Viktoria with a worried frown, 'Why don't you go upstairs and lie down for a bit? I must go and see to our guests. They must be wondering what on earth is happening.'

At that moment, Goering appeared in the doorway. 'Oh, dear,' he exclaimed, blandly, 'don't say you've been having trouble with the communists? I am sorry. I do hope they haven't done too much harm.'

Benno hurried across to him. 'Herr Goering, I'm very sorry if your dinner was disturbed, but the matter is quite sorted out now.'

Goering put his arm round Benno's shoulder. 'Don't worry, my dear Herr Kraus. When we are in power, there will be no communists to trouble us.'

Viktoria stayed to hear no more. Still numb with fear, she made her way across the foyer, then slowly mounted the stairs. Suddenly, she was aware of Stefan sitting at the top of them, his brown eyes big in a face that was white as a sheet. 'Stefi,' she cried, rushing up to him. 'Stefi, how long have you been here?'

'All the time. I saw it all.' She sat down beside him, putting an arm round his shoulders. He was silent for a moment, then said, 'That blackshirt killed the waiter, didn't he?'

She bit her lip. The police officer might lie to her, but she couldn't lie to Stefan.

'The stormtroopers were here first,' Stefan went on, 'I saw them come with Goering and I think they were looking for a fight. But none of them were arrested, were they, Mama? Not even the one who committed murder. I think the police are on the side of the Nazis.' He stared at her. 'I hate the Nazis.'

One after another, factories and small businesses were forced to shut their doors that winter, adding to the ranks of the unemployed, who rose in number from three million to four million. But no statistics could portray the misery of these people, who bitterly labelled Bruening 'the Hunger Chancellor', so pitiful was the unemployment relief system operated by his government. They shuffled through the streets of Berlin, forming queues miles long, when a job was rumoured to be vacant, and begging outside the kitchen doors of the Hotel Quadriga for scraps of food.

It was the plight of these people as much as anything that persuaded Max Patschke to give in gracefully and accept that the time had come for him to retire. 'Yes,' he said, after Benno tactfully raised the matter with him at the end of April, 'it's better that a young man takes over my job, someone with a family to keep.'

'If you don't mind,' Benno said, 'we'd like you to remain for a while and train your successor. And, of course, Max, once you retire, you'll always be welcome to come back and see us whenever you want.'

'Thank you, Herr Benno.'

But Max's heart was heavy. 'I hate the thought of leaving,' he confessed to Ricarda. 'The Quadriga has always been my life. I don't know what I'm going to do without it.'

'I've been retired now for a long time,' she consoled him, 'and I must admit I'm enjoying it. After all, you and I are both getting on, and we must give the young people their opportunity. Are you still going to buy a cottage in the country?'

His eyes brighted. 'I've found another pretty little house near Potsdam. The money's in the Darmstaedter Bank and the lawyers are preparing to exchange contracts. I don't think anything can go wrong this time.'

Even when he learned of the collapse of the Austrian bank, the Kreditanstalt, Max did not really worry. He watched long queues forming outside German banks, as people hurried to withdraw their money and keep it where they could see it and touch it, hidden in makeshift safes in cowsheds, inside mattresses or buried in waterproof bags in the garden. He watched the panic with growing alarm, but consoled himself that if any failed, it would be one of the smaller, private ones, like the Arendt Bank, not a giant like the Darmstaedter. The thousands of marks he had saved for his country cottage must surely be safer there than crammed into his wallet or left in his room where somebody might steal them.

With great relief, he eventually heard from his solicitor that the purchase would be completed on 13 July and, leaving his young successor to look after the restaurant, Max set out to the bank to collect the bank draft he had ordered. As he turned the corner, a terrifying sight met his eyes. The doors of the Darmstaedter Bank were not only locked, barred and guarded by policemen, but an angry, shouting mob was trying to force its way into the building. Max stopped and stared at them, his blood running cold.

'Don't bother to go there,' a passer-by said, bitterly, 'the bank's run out of money.'

Max caught hold of his sleeve. 'What's happened?'

'It's closed. Everybody's been withdrawing their money, and now the bank's got no more cash.'

'But can't it borrow some?' Max asked desperately.

'Where from? The whole bloody country's bankrupt!'

At last, a bank official appeared at an upper window and confirmed everything the stranger had said. And at that moment, Max knew life had no further meaning for him. His job at the Hotel Quadriga was finished, and his savings gone. Heavy-heartedly, he returned to the hotel, and without saying a word to anybody, went up to his room. He took the heavy cord that secured his travelling trunk and knotted it securely round the sturdy curtain rail, forming it into a noose. Then, with one last look down Unter den Linden towards the Brandenburg Gate, he pulled the curtains.

Finally, after sadly glancing round the room that had been his home for thirty-seven years, Max Patschke stood on a chair, put his head into the rope, kicked the chair away and hanged himself.

Max's death devastated everyone, family and guests alike. 'If only we'd known,' Ricarda kept saying, 'if only he had come and talked to me before he did it, we might have been able to help him.'

'Poor Max,' Luise cried, 'if Benno hadn't told him he had to retire, he probably wouldn't have killed himself. He simply didn't have anything to live for any more.'

'He thought his money was safe in the bank and it wasn't,' Viktoria said in bewilderment. 'It's terrible, to work as hard as he did all his life and then lose everything. Oh, if only we'd had some warning. But you'd have thought the Darmstaedter was safe as houses.' She felt terribly guilty, convinced they could and should have done something to help Max and had let him down in his moment of greatest need.

'Nothing is safe any more,' Benno told them, sadly. 'You mustn't blame yourselves. After all, Max was nearly seventy and he couldn't do his job properly any more. And it isn't our fault that the banks are in trouble.'

As various of the hotel's guests who had known Max for a long time came to offer their condolences, it grew very apparent whom they blamed. One of them, a ball bearing manufacturer from Schweinfurt, told Viktoria bluntly, 'It's the Jews, Frau Jochum-Kraus. I've heard say that Jakob Goldschmidt, the chairman of the Darmstaedter Bank, deliberately manipulated the collapse of his bank to avoid paying his creditors. Like Dr Goebbels says, the Jews are our greatest curse. The sooner they get out of Germany the better.'

There was a chorus of assent at this. 'Yes, it's the Jews.'

'Goldschmidt hasn't hanged himself, has he?'

'I agree with Hitler and Goebbels. Get rid of the Jews!'

Still stunned by Max's death, Viktoria did not know what to think. She longed to find somebody else to blame and so shift her burden of guilt onto their shoulders, but to hold the entire Jewish race responsible seemed too facile an escape.

A couple of days later, Baron Heinrich arrived in Berlin. 'Sorry to hear about Patschke,' he said, as he joined Benno and Viktoria for a drink in the bar that evening, 'but these things happen, don't they? Well, he'd probably have been bored stiff in the country.'

Then, evidently satisfied he had settled that matter once and for all, he went on, 'I'm actually here to see Theo Arendt.'

'Do you think the Arendt Bank is in difficulties?' Benno asked anxiously. 'You know we do nearly all our business through it?'

'No more than any of the others. Despite the depression, Theo Arendt is still one of the wealthiest men in Berlin, if not in all Germany.' He paused. 'I'm glad to say Kraus is doing very well at the moment. Ernst is helping us make a lot of money in America, using the gold we bought a couple of years ago to buy into what is still a very depressed share market. American railways, the Bell Company, public utilities, blue-chip companies that can't go wrong. Of course, in Germany, things aren't so good. We do badly need someone to set this country back on its feet.'

While Benno nodded enthusiastically, Viktoria stared hostilely at her father-in-law. If he were a Jew he wouldn't dare talk like that. Apparently, it was all right for a Kraus to make money during a depression — but not for a Goldschmidt or an Arendt.

Theo Arendt was fifty-one that year, an elegant man with silver hair, an aquiline nose and refined features, bearing scant physical resemblance even to his ancestors, whose portraits hung on the dark, panelled walls of the bank's first-floor conference room. Yet, that day, as he listened to Baron Heinrich von Kraus talking, he was more than ever aware of the ties that bound him to those forebears, ties of race, blood, infinite respect and deep, deep affection.

He observed with distaste the Baron's gross body, his broad red hand clamped round a fat cigar, the broken veins that mottled his nose and cheeks and the cold eyes behind steel-rimmed spectacles. 'What I'm proposing to you, Herr Arendt,' he was saying, 'is that I buy your Berlin bank, not with money, but with an extremely good portfolio of shares in some very sound overseas companies, which will help you consolidate the assets of your London bank. My lawyer's gone into the international tax situation and I can assure you, it's very favourable indeed. In short, my dear Herr Arendt, I'm making you an offer you can't refuse. The problems of getting the sale proceeds out of Germany are all obviated and you'll have some solid securities as assets for your London bank.' He indicated the folder on the table. 'I think when you read through those, you'll see just how generous I'm being.'

Theo leaned his chin on his hand. What, he wondered, would his father Isaak, or his grandfather Abel, have done in his situation now? But he was in no doubt as to his reply. 'I can see the advantages of this deal to yourself, Herr Baron. In your position, I should very much like to own an established private bank. But I am not quite clear why you believe I am so ready to sell. We still have credits with foreign banks, albeit at extremely high interest rates, and we are still able to cover all our customers' deposits. Unlike the Darmstaedter, we are not on the brink of insolvency.'

The Baron leaned back in his chair, blowing a cloud of blue cigar smoke into the air. 'You don't need me to tell you that Germany is in a devil of a mess. Factories are shutting down left, right and centre and we've nearly four and a half million unemployed. Our agriculture is in almost as bad a state as our industry, for the socialists have done nothing during their years of misrule to help either farmers or peasants, and Bruening's agrarian policies aren't going to do a damned thing to rectify matters. We need a strong leader to sort out this country and the only person I can see who's going to do this is Adolf Hitler.'

Unblinkingly, Theo stared at him, knowing full well what the point of his argument was going to be.

'You know Hitler's feelings regarding the Jews,' the Baron continued. 'Now, I'm not saying I agree with him, Herr Arendt, but a lot of people do. In your situation, I'd be thinking very seriously about leaving Germany.'

Theo stood up, trying to conceal his repugnance. 'Thank you for your concern, Herr Baron, but I do try to keep myself fully informed of the political situation in this country. However, at this moment, I see no necessity to sell the Arendt Bank. Should the situation change significantly, I shall remember your generous offer.'

Yet after the Baron had left, Theo could not help wondering if he had made the right decision. There was not just himself to think of, but his two sons and Minna. And not just their future either, but the futures of their children and their children's children. With a terrible sense of foreboding, he feared that he might yet have to accept the Baron's offer.

Chapter Twenty

As 1931 drew towards its close, with the third winter of the depression approaching and unemployment soaring towards five million, Luise had the sensation that her life was gradually disintegrating around her. It was not only in the riots between stormtroopers and communists that the differences splitting the country made themselves felt, but increasingly the battle was reaching nearer home.

At the hotel, her sister and Benno seemed to be at loggerheads for no other reason Luise could see than that Benno was in favour of the Nazis and Vicki was not. At Café Jochum, the same thing was happening. Every day, bitter arguments flared up and customers stormed out, long-standing friendships were dissolved and strange new allegiances formed, love affairs broke up and professional relationships were severed. All because of politics.

It was over Café Jochum that Luise had her first conflict with Benno. One December evening, he said worriedly, 'Luise, I'm not at all sure that Emmy should perform at the café this New Year's Eve.'

Luise stared at him, aghast. 'Not sure? But Emmy has become a tradition. New Year's Eve wouldn't be the same without her!'

'I realize that, but you see, Luise, some of the concerts and musicians you have been choosing, particularly here at the hotel, have been giving rise to rather unpleasant comments from our guests.'

'What on earth is the matter with them?'

'They're not seen as being quite patriotic enough. We're increasingly being asked for more traditional music, something with a proper tune, more folk songs, that sort of thing. Certainly, the New Year's Eve Ball here is going to have a totally conventional flavour, waltzes, foxtrots, quicksteps, none of your American music.'

'And that's why you don't want Emmy at Café Jochum?'

He looked somewhat embarrassed. 'Luise, she isn't Aryan, and the songs Georg wrote aren't German. We don't want to attract any adverse attention to ourselves.'

To Luise, his argument was not only incomprehensible, it was tragic. 'Aryan! I don't know what you're talking about, Benno. She can sing and that's all that concerns me.'

Next day, after describing the incident, she asked Lothar, 'Who's crazy? Me or Benno?'

He did not smile. 'Poor Luise, you've never been a political person, have you?'

'Politics just don't interest me,' she admitted, 'but people do. I think there are good people and bad people — and that's that.'

'If you don't mind my saying so, I think you're being rather naïve. Politics are a fact of life, Luise, and one you'd be wise to face up to. You know what happened at the première of *Café Berlin*. Yes, I must confess that, these days, I'm glad I'm Swiss.'

Fear gripped her heart. 'Lothar, you aren't thinking of returning to Switzerland?'

'Maybe. You must remember, I have other interests and responsibilities, including a collection of Impressionist paintings and a sausage factory! I've neglected them for far too long.' Then he gave a ghost of a smile. 'Of course, if I do go, you could always come with me.'

They were almost the same words as Sepp had uttered ten years earlier and, just as Luise had known then that she could not accept his proposal, so she knew that she must refuse Lothar. 'I'm sorry, Lothar, but ...'

He patted her hand. 'It's all right. I understand.'

Luise gazed at him, conscious that she was witnessing the end of her most precious remaining friendship and helplessly aware that there was nothing she could do about it.

As New Year's Eve approached, she became increasingly nervous. The posters they put up advertising *EMMY ANDERS SINGS SONGS BY GEORG JANKOWSKI* were defaced, with crude swastikas painted across them. Over Emmy's name the words *African whore!* were scrawled and by Georg's *Jewish pig!* Several old customers of the café cancelled their bookings.

On the evening itself, unaware of the commotion her visit was causing, Emmy arrived at the café in a magnificent white Rolls Royce with no fewer than six white poodles in tow. When Luise hurried out to greet her, she said, 'Meet Mimi, Fifi, Frou-frou, Bijou, Cha-cha and Bubi. Aren't they darlings?' Then she held her hand out to the handsome young man who was holding open the door. 'And meet Jean-Pierre David.' She smiled knowingly. 'He came with the car.'

Emmy's happiness was so infectious that Luise started to relax and, as the first guests drifted in, she decided she had been foolish to allow Benno and Lothar to unnerve her. Despite the fact that some well-known faces were noticeably absent, there were more than enough other people to make up for them, many gorgeously clad in outrageous fancy dress, all intent on enjoying themselves and forgetting, for one evening at least, the troubles going on around them. In addition to Emmy, Luise had engaged two jazz bands for their entertainment and, as the tempo hotted up, the atmosphere grew more abandoned and the dancing more frenetic. Suddenly, it seemed once more like the old days of Café Jochum, when nobody seemed to have a care in the world.

Just after eleven, Emmy made her appearance on the stage, and, as always, there was not a sound to be heard in the café, as the lights dimmed and a spotlight shone on her slender figure. 'Ladies and gentlemen,' she said huskily, 'it is with great pleasure that I sing to you for the first time the latest songs written by Georg Jankowski, specially sent over from America.' Provocatively, she placed one foot on a chair, leaning her elbow on her knee and cupping her chin in her hand, so that her dusky legs and arms were fully exposed to her audience.

'Eh, she is so beautiful,' Jean-Pierre murmured in Luise's ear. But Luise scarcely heard him, so enthralled was she by the music being played by the accompanying jazz band, music so distinctively Georg, that it seemed he must almost be in the room with them. It conjured up memories of distant days in Lothar's apartment, on the shore at Heiligensee, of the Palm Garden Room, of happier times when he and she had been one person and their love all that mattered in the world.

So engrossed was she that she was unaware that newcomers had entered the café until she heard catcalls and whistles from the back of the room. Annoyed, she looked round and then she saw them, a dozen or so brownshirts leaning arrogantly against the doors, smoking, bottles of beer in their hands. By then, heads were turning all round the café and, confident now of their audience, the stormtroopers broke into an obnoxious Nazi anthem written by a stormtrooper called Horst Wessel who had been killed the previous year in a SA brawl.

Obviously perturbed, but ever the true professional, Emmy went on to the end of her song, at which point the brownshirts pushed their way roughly through the tables, booing, hissing and yelling obscene remarks, knocking over glasses, kicking at table legs and lurching against guests. From all around them, people shouted at them to be quiet and get out, but it was obvious that now they were in, they had no intention of leaving. Helplessly, Emmy stood on the podium, her hands loosely to her sides, staring at them with frightened eyes.

While Luise was still wondering what to do, Lothar hurried up to her, took her hand and led her off-stage, while Oskar Braun, a grim look on his face, marched over to one of the stormtroopers, grasped him by the lapels of his jacket and muttered something fiercely to him. To her surprise, she saw a look of doubt flicker across the young man's face. Then she heard the manager say, 'Herr Kraus is a personal friend of Herr Goering ...' To her relief, the brownshirt shouted to his companions, 'Let's get out of this shit-heap!' At the door, however, he bawled one last message, 'Any more of that Jew music in here and we'll smash the whole bloody place up.'

When they had gone, Oskar Braun walked onto the stage. 'Ladies and gentlemen,' he said, smoothly, 'I am very sorry for that most unwelcome intrusion and would like to invite you all to a glass of champagne on the house to steady your nerves.' There was a weak round of applause. He looked at his watch and continued, 'In view of the fact that it is almost midnight, I suggest we allow Fraeulein Anders to relax for the rest of the evening after her ordeal and content ourselves with dancing.'

As the band broke into a rather ragged tango, Lothar brought a very shaken Emmy back to their table. 'They looked so threatening,' she whispered. 'Oh, Fraeulein Luise, what did they want?'

Trying not to betray her own disquiet, Luise laid a hand on hers. 'They're just thugs, out to make trouble. Forget them.' But for the second time, very clearly, she had personally witnessed the full implications of Dr Goebbels.

When midnight struck and they all clinked glasses, there was a drawn look on Lothar's face as he wished them a happy New Year.

'I think we'll go now,' Emmy said in a tiny voice, sitting very close to Jean-Pierre. Very soon afterwards, other guests asked for their bills and started to leave. By one o'clock the café was completely empty except for the staff.

573

It did not take long for Benno to learn of the incident and the following evening at supper he announced, 'We're going to have to do something about Café Jochum, get rid of some of the layabouts who sit round there all day. Perhaps we should replace Oskar Braun and put in a new manager, someone who will attract the right sort of clientele, not all these artists and actors. Café Jochum should be respectable, as it was in your father's day.'

Blood rushed to Luise's cheeks. 'I suppose you think stormtroopers are the right sort of people.'

'The reason they broke in is because Café Jochum is getting a bad reputation,' Benno retorted, in a reasonable tone. 'It's always been a meeting place for left-wing radicals and it's about time it stopped.'

'No,' Luise said furiously, 'you know very well that it's one of the most popular rendezvous in the city for artists and intellectuals, regardless of their politics, and that's what you and I and Oskar Braun intended it to be. God almighty, that's why Erich Grossmarck based his film on it.'

'And I think that I made a mistake in allowing Grossmarck to film *Café Berlin*.'

'You didn't think so then. Something seems to have happened in the meantime to change your mind.'

'The Nazis,' Viktoria told her bitterly. 'Surely you realize by now, Luise, that the Nazis are against everything that Café Jochum represents.'

Benno sighed in exasperation. 'What can I do to make you two see sense? It's true, I do agree with the Nazis in very many things, but I can also see with my own two eyes that Café Jochum is degenerating.'

'Benno, I think you should realize that decisions as to how Café Jochum — and the hotel, for that matter — are run, are not solely your responsibility,' Viktoria said acidly. 'Luise and I, as well as Mama, are entitled to have some say in the matter. So, may I suggest that we leave Café Jochum just as it is for the moment?'

He shrugged resignedly. 'I'm only trying to help you. However, I warn you that if you have any more visits from the stormtroopers, there will be no Café Jochum left to run.'

Emmy paid a brief, daylight visit to Café Jochum before she and Jean-Pierre left for her next engagement in Zurich. She seemed to have recovered from her ordeal and promised that, despite the stormtroopers, she would be back next New Year's Eve.

574

That evening, Lothar dropped his bombshell. 'I'm going back with them to Switzerland,' he told Luise, as they sat at their *Stammtisch*. Although his tone was light, there were worry lines round his eyes. 'After all, who could refuse a ride in a white Rolls Royce?'

Suddenly, Luise recalled that other occasion Lothar had left Berlin precipitately, after the Free Corps had broken up *Hurra! Dada!* 'You will return, won't you?'

He chucked her affectionately under the chin. 'I should think so.' But there was no confidence in his voice and she could not help wondering whether she would ever see him again. They talked desultorily for a while, then Lothar pushed his cup away and stood up. 'Goodbye, Luischen, take care of yourself while I'm away.'

She felt he was almost relieved to be escaping — not from her — but from Café Jochum and Berlin and the life he had loved for so long. She accompanied him to the door and watched him get into his car, a short, plump, rather ridiculous and undeniably middle-aged character, and felt tears spring to her eyes. She and Lothar had shared so much together — Sepp, Georg, Pipsi, Emmy, Grossmarck and *Café Berlin*, Café Jochum itself ... And now he had gone ...

She brushed her hand across her eyes and turned back to the black and chrome interior of Café Jochum, which now seemed to represent all she had left in the world. And, even that, Benno was trying to take from her. She was suddenly filled with a desperate determination not to let Café Jochum go, for now, more than ever, it represented her entire existence. She did not dare consider what would happen if she lost it as well.

That February, to Viktoria's dismay, Benno wore a Nazi Party badge in his lapel. 'Dr Goebbels has announced that Hitler is going to run against Hindenburg for the Presidency next month. Joining the Party is the best way I know of showing my support,' he explained.

'What does that mean, being a party member?' she asked fearfully.

'Nothing more than that I pay a subscription, really. But I feel I'm doing something.'

She grasped at a small straw. 'How can Hitler run for President? Isn't he an Austrian?'

Benno dismissed her objection. 'Your grandfather obtained

German citizenship, so I'm sure Hitler will manage to overcome that small obstacle, too.' A couple of days later, he informed her that by becoming an attaché of the legation of Brunswick in Berlin, Hitler had been made a German citizen. 'Now we stand a chance of getting a President who will do something positive for Germany, a strong leader to set us straight and to make us powerful again.'

Benno might be certain on this score, but to Viktoria's relief, she learned that both Chancellor Bruening's Centre Party and the Social Democrats were firmly supporting the aged President, while the communists, disgusted by this betrayal, were putting forward their own candidate. So, too, was Dr Hugenberg's Nationalist Party, making four contenders in all for the presidency.

It was the bitterest election campaign they had ever experienced. Nazi trucks roared through the city, carrying loudspeakers, blaring forth slogans and incitements. Their posters were plastered over walls and millions of copies of pamphlets and Nazi newspapers were distributed to houses, offices and on street corners. Hitler himself flew backwards and forwards incessantly across the country, addressing huge rallies. And through the streets marched the swelling ranks of the SA and the SS, chanting the Horst Wessel Song. Everywhere, their campaign cry was heard, 'Down with the Republic!' Through the streets, too, marched thousands upon thousands of communist supporters, so that every day witnessed bloody street battles in which the police appeared powerless to intervene.

During those fearsome weeks, few people left the hotel after dark and every morning Viktoria woke up convinced that this was the day Otto would march back into the hotel and carry out his threat to get even with her. Possibly Hitler was the right man to save Germany, but so long as Otto Tobisch was part of the movement, she would never vote for him.

When the votes were counted, they learned to their dismay that, although Hindenburg had polled the most, he had fallen short of an absolute majority and that a second election had to be held. So, in order to support Hitler, the Nationalists withdrew their candidate and the campaigning recommenced.

This time, the Nazi campaign had a new tone. In no uncertain terms, it identified who was to blame for the current situation — the communists, the socialists and the Jews — and promised to rid the country of those 'evil forces'. However, Hitler did not merely blame, he also offered a message of hope. He promised work for the unemployed, business for the industrialists, an agricultural policy that would bring wealth back to farmers and peasants, and the restoration of a great German army.

'The Nazis certainly seem to be the only party offering a positive programme of recovery,' Ricarda said thoughtfully one evening. 'I agree with you, Viktoria, that I don't like the stormtroopers, but I do think we need a younger man than Field Marshal Hindenburg in charge and Hitler would seem to be our only choice.'

After that, his mother-in-law could do no wrong in Benno's eyes. But although Hitler's powerful message convinced not only Ricarda, but over thirteen million other people, it still failed to convince the nineteen million — including Viktoria — who voted for Hindenburg in the second election held on 10 April.

Almost immediately after the elections, to everyone's great relief, the President issued a decree banning Hitler's private armies. For the first time in months, an uneasy peace settled over the country and Viktoria woke in the morning without a feeling of dread. Even she, however, did not need her mother and Benno to tell her that, apart from this, nothing else had changed. There were nearly five and a half million unemployed, with shops and factories closing by the day, while prices continued to rise steadily. Neither the President nor the Chancellor had made much attempt to rectify the situation before. Why should anything be different now?

In May, Bruening, the 'Hunger Chancellor', was forced to resign and was replaced by an almost unknown Centre Party politician, an aristocrat and industrialist, called Franz von Papen, who appointed a cabinet composed almost exclusively of members of the nobility, rapidly christened by a discontented public 'the barons' cabinet'. The first thing Papen did was to call upon the President to dissolve parliament, call new elections for the end of July and to lift the ban on the SA.

It was the beginning of the most violent and bloody campaign they had ever experienced, beside which the previous two elections that year appeared almost peaceful. So far as both Nazi and communist supporters were concerned, the message of the campaign appeared to be murder and death. Every day the newspapers reported fights in which hundreds of people were killed, but, although communists were often arrested, the police appeared to be offering the Nazis protection. As Stefan had so rightly observed two years earlier, they were on the side of the stormtroopers.

Lothar did not return that summer and, in his absence, Viktoria and Luise grew closer than they had ever been before, for both could see the things they loved altering before their very eyes, while they remained powerless to do anything about them. Although Benno had not carried out his threat to dismiss Oskar Braun from Café Jochum, the character of the café was gradually changing of its own accord. Many left-wing writers, producers and artists found new haunts, leaving Café Jochum the domain of their former friends who were becoming increasingly outspoken in support of the Nazis. Luise, who had always found the communists boring and rather naïve, tried to console herself with the thought that her café still remained the kernel of Berlin's artistic community.

A similar transformation was taking place in the Hotel Quadriga. It was not that any of their guests formally announced their intention of not returning, more that, after several months, Viktoria noticed that certain familiar names no longer appeared in the register, and that various well-known faces were no longer seen in the restaurant and foyer. Then, one day, she would hear, 'Incidentally, did you know that Herr Abraham has sold his business and emigrated to America?'

In their place, new figures became prominent, industrialist friends of Baron Heinrich, together with up-and-coming Nazi politicians, men called Gregor Strasser, Wilhelm Frick, Dr Robert Ley, Hans Frank and Dr Hjalmar Schacht, whom the Baron appeared to hold in very high regard. Old friends, like Theo Arendt and Professor Ascher, no longer casually dropped in for a drink on their way home from work.

When Baron Heinrich von Kraus renewed his offer to buy the Arendt Bank that summer, Theo was faced with the most difficult decision of his life. It was one that could be deferred until after the result of the July election was known, but if this turned out as Theo expected, then the sale should be effected as quickly as possible.

He knew he was not alone in his distrust of the course von Papen appeared to be taking, for merely unleashing the SA again proved that he, Hindenburg and Hitler had formed some uneasy kind of alliance, from which it was not hard to prophesy that Hitler would come out on top. Many of his Jewish friends in Grunewald who held prominent positions in the business and financial world, were murmuring anxiously, 'If the Nazis gain more seats in the next election, then there is no future for us in Germany.'

Every day, when Theo reached the Arendt Bank, there were brownshirts and blackshirts waiting for him, shouting, 'Dirty Jew!', 'Jewish swine!' and '*Juden 'raus! Juden 'raus!*' 'Jews out!'

It was the same at the university, Professor Ascher told him. 'A lot of our students, and even some lecturers, support the Nazis. On occasions, it is almost impossible to complete a lesson, so intent are these thugs on causing total disruption. Einstein has been offered a teaching post in California, which he's going to accept.' He shook his head of white hair sadly. 'Imagine, Einstein was a national hero when he was awarded the Nobel Prize; now he is just a Jewish pig.'

Theo looked around the elegant living room of his villa, out across the small park of his garden. It was hard to conceive leaving all this, to start a new life in London at the age of fifty-two. Yet was it not better to go now of his own volition than to be forced out later, after the Nazis had perhaps even expropriated not only his bank but also his home? 'If I accept Baron Heinrich's offer and we go to London, will you come with us, Bethel?'

Professor Ascher hesitated for a moment, then he said slowly, 'I believe that you should accept the Baron's offer, for the sake of the children as much as for anything else. They are the Jews of the future, Theo, and it is our duty to keep them safe. But I shall not come with you.' As Theo opened his mouth to interrupt, he smiled gently and went on, 'No, hear me out, please. I am an old man, I am sixty-six, my working life is nearly over. But I believe I still have a task to perform and a duty to my people, for not all Jews are as fortunate as you and I. Somebody must remain to protect them and fight against injustice, intolerance and hatred.'

His answer did not surprise Theo, but it saddened him, for he hated the thought of leaving him alone. 'I respect your decision, Bethel, but I wish you would reconsider it.'

Professor Ascher inclined his head. 'In the Diaspora, the Jews were dispersed from Palestine and settled throughout the world, without a country of their own, and many times since then they have been forced to flee again, as is starting even now in Germany. It is my dearest dream that our settlers in modern Palestine will one day create a Jewish homeland, but in the meantime, we must continue to fight adversity. There is nothing that Hitler can do to me that I cannot face and overcome.'

'Perhaps the people will show more perspicacity than we give

579

them credit for,' Theo suggested hopefully.

'Hitler is the only political leader to offer any hope, Theo. If you were not a Jew, wouldn't you vote for him? I am sure I would. I don't blame the German people.'

Later that afternoon, when Professor Ascher left for his own home in Dahlem, Theo accompanied him to the front door. Through the still air of the sunny July afternoon they could hear strident military marches and voices blaring through loudspeakers from the huge Nazi rally being held in the nearby Grunewald stadium, followed by ecstatic cheering and shouts of '*Sieg Heil! Sieg Heil! Sieg Heil!*'

Bethel Ascher took his son-in-law's hand. 'Go to England.'

On 20 July, the most ominous event yet took place. To stop a violence that was reaching almost the proportions of civil war, Chancellor von Papen banned all political parades and proclaimed martial law in Berlin; then, by evoking emergency decrees, dismissed the Prussian government and appointed himself Reich Commissioner for Prussia. It was an obvious attempt to appease the Nazis and it was an open violation of the Constitution. To Theo it heralded, not only the beginning of the end of the Republic, but also of democracy in Germany.

In an atmosphere more tense than ever before, the people went to the polls and, although the Nazis failed to obtain their hoped-for majority, they totalled thirty-seven per cent of the vote to become the largest party in the Reichstag with two hundred and thirty seats.

Theo knew his decision had been made for him. After talking things over with Sophie, lengthy telephone conversations with his cousin Hugo in London, and several discussions with Oskar Duschek, he wrote to Baron Heinrich von Kraus and told him that he was prepared to sell the Arendt Bank.

They spoke only once on the telephone while their lawyers were negotiating, and that was when the Baron rang to ask him, 'Herr Arendt, presumably you are also going to sell your villa? If you don't already have a purchaser for it, I should be interested in buying it. My son, Ernst, will soon be returning from America. It would be useful for us to have a pied-à-terre in Berlin.'

It was as simple a solution as any, although it pained Theo to think of his beautiful house being lived in by a Kraus who would have scant appreciation for its elegant rooms and lovely grounds. Reluctantly, he gave his consent.

Now the dreadful moment had come, he discovered he wanted nothing more than to leave as quickly as possible. 'I think it best that you and the children go ahead of me to London,' he told Sophie, 'and I'll follow you as soon as the sales are completed. It shouldn't take long, because Baron Heinrich's lawyers tell us they want everything finalized by the end of August.'

After his family had left, removals experts started packing their precious pictures, furniture and other belongings into cases for shipment to England. Theo watched them sadly. It took so long to build a home and so little time to destroy it. So long to build a life. So few minutes to see it demolished.

At the end of August, when the lawyers had concluded their negotiations, Theo and the Baron finally met again in Berlin to sign the final agreements. Then, the formalities completed, Baron Heinrich stated blandly, 'We shall, of course, rename the bank. Since my family originally came from Liegnitz in Silesia, I have decided to call it the Liegnitzer Bank. All our customers will be advised.'

Theo nodded. Of course, all memories of the bank's Jewish origins should be destroyed. 'I shall tell the personnel what has happened. And I shall leave Berlin this evening.'

The Baron looked at him closely. 'Herr Arendt, you've lost nothing through our deal and you know it.'

When he had gone, Theo remained standing for a long time, looking round the office that had been his and his father's and his grandfather's before that. The portraits of the Arendt ancestors had already been removed from the walls and shipped to London, and, outside, workmen were already taking down the sign *ARENDT BANK*, preparatory to replacing it with the new one. It scarcely seemed possible that two centuries of Arendt banking tradition in Germany should come to an end.

He clenched his fist into a ball. For as long as he lived, he would never forgive the Germans, nor would his children, nor his children's children, nor his children's children's children.

Viktoria and Luise were sitting together at their corner table in the hotel bar that August evening in 1932, when Baron Heinrich made his triumphant appearance, with Benno at his side. He kissed both sisters enthusiastically on the cheek, then announced, 'Splendid news! I'm sure you'll both be delighted to hear that our family now owns the Arendt Bank! The agreement was signed today.'

Viktoria felt the colour drain from her cheeks. 'You've bought the Arendt Bank?' she asked incredulously.

'It was only a matter of time. Theo Arendt is not a stupid man. He could see how the wind is blowing and knew that, if he left his decision much longer until Hitler becomes Chancellor, his bank might be expropriated by the state. After all, he is a Jew and the Nazis do not like the Jews.'

'But Theo isn't just a Jew,' Viktoria cried, 'he's our friend!'

'And mine, too. My dear Viktoria, I have nothing against the Jews. This was purely a business transaction, from which both parties have profited. I offered him a very good price for his bank and his villa and he was wise enough to accept. What's more, I have every intention that Kraus Industries will continue to do business with his London, French and American offices.'

Luise was also staring at the Baron white-faced. 'You've bought his house as well? So where are Theo and his family now?'

'His wife and children moved to London several weeks ago. He is travelling to join them this evening.'

'You mean they've gone without saying goodbye?' Luise's eyes were enormous in her thin face.

'It would have been rather embarrassing for him to come to see you, under the circumstances,' Benno commented gently.

Impervious to the obvious distress of the two women, the Baron went on, 'Now for my other piece of news. Benno, our old friend, Herr Goering, has been appointed Speaker of the Reichstag! The news will be in all the papers tomorrow. He'll chivvy them all up and make them come to their senses. At long last, there's a Nazi in the chair!'

Still reeling from the shock of learning that Theo had left Germany, Viktoria stared from the Baron to her husband, appalled that Goering should suddenly have been given such power.

Benno was smiling happily. 'That's wonderful news. Goering won't stand for any nonsense from the communists or any of the other parties. What do you think he will do?'

'I don't know, but of one thing you can be sure, he'll find a way of discrediting that jackass Papen pretty quickly.'

Viktoria glanced at her sister, then stood up. 'If you'll excuse me, I should go and look at the children. Luischen, will you come with me?'

In the safety of their apartment, she took her in her arms. 'Darling, I'm sorry. What dreadful news.'

Luise laid her head on Viktoria's shoulder, her body trembling. 'I don't understand what's happening. All our friends are leaving us. Soon, there will be only you and me left.'

Viktoria stroked her hair, gazing blindly across the room. 'Then we must stick together. Do you see what the Nazis are doing to us, Luischen? They're forcing people apart, making them distrustful and afraid of each other, even to the extent of making dear friends like the Arendts flee the country. I can't blame Theo for going and I don't blame him for not telling us. But, I do so wish . . .'

They were both silent for a moment, then Luise asked in a small voice, 'Vicki, where will it end? Benno and his father obviously think the Nazis are right, while you equally obviously don't. They're driving a wedge even between you and Benno.'

Horrified, Viktoria stared at her. It was true. Gradually, she and Benno were becoming strangers to each other — and all because of their disagreement over the Nazis. She had to make it up with Benno, quickly, before they were totally lost to each other.

At that moment, the door opened and Stefan appeared. 'Mama, Aunt Luise, what's the matter?' His eyes were full of concern and his chin jutted obstinately. In a sudden flash of perception, Viktoria realized her son was no longer a child. He came to them, not in search of protection, but to protect.

'Theo Arendt and his family have gone to London,' she said.

An expression flickered across his face, that reminded her strangely of her father when his path was crossed. 'Why?'

'Because they are Jews, because they believe they are no longer wanted here, because your grandfather has bought their bank.' She could not conceal her bitterness.

'Has Minna gone with them?'

Viktoria had forgotten their childhood friendship. 'Yes.'

Stefan bit his lip in another characteristic Jochum gesture. 'So Herr Arendt has sold his bank because he is frightened by Hitler,' he said slowly. 'He's gone, like Herr Jankowski and Herr Lorenz.' Then he stood suddenly straight, pushing back his shoulders. 'Mama, would you give up the Hotel Quadriga because of the threats of someone like Hitler?'

Or someone like Otto Tobisch, she added mentally, and had no need to consider her answer. 'No, I'd stay and fight.' She sensed Luise stop shaking and look up at her. She forced her voice to sound confident. 'You and Aunt Luise, Monika, your grand-mother and your father are the most important people in my world, Stefi, and after you comes the Quadriga. I would fight tooth and nail to save you, for without you all my life would be worth nothing.'

It was a simple statement of fact. The love she felt for them transcended everything else, even her contempt for the Baron and Goering, even her fear of Otto.

There had never been any doubt in Olga Meyer's mind that the only way to put a stop to the evils that threatened Germany, be they monarchism, socialism, capitalism or nationalism, was to fight them, with words, guns — or, if all else failed, with bare fists. And, throughout her life, she had been doing just that. Yet, that autumn of 1932, Olga had the dreadful feeling that the fight had been in vain, that the instinct of the people had still not reached the stage of revolutionary class-consciousness.

Almost as soon as the Reichstag was reconvened in the middle of September, it announced its dissolution, and the fourth election in a year was set for 6 November. Again, Olga prepared for battle, this time with a sense of impotent rage, for Hitler's appeal to the masses was gaining in strength. Even in Wedding, that loyal heart of the labour movement, some people — under the misguided belief that National Socialism actually meant socialism and not nationalism — were succumbing to Hitler's promises of bread, work, and uniforms.

One evening in late October, as she and thirteen-year-old Basili made their way towards the hall where she was to address a mass meeting, her son asked, 'Mother, do you think Hitler will come to power?'

Her first instinct was to say no. But she could not lie to him. 'Yes, I think it's possible.' Then she looked up at the tall walls of Kraus Chemie and found a grain of hope from an unexpected source. 'But I don't believe he will last for long. You see, Basili, the Nazis are financed by industrialists like Baron Kraus, because they want to be free of the trade unions and the Republic. But Baron Kraus won't allow Hitler to stay in power for long. He won't allow a jumped-up corporal to dictate to him. Nor will the people, for that matter. They'll soon learn that waving flags won't fill their bellies and shouting slogans won't bring them jobs. They'll send Hitler packing and then, it will be our turn.'

The hall was packed with people, thin women dressed in rags, men with careworn faces, children with pinched cheeks who had never eaten a proper meal. No longer could she exhort the workers of Wedding to strike, for the unemployed had no labour to withdraw, but she could incite them to fight for their rights as free human beings.

As Basili took his place in the audience, she stood on the podium, a small, almost insignificant-looking woman of forty-one, her grey hair pulled back in a bun and her face lined beyond her years. She targeted her speech at those whom she considered her greatest enemies — the Weimar coalition government and Franz von Papen. 'Attack in all streets, in factories, in meetings. Down with the government of Herr von Papen and his barons' cabinet who think they can rule and reign over us! Fight Papen, who, by proclaiming martial law and dismissing the Prussian government, has violated the Constitution!'

Then she directed her attack towards the Nazis. 'Fight the demagogues and adventurers who are leading the nationalistic movement. Fight for freedom! Comrades, we are in the midst of a counter-revolution. History is on the side of freedom and freedom will be with you as long as you fight for it. And we shall fight to the end. We are German workers! We shall never be enslaved!'

Once more, to her joy, she saw the light of battle shine in the eyes of her listeners, watched them as they stood *en masse* and cheered her words, their clenched fists waving in the air. Throughout the hall, they shouted, 'Fight! Fight! Fight!'

At that moment, the doors burst open and a mob of SA men surged in, booing and jeering, brandishing truncheons and coshes. The workers of Wedding were ready for them. With their bare hands, men, women and children fought back at the armed brownshirts, until all Olga could see from her vantage point on the stage was a struggling, shouting mass of human bodies, somewhere in the midst of which was Basili. Jumping down off the stage, she forced her way through the mêlée towards the place where he had been sitting, pushing people roughly out of her way, calling out his name.

Suddenly, her arms were seized from behind and a man growled, 'This time you won't get away from me.'

She had never before heard his voice close to, but Olga knew without any shadow of doubt to whom it belonged. With a strength she didn't know she possessed, she pulled free from his grasp and stared up into the hated features of Otto Tobisch. For a minute, perhaps, their eyes remained interlocked, his glacially blue, hers full of passionate hatred, then, deliberately, she spat in his face.

His hand lashed out, cutting across her face, his gold ring drawing blood from her cheek. So intense was her rage, she hardly felt the blow. She kicked out at him and, as she did so, she saw a movement behind him, saw her young son grab hold of a chair and smash it down on Otto Tobisch's head.

It did little more than stun him, but it gave her sufficient time to grab hold of Basili's hand, pull him onto the stage and out of the back exit. Behind her, she heard Otto's infuriated orders for his men to follow them.

As she ran through the grey, silent streets of Wedding, the dark tenement blocks looming in on her, Olga suddenly remembered that other occasion when she had fled from Otto, after Reinhardt's death, before Basili was born. Then, she had found refuge in the Hotel Quadriga but tonight, there was nowhere for them to claim sanctuary. The sound of running footsteps drew nearer and she dragged Basili into a dark alleyway, holding him against her, concealed in her thin coat. Flashlights waving in their hands, the stormtroopers rushed past them.

They dared not return to their own flat, but hid in a cellar belonging to some safe comrades in the suburb of Pankow, where they eventually heard the results of the elections. To Olga's joy, the Nazis lost nearly two million votes, which went to Hugenberg's Nationalists — and to the communists. A few days later, Chancellor von Papen and his barons' cabinet resigned. That night, they returned to their own flat.

For the next few weeks, they lived in a state of constant uncertainty. Twice Hitler was summoned to meet President Hindenburg and Olga feared the worst could happen. On 2 December, however, the President named his new Chancellor — General Kurt von Schleicher, Minister of Defence in Papen's barons' cabinet. It was a dreadful decision, for not only did Schleicher represent Prussian militarism at its most extreme, he was also a conniving power politician who would stop at nothing to achieve his own ends.

Yet for all that, she did not give up hope. In a radio broadcast to the nation, the new Chancellor announced that he wanted to cooperate with the trade unions and that he was going to help impoverished farmers. And, at the same time, rumours circulated throughout the city that the Nazi Party was bankrupt. It was said to have no more funds to pay its officials, no more money to support its massive army of stormtroopers.

Olga's fight had not ended yet.

When Luise wrote to Emmy in Paris, confirming her appearance at Café Jochum on New Year's Eve, it was a very deliberate decision. Fearful of Benno's reaction, Oskar Braun tried to persuade her against it, but Luise was adamant. 'The posters will go up. Emmy will sing here.' No matter what the consequences, she was prepared to fight to the bitter end for the thing that mattered most in the world to her — Café Jochum. Only after all the arrangements had been made, did she tell Viktoria and Benno.

Benno turned on her in dismay. 'Where is she at the moment?'

'In Paris.'

'Then she should stay there. Luise, are you out of your mind? Don't you remember what happened last year?'

'Benno, what have you got against Emmy?' Luise's eyes glittered dangerously.

'I've got nothing against her personally,' Benno replied wearily. 'She's a nice kid, but she isn't wanted here. Listen, Luise, my father is coming here for the New Year and he will undoubtedly be holding a number of very important meetings, including some with Nazi politicians. If somebody like Dr Goebbels discovers Emmy is singing at the café, it will not only discredit ourselves and my father, but also do untold harm to Café Jochum. He'll just let his stormtroopers loose on it. That concert mustn't take place.'

'If people want to hear Emmy, they should be allowed to,' Luise said adamantly. 'This is still a free country, whatever you and your precious Dr Goebbels may think. I am a Jochum and Café Jochum belongs to my family. And if I say Emmy Anders is going to appear at our café on New Year's Eve, she will!'

Helplessly convinced that Benno was right, Viktoria pleaded, 'Do what Benno asks, Luischen. If the stormtroopers learn Emmy's at Café Jochum, they could tear it apart.'

Luise stood up, her chin jutting obstinately. 'Vicki, you mind your own business and I'll mind mine. The arrangements are all made. It's too late to change them.' She turned on her heel and slammed out of the room.

In the silence she left behind her, Viktoria and Benno stared down at the table top, avoiding each other's eyes. Finally, Benno sighed, 'We can't afford to run this risk. I'll send Emmy a cable in Paris, telling her the concert is cancelled.'

Viktoria nodded miserably, horribly conscious that she had somehow betrayed Luise, but also desperately wanting to be friends with Benno again. She put her hand on his arm. 'Benno,

I'm sorry, I don't mean to fight with you all the time. It's just that I'm so tired of elections, I'm tired of endless demonstrations, strikes and talk about revolution. I'm tired of prices going up and seeing the grey faces of millions of people out of work. I'm tired of brownshirts and blackshirts and communists and socialists and politicians who can't make up their stupid minds about anything. Oh, and I'm so sad that we are always quarrelling amongst ourselves.'

For the first time in months, he drew her to him and kissed her on the forehead. 'Vicki, I do understand, my dear. I know you're tired. We're all tired. But someday, soon, things must be resolved.'

But by the time Benno's cable reached Paris, Emmy had arrived in Berlin. Jean-Pierre parked the Rolls Royce in the road outside her apartment in Wilmersdorf, then hurried ahead carrying some of her suitcases, while she followed with Mimi, Fifi, Frou-frou, Bijou, Cha-cha and Bubi, all yapping with delight. When she reached the top of the stairs, Jean-Pierre was standing in the doorway. 'The lock is smashed. Emmy, I think you have had the burglary.'

She pushed past him, switched on a light, then screamed in horror, as a scene of total chaos met her eyes. Not a piece of furniture seemed to be intact. Cushions were ripped open, their feathers lifting slightly in the draft. Lamps had been knocked over, photograph frames smashed and pictures defaced. Her feet crunched over broken glass and china.

Apprehensively, Jean-Pierre made his way into the bedroom. Trembling, she followed him to find a message crudely smeared on the pink wallpaper. *Emmy Anders! Get out of Germany! Go home to Africa!* To either side of it were two huge, black swastikas.

Emmy knew the most terrible fear of her life and tears started to pour down her cheeks. This was no wanton burglary, this was deliberate vandalism, directed personally at her. Suddenly, she remembered the brownshirts who had invaded Café Jochum during her last concert there and knew that this was a message from them. 'Oh, Jean-Pierre, what shall I do? Where shall I go? They've ruined my home! They'll kill me if they find me.' She threw her arms desperately round his neck.

He shook his head in disbelief, stunned by the devastated apartment, then finally asked, 'Your friend, Mademoiselle Luise, can she help you? Can you stay at her hotel?'

The thought of Luise was like a lifeline. 'Yes, we'll go to the Hotel Quadriga. Luise will know what to do.'

Jean-Pierre picked up the suitcases and carried them out to the Rolls Royce, while Emmy and the poodles got into the back. Neither she nor Jean-Pierre said a word as they drove round the Brandenburg Gate and pulled up outside the Hotel Quadriga. Then, once again, she clipped six leads onto six diamante collars, and, with her head held high, she walked up the white steps into the hotel. The commissionaires stood stiffly to attention, but showed no sign of recognition. The hall porter stared at her, in what seemed to be shocked surprise, and a page boy muttered something to a colleague. A terrible premonition seized her, but she continued resolutely on her way. In the distance, she saw Herr Fromm pick up his phone, dial a number, ask a quick question, then put down the receiver. Guests, sitting in the foyer, glanced at her curiously, as she made her way towards the reception desk, her six dogs trotting obediently at her heels. 'Good evening, Herr Fromm. Is it possible for me to speak to Fraeulein Luise?'

He looked at his watch. 'But, Fraeulein Anders, it is midnight. Perhaps, tomorrow . . .'

At that moment, Benno appeared. He did not shake her hand or kiss her, but just stood there, a serious expression on his face. 'Why, Emmy. I didn't expect to see you.'

'What do you mean?' she asked, drawing her poodles closer to her.

'Didn't you receive my cable, cancelling your engagement?'

'No,' she said anxiously. 'I must have left before it arrived. Oh, Herr Benno, what am I going to do? My flat has been wrecked and I've got nowhere to go. Can I stay here tonight?'

Suddenly, from the Jubilee Room, music broke out, the pianist's foot heavy on the loud pedal and men's voices lifted in the Horst Wessel song, the same anthem the stormtroopers had sung a year ago when they burst in on her concert. Benno glanced nervously towards the door, then said, 'Emmy, we can't give you a room. I'm sorry, but we can't.'

'Why? What have I done?'

He stared down at his hands, interlocking his fingers so that his knuckles gleamed white then, avoiding her eyes, replied, 'Let's just say the hotel is full.'

Dully, Emmy began to understand. Benno Kraus was on the side of the Nazis — and against her. 'But where shall I go?'

He was silent for a long while, then he said gently, 'In your position, Emmy, I'd leave Berlin and I'd leave Germany.'

She made one last, valiant attempt. 'And you won't let me see Fraeulein Luise?'

'Emmy, there's nothing she can do.'

She nodded and with all the dignity she could muster, said, 'Thank you, Herr Benno.'

It was a long, lonely walk across that vast area of Savonnerie carpet, over the Tuscan marble floor of the hotel where she had sprung to fame and at which there was suddenly no room for her. The hall porter rushed to open the door to let her and her poodles out into the night. As Jean-Pierre hurried towards her, the last vestige of self-control deserted her. Throwing her arms round his neck, she wailed, 'Herr Benno says the hotel is fully booked. What shall I do?'

He bundled the six poodles into the back of the car, then pushed her into the front seat beside him. 'First, we're going to get out of Berlin and find somewhere to sleep along the road. Then we are going back to Paris, Emmy.'

Tears were streaming down her face now. 'I don't care if I never see Berlin again,' she howled.

Luise was furious when she learned at breakfast next morning that Benno had turned Emmy away. 'Her flat had been ransacked and you wouldn't give her a bed for the night?'

Stefan also looked at him in horror. 'You refused to help Emmy Anders? Why?'

Benno took a deep breath. 'It would have been dangerous for her, Stefan. She's a jazz singer and in the eyes of the Nazis, she's decadent and racially impure. That's why I cabled to cancel her performance. It would have been madness to let her stay here, with a Nazi function going on in the Jubilee Room.'

In words terribly reminiscent of his grandfather, Stefan demanded coldly, 'Surely we should be the ones who determine who can or can't stay in our hotel, not the brownshirts? Papa, I don't understand why you allow yourself to be intimidated by them.'

Surrounded by his family's angry faces, Benno struggled to control his temper. 'Stefan, you are still a child and have no idea what you are saying. I, and a very great number of other sensible people, happen to believe that the policies of the Nazi Party are right for our country and that the stormtroopers are a necessary force to uphold law and order.'

Stefan looked at him sceptically. 'In my experience, the storm-troopers have done nothing except disrupt law and order.'

'Emmy has certainly committed no crime,' Luise added.

'Perhaps they mistook her flat for someone else's,' Viktoria suggested doubtfully. 'Possibly they thought she was a communist?'

'Whatever happened, Emmy's gone,' Benno said. 'And the sooner you all recognize that the stormtroopers are a fact of life, the easier you will find things. My advice to all of you is to look to the future of your country — and that future depends on patriots, men of courage and determination, like Hitler. Once he's rid Germany of its disruptive elements, he'll subdue his stormtroopers.'

'I can't think there are many disruptive elements left,' Luise commented in a small voice.

Superficially, that New Year's Eve was no different from all the others the hotel had celebrated during its long and distinguished history. A gala banquet was given, after which Viktoria and Benno, elegantly dressed in evening gown and dinner jacket, welcomed their guests into the magnificent ballroom, where the orchestra was playing Strauss and Lehár. Reichswehr officers mingled with aristocrats, civil servants, industrialists, politicians and financiers, their ladies vying with each other in the splendour and richness of their dress and jewellery. They gossiped, they drank champagne and they danced. It appeared to be an evening in the best tradition of the Hotel Quadriga.

At a prominent table near the dance floor, Baron Heinrich sat with his family around him. Julia and Ricarda were reminiscing quietly together about old times, the many other New Years they had seen in, when Karl and Ewald were still alive. Women, the Baron thought impatiently, always living in the past, unable to understand it was the future that mattered, not a sensible thought in their heads. His daughter-in-law, Trudi, was just the same. A lump of a woman, but nevertheless a Biederstein, she was gazing vacantly into space, probably thinking of Ernst, due back from America within the next month or so. Marriage, children and servants, that was all she ever talked about.

His glance fell on Luise Jochum. When she had helped fit out the *Countess Julia*, she had seemed to have her wits about her. But look at her now! Her green eyes huge in her white face, she was

591

playing nervously with a gold cigarette case, the ashtray in front of her already full. Apparently upset about some cabaret singer. Neurotic!

His spirits rose as he studied his four grandchildren. Ernst's two sons, Werner and Norbert, were carrying on a desultory conversation with Benno's couple, Stefan and Monika. Three good lads, the Baron thought proudly, and even the girl promised well, blonde and down-to-earth. But strange the difference between her and her brother. The Biederstein strain so strong in Stefan, while it was not at all evident in Monika.

Thinking of the Biedersteins, the Baron was reminded again of the visit he and Julia had paid to Fuerstenmark just before Christmas. Poor old Johann was not at all well and Anna was talking seriously about asking Peter to return from London, where he was now Military Attaché. That was grave news, but not as serious as the subject that had dominated their conversation — Chancellor General von Schleicher's agricultural reforms. The Baron would not have been surprised if the worry caused by this threat to his estates was not as damaging to Johann's health as the arteriosclerosis the doctors said could cause a heart attack at any moment.

Ponderously, Baron Heinrich raised his massive bulk, reached for the cane he now needed to balance himself and set out across the room. He cared nothing for the festivities themselves but they offered excellent camouflage for discreet discussions with likeminded colleagues. Circumspectly, he gathered them together, a small but immensely powerful group of men united by their hostility to one individual — General von Schleicher. Under cover of the music, they sipped champagne, smoked cigars — and hatched a plot.

'Schleicher's a lunatic,' a factory owner said. 'Negotiating with the trade unions! What we need is a lessening of union power.'

'Talking of dividing up the estates in the east and giving them to the peasants, that's little short of Bolshevism!' an irate landowner complained.

'He won't last long,' a private banker from Cologne prophesied. 'Don't forget Hindenburg himself has massive estates. He's not going to relinquish them on some whim of Schleicher's. He'll force Schleicher out of office.'

'But who will replace him? It's common knowledge Hindenburg can't stand Hitler and I'm not at all sure about him myself. Some of his policies are too radical for me,' an influential Berlin businessman declared.

The Baron shook his head. 'Bah! Hitler is a politician. He doesn't mean what he says. But he needs the support of the working and middle classes and, to win their votes, he has to make these radical promises. As soon as he's in power, he'll forget them!'

'Perhaps if Papen and Hitler could reach some kind of agreement, they could discredit Schleicher together,' the landowner suggested, cunningly. 'Maybe if a meeting were arranged ...'

'And if Hitler could somehow inveigle himself into Hindenburg's good graces ...' the factory owner said thoughtfully. 'Possibly with Papen's help?'

'Gentlemen,' the banker said quietly, 'I think you are forgetting one thing. It isn't just a rumour, it's true that the Nazi Party is bankrupt. It has already incurred massive debts and few of its functionaries or stormtroopers have been paid since before Christmas.'

'What sort of money are we talking about?' the businessman asked.

The banker shrugged. 'It takes about two and a half million a week to pay the stormtroopers. Then there are newspapers, office rents, salaries, electioneering expenses ...'

'If we helped Hitler out of his mess, he'd be in our debt,' the businessman mused.

'And he's already promised to get rid of the trade unions and the communists ...' Baron Heinrich added.

At that moment, the orchestra stopped playing and Benno jumped onto the podium. 'Ladies and gentlemen,' he announced, 'it is midnight. On behalf of the Hotel Quadriga, I wish you a very happy and prosperous New Year.'

Baron Heinrich raised his glass to his fellow conspirators. 'To a prosperous New Year! And' he added blandly, 'let us not forget that whoever holds the purse strings holds ultimate power in any country.'

Although the rest of his family returned to Essen the following day, the Baron remained in Berlin, for he had much confidential business to transact. Five days later, he learned with great satisfaction that Hitler and Papen had met in Cologne, apparently coming to some sort of deal. Further meetings were due to take place between them and President Hindenburg's son. Baron Heinrich's colleagues had done their part. It would not be long before Schleicher was hounded out of office. Now it was time for the Baron to keep his side of the bargain.

'I think it might be wise if you were to prepare for Hitler's appointment as Chancellor,' he warned Benno. 'When the moment occurs, we don't want the Hotel Quadriga to appear lacking in fervour or patriotic feeling. Organize flags, bunting, that sort of thing, maybe even a portrait of Hitler to go in the bar.'

'Are you that confident?' Benno asked doubtfully, for the future had never seemed less certain to him.

'Have you ever known me to be wrong, boy?'

When Benno had gone, the Baron opened a Liegnitzer Bank cheque book and wrote out a cheque to the Nazi Party for two and a half million marks. After sealing it in an envelope with the Kraus crest, he pressed a bell and a page boy instantly knocked on the door. 'Take this to Deputy Goering at the Palace of the Reichstag President,' he ordered. A week later, Goering wrote a personal note to thank him and intimated that, because of the Baron's and other supporters' generosity, the financial situation of the Party had improved beyond all recognition.

The weeks that followed were rife with speculation, but it was obvious even to the most uninformed that Schleicher's days were numbered, that some kind of unnatural alliance had been formed between Papen and Hitler, and that the stormtroopers — far from being disbanded through lack of funds — were on the increase.

Then, on Saturday 28 January came the report that Hindenburg had summarily dismissed Schleicher. Feelings in the city reached tinder pitch. Ever wilder rumours abounded. Some people claimed President Hindenburg was going to reinstate Franz von Papen, others that Schleicher had persuaded the Reichswehr to stage a coup d'état, arrest the President and establish a military dictatorship. Swelling numbers of stormtroopers in Berlin induced many to believe the Nazis were preparing their own putsch and that if Hitler was not made head of a new government, his troops would seize the Chancellery.

In a last desperate bid to save their country from National Socialism, the workers of Berlin rallied to the call of their leaders. On Sunday morning, they marched into the city centre. From the furthest outlying districts, they set out at dawn to demonstrate their opposition to Adolf Hitler. They came from Lichtenberg, Wartenberg and Friedrichsfelde. They walked from Weissensee, Kreuzberg and Schoeneberg. They marched from Reinickendorf, Pankow and Wedding. In front of the Imperial Palace where Hindenburg resided, down Unter den Linden to the Brandenburg Gate, they poured, singing the *Red Flag*, the *Internationale* and chanting anti-fascist slogans. Ten, twenty, fifty, a hundred thousand of them, united in a common cause.

With Basili at her side, Olga looked down from the hastily erected stage at the sea of faces beneath her, inciting them once more to rise against the evil forces that confronted them. There was so little time and so little they could do. 'Once before, these Free Corps soldiers, these brownshirts, tried to stage a putsch here in Berlin — the Kapp Putsch!' she screamed derisively. 'Comrades, how was that pitiful coup averted? I will remind you! It was stopped, not by the Reichswehr, not by the politicians, but by the workers of Germany! A general strike prevented the nationalists seizing power! Comrades, our labour is our most valuable weapon! Fight for freedom! Strike for freedom! Bring the country to a halt! Strangle Nazism before it strangles you.'

As her cry resounded across the Pariser Platz and was taken up by the multitude, Olga clasped Basili's fist in hers and waved it in the air. 'I am the wife and this is the son of Reinhardt Meyer, who was murdered by those same evil stormtroopers. We vow to you, that for so long as we live, we shall continue to fight for Reinhardt's dream that, one day, the Communist Party will rule in Berlin! We shall fight for your future! We shall fight for Germany!'

Her words only faintly reached the people standing on the balcony of the Hotel Quadriga. 'Strike, strike, strike,' Baron Heinrich muttered. 'That's all that bloody woman has ever been able to suggest. The sooner she's put away the better.'

'Poor Olga,' Ricarda sighed, 'she's had such a hard life. I know I shouldn't feel sorry for her, but I do.'

Luise shook her head impatiently. 'If only she'd done something. The communists are so stupid. They've had so many opportunities but all they've ever done is talk ...'

'Thank God,' Benno retorted acidly. 'I hate to think what state the country would be in if Olga were in charge.'

'Who is that boy beside her?' Stefan asked. 'Is he her son?'

Viktoria stared at the distant figure, trying to discern his features, but he was too far away. As if it were yesterday, she recalled her meeting with Olga at Heiligensee, after her father's death. 'The future of Germany depends upon children like the one I am bearing, for they will be the children of the revolution,' Olga had said. 'One day, your son and mine will meet and then we'll see which of them has turned out best.'

'Yes,' Viktoria told her son, 'that is Olga's son.' At that moment, she did not know which she feared most — Olga's fanatical hatred or Otto's vindictive thirst for revenge.

The following day, they awoke to rumours that, under Hitler's orders, the SA had completely cordoned off Berlin and was preparing, with the aid of the police, to overpower the army and seize the Chancellery by force. It seemed that Olga's fears might have been justified.

The morning passed in an agony of suspense. The ground floor of the hotel, by that time, was a seething mass of humanity, including journalists from all over the world, vying with each other to be the first to be able to inform their readers that Hitler had finally become Chancellor. A constant procession of people made their way up Unter den Linden to the Wilhelmstrasse and all reported large numbers of stormtroopers marching through the streets, with SS guards standing alert at strategic points. The radio played constantly.

At noon, a news bulletin gave the long-awaited announcement. In full compliance with the constitution of Germany, President Hindenburg had named Adolf Hitler as the new Chancellor. Franz von Papen had been appointed his Vice-Chancellor. In silence, the assembled guests listened to the details of the new cabinet and to the news that a huge torchlight procession of SA and SS men would parade through the streets at eight that evening. Then a frenzied uproar broke out.

'A sound cabinet in my opinion,' one man said. 'He's made von Papen Vice-Chancellor to counteract any of Hitler's excesses.'

'Surprised Goebbels hasn't got a place ...'

'General von Blomberg as Minister of Defence ...'

'Dr Hugenberg is Minister of Agriculture ...'

'Only three Nazi cabinet posts out of eleven,' someone sneered.

'It seems a very good compromise,' Ricarda said quietly. 'There are a reassuring number of old conservatives in the cabinet and the most important post of Chancellor has gone to Hitler. You see, Benno was right all the time, Vicki dear.'

'Excellent,' Baron Heinrich exclaimed, pumping Benno's hand. 'Hitler as Chancellor and my good friend Goering as Minister of the Interior of Prussia and Minister of Aviation, which can only mean that we shall soon have an air force. Splendid news for Kraus Industries.'

Viktoria stared at him. Certainly, Hitler had achieved his revolution by seemingly democratic methods. The stormtroopers had not seized the Chancellery. There had been no repetition of the Kapp fiasco or the Munich Beer Hall Putsch. But there was something in her father-in-law's complacent tone that raised her suspicions. It seemed scarcely conceivable that he had been influential in Hindenburg's decision — and yet ...'

'Vicki,' Luise asked, 'this torchlight parade? Does it mean more trouble?'

'Of course not,' Benno said briskly, 'it's a celebration, an old-fashioned, patriotic procession! Vicki, I'm afraid I've got rather a lot to see to. Please help Herr Fromm at reception, he looks totally distraught.'

Viktoria hurried to his aid. Throughout the entire afternoon, the telephone did not stop ringing, as people from all over the country tried to reserve rooms. Priority was, as always, given to their regular guests, but there were many whom they had to disappoint. Could there really be so many ardent supporters of Hitler among the hotel's clientele? Could it be that she was the only one out of step? Were they, Baron Heinrich, her mother and Benno right?

Already huge crowds had begun to line the pavement outside, so that Unter den Linden appeared to be a sea of waving swastikas. With a worried frown, Herr Brandt expressed concern at the number of strangers who were already taking up position in the bar in order to view the procession. 'It just needs one or two communists to get in among them and we could find ourselves with another riot on our hands. Frau Viktoria, with your consent I'll ask for a police guard.' Recognising the sense in his proposals, she unwillingly agreed.

Benno, in the meantime, quietly began to organize other members of staff. Out from the boxes he had stored in the cellars came the blood-red banners emblazoned with swastikas, with which the maintenance men hurried to festoon the foyer and, along the full length of the portico, smaller Nazi flags were hung in riotous jubilation. Viktoria watched the transfiguration and felt an ever deepening sense of oppression. In the past, they had garlanded it with flowers and laurel wreaths, now it was adorned with her hated symbol of the swastika. Her beloved hotel seemed to have become a shrine to Otto Tobisch.

At six o'clock the hotel doors were locked and barred, with a chain of policemen posted outside. If this were an omen of things to come, it could hardly have been less optimistic.

Under the Brandenburg Gate, they marched in triumphant procession that wintry evening in January 1933, rank upon serried rank of brown-uniformed SA and black-uniformed SS men, the black insignia of the swastika within a white circle upon their blood-red armbands and the gigantic standards borne before them. Drums rolled, trumpets blared and blazing torches were brandished in the air. Voices roared the old, patriotic songs of Germany. In steady tempo, burnished black boots goose-stepped over the cobbled roadway, thousands upon thousands of them, hour after hour after hour, while the crowds that packed the pavements raised their arms high in the Nazi salute, roaring deliriously, '*Sieg Heil! Sieg Heil! Sieg Heil!*'

At the head of one of the columns marched Sturmfuehrer Otto Tobisch, supremely conscious that this display of their own military strength conclusively proved to Berliners — and to the rest of the world — that Germany need no longer bow her head in shame for having lost the war and need suffer no more under the humiliations of the Versailles Treaty. She might still have only a one hundred thousand man army, but the legions of Hitler's stormtroopers who proudly strode before them made a mockery of that myth.

He glanced up at the Hotel Quadriga and his lips sent a silent message to Viktoria Jochum-Kraus. 'From now on I shall have the right to do whatever I want with your hotel, because from now on, we are the masters of Germany!' It seemed he had spent his entire life working towards this day and finally, it had arrived!

No faces were visible to the people densely packed onto the balcony of the Hotel Quadriga. All they could see were the flaming torches, a moving river of fire, lava from a volcano flowing over streets of molten snow. The collar of her sable coat turned up against the bitter night air, framing her pale face, crowned with its coronet of golden braids, Viktoria stared apprehensively at them. Somewhere in their midst, marched Otto, the reason for her fighting Benno so long and so bitterly over Hitler. Otto, striding triumphantly through the central arch of the gate where her father had lost his life under the wheels of a Free Corps lorry, almost exactly fourteen years earlier.

They were chanting the Horst Wessel Song:

'Raise high the flags! Stand rank on rank together.

Stormtroopers march with steady, quiet tread ...'

'That's what they sang the night they broke up Emmy's last concert,' Luise muttered. 'For as long as I live, I shall hate that song.' She clutched Viktoria's arm. 'How many of them are there?'

'If you include the Stahlhelm, I would estimate that there are well over two million stormtroopers in the whole of Germany,' Baron Heinrich pronounced portentously, a cloud of blue smoke from his cigar gusting into their faces. 'Your cousin Olga doesn't stand a chance against them.'

'And us?' Luise whispered. 'What sort of chance do we stand?'

Viktoria squeezed her hand comfortingly.

'Doesn't it make you feel proud to be a German?' Benno asked Monika. Viktoria could see he was deeply moved by the parade, the military music, the flags and the patriotic fervour of the crowds. She could almost read his thoughts. Germany was strong again! Germany was, once again, a force to contend with!

Their twelve-year-old daughter frenziedly waved her swastika flag, her grey eyes shining and her voice hoarse with excitement. 'I wish I were a man,' she sighed wistfully, 'then I could join them.' She turned to Stefan. 'Stefi, wouldn't you love to be a soldier?'

Stefan tugged her thick, blonde pigtails affectionately, and Viktoria wondered, not for the first time, how her two children could be so dissimilar. 'Not really,' he replied, 'and I certainly don't want to belong to the SA.'

'Victoriously, we shall defeat France ...' the voices of the stormtroopers passing beneath them roared the old battlesong, dating back to the Napoleonic wars. In a fever of excitement, the crowds joined in, lifting their voices in a triumphant crescendo. '*Sieg Heil! Sieg Heil! Sieg Heil!*'

'That slogan, "Hail Victory!" and these crowds, don't they seem menacing to you?' Stefan asked.

Ricarda put her arm around his shoulder. 'Stefi, you're a Berliner, born and bred, and you should understand the Berliners. In the past, we lined the streets in our thousands, to catch a sight of our Kaiser, to watch wedding processions and funeral cortèges. Yesterday, it was to see the communists. Tonight, it is the storm-troopers. But the wonderful thing about us Berliners, as I realized a long time ago, is that deep down inside us we always retain a native scepticism. None of us like the stormtroopers, but we'll put up with them for a bit longer, while we give Hitler a chance.'

Viktoria experienced a sudden, overwhelming sense of gratitude at her mother's serene level-headedness. Perhaps she had been allowing her fear of Otto to prey so much on her mind that it was robbing her of her common sense. 'I'm sure your grandmother's right,' she assured Stefan, but there was still an edge of uncertainty in her voice. 'And after all, darling, if we don't like what Hitler does, we can always vote him out of power.'

Her words were almost drowned by a roll of drums in the street below, followed by a powerful rendition, by percussion and voice, of Germany's national anthem, *Deutschland, Deutschland ueber alles* . . .

It was past midnight before the torchlight procession ended. The crowds slowly dispersed, the policemen were sent off-duty and the guests of the Hotel Quadriga made their way to the bar for a well-earned nightcap. Gradually, congratulating each other on an extremely satisfactory day, they retired to their rooms. One by one, the hotel's lamps were extinguished, until only the foyer lights shone out onto Unter den Linden, a welcoming beacon in the darkened city.

Little white flakes obliterated the slushy imprints of the storm-troopers' boots beneath the Brandenburg Gate, cloaking the statue of the Quadriga and the four prancing horses with a caparison of snow. Her arm valiantly raised, Viktoria, Goddess of Victory, kept solitary vigil over the streets of Berlin.